THE THRESHER

THE THRESHER

by

HERBERT KRAUSE

Author of
WIND WITHOUT RAIN

THE BOBBS-MERRILL COMPANY
PUBLISHERS
INDIANAPOLIS　　　-　　　NEW YORK

To
GEORGE WEIDA SPOHN
and
LUCY TYLER SPOHN
whom their boys and girls called
POP AND MUDDIE

CONTENTS

Part 1

THE SEASON OF GROWING WEATHER

My friend! My friend! I yearn toward thee, but I know not how it is that our distrust, our hate, is stronger than our love. It is of no use to speak the truth to you. You will not hear it. You keep me at distance. I will not endeavor to blame you. There is nothing to be said about it. You are on one side, I on the other.

My friend! If my coming hinders him in the least conceivable degree, I will exert myself to the utmost to stay away. If my coming casts but the shadow of a shadow, I will retreat swifter than the wind. I will be gone irrevocably before he fears that I am coming.

For a long time you have appeared further and further off to me. I see that you will at length disappear altogether. The memory of me is steadily passing away. The meadows are like barren ground. My path grows steeper. My heart is full. Morning, noon, and night, I suffer a physical pain, an aching of the breast which unfits me for my tasks. I knock on the earth expecting my friend, I expect to meet him at every turn, but no friend appears. The night is approaching. I walk alone.

Thoreau's *Journals.*

1

CLEAR as a cowbell tinkling in dusk, the *s'rum-s'rum—rum-s'rum* of the separator and the "G'up, there; g-up" of the driver rode over the fields. It crowded echoingly against the walls of the railroad station, stopping the ears with a broad sound of rush-and-tear, until Johnny, eyes red with the salt of grief, looked up and away. He scarcely saw Uncle Herm striding restlessly over the platform. Wide acres in stubble stretching out until they washed around an island of trees in which a huddle of buildings and a bulge of yellow straw pile were nearly hidden—these his eyes took in. Not many mornings ago wheat in yellow waves under a quartering wind had rolled over these acres and beyond; stems arched and heads bowed with the weight of sustenance. Most of the fields were empty now except for the wagon trails that rambled in long easy turns back to the island of trees.

From its farther side curved the shouts and the low grumble of machinery. Johnny heard them. And Uncle Herm, hiding pain in the scraggle of his mustache, saw with a heft of gladness at the heart that a little of the droop unkinked itself from Johnny's lip and that his head lifted at the sound. He muttered under his tongue, "Moses Almighty blast that train, anyway, late at a time like this; I'm glad Marchen brought the team to Mary's Hill." He jabbed the silver watch fiercely into the pocket of his square-cut vest. Aloud he said with heartiness, "They're thrashing there, Johnny. All through the ridges you'll see them—horses circling around the driver and men pitchin' bundles into the thrasher. All over the Valley, too. This here's only the fringe. We're finished, though, at our place."

For a moment of tight breath, Johnny, twisting around, let the hills to the north and east take him with their tree-green friendliness. Blue distances gathered deeply between their jutty shoulders. They crinkled the prairie gently into rolling land at first, above which they humped in broken upthrusts. They ran with red fire in a sun no more than three hours high. One long ridge, knotty with oak clumps, sprawled like a slanting leg out onto the prairie. Pockerbrush, Uncle Herm called those hills, and up there a homestead in a valley, shadow-haunted; Aunt Phrena there, and the

11

heavy-bodied Kurt. . . . He swung quickly back to the acres in stubble and the island where the threshers hid.

Once a smoke of dust billowed above the trees and once a cart, lugged ponderously by a yoke of oxen, dragged its way near the straw pile. Johnny followed its slow crawl with quick twists of his body, and in his eyes, sorrow-pinched, there grew a sort of shining that was like a candle brightening through a foggy pane. Then cart and oxen inched back among the trees and were gone.

There was only the prairie, dying in autumn, the far reaches of its unbroken floor gathering loneliness as a storm does darkness. No bird lazed on a wing. Marching lines of cottonwood were so far away the eyes hurt to bring them clear. Even the neighborly drone of threshing faded, drawn thin as spider-thread. The candle behind his lashes dimmed. He shivered as though he were alone in this emptiness. Around him the station platform was cluttered with boxes and bales and cradle bows and sickles. His valise like a brown dog sat at his side. The empty ladder of the railroad track lifted into the skyline. There was only Uncle Herm squeaking impatiently in his boots: no mothering voice, no kitchen with the smell of cookies; only the awful emptiness of sorrow—emptiness that was like a weight laid more on the stomach than on the heart; grief like a hound at the throat, gripping hard, so that even the tears hurt. Fields and the island of trees slid out of focus in a rush of water that blurred his sight.

Uncle Herm was saying, "We'll soon be in Mary's Hill, now; and then home—home in Pockerbrush, boy," when Johnny ran to him and clung to his coat sleeve, all his nine years crying in his voice, "Mother, Mother. Oh, Uncle Herm, she won't ever sing me to sleep again."

Uncle Herm knelt down to hush him. "Now, now, boy. Your ma would want you to be a big man; and men don't cry, boy." Suddenly, with longing in the circle of his arms, Uncle Herm hugged him fiercely as if this were seed from his own loins—or, by rights, ought to be. His face twisted as though he wished that it were night and in the darkness men could cry.

2

In those years until the farm became hard under his feet and familiar as a hole in his pocket, he mulled over the black hours before he came to the homestead in the hills and the first long growing days after. Some things grew misty with the shadowiness of forgetting; some remained full of hidden meanings he didn't understand. Not then, at least. But always he remembered with a quick breath how Uncle Herm came out of nowhere, it seemed, and put a warm hand on his loneliness, quieting him.

"You come now with me and Phrena," Uncle Herm said. "We got an old dog named Sport and a thrashing rig up there." And Uncle Herm showed him a silver watch, thick and shiny with wear and larger than the palm of a hand, and the brassy square-ended key that wound it. "Listen. Hear it go *tick-tick-tick?*"

With Uncle Herm came the forlorn, forgotten-sounding name Pockerbrush. With him came Kurt—Kurt, a year older than Johnny. In odd unexpected moments Johnny recalled how Kurt stood near a window just before they went to the cemetery, pursed of lip and heavy in his legs, absently crushing a bluebottle fly between thumb and forefinger and wiping the smear on his pants. And then he'd hear again Uncle Herm saying, "You go home now, Phrena, and see how things are up in Pockerbrush. I'll come with him. Maybe in a couple of days. I'll see that everything's settled."

In remembering the agony of that hour, he would shut his eyes, now over a feeding of chickens, now over a slopping of hogs, thinking, thinking how in desperate woe he had looked despairingly for a door to run through and escape. Pockerbrush, lonely name. That's where they were taking him. Pockerbrush, a place lost in distance, miles from the picture of Mother and the silent room still sweet with her laughter. But Aunt Phrena he remembered only as a shapelessness in black, dampish with sobs, rushing into a room and crying, "Poor dear sister! Poor little dove!" Over and over.

Some things, like that first night at the farm, were cut deep as brand marks in his mind. But these were mixed up with others, half blotted away, and he saw them as one looking through a window streaked with rain: the bumpy railroad cars with the hard seats thrust against his back and rump, and the conductor, whisky sour on his breath, lighting oil lamps in the coach; the station where they stopped and he heard for the first time the sound of the threshing machine; the trip in the dark over the ridges from Mary's Hill, the wagon banging sparks from the iron of its wheels against stone; the splash and grind as they forded a creek; the moon now on one hilltop, now on another as they followed the curvy road; and at last the farm in the woods, the black loom of the house and red eye of the coal-oil light blinking out of it; lamplight and house warmth coming in a rush of welcome over the step for the scared trembles in him.

Kurt was sitting popeyed near the stove when he entered. Aunt Phrena, fat and bulging as dough in a pan, peeped at him through wobbly lids and cried, "Kurt, get me the Comfort Book." She flung her apron over her head, howling into the crocheted edges, "The poor sweet dove, sweet as my sister, my poor dead sister. Come in, Johnny, come in. Ach, the Lord giveth and the Lord taketh away."

Uncle Herm, pulling his whiskers, tried to interfere. "Bull wheels of Moses Almighty, Phrena! He ain't no dove. He's cold, that's what he is; pinched blue." Then he shouted, "Get me the lantern, Kurt. The team is waiting to be unhooked."

Johnny had milk and mush that night mixed with Aunt Phrena's reading, " 'He feedeth his sheep like a gentle shepherd.' Eat your mush, Johnny. 'Yea, like a gentle shepherd' "; on and on. Once she interrupted herself to say, "Kurt, you go outside now first, before you fall asleep and wet your pants." Then she continued, " 'Like a good shepherd he watcheth over his flock.' You hear that, Johnny?"

He nodded, choking over a spoonful.

Uncle Herm hitched about as if nettle-stung. "Almighty, Phrena! Give the boy a chance. His stomach's empty; let him eat. Talk later."

Aunt Phrena replied with bitterness, "That's right, Herm Barewolf. Stuff his miserable sinful body; stuff it full of corruptible food and forget his poor starving soul—his poor, skinny soul." For a moment her round, chubby face was rigid; then it crinkled into grief and she wept gulpily. "I try so hard to be good, and you're all against me; all of you." She lumbered from her chair and into the bedroom, closing the door squeakily. Uncle Herm muttered in his whiskers. All at once he went out of the house. But Johnny sat scared and hardly breathing, until Kurt's heavy lips folded back in a grin. "Let's go to bed," he yawned.

Johnny was still wide-eyed with wakefulness though Kurt snored beside him when Uncle Herm came back. He heard the bedroom door downstairs squeak again. There was a jumbled sound of talk, heard but not understood, over which Aunt Phrena's voice rose once: "Such a man. That boy's marked." And Uncle Herm's: "Phrena——" And Aunt Phrena's: "Don't you tell him. For my sister's sake I'll save him and——" Then the jumble again.

In the rustling quiet of the dark, gnawed at screekily by a mouse in the studding, he lay, brain in a roil, the pieces of yesterday and today large in his mind, each thought a worry so black and oversized that Aunt Phrena's words were dwarfed into nothingness. But they remained, dark seeds for tomorrow's growing.

After a while the wall above the stairs glowed and Uncle Herm tiptoed up, the candle shining in his whiskers. "Sleep well, boy," he muttered, patting the pillow awkwardly. Then he whispered as if to himself, "So like your ma you look." He cleared his throat. "You're home now with me—with us," he added quickly, and creaked downstairs.

In time Johnny would get used to what he had seen this night, for he would be a part of it then—Aunt Phrena bawling suddenly and Uncle Herm grouching from the house, mutters drawing at his lips. Long afterward Johnny would think about Uncle Herm's saying once as something held back so long it had to be said, "Diff'rent as pig and porcupine, your ma and her sister Phrena. I liked one of them and, darn me, I married the other. That Albert Schwartz was a lucky plug." Which didn't say much. But that was before Johnny put the two and two of the puzzle together and figured out that Phrena was Uncle Herm's second wife and Uncle Herm was Aunt Phrena's second husband. "We tried it twice," Uncle Herm used to say; "yep, twice we tried it, both of us. Never learned a damned thing, either."

But this night Johnny breathed jerkily and wondered how skinny his soul really was. Was it like the scrawny, rib-marked cat his mother—— His mother. All other thought cracked to bits. He wanted to call, "Where are you, Mother, where are you?" but Kurt slept moistly beside him, shoulder near. Under this strange roof, he crowded back the gulps that pressed against his lungs. Tears came and with mouth against a pillow he cried wetly into sleep.

3

Uncle Herm had a hundred and twenty acres, homesteaded years before by his brother, now dusting to earth in the churchyard. It was a good piece, the eastern edge humped up into a ridge of pasture land, the rest in timber where it wasn't under plow. The south side, mostly low land, was part in trees and part in meadow. Through its clumps of willows and its shady places where Johnny hunted for acorns, the creek snaked its silver body, vanishing at last into the darkness of Norton's woods south. It was silent in the pools and rushy over stones. Here, in warm seasons as they grew to middling size, they came, he and Kurt and Snoose, and dived from the black rocks into the deep holes where bass bugged their red eyes at them. Once hate flashed here in an upthrust of water that all three remembered.

But at first Johnny remained close to the buildings and the clearings, half-fearful of the shadows crowding in from the south woods and the owls screeching in the dusk, although Kurt laughed at him and Aunt Phrena watched teary-lidded. The ridge was different, he decided. It lifted high above the farm and the farms of the neighbors, and took the last fire of the day. He'd have the beginning of a grin pulling at his lips when Uncle Herm took him there for a load of windfalls. Bully and Bill, the oxen, puffed by the time they drew the wagon into the clearing. It was a place bright with sun, where finches in autumn clawed in the white hair of the bull-thistle heads, feasting on the dark seeds, and fleabane lifted their frilly white faces above the stumps. Fox slunk here, eyes almost topaz with suspicion, scenting the air for dog or man-smell, and chipmunks flicked their tails in the underbrush.

The first time they stopped in this place, Uncle Herm said, "Look; look down there." He leaned his back against a young ironwood tree, one arm sagged about Johnny, the other pointing. "That's Pockerbrush—what you can see of it; hills and woods and clearings. That's my field not far from the crick—forty acres of new breaking. Over there's the Diemer Hills and there—see the tamaracks sticking up? That's the swamp. There's deer there, and bear, too. They got my spotted calf last fall. And 'way over there—see the smoky blue on the other side of the hills?" He bent forward as if to follow his index finger pointing. Johnny blinked fast to see better. "That's the Valley. There's Dakota flats beyond—miles and miles, thousands, for all I know. And a big river they call the Red. I've seen it—wider'n my field and boats full of wheat and timber ridin' north to Fort Garry."

It was a white minute to lay among the black hours of day and night and the blacker mound in the churchyard far and ridges away from these hills and this level place where quiet slanted down with the shadows.

He came here alone after a while, following the open woods road around a corner where no shadows hid. He looked down on the yard below, the square house of boards instead of logs (Aunt Phrena could say proudly it was the only frame house in miles), the barn with the lean-to, the sheds and the oaks blackening the pigpen with shade. There was a kind of safety lodged in those sturdy rafters and behind those stout walls—timbers Uncle Herm had raised and hammered into place with neighbors' help. Something of Uncle Herm, strong and reliable, jutted out with the square, sharp angle of the eaves. But there was Aunt Phrena with her short tubby stares, slapping into silence what might have been a laugh upon his lips.

Over west across the seven-acre patch lay the Marchens' place, hidden by a strip of trees, their fields to the north. Snoose lived there and his big-boned sister Sophie. To the south of them the Dunkel barn pointed a red gable above the clearing. Mr. Nussbaum and his narrow acres were next, the one as dour as the others were stony. Beyond the creek was Mr. Schadel's place, a small blacksmith shop on his yard where the threshing rig stood the summer long. And lost somewhere in the oaks on the other side of the Schadels' was the Hukelpoke farm. Alb was the best horse

jockey and pigsticker in the ridges: so the folks said. There was none
his like on the horsepower at threshing time: so he bragged. Uncle
Herm's neighbors these were, folding their talk and ways stripwise into
the growing matter of Johnny's thought.

But there were hours when the loneliness welling up irresistibly as
springs in a well couldn't be held back and, young as he was, he felt
haltered and bridled. There was yet much of his mother snagged in the
tangles of his memory. And what wasn't there he built with his fancy, out
of emptiness. He'd be carrying lunch to Uncle Herm, one hand caught
in old Sport's brown ear, the other fast on the handle of the half-gallon
bucket, trotting along, when a cowbell lost in the ravine or a stretch of
pathway losing itself in the lonely swamp would bring back sweet as
wild-rose petals her voice:

> "Johnny-behind-the-rocking-chair,
> Oh, where do you go, where, oh, where?
> To the brook for water so clear, so clear
> And the honeycomb sweet and golden fair."

He'd rump down to earth bawling quietly, head on one side, hopelessly,
with a depth of sorrow that left him hiccoughing; until Sport whined and
he got up, ashamed of tears even before the dog, and dried his eyes so
that Uncle Herm wouldn't see.

One evening he left Uncle Herm and Aunt Phrena over their milk
pails and ran wild down the road, blind to the woods that were dimming
tree by tree in the dusk, blind to everything but the sharp necessity of
running, running home to Mother. He came back screaming, his brain
hurting with the dreadful shriek that had prickled into his ears out of the
shadows. He legged it straight for Uncle Herm, never seeing Aunt
Phrena and the arms she stretched out. He almost upset him in a wild
rush to shut away what slunk behind tree and bush.

Kurt teased him for that. "Little tit-baby, that's what you are. Scared
of a screech owl." But Aunt Phrena, letting drop her out-held arms,
regarded him shortly, as something that had escaped her. She was stern
over the fast and angry way he sprawled off Uncle Herm's knees, black
hair flying, his black eyes bright with tears. He clenched the fists that
were no longer than Indian potatoes, shouting at Kurt, "You'd be
scared, too."

It was that night she put him in a chair and made him repeat the
Comfort passages to her. "About time you learned your Scriptures, hot
temper as you've got. Say after me: 'All we like sheep have gone astray.'"

She spoke soggily but there was sharpness under her tone, rock under wet moss.

Uncle Herm tugged his whiskers, disturbed. Kurt sat listening near by. But Johnny's voice was almost lost under the table, he scrouged so low in his chair: "'All we like sheep . . .'" Afterward, before Kurt came up to bed, he dragged into the candlelight the wooden box with the Indian face painted on it, and from the boy's clutter within brought out a doll with a china head and a scarlet ribbon round its neck. A girl's plaything, he admitted with shame, but precious because Mother had smiled from her bed when she put it into his hands. Over and over, he ran a finger along the red ribbon, a kind of solace for him then. Later, when Kurt's foot came on the stairs, he put the doll away quickly and shoved the box under the bed.

With farm truck he was at first awkward as a new-dropped calf so that Kurt used to hoot him into rages over fork and rake. Grass stubble in the hay fields, sharp as splinters, punched his toes bloody. He'd get his fingers cramped from the round of the hoe or his legs stiff from crouching over a bundle of corn, ripping the husks from the ears with a slender tip of cow horn scrapped down to a size smaller than a little finger.

Evenings, he'd struggle in to supper, weary to the final knuckle, and fall asleep with the last prune in the dish half-divided. It was then that Aunt Phrena, as though caught unawares, would regard his huddled shoulders with a kind of longing in her eyes, the tears not far. Once his black eyes fluttered into wakefulness before she knew, and the yearning he saw in her face, tender with dreams that echoed memory, brought back his mother in a rush. She put out a hand, intensity in the solidness of her fingers, as if in a moment she'd scissor away all the wasted years of waiting and take him as something rightfully hers into the hungry circle of her arms. She drew aside quickly at his startled jerk; folded her lips primly and clattered a plate. He slid from his chair, sleep falling from his body in swift uneasiness.

But she was alien to tenderness the evening the egg basket slipped from his hand. There was a sick look about him as he pulled his foot back from a mess of shells and yolk running yellow in the grass. A spatter lay on his ankles.

"Reg'lar fumble-fist, ain't you? Moon-eyed as Snoose Marchen," Kurt snickered, as if he enjoyed this. "Gonna be a long spell before you'll milk the red heifer."

Aunt Phrena said when she heard, "Dry bread for a week, that'll take the clumsiness out of you. What you do, you do wrong, don't you?" Yet she put a boiled egg on his plate the next morning and the hog-lard for butter within reach, though why, he couldn't make out, for she muttered that he could smash all the eggs in the henhouse, if he wanted to, her cakes could go without; but no child of her poor sister was going to starve, no matter what he was like. She sopped a tear with her apron, asking, "Boiled too hard, the egg?"

He was hangdog under her blame; confused, too, and wishing that Uncle Herm, away threshing, were here. With hunger crawling in his belly, however, he spooned the egg with more relish than he knew, considering how Kurt glowered over his mush. But remember her words he would—words spiky and heavy as weights: "What you do, you do wrong, don't you?" It was the beginning of doubt and rebellion, though he didn't know it.

He remembered the afternoon Mr. Marchen brought the heifer because of the cows and the boy who played at threshing. Uncle Herm was at the Peisers' with the rig; he and Kurt were in the garden with Aunt Phrena when Mr. Marchen drove up, the heifer stubborn and bulge-eyed at the rope's end.

"Where's your bull, Phrena?" he shouted. "I've had enough of this heifer bullin' around." A lean man, with a limp in his knee, Mr. Marchen, tall as Uncle Herm, whiskery and tough as tug leather, with a temper like hot coals whipping out sudden and fierce as the blacksnake that curled in his fist. Yet in moments when nothing crossed his ire, he was jovial and brimming with rough laughter. He had a way of hitching up his suspenders that made Alb Hukelpoke grunt, "No wonder his pants won't stay, his wife takes 'em down so much." But his cattle and his kids bore the hard scars of his swift and unpredictable humor.

He took Johnny with a measuring look and a kind of snicker. "Well, so you're little Johnny Schwartz: a little Schwartzie, all right, hair and eyes and all. Does he take after his old man any?" he asked, lugging at the heifer; and was unaware of Aunt Phrena's quick movement and stiffening back—as though he'd pried into her back closets and snuffed at that which she wanted to hide. Strident as a cicada in the dog days, his voice wriggled into Johnny's ears as snakily as his whip did over the nervous team. Something in Mr. Marchen's tone—— Johnny didn't know why, but a kind of shame arose and lay red on his cheeks. Nobody had ever spoken his name that way. The rope gripped in his hands, Marchen was demanding, "Where's your bull, Phrena; in the pasture?"

Aunt Phrena hid outrage in her sunbonnet. Such talk before kids and women. She ordered, "Go to the house both of you," and pointed Mr. Marchen to the barn.

Indoors Johnny itched with curiosity over Kurt's sniggering, "Ma—

she says kids ain't supposed to know about things; not till they're grown up. Huh! I know what the bull does."

"With the heifer?" Johnny was eager.

But Kurt gurgled mysteriously, "That's for me to know and you to find out." The lever of no argument could pry more than that out of him.

Johnny left him to his secret and sneaked through the back door, his mind on the shiners in the creek. He crossed the seven-acre patch: let Aunt Phrena gather dill seed herself, or get Kurt to do it. He was restive when she stood and watched him, tears welling and her chin wobbling. Over the strip of plum hedge lay Mr. Marchen's field. A cowbell *clunk-clunk-clunked* near by.

As he entered the meadow, a *r-r-r-r* and a *hum-m-m-m-m* burst through the plums, high-pitched and vigorous. With rapid heartbeat, he wondered whether this was the grumphus gopher, that monster Alb Hukelpoke told about only last Sunday: "I got one in my back pasture. Worst animal I ever seen. It's got an auger for a mouth and his hole's so deep a cow'd fall in and be lost. Kids? Sheetin' Judas, he eats 'em like cranberry sauce." Johnny listened now, breath drawn. Then a voice yelled, "G-up, there, Jerusalem." Again came the *r-r-r-r* and the *hum-m-m-m-m*. Silence then, until somebody called, "I see you standing there. Come on over." There was a chuckle. "I'm thrashing my wheat. Want to help?"

Afterward Johnny felt that he must have known Snoose long before that afternoon, they pitched into the play of harvest together with so little questioning. At once horsepower and separator, Snoose was the thresher, his gray eyes dreamy over the piles of grain and his hair tousled. His small sad face had a kind of longing in it, as if it were looking for something that was lost just over the hill. Neither of them saw how the cows drifted westward, nor Mr. Marchen's long shadow.

All within an hour they sowed their grain in grass, enduring floods; cradled it from the stem before the teeth of storms; and gathered it for the thresher. Snoose showed him how to pull fistfuls of long stems. With a blade of grass he tied them into bundles. So Mr. Dunkel did with straw, whistling behind Uncle Herm's cradle in the exchange of harvest. These bunches they piled circlewise in stacks, cone-shaped like small beehives—not far different except for size from those Uncle Herm piled in the yard. Uncle Herm was no more careful over the placing of each bundle or the shaping of the bulge and slant of the stack than Snoose was.

Johnny was the pitcher of the rig. Snoose threshed the bundles, tearing them to pieces by scratching them furiously dog-fashion over his knees, the *r-r-r-r* of the horsepower between his teeth and the *hum-m-m-m-m* of the separator on his lips. Sometimes he yelled, "G-up, there, Jer-u-s'lem," as

Alb Hukelpoke did to the circling horses, and kicked up grass until green ribbons stuck in Johnny's black hair.

"I'm gonna be a thrasher when I grow up," Snoose crowed. Charley he had been baptized but they called him Snoose ever since the day Mr. Marchen, giving him a pinch of snuff, had laughed as over a joke and whooped, "Little Snoose-Charley," when, puke-sick and vomiting, Charley had rolled on the ground. "A big thrasher," Snoose vowed. Once he said strangely, "If we had a long straw carrier—long enough to reach the sky— we could carry straw to heaven. St. Peter's there, Gramma says."

Gladness warm as spring rain washed over Johnny for this hour, this hour that touched gently the bruised edges of his loneliness. But when Snoose said, "I guess you can thrash my oats next," he hunched down, eagerness shoving his knees forward, his grin white. He waited for Snoose to pitch the bundles on his knee. A queer silence fell.

Before a stalk dropped, there was a burst of feet across the stubbles and Mr. Marchen towered over them, eyes white-rimmed with rage, the blacksnake wriggling. "Monkeying," he yelled; "and the cows eating themselves sick in the corn. You damn little——"

His arm shot down. The blacksnake crackled. Grass bundles tipped where the lash struck, inches from Johnny's knees. The whistled swish of leather was sharp. Johnny gripped his pants. But Snoose wasn't there. Even while his father trod the stubble, he had sucked in his breath, as one long practiced: a crash in the plums and he was running like a singed fox, the hedge between him and the whip.

Mr. Marchen was ready to spit wrath and rip into Johnny, or anything in his path, stump or dog. Johnny felt his belly go numb. But with a "Damn it all, anyway," Mr. Marchen swung and limped away, the blacksnake slithering behind him.

Scared to his inner backbone, Johnny slunk off. Weeks later he'd wake up in the dark, sweaty and bound by a spell of fear, sure that Mr. Marchen was lashing a red whip out of the night. Now as he trotted along, following the hedge into the trees, he twisted backward in raw uneasiness.

He almost jumped when a basswood limb jiggled overhead and Snoose's sad face grinned wryly at him, a part of the leaves almost. "This's my linden tree. Nobody finds me here. I'm gonna build me a house up high someday."

But Johnny was pin-stuck with anxiety. "Your pa—he's mad. Won't he lick you?"

"I guess so," Snoose answered mournfully, as one who knows that reward is worm-holed with agony. "He kicked me once so I couldn't sit for two days." There was a kind of pride in his father's achievement. "Your pa lick you?"

"I—" Johnny hesitated—"never saw my pa. He died long ago, my mo-mother says. She's dead, too." Loneliness almost smothered him.

"Then she's walked up Jacob's ladder," Snoose said excitedly. "Didn't you know?" And when Johnny shook his head, wordless, Snoose explained, "My gramma told me. When you die, you walk up——"

"Snoose-Charley!" Mr. Marchen's voice roared over the fields and rattled in the basswood leaves. Johnny moved restlessly. Snoose began climbing sadly down. "S'long. Guess I'll catch it again."

Johnny had a sort of rebellion in him, watching Snoose go. That Mr. Marchen—— His fist doubled. Then he saw the whip again. Hastily he dodged into the seven-acre patch, emptied of assurance. With instinctive blind-mole faith, he crept home and upstairs and cooled his fist on the china head of the doll with the red ribbon. That Mr. Marchen—— Whip or no whip, this wasn't the last hour he'd spin off with Snoose. The ribbon waved from his tight fingers.

But one day Aunt Phrena "cleared up his truck." She put his stuff on a wall shelf and flung the box with the Indian head into the woodshed. "Makes good kindling for the kitchen stove," she said. She held the doll in her fist awhile, her face caught in a moment of struggle between a tear and a snort. Then she put it gently on the shelf, a kind of scorn large on her lips. He found it there.

When Kurt laughed, Johnny thrust it from sight. No matter in what cranny he hid it, however, the doll would be there again, white-faced and black-haired on the shelf, whenever she finished tidying the room. Aunt Phrena always felt better when she came upon the doll where he had hidden it and could put it on the shelf where he'd see it the first thing. It became a sort of joke at last. That is, outwardly. Underneath there moved in him even then a hot breathlessness that made him shiver and choked his giggle. But Kurt laughed loudly.

Perhaps it was this, perhaps something else, rooted in his bone and indefinable, that began to grow and push gently between him and Kurt; in a way, between him and Aunt Phrena, too.

4

By degrees no sharper than the inevitable shift of darkness into light and one day into another, the farm and the neighborhood grew around his memory like dodder around a wheat stalk. What was new and rough-cornered with strangeness when he arrived, like Uncle Herm's cradling wheat, became worn with familiarity and common as dishrags: almost forgotten after Uncle Herm brought a reaper home and there were two machines, his and Mr. Nussbaum's, to clatter in the ridges. Johnny bounced with curiosity over hearing about Mr. Dunkel's feud with Old Geppert but accepted it at last as an old tale thrice told and now a part of neighborhood lore. Uncle Herm's standing tall and bent forward a little on the separator—that he kept in memory as he did his first stick-knife, a precious memory.

There was the farm, once no larger in the woods than the space a man needed to swing an ax in. It was growing now and spreading—acres that pushed blackly against the towers of oak and pine where the plow had shoved a blunt nose under the thin hide of forest land and turned needle-and-leaf mold into furrows of darkly shining soil. There was the creek where the red-eyed sandfish hid and over northeast beyond the ridge the lake which mirrored hill and field and the cows in the slanted woods. With willow poles light on their shoulders and shiners from the creek in their bucket, he and Kurt would go fishing there, swinging their home-braided lines from the rocky ledges. In quiet bays water lilies spread their white petals like feathers around their golden hearts and flag lifted its purple blossoms. Rock bass hungrily struggled at shiner and hook, and the loons called the season's weather.

They brought home messes of fish on the crotch of a willow. If she were cheerful, Aunt Phrena would say, "Ach, so many fish. Who caught the most?" and set them down to cookies and barley coffee fresh from the stove.

"We smelled it, the coffee, clean over in the pasture," Johnny'd tell her, crinkling into his white smile. "Shall I call Uncle Herm to lunch?"

In such a moment sweet with the cinnamon of the *Kaffeekuchen* she was making, he regarded her shapelessness awhile and asked, "Was Mother—my ma—young once and pretty like—like Gatha Blumen, maybe?"

She wheeled quickly for one of her bulk. Her eyes like hands explored his face. "That sounded like Schwartz." Her tone was only half-audible. Then she clattered a pan. "Can't you see I'm busy?" She was snappish. "And don't smear the table with syrup, either."

But if she had a moody streak showing when they brought the fish, she'd squeal, "Haven't I enough to do without cleaning fish? Get those stinkin' things outside. They're dirty as thrashers. Clean them yourselves." He never knew any more than Uncle Herm what to expect in her and wished he could remain as unfluttered as Kurt, or had a storm glass to measure her weather shift like the barometer Uncle Herm used to predict fair days or blustery outside.

He liked to wait at the patch-end and watch Uncle Herm at seedtime striding across the field and leaving tracks a scatter-width apart, flinging wheat with a bold sweep of his arm. He'd catch up a handful and toss the kernels far, though Kurt yelled, "Don't waste wheat like that."

At harvest time he was pucker-lipped over getting his fingers smeary while Uncle Herm, tinkering with the reaper, grumbled, "Moses Almighty, half the time this damn contraption don't work." Later on there'd be a ribble of wheels and Uncle Herm would start for Mary's Hill to fetch out the "expert" with his bag of tools and his talk about a "harvester" which the machine companies were manufacturing. "Elevates your grain onto a platform right on the machine," the expert would tell excitedly. "You bind it there, not on the ground, as you do now." Uncle Herm only snorted, "Harvester! More pieces to break and fly around. You fix this one first."

Mr. Dunkel, still harvesting his grain with a cradle, would stop sometimes and regard Uncle Herm with neighborly commiseration. "Old ways is the best ways," he'd say, for all that he was seasons younger than Uncle Herm. "I'll stick to my sickle." The year Uncle Herm bought a seeder and a reaper, Dunkel spoke out bluntly. "You and Nussbaum, you run your noses deeper into debt, Herman, all that new machinery. Nope. Whoop-Jinny-and-fall-down, I'll cradle my wheat and know it's right; stick to my oxen, too." His friendly, round face said plainly, crease by crease, "How much you owe Norton by now?" With a wrinkle on his brow, Johnny saw that Uncle Herm uneasily trod a dirt lump. He yearned someway to put a hand against the slump in Uncle Herm's shoulder.

The come-and-go of country ways, the curve of fork, the depth of a milk pail—these Johnny learned fast. Even Kurt admitted that at potato picking he was fairish. "He's quick, Johnny is, but he's dirty; more dirt than spuds in his pail." At ten he milked the red heifer though she swiped his nose and left it bloody. He was so braggy that night that Kurt pinched heavy lips. He soon liked the lazy restfulness that crept over him, head against the cow's warm side and the teats soft in his hands. He squirted milk under the pressure of his fingers, laughing at Kurt's dislike of the job. "Couldn't you push a straw up her teat and let the milk down that way?" Kurt wanted to know, and tried it once. But Uncle Herm caught him and Kurt came near getting a hiding. Sometimes on rainy fall mornings, when even the rooster's arching tail dragged in the mud and the cattle in the yard were lying huddled, heads to their middles for comfort, Johnny came teetering, his bare feet shrinking from the chill grass and ice-cold. He scared up a cow where she lay and burrowed his toes and heels in the loose earth, body-warm from her ribs and belly. He'd shiver, feeling the warmth soak into his soles and spread through his toes, as he waited for Kurt.

The last cow stripped, he and Kurt brought their cups and drank the milk, fresh and steaming. The animal heat of the udder was as warm as the blood in their lips, and the froth a mustache under their noses, white against the summer-brown of their skin. Mrs. Dunkel used to say that milk hot from the heifer brought on rheumatism but so far neither complained of cricks in the joints.

They hung their cups on nails driven into the milk stand. After a loud quarrel one night, Johnny sure that Kurt had put his mouth to the wrong cup, they had dug eightpenny nails out of their pants and gouged their names deep in the tin on the bottom of the cups. The "Johnny Schwartz" on the one was scrawly and impatient, with the tail of the 'y' running almost to the rim, a silver streak where Johnny pressed hard and the nail slipped. The "Kurt Barewolf" in the other was as neat and orderly as Aunt Phrena's sewing basket, the letters, as if measured, squarely in the center of the bottom.

After milking they'd slosh the tins in the water trough. When he was at home, Uncle Herm showed them how to tell fortunes. They'd try it, Kurt lucky, Johnny peevish over his luckless cup, spilling the water pettishly. But Aunt Phrena sputtered, "Herman Barewolf, don't you know no better than that? And you kids—you should better read your Comfort Books."

In spite of Mr. Marchen's whip and the loud voice yelling, "Hey, Schwartzie," suddenly in his ear and the louder laughter, Johnny wore a path through the seven-acre patch, going to Snoose's. He was ear-plugged to Aunt Phrena's, "Can't stay home, no?" Once she added, "Like somebody else," and his head shot up.

He only growled at Kurt's noisy "Don't know how to spell 'work,' you do so little of it," and flung back, "Who bedded the oxen last night?" Usually, he'd sweat over a chore Uncle Herm set him at and finish it without a murmur. But when he could he kicked over the pole and wasted half a day's work with Snoose. Like two wolves they slipped through brush where at mating time cock partridge strutted before his mate and the veery lamented from the swamp. They crept slow as lynx shadows up on beaver slapping mud on a dam in the creek and waited while one, brown as a cinnamon stick and flat of tail, chewed round and round a popple until the tree tottered and swayed reluctantly to earth, sawed to the heart by white woods' teeth.

When prairie gophers squeaked in their holes, they found buckets and on Sunday afternoons "drownd-ed them out," Johnny explained to Uncle Herm. But Kurt held aloof from soiling the Sabbath. Of this Aunt Phrena approved.

Snoose carried the water and Johnny waited, willow stick poised above the hole. As the striped animals, sneezing moistly, popped from the grass roots, Johnny pounded them into limpness. Blood incredibly scarlet swelled at their nose-ends. "They waste grain by the bushel," Johnny scolded, poking at the shattered heads. Snoose wouldn't touch them. A kind of sorrow deepened his sad face. But he joined the drowning with enthusiasm and his bucket was never empty. Afterward they wolfed hungrily the slabs of bread, thick and dark, which Sophie buttered for them. One Sunday she had a kettle boiling and fished fried cakes from the sizzling grease—"doughnuts," Mrs. Edgely called them; but she was Yankee and could be forgiven such foreign and outlandish notions.

Over a lardy circle he was munching he watched Sophie, her big body and her heavy breasts, arms stretching her sleeves until they shone with smoothness. There was no fat like Aunt Phrena's on her bones, but muscle like Mr. Dunkel's or Heinie Beerwagon's. She was the only girl in the hills who dared to step into a pair of pants in the sun of daylight. "Na, that Sophie Marchen—more man than woman," the neighbors said. She whistled waltzes and polkas, the tunes clear as a loon's call on quiet nights, so that Johnny, hearing, stopped in his steps, though Aunt Phrena sniffed and Uncle Herm laughed. At the dances Uncle Herm slapped Sophie on the buttocks when Aunt Phrena wasn't looking and teased her into a square dance whenever he could. She sang alto in the choir later on, and Johnny thought she sounded more bass than Rob Nussbaum.

"More cakes?" She offered the dish and scratched the lobe of his ear so that he nickled his head to his shoulder but liked it. He laughed in her face when she complained, "You boys got it handy: two pushes and you're in your pants, mornings. But girls—they got to hook and button and fuss with eyes. My skirt-tails tangle my ankles. Pants is the best, anyhow." She teased the red into his face with a verse:

> "Here comes that laughing Johnny Schwartz;
> Girlies, run; he's coming for your hearts."

His teeth shone as he finished the doughnut, though he didn't half like the song.

Unaware of grease rings they left on the table, he and Snoose banged from the house. From the window she saw them go, boy arm on boy shoulder. "Two kids like that, a black head and a sandy head—that would be good to see in my cradle. Clymy, Clymy, don't run away from me," she murmured. The boys closed the barn door behind them.

They talked boy matters in man fashion, Snoose's gray eyes with the long fringes dreaming away over the hills so that at times Johnny was sure he wasn't there at all except in body and nudged his ribs to bring his mind back. Snoose had a queer way of poking into notions as mysterious to Johnny as the fairy tales Mrs. Sperry read at school. "I'll see you at midnight," he'd tell Johnny when they were ready to part for home.

"Huh, by that time you couldn't wake me with a sledge hammer," Johnny'd answer, matter-of-factly.

"I'll come anyway." Seeing the expression on Johnny's face, he'd chuckle. "I'll kick against your bedstead." Or he'd say, "I was born on the lick-end of leap year; pretty near came not being born at all, Gramma says," as if there were a joker in this.

There was the summer's day when Johnny hobbled in the yard, itchy with poison ivy. Nothing in Aunt Phrena's medicine bottles did more then redden the skin; her scolding hardly eased the burning: "Run with Charley Marchen, no wonder you get into such stuff."

He protested, "Don't know where I got it. Oh, I could scratch the hide off."

Snoose made fun of him gently. "This'll learn you to watch before you sit down in the brush." His laugh was a slow gurgle in his throat. "Next time you grab for a handful of grass, you'll watch out for a three-leaved blister vine. Come on."

Johnny followed him sprawl-leggedly to a willowy place on the creek. Touch-me-not hung orange-and-brown-spotted jewels here. "Old Man Fleischer showed me." Snoose reached a hand toward the rank growth. "It's good for the itches, he says. Maybe he has got a hex, like they say, but he's good and he knows things."

From a fistful of dripping stems, lush as lily stalks, he squirted juice on the pimples. In a day, it seemed, Johnny ran free of the scratching. He had no words of gratitude and Snoose wouldn't have known what to say, if thank words had been spoken. They accepted their friendship as they did the black haws they shared, respect in each for what the other had a fancy about, whether it was Snoose gawking at an October wasp nestled in the fold of a leaf or Johnny hammering a bean thresher out of a box, with an armful of barrel staves for concaves.

Thereafter from a skein of memory Johnny untangled talk about his mother. Added up, there wasn't much to tell. Once he ventured, "She

never said a word about my pa. Not even when I asked; only looked so—
so sad. You s'pose——" He didn't finish his thought. Whatever it was, it
brought such black loneliness that Snoose cried, "Don't, Johnny; don't
look so," and put a hand on his knee.

5

He took Uncle Herm as he took meat, sufficient for emptiness and more
than emptiness; took him as he did Snoose. He'd desert the warmth of
bed with the first rattle of the stove downstairs and leave Kurt snoring in
a tumble of pillows in order to join Uncle Herm in the barn. He got
the feel early of leather tugging in his palms and gee-upped the team like
Alb Hukelpoke so that Uncle Herm exclaimed, "That's the stuff; hit
'em on the tail." But with Bully and Bill the oxen he was short of
patience; jerked their yokes and jabbed them with the goad, disregardful of
gall sores on their shoulders where the curved wood lay. "Might as well
harness a worm. I got to get faster," he'd tell Uncle Herm. There was
more than leather beginning to bind them together, these two, side by
side, stiff-legged against the bump of a wagon.

Going after the cows, he'd grumble aloud to himself as Uncle Herm
did, over the price of wheat and butter and the cost of a harness or a
plow: "Got us where the hide is short, the damn skin-flint merchants."
He knew only a quarter of what he was mouthing and that not clearly,
disturbed because Uncle Herm was disturbed. And one time Uncle Herm
caught him swinging a bullwhip in the upper pasture, whaling the shreds
off a young oak tree. "What in tarnation Moses Almighty—" he demanded,
and Johnny, face red and hang-dog in his shoulders, muttered, "He's a
railroad man, the oak. Didn't you say the God-damn thieves ought to be
rawhided?" Uncle Herm wanted to laugh so hard his belly hurt but
didn't. Aunt Phrena would be saddened to tears over the swearing if she
found out.

It helped, though, this sharing a burden, and made Johnny feel that
the farm was not alien soil and that the problems that speared up like
weeds with the wheat were his to tackle as much as the wild mustard or
the cockle.

But under his ribs he was afraid of Aunt Phrena and in a queer fashion.
This was true especially after the spring evening he ripped a finger on a
rusty nail and the blood spurted. He was afraid not of her hands as

Snoose was of his father's fists and the rawhide twisting, but fearful of her moist droopiness and her tongue. He'd rather have taken a birching twice over than one of her teary "search-your-soul talks," as she called them, when she laid his misdeeds bare with mournings and then with gushing cheeriness covered every black patch with white assurances out of the Precious Comfort Book. He wanted to believe them and her, jot and tittle, but wallowed in uncertainty instead. He'd look at her and cringe, her roundness made rounder by the nobility of Christian duty.

He wished more than once that the mice would get at the Precious Comfort Book, that volume with the split back and the finger-worn covers which contained verses from the Scriptures ripped out of context for the kernel of the promise they contained, soothing as the syrup-of-figs Mrs. Dunkel fed her Gretel when she cried. Verse by verse they were gathered, from Genesis to Habakkuk, from Matthew to John, under headings like "God's Blessing on Fields and Flocks," and "Food Never Failing for the Lord's Children." Some pages were smeary with wetted finger stains, especially those covering "Prosperity in Business and Finance" and "Healing and Health Promised." And several leaves were wrinkled to tissue from use and falling apart, so often had Aunt Phrena turned to the portions that held the sure word on "Pious Christians Triumphant in Victory over Enemies and Trouble."

"Read the Book," Aunt Phrena would say stoutly. "Nothing you can name ain't there."

Uncle Herm ventured one time that there was hardly much sense in trying to get anything any more, we already as good as had more than we deserved, guaranteed and all. Aunt Phrena snapped the covers shut and moaned that that was blasphemous and came from the Devil's tongue. She waddled out of the room, weeping. Johnny gazed after her miserably.

Aunt Phrena said little about her first husband, Kurt's father; called him a good man and left it at that, out of respect for Uncle Herm, perhaps; but saw to it that Kurt was called Barewolf for last name and that Herman Barewolf was Uncle Herm to Kurt and not Pa Barewolf. Afterward Uncle Herm used to say with a kind of wistfulness, "Funny, all right; I got two kids on my place and none of my own."

She was slow-moving as a stoneboat and heavy on her feet and where she walked in the house the boards creaked a little and tiny shudders disturbed the skin over the water in the pails. She couldn't forget that she was a judge's daughter from Fergus and had married a farmer—a farmer who bought a half-share in a threshing rig and went into debt and turned thresher ("a dirty thrasher," she said). Now that she had married him, however, she'd stick to him. It was her bounden duty, she said, though she made it sound more like a cross.

The house was full of her family, pictured in sad poses on the wall, all of them large as to bust in the women and shaggy as to whiskers in the men. But right in the center place on the bureau where it struck the gaze the moment the sitting room door was opened was a picture of Uncle Herm's first wife, a vague, egg-shell-fragile looking woman whom Johnny had never heard Uncle Herm speak of—a part of his life too sacred for words. Aunt Phrena had put it there as if to remind herself with bittersweet wryness that she was only second mistress in this house of four rooms with an upstairs still unplastered.

She put hairwreath behind glass on one wall; on a shelf beside the mirror on the bureau, winter and summer, she had strawflowers in a beer stein that had leering faces on it, one with a long nose projecting above a wide mouth where a frost of dust gathered. Johnny liked the smooth feel of the nose between his thumb and forefinger as he wiped away the dust. She hung branches of black-oak leaves, fired red by autumn, on the walls, which let fall showers of color when Johnny and Kurt wrestled upstairs and shook the ceiling with their tumbles.

When she was happy she sang "Nearer, My God, to Thee" and rattled the house into order with energy. She set up a table steaming with odors to tickle smell and taste so that Johnny, hungry from an afternoon's planting of potatoes, felt the water flood over his tongue and his belly muscles crawl. She hoed in the garden and planted beds of bachelor's-buttons and love-in-a mist flowers (which Uncle Herm called Devil-in-the-woods). But when the sour days came, and they frequently did, she laid her tongue in soggy twists upon her household. Then the love-in-a-mist flowers became dirty with weeds.

The pale lemon of burnt-out day was thinning to duskiness one spring evening, when Johnny came running. The blood spurted from the torn finger. He was past ten years then; scared wide-eyed but clamping his jaw on the pain.

He rushed into the kitchen, blood punctuating each step redly. The jar of sauerkraut slipped from Aunt Phrena's fingers to the table. She clutched him hungrily in the extremity of her emotion, all the hard scrutiny of suspicion soft with compassion. "Poor little dove," she cooed; "my sister's own, don't cry. Aunt Phrena'll fix the finger." He wasn't crying but she was; tears squeezed between her stubby lids. He felt himself pressed into the pillow-soft yieldingness of her breasts as one day he had thrust his fists deep between two loaves of dough in a pan. He struggled like a collared puppy, real tears coming with a wave of something that made his stomach move. He screamed, "Don't touch me. Don't. You're—you're fat."

For a moment she was very quiet, holding him. Then she pushed him away gently, her eyes wide, soaked in water, but with a dreadful calm as if she saw renewed here in this young sprig that which she longed to forget. "Fat," she repeated, breathing out slowly. "So it is. I hear it yet again. Like Schwartz—his words almost."

He stood staring, fogged in amazement mixed with a sort of awe, her meaning dark and concealed from him. After a moment she waddled to the pantry for skunk oil and bandages. "Reach here, your hand," she ordered, her voice soft. But there was iron under it that he understood. He came fast. Her hands were deft and he felt ashamed but didn't know how to say he was sorry, not then or later, already gripped by a silence that was neither stubbornness nor indifference but a feeling that overwhelmed him into wordlessness whenever the tortured face of emotion came within his finger's reach.

Never again did Aunt Phrena put out a hand in caress upon him. From that day on she laid Schwartz in his mind like a blame-word.

Johnny never forgot how Uncle Herm looked the first time Aunt Phrena said bluntly, "There, Johnny; just like Schwartz." They were at table, Aunt Phrena poking at her meat with a fork and Uncle Herm reaching with his knife for a thin dab of butter. In a shift of hands Johnny dropped the slice of bread he held. He went after it, grumbling, "Devil take it, anyway."

"There, Johnny." Aunt Phrena spoke quickly. "Bad words in your mouth and you not yet eleven. Just like Schwartz."

Johnny came up with a red face. He saw Uncle Herm hold the knife to the butter rigidly for an instant. "Phrena, is it right that—" he began and broke off. Aunt Phrena's fork pricked the meat. There was a moment when it seemed knife and fork clattered like blades together in their glances. Then Uncle Herm put his knife down. A kind of futile regret deepened the wrinkles on his face; pain misted his eyes. He ate his bread unbuttered. Aunt Phrena smiled.

How often on a later day Uncle Herm's sad face over that supper table would come between the questions swelling Johnny's tongue and the answers Johnny urgently desired. But the queries would stop on the lip and he would let his inner longing feed upon dark scraps of doubt and uncertainty.

Young as he was, he twisted around sometimes to trap Aunt Phrena's hawklike vigilance or catch Uncle Herm's sidewise regard. Before long he began to lower his head over a persistent notion. "It's something about

my pa—something I ain't s'posed to know. Just like my pa I am, she says.
I wonder——" These were like shadows at first, elusive as minnows in
the creek. But they grew, wriggly as eels in his mind.

6

With September and the season circling round where darkness caught
up and ran upon the heels of daylight, Uncle Herm's eyes brightened with
thresher's fever. Before rooster cry he arose and worked restlessly in the
dawn. Peat smoke gathered in the valleys and thinned on the hills. In
his ears the hum of cylinders wound a lureful skein. The lean of a hill
was no barrier to the fields and stacks of grain beyond.

On one such a morning Johnny and Kurt helped him gather hog-rind
for packing and oak stakes for the power and saw him get ready to go to
Mr. Schadel's. "Me and Schadel and Hukelpoke—we got to tune up the
rig," he chortled over his breakfast egg and potatoes.

Aunt Phrena sniffed. "Running over to Schadels'. It's a wonder the
thrasher couldn't set in our yard one year."

Uncle Herm shrugged, knowing the futility of argument. The rig
never came to stay at the Barewolfs' after the season. Mr. Schadel, owner
of the one-quarter share, had a blacksmith shop on his place and fixed his
neighbors' smashed wheels and irons. In his yard where fire and forge
were handy to repair broken shaker rods and cracked braces, the separator
and the power usually remained. To this Uncle Herm and Alb Hukelpoke
(who owned the last quarter share) had no more objection than kids
let out on a hazelnut hunt. For ten months of the year, the rig was
something more talked about than seen. When Uncle Herm brought work
home, however, and in the granary riveted slats on the belt of the straw
carrier, Kurt hung near and Johnny all but crowded under the hammer.
He had a thumb smashed once when he swung at a rivet and missed.
For a week the nail was as purple as if it had been dipped into wild-grape
jelly.

After breakfast and the last crumb wiped away, Uncle Herm pitched
his tools into the old red toolbox he dragged from the granary. Eager-
limbed as if a polka danced in his legs, he grumbled jovially, searching
among the irons. "Now where in Moses Almighty is that S-wrench?" He
turned to Johnny and Kurt. "Did either of you kids——" But before they
could utter the "no's" in their heads, he banged a hammer down dully.
"Marchen. I remember. He borrowed it for his mower." He tugged at a
whisker. "Now, Johnny, you got long legs. Run over and ask Marchen
for that wrench, will ya? And put a little hustle in your knees."

Johnny wanted to say, "Let Kurt go," but he went. His legs had reluctant hustle, however. Even though the yard was empty of Marchens when he got there, he cringed in expectation of Mr. Marchen's "Hey, Schwartzie, how's the little-peter today?" That Mr. Marchen—he had a muddy tongue, all right.

Johnny thought: "Sophie or Mrs. Marchen—I'll ask them at the house." Then he heard a banging in the machine shed where Mr. Marchen kept his tools. Probably Mr. Marchen fixing something, he decided, going there hesitantly.

But it wasn't. It was Sophie, big-armed Sophie, bowed against a bench, one hand still fisted about the handle of a slop pail, the other pressed across her face, crying so that her shoulders swayed with inner tumult. He shuffled his feet, wanting to run. Then he came gently and silently. She let him take the bucket away as if she didn't care.

He felt cold and shaky. Sophie, big Sophie, twenty now, the oldest child in the Marchen family, and weeping here alone in the machine shed. She was the only one of his kids that Mr. Marchen didn't dare whip after the twelfth birthday. He tried it once when she was thirteen, overgrown and taller than he was and with arms that ripped her seams when she lifted a forkful of manure or a can of milk. He gave her one swipe of the rawhide. With rage grinding her teeth together she got the splitting ax from the woodpile and chased him across the yard and into the haymow where from a crossbeam he chattered and threatened for an hour before she cooled down. He left her alone after that; bragged of her strength, how she could shovel two men's work in the wheat at threshing time. She grew up a horse-legged, rangy woman with a large mouth and bony cheeks, her words as direct as a punch from the shoulder. She and Alb Hukelpoke used to wrestle like young men when she was over at his place, helping his wife. They did yet, when they got a chance. "Sheetin' Judas," Alb used to say: "she's got a holt on like a pair of pincers." The boys ragged him. "Can't put a girl down on the floor, can you? What a bull you are. Does your wife take you down in bed, Alb?" But when he growled, "Try it once," nobody did, afraid of her solid hands.

And here she was crying so that it hurt Johnny to hear her: Sophie, she who wore pants with red-braided suspenders and joked with the men, story for story. Why, only last Saturday night at the dance (Johnny heard it buzzed at church on Sunday morning), she had whistled and waltzed and softened her gray eyes for Clymy Humber. When the dance roughened after midnight and Alb got drunk and fresh, she grabbed him by the collar, dragged him to the center of the barn and knocked his head on a post until the blood spurted from his nose. Then she dumped him in front of Mrs. Hukelpoke and Alb's squealing kids. "Take that pig-eared man of yours and watch him," she yelled. "Next time he reaches in my dress, I'll break an arm off him." (How the congregation buzzed over this, the Pastor's vinegary jeremiads forgotten.) Mrs. Hukelpoke, bantam for size but wolf cub for spirit, flew at Sophie's hair and the crowd "ah-ed" into a circle, eager for a woman-fight. Sophie picked up Alb's wife and set her among her children kindly but with a bump. She waltzed away whistling, no grudge in her heart against Alb or his wife, knowing that none would be returned. She let her gaze follow a boy not half her size, Clymy Humber, who scuttled to the barn's end with a rabbity look.

And here she was, leaning over the bench, as tear-smeary, Johnny thought, as Gatha Blumen over a broken plaything at school. (But Sophie's tears were different from Aunt Phrena's.) "Oh, Johnny, Johnny," she moaned, rubbing her forehead. Ground oats from the slop pail dried on her nose. "Big and clumsy as an ox, that's what they say about me. Old she-bull Sophie." Her voice spilled bitterness.

"Clymy Humber?" he ventured, not knowing what else to say.

"Not him. The others. But he's scared of me. I ought to be ashamed, running after him. But I'm not; never will be, and that's why—why I'm bawling." Johnny was so muddled that she laughed wryly. "Jabbering such stuff to a ten-yearer. I'll be——"

"I'm eleven," he protested stoutly. "Next month, anyway."

"Bless the man's buttons," she began, a grin relaxing the tenseness. But he was serious and wouldn't be put off, the tears on her cheeks stirring what roiled in him.

He burst out, "Why do they call me Schwartzie? That name—it's—it's—oh, I don't know."

Her grin vanished. "So the hawks are at you too, and you no more than a little shaver. What you care?" she demanded fiercely. "A name—it's not inside you. It's like preacher's lice; it's on the outside of you somewhere." Softly she added for herself, "I'm not stopped yet. Nobody's going to, either." She thumped the slop bucket against the bench, thinking of Clymy. Tools rattled metallically. In his disturbance Johnny remembered the wrench.

Uncle Herm had hitched the team to the wagon by the time he returned, gaspy from running. "I'm scratching myself, waiting," Uncle Herm called, hiding impatience.

Johnny tossed the wrench. "Sophie found it for me."

Uncle Herm slammed the toolbox lid. "I'll be back Saturday and bring you a new slate for school," he said, stooping to touch Johnny's shoulder, one eye guardedly on the house where Aunt Phrena watched. "Giddap," he shouted eagerly.

When distance took the last rattle of his wagon into silence, Johnny slouched to the granary, as much disturbed by Sophie's grief as by Uncle Herm's leaving. He had a sagging weight in his stomach, for the wolf of loneliness snuffed at his heels when Uncle Herm's chair stayed unwarmed and empty and Aunt Phrena puffed at the head of the table. Forlornly he stepped on the rectangle white in the dust where the red toolbox had stood, mouse-nibbled these months of spring and summer. That much of the thresher Uncle Herm kept on his yard.

Balanced on one foot, Johnny marked in the dust with his big toe an H—two straight lines with a cross-bar—as if it were a mystic sign by which to hurry Saturday night along and bring Uncle Herm back for Sunday; or to bring a drizzle-mist to stop the rig for an afternoon, though threshing hadn't yet begun.

The rig would begin at the Pastor's (a sort of proper tithing) and thresh his small beehive of a stack or two, fashioned in the hot dog days by Mr. Whiteland. It was he who plowed the church land and seeded it to kernels different from those which the Pastor broadcast. And so there was about the Pastor's threshing the freshness of the field while the stacks of others weathered into grayness.

Sometimes the season was long, dragged on by contrary weather, so that winter set in and a drift of snow had to be shoveled away before the separator could be squeezed between the stacks. Once, so Uncle Herm told Johnny, stacks were dark and weather-worn at Christmas. The last of them weren't pounded out until January that year. The circle where the horses moved under Hukelpoke's red-hot tongue was tramped so hard a scab of crusted ice remained after all other snow had soaked away among the grass roots. The kids whooped in their games, following the smooth curved path.

7

With Uncle Herm gone six days of the week and blundering home late on Saturday night, the wind in Aunt Phrena changed and she seemed to have a private quarrel with God. "Sakes and days alive, now it starts. Cookin' and bakin' and messin' for thrashers." She thumped the Precious Comfort Book in a corner of the bureau and banged the kitchen stove. It was then that Johnny hitched off to school with zeal, though usually no bright fire of haste was struck from his plodding heels. Old Sport kept to the doggy shadows under the porch and even Kurt stepped lightly.

The Monday morning school began, he left Kurt fussing over his boots and was early at Snoose's gate, the new slate under his arm. He puffed air out of his mouth as if emptying his lungs of a smell. Autumn burned like brush fire on the ridges and vervain stuck purple spikes into the hazy air.

Snoose joined him. Leaving Kurt behind, they set off, half-gallon lunch buckets swinging at their sides. "Jackie and Bill don't have to go for two weeks," Snoose reported half enviously. "Pa needs 'em for thrashing and corn cutting." Johnny sighed with Snoose's envy.

They went northeast and left the print of bare toes in the path, faintly marked in the sand over the hill, deeply grooved in the moist dark earth of the hollow. Here jack-in-the-pulpit wrapped his withered canopy like a scarf about his bright cluster of berries. Johnny hated the tight pull of boot-leather on his ankles and went naked of foot even after frost laid a crinkly black cover on Aunt Phrena's cucumber bed. "Keep your boots on," she scolded. "You're like a horse—you like to stay unshod till freeze-up time." But Kurt seldom ran barefoot, even in summer. The stove polish was never black enough on his boots.

Aunt Phrena had her notions about the District School and said them. "Heathen and Hottentots go there; no Bible nor nothing. Not even a *Vater Unser* do they say there."

"It's the law," Uncle Herm tried to explain. "Church prayers and such in public schools ain't allowed and——"

"That Mrs. Sperry is a God-fearing woman, I know," interrupted Aunt Phrena. "Where is the wrong in a nice holy hymn? I'm glad our boys go to Pastor Steuber's next year and study catechism. Especially——" She let the word hang in Johnny's ears. Her look over him was slippery.

The schoolhouse was small and dirty cat-yellow. Boys and girls were buzzing in clusters like bees when Johnny and Snoose arrived. Gatha Blumen yelled, "Hello," and bounced over to see them, Em'ly Musser trailing behind her. Gatha was long-legged and rompy, a year younger than Johnny—about ten or so—and spiny with pigtails. "I heard a rhyme about you, Johnny," she said abruptly, her voice lowered breathlessly. "Listen once. 'Here comes that laughing—'"

He pulled Snoose away, red-eared and furious all at once, not at Gatha so much as at the laughter of the rest, should they hear. For they were all there, the neighbor kids: the Nussbaums, the Schadels, the Peisers, the Beerwagons (except Heinie who attended parochial school). For many of them this was the last year before confirmation study. The winter following they would struggle with the Catechism and chase Moses through the wilderness under the Pastor and his ministering yellow-birch stick.

There was much noise and running this morning. Already Mosey Fritz was scaring the girls with a toad he kept in his pocket, his weaselish face alive with trickiness. Lornas Tetzell egged him on. "He's a stinker from 'way back, that Mosey Fritz is," Snoose muttered to Johnny. Johnny nodded, jerking a thumb at Kurt, who was just then stalking up the path.

They trooped in when Mrs. Sperry tinkled her bell. She stood back of the desk, a welcome smile perched on her lips. She was short and wide in the hips and most of her weight was bunched where the Lord never intended it. Alb Hukelpoke used to say that most folks had a breadbasket in front but Mrs. Sperry had it behind. She wore the largest bustle in the ridges, a massive projection which everyone was sure must be of wire and springs. Lornas Tetzell swore it was; he heard the *zing* of metal, he said. When she paraded down the aisle at church, folks nudged one another. The bustle looked so like a saddle bouncing along that once Alb Hukelpoke muttered, "Where's the horse?" and added, "Jump on there, somebody, and ride." With one swift look Mrs. Sperry thrust him behind a hymnbook.

She held up her record book, ready to take roll, saying, "On this autumnal morning——" when there was trouble. Johnny had gone to the desk with the dog's head carved near the inkwell. But Mosey Fritz was there, a leg thrust across the seat. "Beat you to it, hey?" His lower lip was stuck out with elation.

"It's mine. I had it last year." Johnny's fist began doubling.

"S'pose you did? First come, first seated." Mosey's smile was large. "Lornas sits with me. Me and him want to be together."

Johnny hesitated, baffled by Mosey's right of possession, jumpy with ire at being thwarted, his teeth on edge in uncertainty. He might have turned away, had not Mosey, arrogant in triumph, demanded smuckily, "Order me around, hey? And you so poor your kinfolks have to take care of you."

Rage in a sudden thin fog webbed Johnny's sight. His hands reached for something—something with which to strike. His fingers closed over an object hard and cool. He lunged toward Mosey.

Snoose pulled him back. "Keep your britchin's up," Snoose yelled.

Johnny's sight cleared and he saw that he was holding Mosey's ruler ready to strike. It clattered from his fingers. Mosey crouched at the end of the seat.

Then Mrs. Sperry was saying, "I'll have no fisticuffs in my department of learning. You understand that?"

Johnny was shaking and weak all at once; stumbled after Snoose and slid into a seat beside him near a window, knowing how the school would titter. His tail had been lowered this day, all right, and by Mosey Fritz at that. But there'd be other days, the hours of other afternoons.

"I told you he was a stinker, that Mosey," Snoose said when they were ready to start for home. "Where's Kurt?"

"Staying behind again. He's getting a book on soils or something." Scorn tinged Johnny's tone. "First thing you know he's going to grow spuds on a rock pile. Let's go."

When they came to the lip of the hollow where the path straggled into the twisty raspberry vines and the shadows lay before them, Snoose looked back at the bright meadow they'd crossed. He always did, Johnny noticed, even in winter when the trees were naked. It was as if he were leaving flower-heat and sun in the roots for a moment of death in the gloom under the vaulty branches of the hollow. They entered a twilight so thick it deceived the owls into muffled lamentations at midday. They pushed aside the branches that interleaved across their way and brushed the rusty spikenard and withering sarsaparilla with their knees.

The hollow was cool on their shoulders and dusky. Somewhere a woods drum began its hooded beat, slowly, slowly at first with deliberation, swiftly in a blended ruffle at last: a partridge on a weather-stripped log, rub-a-dub-dub-ing the brief flight of autumn before the plunge into winter darkness. Snoose shivered, touched by the cold fingers of his own dark fancies, and pointed. Beyond a hazel bush jutted an oak stump, its tortured body wrapped in the charry coal of the flames' roar. "That could be a Crooked One, like Old Man Fleischer sees." His voice held a sort of quaver. "Or maybe a *Huldrekall*. But they're not black, Torsten says."

Johnny wanted to say, "It's only an old dead stump that's half burned," but he didn't, not because a shadow crossed him with its fear but because Snoose had a strange look when he hurried past this place. Johnny wasn't sure how to take him. But he accepted without resentment what he couldn't understand—something he found impossible to do toward Kurt. He knew that Snoose no more doubted omens and spells and the existence of goblins than Torsten Torgrimson, the hired man at the Peisers', disbelieved in the *hulder* of his boyhood Nordland. "Torsten says he saw a *Huldrekall* once, back in Norway. He was a little man in a blue suit with big brass buttons."

"Oh, like fun," Johnny scoffed.. "Such Noree-gian stuff."

"Don't know about that." Snoose spoke more easily now. The hollow had been left behind and they were on higher ground. The late afternoon sifted down brightly and the sun flicked reddish spots on a tree crotch over-

head. "My gramma—she remembers his story from the old country.
There were four men playing cards. They got drunk and swore something
awful and banged on the table, trumping their cards. And one man dropped
a card and went under the table to pick it up. It was the ace of spades.
And when he looked, he saw another leg under the table and it had a hoof
and was split in the middle like a cow's."

"Oh, Snoose——" Johnny began, wriggling away from the cloak of
uneasiness that hung on the edge of his mind.

"And Old Man Fleischer—he picked up some spitfire once." Snoose
hurried on, pursued by the lean phantoms of a heritage, dark on the bone,
that derived from his mother and his mother's mother and the faraway,
troll-haunted isles of the Rhineland. "He was near the swamp where
the ridge slants down. It's a dreary, dreary place there, anyway." He
shrugged a shoulder, remembering. "It was drizzle weather, hot and
muggy. That's when you can see the Crooked Ones, Old Fleischer says.
He heard a noise in the bushes and was sure that they must have been
dancing or something. Well, there on an old rotted stump he saw some
burning stuff. Like swamp fire it was; you know?"

Johnny nodded, though he didn't know.

Snoose said, "He picked up a handful and it was spit, all right; burning
spit. The Crooked Ones, so mad they were, they spit all over the stump,
and it burned. White and spooky, it was. It didn't hurt him, though,
because he prayed the Lord's Prayer quick." Snoose's voice sank in the
telling. "But when he got into the light, up on the hill, the fire was gone
and all he had was a handful of rotten stump."

"Gee-gods, Snoose, you s'pose that's really true?" Johnny wriggled in
uncertainty, more than half beginning to believe this, but doubtful nevertheless.

Snoose poked a stick along the root of a basswood. "I don't know.
But I'd like to see a spook just once." Johnny let things rest there.

On the hill they waited for Kurt. The path edged a clearing under
plow. It was like a square cut to the dark ground out of solid elm and
popple. Nightshade hung its small black tomatolike berries in the stubble.
Kurt came puffing. They turned to go when they heard it clearly: the
s'rum-rum-s'rum of the separator at the Nussbaums'. Over the valley it
came while they listened. It was as if a door into distance had been swung
open slowly and for a moment a far sound let in. Johnny's eyes shone
blackly. He hopped in the path. The sound faded. He wanted to climb
an elm. "Maybe we can see the rig," he clattered excitedly.

Kurt objected. "There's chores to do. And school work after supper."

"Oh, school truck." Johnny was ready to kick over the traces. But

Snoose had wood to gather, he said, and had to hurry home. Johnny thought of Mr. Marchen and his hard hands. They wandered on. Johnny was restless.

Snoose said, "That Lornas Tetzell—he's no better than Mosey. He likes to sick Mosey on to somebody, like Mosey was a dog. But when trouble gets bad, Lornas ain't around."

"He's got a brother that runs a thrasher over Loon Lake way," Kurt said, as if that put a better stripe on Lornas' breeding. "Bory Tetzell's his name. He's always talking about getting a steam engine for thrashing."

Johnny skipped over a rock. "I bet Alb Hukelpoke's teams and power would thrash twice as much as Bory Tetzell's old steam engine."

"Horses—they're too slow." Kurt spoke in a positive way.

Johnny wondered from what paper he'd filched that notion, the *Prairie Farmer* or the Lincoln *Freie Presse*. He answered doubtfully, "A stinker, all right. A buggy stinker." They descended the slant and entered the valley.

By the time he was at chores and the bread and barley coffee of lunch had pushed hunger out of his belly, he let this day's disturbance plague him no more than the switching tail of the heifer he was milking. There was a measured sway to his body as his hands fisted on the downward stroke, relaxed on the upward; right hand, left hand, muscles tightening, then slacking. He breathed as deeply as in sleep, eyes almost closed, his thought far away from the plunge of his hands, as if his mind stood on a hill and his fingers were lost in a valley. If rain hopped on the barn doorsill and Uncle Herm were home, grunting audibly over the lifting of a harness to a peg, Johnny was as brimful of content as later his cup was of milk. He swayed into forgetfulness, the milk on the metal of the bucket warming languorously the flesh of his thighs through his pants legs. So it was in those days and long thereafter: the furrows of distraction were harrowed into smoothness by the cadences of rhythmic motion, whether of flesh or of iron.

Even Aunt Phrena and her hints and the slow curl of doubt untwisting in him were then only echoes, like brawls at a neighbor's, too far away for the moment to have personal meaning. Then if ever he began to feel that he was a part of the farm; that he was crowding out a place for himself as a partridge hen does a nest in the leaves, not easily but with hardiness. Even at church the congregation no longer creaked in its benches to auger him with stares, as it used to. He added his shoulder muscle (knot-sized though it was, but growing) to the man-woman-and-animal strength on the place—strength that brought milk from barn to house and grain from the field to the bin and so kept the round of labor going even as the teams on the sweep kept the power running and the separator threshing.

Sometimes, however, this sense of belonging smashed as dropped skim-ice does. He'd toss aside a feed can and rush through the pasture to the cleared space on the ridge, loneliness like a hand gripping his throat, unconcerned that Aunt Phrena scolded or Uncle Herm cared. He'd stand where he and Uncle Herm had stood and see a hawk dip crazily in his tears. He longed for wings to carry him—where? Where? He didn't know.

Or evenings, when Kurt was nose-deep in the Fourth Reader and Johnny was supposed to be, he'd come upstairs, candle in hand, and hold the doll with the china head in a hot fist, the red ribbon dangling between moist fingers. Though he didn't know it, the memory of his mother was shrinking and fading beside a shadow that was beginning to form—the shadow of a father he'd never seen, a dark figure that troubled the bright-ness of his play whenever Aunt Phrena spoke his name; a man made up of the hints and the unsaid meanings in her words. And as he sat there, his breath came jerkily, as if he were sobbing, though he wasn't.

But squarely in the middle of his loneliness would come a thought, soothing as a cool stone laid on a bumped forehead: "Uncle Herm—he'll take care of me. And Snoose and Sophie Marchen; she'll be handy, too" (never Aunt Phrena or Kurt); and he'd leave the cleared space on the ridge or hide the doll where he hoped Aunt Phrena wouldn't look, and come to sit near Uncle Herm's craggy shoulders or sneak over to wrestle with Snoose and eat the cookies Sophie dragged from the oven.

And so, under the pull of the farm and its rooted life, of neighbors' ways spinning out the threads which wove and interwove darkly or brightly through his life, some of the loneliness ebbed slowly. But this new disturbance—that began to grow and spread like wild oats in a field.

It came to him, years later, not as something he had learned but as something that was a part of him, that the pang of grief or the bite of trouble is best blunted with the opiate of action, strength in motion, whether of a span of oxen or an engine, steam-wet with the surge of power.

8

That year the threshers came near midafternoon in late October. As long as they remained, Johnny and Kurt stayed home and the school lunch pails stood empty in the pantry. Always in this season one seat or another at school was vacant and Mrs. Sperry would observe with patience, "Well, the Nussbaum children are absent today. They're

threshing, I suppose"; or, "The threshers finally arrived at the Peisers'
Nobody here from their house."

Johnny crawled with eagerness when Alb Hukelpoke drove the power
near the barn, the team spanking under the harness. Uncle Herm followed
with the separator, one foot on the feeder head, shouting, "I'm back.
Chase the hens off the stacks, Johnny. We want to keep a little wheat
for flour." Johnny ran to meet him, trotting beside the machine and trying
to find a place to catch on and ride. He was glad that Uncle Herm would
eat supper from his own plates again for two or three days in a row; as glad
as he was over the threshing and the piling of wheat in the granary.

Mr. Schadel rumbled up with the grain wagon, sacks flung over the
box edge and flapping. His two boys balanced their pitchforks against
the sway of the wagon. After that Mr. Dunkel came, slow with his oxen;
with him Mr. Marchen with Snoose and the two older brothers, Jack
and Bill, in a wide-tired wagon. Behind them drove Mr. Nussbaum and
his boys, proud of their sorrels, and sometimes a hired hand—a small
circle of neighbors then who gathered to set the machine and stake down
the power. Uncle Herm giddapped the team and pulled the separator
between the stacks.

Meanwhile in a grassless place, Alb "unlimbered the engine," he said.
The power, a bull wheel with a nest of gears in it, held together by a
cage of iron, was mounted on a rectangular wooden frame on four wheels.
From a rack Alb flung braces and brace rods. They hit the ground with a
thud and a jangle. "Stake 'er down, boys!" he shouted. Johnny ran for ·
the maul, yelling at Kurt to come and help. Under Alb's shaggy gaze, the
Nussbaum boys steadied the frame into position and kept it propped there
with braces inclined to the ground. These braces they anchored firmly with
a dozen links of chain and two stakes driven into earth.

"That maul handle of yours is slicker'n a calf's pizzle, Alb," said Rob
Nussbaum, hefting the iron.

Alb laughed. He was the kingpin of the crew, Johnny could see. Uncle
Herm was a good separator man, as was Mr. Schadel; but the way Alb
drove the horses determined how well the cylinder hulled the grain and
separated wheat from chaff. The feeder-man had his share in threshing
the stacks cleanly. But he, too, waited on the power. The neighbors
agreed with Old Geppert: "The man who stands on the power—he puts
a farmer's crop in the granary, or in the straw pile. And Alb keeps one
eye on the straw pile." No one but Mr. Nussbaum fussed over Alb's
handling of the four teams on the sweeps.

He was a tall man, Alb was; lean and scraggly whiskered, with a voice
high in his throat. He grunted with a catch in his back when he stooped

over his work. "Cracked kidneys," he said wryly. On the bull wheel he fastened the sweeps, four twelve-foot lengths of pole, and the stay rods which opposed the strain of the horses pulling on the sweeps. "Yep, smoother'n a cat's knuckle, that maul, all right. Nothing like sweat to polish 'er up." He attached the equalizer rods. "There; guess that will even up the pull of the tugs, eh, Johnny? That gray mare of Schadel's— I'm gonna poke her behind with a pitchfork, if she doesn't limber her legs a little."

"Sweat," grumbled Mr. Nussbaum. "'Bout what a farmer can expect for a year's work." He slipped a coupler on the end of a tumbling rod which Johnny held for him. Grease smeared over his fingers. "Ach, corruption," he growled and wiped them on his pants. Johnny felt a laugh starting but squeezed it back, Mr. Nussbaum's face was so dour.

"My old man used to plant wheat when we lived down in Nicollet County." Mr. Dunkel's round face creased with recollection. "I wasn't no bigger than you kids." He nodded at Kurt and Johnny. "Each fall, 'bout every dollar Pa could depend on was piled in those stacks of wheat."

"Some of them counties down there is all wore out for wheat," said Mr. Marchen, pushing his suspenders up his shoulder. "Prices is down, too. Like Old Geppert says, it's them fellers from Egypt and them Rooshyans. They dumped such a muck of wheat on the market, they kicked the prices down to hell and gone."

"Geppert!" snorted Mr. Dunkel. "That blowhard! Only thing he knows is oxen and wheat cradling. There he's got a loud mouth."

Johnny listened, arms heavy with a tumbling buck, but Kurt wondered about the "fellers from Egypt." ("It ain't 'feller.' It's 'fellah.'" he told Johnny next day, after he had poked in Aunt Phrena's dictionary. "And he's a farmer; an Egyptian farmer." To which Johnny answered grandly, "To hell ya say," in Hukelpoke's high-pitched voice, liking the sound of Alb's words. Then he jerked around quickly; Aunt Phrena might be near.)

And in the house Aunt Phrena "how-dee-do-ed" Mrs. Marchen and Sophie and helped unpack the baskets they brought. Sophie was pettish over a rip in her dress. "Men got everything handy; no long skirts to catch in a stump and tear." She pushed the curtains aside and wished that Clymy Humber were among the men in the yard.

Johnny poked at a wasp, bumping uncertainly along a board, drunken with autumn, lively in old age.

Alb hooked a doubletree to a chain before he said, "'Tain't them foreigners alone that raise the devil with prices. It's them crooked elevator men and the spec-alators right here in this state. They got more grades of wheat to go by than tits on a sow. No. 1 hard and No. 2 Northern and No. 3 spring. Sheetin' Judas! It's all the same wheat, only the price is different, seems to me. And dockage?" He straightened a singletree. "That bastard of a Meyer at the elevator in Mary's Hill—he docked me six pounds on the bushel, couple of falls ago. Ain't forgot it, nuther. No wonder folks don't plant wheat."

"Well, Alb, that patch of your'n was pretty weedy." Mr. Dunkel spoke judicially. He laid the tumbling rods end-to-end between the power and the separator.

"Sure thing," Alb agreed. "But not six, seven pounds to the bushel; nope. Some people got beat worse than that." He stepped back, squinting over the top of the bull wheel. "Wonder whether the old bitch is in line with the cylinder gear now? She was a little outa whack at Schadels' and the knuckles howled." He grinned at Johnny. "Think she's in line, young shaver?"

They connected the power with the separator by means of couplers or "elbows" joining the ends of the tumbling rods. Alb covered the rod nearest the power with a box, saying, "We never *would* get Nussbaum's sorrel horse to step over that turning shaft. We have to hide it from him or the hames'll fly, he's that snickety." He laughed, none too neighborly with Nussbaum, and took a chew of Indian Twist; offered it to Johnny with a wink and then to Snoose.

"Old Geppert is right. It was crazy, planting wheat, spring in, spring out." Mr. Nussbaum tamped his pipe severely. "S'posing you get a bad year or the damned grasshoppers take it? It's root-hog-or-die for the farmer then, by jippers. Or fire gets into your stacks and you get burnt out." He helped Alb with the tumbling rods. There were four of them: a short one inclining from the gears; one under the sheltering box over which the horses passed; a third slanting up, supported in a notch on a tumbling block, a three-legged frame with one of the legs at a gentler pitch than the other two and notched to vary the angle of the rods; a fourth continuing the slant at a sharper angle and attached to the cylinder gear on the separator.

"It don't pay to depend on wheat alone." Mr. Dunkel smiled speculatively. "You get yourself a bunch of cattle and some pigs and plant you some oats and barley, and whoop-Jinny-and-fall-down, you can feed the stuff to the critters and tell them elevator crooks to go suck a thumb." Under a puff of breeze, chaff lifted from a corner on the separator and scattered, and the manure pile came strongly to their noses.

"Tell ya." Uncle Herm spoke from the feeder. "A good stand of wheat—she's a purty sight. And the clink of dollars—it warms your insides the whole winter. But it's a poor crop this year."

"With prices good now, they're going in for it again, up here," said Mr. Marchen. "Old Man Rose—he put wheat on every last acre he's got. 'Course, a cripple like that—it's the easiest crop for him."

"He got it hard, farming alone like that; him on crutches and his boy doing most of the work," sympathized Mr. Dunkel. "His family's living in town till he gets the place fixed up."

"They're moving out this winter, I hear," said Mr. Marchen. "Wonder how his missus will like a log house. She's a schoolteacher, or was. They got a little girl too."

"No church members, them Roses," pronounced Mr. Nussbaum grimly, as if that had dire significance. "Not one of the family is baptized."

Mr. Marchen swung his long arms with the stubby fingers. "Hand me that wrench there, Schwartzie."

Johnny hesitated, teeth all at once on edge; then obeyed, wanting to howl, "My name ain't Schwartzie," but shutting his mouth, remembering the bruise on Snoose's cheek.

"A farmer surely is a dumb fool." Mr. Nussbaum lit his pipe gloomily. "He risks the pockets in his pants on the seeds he scratches in the ground. And, by jippers, only God knows what's between seedtime and harvest— frost and stones and dry weather and chinch-bugs and grasshoppers—ach, corruption. If the grain don't fill out in the head, where is he then? Where's the money for shoes and flour and clothes——"

"And another kid, maybe, once a year or so," Alb broke in, wiping the sweat.

"Ya, that missus of mine—she don't need much pushing." Mr. Nussbaum grinned broadly, stiffness lost for once. "Well, I allus did like to furrow a soft, loamy field." Then, noticing Johnny's expression, he said, "Ho, got your ears up like a rabbit, eh, kid?"

Johnny's neck felt red and he sidled over to Mr. Dunkel, for Mr. Nussbaum had a way of pinching a feller where it was embarrassing. He liked Mr. Dunkel's smooth round face and lively eyes and the determined manner in which he moved. He wasn't as muscled as Mr. Marchen or as tall as Alb but in-between; solid in bone and thew as the oxen he "gee-ed" on the wagon. Looking on him, Johnny felt a glow which faded whenever Mr. Nussbaum came near.

"Well, she's tied down. We're ready to hook up," Alb yelled. "Get my team, Johnny."

Johnny brought up Alb's horses, guiding them smartly to the singletrees with a "Step over there now, Jerusalem." Excitedly he ran for Mr. Nussbaum's team. But Mr. Nussbaum shouted, "You leave them horses be; ain't gonna have my team spoiled by a little hind-end like you." Johnny dropped the lines as if they were red-hot pennies. His throat wobbled, a bubbling inside him that made him walk stiff-leggedly past Mr. Nussbaum's glare.

Kurt sniggered, "Always getting your nose in trouble, ain't ya?"

But Snoose, putting a hand on Johnny's shoulder, said, "You got a good driving fist."

Alb, overhearing, leaned near and added, "Sure thing, Johnny; best for your age I ever seen. Never mind Old Nussbaum. He was born with a crab in his teeth. Some day me and him are going to have trouble." The bubbling died down.

Before a gear moved, Uncle Herm squinted at the weather and pointed. A ridge of cloud piled darkly under the sun. "There won't be many bundles pitched before it wets down. But let 'er fly, boys," he ordered. "We'll thrash what we got, poor as it is."

Johnny felt the blood under his skin run faster. There was much shouting in the yard. Uncle Herm trotted, oil dribbling from a can. Alb roared, "Jeru-s'lem, you sawed off, runt-legged son of a blister, you, lag into the leather." Mr. Dunkel bellowed at his team, backing the wagon near the grain tally. With a great clatter, the machine got into motion. (Years later, with the throttle of the steam engine rattling under his hand, Johnny would remember with yearning the *clitter-clatter-clitter* of the couplers— "knuckles," Alb called them: elbows of iron on the ends of the tumbling rods which slanted up to the separator. The strength of horses transformed by gears traveled along this dark shaft to the bevel wheel on the cylinder pinion.)

With excitement stirring his toes, Johnny ran restlessly nowhere and everywhere, sometimes alone, sometimes with Snoose and Kurt. They goggled at the figure-eights of belts, the spurt of dust from the fan, the gray blur of a wheel yellowed by straws whirling with the spokes. Johnny leaned to hear the click of the grain register as Mr. Dunkel slid another half-bushel basket through the measuring box.

A greasy, horny hand shoved him aside. "You get away from that tally box, now," Mr. Schadel yelled at his ear. He ran to climb a grain wagon where Kurt and Snoose perched on the box edges like hawks and watched the bandcutters thrust their knives into the bundles and the feeder catch at the loosened straw; watched Alb Hukelpoke stand on the platform of the power and shoot a curl along the length of his snaky bullwhip—a curl that exploded into a "crack" over the horses' rumps.

Sometimes he and Kurt carried water from the spring, cool and beading on the jug. Johnny was proud when Alb or a feeder called to him. Once he ran to ask Aunt Phrena for a tumbler of vinegar. Mr. Schadel and Mr.

Dunkel liked their drink pungent with acid. They sloshed the brown liquid into the clear. He scampered to the granary where the wheat piled warmly in the bins.

But always (so it seemed to him) just before a cylinder choked with straw or a carrier stopped with a broken chain or a minor catastrophe brought quiet to the rig, Aunt Phrena shrieked, "Johnny! Johnn-ee! The woodbox is empty," or "Kurt and Johnny! The cows broke out of the pasture. Run quick, or they'll be in the corn." He'd leave, eyes bobbling over his shoulder, reluctant, and miss the quickening flurry that ruffled over the crew, the calls flung from stack to stack: "What did he say got broke?"— "The shaker arm."—"It was the shaker arm."—"No, not the shaker arm; the straw rakes. They only got stuffed up."—"Oh, hell! I thought we'd get a minute, anyway. My tail end aches."

Dusk ended the threshing in the middle of a stack. The pitchers heaped the bundles against the prophecy of rain. Johnny milked in the dark, his eyes on the black hulk of the separator in the yard. A moon sailed before storm. From the haymow where some of the threshers bunked a moment of laughter lifted wildly in the night. Old Sport whoofed softly. Johnny carried the milk to the house. Afterward he left the chips he was gathering for kindling and came slowly to the power. And in the ring where the earth was ground to powder by the circling hoofs, he dragged his bare feet, the dust puffing coolly up between his warm toes. As he scrogged along under a moon riding suddenly into a clear space, he had a cloud of silver on his heels.

9

The rain Uncle Herm promised fell in Johnny's sleep. Next morning, what threshers had remained the night ate breakfast peppered with Aunt Phrena's grumblings. "For the thrashers rain means rest. But for me, it is an extra breakfast and dishes." They left for home or Mary's Hill early.

"It's bad, wet in the stacks like this," Uncle Herm gloomed. "But now I can get that sloo grass cut. It's late but it'll fill the bull's belly."

They tinkered into the forenoon on the mower. Johnny was helpful with a wrench Uncle Herm needed, or he became absorbed in screwing or unscrewing a nut or a bolt. The feel of iron sliding over oil-slippery iron was pleasant to his finger ends, though he got sweaty with wrath over a rusty stubborn screw. He sucked in his belly when Uncle Herm said, "Crawl under the frame now once, Johnny, and screw me that bur on. Little stinker like you can get under there easy." He bloated with ego: nobody could tell him anything, not even Old Geppert or a machine expert

like the one that came to fix Mr. Nussbaum's reaper. His grin at Kurt
was wide and catlike.

Not far from noon Mr. Dunkel, on his way to Mr. Edgely's with a load
of feed, drove up to say, "What do you know about them doctors' laws,
Herman?" With him was Mr. Peiser, a short dark man with a hairy face
that defied a razor. "Peiser says they're going to kick Doc Huber out of
his office." Mr. Dunkel curled a strap unbelievingly. "Doc's helped the
stork with a lot of babies hereabouts; brought my little Gretel safe——"
He glanced at Johnny.

"It's the law, though," interrupted Mr. Peiser. "It's been so for some
years now, they say in town. A doctor's got to have a *cert*'ficate from the
medical board. And Doc Huber ain't got a *cert*'ficate." Mr. Peiser liked the
sound of the word in his mouth.

Said Uncle Herm in wonder, "'Salmighty! You mean Old Doc can't
give me a pill because he ain't got no papers from the medical board, or
what the hell they call themselves."

"Yep, that's right. He can't. He's got to get papers from St. Paul."

"Getting so a feller can't cure a bellyache without the gover'ment's
say-so." Uncle Herm had a trace of sourness in his voice.

"What's more——" Mr. Peiser was triumphantly dismal—"They got a
law that says if you got a sick critter, cow or pig, you have to get rid of
it or they'll come out and shoot it for you."

"Moses!" exploded Uncle Herm. "Seems to me I got a rusty shotgun
around here somewheres." After a moment he said, "About Doc, though.
Maybe it would help if we asked Old Geppert. He's——"

"Old Geppert!" Mr. Dunkel was quick to bristle. "What can he do
that we can't?"

"Well——" Uncle Herm tried to be fair—"he's chairman of the town
board and clerk of the school district and head elder of the church and——"

"—and the fifth teat on the old heifer." Scorn blistered Mr. Dunkel's
tone.

"Sure," Mr. Peiser broke in; "but Old Geppert and Norton are the
biggest fellers in the——"

"'Old Geppert, Old Geppert,'" mimicked Mr. Dunkel. "Whoop-Jinny-
and-fall-down, do you fellers ask him leave when you want to take your
pants down?" Then, grinning in apology, he said, "'Course Geppert's a
smart man. But I got ideas, too. Like I was telling Peiser. If Doc Huber's
kicked out, that's the law's business. We can't do a thing. And it don't
matter what Geppert says."

They drove away. Uncle Herm and the boys went in for dinner, grime-
smeared of hands and face, Johnny the dirtiest of the three, so that Aunt

Phrena screeched, "Don't you touch that towel; not till you've scrubbed off every lick of that grease. And don't waste soap."

Uncle Herm chuckled, smoothing her over. "Na, Phrena, we're not likely to peter out of soap; not with pig scraps for fat and a whole woods to burn for ashes."

She wailed. "I try so hard. Why he sticks himself into dirt all the time, I can't tell. Schwartz was like that, too."

Johnny swooshed alongside of Kurt, his face burning in the towel (it would burn for an hour afterward) with the harsh, skin-peeling suds, his ears full of Schwartz, if clean of lather.

Over a forkful of potatoes Uncle Herm said, "That Wilhelm Dunkel— I wouldn't give a three-cent nickel for what he thinks of Old Geppert. Funny how they agree on oxen, though. Only two farmers around here who stick to their oxen."

"A pair of fools, though I don't blame Dunkel." Aunt Phrena was snappish.

Johnny set his cup down slowly, thinking about Old Geppert, that tall, gaunt man who sat beside Mr. Norton on the elders' bench at church: a farmer of many acres, the best cradler in the neighborhood (though Mr. Dunkel disputed that), who doctored horses and cows and was the ear into which folks grumbled their woes and the tongue that gave them sought-for advice. All the valley knew (or thought it knew) how he had coaxed Mr. Dunkel up from Nicollet County with reports about a farm where wheat grew like wild ducks, unrestrained and plentiful; how Mr. Dunkel came with his wife, new married, to take the farm, and found one of Old Geppert's neighbors on it. But Geppert with loud remorse found another place for the Dunkels—a place that was a bramble of bushes and jutting with stone. Some folks hinted that Old Geppert made a pocketful of money and laughed at Dunkel in the bargain. Others said "no" and thought that Dunkel was lucky to have so neighborly a friend.

But all agreed that Dunkel had done well: he had cleared his acres with patience, and now his farm, as good as any in the valley, was wide enough for him and his wife and the small, brown-haired, big-eyed Gretel. But Aunt Phrena insisted that old quarrels down south lay between them and that Dunkel only waited and waited. "He'll claw into Geppert yet," she prophesied.

"It's more than a land deal," Uncle Herm was sure. "That Dunkel, he cradles his wheat and uses oxen, sure. But he's sproutful of notions. He wants to change things, like that road on the town line. But Geppert, now—when Geppert puts down a post for a fence, he wants it to stay there."

With his fork Johnny absently paddled in a patch of gravy.

More rain spilled over the ridges in the night and fell the next day long. Uncle Herm stomped impatiently in the puddles. But Aunt Phrena, as if shifting by contraries, became unexpectedly cheerful and set them down to apple pie at supper. "Two days' rain and you scold, Herm," she rebuked him briskly, clearing away the dishes. "Let it rain forty days and nights, once." She brought Uncle Herm's long coat and flung it on Johnny's shoulders. "Run to the henhouse and fetch me the eggs. I didn't get them. Think I'll stir up a batch of doughnuts tonight."

He came from the chicken shed, carrying the eggs, and for a moment of shining eyes regarded the rig, so noisy with clamor yesterday, so fixed and frozen into silence now, with the teams gone and the gears still. There was the power, its four sweep poles thrusting spearlike to the four horizons from the bull wheel in the center. The equalizer chains hung indolently; drops of rain gathered and fell from one link to another. The circle around the power where the horses trod was slippery, and plugs of mud squeezed up between his toes. From the power the black line of the tumbling rods slanted upward to the separator, the line sagging where the rods were held together by the couplers. Water bunched like whitish tits on its underside and rilled down.

And there was the separator itself, a box on four wheels. Its feeding table jutted from the level of the cylinder in front; its straw carrier slanted upward in the back. Yesterday the machine had trembled with exertion over the parting of kernel and husk, fan and shaker in motion. Now it was sodden. A faint tarnish of rust burned on the silvery teeth of the cylinder. Rain crawled down the long stems of wheat hanging from the carrier slats and dripped off. Under the separator Johnny saw a feather-soaked rooster lowering its tail to the ground and standing on one foot. He went to the house, shaking drops on the eggs from his wet coat.

10

What lay between him and Kurt, as intangible at first as a thistle needle in April, soft and thin but hinting of the prick, began to grow that fall and winter. It came out even in scufflings, a wolf-cub anger showing its teeth in the hard way Johnny flung against him, striking wildly without thinking though not intending to hurt. His fists, gentle with Snoose, left blue marks on Kurt's skin. Irritation edged in him when Kurt got up with an ear torn though never quite worsted. Kurt would never shrill "King's X" in a game, or grunt "I give up" when he was beaten. Stubbornly he kept his silence, no matter how much his lip was squashed.

He was a heavy boy with a shifty grin and a roving eye. There was a weightiness in his gait and speech that he borrowed from his mother, a calm strength in him. Even at twelve he had grown an inner hide that was almost proof against her. Whether she was cheerful or in tantrums, he accepted her with an indifference that hid but did not alter a fierce loyalty burrowing deep like a current under a placid stream, which now and again boils to the surface. But there was that in Kurt which made Johnny as he grew older step aside; an uncertainty that bothered Johnny as anything always did when he couldn't put it in a drawer, safely labeled and understood.

It came out in a slow uncoiling the Sunday evening Aunt Phrena said, "A week from tomorrow the Pastor begins religious school. It's time Kurt goes." She pulled a slip of paper from a drawer. "On Saturday we go to town and get him a new suit. I always say, a boy should have a new suit when he starts reading for the Pastor, and another one when he gets confirmed."

Something in the triumphant manner she spoke rubbed Johnny with the salt of ire, he wasn't sure why. Kurt squinted uneasily, not happy over leaving District School in the beginning of the Sixth Reader, but said nothing. Uncle Herm looked at his hands quietly.

Outside, Kurt sniggered, "I'll get a new suit for Sundays, anyway." Meaning plainly, "And you won't."

"Oh, well, there's plenty time for me to get one next year," Johnny tried to say comfortably but he couldn't. His fingers closed in spite of himself.

"It riles you, don't it?" prodded Kurt with an understanding thrust.

"No," Johnny yelled violently. "And you don't hanker much for the Pastor either."

"Maybe not. But we got to study Catechism sooner or later." Kurt pronounced judgment with a flighty air, Johnny thought, but knew that Kurt was right. The congregation was growing. There was a house for the Pastor near the church now. No longer did he need to drive from Mary's Hill to hold services here. His black buggy stood in the yard, his ponies were stabled in a small barn at the end of a path. There was talk of building a new church, too, but the log house remained as an altar. Here the congregation gathered; here the Pastor broke the head of Satan anew each Sabbath morning; here Kurt would join the kids who came for Catechism.

Late on the next Friday afternoon, Johnny was upstairs, changing from school pants into dirt-stiffened overalls and waiting for Kurt, when he heard Uncle Herm's voice saying below: " . . . Johnny and Kurt together—

like brothers." They were just coming in, he and Aunt Phrena. The door closed.

Johnny would have run down to greet Uncle Herm but Aunt Phrena's cry stopped him. "Brothers!" He could hear the water in her voice. "Brothers! My boy and that——"

"Phrena, what's gone by is gone by." Uncle Herm's voice hurried. Johnny flattened against the wall, feeling the past twisting snakily in its lair. "Kurt—he can wait a year before he goes to the Pastor. Then he and Johnny can go together."

"You left your thrashing to tell me this?" Aunt Phrena spoke bitterly.

"It's three miles to the church; too far for a kid to go alone, winter storms and all." Uncle Herm's tone was shaky as if the words were jerked from him.

"Winter storms," Aunt Phrena said as if she had suspicion in her eye. "Is is Kurt you are thinking of or——"

"Phrena. All I want is this. I want them two kids to be together and forget what's done." Uncle Herm was patient. Johnny's throat tightened and he shivered, as though a chill warned him of the black frost to come.

"I see it. I see it." Aunt Phrena began crying. "You want to deny me and my boy, don't you? And you favor him——"

"I favor nobody," Uncle Herm shouted. "Not even the son of Albert Schwartz. It's not my fault you wanted to marry him. I told you I'd forget the whole——"

Johnny felt himself moving. How he got downstairs, whether by crawling or walking, he didn't know. But suddenly he saw them as in a mist and heard his own voice asking almost sadly, the loneliness like a cloud on him, "You talk and talk about my pa. But you never tell me anything." They stood icicled into silence. "You whisper behind your hands." He almost choked with the want of air in his lungs. The water kettle bubbled loudly.

Uncle Herm broke the stillness. "Johnny, Johnny, you must believe this. I—we—this is not meant against you. It——"

But Aunt Phrena cried, "Herman Barewolf, you gave me your word you'd let me handle this. He is my sister's child."

Uncle Herm muttered as he turned toward the window. Johnny gulped. Rage against Aunt Phrena flared in him: ordering Uncle Herm around like a puppy in a corner. All at once he screamed at her, "What you got against my pa?"

Aunt Phrena's chin stiffened. "Such truck is not for kids' ears to hear; not till he's older." She spoke as if Johnny were in the barn and not before her, white-faced and trembling. "You ought to know that, Herm." And when Johnny blubbered incoherencies, she said firmly but gently, "The ox stall needs bedding. Go and do it."

Johnny's dark look begged Uncle Herm to push her aside. But Uncle Herm stayed at the window, twisting his mustaches. Sullenly, Johnny went down to the barn, leaving them with the past in which he was entangled, unsolved and large between them.

That Aunt Phrena gave in about the parochial school Johnny learned when Kurt came to help with the chores. She had reasons of her own for yielding and added them to those she held against Uncle Herm.

Kurt stepped lightly in the straw, saying, "I get to go to District School this year, after all."

"Well, I guess you don't get the new suit then, do ya?" Johnny couldn't stop a lashing meanness.

"Don't mind." Kurt shrugged tranquilly. "It works out good either way. If I go to the Pastor, I finish confirmation faster. If I go to District School, I'll beat you in spelling and arithmetic." Kurt climbed into the haymow. He called back, "I can get a new suit any time. Ma says so."

Johnny swung away abruptly. He was hangdog with a sense of defeat yet smoking with anger, too. Aunt Phrena's words were loud in his ears. He wanted to ball fists and smash into something. As though this moment of bitterness were shaping a notion lying somewhere deep, he muttered, "If I were a thrasher like Alb Hukelpoke, she wouldn't *dare* talk to me like that. She wouldn't *dare*." It was as if Aunt Phrena and Kurt were twin trees in his path and growing from the same stump and he helpless to root them up. "Schwartz, Schwartz." He wanted to vomit with the dreadful ache that pulled his stomach at the thought of this man, his father, unknown but there. A taste of bitter weed was on his tongue.

He grabbed a pitchfork. Blindly he prodded Bully the ox until the animal snorted. After a while he went to the straw pile for bedding, longing with all his young-pup strength for a moment when he could crush and rip apart all that opposed him, bodies or wills.

He returned and was staggering past the ox stall under a forkful of straw when black Bully lifted a sharp and newly shod hoof, the calks gleaming, and kicked a streak of black lightning. All the torments of uncounted seasons of yoke and goad seemed to burst in one desperate reckoning of accounts. There was an iron *bu-ung*, like a hammer glancing from a spike and slamming on wood. In the pine wall stuck the shoe, torn from the hoof, the calks buried and the nails pointing outward, driven in so hard that manure on the iron sprayed on the wood. Bully stopped pawing though he snorted angrily into the manger. Johnny saw grayish pieces splintered from the hoof.

White with a sickness at his stomach, he fingered a six-inch rip in his coat and a numb place on his ribs. He got a chisel and needed force to pry the shoe away. Then he found a length of tug and, for all of Bully's lunges, raised welts thumb-high on the ox's black hide. "Kick, will ya? And over nothing?" he panted, hoarse with words that were more inside than outside. "I'll lick you so long, you won't think of liftin' a foot again."

It vented his steam but did little else. The ox would do this again, as Uncle Herm plainly said, mild anger in his voice, as he came with the liniment bottle. Johnny hated to admit it, not yet knowing that there are some things beyond a fist or a club to work a change. He grouched in the house, pretending he was blind to Kurt's lidded stare. But Aunt Phrena said, "I think you got a piece of Satan in you, Johnny."

With rain and soggy roads to mire the rig, the threshing season dragged on longer than the chaffy heads and meager yield warranted. Johnny dug potatoes and tied corn in the shock as though these were charms to rouse fair weather and hold away the first rush of winter. When his warts itched, more now than in summer, he tied knots in a string and buried it in the mud near an ooze of standing water, mumbling Snoose's incantation with a half-grin over his shoulder:

> "Wartman, wartman, hither hie
> And see the knots I tightly tie.
> A knot for a wart, a wart for a knot;
> Cut it or burn or tear or rot,
> Spit three times on the knotted string
> And bury it deep in a lizard spring."

At night, however, he used the bottle of caustic which Mrs. Dunkel strongly advised for warts.

When Uncle Herm drove home for Sundays, Johnny noticed the worry-crease above his nose and was disturbed. What with the late cold spring retarding the sprout and the stem, and in some areas chinch bugs stinking in the field, threshers had little more than chaff with which to fill their pocketbooks. Bory Tetzell up at Loon Lake reported he'd be lucky if the season brought him enough to pay for grease and oil.

December blew in with a snowstorm before Uncle Herm warmed the emptiness of his chair for good, the run at last finished. "I'm home for Christmas." He grinned, his hands caked with tarry calluses and a hide of dirt on his lumbering body. Aunt Phrena scolded: "Look at them pants; so stiff with grease they'd stand in a corner by themselves."

Johnny remembered that winter for the evening when Uncle Herm reckoned his accounts. During those snowy days Uncle Herm chopped and sawed and hammered a bobsled from elm and birch. Later on he planned to yoke a pair of bull calves to the oak whippletrees. He left the shaving of a runner one night, gathered a heap of papers at his elbow and hunched over Johnny's slate. The slate was clean now. There wasn't a scratch to show that, hours before, "I pulled Gatha Blumen's hair" had been written at the top in Mrs. Sperry's neat script and below her sentence, Johnny's unrepentant scrawl fifty times over.

Worry-nipped and long-jawed in the lamplight, Uncle Herm pondered, his pencil slow upon the way a year's sweat on farm and on threshing rig sieved down to pennies. The black stone of the slate grayed with the digits of obligation. He spat on it and wiped the figures clear with a drag of his shirt sleeve. Aunt Phrena pinched her lips.

"Not much left for the pantry shelves," he muttered at last, crumpling the papers. There was a droop to his shoulders.

"Thrashers!" Aunt Phrena sniffed scornfully. "That Norton fattens on you."

Uncle Herm dropped the pencil. "The rig brings in almost as much as the farm, even with three fellers to share it," he said quickly. "I'm not the only one in debt to Norton. Long as we pay the interest, Norton won't——"

"The interest!" Aunt Phrena was abrupt. "It eats and eats—like sin," she added softly.

Kurt squeaked sums on his slate. Uncle Herm pushed at the pencil with a long horny finger. "That's done—for another year. Figures give me a stomach-ache." He straightened, relieved. "I'm glad I know what I haven't got." He shrugged quizzically. In a week he had forgotten Norton, or so it seemed; and the gray sums on the slate irritated him no more than the dust under his suspenders. But Johnny remembered how he looked that night—like a cornered rooster, mouth open and the proud fight running from its body.

At church sometimes that winter Johnny peeked over his hymnbook for glances at Norton, the wide shoulders bulging over the top of the bench-back, the thick neck that reminded him of the bull-calf ox at home. "Four Oaks Farm," Norton called his four hundred acres near Mary's Hill and the river. A farmer with money in his seams, they said, though his coat was lint-flecked and frayed to whiskers at the cuff. He came to services in a top-buggy with a spanking gray team and sat in the front row with Old Geppert. "He belongs to our church, not the one in Mary's Hill," the folks crowed. "Rich man like that." The barn which stabled the

Pastor's ponies came from his pocket. He headed the deacons and his pledge would be a stout lever to raise a new church. Aunt Phrena, untying her Sunday bonnet, said once that she could give a peck of silver too, if she squeezed blood out of other people's turnips. With that Uncle Herm disagreed. "Norton's worked for what he's got. And I did hire the money from him. It was a fair deal." His grin was rueful, nevertheless. Johnny wondered whether the blood would run if he jabbed a pin into Norton's heavy neck.

Storms shrieked over the ridges. With the bull-calf team he and Kurt hauled bags of feed from the granary and snaked trunks of fallen black oak from the pastures—the last span of oxen Uncle Herm broke. Along the creek Johnny hunted weasel and mink.

By and by April came with a hint of spring though the drifts lay deep. At school he heard that Old Man Rose had brought his wife and his girl from Mary's Hill. With them he brought a piano. They lived south of the creek near Norton's woods. Queer folk, sparing of their presence and not very friendly, the neighbors gabbled.

He was a big man, they said, but helpless now, chained in the house. Even with crutches his legs were almost useless. It was lucky the boy was big for his age, sixteen or seventeen. The girl was younger but neither had been touched with the water of baptism.

Aunt Phrena shook her head. "It's tempting the worst to happen, not being baptized."

"Pretty good farmer, though," Uncle Herm remarked. "A poor year, but his wheat went twelve bushels. 'Bout all he wants is wheat."

Johnny hadn't seen them. The girl wouldn't start school this spring, late, as it was and they busy.

Before the snow melted he and Kurt hauled more wood for the summer supply. He tossed a last limb of firewood one day, proud of the knotty pile they'd gathered. He glowed in the chill April wind when Uncle Herm chortled, "You fellers handled the wood job so good, I guess I'll have to give you a calf apiece to raise."

Kurt grunted. Johnny bit the thumb of his mitten awhile before he said with earnestness not yet tempered with experience, "Couldn't we haul a couple of loads to Mary's Hill? Snoose tells they're paying fancy prices for black oak." He didn't dare risk a glance. He feared what he had in mind might slip bare into light for Uncle Herm to see. "Little extra money——"
He stopped in confusion, struggling with an idea too large for his tongue. "Heinie Beerwagon—he's getting a job, as soon's he's confirmed. I——"

Kurt broke in, "If you want a job, there's more oak to haul."

Uncle Herm stared like a barn owl dragged into lantern glimmer, not understanding then. "Never you mind, Johnny. You'll get your penny for the church collection and your two nickels when you go to town. We'll keep the firewood." He patted Johnny's shoulder.

Johnny looked away from him in a sort of misery, his tongue stone-tied. He glowered when Kurt jeered, "That little pig pile of wood? It wouldn't bring enough silver to jingle in a pocket." He yelled, "G'up along there," at the ungalled ox team. On the path to the barn he thought, "A calf of my own—I wonder how much a whole cow would bring?"

11

That summer fled on long grasshopper legs. October rushed up with his birthday, and then November and the Pastor's school. The Monday morning came when he and Kurt reluctantly trudged to the log church. Thereafter, winters of days, they went to Pastor Steuber and his Catechism, two miles away by the short cut, three in spring when the creek became honeycombed and unsafe.

A small place, though much larger than the District School, it had an altar made of boards and covered with hangings. Above the altar hung a cross. There was a narrow aisle up which on stormy days they played tag or skip-to-mallew. Many who attended District School the year before were here now—Em'ly Musser, Lornas Tetzell, Mosey Fritz, as weaselish as ever. Once Johnny and Snoose swayed to an awkward waltz beside the pulpit, Heinie Beerwagon making noises on a comb and a piece of paper and Gatha Blumen looking on longingly; until Kurt, on guard, called, "Pop to your seats. Here comes the Pastor." They were straight-backed and unsmiling in the benches when he strode in.

Here they chewed over the rags of knowledge the Pastor sorted out of his head—the reading, writing and arithmetic that were lined with the prickly hide of personal doctrine. "I feel better, you kids out of that District School." Aunt Phrena closed the lunch pails with a tap of satis-faction. "Now you'll get your *Vater Unser*."

The Lord's Prayer they got and theology by the yard if little religion, learning Catechism and Bible history by rote though not by understanding. Night after night Kurt and Johnny would sway on their chairs by the heater, their bodies penduluming a rhythm to chapter and verse, adding thread by careful thread to the fabric they were weaving for the morrow and for confirmation. "Hope I can keep this in my head till confirmation time," Snoose said gloomily once. "Guess I'll go fishing then and rest my thinker." Johnny agreed. They squeezed out precious little meaning for their daily lives.

The Pastor droned over Moses receiving the Ten Commandments one day. "I the Lord thy God am a jealous God—" the Pastor held a moment of silence for emphasis—"a jealous God visiting the sins of the fathers upon the children unto the third . . ."

The reading went on but Johnny wasn't listening. "Sins of the fathers . . ." The words speared out of the Pastor's droning and hooked themselves into his head. ". . . upon the children . . ." The rest was meaningless but those phrases dug into him. My father, he thought and it hurt to think. A bad one. That's what Aunt Phrena means. Is it coming out in me, like cold sores? He swiveled a glance at Snoose and Kurt. Could they see anything in his face? In panic he thought, Is there something wrong with me? If Uncle Herm would tell me. . . . Even then he almost feared treading on truth in the open and recognizing it.

It was that day a Nussbaum boy was whipped for cutting a hole in the partition which separated the girls' part of the backhouse from the boys'. Everybody knew that Mosey Fritz's knife had whittled the hole but no one spoke a defensive syllable. Johnny watched almost absorbedly while the Nussbaum boy writhed over the bench and jerked as the birch stick leaped into his flesh. The cloth stretched over his buttocks jumped with each stroke. In a kind of revulsion Johnny paged in the Bible history. He stopped at a picture showing Christ gathering the children in His arms.

Beside the church was the graveyard, a cleared patch with now and again a stump of oak or elm among the tombstones. It was a small acre of God's wrath. Here a lonely few rested under sod, pioneers on a darker frontier. But it was growing. Under the evergreen that spired like a steeple, the kids often came, spilled over from play in the yard.

In the wintertime the headstones were thin and gray, some half buried in slants of snow, except the iron ones. These were black in the drifts and shaped like a cross with scrolls to soften the shadows they threw. Johnny screwed up his lips over the inscriptions. On one was written in words of gold:

> *Augustus Bhaerwulff*
> *A chil of sin becom*
> *A lamb of God*
> *18*

But the letters were worn with the rub of weather and some were as lost as he who lay beneath them. Many times Johnny had put his thumb on that name, Bhaerwulff: Augustus Bhaerwulff, Uncle Herm's older brother who had staked the claim that was now the farm. He wondered how Uncle

Herm lost the *h*, the *u* and the extra *f* in his name and how the *e* switched places with the *r*: Barewolf. There were folks south of the church who called themselves Whiteland though the gravestone of their father was plainly marked "Weisslandt." He must ask Uncle Herm about this.

Not far from the church stood the store where the stage rattled to a stop, bringing the mail from Fergus and taking passengers over the ridges. "I want nobody of you to be seen over there, noons and recesses," the Pastor thundered. As a predictive gesture he banged his desk with a length of birch. But his warning only lent a fragrance to adventure. They went to the store, the daring ones, led by Heinie and Lornas, Johnny and Snoose tagging them, swinging their lunch pails. They kept the hedge of woods between themselves and the Pastor's house. In the store with the smell of coal oil and new print cloth strong in their noses, they munched their icy sandwiches and tossed scraps at the storekeeper's dogs. Mr. Jimpson had only to turn his back and they stole raisins and filched crackers. With a pointed splinter from the wood box near the stove, Heinie tried to spear the herring in the keg. "Crackers and herring and beer— tasty," he told Johnny.

On three days of the week the neighbors gathered for letters or packages. Old Man Dresser was usually there, his wooden shoes *klip-klop-klipping* on the floor. "No letters yet for me and mine girls—from the old country?" he'd question wistfully. Johnny wondered what curl of toes it was that kept those shoes on. He flexed his own in his good leather boots.

The folks bought their coffee sticks and coal oil here. In cold weather they warmed their rumps on the rust-sided stove. They folded in their pockets copies of the Fergus *Weekly Telegram* and the *Tageblatt*, their grumbles rattling over their lips: "Butter twenty cents again. And eggs—— We get sixteen the dozen. But Jimpson here turns round and sells them for a shilling. Damned merchants!" The Norwegians came for the *Decorah Posten:* Mr. Muri, Tjöstöl Skjelle, Tor Gjevsjö. Solid Northland names. One season Torgrim Torgrimson met the stage half a mile from the store, impatiently asking for the back copies of the *Posten* which his aunt was sending him in bundles; he could hardly drink his coffee, he said, for worrying about the continued story. Mr. Dunkel always tramped over for his *Prairie Farmer.* Folks said with a simmer of envy, "They take the *Prairie Farmer.* Regular come-uppers, them."

There was a tang of danger in knowing that the Pastor might roar in any second in search of them. Eyes vigilant, the boys listened with half an ear to the grumblings of one neighbor to another. "Didn't make a damn cent last year. Railroads took it all and what they didn't the merchants do. Lick the last drop off the cow's teat, give 'em half a chance."

"That's a fact," somebody said. "Wheat fifty-eight cents. Not much left after *they* take their bite. Saw in the paper where freight from Mary's Hill to Minneapolis is seventeen cents and going up."

"Seventeen?" somebody else half yelled. "And wheat fifty-eight? That's paying just as much freight now as when wheat was a dollar."

"Sure," Mr. Schadel said once. "Big bugs own the elevators and the railroads, the whole shooting match. The state inspectors are playing with them thicker'n he-dogs and bitches. And us farmers? Huh!" He spat disgust with his tobacco. "They set the price and we gotta take it and be damned glad, or eat hazelnuts next winter."

That sounds exactly like Uncle Herm talking, Johnny thought, edging to a window. He'd better keep an eye open for the Pastor.

Sometimes Adam Schramff was there and Johnny would listen to the melodies he pulled sadly from the white-toothed accordion, though the rest paid little heed. With eyes half shut, Adam would sit on the edge of the herring keg. He was a fat, gloomy-eyed man with slack suspenders. So generous was he, his pocketbook never snapped shut on what he had to give. "He's got three ways of making money," people said, "and a hundred ways of spending it." He had kinfolk in Minneapolis, far away. But his playing brought Johnny to a pause within a haunted ring of melody. Once, bending backward under the swell of a tune, mournful and slow, Adam tumbled into the herring brine. He arose, smelling of bay leaves and spices, the white circles of onions sticking to his wet seat. Mr. Jimpson said even the Pastor's dog followed Adam home that time.

But the moment a black coat moved down the path toward the pond that lay between the parsonage and the church, there would be a cry from a watcher—Heinie or Kurt or Snoose, alert as minks: "He's starting now. Let's get." The Pastor would find them unblushingly deep in their Catechisms.

To be sure, some of the things which the Pastor thrust at them stuck in their minds, as crumbs to a cloth wherein broken bread has been wrapped. But much of what they recited might as well have been jabbered in Indian, for all the good they got from it. "Thou Shalt Not Steal" was undoubtedly marked on tablets of stone by the bright finger of God but it never stopped the kids' snitching watermelons from a neighbor or a knife from an unguarded pocket.

It didn't stop their parents, for that matter. Only the fall before, a dozen long melons vanished from Mr. Fleischer's patch and Mr. Peiser openly admitted that melon rind was his favorite pickle, though he grew no melons. Right afterward one morning, Mr. Peiser's single apple tree stood empty of its late, drag-heavy crop. That winter the Peisers had melon-rind pickle and the Fleischers had apple pie: a fair exchange, said the neighborhood. Johnny laughed over the story, defiant at Aunt Phrena's sniffings. Even Uncle Herm wasn't stricken by the birch of conscience over purloining a canful of Mr. Marchen's pasture plums. "The way I look at it," he said, "I'd maybe swipe a feller's plums, all right, but I'd never steal a sack of potatoes."

Johnny learned "Thou Shalt Not Lie" but it never entered his mind that it had anything to do with telling truth in all weathers, most of all when caught in a fault. He spun falsehoods like a spider with the rest the day the Pastor fell into the pond. The boys cut a hole in the ice where he walked, concealing their work with snow. They had planned to run and hide but his yells brought them scuttling. There he was, in water up to the neck. They pulled him out, icicles in his chin whiskers, or he'd have brought early hell to the turtles under the ice, Alb Hukelpoke said when he heard. The Pastor racked them inquisitorially but they were prepared and agilely twisted themselves into safety.

True, on Thursdays, when he waved his hands over telling about the fires of Gehenna that sizzled for the wicked, and other pleasantly edifying Bible stories, they squirmed in their seats. But Johnny, emboldened by a talk with Uncle Herm, spoke up one day and asked about the Lord's Shepherd and the cool waters He led His sheep by, and wasn't there one drop of spring water in all the acres of hell? The Pastor, glad that the Lord had given his servant opportunity to slash the stalk of iniquity to the stem, coughed grimly and dived at him with the stick.

Johnny remembered how the dark birch whistled; remembered the shock, more of surprise than pain, that was thrust through his body. No one had ever struck him like this before. The breath tightened in his lungs. Blindly he groped for the stick.

"So, you reach for more, do you?" the Pastor crowed, evading him. His voice was oily. Then he rasped, "Good! I have an excellent supply for you." He lashed with an inspired arm. Pieces of bark, ripping from the birch, flew from Johnny's shoulders. Under a drift of dizziness that swirled from rebellion more than pain, Johnny closed his eyes, steady but sick.

Then Gatha Blumen's voice shrilled suddenly. "Quit that! Quit that!" She was scared and crying but defiant where she sat. "If I was a man I'd— I'd maul you down."

From his seat Snoose gasped, determination almost subduing fright, "Can't we even ask questions any more?"

The Pastor hesitated, astonished, his breathing heavy. This insurrection in the house of God. Then he fired a virtuous zeal. "So, it is catching, is it,

this Satan's revolt against the word of God? Lay over, Charlie Marchen."
Snoose grunted as the black arm whipped down. Johnny's knuckles were
white with the pressure of his fingers.

But when he heard the first blow thud on Snoose's shoulders, Johnny
began to cry. Straight of back he sat there, the muscles in his face hard
and unmoving except where the nostrils thinned and whitened with the
short breaths he drew. Tears crooked down his cheeks and over his
pinched-together lips—tears that never ran for pain but something lying
deep as bone. Between the first unreasonable fall of club or hand and the
incredible realization, the wild hawk dies in the blood, the wild hawk's
way is shattered, a boy's way lost. The spirit molts its pride desperately,
aware of the inevitableness of decay. The shackled animal slinks forward,
divine erectness gone, and shambles into maturity. Over its shoulder it
yearns for the green avenues of youth and the wild hawk unfettered there.
With snarling defiance, face to earth, it slouches furtively through the
scabby alleys of the world it calls its own; it hugs its chains and squeals,
"I'm free, I'm free: I am a man."

Gatha howled even before the Pastor switched her. But Johnny didn't
hear. He slumped down, head in elbows, feeling the neighbor eyes like
fishhooks barbing into his naked flesh. Clean and purified, the Pastor ordered, "The story of David and Bathsheba—memorize it for tomorrow, all
three of you. Now we'll take up the Catechism—the Mercies of God and
the Forgiving of Sin."

On the way home Johnny nudged Kurt's arm fiercely. "You know what
I mean," he muttered fiercely. "If *they* find out——"

"Why should I spill your beans?" Kurt demanded scornfully. Then he
remarked with hardness, "That Pastor—he ought to be whaled to the
bone himself." Johnny dropped his hand. He regarded Kurt with a long
stare that night.

He had no words of gratitude for Gatha, only a twisting mouth the next
day. Before her wide smile he was silent, though his black eyes gleamed.
At home he was shy over Uncle Herm's finding out. He didn't need
prophecy to know what Aunt Phrena would say.

The Pastor's words, the smoky sternness of the Biblical injunction, "The
sins of the fathers . . . upon the children . . ." His hands slowed over the
milking more than once. Sometimes he'd turn swiftly on the stool, questions
big in his mouth, as though he'd stop Uncle Herm in his tracks and ask.
But he didn't. He couldn't, he told himself desperately, and was sad in a
kind of frustration, only half knowing that there are places in our lives
where touch and footstep are a violation.

There was that about Uncle Herm which was solid as the rock sticking through the hide of grass on a pasture slant, unshaken even by thunderstroke; more of patience in him, in one elbow of him, Johnny decided, than in any neighbor he could name. It was sand under his tongue whenever he heard the neighbors loose-lipped in talk about "that thrasherman, Barewolf." "Devil take them, anyway!" he'd mutter, lowering his head. But he enjoyed the big sound of the words.

He wanted to vomit the winter's morning he came to the barn and smelt birthing raw as fresh meat. He saw the calf new-dropped and Uncle Herm ripping with his bare hands the birth sheath, warm and smoking in the icy air. Slow-voiced Uncle Herm unplugged the calf's nose so that it snorted with the first breath bitter and almost unwelcome in its nostrils, used as it was to the quiescence of mother heat. Johnny felt the retch in his throat but had his stomach in a minute. There was gentleness in the way Uncle Herm soothed the cow. "Sho-boss, sho-boss, easy now." He shook his hands in a wide circle, scattering the birth drops as he did wheat in seeding. Johnny bent over to touch the animal, a red one with white spots.

It was the next Sunday that he heard Mr. Blumen say to Mr. Fleischer, "Ya, good neighbor, Barewolf. Better than most thrashermen. Keeps his land clean. But he's softhearted as cheese."

Mr. Fleischer answered, "A good man if he'd keep his woman out of his britches. A second wife, you know. She's the rooster in his henhouse, all right."

Johnny longed to shout, "It's a lie, a stinkin' lie." He jerked his hand clumsily in his coat pocket, almost crying in young-pup rage. It was true and he knew it. Aunt Phrena *did* get her way and got it by sniffling into Uncle Herm's web-wrinkled face. She got her way, or the house might as well be pitched into the cellar for all the care it would get.

He was prickly, going home from church, and short with Kurt, who wondered how the Israelites made the slingshot which David in the Bible story used.

"Not much use you'll have for a slingshot. You can't even shoot a gun straight." Johnny was surly.

Aunt Phrena, sorrow thick on her lips, sighed, "Ach ya, Johnny, didn't you hear what the Pastor said? Like brothers and sisters we should live; not in hard words. It's all in the Comfort Book. But you never read it," she moaned. "There is such stiff-neckedness in you."

"Moses Almighty—" Uncle Herm began but she pushed him off: "In you too, Herman Barewolf."

It was the next morning that Johnny said unexpectedly to Uncle Herm, "I think you would—you'd make a good pa for me." He said it with all of his boy faith strong in his eyes. The granary where they stood seemed to echo with the words.

As if understanding much that was dark before, Uncle Herm said softly, "Is that why you keep asking about the calf?" Johnny didn't dare nod even, the tears were so fiercely near. Uncle Herm laid the hammer quietly aside, a queer strangling in his chest. There was this much heaped between them, at any rate.

12

In February the Pastor added new brightness to the Golden Rule by assigning for memory work the story of the Good Samaritan. He was loving over the compassion of the outcast. The tale was obediently put to memory. One afternoon Johnny clacked off pieces in recitation so smoothly (and with so little comprehension) that the Pastor was pleased and had a vaguely beatific notion that of this the recording angel ought to take golden notice. For years, once he got going, Johnny could rattle off rods of the Catechism or Bible history. But let a laugh interrupt and stop him and he had to make a fresh start before he swung down the groove worn familiar in his recollection.

Thick with virtue, the kids trooped off home, Johnny among them. On the road they met a young Norwegian from over the river and beat him into unresisting jelly, leaving him to soak snow with blood. "Teach him how to take it like a man," they bragged the rest of the way. Johnny was almost a hero among the girls, Gatha Blumen especially, the scab on his knuckles was so thick and hard.

Afterward he couldn't have said why his fist plunged out or over what argument. But he didn't forget in a hurry the queer feeling that stiffened his arms and snapped back his head when his notched fist struck the jaw of the Norwegian. A rush of blood scorched through his skin and a dizziness of pride shook him. It was heady as a drink of Mrs. Dunkel's chokecherry wine, this meeting for the first time with brute victory over a fellow being and savoring it. He kicked snow all the road home but was careful to hide his knuckles from Aunt Phrena. Her ideas on fisticuffs were short and simple: "Kids that fight at school should get a licking at home." Her double chins were firm over the pronouncement.

So fiery was the raciness in his blood, however, that next day he chased the girls and twice put snow down Em'ly Musser's neck. (He didn't bother Gatha though she looked as if she wanted him to.) As though he'd eaten snakeweed and run mad, at the first recess he knocked Mosey Fritz into a puddle of thawed snow; hounded him thereafter until Mosey locked himself in the outhouse, breathless and for once a little scared. The Pastor returned early. Mosey sneaked in late and was caught in the middle of the prayers. Johnny tittered over the birching until the Pastor threatened to stretch his pants, too.

He strutted at recess until Snoose chuckled, "Britches too big, eh, Johnny? Guess we'll have to give you 'lap jacket'." So astray in error was he that at noon he picked a fight with Heinie Beerwagon, older than he was and quick on his toes, though on ordinary days they were friends. When it was over Heinie pulled him to his wobbly feet and Snoose wiped the blood from his broken lips. There was little either could do about a loose tooth and one eye that was rapidly darkening to the color of raspberry jam. All three looked at each other: the Pastor!

The Pastor glanced at Johnny's battered face and said briefly: "I said no more fighting or I'd use the stick. Who started this?" He banged the birch to hasten their memories.

Mosey began giggling excitedly, pleasantly anticipating the whipping Johnny would get. But the Pastor swung the tip of the birch. "So, Mosey. I might have known. Lay over the bench."

In frightened outrage Mosey shrilled, "I didn't." Johnny laughed inside himself in spite of thickening eye and lip.

"If there's a fight here, I always find you stirring at the bottom of it. Lay over, Mosey."

Johnny thought, this is as good as beefsteak.

"Herr Pastor, I didn't fight." With a vomity look Mosey began to rise.

"No? I'll start with you anyway." The Pastor was nicely impartial. "I couldn't make a better beginning."

Johnny leaned back to hear the first *zipple-swish* over Mosey's rump when Kurt spoke up calmly, "Herr Pastor, Mosey wasn't even around here. He was locked in the outhouse."

Johnny turned to glare, thinking, what's he butting in for? I'll crack his teeth if he tells.

"Then who started this?" shouted the Pastor, bouncing irritably to a new attack. "I ask for the last time. Tell me at once, Kurt Barewolf."

Johnny went cold. If he tells on Heinie——

Slow astonishment pushed over Kurt's heavy face. "Why, Herr Pastor—" he began as if he couldn't believe what he had heard.

"At once!" The birch snapped down.

"Herr Pastor—" Kurt arose deferentially—"a minister like you stands for fair play." His words were distinct. "And the Herr Pastor would be right to punish me, if I turned cowardly snitcher." He sat down.

The Pastor's hands trembled. There was a scornful steadiness in Kurt's eyes that enraged yet baffled him. "Yes, of course, of course," he muttered, flinging the stick on his desk.

Mosey sent Kurt a quick glance, soft with gratitude. But Kurt was already deep in The Fall of Jericho.

Johnny felt more shame than he ever acknowledged. Furiously he sputtered at Kurt after school, "What did you put your oar in for? Mosey had it coming. Time and again he's let somebody else catch a licking while he got out of it. And he'd laugh, too. You must like that Mosey Fritz."

"I don't care how many lickings Mosey gets, fair or unfair." Kurt was unruffled. "Or how many you get. You had yours coming too, scrapping over nothing. But the Pastor—he likes to feel the stick hit the bone. I thought I'd just spoil his little fun, for once."

"Oh, you—you're——" Johnny choked and his lip hurt.

Aunt Phrena clattered a spoon when she saw him. Without lifting a finger against him, she punished him with words and tears and a cool knife and a piece of meat slapped over his eye, not so much to ease his swelling as to erase a mark that was, in her sight, a disgrace in the neighborhood. "Fighting like a crazy thrasher," she scolded, angry water glinting in her eyes, though her hands were gentle on his cringing flesh. "What will become of you, Johnny, starting off bad like this, and you so young? I promised my sister, poor dove, that I'd bring you up good, and now fighting."

She wanted Uncle Herm to give him a hiding with a leather strap then and there. When Uncle Herm answered, "Na, Phrena, wrong maybe it is, but not so worse as that," she wailed into tears. "My poor sister; in heaven she's blaming me, I know she is." Uncle Herm stomped outside. Johnny huddled in his chair, beaten more by this than by Heinie Beerwagon's fists or by any strapping Uncle Herm could give him. But Aunt Phrena leaved in the Precious Comfort Book as if out of its thumb-smeared pages might flutter a plan to save him, her sister's son, from the rabbit snares of sin.

For a week Johnny's feathers, arched proudly before, dragged on the ground. Between him and Heinie were the upthrusts of chilly shoulders. It wasn't the black eye that irked him; he was proud of the pummeling Heinie had given him. But he did want to stand beside Heinie as the headman in school; and Heinie had lowered the high-tail of his importance, and that rankled. But one day Gatha Blumen winked at him, friendliness running along her thin boyish body, and offered to share a piece of her juiciest molasses cake, dark and smelling of cloves. He was grateful, at least gastronomically.

The irritation remained, however, and even this gratitude ebbed when he heard a flock of girls caroling:

"Here comes that *fighting* Johnny Schwartz;
Run, girlies; he's coming for your hearts."

Gatha joined them. It was Sophie's verse but changed now, prickly with teasing. He glared around. Sophie's playfulness he didn't mind any more than Snoose's. This was different. These voices tonguing his name. It was something like the feeling he had about Kurt these days. His hands twisted.

The boys joined the chorus gleefully, Mosey Fritz with doglike howling. All of them jeered except Snoose, who bothered his lip with a disturbed finger. Even Gatha Blumen chirped, mirth in her clear smile. Johnny spat out the reminiscence of chewed molasses cake. He wanted to ball fists again but his scabby lip was a caution he couldn't avoid. Besides, Heinie stood there swaying his hulking shoulders; and Lornas Tetzell waited with his slouchy body. Johnny swung away, calling to Snoose, swearing that he'd sooner keep company with Bully the black ox than with people so crooked-mouthed as these, even Gatha Blumen: who were clap-shoulder friends one moment and stuck out their tongues at you the next.

"Why do you fire up so?" Snoose asked, once they had put a length of dirt road between them and the churchyard. "They mean only fun."

"It's—it's—oh, I don't know, Snoose," Johnny stammered helplessly. "Why don't they leave my name alone?"

"They make fun of everybody's name, when they can."

"I know." Johnny worried a cuff on his coat. He couldn't say, "It's got something to do with my pa; with my ma, too." He couldn't say, "I'd like to kick my foot into their teeth when they laugh at me." He could only mutter, "They make it sound—oh, like spit and smuck."

"Oh!" Snoose glanced up swiftly. "Ya, I know, *that* I know. Like what they call me." They looked at each other in quick understanding, sharing this Job's lot of trouble like bread. Then they started back in a sudden run. They were late and the Pastor pointed to them as a timely example of the Foolish Virgins who were tardy.

Two Fridays later, during a thaw, Johnny and Heinie Beerwagon fell into the pond together, friends once more. And Gatha Blumen held out her hoarhound candy stick. He was huffy at first and barked that he'd just knocked out his sugar tooth and thrown it into a brush pile. He came around however and almost eagerly nibbled the tangy sweet.

Drifts in a howling March storm piled high near the rail fences, higher where the wind dropped its sky-sifted burden in a sheltered place. Shocks in the cornfield had an arc licked clear of snow on the northerly side, wind-

wells dug by the sweep of the blizzard. And another calf was dropped in
the barn, a black one with silky hair. Johnny looked his question: "Is it
this year I get a calf for my own? But he let it go at that. Uncle Herm took
his time.

In those blustery days some things began to take shape and form in
Johnny's mind, especially about Kurt. He'd plod from school through snow
boot-high, his gaze on Kurt's heavy shoulders ahead of him and his teeth
edged together. He could pin those chunky muscles to the ground, yes;
but he'd have given the good stick-knife in his pocket if he could have
forced one cry between those thick lips. Sometimes at skating parties he
felt that he never could get his skates sharp enough to carry him zipping
across the ice away from Kurt's lumbering body or his sticky laugh.

He'd watch Kurt pitch corn bundles when they went to the field on
Saturdays. They pried the corn from its frozen moorings, sometimes stalk
by stalk, sledloads of it. Uncle Herm would watch the mice scuttling away
among the pigeon-grass seeds. "Stubtails again," he'd say. "Gonna be a
short-crop year, kids." Or: "Bull wheels of Moses, look at those long tails;
reg'lar whippers. Looks like a good crop, this season." (In spring after the
last freeze, he'd thrust a stick of weed into an ant pile. If the ants swarmed
up and over the end, he'd be sure it was a yielding season. If they came
only halfway up and then turned down, 'he'd grumble, "Huh! Half-crop
year again.")

Kurt remained serene. Once in a while, however, an impatient plunge of
his arm betrayed a current of disquiet underneath his placidity.

At shindandies and socials too there was this stubby growth between
them. Like that night at the Dunkels'. They went there to help eat Mrs.
Dunkel's birthday cake and say, "My, you ain't a day older than last year."
Aunt Phrena brought a batch of cookies and Uncle Herm his thirst for
the Dunkel chokecherry wine.

Johnny left Kurt quickly and hung in the corners with Snoose, com-
pany-shy until Mr. Dunkel said to him, "Growing fast, Johnny. Almost
big enough to come with me to Fergus after grain-cutting this fall."
Anders Stramff nodded, his accordion like a hunched animal back of his
chair.

Johnny became so loud of voice then and rough-horse in play that Aunt
Phrena had to call, her warning stiff as a scrub brush. Uncle Herm tugged
his whiskers. Johnny swaggered a little when he noticed how folks glanced
at him. He made faces at the tongue Gatha Blumen popped at him, girl-
wise but not unfriendly. Kurt stretched himself lazily, important in the
talk with the older Nussbaum boys. Sophie laid her sharp glances on
Clymy Humber, and Clymy knew it. He sat dwarfed and timorous, half

fascinated, half frightened at the muscle of her arms and the ampleness of her young breasts. Sophie hardly dared move her head; he might be scared away.

After lunch Alb Hukelpoke said, "Old Geppert—he's sure talking how much French Imperial wheat he's gonna plant."

"I'm planting a good-sized patch myself." Mr. Dunkel was suddenly testy. "Old blowhard, bragging about his wheat and how good he is at cradling. Whoop-Jinny-and-fall-down, I'll cradle him two lengths of grain before he can spit."

Adam Schramff began tweedling a lonely waltz just then. The little Gretel danced at his knee. And how she whirled! Mr. Dunkel forgot Old Geppert, tapping the rhythm pridefully. Mrs. Dunkel mother-smiled near by. "Ought to call her Gretel-behind-the-brush-pile, the way she runs and hides; in the wheat, last summer." Johnny and Snoose touched shoulders, sitting on the floor.

The little Gretel was big-eyed and brown-haired and white of skin as a lily throat. The women "Oh-ed" and said "Angel" when she trotted into church beside Mrs. Dunkel. The Pastor, undeterred by innocence, had once pronounced, "The good die young." She lifted her chin, confidence in her four-year-old smile, and danced, the white dress with the scarlet rosettes and ribbons a blur of snow streaked with red. "She's pretty sweet," Johnny told Snoose without condescension. "But she'll probably spindle up and be as mean and cross-sticked as the rest of the girls."

The dance ended. In the pause between pieces, Johnny, still excited by Mr. Dunkel's words, exclaimed more noisily than he intended, "I'd like to take a trip to Fergus."

Kurt smiled stickily. "Would you really? And what would you do there?" His question was deliberately loud. "Stand on the street corner and suck your thumb?" The folks guffawed roundly. Johnny flushed and tried to hide behind Snoose.

The hedges of their ire thickened the morning Uncle Herm, striding in from the barn, said, "There's now two calves in the pen." He hesitated, glancing cautiously at Aunt Phrena. "Kurt's already made his choice. I s'posed he ought to have the first say." He didn't explain why. "He has a hankering for the black one. And the black's a good one to raise. There's the red one with the white spots for you, Johnny. It's a heifer. Take care of them, boys. The money you get for them is yours."

Whooping, Johnny ran to the barn. He was glad Kurt had chosen the black. The red spotted calf was straight of back and wide of hip and had a tongue that folded like a leaf around his finger when she suckled it, her head down in the pail. She's gonna grow up big as a bull, he thought, jauntily entering the barn. "Ain't ya?" The calf *maw*-ed protestingly at the rope's end. She'll bring, oh, loads of money. I can get the mushrat traps and—— His bubbling eagerness flattened before a sober notion. Nope. Uncle Herm; it's him that needs the money. Worse'n me.

When he untied the calf and led her on the rope, she ran her tether and kicked manure to the ceiling, deluded as men are into the belief that those eight feet of liberty were equal to the freedom of earth and sky. Laughing, Johnny patted her. "Old Kickin' Bessy, that's what we'll call ya. Bessy." Then he saw Kurt watching lazily from the horse stall.

Kurt said, "Think I'll take the red one after all, seeing Uncle Herm gave me first say."

The rope slipped in Johnny's hands. "You can't. Uncle Herm said you wanted the black one and——"

"Uncle Herm gave me the first chance." Kurt was stubborn. "I didn't exactly decide on the black. I just didn't say."

"The red one's mine. You had your chance."

"Feller with the first say gets the one he wants. That red one there, strikes me she's——" Kurt let his words drag slowly into silence. He leaned against a post, so slack-boned and easy that Johnny began to simmer.

Johnny flung the rope over the manger bar, anger in his throw. "Uncle Herm is going to settle this."

But when he brought Uncle Herm from the hen house, he found Kurt bedding the black calf with new straw and whistling with relish, "Boys, Keep Away from the Girls," knowing that Mosey Fritz had yammered it cat-fashion at school and that Johnny hated it. Before Johnny could spit out a word, Kurt spoke in a slow unhurried drawl: "Don't know what you're makin' such a howl for. The black calf is a good one."

Uncle Herm stared at Johnny. "Thought you said Kurt wanted the red one now."

"He did." Johnny jumped about. "He said it, a while back there. He said he wanted the red one, not the black."

"I said I *thought* I'd take her." Kurt was tranquil. "Didn't say I *would*."

"Don't know what you want, do you?" Johnny yelled. "You *thought* and you *would*. Which is it now?"

Uncle Herm turned from one to the other.

"Oh, the red one is nice." Kurt rubbed a mittened hand along the calf's spine, not ready to give up anything yet, laying down time as Old Geppert did money, with care and in no hurry. "But I *think* the black one——"

"Think?" Johnny shrilled and stood still. He couldn't hold back the anger hopping like a firecracker in him. In blind fury, half his forehead wrinkled in rage, half clear, he grabbed a tug and piled into Kurt, arms flying, forgetful of everything except to smash what barred his will and way.

He came out of a red mist to find Uncle Herm shaking him, holding him off, and shouting, "Johnny, let go that tug. Let it go, or I'll crack a rib of yourn."

He gave in. Cold like the chill after sweat crawled over him. Water rushed to his eyes at Kurt's grin, still tantalizing, although Kurt was whiter around the ears than usual. Kurt's grin said plainly, "Baby-tit had to run and tattle." And in his swift unthinking anger, he *had* run to Uncle Herm. He knew it and knowing wasn't ointment for his wrath. Realizing all at once how helpless he was before Kurt's goading and how Uncle Herm stood, not yet sure which way the wind rode; feeling unreasonably that Uncle Herm, for the moment, must be against him since he wasn't for him—Johnny felt the sour of curdled milk in his mouth and flung away bitterly. "Kurt can have the red one, too; both of them. Don't want none of 'em now," he muttered sullenly and stumbled from the barn.

He left Kurt with a slow grin spreading and Uncle Herm growling, "What in tarnation got into him?"

Aunt Phrena regarded him with sorrow when she heard, as if he'd budded a new sprout of evil and she must hasten to snip it before it branched and flowered. "Sometimes, Johnny," she sighed, "I think you got the Devil right in you."

All that spring and early summer she rummaged in the closets of her mind and leaved in the Comfort Book, hunting a way by which she could tether him on the sheepy pastures of salvation and so guard him against the gentle slopes of error; and perhaps—she recognized the quandary into which the quarrel with Kurt had flung Uncle Herm—perhaps she could tenderly unseat him from a kind of favor she was sure he was gaining in Uncle Herm's eyes. Reading one day about the conversion of St. Paul, she pounced upon an idea that wriggled on the edge of her contriving. "Ach, sakes and days alive, ya! Why didn't I think of that before?" A seraphic glow parted her full lips. She'd see the Pastor the next Sunday and wait for the fit occasion.

That season Kurt fed two calves. Johnny helped him now and again, letting that matter cool, though once he said grudgingly, "You sorta planned this, didn't you, Kurt? You wanted both calves from the start, huh?"

Kurt answered with all the slyness gone and in unsmiling seriousness, "No, no, Johnny. You're the one that settled the matter. I didn't care, one was as good as the other. I just changed because—well, you got to change your mind as you go along. You got mad and then you didn't want either one, finally."

Over this Johnny clamped his jaw, anger welling again because he couldn't say anything but a helpless "So. It's my fault. After all your gabbin' and shootin' your tongue, it turns out to be this—I'm to blame." It hurt that he couldn't share some of the burden which Uncle Herm shouldered on account of Norton and the threshing rig and the year's unpredictable yield. Even the sale of a calf would help, he was sure.

Restlessness that was not far from lonely grief ran in his veins and he'd plow through the woods to the cleared space on the hillside and let forlornness drench him like a sponge. Without tears these days, crinkle-eyed, he'd stand there, looking blindly at the valley. Over and over he'd hear: "Just like your pa. . . . By its fruit the tree is known. . . . Sins of the fathers . . ." It must be true. The Bible couldn't lie. In trembling sweat he'd mutter, "It's in me; I'm bad—from *him*." So he called his father: "*Him*."

And out of Aunt Phrena's hintings and stabbing innuendoes, out of Uncle Herm's reticences, out of the Pastor's white-edged exhortations, the shadow grew, a darkness thicker than any cast by oak or elm. Hate began to glare. *Him, him.* Is it my fault? A past he wasn't asked to choose, a yesterday he was powerless to avoid? *Him.* If I had *him* here, I'd—he kicked at a stump as though it were a cat and alive—I'd push his face in a pile of cowflop.

But even hate couldn't overlay the sense of humiliation, long dormantly felt, that spread over him. Schwartzie—shame, that's what *she* means; until he felt uneasy redness on his ears when his name rolled over somebody's tongue, even the Pastor's at recitation call. He'd jerk up quickly as though he heard a joke at the back of the sound.

He wished sometimes that he could set off like a dog and leave Aunt Phrena and the valley miles behind. The memory of his mother's face was dimmer now, crowded out, but sweeter for its shadowiness, as ecstatic dreams in fading leave behind a longing for their sweet fulfillment. Curiously, her smile was becoming more like the smile on the face of the china doll and her voice was thinning to a thread of melody—a thinness like the red ribbon around the doll's neck.

He shut his eyes and felt again the panic leaping in him: Bad, that's what I am. Scrapping and getting into trouble. That's what *she* says. Bad . . .

13

In April Old Geppert's ox (a red one called Gehenna—G'henna for short) sickened to raggy bones. The neighbors unstuck the pages of their doctor books. Whether the ailment resulted from the poison of the warble-fly stings in the season before (as Mr. Dunkel insisted) or from the leaves of the deadly snakeroot dried in the hay (as Old Geppert supposed), no one was ready to say.

"It's the wormils," Mr. Dunkel told Uncle Herm. "He didn't squeeze the worms out of the bumps on the ox's back, like I told him in Feb'ry."

"Wormils!" snorted Old Geppert. "I've forgotten more about oxen than Dunkel will ever learn. It's something G'henna et, I tell you."

Mr. Nussbaum said dourly, "Oxen, oxen; nothing but trouble. By jippers, why don't Geppert sell his bullies and get hisself horses; Dunkel, too?" But Mr. Dunkel shook his head and Old Geppert doctored his Gehenna.

The neighbors came to prod the red ox grunting in the stall. Some (favoring Dunkel) brought hide-searing stuff for his insides; some (favoring Geppert) gut-smelling stuff for his outsides. Often enough Geppert had given remedies to his neighbors; now he was receiving them. Carefully he threw away bottle and jar. But the pain of Gehenna waxed until the valley agonized in human grief.

Long winds sucked away the last of the snowdrifts facing north and rubbed the scummy hide of ponds. The creek burst into foamy wreaths among the rocks. Spring-warm rains swished broomlike over the May ridges, leaving tree and greening blade clean of winter grit. Johnny and Snoose prowled in the moist woods coming from school and after, forgetting chores and spring work at home. They pushed aside the heavy thickness of the hazels to find bloodroots, yellow-centered and snowy-winged. In damp leaf-rich places they touched the trillium, its waxy petals lifted by a forward May whitely above the cushions of its three leaves, green and deeply ribbed. Where June bogs held coolness from the swamps they stumbled on marsh calla drawing its glossy pink-white sheath around the green club of its flowers.

"If G'henna kicks the bucket," Johnny said casually one day, resting on a grassy bank, "where will Old Geppert get another ox?"

"Don't know exactly." Snoose ran violets disregardfully through his fingers. "Dunkel's the only man left around here that's got *decent* oxen. Pa says Geppert and Dunkel will prob'ly make a trade." Absently he tied the violets in bunches with hair jerked from his head. He could name many flowers, but Johnny didn't know a bellwort from a cowslip and was prideful in saying it.

Geppert dealt with Mr. Dunkel finally, Johnny heard. He got the new ox in time for spring planting. It was a sensible deal, Uncle Herm maintained. "If they want oxen and no horses, they'll have to trade where they

can, even if they can't get along." His own oxen Uncle Herm used only
for the weighty hauls, and then rarely.

At once there were whispers of an underhanded deal. Mr. Dunkel,
saying nothing, whistled over his spring planting as sprightly as a grosbeak.
But there was talk that Geppert had toothed a lower lip grimly and called
Dunkel names.

Bellwort hung yellow flowers in the high shadowy woods; jack-in-the-
pulpit stood erect and green under his brown-striped canopy. And one day
Johnny exploded through the scented plum hedges into the field where
Snoose was hoeing corn. "I'm going, I'm going," he shouted, shaking like
jelly in his excitement. "To Fergus this fall, with Mr. Dunkel. He's giving
me a new stick-knife—with silver on the——"

"Settle down," Snoose chuckled, poking at Johnny's middle with the hoe
handle. "You'll start kittening all over the place, first thing you know."

"Uncle Herm says I can." Johnny calmed a little. "And Aunt Phrena—
well, you know how she is. But she says yes too. Mr. Dunkel's going to
take Mr. Peiser's team and spring wagon. We're gonna stay all night—*all*
night." He swallowed happily. "He's got lots of business to do. I'm gonna
help with the horses. And Kurt can't go," he finished gleefully.

Snoose's gray eyes were unenviously warm.

The spring began in trillium and bloodroot. Nobody guessed how
fiercely red the flower of wheat would grow before the harvest time.

By early summer Old Geppert began to grumble; made remarks at the
store from the corner of his mouth about the scabby animals Dunkel had.
Mr. Dunkel heard but never stopped his whistle curving sweetly over the
fields. Some folks wondered, "You s'pose Dunkel beat him in the deal?"
Others spoke brusquely: "That Dunkel—a come-upper. Needs a trimming
down." Aunt Phrena said, "Ach, I expected this. A man like Geppert." The
neighborhood settled down like a dog, expectantly.

Before midsummer everybody was talking about the ox trade. Folks
guessed at who had worsted whom. They took sides, most of them Geppert's, until Mr. Dunkel's temper began to be edgy. Dissension like heat
lightning flickered over valley and ridge, ominous and portending storm.
Whether the ox was worthless as Geppert maintained was never really
proved. How much of the trouble came because of this quarrel, how much
because of rancor begun long before the neighbors knew either Dunkel
or Geppert, how much because of neighborhood goading, nobody stopped
to ask until the wheat had been cut and the grave dug. And little good it
did to ask then. Johnny was disturbed for Mr. Dunkel's sake. But he had
misery of his own crashing about his ears. It came at the beginning of the
next week.

Out of what hidden pocket of her mind Aunt Phrena hauled the notion that he ought to study for preaching, Johnny never learned. She let him know about it over Sunday's kraut and sowbelly. Usually, meals at the Barewolf table were silent and only sprinkled with talk. No useless chatter hindered the lifting of a knife or spoon. There was hardly more said than "Pass the meat," between the first helping of potatoes and the second; little more uttered than "Pitch me a hunk of bread" before they put knives to the butter. (It was hog-lard mostly. Butter in Mary's Hill paid the grocer's bill.) When they scooped into the second helping, talk began to liven up.

Aunt Phrena always seasoned her meals with grace. "Sakes and days alive, I won't have my family go to the table like hogs to a trough," she proclaimed. Although he couldn't remember half the time, it was Uncle Herm's duty to fold hands and begin the prayer, Kurt and Johnny by turns adding their short petitions. Often Uncle Herm would forget and shove a piece of bread between his teeth before he caught Aunt Phrena's long and weighty stare. Then he'd begin to choke over "Come, Lord Jesus," bread and his words getting mixed in his throat. Even at threshing time Aunt Phrena stood at his shoulder, holding the soup ladle in her hand and out of reach. No soup was ladled until grace was finished. "The blessing won't hurt them, all the swearing they do outside."

They strung neighbor talk with the kraut on their forks this Sunday. Geppert was getting louder about the ox and even Mr. Dunkel uttered sharp-sided words. . . .

The walking preacher was coming to the Edgelys' again, to hold revivals and send the Pastor into spasms of wrath over false prophets and the deceivers out of darkness. Aunt Phrena, disturbed by the Pastor's recent sermons, thought she'd like to see what the walking preacher was like. Not that she really would, since she was a God-fearing soul and Uncle Herm was a member of the Pockerbrush congregation. . . .

Anders Stramff was going to live at Alb Hukelpoke's house, done at last with working from place to place, season after season, lonely and kinless, his folks in Minneapolis forgetfully far away. . . .

Bory Tetzell over at Loon Lake was talking about getting a steam engine for his separator—a "bull traction" engine he called it because oxen were used to lug it from one farm to another. Bory had a new team now, a pair of trippers, which he'd like to hook to the engine. "Cripes, that's just like a Loon Laker. Crazy in the noodle," Mr. Schadel had snorted. "Heavy chunk of iron like that. He'll bog hisself down in the swamp roads. That corduroy won't hold him. It shakes like jelly now when the teams go over it and the horsepower." Uncle Herm, reporting this, agreed. Johnny chewed sowbelly, uncertain, but Kurt wondered whether the horses would get used to the smoke from the stack as they pulled the engine along. . . .

That girl Sophie Marchen, the shameless way she chased Clymy Humber, scolded Aunt Phrena; but Uncle Herm prophesied they'd be married before Clymy knew she had a finger on him.

The Sunday meal went on. All at once while she set the coffeepot down for emphasis Aunt Phrena observed, "The Pastor says you're doing real well in Sunday school and in Catechism, Johnny. You ought to dig in with a will this fall, and show him. You could be a preacher some day."

"Preacher?" Astonishment choked the coffee in his throat. "Me?" Kurt put down his knife. Uncle Herm forgot to chew.

"Like my brother Zacharias, dear good Zacharias. He looked so nice in his white collar." Aunt Phrena sighed over the thought.

"Leave the place and go to preacher school?" Johnny grabbed a piece of bread so hard it broke. He didn't know how serious she was but a dimness slithered over his mind when he thought of the Pastor and his long black gown. Not even the thought of a white collar gave him any pleasure.

"Is it so terrible then, to study godly things?" Aunt Phrena soothed him.

Johnny clutched desperately at the first moving thought. "I'm going to run a lumber boat on the Red River, like Mr. Beerwagon used to do. That's what Snoose is going to do when he grows up." He blinked at Uncle Herm: "Or get a thrashing rig." As if this were a secret between them. "We figure——"

"Charley Marchen." Aunt Phrena nodded her head, satisfied with her worst fears. "Mrs. Marchen should better watch out for her boy. So lazy he smells. Mrs. Fleischer says she saw him back of the church after service today, monkeying around instead of remembering what the Pastor——"

"It was a squirrel," Kurt broke in to defend Snoose before Johnny could. "It had a broken leg. Lornas Tetzell wanted to kill it."

"I s'pose it is so nowadays." She threw him a sad, sick kind of look: her own son putting an extra ox weight on her shoulders. "A squirrel now. That's more important than a starving, dying soul." She gulped coffee. Uncle Herm tweaked his mustache. Johnny licked lard from his fingers, glad that Kurt had spoken up.

Aunt Phrena tried again. "Your ma, Johnny—poor sweet dove, how proud she'd be, you a minister and folks driving buggies for miles to hear you." Her fat lips uncurved beamingly.

"Don't want to be a preacher." Johnny didn't know where to look. He flung the words like stones, careless where they struck. "Have to go ten years to a darn old preacher school——"

"There. Swearing." Aunt Phrena pounced on the bone of sin triumphantly. "That's Schwartz coming out again. Soaked to the marrow you are with him."

"Na, Phrena." Uncle Herm licked his fork in protest. "The boy should wait for a call, shouldn't he? From heaven or wherever it is a preacher gets it. He's too young——"

"I don't blame Johnny, I don't." Kurt looked as if he were surprised at his own boldness. "Wouldn't want to be a preacher either."

"That's right, stick up for Johnny. My own son, too." Aunt Phrena began to wail.

Said Uncle Herm in innocent haste, "Maybe Kurt, too—both of them could study for——"

"I won't," howled Kurt, clattering his knife so hard the coffee spilled. "I'm sick to my belly of the Precious Comfort Book, too."

"There, now. That's all the thanks I get," she hiccoughed, pushing her plate away. "It's hard enough, bringing up my own boy. But I promised her, poor sweet dove; with her dying breath she heard me. I said I'd bring *him* up—" she flung a nod sidewise at Johnny—"like my own. All I get is blame."

"You hate me, don't you?" Johnny pushed his chair back sharply; stood beside it.

She leaned back, a kind of dismay freezing her saggy mouth. Out of shocked amazement Uncle Herm protested, "Na, Johnny, what you say?" Kurt stiffened.

"Don't you?" Johnny raised a quavering voice. "On account of my pa?"

"No, no, Johnny," she muttered. "You're my sister's boy. You should grow up fine and——"

He wanted to shout, "Tell me, can't you?" but the youth in him, like sapling before oak, failed in the smart of approaching tears. He crept miserably from the house. Uncle Herm shoved his chair aside, growling, "Moses Almighty!" and went to the barn.

But when the kitchen was empty of menfolk and the kettle loud with water, Aunt Phrena waddled to the bedroom, whispering "It is not so. I do not hate." Her fingers trembled when she wet them, paging in the Comfort Book, until she came to the portion on "Evil and Iniquity Forgiven."

14

For a week Johnny grouched over his work. He might have remained moody-spirited and sullen longer, had not Snoose drawn the trouble from him as gently as he removed the stings of bees, or splinters. For a while Johnny dared not tell him about the preacher school, resentful even of Snoose's chuckle. But one evening he couldn't hold back. They were walking along a cowpath, Snoose listening, drops of water on the cheeks of both from a swim in the creek. It rushed out like sticks and stones dumped from a wagon. "I won't be a preacher." Johnny kicked dust in the path until it arose gray in the twilight. "She can't make me."

"'Course she can't. Nobody can," Snoose answered comfortably, more to quiet him than from conviction, for both knew that Aunt Phrena would have her way finally. They couldn't imagine a stratagem desperate enough to evade her determination; not then, at least. "And your Uncle Herm—" Snoose went on—"he don't want you to go to preacher school either, does he?"

"No. But Uncle Herm—even he collared me," Johnny mourned dispiritedly, as if this were the worst. "He said I was wrong, Aunt Phrena ain't against me. She's trying to do the best for me. Even Uncle Herm." He stamped a heel rebelliously. "Oh, Snoose, I could run away."

"And leave me?" chuckled Snoose. "Sometimes you're as smart as a porcupine and that ain't smart." He put an arm about Johnny's shoulders.

Since the fight with Heinie Beerwagon and their talk in the road near the church, Johnny and Snoose had felt a greater need than ever one for the other. They were together by the hour, working or playing, whenever time or occasion offered opportunity, until Aunt Phrena sniffed about folks being strangers in their own houses. Until Kurt was waspish and even Uncle Herm frowned.

They baggled over this and that mouthful: where bullheads in the creek spent the winter when ice sealed crook and inlet with bubbled glass; who invented girls anyway, Snoose confessing, ear lobes red and chuckling loudly, that it was fun kissing Em'ly Musser, she wanted it so. Which set Johnny to wriggling. He vowed with his hand on a cake of mud that he'd try it the first thing, maybe with Gatha Blumen.

Once Snoose burst out after a while of silence, "'Snoose.' What a name to call a kid. Might as well call him Devil." Charley Marchen: that was a name the Lord would recognize, once he got to heaven. So his gramma told him. But "Snoose." That sounded like somebody who'd got in by mistake and really belonged in the other place. Maybe he'd go there anyway, Snoose muttered darkly.

Johnny shook his head. "Ma used to say that the Lord saw through you like a pane of glass—even a spotty pane." They sighed together, each savoring the other's thought like tart-sweet cranberry juice. In those hours Johnny shrugged away the thought of the preacher school.

They came upon unsuspected depths in themselves one afternoon which left them shy of each other for days. Johnny was in the garden, Snoose with him. Snoose had come over to borrow a rake. It was a hot day, a weather breeder, with butterflies darting in mad soaring curves from plant to plant. Johnny was hoeing, his shirt off in spite of Aunt Phrena's warning, "Sun's bad for your ribs." He was going into his thirteenth year with a body stained the color of old leaves. Snoose was nibbling bits of cabbage leaf, his spit greenish, and trying to catch the butterflies that were to Johnny no more than blobs of white wings and dusty gray bodies.

Johnny offered, "You can have my old stick-knife, Snoose, just as soon as Mr. Dunkel gives me the new one. There's to be silver in the handle. Mr. Dunkel says the stores in Fergus got lots; more than in Mary's Hill." He hoed a while. "Kurt wants the old one, but I won't give it to him."

Snoose called, "Come arunnin', quick." Johnny came and found him with a captured insect. "That's a she," Snoose said, holding the insect by the wings. Johnny kneed down in the soft dirt. Snoose thrust his hand through a pea bush. The vines concealed all except his finger and thumb and the insect between them. The insect twisted its pale gray body like a worm. Snoose murmured, "Now watch them."

Johnny did, an edge of excitement stirring in him unaccountably. Out of a dozen butterflies tumbling about the cabbages, three or four darted near. One came zigzagging. "That's a he," whispered Snoose, breath-drawn. "Sit still." Lured by the lodestone of attraction, it fluttered wildly above the captive, then settled down, the end of its curving body touching and at last holding the other. "Now—now they are—it is like a wedding, a wedding night." Snoose's lips were wet and his eyes lost in gray wells of dreaminess.

Johnny sat hammer-struck, his breath coming faster, his blood stirred into tingling by strange and awful ferments whose urge lies with bedrock and the first dividing cell. His muscles flicked but he stayed like a stone when Snoose, releasing the butterfly, nudged closer to him. Webbed with something beyond him to understand, Snoose put his hand on Johnny's bare side, fingers on ribs. He bent forward and slowly thrust his hand deep into Johnny's pocket. For a moment both were locked in the ice of discovery, moveless of body, a great roaring in their ears. Then Snoose got up, panic darkening his eyes. Johnny rose with him, aware from that day of currents wild and untamable as rivers swirling under his skin, welling up from the unfathomable deeps of his being. Together they walked to the spring for a long drink of water.

15

The oats were ready to cut, ripely heavy, when Uncle Herm opened the door and said at lunchtime, "Well, they've done it. Dunkel and Geppert— they're going to have a cradling match. Two swaths across and two back in Dunkel's wheat field. Best man wins and the loser pays for the beer."

Johnny and Snoose chattered like red squirrels disturbed by a cat. The strife between the two neighbors, crackling like fat pine wood all spring, had exploded into raw flame that was to roar through their memories like fire through brush. Up and down the ridges folks tossed words from lip to lip about the match. Some were on Dunkel's side but more on Geppert's, seeing that he was bone-breed to the hills (as the saying went), while Dunkel was all but new-come and sproutful of notions. Kurt decided that Old Geppert had a good swing to his arm. He was called "old" because he had a son everybody called "young." The designation "old" had nothing to do with his age or his cradling abilities. It was a way the folks had of separating the father from the son in their minds. Johnny, anxious for Mr. Dunkel, said you had to have more than swing.

Alb Hukelpoke drove over to the Barewolfs' with a heifer in heat struggling at the gate of his wagon. He brought his opinion. "I've seen Dunkel cradle. Sheetin' Judas, Old Geppert better take a back seat 'fore he starts!"

But Mr. Nussbaum said at the store, "You ought to see Geppert. He goes through wheat like a greased pig."

Old Mr. Buckholtz, shaky with his more than eighty years, was glad. "Didn't think to see a cradlin' match before I went to the graveyard."

Folks who had cradled and seen cradling for years, common as ragweed, suddenly discovered art and science in the job and discoursed learnedly on the subject, although most of them regarded the work as irksome and old-fashioned, now that reapers and harvesters were being used and binders talked about.

Johnny, pestered by doubt, made up his mind that Mr. Dunkel must win the match. He tugged at the brass-wire band which Snoose had got from Old Man Fleischer to keep off the warts. He wondered whether its magic would put limberness in Mr. Dunkel's arms.

Aunt Phrena was sharp over the talk. "Them two, Dunkel and Geppert. Mad about an ox trade. It serves that old fool of a Geppert right he got beat in the deal. But to even it up with a cradling match——" She had no patience with the idea.

"Well," Uncle Herm tried to explain, "Old Geppert got mouthy. He figures Dunkel's bull is no good and says so; rubs it in. Dunkel, he got sore and said Geppert's talk was like his cradlin', a lot of swing and little to show. Well, the kitten led to the cat and before you knew it, they set a match."

"It's a spite match, all right." Aunt Phrena had dolor in her voice.

"'Tain't that exactly. It's—well, it's——" Uncle Herm tried to scratch the right word out of his mustache. "It's like two bulls in a pasture. They beller at each other a spell, they're that full of zip and peppermint. Then they're at it. That's when dirt and the bull wheels of Moses flies around."

"No." Aunt Phrena was firm. "No, the Pastor says it right. It's a spite match and it wasn't made yesterday. It has long roots and that's a mighty good poker to stir up trouble." But she decided to make pans of *Apful Kuchen* squares just the same and frizz her hair for the coming-together.

The harvest that year was lightened by the quick flame of anticipation running under the sweat and the exertion. And in Old Geppert's stall the red bull grunted. He was less ill now. One discomfort waned while another waxed.

Johnny felt the prod of excitement. Sleepy as he usually was in the morning, he crowded into his shoes with haste these days. Between wearing the path to Snoose's house a little deeper and fretting over Mr. Dunkel he almost broke into a rash. Once he thought, "If *he* loses, I won't get the silver-handled knife." He slapped his thigh quickly, ashamed of himself.

He raked cut grass one afternoon—a job Uncle Herm set him to do. But when he saw Mr. Dunkel lay the sickle of his cradle against a stand of oats and Mrs. Dunkel binding, he left the rake and walked over as if to assure himself that Mr. Dunkel still swung with a clean stroke. By the time he climbed the popple-rail fence into the field, Mr. Dunkel was resting over his cradle. On the acres beyond he could see Mr. Nussbaum beside his reaper, the vanes glinting in the sun.

Mr. Dunkel lifted a leg in welcome. They talked about nothing, neither speaking of that which lay heavy on their tongues, Johnny out of respect, Mr. Dunkel out of a kind of modesty. A quarter of an acre of oats lay in swaths behind him, still fresh from the stem and green-yellow in the stalk though washed-out-lemon color in the head.

With one eye on the little Gretel mixing sleep with shadows on the cool side of a shock, Mrs. Dunkel bound the oats close by. Her back curved like a spring to the ground. She picked a fistful of stalks, pushed and pulled them straight. With a supple twist that Johnny never could master, try as he would, she knotted the heads together and shook out a long string—a rope of oats. Seeing Johnny she waved it and said, "In a minute you can have a swallow, so hot it is. We got plenty water." The callus on her thumb knuckle was not yet thick. It was red from the rasp of straw, sharp-edged and brittle. In one hand she held the band; with the other she gathered the grain in the angle of an elbow, heaping it against the fulness of her breast, fruit against fruit, the heads sweeping like curls over her arm—curls like her little Gretel's. She pressed the bundle tightly about the middle so that butt and drooping heads spread out circlewise, the one as empty as the other was skinful of life.

Johnny saw kernels stuck in the sweat of her neck and felt shy when she put her hand inside her dress and pulled out a head of oats. "Scratchy old thing," she said. She bound the straw firmly with the cord of grain, slipping the free ends under the band. She let the firmly packed and tied stalks slide to her knees. With a rustle that was like a sigh, the bundle expanded against the band and was securely held.

He wished he could bind like that. He had wasted more than one handful of oats in trying. Time and again Uncle Herm stopped the reaper to show him how the thumb was a kind of knotter around which you wound the cord of grain to make a knot. Kurt learned easily and would repeat, scorn in his slow words, "No, this way. Can't you do it?"

"No, I can't," Johnny'd squeal. "It slips, and besides, it's so slow." All he got for his trouble was blisters on the knuckles of his thumbs. Neither of them bound much, for Mr. Marchen usually came, or Uncle Herm would exchange a day's binding with Mr. Dunkel. Aunt Phrena seldom put her foot on the field. She had a backful to carry in the garden, she said; it was enough that she sent coffee and bread to the fields for them. And so the grain was bound with neighbor muscle, Johnny watching while he gathered stray and scattered stalks, envious of hands that twisted deftly the straw into cord.

Mrs. Dunkel brought the jug. Johnny looked on warmly. The brown of her sunburned neck shading to white below the edge of her dress was good to see, he decided suddenly, although he couldn't have told why, unless it had something to do with his mother and her arms holding him from hurt. For all that sweat fell and a drop splashed on her bare foot, drawing the dust on her skin raggedly to its edges, no one could twinkle a heel lighter than Mrs. Dunkel, in polkas or schottisches at the barn dances.

"Here is water, Wilhelm." She put the jug in his hands. "I should go home soon now with Gretel. She crawled into the bushes again yesterday and went to sleep."

Mr. Dunkel took a long pull of a drink, his throat gurgling. Then he sighed, complaining, "It gets me here—cricks in the legs and in front of the shoulders, cradling does." He handed over the stone jug, cool with water beads. "Take a good one, Johnny." He brought the whetstone, spat on it and began moving it slither-slather across the blade. A grasshopper nibbled at a handle of the cradle, greedy for the salt where Mr. Dunkel's sweaty hands had darkened the wood. He snapped his finger at it. "Go away, you long-legged bastard, you! Wonder if we'll have those devils back again. They cleaned me and Pa in '77, slick as a whistle down in Nicollet County. We didn't have enough green stuff left on the place to fill a shovel."

He sharpened awhile, s'mira, s'mira, stone over iron. There was gentleness in his stroke, Johnny saw. Mr. Dunkel said, "Good many bundles I've laid in a row with this old cradle. It was my pa's. Old Geppert thinks he can really handle the sickle." It was out, what Johnny wanted to hear. He wriggled hopefully. Mr. Dunkel went on, "I'll mow him ten paces while he's still spittin' on the handle." He passed a hand like a caress along the top of the bow, which was curved like a finger with the sickle, as were the three other bows. Johnny saw how smooth the tips were, rounded like a cow's horns with the rub of stems. "You wait till the cradlin' shindandy next Sunday," promised Mr. Dunkel. "I'll shorten that tongue of his."

"Geppert is an old hand at it, Marchen says." Johnny was hesitant with the information.

"Oh, he can handle a brush hook, all right; but cradling——" Mr. Dunkel let it pass.

Mrs. Dunkel shook her head at Johnny. "It's been itchin' long in him, this wanting to cradle against Geppert; since young Nussbaum backed down, I guess, three or four years ago." She reached for the jug. "Now he can try. If he gets beat, I hope he's satisfied."

Mr. Dunkel waved his hand over this woman truck. Then he asked Johnny: "You coming, ain't you?"

"You betcha britches," Johnny answered sturdily as man to man with Mr. Dunkel, now that he was nearly thirteen and would be confirmed before many years. "There's going to be a whopper of a crowd, I hear."

"Ya." Mr. Dunkel wasn't complaining. "My house ain't big, but it'll hold 'em, or we'll put 'em in the outhouse. Ma, there—she's been bakin' stuff all week."

"I got the m'lasses cake yet to make. And not half enough to go around." Mrs. Dunkel was heavy with doubt. "And now there's this binding to do. Of course, if we had the money——"

Mrs. Dunkel was careful with her words, but Mr. Dunkel finished, as if he knew what she had in mind. "Not as fast as a reaper, maybe, this cradlin'. But a reaper now—does it always work?" He pointed with a whetstone. "Look, there. There's Nussbaum, stopping again. He spends half

the day fixing the damn critter. Digs oat straw out of the gears, or has to
run to the woods for a willow stick for teeth in the fans. Heavy grain comes
along or there's a bush oak he don't see and, whoop-Jinny-and-fall-down,
his reaper is out of teeth, that's all." He wiped the blade free of spittle.
"Couple days ago the horses ran away for him and smashed a wheel. Na,
na, I don't have to hitch up a team to make my cradle go. I ain't in no
hurry to throw money after the dog." He rose and lifted the cradle. Afterward Johnny remembered how the whetted sickle was an arch of brightness
in the sun.

He left the Dunkels to wade through the uncut meadow, grass shoulder-
high, like swimming, he thought. After a while, he saw Mr. Nussbaum and
the reaper. He put hands before him to bend the heavy growth apart.
Once he sprawled to the ground over a hummock and was lost in rank
meadow stalks. The minty smell of crushed motherwort was like balm in
his nose. Looking up the green well of grass, he saw a cloud like a tower
white against the blue. A song sparrow fluttered away and after a moment
of poking, he found the nest in the lee of a budding sneezeweed, the
youngsters feathered and hopping over the edge the moment he reached
down. And there was a butterfly he chased from an early joe-pye weed
nodding its dull pink head. A butterfly wing of brick-red brown with whitish spots pinned to his Sunday cap would make the kids in church open
their eyes. But it escaped him.

He sat on a rock, resting and watching Mr. Nussbaum drive down a
reaper-width of grain. The five vanes made a circle that was tilted like a
windmill wheel on a slant. They swooped low over the sickle, forcing the
oats against the blades. The fifth vane, setting its teeth, raked a bundle heap
off the platform to the stubbles. Round and round went the vanes, teeth
dribbling oat stems and trailing wild morning-glory vines. Armfuls of grain
fell, left for the binders. Johnny saw the Nussbaum boys, tall and angular
as their father, catching up straws for oat strings to bind the grain as Mrs.
Dunkel did. But he ventured no closer, for Mr. Nussbaum was sharp with
talk, and he didn't spare names on his horses.

Just then there came the sound of crashing wood, and he saw Mr. Nussbaum dancing in the oat swath, hopping mad, and heard cuss words bouncing over the stubble. Something broke again. Johnny slid off the rock, a
fork of uneasiness prodding him. There was the sloo grass, he remembered,
and in the west a cloud of rain. He legged it back and crawled over the
popple-rail fence. Furiously he worked in the hay till sun laid sweat like
oil on his arms. But there were more winnows than cocks of hay when Kurt
shouted at him to come home.

Uncle Herm, folding his lips, only looked at the sky and the rain threatening and said nothing. He shamed Johnny by going out after dark and cocking hay by moonlight. Aunt Phrena shook her head, eyes running. "That poor sister of mine! Poor thing! Think of her looking from heaven and seeing you run around like this. Like a yearling. Worse than thrashers." She blinked a tear, in sympathy with her thought. "Never at home. It runs in the blood." He was glad to be rid of her sticky tongue; left his barley coffee half drunk, and followed Uncle Herm to the sloo. Kurt stayed home. "He should read his Precious Comfort chapter tonight," Aunt Phrena ordered, pointed as a scissor.

Silently they raked under a watery moon. The sweat ran. Johnny piled hay until, slouching on a cock for a moment of labored breath, his sight fogged. The sweat of day and the wear of muscles slid over him. He fell into sleep like a dropped stone. He woke to find Uncle Herm lifting him to his unsteady legs and sighed, drowsiness like salt under his lids, "Mother, are the raisins in the pudding?" He grabbed Uncle Herm's hand as if it were Sport's brown ear and lagged home, too sleepy to notice how fast Uncle Herm's bony fingers closed over his sweaty palm.

<h1 style="text-align:center">16</h1>

They started for the Dunkels' the Sunday of the match late as usual, for Aunt Phrena discovered a rip in her flounces at the moment when Johnny drove the spring wagon past the door. She wouldn't move until she had threaded a needle and repaired it. They were no later than others. Uncle Herm remarked on the way, "His wheat's heavy, Dunkel's."

Johnny and Kurt were stiff-backed with loftiness at wearing new button shoes, though their toes ached. Aunt Phrena sighed, solemn over their vanity: "Ach, the harvest is great but where are the laborers, as the Bible says?" Her look was so brimful of meaning that Johnny felt "preacher school" in the air again. But stubbornness set his jaw. He sealed his ears in a plan to make Mosey Fritz ride the Dunkels' mad sheep buck.

The Dunkels' yard crawled with people—the Nussbaums, the Schadels, the Hukelpokes, the Marchens. Snoose ran to help Johnny unhook the team and whispered, "They got the beer keg by the machine shed."

Folks from over Jenny's Peak way and others to the north, ten miles over ridges, were there, and folks unknown in the hills, strange as a new waltz tune. There were the Habers, just come from Wisconsin, with most of their chairs and the baby's cradle and the boxes still piled in the wagon in which they came, now staying with the Fleischers until Mr. Haber cleared a patch and dug a cellar for a house. ("Not that we mind, I'm sure," Mrs. Fleischer told Aunt Phrena; "but eleven people usin' five spoons, and your buttonhooks gettin' mixed up with theirs—well, when the shoe gets crowded, the toe comes out, that's all.") And there was Mr. Krumlich, whose family stayed in Fergus while he hewed black oak for a log house up in section three, that place, wild and rock-scattered, where, Alb Hukelpoke said, God kicked together stone and brush for a place to spit and called it section three. They were all there, most of them already chewing food.

Geppert with a plate of pumpernickel and rye bread was bragging, "Yep, laid me down three acres of oats the other day; went at it so hard, the old cradle nearly got me hot on the stones." His tongue came out in a laugh. He was lean and tough with hardly a gray hair on his head.

Mr. Dunkel, disbelief in the hunch of his shoulders, pushed his fork tinnily against his plate. "That will be something to see." He was definite but polite; he didn't want to cast stones at a neighbor, even at a match.

Carrying their plates, Johnny and Kurt with Snoose drifted to a spot behind Mr. Mercer, who was grumbling, "I need a new grain cultivator the worst way. Getting tired of chopping down a dry oak to drag my grain under the ground. I can't buy, though. Elevator man beat me out of most of my wheat last fall."

"Just like them," Mr. Peiser said, hitching his belt. "But what can you do? I'd like to build me a house for once. Ma sure needs it. Old shack of ours, wind blows in, winters, so's her skirts flap. It was all right for a home-stead shanty but now, with the kids——" He sighed through his whiskers. "My youngest died two winters ago; caught cold—— Well!" He shrugged a suspender. "But what can you do?"

Folks talked. With side glances they appraised now Geppert, now Dunkel, those two who appeared so calm under their blue shirts and were so full of seething under their skins. "Had a letter lately from my sister in Olmstead County." Mr. Schadel rubbed his buttock exasperatedly. "The prices they pay there! Cream's selling twenty cents the inch, she says."

Kurt listened, forgetting his potatoes, ears wide as cupboard doors, but Johnny, only half paying attention, put a dandelion tube in Snoose's cup and sucked coffee when Snoose wasn't looking.

Mr. Nussbaum, coddling his whiskery jaw, said, "By jippers, we oughta have farmers in the wagon seat, that's what, and tell those pants warmers in St. Paul a thing or two. Oughta own the elevators and stores. From what I learn, they're going to start a Farmers' Elevator in Mary's Hill next year."

"Aw, hell! They tried that before." Mr. Schadel wasn't hopeful. "Always go broke. Big fellers laugh when a farmer puts on Sunday pants."

Old Geppert hefted his cradle and bellowed, "Feel fine—like a yearling with his first heifer," when somebody asked. He roared over his teeth at the joke. Johnny, refusing a third helping of cabbage and sour cream, overheard Mrs. Dunkel: "You find Gretel, Mrs. Beerwagon. She's had her meal; time for her after-dinner sleep, company or no company. Otherwise she'll be snippy as a crab tonight."

Leaning against the popple fence, a bunch of older boys, seventeen and after and dangerously close to dark fuzziness on their upper lips, guffawed over slippery tongues, their mouths puffed with stories of last night's barn dance. From the way Jack and Bill Marchen grabbed at their belt buckles and threw back heads in mirth, Johnny knew that the telling must be good, full of girl stuff. He ached to run and hear but didn't, knowing how they'd chase him off with scorn: "Can't hold it in, can you, you peashooter, you? Gotta get your ears full." One of these days he'd be with them; wait till he was confirmed.

Half hidden by lilacs, a Peiser girl let young Kory Mercer hold her plate and look at her ankle, plain in sight below the heavy hem of her skirt. Once he caught her hand (Johnny saw this with a start of blood), making sheep's lips at her, and she struggled but not more than would encourage him. Johnny nudged Snoose.

"Them two—rabbiting in the bushes and don't care who sees." He speared a crinkle of cabbage leaf, feeling that he wouldn't mind sitting in the bushes with a girl, some way, but was half uncomfortable at the thought.

Then he noticed Sophie Marchen swinging past on long legs. She cornered Clymy Humber before he knew, secure in the angle where the rail fence met the granary wall. Clymy hunched his shoulders as if somehow trapped. She had her fingers on his trouser belt now, folks said; they'd be married before many snows. Johnny regarded them, ruffled at such behavior. That a man should run away from a girl—— He speared a cabbage strip that had crawled over the plate and was getting away.

Talk spread after eating, but there was the beginning of expectancy. Mrs. Nussbaum told Mrs. Beerwagon, gathering the plates, "Well, I take leftovers from pigs' heads and livers and such; stiffen it with buckwheat stirred in, and bake it. That makes the best scrapple. Cut it cold and use plenty of mustard."

Young Matt Dornhover, pleased with his new wife and his new twenty acres cleared of stumps, ventured: "Next year, I'm going to buy me a selfbinder; one with wire to bind the bundles. It's secondhanded but my pocketbook's too flabby for a new one." He added, "Cradles and reapers—pretty well played out."

Mr. Dunkel answered him, "Don't know about that. You always have to have sickles. I got a piece up there, full of brush and all. You couldn't get around those stones with a reaper, nohow." He arose quickly without waiting for reply. Jumpy as a chipmunk's nose, the neighbors thought but said nothing, watching him sit alone on a box and grope in a pocket for his pipe.

Over near the woodpile, Mr. Lorimer let it be known, "Brine, that'll kill smut—dries it up. Old Willis says his fertilizin' salt is just the thing. You sow it with the wheat, maybe three bushels to the acre."

Almost shyly Johnny approached Mr. Dunkel. For Mr. Dunkel had his eyes on Old Geppert whetting his scythe and on the wheat field bordered by lilacs near the house. Thoughtfully he tamped his pipe. His fingers shook when he lifted the sulphur match. It was a kind of sign, that match; a sign of his newness and of his dipping a finger in tomorrow. Some of the men there, steeped in accustomed ways, still held a bit of stone beside the pipe in the round of their curved fingers and thumb. They struck the stone with steel grasped in the other fist, catching the sparks in the bowl to start the tobacco. Johnny often watched the spark in Old Geppert's pipe spread to a scab of red ember.

Then Mr. Dunkel saw him. "Na, Johnny. You here to see me get licked? If I lose, maybe I'll feel so bad I'll have to take back what I promised you. And we won't go to Fergus after all. That would be a high price." He laughed at his own seriousness.

"I made a cross in the dust and spit on it," Johnny told him.

"That should settle it." Mr. Dunkel arose, a hand on Johnny's shoulder.

Around the beer keg men smacked their lips in the foam. Waves of gibble-gabble washed now against the straw barn, now against the tar-paper-roofed house, voices heard brightly for a moment and fading the next. Dishes clinked against pans in the house.

Clots of kids gathered in a game and broke to pieces; collected in another. Johnny and Snoose joined the circle for "needle's eye," marching under the upraised bridge of hands:

> "There's many a lass
> That I let pass . . ."

He felt prickles of delight on his skin when Gatha Blumen, shrilling,

> "Because I wanted you,"

pulled the bridge down on his shoulders and made him her partner.

She was tall with legs skinny as a deer's but with a boyish swing to her body and a smile as clean-cut as if whittled. She burst out to him boldly today, "Just look at my cold sore," holding Johnny's hand tightly. "They tease me. They say it's where you kissed me." She giggled until her eyes closed.

He went hot and cold as an April day, flushed over being her partner, chilled at her chatter there before Snoose and the rest. "Gee-god, Gatha—" he began but at once Mosey Fritz, short-legged and pudgy of belly and shoulder, squealed,

"Here comes that stinking Johnny——"

Johnny tore away, half his forehead wrinkled, arms out to grab. But Aunt Phrena's throaty "John-ee! Johnny Schwartz! I've been watching you" slowed him to a walk, sullenly, for he knew how Mosey was making faces at him and how Gatha was looking at his back with brightness in her eyes. Snoose at his heels, he went back to Kurt.

Old Geppert put the whetstone into his pocket and arose. Now it's coming, Johnny thought, excitement in him. Now the tussle begins. But Geppert only took a plug of twist, looked at it, and then joined the others around the keg, saying to Mrs. Dunkel, "No, I don't," when she came by scolding, "If that ain't the beatenest. That Gretel—wonder where she's gone this time?"

"When they going to start cradling?" Johnny asked Uncle Herm, humping in impatience.

"Keep your brichin's up. No hurry. Afternoon's that young yet, it's hardly got a whisker on."

Johnny went with a string of boys, noticing how Gatha Blumen peeped at him over a sister's head. He put a strut in his heels. They passed the horseshoe game where Alb Hukelpoke had just made a ringer. They stopped by the barn and patted Mr. Dunkel's oxen. At the last minute, Lornas Tetzell, grabbing a fork, poked the handle between one bull's legs—"to see it wrinkle up," he said.

Snoose twisted the fork away quickly. "Want me to do that to you? You'd be sore, too, guess." And Johnny agreed, soberly.

They strung out to the pasture where on a level place the circle worn by last year's horse power was not yet erased by this year's grass. Like the round for fox and geese which the kids made in winter snow at school the circle lay, a scar marked in shorter grass, where the teams had followed one the tails of the other, round and round, in last season's threshing. Near by was the straw butt where ragweed flourished and where Mr. Dunkel forked up white grubworms for fishing.

Johnny was ready for a game of circle tag but the rest were too afraid of missing the start of the cradling match and soon they returned to the yard, restive as a brood of wood ducklings.

They passed the horseshoe players and saw Alb stepping back from the peg, his eyes on the iron whirling its own revolutions while it arced through the air and fell in an explosion of dust. "Sheets! Only a leaner." They paused to hear him say in the while between throws, "Yep, he was a feeder, that Carlie Homberg. Couldn't beat him in the hull of Nicollet County. The more dust he could eat, the harder he'd shove in the straw. Once he wore out six pair of bandcutters in a day. Then he walked ten miles to a shindandy and square-danced to near sunup. Back he come and he was waiting for bundles when the bandcutters finished sharpenin' their knives. Oh, he was a feeder——"

They moved on, Johnny wrinkle-browed over thinking that Carlie was a feller, all right; a feeder always was. Someday he'd be up there, between the bandcutters, face in the dust that rolled from the whirl of the cylinders, his shoulders swaying as he reached now to this side, now to that for the bundles spreading out under his hand. . . . He jerked up, stumbling over his own feet and out of his thought.

"What's the trouble?" Kurt wanted to know. "Gettin' duck-footed? That Hukelpoke lies so fast, it's a wonder he don't snag himself."

A boy among the men clogging the machine-shed door yelled, "By cripes, she's runnin' dry." They turned. The beer keg sputtered in the faucet and gurgled in its bowels. "She's empty; empty as a sucked egg."

Old Geppert had his last tin cup full and hoisted his suspenders a notch, flexing his muscles boastfully. He nodded. "I see Dunkel's sharpening his sickle. Well, let him." Once somebody in an alcoholic tenor lagged over the last verse of "Old Man's Drunk Again."

In a quickening moment, Johnny said, "Betcha ten dollars, Snoose, Dunkel wins first time around," though his pocket rattled with only six pennies. Mr. Nussbaum was saying, "Soapsuds—that's pretty good for hog sickness. I use——" but he broke off and got up when the others did. And Mrs. Beerwagon didn't get an answer when she questioned, "How do you make macaroni, Mrs. Hohmeyer? My old dunce of a man brought home a box, and now it sets in the cupboard, for I don't know how——"

Folks moved faster, the men slapping grass stems from their pants, the women uncreasing their skirts, leaving the dishes clean in the house, the neighbor tasks finished. The group around the keg thinned to nobody but the Haber twins sucking the last drops from the faucet and a rooster getting tipsy on a cob of corn that had got soaked in beer.

Mr. Dunkel wiped the blade and tested the edge with a critical thumb.

He answered Johnny, "Sure, boy, I'll watch him at the end of the field. He'll not beat me at crossing over and exchanging sides, not me."

Old Geppert flung the cradle to his shoulders. Excitement began running like a current among the crowd, catching them and drawing them together like a drawstring.

Then the Pastor was among them. His black team and his black buggy plowed a ditch through the crowd. The kids scrouged from the darkness of his black coat, stepping high and careful as roosters in a strange pen. Talk in the yard hushed a little so that the horseshoe players, coming from the barn, were noisy. "Why didn't you stick a ringer on 'er, Alb?" asked one.

Hukelpoke's loud, "Aw, sheets, can't lay an egg all the time, fellers," was clear on the air. He continued: "Put them shoes by the shed careful. Dunkel brought 'em clear from Nicollet County and he'd be madder'n hell if——" He stopped red-faced at Jake Peiser's nudge.

The Pastor's long legs stalked past the players and toward Mr. Dunkel. His voice boomed so that Old Geppert paused. "*Brüder*, what is this that you are doing? An abomination before the Lord, that's what it is. Neighbors' jealousies—they cannot be settled by a spite contest. Beware that you do not tempt the anger of the Lord." He dived into a sermon on profaning the Sabbath. "Like threshers." He glared at Uncle Herm and Hukelpoke. "And those godless men in the cities who befoul the Lord's day like cattle. For them is prepared a fiery doom, my brethren."

With a lowered pointing finger he tried to stop them. But Mr. Dunkel set his jaw and Old Geppert merely shifted his cradle, both deaf, as was the excited crowd, awed by the minister's stern gaze but heedless of his chapter and verse. His beard ends shook with wrath. Like handwritings on a wall there appeared in his mind blazing texts for a month of sermons, illustrated by neighborly stubbornness.

The crowd swirled away from him (let him follow), Mr. Dunkel and Geppert in the lead. They swarmed out to the field, Mrs. Dunkel pulling Johnny's arm and asking, "Did you see Gretel anywhere? I can't find her," he shaking his head, impatient to be with Kurt and Snoose, who were just in front of him.

Afterward Johnny would run this day through the runways of his mind with a sugar-and-salt feeling for the crusty sweetness of neighbors and with a kind of acridness which slow horror pricked in him, blotting out some things, leaving others scissor-cut and sharp: the field of wheat stretching its length of golden heads from the lilacs near the house to the wall of pine trees . . . the two men plunging forward like unbroken colts . . . the wide rhythmic swing of the scythes, whetted keen as knives for butchering.

shearing stem and stalk with dull, thudding, thunking sounds . . . the wheat heads shaking for a trembling space under the wind of death as the iron struck . . . the grain gathering for a swift moment above the blade and leaning against the bows before it fell with the outward pull at the end of the sweep, dropping in rows, heads away from standing grain . . . the two men swaying in the wheat, harvesting this grain for more than money in a pocket or shoes for the family . . . across the field and back they must go, across and back again. A bird darted away and Johnny, stumbling in the morning-glory vines, wondered about a nest and the young.

There was Mr. Dunkel with his shirt off, his underwear, new for Sunday, white against the yellow of grain at the start but turning dark with sweat that stained it, chest and shoulders and underarms, before he finished half a length of mowing. Old Geppert was ahead of him, practice in each swing of the blade. The neighbors were noisy. Snoose jumped over a stone, Kurt near him. Johnny shouted, "He's gaining, Mr. Dunkel; hit yourself on the tail."

Once fire flew as Mr. Dunkel's blade met a hidden rock, sparks winking in the wheat. Folks gasped and a sound like a storm troubling a ridge of oaks rose from the lines straggling alongside the cradlers. Johnny felt his heart go to rags and heard Snoose say between steps, "Wonder he didn't break the sickle." But Mr. Dunkel tore the whetstone from his pocket and swiftly edged his iron with sharpness, though Geppert wasted his breath in a croupy laugh of triumph.

Folks pitched courage and hope to the cradlers. Johnny, caught in a knot of people, bumped against Mr. Nussbaum and bounced away, elbowing Kurt and grabbing Snoose by the shoulder: "Wait for me, can't you?"

The cradlers came back to the lilacs where they had started, completing the first round. Geppert was more than two wagon-lengths ahead of Mr. Dunkel. Behind them unrolled a double width of swaths and cleared spaces. They pointed their flaring nostrils at the pine wall. This was the second, the last round.

The crowd bunched and stretched along again. Little by precious little Mr. Dunkel regained the steps he had lost. Though Old Geppert had custom to show him where to lay the sickle and that certainty which comes to those who speak with authority among the tongues of neighbors, nevertheless Dunkel gained, for he had the lesser drag of fewer years and the confidence of one not yet old enough to be fearful of established neighbor ways—those ways unchangeable by anything except the ruthless smashing and the patient reassembling of the parts.

A flash of gray and a rabbit, confused by trampling feet, zigzagged among the treading shoes until, terrified and lost, it froze to the ground and let a Schadel boy pick it up before it screamed the fear of the dying. Then Johnny saw Mr. Dunkel step ahead and noticed that Old Geppert was tiring, rage paring his nose to pointedness. The shadows of these two, monstrous and black, struck at the ground ahead of them futilely. The pine wall towered just before them. Their breaths were getting thin now, their shoulders pushed ahead with the pumping of belly and chest muscles, their clothes soaked with sweat. They reached the pines. Half a round left.

They turned at the pines, the last turn. In front lay the stretch for home and the lilacs there. They swung into the wheat. Sickles flew faster. Mr. Dunkel crawled ahead now and Geppert, his breath hoarse and choked, teeth biting lip till the blood came, knew the bitter tears of those who see their honored place forgotten and their words flung to a common level.

Something like a glow came to Mr. Dunkel's eyes as he gathered his steps ahead, though his face was blotched red, and the white of tiredness grew about his mouth. His ribs, sharply marked on his wet underclothes, pulled at air that rushed through his throat in ragged, gulpy gurgles. His sickle was like lightning in the grain. His eyes became blind—blind to all but the wheat before him and the steel in his swinging arms. He lunged forward with steadiness in his arches though aches wrenched sinew and bone. He was going forward, going home, coming to his lilac bushes at the end of the piece. Geppert was behind him now, the loser, and he was the victor. There were the lilacs, there the end of the piece, the last of exertion, two rods ahead. Sway with the sickle, faster, faster; wield the bright edge, faster, faster, faster. . . .

Then a dreadful croaking shout dragged over his lips as if he were one who looked unexpectedly upon the toothy grin of death. He seemed to put shoulders back with all his strength like a brake against a forward lunge, the urgency of despair in his arms, desperately—and failed.

The scythe leaped forward blithely into a sickle-width of grain, into a small willow with shade. . . . A scream, high and childish and in agony, tore through the wheat and twisted itself corkscrew fashion into Johnny's ears. The folks stood in a hush, lips sewed with the needle and thread of unbelievingness—this couldn't be true; this couldn't happen in Pockerbrush, not to them. The Pastor shoved forward, all his anger gone, a shepherd of his sheep in mercy for this moment once again, praying "Father in Heaven."

Night after night Johnny, mulling over that awful hour, would squirm on the pillow as if the edge of the scythe with thrust and glitter were driving into his brain. He'd draw breath deeply as now he drew breath, horror like a vine crawling up his legs and holding him stiff and hardly moving, his eyes wide. He didn't know whether he cried aloud, though his head racketed with the words: "Oh, Mr. Dunkel, Mr. Dunkel, take your promise back, take it back. I don't want to go to Fergus. I don't want the silver-handled knife."

There was Mr. Dunkel, cradle thrown wide, hands clawing into the stalks. And there was Mrs. Dunkel running, a cry white on her lips but remaining unuttered. She paused, as if held back, and stood beside Old Geppert who sank panting to the stubbles. And then Mr. Dunkel came toward them, Gretel in his arms. He swayed to staggering—swayed as an oak does, hammered with thunder; his face broke, tears mixing with his rattly puffing, "Gretel, Gretel, my Gretel!"

Part 2

THE SEASON OF
MILK IN THE EAR

1

THERE was dolor in the binding of the sheaves and the finishing of the harvest that autumn. Johnny's birthday would have slipped by, unnoticed, if Snoose hadn't surprised Johnny by mentioning it. "Thirteen, ha? I'm keeping up with you, two months behind. They say it's a bad-luck year."

From the road on their way to Mary's Hill, folks saw with commiseration how Mr. Dunkel finished his wheat and tied his bundles alone. Mrs. Dunkel sat numb in the shadows. For a while no whistle rode over the fields. Then one evening the neighbors heard it again—a scrap of melody with ragged trills like a robin in fall sluggishly remembering his May-twilight notes: Mr. Dunkel beating sorrow into a tune with his lips. They sighed but felt better.

Threshing began and the shrilling of the cylinder had in it sharp reminders nobody could avoid. Johnny saw Uncle Herm start the rig at the Pastor's with dismal heaviness in his feet. The cradling match clung like a beggar's tick in the folds of his brain. Right in the middle of a bucketful of potatoes he was scratching together, he'd stop, pulled to a halt by a mind picture of that afternoon . . . of Mr. Nussbaum carrying the cradle to the barn, its blade edged with a small stain like cranberry juice . . . of Mrs. Dunkel almost falling into Aunt Phrena's arms and a Musser girl fainting whitely away.

It wasn't only the queer dread that settled down solidly after the first shock while folks hitched their teams almost repentantly to buggies and wagons. There were the smaller and less important knots in the solemnness that wove itself in him: Mr. Dunkel patting the dog that ran to him, saying over and over, "Gretel won't take off your collar again, puppy; not any more." . . . Old Geppert with tears on his hard cheeks: tears not for the Dunkels but for himself.

The thought of Geppert pestered Johnny until he forgot picking altogether and needed Aunt Phrena's shriek from the garden, "Hurry up there a little, can't you once?" He had wanted Mr. Dunkel to win. But he saw that Old Geppert had lost more than the cradling match. The niche of favor, his these years, belonged to Mr. Dunkel now. Less and less would his word bear the weight of opinion about an ox trade or a township dispute. Already Johnny heard the neighbors saying with a shrug, "Oh, well. Geppert, he ain't got the sap he used to have. You can't sit in the saddle all the time." The very folks who used to grumble, "That Dunkel— a puppy-come-up, for sure," were now glowing over him. "Jippers, how that man can swing an edge on the wheat! Tough, though, losing his kid, and in such a way, too." They seasoned their admiration with pity. Johnny never thought of the silver-handled knife without shrinking under a thrust of brightness.

Whether she knew it or not, Aunt Phrena added to the confusion snarling in his thought. "There. There you have it," she said, clutching the Precious Comfort Book as if it were a shield against imminent destruction. "That's what Wilhelm Dunkel gets for big-headedness. A spite match— ach, ya!"

Johnny was silenced but Kurt spoke. "It could have happened to any- body, couldn't it?"

"No." Aunt Phrena snapped the book open. "No, *Yunge*. It is the anger of God on those who won't listen to His word, that's what it is." She sighed blowsily. "Think once. If this terribleness happens to church mem- bers, what couldn't happen to those who don't belong, those who sit in darkness? Like the Roses, over there. No church members in that family; nobody of theirs confirmed, nobody baptized. They're named like cows and calves. Awful, awful, that's what it is. Poor Mrs. Dunkel." She flipped a page hastily to fan off contamination. But for once she was outraged over the Pastor's unrelenting harshness.

At the funeral he had taken the handle of the law once more firmly in his grasp. He swept down on the congregation with the flail of the Lord's word and shook the backbone of the stoutest with his thunders about abom- ination on the Sabbath and the swift hammer of vengeance that fell and crushed the sinner and his blasphemies.

At home Aunt Phrena waved a spoon indignantly over a kettle. "Steuber ought to have better sense. That's just like a man, though. No sense for other's feelings. And poor Mrs. Dunkel cut to pieces." She added prac- tically, "It wouldn't hurt the Pastor none to read the Comfort Book more often."

Johnny shuddered over the sermon and the way Mrs. Dunkel had screamed during a hymn. He was sad in his heart for the Dunkels, their home darkened forever, it seemed. The rest of that winter the clovey smell of pinks was like the odor of medicine in his nostrils, sickening him, there had been so many bunches of them on the altar.

His breath was long in relief, that funeral day, when the black casket moved finally down the aisle and the congregation pushed for the door. As he squeezed between Uncle Herm and Mr. Nussbaum, he saw a girl's face—a girl with honey-colored hair and a curvy mouth that pinned the button of a dimple to her lip ends when she smiled. She was smiling now, subduedly, hearing someone speak to her. His eyes crinkled and he stopped so that Mr. Peiser bumped into him. Then Alb Hukelpoke's lean body thrust her face away. Johnny wondered who she was—and shame flooded him. It was just as Aunt Phrena had said: how could he be so heartless when the Dunkels were shoulder-drooped and broken? For a week at least, his face wore gravity as Hukelpoke wore a beard.

He couldn't understand why Kurt was unmoved as a log. "Those poor Dunkels——"

"Ain't gonna bawl over them," Kurt said as if he saw that sympathy for another's grief comes not out of kinship with the broken but out of relief at being spared ourselves. "What happened to them ain't my fault." And Johnny had to admit that maybe he was right. Certainly no horse remained unwatered nor a dishrag unwrung because a new earth heap scarred the green of the cemetery; no breathing stopped.

Threshing continued. Aunt Phrena kept him and Kurt busy as she usually did at this time of fall, helping her shred cabbage for sauerkraut. But it nagged him: so much noon sun spangling brightly under Uncle Herm's trees and so much darkness thick as dust clouding another man's house. Absently he moved the shredding board into position above the keg.

He surprised himself vaguely at discovering that now and again he recalled the smile of the girl at the church; the Rose girl, he learned she was. Uncle Herm had said after the service, "Mrs. Rose was there—her and her girl. Pretty little critter."

"A funeral always brings them." Aunt Phrena sniffed grimly. "They know they got to die, baptized or not."

"Well, it was neighborly and thoughtful of her." Uncle Herm was mildly resolute. "For the Dunkels' sakes."

Johnny wondered about the unbaptized woman. He'd never seen one, he was sure. Could you see it on her face the way you could the freckles on Gatha Blumen's nose? At the notion he stopped shredding altogether until Aunt Phrena bustled from the garden. He bent hurriedly over his work.

With shove and pull he moved a cabbage-sized box over knives in a board and watched the smooth-leaved heads sink through the sharp blades. In long strips and fragments they fell into the ten-gallon keg underneath. The pale-green and white curls smelled of coolness and summer sun kinked in their crooks. Three times the keg was filled and emptied into a barrel before Aunt Phrena was satisfied and brought the salt from the pantry. In the house the pickles and the beans were already gently gathering scum, the brine on them strong enough to carry an egg.

Johnny's fingers had ached over the beans—"half stickers," Aunt Phrena called the long narrow pods that hung among the vines clinging to poles. By the hour he whittled pods slantwise into pieces until he owned that another bean would make him puke. But in January when Aunt Phrena soaked these overnight and cooked them with a slab of sowbelly, he gobbled platefuls, "like a thrasher with a hollow for a stomach," she reminded him acridly. No farmer, Uncle Herm was fond of saying, was ready for winter until he had a barrel of sauerkraut, a barrel of beans and a barrel of pickles in his house. When he had in addition a pig in brine in the cellar and a steer frozen in the granary and under lock and key, he was prepared for the worst that January could do to a stomach.

Aunt Phrena didn't forget the preacher school. Once she unearthed the bone of the idea, she worried it like a teething puppy. With the cradling match an opportune exhortation to virtue, she tried to hurry him into religion, though he held back stiff-legged as a calf on the end of a rope. So she told him once. All that autumn whenever she could corner him in a spare moment and find him out of excuses, she put the Comfort Book in his hands and made him learn prayer and petition yard on yard, preparing him for godliness by recipe. She stood over him, quick to sniff into tears; and her pulings were worse to him than the lashing tongue the Pastor used or Mr. Marchen's rawhide. "God's sakes!" he burst out to Snoose. "If she'd only larrup me like your pa does. But she only sniffles and gets weepy at the nose. I won't go to preacher school."

Uncle Herm looked purse-mouthed but said nothing, feeling that here Aunt Phrena really had the heft of him. For who could argue against godliness or the glory crown that surely came at the end of a preacher's road? If folks rebelled and wanted threshing rigs instead of heavenly harps, that was, without a doubt, Devil's stuff fresh from the ovens of Satan.

Kurt snickered, partly in sympathy. He talked and the kids in the neighborhood heard and Johnny thought he'd rather walk barefoot over thistles than start school that fall.

His mind half in the book, half out the window, he mumbled over petitions for church, for home, for health, for good crops. Once when he was repeating absently, "Lord, protect and increase the fruit of the field and the fold, the cattle and the sheep" (though they had no sheep), he started a ripple of fright through all the layers of her fat by yelling, "Aunt Phrena, the bull is in the corn, bull's in the corn." He left the last verse for another day by rushing to the yard. He kept from her sight until chore time.

She threw Schwartz at him now as if this would help change evil to good as sour milk is turned to cheese. She said, "You keep your clothes on," when he wanted to strip off shirt and run free in the autumn sun, wind paddling his armpits cool. She said it as if this were a sign of taint in his body. When he didn't obey and his shirt came off, she moaned, "Like your pa all over again. That man'd go swimming—ach, my!—almost naked, no more than his underwear on, right in plain sight. There's a terrible lot of your pa in you, Johnny."

He didn't care, though he raged silently, "Wait till I'm confirmed, Aunt Phrena. You just wait." Let Kurt remain white-skinned as flour if he wanted to; let the other boys wear shoes. *He'd* go barefoot to school if there wasn't another unshod foot under the desks. The touch of wind slipping under his work-dampened arm and across his chest sent quivers through his body. It was like—well, like (years later, with more experience, he'd say this) it was like a girl's fingers sliding over his ribs.

She shook her head with sour Jeremiah patience, watchful as a marsh hawk over the sprouts of sin. She was especially watchful after the threshers came and she found him in the haymow with the bundle pitchers. "He was listening to their dirty stories," she told Uncle Herm, pinching her lips as if somebody had splashed mud on her face.

Johnny insisted, "I didn't hear nothing bad." Uncle Herm choked over a laugh.

Kurt said in a mildly objective moment, "The way she looks, guess she'd like to hear those stories herself."

But some of her chidings, sticky as cobwebs, stayed in his mind, stuck there, as those did the day she opened the granary door and caught him naked in the wheat.

The threshers arrived early that fall. They pulled into the yard, the horses straining on the power and on the separator, the rims of their nostrils stiffening as they corded their hamstrings. You needed a good team for that job, Johnny decided. A good team. Yet how fast things changed before your very nose. Why, only two, three years before, Mr. Dunkel's oxen drew the separator and another span pulled the power along the roads and over the corduroy spots in the swamps. And then one day—so the story went—Alb Hukelpoke, in a hurry to get somewhere, hooked his bay horses to the power. He pulled it over to Mr. Nussbaum's place, making good time, and chewed Indian Twist for an hour (so he said) before Mr. Dunkel's oxen crawled into the yard, the separator at their tails.

"You break everything to pieces, driving so fast, Alb," Mr. Schadel had grumbled that time. "Oxen is the only way to haul a thrashing rig. Horses clip along too goldang fast."

Alb hooted, proud of himself. "Sheetin' Judas! I can't waste all day waiting for a couple of steers."

Most of the neighbors agreed: no use in waiting until October rains chilled into snow and turned stacks into cones of ice. Thereafter, horses, Alb's or Mr. Schadel's or Uncle Herm's, were hitched to separator and to power. Oxen were hooked to slower work. Uncle Herm was even talking about selling Bully and Bill.

Sometimes, though, the power bogged down in a stretch of corduroy. Once Mr. Schadel's grays, afraid of the pine lengths undergirding the trembling road in the swamp peat, balked and snorted but refused to budge. Johnny remembered how gleefully Mr. Dunkel used to tell and retell that story to the men listening in a circle over their afternoon lunch. "There they were stuck, whoop-Jinny-and-fall-down, hub-deep in the mud. Schadel's grays were so skittery they couldn't pull a hen off a nest. Well, sir, Barewolf, there—it was you, wasn't it, Herman?—well, sure it was. Barewolf there walked two miles to my place for my oxen. I shoulda told 'em where to go, them fellers so proud of their nags." Mr. Dunkel would tamp his pipe, his smooth face crinkled. "Well, I got my bulls over there and hooked 'em up and, say, that swamp ground shivered for half a mile around. But you can't scare an ox that way. They stepped that separator right out of that sloo hole like a damn." And Mr. Dunkel would chuckle emphatically, "No sir, I'll stick to the old cradle and my bullies and they'll stick by me."

He had to admit that horses were handier in threshing but added, "What's the hurry? Wheat cured in the stack a couple of weeks longer is harder and makes you a better grist of flour. What's the tearing hurry?" Even Alb Hukelpoke didn't try to answer that. But horses tugged the leather now, and more and more ox yokes were being hung to weather in the machine sheds.

Johnny sighed, full of the story, knowing how Mr. Dunkel had enjoyed savoring it in seasons past. But not this year; not this day, his rooftree loud with emptiness. At lunchtime he stood at the circle edge, his hands unsteady with tiredness and his coffee spilling from the cup.

After supper the threshers trooped by lanternlight to the haymow, a place fragrant with minty sloo grass and the pine smell of boards in the new lean-to. Johnny followed them, in spite of Aunt Phrena's wanting shavings in the wood box. He climbed the ladder and hid behind the shoulders of Alb Hukelpoke, who was ready for "a snort or two," he said. "Sheetin' Judas, but that oats was smutty!" He leaned to listen, Johnny with him, to a song Anders Stramff was starting, the accordion a soft undertone:

> "I was born in old Ocanto, boys,
> Where the streetcars never run;
> The doctor said I could not live
> For I was born too young.
> I was brought up on the bottle, boys,
> Till I became a man;
> And then my mother took the bottle, boys,
> And now I am—"

The tune scattered away. Bennie Laufslang was telling, "She was a bitchin' woman, all right," when a strawfork, silver tines running red fire in the kerosene light, was thrust weirdly up through the trap-door opening. It bang-banged on the wall. Aunt Phrena's voice, thick with zeal to snatch this brand from the burning, even if she had to come near the fire of destruction itself, boomed, "John-nee! Johnny Schwartz! You come right down here. And wash your ears with soap, all the dirty stuff you've been hearing."

His ears went red when the threshers laughed and teased him the next day. "Got the soap out of your ears yet, Johnny?" He ran to the safety of Uncle Herm and the granary, where shovel after shovel of wheat avalanched from the chute. A safe place, this granary.

The threshers pulled the rig away. The yard seemed crowded with the bulging straw pile. In a kind of restlessness, remembering other autumns, Johnny came to the granary to feel the earthy touch of wheat upon his flesh. Slipping naked out of shirt and pants, he poured handfuls of cool wheat down his bare chest and over his belly. It fell in a brown rain upon his thighs. A palm heaped full and laid against his ribs was no browner than his skin. A queer sort of longing would ride over him, tugging at the marrow and deeper, and filling him with a strange unease. By the half hour he spilled grain, heedless of time whittling at the stick of his young being. He paddled up a slant of wheat as carp did over the rapids in spring, the kernels inching coolly along his belly and down between his legs. He pressed his face firmly into grain, wiggled and flexed his muscles, settling like a nesting hen, fingers deep. Then he stepped up and away swiftly, kernels hanging on lips and nose, to see wheat holding the print of his body as butter did the pattern of moon and stars Aunt Phrena stamped on every jar. There was his face, the hardly noticeable round of his breasts, his stomach, the cups of his knees.

He came here alone, shrinking from Kurt's heavy eyes, and would not have invited Snoose had he dared. But one day Aunt Phrena opened the granary door suddenly and let in a flood of sun with her own inquisitive nose. She caught him lying there. He was acorn-bronze melting into the gold of grain, his lower half from navel to kneecap dough-white against the darker wheat. She screeched tongue over tooth and tumbled back. The door swung half shut on her scoldings.

At dinner her mouth waggled—and for the week, too—about heathen in Pockerbrush who wanted to live like Negroes and Hottentots (though she'd never seen one). Uncle Herm held a laugh in his throat so long that he choked in his coffee cup.

Glad for the excuse, she spun on him like a pestered cluck-hen, and with that woman logic which defies rule and square and is beyond the measured grasp of man, she howled, "Take his part, then. I'm trying so hard to bring him up in the way of the Lord. And it's your fault, Herman Barewolf. All your fault. You wanted to marry me."

At which Uncle Herm took fire. "Phrena, when I——" But she flung her apron over head and sagged out of the room. They could get the coffee and pie from the stove themselves, if they wanted it, or have none—she didn't care. The door closed but did not end her thin clamor. Uncle Herm dropped dejected shoulders. "What is a person——"

"Why do you do it?" Out of nowhere Kurt gathered his spite and barked, "Why do you like to make her mad? You do—purposely."

"I?" Uncle Herm sucked in his breath defensively, the hair on his chin moving. "I make her mad? She's made me so mad, I——"

"It ain't fair." Kurt interrupted, angry enough to cry, only half of what he said making sense. "It ain't fair, when my pa's dead and gone, and I——" The rest failed on trembling lips.

Johnny, hackles up, flung at him, "Keep your nose out of Uncle Herm." His fist closed on a cup and lifted it from the saucer. "Aunt Phrena scolds all the time; nags and scolds." The two glared, the table between them. "Shut your mouth, Kurt. That's what you can do. I ain't got a pa; and no— no ma either." With that thought, his words slackened, and loneliness hurt in his throat. Prickle anger fell away. He sagged and the cup shattered to the floor. They shifted glances, one to the other, uncertainly, like two unfeathered roosters ready to spring but forgetting all at once what they were to fight about.

They were sullen, both of them, filling the room with their dismalness, adding to Aunt Phrena's hiccupy sobs, so that Uncle Herm, nettle-bitten by this household nagging, yelled out sharply, "Damn such a family any-way," and banged out of the kitchen.

Aunt Phrena was tear-sodden for a day. She left the dishes dirty overnight and chewed mistily what crumbs she could find in the Precious Comfort Book. But shame in a red flood washed over Johnny whenever he thought of this, and thereafter, if he went swimming in the granary at all, he thumped the hook of the door solidly into the staple, locking out intruders with oak and pine, before he put a hand to the buttons of his pants.

In spite of locks, however, eyes with "Shame, shame" in them seemed to be there, eyes in the corners. He was tense as a weasel for unfriendly sound. A mouse slithering down the studding startled him into a grab for his shirt. It came to him then that nakedness was shame, crawly as worms with evil. But no amount of putting two and three together could answer his loud inner insistence: Why? I didn't do nothin' wrong. Nor could it banish a kind of sadness dragging sweetly at his being when he went to the granary no more. It was sadness like that which filled him when finally he gave away the doll with the china head and the black hair and the red ribbon tied around its neck.

He gave it to the Schadel children one day because Aunt Phrena insisted, and sharply. He was too big to play with kids' things—and little girls' things, at that—Aunt Phrena said with derision. He wanted to cry, "It's—it's my mother's," but there was a tightness about Aunt Phrena's mouth that might have been malice. And there were Mrs. Schadel and the little Schadels, expectant as cats for a dish of milk.

Slowly he had brought the doll. But on the way downstairs, of a sudden, he ripped off the red ribbon and stuck it in his pocket. When she saw that it was gone, Aunt Phrena remarked acidly, "Kept the ribbon back, so? Hope it does you some good."

He gave the doll reluctantly and wondered why his lips stuck so tightly to his teeth, hurting him, and why he ran quickly to the outhouse to get away from the sight of everyone, the ribbon damp in his fist, unaware then how youth drifts from sea to further sea and leaves its laughter desolately behind to haunt the far deserted isles of boyhood.

With the pain of that hour came a thought that made him pause more than once over a job. This wanting to run half naked, this desire to bury his flesh in grain, this pleasure in stripping off clothes and in swimming in the creek with Snoose—is that *him* again, coming out in me? Like cat, like kitten, Aunt Phrena said. But why, why? Why is it my fault? he asked. The trees dropping their leaves had no reply. Hate flooded him again, half defined and cloudy, but hate against the dead, the buried dead who wouldn't remain dust and moldy ashes but came creeping back to rise within his own flesh, to mar the proud vision of himself which he carried like a crest.

For a week after the day Aunt Phrena caught him in the granary, he buttoned his shirt tightly to his neck. He'd be skun with a dull knife if anybody'd catch him peeled to the skin again. In another week he forgot most of it. Shirt off, armpits catching at the wind, he lifted fork or ran for the cows, free to the play of weather, let Aunt Phrena roll what thoughts she wanted pepperlike over her tongue. Thereafter, however, when he went to the granary, he went brusquely, manlike, heaping the bucket with feed or helping Uncle Herm sack oats. The grain stayed smooth for the tracks of mice, unstirred by his wriggling muscles. The wheat held never again the imprint of his body all its boyish length.

2

He set off to parochial school beside Kurt with something more than uneasiness flapping at his footsteps. Aunt Phrena had talked with the Pastor. Of that he was sure, her chin had so much of triumph in every fold.

And the Pastor—would he beckon with a curved bony finger and ask questions the moment school opened? Suppose he asked whether Johnny had received a call? Aunt Phrena's brother Zacharias had—right out of heaven while he was digging potatoes. The only call Johnny remembered at potato-digging time was the yearning to grab a gun and get himself a mess of mallards from the sloo. Had Johnny heard the voice of God plain? Zacharias had. And had he felt the inner sign? Zacharias—— He squirmed. All those questions and the kids listening! It was bad enough to have the Pastor catch him shooting spitballs with a springy willow twig; or gluing Hattie Nussbaum's pigtail to a bench back with a wad of sticky pine resin he scraped from a slab. But this—this was enough to set a young pup howling. Nope! He'd be switched if the Pastor would get him into a black coat and send him off to preacher school, let Aunt Phrena cry the pillow wet, if she wanted to. He'd tell the Pastor—well, he'd tell him something; truth if possible, a lie if necessary, such was his desperation.

Beyond a quick glance that first day, the Pastor did nothing. For a week Johnny quaked, no whit eased by the jibes of the older boys. "What text you gonna preach on, Johnny, when you're a minister—Matthew, chapter twenty-nine?" They laughed loudly. Mosey Fritz explained with weighty emphasis, "There ain't no chapter twenty-nine in Matthew; see, Johnny? See?"

But one day the Pastor singled out Johnny's reading with a word of praise and the boards creaked as the boys nudged one another. Johnny swore then and there he'd muddle every page of reading with mistakes from then on—worse than Mosey Fritz. Let the Pastor use the willow. He wondered why he hadn't thought of that before. But the Pastor remained silent.

All that winter and into the following spring he put Johnny on the bull thistles of probation, his beard a kind of pointer at tomorrow under his shut mouth. Johnny memorized until his forehead ached, Aunt Phrena solicitously near. He rocked in his chair as if rhythm oiled question and answer in his brain and brought them less creakingly together But there were days when his muscles rebelled. He fled from precept and Bible reference then as if hounds yelped at his heels, and escaped to the freedom of the barn and pitching manure.

In winter drifts he beat paths knee-deep between the yard and Snoose's house, and in seasons of the growing moon spent evenings there, "studying Catechism," he told Aunt Phrena. Snow tumbled from the folds of his pants in hard-pressed, soaplike slabs when in the Marchen house he took off heavy shoes.

He discovered a warmth there that held a rosiness he never found in Aunt Phrena's house though occasionally he felt it in the granary, in talk with Uncle Herm. In the Marchen house after dark, light from the lamps on the wall brackets showered down and left a friendly yellow on the heads and shoulders of the Marchen men as they eased off the aches of work with their extra shirts and pants. It was good to be here. Talk galloped bridleless from chair to chair, Snoose listening dreamily, chin cupped in one hand. Bill, confirmed in the last spring, slouched near the stove. Jackie was full of mumbles over his final season with the Pastor. Sophie clattered a rawboned way from table to cupboard. But there was a sort of blackness where Mr. Marchen in stocking feet rocked in a corner. Johnny felt his laugh coming easier after Mr. Marchen yawned to bed. The fun usually livened then, the half-choked snores in the bedroom never disturbing a game of pinochle or a tussle on the floor.

Often Mrs. Marchen wheedled a tune from the old reed organ and they sang "The Three Sailors" or "The Mill Wheel Clatters in the Stream," Johnny in a ragged tenor that frequently and unexpectedly pitched into rough bass. In these moments of well-being Sophie dreamed over the music, her bulkiness relaxed, her low syrupy voice heavy with longing for Clymy Humber. What queer law of opposites made her gray eyes soften when she spotted Clymy no one stopped to ask. For he was small and spindleshanked, with a worried blue gaze, nearsighted as a gopher, who would scamper half a mile to avoid a quarrel. He kept out of her way when he could and was half proud, half scared when he couldn't. And in this winter she dogged him at party and shindandy with a persistence that left him dizzy and aroused gruff mirth in the menfolks and scandalized gabblings in the women. If she minded, she hid her torment well.

Once in a reckless mood when Mrs. Marchen was pumping forth a marching song and they were gusty with the rhythm, she cried, "Play us a waltz, Ma," and dragged Johnny to the middle of the room. "I'll show you how to dance." Her voice rang determinedly.

"Aw, I can't; never," he yelped, hunch-shouldered in an ecstasy of embar-rassment. Bill and Jackie guffawed but Snoose watched.

Sophie's arm was hard with insistence as if she held for a moment, not Johnny half grown as he was, but Clymy safe in the embrace of her yearn-ing. Mrs. Marchen tweedled into liveliness. Johnny fell into the dance. He lumbered through the steps, clumsy as a bull calf, knocking against her knees and stepping on her toes until he was sprawl-legged with panic. He finished in despair but Jackie clapped and Snoose chuckled, "You're getting the hang of it fast." Before he could escape, Sophie swept him into a second round that left him breathless and curiously elated. He began to grin broadly.

He went home on tiptoes, though unwillingly, echoes of the evening clamorously sweet in his ears. How agreeably far away the Pastor seemed when the Marchens laughed around their red-checkered table, how near he was in Aunt Phrena's sitting room. The Marchens never wrestled with the flesh as Aunt Phrena did. When they read passages aloud one to the other, it wasn't from the Precious Comfort Book but from the *Bauchweh-lachen Buch*—a jokebook called "Laugh Until Your Belly Aches." Once in a while, however, Johnny was primly shocked at the stories Mr. Marchen told, and right before his wife, too. There was a frosty dignity about Aunt Phrena's behavior he couldn't deny. But this evening of waltzing with Sophie—it was like the meaty taste of blackhaws in autumn. It was long before he forgot the boniness of her knees striking against him.

Cold dragged the winter like an ugly harrow through the weeks. The Pastor shouted at the confirmands but held his tongue about that which Johnny burned to hear. Most things waited until spring for new growth but gossip flourished among the icicles. The Mercer girl was going to have a baby and tongues clacked over the names of boys in the hills who might be the father. Aunt Phrena tried to keep from Johnny and Kurt what everyone was gabbling over. "It is not seemly, such talk for kids to hear. It rots them inside," she said. When they found out, she was horrified. "Stop your thinking about that Mercer girl," she commanded. "You want to help the Devil drag you to hell? It makes you bad inside—badder than you are already." She emphasized with sourness, "It is only bad boys who get into such trouble—bad-hearted, wicked boys." (She felt cheated when during the summer the truth came out and the Mercer girl sent the sheriff to arrest Lornas Tetzell's uncle, a man of forty with a wife and eight kids and a member of the church.)

And Mrs. Dunkel scarcely lifted a broom in the house, Mrs. Peiser told. Several times Mrs. Rose had come to scrub Mr. Dunkel's floor and brush the spiderwebs from the corners; which was more than Aunt Phrena had done, Johnny said to Snoose. Uncle Herm said, "It was neighborly of her, her husband crippled as he is." But Mrs. Rose always found Mr. Dunkel cheerful as his snapping fire and talking as briskly as if Mrs. Dunkel answered from her vacant lips.

And Em'ly Musser was taking *pie*-ano lessons from Mrs. Rose, though Em'ly had only a reed organ at home, Mrs. Peiser chattered. And the Rose girl—my, but she could play! Old Man Fleischer said she played mournful pieces until you were like to have your heart busted with loneliness.

Aunt Phrena only rattled the poker on the stove lid. "A piece of the Catechism, that would do her more good than a piano," she muttered.

Johnny regarded the news about the Mercer girl with interest and a poking curiosity but with no slaverings at the mouth, as he might have expected from Aunt Phrena's warnings. Sometimes he was experimental and deliberately thought about her, wondering where the taint would first appear. Afterward he examined with alert gruntings the crevices of his body to observe the progress of decay. When his pinchings brought only blue marks, he gave up in disgust. Besides, the Pastor's questions were growing more searching. Any day now he might ask Johnny to stay after recess and announce brusquely, "Next fall you go to preacher school." Johnny didn't know what'd he do, there was such tightness throbbing in his ears.

3

Sophie was married in October of a fall so drizzly the threshers remained idle at the farms and ate more than their weight in grain, Mr. Peiser growled; and the bundles were whitish with mold at the bands. Snoose whispered the news early but by late summer the Barewolfs were told, for Aunt Phrena was to make the wedding cake. Over lunch and dinner they tossed Sophie from tongue to lip, their anticipation as fragrant as the coffee beans Aunt Phrena placed green in the oven and took out brown, filling the room with a cozy peanutty odor. The smell was warm as newsawed oak dust but the taste was somehow burned.

"Clymy Humber's going to hop and fast, once Sophie gets him by the pants." Uncle Herm scratched his whiskers. "It'll be a big wedding."

"That Sophie—she'll rip her seams if she wears that tight waist," Aunt Phrena said. "But she don't care, big man-thing that she is."

Only that day Sophie had been over. She had laughed at the picture of Uncle Herm's first wife. (Johnny was glad Uncle Herm was nowhere near.) "She's a perfect size, all right," Sophie had haw-hawed.

> " 'Twice around the thumb,
> Once around the wrist;
> Twice around the wrist,
> Once around the neck;
> Twice around the neck,
> Once around the waist.'

That's what Ma says. But me, I'm a slop bucket beside that one." She had scandalized Aunt Phrena by insisting, "I'd like to get married in britches, that's what I'd like." She left Aunt Phrena shaking her head.

They laughed and knew liveliness in this September and October, in spite of the cloud that shadowed their minds when they saw the Dunkels. Folks said, "Ya, he takes it with good heart," when Mr. Dunkel at his work whistled the emptiness from his house; but they were gloomy over Mrs. Dunkel, over her dim broken eyes and her nose thinning from the pinch of grief. She was taking the baby's clothes to bed with her, Mrs. Peiser gossiped to Mrs. Marchen.

I don't see how Mr. Dunkel takes it so—so calm, puzzled Johnny. He liked that little Gretel so much.

Once it was announced, the wedding was a kind of ferment to bubble and put sweetness into the commonness of their coming and going. Aunt Phrena picked hops in the lower pasture for yeast, gathering the pale, honey-hued cones before frost spoiled them. These she boiled and drained. With the juice of the hops she mixed potato water and corn meal and yeast from the last batch, sprinkled with salt. Johnny would come in to find the house bitter with hop smell—it clung even to the rafters upstairs—and see the corn-meal-colored balls of yeast drying on a board. Once when Kurt wanted to know where yeast came from in the first place, since she needed a ball or so from the last batch, Aunt Phrena said tiredly, ready to bawl, "Do you have to bother me?"

Johnny thought about Sophie's having a man, though she wouldn't have a home until Clymy grubbed the eighty north of the Marchens' and built a house. He had a tickle of mirth at the idea of Clymy's being her man and sitting at the head of the table, frightened as he was most of the time. It was ridge talk that he had been as scared of asking her to marry him as she was glad to have him, and that he galloped ahead of her, one step beyond her reach—until she snagged him with a grub hoe, Alb Hukelpoke said. Soon now she would marry him.

Anyway, Clymy wouldn't shout at Sophie the way crippled old Mr. Rose did at his wife—Mr. Rose who was tied to his chair with useless legs and cursed the threshing machine that had smashed his bones. They lived across the creek south. Johnny remembered the girl with the curvy smile.

September ran into October. Kinnikinnick berries, dirty-white and pea-like, vanished. The last of the robins feasted on them, leaving the crimson stems like little birds' red feet, stiffly outstretched in the sunup frost. It was a damp fall. Rain hissed in the grass with a sound like wheat poured in a thin cascade from the bag to the ground. Stacks of grain stood un-threshed, Old Mr. Rose's among them, and green began to tinge the black straw.

For all their expectations, the wedding was small and sloppy. Aunt Phrena fussed over the doughnuts she was taking, sure that the damp would make them soggy, and was glad the wedding cake was safely in the Marchen cupboard. Johnny bumped into the kitchen to hear her ex-claiming, "Now where did I put the cooky cutter? Sakes and days alive! The Devil is surely covering it with his tail. He will until I scold and get mad. Then I'll find it." She clattered a pan fiercely. "Ach, I could say something *really* bad." He didn't ask for the cooky he saw on the board but grabbed a drink and ran.

All forenoon of the wedding day, drizzles misted over the ridges and geese rode the wind waves south. "Moses, but there's a lot of nice roasts flying loose up there." Uncle Herm pointed past the eaves.

Aunt Phrena, stepping out, allowed the geese to fly; she got a stiff neck whenever she put her head back to look upward. Besides, she was uneasy. "Wonder if they'll have the dance, in this wet?" Ordinarily, fired by a memory long gone to smoldering ashes, her eyes would have brightened a little over a waltz or a two-step, in spite of herself. Whatever her feelings, her words were plain: "Old fools hopping around. What can you expect of the young?" She went to dances because Uncle Herm did; frowned on Saturday night shindandies where kitten, cat and heifer gathered together, she scolded; and refused to stay in the room with the music, remaining instead in the kitchen or the bedroom or the dim, night-lamplit upstairs, declaring, "Let them hop till they fall on their faces. I don't want to see it."

But now with Johnny plainly measured for the cloth, she fully intended to avoid anything as risky as a fiddle or an accordion. Johnny was restive enough as it was. Very soon, now, the Pastor would decide. He had hinted already and she was content. She thought of corralling her family after the wedding supper and bringing them home but gave it up. Uncle Herm could be stubborn, specially over a fourth or a fifth schooner of beer. She'd keep a stiff eye on Johnny, she promised herself, and was glad that the waltz hadn't yet untangled joy in his legs. She never guessed that Sophie was partnering him in awkward dances.

It was a queer wedding afternoon and evening. A chill after dark changed the drizzle to snow, for all that thunder racked the zenith. Reddish lightning touched the flakes pink-white, fire and snow together. And in between the thunder rumbles came the honk of wild geese. But Johnny remembered the day mostly because of the fire and Sophie's white face.

In a moment before the wedding supper Clymy, asserting his manhood with whisky-cherry wine, had refused to kiss his wife, new and inviolate as the veil showering from her head. Pale as the beads about her neck, she had picked him up bodily and carried him kicking like a day-old heifer upstairs to her room, a bridegroom lifted across a threshold by the bride. Johnny saw the veil flutter over Clymy's face and hide it. The door banged. The crowd sputtered into guffaws. Bride and bridegroom returned before the meal, Clymy wild-eyed though not yet sober. But Sophie's face was soap-white.

After supper the crowd was jovial, belly-hunger dulled with noodles and beef. Springy in the heels from beer and schnapps, couples were pairing off for a square dance. Johnny and Snoose watched Clymy trying to make himself taller with big words. Steadier now, he stood in the circle of jostling neighbors who poked at him with itchy fingers, envious with desire. They were telling him to get a good holt of her, big as she was, or she'd throw him out of bed, though maybe, small as he was, he couldn't hurt her anyway.

They were gabbling, bright-eyed with drink, when the black hide of night was slashed open with a jagged blade of flame. Thunder banged and racketed among the ridges and jiggled the lamps in the brackets. Windows became squares of red fire. In the hush that froze them, Mr. Nussbaum's voice was queerly loud: "Jippers, that was a close one. Hope it didn't strike my cow barn." The crowd-babble started again, in relief at being spared for this time the hammer of doom.

They were in the second polka when Mr. Schadel rushed in, shouting, "Hey, everybody! Old Man Rose's place is on fire." He had just come, late with chores. His wagon still stood hitched in the yard. "Seen the lightning fall. I was on the big hill. Fire like a house fell down."

Music scraped to nothing, voices tangled into senseless noise, heels trod on toes in a rush for the door. From the step they saw an angry glow inflaming the dark south. "It'll take more than a snowstorm to dampen this," folks said.

Afterward Johnny wasn't clear how he and Snoose got into Mr. Schadel's wagon, already loaded with people. Nobody noticed them in the excitement. But he remembered how Mr. Schadel yelled his team through the dark and the wind and the snow-rain in their faces. Back of them other wagons and buggies followed. They crossed the creek, the fire a bulge of light behind a hill, a bulge that stretched as they watched and shrank again and burst suddenly into a vast fan of sparks. "That must have been the barn fell just then," somebody guessed. But it was the cowshed, they found when they topped a hill. A scarlet tinge like a radiance lay on the white of knollside and field.

They came into the yard, their cheeks touched with crimson from the brightness, in their ears a roar. The cowshed was gone to black ribs, stubby and spurting bluish spirals. The wind stank of burned hide and hair and smoldering bone. Horses snorted, panic-ridden, and one reared, falling sidewise. There was a crash of wood and a man's yell. Johnny, taking a lungful of air, gulped and wished he hadn't touched the last of the duck soup.

The barn, its front redly kindled, was partly hidden in a dark bag of smoke flattened by wind. But the stacks were cones of fire, all their solid hearts of grain. As the neighbors milled into the yard, Johnny saw a beard of ragged flame brush the girth of the last stack and sink greedily out of sight a moment before it swished out again, grown-up and full-fierce.

Snoose and he rounded a corner of the house and there was Old Mr. Rose crouched on the black rock that was doorstep to his house—crouched there, in the snow, where his son and the hired man had carried him, his legs loose bundles of rags limply hanging, his white hair and his fist lifted to heaven. Calmly as if this were an invocation and slowly he spoke: "Damn, damn you, God; double damn you, God," over and over, his words a dash of cold spring water in Johnny's face.

All at once at the old man's side stood a girl, hair wild about her cap, terror scrawls plain on her face, crying, "Bruno's in the barn, Father; and Adam can't——" Johnny lost her words. But when he saw the honey color of her hair bright beside the dun of her cap, a stain of the fire sheen upon her, he moved aside so abruptly that he bumped into Snoose. Why he felt a rush of gladness at seeing her again, this girl he had noticed at the funeral, he didn't know. But gladness fled, for the button of a

dimple at her lip ends was broken now and she couldn't speak for sorrow.
The old man shoved her away roughly without a break in his litany of
cursing. His icy quiet was worse than shouts.

Prickles of fear shot through Johnny and Snoose. They legged it for the
barn, pushing among the neighbors. As they ran, a drift of air struck them.
Johnny's nose wrinkled. The air was heavy with the odor of burning wheat,
rich and toasty, like the smell of bread baking in a kitchen. He thought
oddly of the salty taste of butter.

Within the reach of searing heat, where snow ran in streams, the old
man's son, Adam Rose, waved a helpless hand toward a horse whinnying
frenziedly on the hillside—the only one saved. "The other bitch ran back
into—into the barn with the pony. I couldn't get 'em out, I couldn't——"
Tears ran out of the corners of his eyes and when he put a hand to his face,
they saw blood smearing his fingers from a cut. "How we going to pay
the mortgage now, I don't know." Near by stood the hired man, a fork in
his hand. From a pocket of his winter coat a rescued kitten poked its head,
frightened but secure if forgotten.

With a quick roar the smoke cleared and the barn stood naked in flame,
gable and eave. Windows exploded in a tinkle of glass. A white chicken
came flying from one, feathers blazing, and fell in a kicking, smoking
tumble on the ground. And above them, strange and almost unfamiliar in
this place, there sounded wild honks. A flock of geese, low on the bursts
of the chill northwester, seemed to pause for a moment as if wanting to
circle before they V-ed by. Johnny saw how red their white breasts were,
painted by the bloody glare.

Then at his shoulder stood the girl—the girl with the honey-colored hair,
her lips broken with tears. "Bruno's in there—my pony. They can't get
him out. He's white with brown spots." She looked at him and his tongue
went to water, the grief in her brown eyes was so mingled with pain. Like
the eyes of the dog that had blundered into Uncle Herm's wolf traps and
waited, broken-boned and howling. Snoose twisted his mittened hands uneasily.

Around them men moved sluggardly. Bewilderment like a sleep was on
their bones before this fury full of tongues lapping with crackles at the
dark bowl of the sky. They looked at the girl and they were helpless to the
last clenched hand. All the misty snow that swept fringelike down was no
more than a bucket of water sloshed against a red-hot stone. Once a man
balled a handful of snow and with swearing anger and a wide swing, flung
it into the roaring mass. There was no sizzle.

And then out of the churning smoke and the twisting rolls of fire came a
scream, high-pitched and quavering, womanlike in its human agony, its

lonely fearfulness stopping the blood—the scream of a horse. The sound crashed shrilly into the brain so that the cords in the leg jerked and the bowels tightened. Snoose went dead-white. With a cry the girl turned as if looking for a place to hide and suddenly Johnny found his arms full of her, her body sagging against him, her head on his shoulder, her hair soft and tangling on his chin and neck. Without thinking his arms tightened around her. For a moment he stood wooden as a block. She moved and a wave of hot confusion flooded him. Snoose stood at his side.

A woman's voice rang among them, calling, "Lilice, Lilice, where are you?" Lileesa, Lileesa. So the name sounded to Johnny. The echo sang in his head. Lileesa Rose. The girl stepped back and with a strange feeling he saw tears large on a cheek.

"Here, Mama." Her brown eyes looked on him solemnly. Then she was gone.

The rest of that night was in Johnny's mind a blur of smoke and collapsing timbers. . . . Old Man Rose saying sag-shoulderedly from his door, "A whole year's work in those stacks; everything. It's smoke now. But the bank won't take that." . . . Aunt Phrena's shrill "Running off like that and me tearing the house over to find you. You can't do that at the preacher school."

Not until he was warm under covers at home did he begin to sort out a few pieces of this night. Again he heard Old Man Rose shout: "Any of you bastards know how to make bread out of ashes?" He felt again the avalanche of heat explode outward when the roof, sagging a moment as if reluctant to leave its gable ends, crashed into a mouth of flame. Most of all he felt the girl in his arms again. A thorn of ire prodded him when he recalled how voiceless he had stood beside her, beside Lilice (her hair was on his chin), Lileesa, so her mother called her, Lilice, smelling someway of flowers and her lips how red—he wondered if he put his finger on them now how soft they'd be—and he was asleep, his thought trailing into dreams.

4

He began cutting bands that fall when he least expected it. Let the Pastor roar! It was good to leave the school at the church and the Bible history and the kids (except Snoose) behind for a while.

The snow that had whitened Sophie's wedding melted under changing weather. Mornings still crackled with the snap of cold nights but noons were warm enough to bring sweat to the forehead of a bundle pitcher. Days continued dry and the threshers strained muscle and horseflesh to finish before winter set his teeth in the straw. Uncle Herm moved the rig by night to save time and said he could use a dozen machines himself, though there were only two in the ridges then, his and Bory Tetzell's.

Johnny and Kurt trudged in from the pasture one schoolless Wednesday—the Pastor was in Fergus on preacher business—to find Uncle Herm pale and pinch-lipped, waiting in the wagon box, the sweat on his face dried into the dust of threshing. Aunt Phrena was sniffling into her apron. The team blew, still windy from the run home.

They ran forward, imagining calamity and destruction. But Uncle Herm called, "Sling another jacket on your back, Johnny, and jump in. You got to cut bands for me at Schimmels'."

Excitement almost sparked from Johnny's heels. Without wasting breath to ask how or why, he flung into the house, scarcely hearing Aunt Phrena's persistent "There's Torsten at the Peisers'. Why can't you get him? Or Anders Stramff. He's so smart with the 'cordion, he could cut bands."

"Torsten's grubbing and Peiser is plowing these three, four days." Uncle Herm was patient but he flipped the lines. "Anders can't be trusted with a knife, he's that flighty. He cuts bands the way he plays—all over the place. I ain't going to have my feeders' hands cut up. Besides, he's pitchin' for me." He added, "Really need two bandcutters. That Jackie Marchen is all right but he gets sloppy."

Aunt Phrena grew tearily stubborn. "You could find someone else. But you have to take him." She nodded saggily at Johnny tearing from the house, jacket under his arm, his jaws working on a mouthful of the slab of bread he had in his hand. "Pastor says he's coming along really well. Spring after next he'll be confirmed and in the fall he could go to preacher school." Johnny, climbing the spokes of the wheel to the wagon box, nearly fell backward under the weight of this news. Aunt Phrena continued: "He got to study hard though, and now you take him away and——"

"Bull wheels of Almighty Moses!" For once Uncle Herm was as stubborn as she. He slapped the lines violently. "Now you open your earholes, Phrena, and listen to me. Young Nussbaum got caught in the tumbling rods and he's hurt; a close call but no bones broke. He's not so bad he won't be cutting in a couple of days." Uncle Herm scratched his mustaches fiercely. "Johnny takes his place, that's all. We got to finish threshing; got to. And if three, four days' work is going to hurt him for being a preacher, then preachers ain't much good."

"You never ask Kurt," Aunt Phrena jealously tried a new attack. "Not that I'd let him go. A Christian boy must——"

"Jump in, then, all of you, by the living cripes!" Uncle Herm yelled, twisting the leather violently. "You, too, Phrena. Jump in! The whole damn fam'ly can help thrash, all I care." He giddapped the team and the wheels rattled over Aunt Phrena's wailing, "I promised her, my sister——"

For half a mile Uncle Herm was grim-faced over his driving. He diddled the lines, aware of the peeks Johnny was giving him. When he swung around and let his lip muscles relax, Johnny whooped, "Get going, there, you tug busters!" Leaning over the edge of the box, Johnny slapped the horses with his hand. In spite of his gladness, however, he kept seeing Kurt in the yard watching them go, firm on his heavy feet and stolid, as if what he wanted, sooner or later, he'd get. Something boiled under *that* skin these days.

The Schimmel yard was loud with the noise of threshing when they came, the tumbling rods *clitter-clattering*. Hukelpoke stood on the power. The horses circled. The separator smoked dust. Herky Morrison, the feeder that year, forced the straw into the whirling teeth of the cylinders. Herky was a peppery man whose long arms curved over the bundles as rhythmically as a swimmer's in water.

Johnny leaped to the ground. Hukelpoke waved his whip in welcome, but his yell was lost in the rattle of knuckles and gears. Jackie Marchen, Snoose's brother, who was cutting bands, slashed a circle in the air with his knife. Herky looked up without stopping, face gray with a cloth of dust, his eyes white blobs. And Mr. Dunkel from his grain wagon flapped a sack. But Mr. Schadel, large with the doubt of one whose familiarity with his work makes him suspect the uninitiated, shouted into the noise, "Think you can handle the knife, kid?"

Johnny nodded, all confidence, and walked to the machine with Uncle Herm. The head of the separator with its open feeder mouth and its long, underslung jaw of a feeder's table, was thrust between the stacks. Herky stood on the platform before the cylinder. On either side, the tables jutted past his hips. Just back and to the right and left side of him were the bandcutters' places where Mr. Nussbaum, taking his hurt son's place, and Jackie Marchen were ready with the knife.

Mr. Nussbaum waved grumpily at Johnny and jumped down. "Jippers, but she's a dusty bastard," he yelled and climbed the stack, glad to be at his old task of pitching bundles. "You can have my job and welcome." Johnny hopped over the tumbling rod. Uncle Herm grinned at him before he went to the grain wagons.

With a queer excitement stirring his flesh, Johnny stepped onto the cutter's platform, a small shelf projecting from the feeder's stand. He grabbed the knife Mr. Nussbaum left for him and waited for the bundles. At his knees the smooth shaft of the tumbling rod spun, carrying power to the bevel wheel and the cylinder. Across from him (with Herky's long body between them) Jackie Marchen slouched against the table, taller than Snoose but lazier in his motions. He bobbed his head.

For a moment of waiting, the cylinder ran free of straw and its whine grew high and thin, impatient to rip the live kernel from the dead husk. Through its heightened drone broke the *rattle-rittle* of the tumbling knuckles and the sharp clack and clang of evener and chain, iron striking iron as the load on the power eased and the tugs slacked.

Then Mr. Nussbaum threw the first bundle. It thudded on the table. Johnny heard the crack and crush of straw in front of him. His eyes caught the band of twine, almost the color of the wheat stems. His hand with the knife thrust forward; the blade touched the band. The stalks, as if alive with release, spread under his knife. Before he knew, a dark hand, fingers curved out, one of them glinting with a gold ring, swooped down. In panic Johnny jerked the blade back. Just in time. Where the knife had been seconds before, the hand was now, catching the bundle and in one sweep, shaking and loosening it. Before the startled blood in him had settled, the hand and the bundle were gone. He saw the loosely gathered straw fed to the teeth in even flows. The cylinder snarled into the wheat, the whine lowered to a steady *hum-m-rum-m*.

He jumped when a voice bellowed into his ear: "Watch that knife, kid! You cut my hands and I'll knock your teeth in." His nose almost bumped Herky's face, so far had the feeder leaned toward him. Herky's tone held no threat; only a promise of fact.

There was a crash and a bundle crackled past his shoulder. Another bundle. Over it Mr. Nussbaum grimaced sardonically. He had a habit of screwing up his lips at the heave of a bundle.

Johnny's knife shot forward and slit the band. He was as alert as a mink now. His cutting edge was gone before the dark hand curved into the straw again. Herky nodded. It was the right stroke. Johnny lifted himself on his toes, satisfaction clean as a freshet in him. He could handle the knife as good as Jackie Marchen; maybe better.

Nerves relaxed but careful he slashed the hours of the lowering sun away. He learned to measure the distance between his severing knife and the falling hand to the neatness of a cord-width. Opposite him Jackie Marchen lazed and gawked about when he could; yelled ununderstandable swearwords at Hukelpoke who answered in mouth twistings but in no sound above the noise of the machine. Jackie waved his fist at the stackers wallowing in the untidy waves of straw which the carrier pushed up its incline and heaped onto the straw pile. He pulled faces behind Herky's back. Once he made Johnny virtuously uncomfortable. With the knife and the fingers of one hand he made the motions of Mr. Humber, the pig gelder, castrating a bull. He acted the fool until Herky straightened up, anger in the jut of a shoulder.

After sundown the clouds of smoky wheat dirt and the dusk were the same gray color. Johnny drove the blade at the band with caution. Suddenly he heard a yell and saw Herky's upflung hand streaked with blood in the afterglow. The next moment Herky's fist smashed into Jackie's mouth. Jackie tumbled off the platform and against the stack. The blow was a "glancer" but it brought red.

For a moment Herky squeezed the wound, shaking the cut finger. With a twist he dived at Jackie, now scrambling up. Johnny leaned on the bundle, taking this in with care. The machine, free again, hummed to a higher pitch. There would have been a fight, for Mr. Marchen jumped from the stack, pitchfork in hand. In defense of Jackie, he was ready to trade fists with Herky then and there. But Mr. Nussbaum and Uncle Herm with others interfered.

That ended the day. The machine slowed under Hukelpoke's "Whoa there, take 'er easy now!" His cries rose as the noises subsided little by little. Mr. Nussbaum ran to pull his team to a gradual halt. The gears grunted; the knuckles clack-clacked, the tumbling blocks shuddered, and the machine jerked to a stop.

With the end of iron din, silence rushed strangely into their heads, almost as if it were a finger thrust into the ears. Herky's voice sounded loud enough to be a scream in the new-made stillness. "Young pricker. He can keep his peepers open, or I'll poke him another one." His tone was harsh but he was no longer flaring.

Jackie spat blood and Herky said, "Give me a chew, Marchen." The fight was over. Nobody was deliberately at fault here. Accidents would happen and tempers, like the quick fire of chaff, would blaze. They'd die, their heat blown with a tussle or two, though a smolder of grudge might be put away and lie in the mind for years.

Johnny stepped down and almost stumbled, caught off guard by the stiffness webbing his legs into unsteadiness. His face muscles broke a mask of dirt when he grinned. The cold that chilled the evening and made the sweaty horses steam sent shivers through him. He wished he'd worn two shirts, as Jackie did. Herky absorbedly chewed the tobacco into a juicy cud. Gently he parted the flesh of his wound. "Deep sucker, this," he said and spat the tobacco drippingly on the cut. Around it he tied a strip torn from a handkerchief he dragged from his pocket and shook free of dust and chaff and kernels of wheat. "There. That'll take the soreness off."

He nodded toward Jackie. "Next time you try that, I'll loosen your belly button." His tone held little animosity. Jackie sheepishly kicked a toe. He understood. Tomorrow they'd be at work again, the one cutting band, the other feeding. Threshing must not stop for rancor or a ripped muscle or a bashed tooth; no, not even for an accident that flung a man on his back. More than one setting of grain was threshed with grudges wide as ditches between this pitcher and that feeder, between this farmer and that thresher. But for the season they were held together by the ropes of need; the farmer to see his acres broaden and to pay the bank; the thresher to meet his duns and keep his rig in oil and good repair; the hired help to lay up money for a farm he planned some day to own, or it may have been for Indian Twist and a bunk to sleep in during the winter.

Mr. Schimmel said, however, "Herky let the Marchen kid off mighty easy. By Gott, I 'member a feeder—this happened on the flats west of Fergus. My brother-in-law's uncle was workin' on the rig. A bandcutter was so unhandy he cut a feeder's thumb off. And the feeder, by Gott, he grabbed that kid and stuck him head first into the cylinder. My brother-in-law, he says there was bones and blood in the wheat. The crew, they took this feeder and hung him on the limb of an oak. . . ."

Johnny stamped a foot for warmth. Tiredness fogged his sight. Even the hot soup and beef Mrs. Schimmel put before him didn't rub it away. He followed Alb and Uncle Herm to the barn, after supper, his breath plain in the cold air. He helped unharness the teams. The collars were sticky with sweat. A strap rubbing against his neck for a moment was moist and clammy. He slapped the horses understandingly when they snorted, heads down, the galling hame and bit gone for the hours of the night. He even rubbed the heads of Tophet and Jeremiah, Mr. Dunkel's oxen, for Mr. Dunkel was staying the night. A neighbor boy was doing his chores. Johnny carried straw to bed the horses and staggered under the load, weary-footed. The stink of leather was acrid in his nose.

After chores, he climbed the ladder to the haymow. His hands felt the grit left on the rungs by another's soles and once the soft squashiness of manure. Ahead of him Alb bellowed, his fingers mucky, "Balls of Holy Judas, some fellers can't help it! If there's a pile of cow flop within a mile, they got to step in it."

Johnny pulled himself through the trap-door opening and wiped his hands on a wisp of sloo grass. The mows were full of hay but the alley space between them was empty from wall to wall. Here quilts and blankets and pillows were spread on hay for resting places. Mrs. Schimmel's star-and-square pattern coverlet was crumpled over the upthrust knee of a bundle pitcher already snoring. Jackie was busy in a corner with his boots. Johnny banged down beside him with a sigh that drooped his shoulders. Lanterns swung on nails in the studding, casting as much shadow as light.

Men were pulling off boots and the smell of sour feet was so strong that Johnny buried his nose in a pillow, glad for the clean odor of soap in the cloth.

Herky, forgetting his cut hand and a feeder's aches in two fingers of whisky, began singing twangily. The tune of "Just before the Battle, Mother" was hardly recognizable but the words were clear:

> "Just before the bottle, darling,
> I am thinking most of you;
> While upon the bar I'm leaning
> With a scotch or rye in view.
> Sober, you may never press me
> To your breast where I have lain.
> But oh, you'll not forget me, darling,
> When I'm in the jug again."

He ended in a hiccup. Anders Stramff wouldn't unpack his accordion. "Too sleepy," he grunted. A long-legged boy was saying, "I figure on doing a little cakewalking with that Humber girl—what's her name?— Josephine, Saturday night. Looks like she could heat a feller up, the little devil."

A pitcher slipped off his pants and shook them free of chaff. His underwear from ankle to shirttail was grayish with sweat and dirt, his legs unexpectedly bony in the lanternlight. A stacker called, "Throw me your stick-knife, Hank. I got a beard under my toenail. Hurts like hell." Mr. Dunkel was arguing: "You can give me a yoke of oxen any time. Horses get ya scared if a girl's skirt flaps; but my sluggies will foller me without a moo, slow and careful, I don't care how stony the field is." And Young Matt Dornover was answering: "Sure thing, but I don't aim to fight stones and brush until my last day; not on my farm. I've cleared twenty acres this year and I'm taking my rail fence down. It don't hold cattle in anyway, it's rotten all the time. And I'm putting up wire and——" Their voices merged. Johnny gnawed a fingernail. That Mr. Dunkel, talking about his oxen, and his wife whispering to an empty chair—— He gave it up.

Two men, as if defying tiredness, wrestled around in brief horseplay. There was a smothered slap of a hand on a buttock and a fun-choked voice, "You look out there; get away with your fingers," and laughter. Johnny kicked his shoes aside. Men began loosening their belts and pushing suspenders off their shoulders with chest-deep yawns and throaty cries of "Oh, ah, ah!" as if they were giving weariness a voice. In early fall they slept in their underwear only. But now in the chill of the year, they went

to rest in the dust and sweat of their woolens and shirts and pants and in
the wetness of their stockings.

Johnny wiggled his toes and crept under beside Jackie, grateful for the
cave of warmth which the other's body made beneath the covers. He eased
his bones into a comfortable tangle. Rich and fragrant, the odor of Jackie's
skin, weeks now unwashed, came in puffs between the folds of the quilts.
Jackie thrust a hand toward him and his whisper on the pillow was loud.
"I can tell you're just come from home. You smell clean."

Somebody blew the lanterns. Blackness fell like a weight upon the sight.
As the lantern blower fumbled to bed, a yell split the dark. "Get your
stinkin' feet out of my face, you gut-livered goose wiper." After a while,
night squeezed through the cracks in the rooftree and through the holes in
the boards where the knots had fallen out—a lighter shade of dark than the
blackness inside.

With silence, drowsiness rode over Johnny. Tired as he was and achy
deep under bone and muscle, sleep danced beyond reach. And in this half
doze, the simple acts of the day swelled to monsters of violence. He tossed
bundles big as barns; the knife in his hand bloated to the size of a filled
grain sack; the set-to between Herky and Jackie became a battle of berserks;
and drowning all was the noise of the machine like the smash and crush of
ice breaking up in the lake and rushing down the river.

When he floated nearer the isles of wakefulness, he sighed in contentment. He was among them, among these threshers; a part of threshing; a
thresher himself, sleeping in his clothes as the threshers did. He could get
a job now, any time; big money too. Then maybe he could pay off Norton,
and Uncle Herm could get a bigger rig. . . . He yawned. True, he itched
between the buttocks and his neck was sore from the scratch of chaff but
he was a bandcutter. Herky's nod was seal and ribbon to his confirmation,
and Hukelpoke's slap on his shoulder the stamp of neighborly acceptance:
"Judas, you cut band like you was born with a knife in your fist. And you
just past fourteen." Alb's words trailed through his sleepiness, a vague
echo from beyond a dream hill. Besides, he was away from Aunt Phrena
and Kurt and the Pastor with his preacher school. . . . He giggled into his
pillow so hard suddenly that he waked himself wide. Jackie whispered,
"What tickled you—a bedbug?"

"Nope," Johnny whispered back. "Wouldn't the Pastor pound the
Book, though, if he slept with us and heard this truck we talk?" Jackie's
nod was a rustle on the pillow.

In the barn below, the teams snortled and sneezed and a calf coughed
drily. For a moment the floor under him shook a little as a horse rubbed a
galled spot against a stud. Then he was asleep or, rather, joggling on the

edge of sleep, for he twitched the night long, his muscles jerking as if he lifted endless knives to hack at dream bundles that swirled like leaves around his waist. Once he pulled open salty lids to hear Jackie snore and somebody fumble in the hay and heard Alb's voice, "Sheets, ain't going down, for that." He felt more than saw how Alb groped his way to a knothole in the wall. A moment later came the dripping sound of water trickling over boards. He heard Alb sigh deeply in relief and scratch an itchy place lustily, nails loud against the stem of hair and tough upper skin. The stamp of a horse's hoof was a small explosion. Men snored or muttered their night longings in tongues that belonged to another world. He felt the cold like a damp cloth against his feet and, drawing his knees up, snuggled closer to Jackie, wishing drowsily that this were Snoose; and slid into outer sleep.

5

By Monday Young Nussbaum returned to the cutter's table and Johnny was on the path to school. In spite of a blister that was becoming a callus, he was reluctant to give up the knife and the curve his fingers had on the handle. Rooster struts were in his heels. Kurt had little to say, though Snoose let the gladness shine in his eyes. Gatha Blumen had such respect for Johnny that she offered, "I'm having a skating party sometime. You want to come?" Mosey Fritz, eaten with jealousy, had his mouth full of jibes. But Johnny was cautious about rubbing folks the wrong way, plugged with brag though he was. He remembered Heinie Beerwagon's fist against his teeth. He found that his white grin and an easy way he was learning softened the struts, so that he could keep just this side of offense and still enjoy his egotism.

Aunt Phrena, distressed to her second chin, saw to it that he made up all the lessons he dropped on the bandcutter's table. That winter she crowded pages of Bible history into the hours he planned to spend seriously on mink in the creek and muskrat in the sloo. In a kind of desperation he went to Snoose's house evenings, as often as he could wiggle away from her vigilance, the books under his arm.

And after the "Healing of the Lepers" was laid away beside the Catechism, Sophie, still at home while Clymy puttered at his eighty, and springier in her long legs than ever since her wedding, spent more than one evening leading him in a waltz or a two-step, with Mrs. Marchen at the organ and Snoose watching dreamily from a pile of coats on the floor. He learned the polka fast, she said teasingly; much faster than he learned the Creed. His slender body, deceptively slim, and his easy-swinging legs twisted in the waltz. Awkwardness soon shed like feathers from a gait that was still inclined to shuffling. Before long, he'd want to take Lilice Rose to a barn dance, Snoose opined, leaning on an elbow. Johnny was ready to pummel him, his face crimsoning. A guilty yet bold sort of pleasure was in his wondering. "You s'pose I could—some day?"

Lilice Rose wasn't going to religious school that year—nor any other, Aunt Phrena prophesied. "That Mrs. Rose—never sending her girl to Catechism. No more baptism in them than in a cat." The congregation agreed, shaking heads.

Johnny puzzled over this. What awfulness there must be in you, if you weren't baptized and confirmed: deep holes of wickedness like the bottomless places in the swamp where the tallest pine, when thrust down, met nothing but the yielding muck of the bog. You came from evil. That was plain enough. Hadn't the Pastor shaken that doom from his threatening fist many a Sunday past? "In iniquity were you shapen; and in sin did your mothers conceive you." ("Conceive." He pulled a lip over the riddle of that word and had a notion he'd learn something new if he dug the meaning out of Aunt Phrena's dictionary.) You broke into life pickled in sin and error. Mr. Nussbaum used to say that babies had horns and the Pastor knocked them off at baptism. Snoose had a little knob on his head, Johnny recalled, though Johnny's own was smooth under the wavy, black hair. But Snoose had been touched with water and word and so the knob no doubt was the evidence of Mr. Marchen's knuckles, not a leftover piece of the Devil.

It must be awful, though, not being baptized or confirmed; like manure on your face for people to see and no water ever to wash it away. Johnny didn't know anyone in the ridges who wasn't a church member and therefore a worthy neighbor, except Mr. Rose and his family. A shiver still crinkled his spine when he remembered how Mr. Rose sat on his doorstep and cursed God to His face. And the barn burned.

He wondered about Mrs. Rose and wasn't sure whether he would run or stay, if ever he met her. But when he thought of Lilice and the leaf-curled wistfulness of her smile, the breath left him in a laugh almost loud: "Horns! Such craziness."

Lilice was attending District School while he went to the Pastor. Maybe he'd meet her sometime and then he'd talk, not remain silent and stumplike, as he had at the fire. He was glad someway that he didn't fall over his ankles in a polka any more.

Mr. Marchen, hitching his suspenders, laughed at him. "Ya, it won't be long now. Give a young stud a can of oats and he thinks he can jump fences and run after the mares. You'll do, Schwartzie." Johnny winced and hunted his cap to go home.

He went to school, moroseness growing in him that winter. The Pastor hadn't mentioned the preacher school in the spring before. Neither had he spoken about it in the fall just past at the school's beginning. He waited while Johnny wriggled—"like a shiner on a hook," Johnny muttered fiercely. The Pastor certainly would speak sometime this winter. He might any day. Johnny wished he could tell him straight to his face, "I won't go to preacher school," but knew he'd never dare. Why, even Mr. Marchen put on bluff and bravado when he went to register for communion. Everybody knew he was scared the Pastor would ask him to recite the Ten Commandments and knew too that Mr. Marchen would probably bog down after the second. No, the pastor would have to find out for himself. If it were a neighborhood dance or a spree, the Pastor would discover it with the swiftness of mink's feet. But not a boy's determination never to go to preacher school. Besides, there was still Aunt Phrena to face.

Beyond a thin nose thrust at him, the Pastor said only when Johnny tripped over a question, "People who go thrashing and waste the blessed Lord's hours of study usually find themselves as blockheaded as an ox on a hill." His voice dripped acid.

At the end of the year his account book worried a new sag into Uncle Herm's shoulder. Norton—that name was clear in his talk as the ice cracks in the pond, yet he never mentioned Norton by name. There were times when, returning from Mary's Hill and the selling of the wheat, he swore among the cows where Johnny was milking. "Bull wheels of Moses Almighty! You know what, Johnny? That double-castrated tomcat of a Meyer cheated me again. 'Damp wheat,' he says and grades me number two. 'And three sacks are frosted,' he says. 'Frosted?' I says. 'What do you mean?' 'They got froze; millers in Saint Paul say it makes a poor grist of flour,' he says. 'Look here, Meyer,' I says to him. 'That wheat's solid as a dollar.' And the bastard—he looks at me and says, 'What dollar, gold or silver?' and tells me I don't have to sell my wheat to him, he's got plenty." Uncle Herm kicked the feed can the length of the barn. "Moses, I'd like to wrap my blacksnake around his neck."

Johnny almost stopped milking, listening while the foam in his nearly full pail hissed softly as it disappeared. "Maybe you would get a better price, hauling it to Fergus." He spoke as man to man. Uncle Herm's gaze softened.

"Don't think so. The elevator men there are hooked up with the bastards in Mary's Hill. Besides, there's the long haul. Nope." Uncle Herm shook his head. "This country's sure headin' for the damnation bowwows, as Edgely says."

Sometimes when Mr. Marchen came over, Uncle Herm agreed that the elevator men were all bunched together with the railroads. "You lick my rump and I'll lick yours, that's their style," Mr. Marchen said.

"Edgely was telling me that it costs more to ship wheat from Mary's Hill to St. Paul than from Mary's Hill to Chicago, and cripes, that's anyways a thousand miles more."

"Well, the *leg*-islater passed *ya* a bill." Uncle Herm leaned against the fence. "Elevator men are s'posed to get licenses. And the law says inspectors must examine things ever so often. But freight rates are as high as ever; and the gradings—Moses Almighty, they'll grade your hind end down to pimples!"

"Cripes, ya!" Mr. Marchen spat. "It makes a feller want to join the 'Liancers." He licked his lips. "Give me a chew, Herman."

"Don't know about them 'Liancers, Johaan." Uncle Herm dug up the tobacco. "Seems like all they want is the gover'ment to run things. Well, I don't want a gover'ment feller telling me how to plant my spuds nor how to nut my pigs, either."

But Mr. Edgely, whose brother in Kansas was a burning Alliance man and sent him bundles of papers, said, "Dumb Dutchmen. They haven't enough sense in those thick skulls to vote for what's good for them. Besides, they're afraid to try any plan that isn't a hundred years old."

"Talk, talk, talk," scorned Aunt Phrena over her sewing. "It never paid a bill yet."

With all this noise echoing about him, Johnny began to long for confirmation and the day he could go securely to a neighbor for a job. Until the Pastor laid hands in blessing on his head, few neighbors would hire him, except as a kid for board and keep. He knew that. But after he'd sipped his first communion wine, they would expect to pay him lodging and wages besides. He'd make good use of these, he promised himself, eying grimly the pile of bills over which Uncle Herm hunched.

That spring Aunt Phrena heard the walking preacher for the first time and caught a beatific fever that racked her bones as the ague did Mr. Fleischer's. It was neither an angel clarion nor a fiery sword that brought her into the smoke and dust of this new and frenzied Armageddon but a setting of goose eggs. Often she had envied Mrs. Peiser. "Such pillows she has—light as air, made all of goose down. Warm feather beds, too. Ach, such lightness!" She had vowed she'd start a lapful of goslings herself sometime. In March she settled the matter. "This year we have geese," she announced, as if that would make her pillows downier at once and her roast more inviting to the tooth. "All the feed you waste in the barn, we can easy raise a flock. Mrs. Edgely has geese's eggs to sell."

The Edgelys lived a ridge over and, one evening after early chores, they drove over there in the spring wagon. Water running from the thawing drifts was slowing in the after-sundown chill and catching the pale light of the afterglow in its rills. The wagon splashed in the watery patches. Melting snow slopped under the wheels, each heap of slush squirting a foot away.

Smoke plumed lazily above the trees near the creek where a home-steader, in haste to set his plow in ages-undisturbed Dakota earth and raise his walls of prairie sod, defied the season's weather with a fire. Or it might be a wagon train. Each spring the homesteaders arrived with the certainty of northward swinging geese, in companies large or small, dreams bumping with iron over stone.

"Early this year, the homesteaders," Uncle Herm observed languidly. "Bet they got stuck in the mud more than once, coming up." Sometimes Uncle Herm spent an evening of firelight in talk with them, Johnny tagging along, and now and again Kurt, their eyes bugging in curiosity over intimate household jars and packages bare to their inquisitiveness. Often the homesteaders came to buy a basket of eggs from Aunt Phrena or carry away a bucket of fresh water.

They gabbled of Devil's Lake and Church's Ferry and wheat in Dakota country that grew like curls on a sheep and sold for a dollar a bushel. Johnny dreamed about the money they spoke of—money clear in the bank. Such talk stirred some folks and rooted them from their places. Mr. Krumlich left his house half built and a tree leaning where he was cutting it and joined them, setting his wife and kids among his truck in the wagon.

"He got Dakota fever bad," Uncle Herm said, shaking his head. Lots of fellers got it bad. But you couldn't trade me all of the Dakota prairies for an inch of this tree land. They'll come back, them fellers, you bet, when the sod dries out and their wheat won't sprout. You gotta have *ya* trees to make rich land." But last year's wagon train never returned and new ones came with spring.

Johnny watched the homesteader's smoke flatten, wondering by what strange waters the caravan would lumber before it stopped to camp again.

Aunt Phrena sighed against the sway of the wagon. "Here it is April again. And next spring both of you get confirmed. Ach, ya, how time flies!"

Her words bumped him into listening. There was so much yearning in her sigh that for a startled moment he thought she was in a hurry to get rid of him, but dismissed the notion. He squirmed on the seat beside Kurt, wishing that the team would move faster. Uncle Herm was hunched over the lines, longing for bed to unkink the knots which the grub hoe had tied in his muscles.

In the Edgely yard they found teams roped to posts and a buggy shadowy in the dusk. The small house burst with light and gathered voices singing. "They got company," Uncle Herm began eagerly, scenting jollity and a pony of beer in so much song. Some of his tiredness faded before this brightness. But Aunt Phrena whispered as if she'd put her foot in the wrong shoe, "The walking preacher again. They got a meetin' tonight." She was ready to cry excitedly, "Turn around, Herman. This is no place for us," in spite of a curiosity hard and bristly that rose in her.

Mr. Edgely bore through the April darkness then. His greeting was hearty. Yes, they had goose eggs for sale, but Mrs. Edgely was busy for a moment with Brother Erdman, the preacher. Wouldn't they step down and set for a spell? Mrs. Edgely would have a clutch of eggs ready in no time.

With eggs and curiosity and neighborliness mixed like wheat and pigeon grass, it was hard to say "No" and swing the team rudely about and leave right in Mr. Edgely's face, although Aunt Phrena stepped down so reluctantly that it was plain she had every nerve alert for the snares of delusion. "You never know what pitfalls the Devil digs for you," she muttered to Johnny. Secretly, she was curious about the meetings, for Mrs. Haber had told her with heaves and sighs of the shoutings and hallelujahs and the joy of the sinner visibly saved by grace. Johnny wished he'd stayed home and gone over to see Snoose.

The Edgely house, small though it was, was large enough for the dozen that crowded in. Among them were those who were newcomers in the hills and those who defied the Pastor and went where they pleased and so were really outside his shepherding care, except as deplorable examples of benighted heathens. The room was full of Brother Erdman's sermon when they pushed in, Aunt Phrena ahead, protectingly. They found seats on a board bridging space from one oak block to another—chunks brought in from the woodpile. Aunt Phrena sat stiffly, a poker in her spine, but Uncle Herm was already nodding to Mr. Haber. With the lights and house warmth and Brother Erdman's ringing voice, Johnny was confused, ears and eyes full of sound but little sense.

After a while of looking he almost gasped when he saw Mr. and Mrs. Dunkel in the front row. In a corner where a bracketed lamp showered light on her honey-colored hair was Lilice Rose and beside her a woman he guessed at once was her mother. He nearly toppled from the board.

That the Dunkels should be here, Mrs. Dunkel humping toward the preacher as if any minute now she'd fall in agonized entreaty—that was wonder enough. But this other—no doubt about it; this was the unbaptized woman!

He gaped at her. She—why, she was—well, pretty. Even with a kind of tiredness drooping on her lips, there was energy in the way she listened, her head lifted as if she knew what she wanted to hear. And when she met his gaze, he found her eyes direct but quiet as the lake at dawn. He dodged her look and for a moment earnestly regarded Lilice, bent over the sermon, the wrapt expression like candleshine on her face, the smile tucked away in seriousness.

Kurt elbowed him then and Aunt Phrena skewered him with a chill stare. He swallowed to gather his wits and listened hard.

Brother Erdman stood by a small table, Bible in hand: a tall man in a frock coat but with no black gown such as the Pastor wore. The red of heartiness was in his cheeks. There was no sign of cringing in the set of his shoulders or the firm stand of his feet on the floor. A woman ahead of Johnny leaned to whisper to a neighbor, "Ah, he's so strong!" There was something boyish in the plumpness of his face, a softness about his jaws. Johnny, seeing only the solidness of flesh, approved inwardly: Looks like he could be a farmer, all right. He let his heel fall sharply. A farmer—like himself—turning minister. . . .

Brother Erdman's voice, low now and sad as the mourning strain of a wood dove, unsnarled itself into meaning for Johnny. He jerked to listen. "Where will you stand, my brothers? Oh, where, my sisters, on that grand morning when the Saviour shuts His lambs forever from the goats? Will you stand on the pitside of fire? God forbid, my brethren. Or on the edge of His green pastures for aye?" The haunting, undulating chant broke with a quick turn into the thunderclap of his yell: "Sinner, make up your mind!"

Johnny pushed in his seat. He heard the board creak as Aunt Phrena moved. Somebody drew breath harshly. Mrs. Dunkel moaned. Stonily Brother Erdman shot at them: "Worms of rottenness, dragging your bellies through the slime of your stinking thoughts. Yes, indeed; yes, indeed. Condemned and lost."

Mrs. Dunkel groaned and swayed forward. Johnny shivered. As if her agony were a signal, Brother Erdman softened to the sweetness of bells heard afar. "Lost you would be, but now you are not. No, indeed. No, indeed. Saved by grace, my brethern, that's what you are. Saved." His voice mellowed as he gave them slices of the unutterable joys of the faithful: burning tongues cooled with water, sorrows changed to laughter, the harlots gamboling in their new radiant innocence to receive the virile, holy strength of men, the prisoners shouting as the shackles slipped from their ankles. A queer sort of glow lighted itself in Johnny. Brother Erdman almost whispered now, his eyes half closed, his breath coming in shorter and shorter gasps, his lips trembling. "The blood—it is the blood that has saved you—blood of Him. Oh, wash in it, all your naked and festering bodies! Rip away your filthy clothes and stand bare in the flood of redemption! Oh, come and be saved! Come in, come in!" he trumpeted all at once, his arms outstretched, cheeks ablaze, his zeal a guide for the faint-hearted and uncertain, as if he would fold them all to his breast in holy passion.

Listening until his back ached with drawn breath and a hunched-over position on the oak plank, Johnny gladly heard that salvation lay in the next field and could be picked up as hay with a fork. The preacher's voice swirled about him in its manliness; his strength flowed in streams. Johnny found himself suddenly trembling as if he had a chill. What was this that lay beyond his finger tips, this something that he could almost feel? Or could he taste it and smell it? An odor like a dream of flowers long forgotten?

He grabbed a knee in a kind of fright. Was this a call, like that which Aunt Phrena's brother had received—a call from God to go forth with scrip and staff? A call like Brother Erdman's, whose muscularity spoke robustly of handling a pitchfork or a shovel? Johnny's breath came faster.

Then he went cold; a kind of weariness seeped into him. For with the preacher's ringing cry, Mrs. Dunkel arose. Like a partridge hen stripped of her brood and doubtfully haunting the nest, she faltered. But she put aside Mr. Dunkel's protesting arm. As if commanded, she tottered up beside Brother Erdman and flung herself on the floor, moaning, "Jesus, Jesus," and beating her fists on the wood. Mr. Haber stood tall beside Uncle Herm and went forward, his face twitching. He knelt and stretched full length near the cupboard. As his body thumped down, a faint music of china and silver clinking rose from Mrs. Edgely's closet shelves.

Over the prostrate penitents Brother Erdman quavered, "Oh, come, my suffering brethern! See the blood running for you; see the spear in the precious side for you; don't cheat your Lord. Come, oh come!" With a great tearing sob in his voice, he sank back against the table as if a crisis had come and gone and he was spent. Tears slid over his rounded cheeks like melting sleet kernels down a window pane.

Johnny shut his face away. A big strong man like that and bawling. The red of shame washed over him from thigh to ears—shame for Mrs. Dunkel knocking her head against Mrs. Edgely's pine floor, though he felt sorry for her; shame for Mr. Haber, belly-flat in plain sight of his neighbors. How could he grovel so, and grunt, "Jesus, Jesus," as if he had a stomach-ache? Shame for the others who were joining him; shame for the preacher, a broken mullein stalk and not a towering oak. Suddenly he wanted to run away and hide, shrinking from this prying into the back cellars and private entries of neighbor lives.

For once he turned to Aunt Phrena with gladness for the sour strength in her, remembering her warnings. He couldn't believe his glance and looked again. Aunt Phrena was close to tears, her eyes winking. The shadow of the beatific was on her face, a foretaste of the grapes of paradise already on her tongue. "So true it is; so true," he heard her whisper.

Desperately he twisted, trying to find a piece of solidness on which he could put a hand. He saw Lilice pressed against her mother, something like horror on her face, and her mother, chin lifted in a kind of pride, shaking her head violently when Brother Erdman, handkerchief to his cheeks, beckoned to her with a limp free hand.

Then Uncle Herm turned to him with his quizzical half-smile and serene regard. Johnny crowded against him, as though this man were not far from being a rock around which a man would throw his anchor rope.

Before Brother Erdman could announce a hymn tune, Mrs. Rose disturbed the spell by gathering her wraps and Lilice, and steering for the door, saying firmly to Mrs. Edgely's protests, "Thank you, Mrs. Edgely. It's good of you, but we'll not come to meeting again. I don't want Lilice ashamed of God."

Brother Erdman's arm lifted, fell. Instead of singing the hymn, he abruptly took up the collection. Outside a buggy—Mrs. Rose's—struck stone as it rattled Lilice away in the night.

6

By the time the Pastor actually opened his mouth on doom about the preacher school, and doom it seemed, Johnny had wound a hard shell of defiance about him. The memory of the evening at the Edgelys' brought nothing edifying, only a bruised sense of outrage, as if someone had put a dirty heel upon a white altar cloth. Mrs. Dunkel. You can't blame her. Gretel left her that way, not right in the head. But a big man like Mr. Haber, he thought bitterly, flopping down like that. And that Erdman. A bull strapper and bawling like a tit-baby. Why, Uncle Herm is worth a dozen of him. Even the Pastor half a dozen.

Unsmilingly he regarded that last thought a moment. It was true. Dignity the Pastor had, stiff and chill as frosty reeds, and an austerity that inspired awe as much as respect. No one could deny that. But this was also true. The gentleness of the shepherd, friendliness and understanding— who in the parish had felt the touch of these?

Not that Johnny cared. In one thing he was as firm as the fork he thrust determinedly into the heaped-up manure. I'm not going to lick dust off the floor. No, nor stand bawling there, either. He climbed the load. Nor wear a sour-milk smile all the time. Not me. He shouted, "Giddap, there," and drove to the field. "Git along." He pitched manure as though salvation lay there. Work, that's what you needed when thinking pressed too hard on you. Work, or a day's hard-muscled fun with Snoose.

But all the manure he pitched and all the ache that lamed his arms couldn't hide what now began to pucker his lips. This jaw-set determination to thwart the Pastor and Aunt Phrena . . . Is it really me that's dead set against the preacher school or—or is it—is it *him?* he wondered. He wiggled sweatily at night over the notion until Kurt complained, "I can't rest with a kicker like you. Go sleep in the barn, you thrasher."

Sometimes he was too tired even for talk with Snoose. After the day's work, he pulled sleep with the quilts over his head as if the covers were the drugged cloths of forgetfulness. He ate Aunt Phrena's soggy bread and scorched potatoes with no more than an evil taste in his mouth. Ever since the meeting at the Edgelys', Aunt Phrena chanted her way about the house, her walk the shuffle of penitents and her housework like an upset sewing basket. She forgot salt in the biscuits and one dinnertime mumbled in the Precious Comfort Book so long that the potatoes cooked dry and stuck to the kettle and the house was acrid with a burned-starch smell. "Pastor Steuber is ya all right," she said over a plate of *schwat suer* after late butchering. "But he likes too much the punishment and not enough the grace. Always it is the fire, the fire. The promises, the precious comforts he forgets."

Uncle Herm nodded, suckily noisy on a spoonful of the soup. After a moment of ladling she ventured as if it were a thought far in her mind and not really important, "I wonder when Brother Erdman comes to the Edgelys' again."

Johnny laid his spoon aside, jaws fallen. How could Aunt Phrena bear it—listening while folks gave testimony and strangled over inner agonies? In the barn he somberly agreed with Uncle Herm's exasperated "Slop religion!" But when his own ponderings began to stumble in circles, whipped by the realization that one day now he'd have to answer to the Pastor, and questions and answers began to whirl senselessly, he yelled, "Devil take it by the hind legs!" and dug more sternly at his work. Occasionally—he didn't stop to ask why—there was healing in the thought of honey-colored hair.

It was May before Johnny struggled through the Marriage at Cana and the Creed, and Heinie Beerwagon and Jackie Marchen received the last pastoral strappings and the final dire instructions before confirmation. His beard jovial with approval, the Pastor said one day, his mouth not far from pleasant, "Na ya, Johnny, that was a good recitation."

Cold dread surged down Johnny's spine. Now it's coming, he thought, panic riddling him in a blast. The benches creaked expectantly. Somebody hissed, "Stinking Johnny Schwartz." Johnny balled a fist. That Mosey Fritz. But the Pastor only patted the book and the lesson continued. Johnny settled back.

Before he could get away to join the pump-pump-pull-away game at recess, the Pastor had him, unaccustomed joviality twisting his spade beard. "So you want to study for the ministry," he clucked before Johnny could deny a syllable. "Na, good."

A gasp stuck in Johnny's throat. He was so steaming full of desire to shout "No! No!" that his ribs felt tight. He finally stammered, desperation clutching at his fingers, that he didn't know . . . there was pretty much work on the place . . . and . . . well . . . Uncle Herm didn't have much money . . . it would take a lot at the preacher school . . . and . . .

He looked so pukishly unlike an eager candidate for the cloth that the Pastor stepped back in perplexity and hooked his tongue over a wisp of beard. He uttered, "So?" with an ominous chesty sound. "But your *Tante* Phrenasobia—she says that you——"

"Aunt Phrena don't—she don't—well, Uncle Herm is the boss. What he says goes," he burst out, armpits wet.

"Your uncle—yes." The Pastor nodded as if this didn't at all surprise him. "A thresherman—what else could you expect?" He continued dourly, "And you? Do you want to go——"

With a frantic swim-dog-or-die sort of expression, Johnny bellowed, "Nope, I'm no good for a preacher. Don't want to be one. I—I got the seven years' itch."

The Pastor said with fearful gravity at such flighty talk, "It is your aunt then who wants you to be a student. Not you. So." He held Johnny trapped for an undecided moment. Never had the doorway seemed so small and squeezed-together to Johnny, never the aisle to the door so many miles long. Then the Pastor nodded his dismissal. Johnny barely missed the doorposts.

The Pastor regarded his haste with frosty disapproval. The willow must be brought home to this young sprig more often hereafter. And as for

Mrs. Phrenasobia and her husband——— He tugged his beard carefully.

But Johnny, gulping the welcome air with a depth of energy known only to wolf or wild dog freed from the deadfall (and accepting release no more seriously), was already whooping in the pump-pump-pull-away game. When Mosey Fritz pried, "What did he want, Johnny—give you a stick of candy?" Johnny snapped, "If he did, you wouldn't get a smell of it." Kurt watched carefully. To the others Johnny said evasively, "Something—something to tell Uncle Herm," and raced into the game. Under his shouts was a kind of song, "No preacher school! No preacher . . . school!" He blew to the farthest horizon of his mind the thought that Aunt Phrena would have more to say than the Pastor. Small but persistent the thought hung cloud-like there and would not be dispelled.

7

In those next days he lived as in a thistle patch, not sure where next to move, the pricks about him. There were Uncle Herm in the field and Aunt Phrena in the garden and Kurt near the barn—and nobody knows but me, me and the Pastor, he thought in amazement. They don't know but they soon will. It was incredibly sweet to realize that he had escaped the teeth of one nagging at least. He wanted to kick over the manger or race with jacket tails flying through plum and hazel. But the sweetness soon changed to wet ashes in his mouth, stale as old cake. Soon now Aunt Phrena would know. The Pastor would tell her, since Johnny's confirmation lay only a year away. Johnny shrank from the moody dampness that would settle then and mildew whatever weak laughter echoed in the Barewolf house.

He could blurt it out to her himself but shivered at the thought. He found solace in even a temporary respite from a future hour of commotion—respite, that fool's Eden for those who trust in the act deferred and the crisis avoided.

Bothered though he was by his own tortured dreams, he felt honest sorrow for Aunt Phrena. In those spring days, when the brown fire of bud case and bursting sprout tip hung cloudlike in the trees and the elms feathered in tufts of hairy, green leaf flowers, he saw her look as if soon now she'd lay aside a burden that was worrying her. He wanted to laugh, too, she was so serious over the Comfort Book and over him, as if she already saw a black gown fall to his ankles and a white collar pale the tan of his neck.

He felt ashamed but knew neither what to do nor what to say. The preacher school—that was her idea from the first and none of his, and he'd fight it now as a calf struggles against the rope haltering it. Here were the farm and Uncle Herm and Snoose and the threshing rig; and what was he to trade for this? Bawling at funerals and scolding from the pulpit; vinegar in the mouth and never having any fun. Nope, he told himself defiantly, rattling the milk pails. Not one thought did he have of the Pastor that wasn't seared by the memory of quick anger and a heavy arm swinging the willow, of harsh words thundered in church, a prickly heaven and a fiery hell. No, no. He was sorry but was sure that, down deep, he'd not so much as uncurl a finger to stop Aunt Phrena's joy from souring.

And that was slinky and two-faced, he raged within himself. "It's weasel-sneaky," he muttered. "Am I acting like—like *him* again?" Had his father too slunk through the underbrush and side roads of the past? "If *he* didn't, why don't I go right up and tell her?" He shook his head quickly, yet a vague sort of guilt pricked him, guilt that left him disquieted.

He stopped beside the milk stand one evening where the tin cups swung from the nails. How many swallows of foamy milk hadn't he emptied since the night Kurt and he had hung them there. They were rusty at the handles now and the names scrawled on the bottoms were no longer metallically bright. Silently he watched the "Schwartz" of his name swing now in, now out of the heavy redness of sun burning through horizon clouds. Slowly he stomped away, vowing, You wait, Aunt Phrena. You wait till after confirmation.

It came to him disturbingly again that she wouldn't mind setting the table just for three and that his absence might be a double joy to her— duty to her sister piously performed and freedom for whatever hopes she guarded secretly. It ruffled him for a while but he shook it out of his head. Yet the shadow remained like a stain.

Bitter loneliness weeviled him, so that sometimes at milking time he left with a bucket half full and stood at the door, a kind of fog blotting from his sight the green hanging like a mist in the brown branches of trees to the south, the box elders a lighter green against the darker olive of the woods. And his mother rose in his throat like a sob and even Uncle Herm's tuneless but friendly *Du, du, liegst Mir im Herzen* had an echo of a sweet, faraway melody. Tears welled. But at their sting he brushed his lashes with an angry swing of his hand, as though with the water he'd like to wipe away memory, too.

One weary night he went upstairs and rummaged the ribbon from the box where he'd hidden it—the red ribbon from the doll with the china head. The doll itself had been smashed by the Schadel children long ago, the pieces scattered like the leaves of the basswood.

He twisted the ribbon about his hand. Crabbed of brow he tried to bring back the memory of the doll's face. But the features that swam mistily back to his mind were shadowy now. (So little left of his mother's smile.) He realized then, though vaguely, that the past of the farm had been laid with sturdy quiet upon the fragile past of his mother. The upthrusts of yesterday remained only here and there to show what seeds had tarried and what roots had sprouted into young and lusty stems. But the past of his father was ragged and murky as the dank hollows in Norton's woods.

Slowly he put the ribbon back, snapping the box cover shut with a jarring stroke of his fist. Forlornness hid in the dark tangles of his young being that spring and summer and the ribbon lay curled and neglected in the box, both like somber threads among his jumbled boy-truck.

With a kind of resignation he waited for Aunt Phrena to pounce on him. Hearing a rattle of wheels in the yard, he'd think, The Pastor, and stir phlegmatically. At church he kept Aunt Phrena in sight before and after services and measured the distance between the place where she sat and the Pastor at the altar. He moved carefully. He almost quarreled with Snoose and over nothing, and he avoided Gatha Blumen. That is, he tried to avoid her, which was easier in decision than in deed. One recess, after he pummeled Mosey Fritz and had his cheek scratched and his lip broken, she bumped against his shoulder.

"Why do you want to fight him?" she asked, softness in her tone, as if she'd like to run a cooling finger over the bruises.

"Oh, he—" Johnny floundered—"I get mad and——"

"Well, he tumbled on his noodle when he was little and don't know any better." She giggled and for a moment her arm was hard as a boy's against his own youthful muscles. He looked at her quickly and intently. She ran ahead.

On the walk from school he told Snoose, "Gatha—she plays ante-high-over like—well, like a boy. Not fumble-fisted like Trudie Peiser and the other girls."

"Gath's got a swing to her arm," Snoose conceded. "Better than most girls." He asked slyly, "You kissed her yet?"

Johnny answered boldly, "Sure," but collared Snoose in embarrassment, knowing that he hadn't, though he wanted to. He remembered how Sophie had squeezed him in the waltz. It would be fun touching lips with girls— girls like Em'ly or Gatha or—he couldn't even pronounce the other name in his mind.

But one Sunday at services just before the school year closed, Aunt Phrena rose after the final "Amen" and elbowed herself to the front where the Pastor had lifted the curtain of his cubicle and vanished within. Johnny straightened a little and dragged his feet, thinking, Devil take it, now she'll bawl! If you had to take a hiding, it was good to know that there was nothing you could do about it.

Almost indifferently he saw the women in their pews wait as they always did until the men, their lords and masters by Scripture and by church edict, crowded through the door into the outside. Then they finished tying their bonnet strings and buttoned their cloaks and moved into the aisle. Outside in a sun that quivered in waves on the road, Johnny waited with Uncle Herm and Kurt, kicking at the mud dried on the wheel of the spring wagon. Aunt Phrena came soon enough. One look at her double chins wobbling with anger and even Uncle Herm ended his words with Mr. Peiser. He had been saying (later Johnny remembered this), "Nothing to stop Tjöstöl Skjelle from changing his name, if he wants to. If he writes down Chester Shelley at 'lections and town meetings, folks'll catch on. Don't blame him. All the trouble we used to have with our name——"

He saw Aunt Phrena then and straightened a line on a horse's back. Without a glance at him, she took his hand helping her into the wagon and sagged into the seat. The springs protested squeakily. Kurt and Johnny sat in the second seat, and all the road home there was silence broken only by the grind of tires on rock or the slow purring of sand lifting with the spokes and pouring back; and there were Aunt Phrena's stiff shoulders.

At home she knocked the key into the lock with a clatter and marched huffily inside. Johnny stuck so close and burlike to Uncle Herm's side that Uncle Herm grinned, though Johnny noticed that in the barn he wasted minutes over the careful hanging of the collars and the unkinking of the straps—more than was necessary.

At last Johnny couldn't keep still. "I told him—told the Pastor I wouldn't go to preacher school," he burst out breathlessly. "Now he's told *her* and—well, she's mad."

Uncle Herm nearly dropped a strap. "She looked it. You must have held your tail high, telling the Pastor you wouldn't go."

Miserably Johnny shook his head. Uncle Herm lifted a tug. "I had a feeling that this was coming on," he said. "My feet this morning in church—Moses, how they itched! I couldn't scratch 'em either, with my boots on."

"Oh, Uncle Herm, don't make me go to preacher school," Johnny entreated. "I'd soon—sooner be caught in a wolf trap."

"I wouldn't make you do anything you've set your mind against, boy." Uncle Herm put a hand on Johnny's arm. "Not for myself, that is," he added with a sigh. Johnny understood.

Uncle Herm said, "If you had more whiskers than you've got——" He stopped abruptly. And suddenly there was silence between them, silence prickly as rose hedges with questions unasked and answers not given. Neither spoke. Aunt Phrena stood guard there, her sogginess more peremptory than a finger on a lip.

Uncle Herm's grip tightened. "Don't look so, boy. Storm always appears blacker'n it really is. Come on. Longer we wait, the more time Phrena's got to get mad."

Aunt Phrena was aproned and plumping potatoes violently into the kettle when they opened the door. Water joggled and splashed. She was complaining to Kurt, who perched on a chair, sullen, with a not-my-kettle-of-fish; tell-Johnny-why-don't-you sort of expression. She turned on Johnny, knife in hand, spiking him in a long stare, a crusty survey, but said no more than "So. Not good enough for you, is it, to be pastor? A thrasher, now—that makes a better man of you." The knife clanged against the kettle rim; anger froze her tears even. "I try so hard. Your poor mother—and this is what I get for it. All I ever get," she continued, dragging Uncle Herm into the net of her blame with a swing of her shoulders. The two of them shuffled, awkward under her reproaches.

But when they went to harness the team, Uncle Herm grabbed Johnny's shoulders and shook him in wordless relief. Johnny clung dumbly to those bony arms, closer to tears than he knew. In the week that followed, all he could do was paean inwardly, She knows; Aunt Phrena knows. Now she'll never get me to go. Breath ran in his nostrils as if oiled. He bragged at school, "I told him right to his teeth. 'Pastor Steuber,' I said, 'I'm not going to preacher school; not me,' and he had to take it." He bubbled. But his voice, loudly boisterous while the Pastor remained in the parish house, lowered to whispers when the black coat strode into sight and it was time to break and rush for the church room.

Kurt's lofty "Betcha you was so scared you wet your pants" made Mosey Fritz guffaw but nettled Johnny no more than the shadows at home.

As for Aunt Phrena, she was sodden for days. Johnny felt like eating with the cows, the table ran so with the dankness of rebuke, sometimes silent, sometimes spoken. To his astonishment, however, her scoldings were less waspish than he had dreaded, as though she couldn't believe a Christian body would accept husks and sweepings and throw Heaven into the creek.

The preacher school was still firm in her mind. She let him know *that* shortly, but with a gentleness that was new running in her talk, as if she'd wear down stubbornness as the creek did rocks, inevitably but without grating. He really didn't know what he wanted, she said, he was that young and without experience. There was plenty of time. He had a year yet to gather his five wits. His mother in heaven—blessed dove—from the portals of eternity she gazed upon her boy. She wouldn't mind waiting even a *whole* year *after* his confirmation, as long as he decided in the right way and put the last sweet jewel in her crown of joy. Neither would Aunt Phrena mind waiting. Johnny only lowered his head stubbornly. She'd explain to the minister how all this happened and——

She stopped there to sniff. "That Pastor Steuber—scolds so much, he can't think about paradise." Ever since her conference with him, she grumbled about the Pastor. Before long it came out that he had fallen as deeply into the meshes of her wrath as Johnny had. "No mercy in that man."

Johnny had a quick lift of heart with wanting to laugh. "Me and the Pastor," he told Snoose. "We're both in the chicken coop. I'd like to tell him that."

Aunt Phrena continued her squabble with the Pastor. "Scolding at the Dunkel funeral, the way he did," she fretted. "Ach, that poor Mrs. Dunkel! It's his fault that she's so queer. Mrs. Peiser was telling me that she goes to the machine shed and throws stones at the cradle that's hanging under the roof. That Pastor. A sermon—it should help folks that are in trouble, not scare them so they don't know where next to turn."

She hinted that she'd be at the Edgelys' the next time Preacher Erdman held meeting, church or no. Her two chins were so grim that Johnny was sure she'd go as much to get even with the Pastor as to find a more downy road to Heaven.

Johnny hardly worried a sliver of care about it. Let her pitchfork part of her spite onto shoulders other than his own. It made him sleep easier.

8

Often he had assured himself, If I get out of preacher school, I'll—I'll kick over the barn. And whoop he did at times, going after the cows in the evening now that his freedom was assured. But there was a worminess in his enthusiasm. He kept hearing Aunt Phrena's favorite admonition, "By its fruit you shall know the tree." This abandoned joy that swirled excitingly over him—was it from his own flesh or was it the rotten fault of . . . a soaring whistle on his lips toppled into silence.

He longed to share with Snoose this inner gnawing but hesitated. There were some webby corners of your life you couldn't open even to a comrade as skin-close as Snoose. He wondered whether rags of the past fluttered phantomlike under the Marchen rooftree as they did here.

In nights that were mellow with a moon of gold, he browsed upon

Snoose's understanding silences. Summer lengthened and the grain, tall and wavy as a woman's hair, entered the milk season and then hardened in the kernel for the harvest. Cutting began. They walked the hillside paths, the day's work pulling like a gentle garment at their shoulders. During those hours Johnny was torn between loneliness and wanting to harden his muscles in grappling with what lay about him.

On such a night of gold and silence they slouched unhurriedly back to the Marchen house from the woods. Johnny could see Aunt Phrena's lamp winking through the thinning grove and across the narrow field that lay between the spot where he stood and Uncle Herm's doorstep. But Uncle Herm was away these days, cutting Hukelpoke's early oats with the new harvester.

Snoose broke his thought. "Pieplant leaves in the garden are big as elephant ears. Your aunt is s'posed to pick some, ain't she?"

But Johnny exploded, thoughts roughly elsewhere, "I get sick to my belly of Aunt Phrena. The way she nags Uncle Herm. Nag, nag; guess she keeps it up in bed, too. Makes a feller want to pack up and go with the homesteaders." He would have set his nose for home but Mrs. Marchen called, "We're having cookies and cold coffee. Come in." He didn't need Snoose's urgings.

They entered just as Mr. Marchen with a "Have some, Schwartzie," and a hitch of his suspenders, went for a second helping. Sophie brought Johnny a cup, blackish to taste and bitter, but cooling. She was in overalls. Clymy grumbled sleepily from the lounge where his small body sprawled tiredly.

"He's getting like an old steer," she complained, swinging her long legs in a waltz step. "I can't move him any more."

Snoose flung himself on a coat or two in a corner, his spot in the house, nibbling the cookies. Said Mrs. Marchen, "Tell Phrena she can have pieplant any time now. I expected her over for an armful today but I guess she gets too tired, gardening." The thin pine ceiling above jarred with scraping noises, the hollow bounce of a shoe, the swift thud of heels, telling that Jackie and Bill were kicking off their clothes for bed, too weary for refreshment.

Mrs. Marchen rocked while she sewed buttonholes on the long-armed-and-legged underwear which Mr. Marchen wore—suits not much different in style and cloth, though smaller, from those which Aunt Phrena bought for Johnny and which he hated to have next to his skin. Now and again Mrs. Marchen sipped coffee or chewed a sliver of cooky over her needle. Hominess and peace hung so from the very pictures on the wall this night that Johnny almost choked. If only he could live here with Snoose, he'd gladly go stockingless and on bread and water, though he knew that Mr. Marchen's temper flew into his fists and meanness crackled like sparks between these walls at times. He didn't care. This was as filling to his empty spaces as coffeecake.

When Sophie proposed a waltz, he hesitated never a moment. Mrs. Marchen jabbed the needle into the seat of Mr. Marchen's underwear and sat at the organ. Johnny put away his cup and joined Sophie, less red of ears than usual. He was careless of Clymy drowsily growling, "Can't sit still five minutes, can you, Sophie?" and remained happily ignorant of Sophie's meaning when she answered Clymy, "Not much time left for me to dance. Gonna be no fun, waiting and doing nothing. Men have all the fun and no pain."

Johnny waltzed her in whirls, firm in his leading for once, so that Sophie tickled his ear and Snoose said, "You slip over the floor like a piece of ice, Johnny." Mr. Marchen, excited into unusual affability, opined that they all ought to go to the barn dance Saturday night.

Johnny polka-ed a stitch into Sophie's ribs. Mr. Marchen was whooping over a third cup of coffee, when the door opened and Aunt Phrena strode in. Her steps were heavy. Anger beaded her eyes. Johnny almost tripped, trying to catch his balance. The organ wheezed into a silence broken by the squeal of the stool as Mrs. Marchen turned.

"So." Aunt Phrena's voice thickened. "That's the catechism you studied last winter." She glared at them circlewise. The clock ticked loudly.

Mr. Marchen smiled in her face. "Na, Phrena. Did you come for the pieplant anyway? Sit down." At her snort over this levity, he arose, playful as if he'd had a drop of schnapps, and held out his arm mockingly. "Maybe a little waltz, then? Ma can play us a——"

Aunt Phrena gasped, the folds of her chin beginning to shake. "Dancing! Like Schwartz!" she almost screamed at Johnny. "It's a blacksnake you need on your hide, you heathen." Gone was the blandness of the past weeks. He was startled at what he saw mirrored in a sort of contortion of her features. Before he knew she had stepped where he stood with Sophie and caught his arm in a fierce pudgy grip. "You get for home, now!" Never had he seen her so angry. "Hear me? Git!" She might as well have been shouting at the dog.

Still gathering the wits that had been scattered by her sudden appearance, Johnny felt her fingers digging at his muscles. He stiffened. Something snapped in him. He tore her grasp from his arm as if he were rubbing off that which had dirtied him. Rage ripped him. The blood hurt to his finger tips. He flung up his arms as if he'd strike her and she almost cowered back before the white heat that fired his black eyes.

"You let me alone, do you hear?" he yelled. "I'll dance if I want to and you can't hold me. All you think of is preacher school and sending me away." Before he could stop he blurted what had rankled these months: "You don't really care if I am a preacher or not, do you? You hate to see me with Uncle Herm, don't you? All you want is to get me out of the way." His voice was shrill. Sophie stood frozen. Mr. Marchen slowly hitched up his pants. Mrs. Marchen half arose and sat again. Snoose uncurled his body swiftly.

Aunt Phrena received the words as if they were slaps. She waited there, unbelief at what she heard growing in fold and wrinkle of her face. He never noticed how her lips formed over "no's" of protest. He screamed, "Morning and night, it is the same old tune. 'Go to preacher school. Study the Catechism. Git going.'"

All at once she sagged, anger and her strength running away. "No, Johnny, I never, never. Your poor mother, I promised her——I meant for the best."

Heedlessly he rushed on: "You want me out of the way, don't you, so that—so that——" He floundered over what was only suspicion after all; ended harshly, with less certainty, "So that I won't take Kurt's place on the farm and he can have everything his way and——" He sputtered into silence at her agonized entreaty. Upstairs there was the rattle of springs as somebody jumped from bed, disturbed at the racket, and the scrape of clothes across the floor.

Crumpled as an old cloak, Aunt Phrena moaned, "No, Johnny, I never. It is a Christian woman I am—a church woman; never would I do that to you." Then, as if she feared that all her inner thought like a pocket had been turned inside out for the neighbors to see, her lips quivered, tears budded between her stubby lids and gushed down her cheeks. "Never, Johnny. A church woman——"

Mrs. Marchen went to her, hands outstretched in comfort. "Phrena, Phrena, don't sorrow yourself like this."

Full of twisted feelings he couldn't name, Johnny didn't know where to crawl or into what hole to hide himself. His arms were suddenly miles too long, his legs awkward and shuffling. Bitterness like tears filled him; he was helplessly sure that this too would be left as blame at his door. Loneliness sharpened the line of his cheeks, so that Snoose came and put a hand on his shoulder. For an icy moment he wanted to shrug off even this token of friendliness. Then gladness for Snoose's hand left him almost weak.

Dully he realized after a while that Aunt Phrena had gone, and that Jackie was poking a sleep-frowzled head from the upstairs door and that Mr. Marchen was calling him, not Schwartzie, as he always did, but Johnny.

"Yep, Johnny; couldn't believe it. Didn't think you had enough belly to stand up to your aunt. Thought she had you under her foot just like Herman." He pulled off a boot slowly. "But you're wrong, Johnny. Phrena's a good woman in her way. She wouldn't treat a flea no way but kindly."

Johnny nodded in agreement. But a voice deep inside him was insistently loud: Not always will it be like this. Some day I'll *make* it right for me, if I have to smash it. Rage stirred him like a mixing rod. He might as well go. He walked through the door as if through a gate. The moon clouded his homeward path. For moments he glared at the crack of light under Aunt Phrena's door, his heart beating loudly in the house-quiet of the night.

By the time he'd finished the last cow the next morning, Johnny made up his mind. At breakfast Aunt Phrena had been folded of lip. Her eyes were puffed with the dark hue of sleeplessness. Johnny wished ardently that Uncle Herm were here to bolster his spine.

Kurt was gruff. Often this summer his wooden face grew tight as he flicked a glance over Johnny. There were bubblings under the surface here that were near the breaking moment. Pitchfork in hand he went to the meadow to see how well the sun was crisping the newly sickled hay. Johnny watched him go, hands clenched in his pocket, then swung to the house.

He found Aunt Phrena over the breakfast dishes. She held a cup for a moment when she saw him; then put it down. When he broke out, "Aunt Phrena," stiff with determination as the broom in the corner, she said, "I know," as if she were expecting this. "Britches won't hold your bigness any more, so?"

"You've no right——" he began hotly.

"Right!" she flared up. "You little table-snipper talking about right. The wrong I have lived with these years—— Much have I forgiven you, Johnny——"

"On account of my pa, I s'pose," he interrupted, goading her.

"On his account, too." She clattered a plate sharply, mounting ire unloosing her tongue. "Ach, ya, on his account. Making a fool of me and laughing behind my back. Schwartz was good at that. And putting your ma early in the grave, he with his smiles." Anger, fired by all the humiliation of the night before (neighbor eyes sticking pins of curiosity into her), all the shame of one whose private life is intimately sacred, blazed into fury. "Look at yourself, Johnny Schwartz. If you want to see what your pa was like, look at yourself."

He tightened like a fiddle bow, wishing that his ears might be stopped against the dread he felt was coming.

"Like the Bible says, a fornicator, that's what your pa was. He was killed in the gutter," Aunt Phrena shouted, hurling the words as if they were blocks of wood. "He got a girl in trouble and laughed at her—like he did to me. And your ma—she died of the shame and slowly." Johnny felt salt on his tongue but none in his eyes.

Then it poured out of her like sour milk from an upended bucket, the years of bitter scourings chewed over in secret, the years of scabby frustration, of second best with Herman Barewolf, all the collected rancidness of her life.

And Johnny saw the shadow take flesh and bone and his father walk between them, the devil-give-a-damn smile and the cap poised at a cocky knock-it-off-if-you-dare angle, the black eyes pupiled with a shining glint . . . the laughter rocking from tavern to tavern, the fists that pounded and left knuckle marks on the flesh of friend and alien alike and the cracking man-strength that hoisted kegs in the brewery, the man-strength of his limbs that was like an odor drifting from him . . . the girl-smiles that faded or bloomed with the sun and rain of his pleasure or his shrugging indifference . . . the girl his wife and the mother of his son who waited grieving beside a curtained window . . .

And then the reckless tryst with one he desired in a moment between a laugh and a curse, the whispered ecstasy . . . the brawl in the beer cellar, the careless wave of a hand to danger . . . the lonely place on the street and the swift feet running, the blunt instrument falling (so the coroner's jury pronounced it) . . . and next morning the face lying downward and the black eyes open in the gutter, all the bright glint and the wild laughter and the memory of fragrantly intoxicating breasts of girls crushed into the nothingness of oblivion . . .

Johnny heard, the red of excitement paling as he listened, and his shoulders slipping from their proud defiance. Water splashed in Aunt Phrena's pan but the sound of no falling drop came to him, so loud was the tavern laughter spilling corrosively into his ears.

Like one blinded by an unexpected glare of light, Johnny groped away. He wished he could drop to the ground and sleep, and never wake up. Stumbling, he followed the path into the woods. His dinner plate stayed unheaped, though Kurt, grumbling to Aunt Phrena, asked, "Where's Johnny? The hay's still too green to haul."

At lunchtime his coffee remained unpoured. Beyond the clearing on the ridge and deep in the undergrowth his toes cracked dry sticks as he plunged heedlessly through the brush, shaking the hazels where the young finches begged monotonously, "Doy-doy-ee, doy-ee, doy-ee." Where coolness gathered under the rustling leaves, he leaned against a young oak, the rough bark painfully sweet on his forehead.

For a moment he stood there, then fiercely whipped off shirt and pants. Under the trees his leaf-dark skin became flecked with sun and shadow like a patchwork cloak. The garlands were dropped away now, however. He felt again the shame that had swept him the day Aunt Phrena caught him paddling in the wheat. This flesh, his inheritance, soaked with his father—— He caught at his body as if to tear away handfuls; pinched and ripped until he stumbled sobbing to the ground.

He came to the barn in the middle of chores, tired and worn as if from a long running. Beyond a steady look, Kurt, half done with milking, said nothing. What Aunt Phrena had told Kurt, Johnny didn't care. Uncle Herm was still away.

He grabbed a pail but waited a moment before he started work. His throat hurt and his tongue was juiceless as an acorn husk. He went to the milk stand where an island of foam settled in a bucket. Quickly he reached for his cup. His fingers touched the bottom and the name scrawled there. The tin clanked against his fingernails. He unhooked the cup and his hand gripped the tin. The foam in the bucket hissed and settled while he stood there. Suddenly he grabbed a staple from his pocket, fingers tense on the iron. Savagely he dragged the point over the "Schwartz" again and again, as if by scraping out each letter, the curl of an s and the crooked bottom of a w, he could hush from his mind a haunting echo. Flecks of metal winked as they fell. He rasped so violently that the sharp point of the staple shot over the rim edge and punctured his thumb. His muscles twitched; blood leaked and a drop spattered on the gouged surface.

He flung the cup to its place. The handle rattled against the nail. He sucked his thumb, blood tinged with salt bitter in his mouth. With thirst fiery on his tongue he began the milking. With ungentle hands he fed the calves that plunged in eager hunger at their tethers. He slammed the buckets against their heads viciously, growling, "Devil take you, anyway!" There was relief in thrusting the sharp edges of ire against something that winced under pain.

9

More than once those harvest days when the bundles of grain were leaned head against head in shocks pointing to the sky and the fields looked like a bivouac of tents, he screwed up his lips over the notion of running away, but didn't. This valley and these ridges, they were all he knew of earth outside of the school geography book. Home and the world were here with Uncle Herm and Snoose and the truck on the farm worn smooth of strangeness by the familiarity of palm and fingers, even though Aunt Phrena had few words for him and let reproach sag from her pale, china-blue eyes like wetness from a dishrag.

Sullen and morose, he avoided Snoose, almost grateful for the harvester and the hard drag of sweat squeezed from him in the press of work. One evening, however, Snoose stood beside him where, flung down, he rested in the grass. Day was only a pale shadow of lemon in the west.

"You might as well hump yourself and come," Snoose said. "I'm going over to—well, to borrow a couple of Schadel's plums. They ought to be sweet about this time."

Johnny was glad to see him, gladder that Snoose had come now. But this evening had no way to offer gratitude except to rise slowly and go with him.

Snoose chattered like a chipmunk. But when they came to the creek, he said softly in the strange fashion he had, as if he were a part of Johnny's thought, "I don't believe it either."

Johnny looked up, startled. "I—how did you know?" He slumped on a water-streaked rock.

"I don't know what your aunt told you. But the way you've been be-having—well, it didn't take much to figure out that you had a fight with her. She was mad, that night, and so were you."

"Oh, Snoose," Johnny cried tiredly. The words unstopped what was pent up in him, down to Aunt Phrena's last harsh syllable. He could speak now, the silence no longer his when the world was one mouth of noise. There was mockery in the three gold dusk notes of a vesper sparrow. Night without a moon gathered the hills from sight.

Snoose crouched beside him, protective, listening, the plums forgotten. Johnny raged, "Black, that's what it means, my name. Black." His hand closed over a stone. He pitched it angrily. Ahead of him the splash was swallowed in darkness. "All right," he muttered. "I'll be black, then, and mean as the Devil."

Snoose's chuckle lazed in the night. "Your uncle depends on you. All of us—we'd never think you mean. And me—I'd feel funny, not having your bullheadedness around. That's why I came over."

Johnny felt warmed but he threatened, "I'd like to show Aunt Phrena a thing or two." Snoose's hand on his shoulder out of darkness was a kind of seal to a promise.

Time and again his words came to Johnny's mind when in moments of turmoil, torn between rage and determination, he howled to himself, Sneaky and two-faced, that's what I'm gonna be, and whose fault is it? Or when he squared shoulders in the pugnacity of his almost fifteen years. I'll make her chew what she's said, you wait and see. Anybody else, too. He felt better after such outbursts.

Some days, however, the hounds of impatience barked in his mind and he was sure that, given an inch of excuse, he would have joined the wagon trains that stopped for the night on the level space near the creek. Or so he thought, without measuring provocation. Often he watched the brush-pile fires of the wagon camp, or from the clearing early in the evening, the circle of wagons with the teams tied to spokes or rims, or staked in the grass. Years after Uncle Herm had broken the campground and put it to seed, that circle, rich with the leavings of migrant man and beast, lifted a darker green and a heavier growth, clean-cut as if a branding iron had smoked a scar there. After harvest a ring of stubbles closely packed in rank growth and yellow in color marked the field where the homesteaders paused.

Some of the wagons were tented with canvas, some were open to the sky, unshielded against rain or hail that might bounce on the kettles and trunks and quilts that were heaped up or tied on or roped under. Late at night he'd hear the bellow of oxen, hoarse and broad, and Uncle Herm's cows in the pasture answering.

A sprinkle of drops they were, these migrants, flung now and again this far north by who knows what random wind from the rush of emigration that was spreading like swirling water over the Red River flats and the Dakota country. Among those who camped here for the night were folks who had shut the doors of old communities forever behind them. Their acres, worn thin and unproductive by endless growing of single crops, they had left for the raw spaces of a land that knew more about the slash of hail and the sharp toes of buffalo than the dip and heave of the cutting share. Johnny saw wagons that had come from Wisconsin, Iowa, the sturdy southern counties.

There were some who had the twang of New England in their noses and others whose guttural throats spoke of forefathers that had dug in the burgomasters' fields. Some were Swedes. Many were Norwegian, long-limbed, heavy-shouldered, with eyes that were haunted by the crags and waterways of the northland, and with hair of that blondness sometimes that made folks turn about and stare: cotters, day laborers, landowners, fragments of a landed society breaking into pieces in the old world and moving into the sunset where a man who had been thumb-pressed by tradition these centuries could mark the limit of his acres, loop his fence about it and say to all who came, "This is mine; all others keep away." But some of them, huddling on the hard planks, bowed their heads as if the price they paid for a dream had been too dear. They built their fires, but the songs under which they loudly hid their longing for saeter and cot floated echoingly to Johnny in the pasture, driving home the cows.

One morning he and Uncle Herm crossed the camping place. They came with ax and hammer and long square spikes to fix the rail of a fence that a heifer had smashed, lowing in the night for a tryst with a homesteader's bull. By good luck she had failed to escape. The circle was smeary with the manure of horses and cattle. The ashes of the fire, water-soaked, stank of warmth and coffee grounds and scorched refuse.

Uncle Herm grunted, measuring a popple with an up-and-down glance. Johnny lifted the pieces of a box he found in a wagon track—a box of pinewood with corners of brass. Small it was and made by fingers that loved a jackknife and a hammer, but crushed now, the splinters grimy where they had been trodden into earth. Not even an odor remained to say what dreams had once lain in its four corners or what store it held, flower or hair or the sparkle of jewels. On a broken panel he saw a name burnt into wood: Brynjolf. His tongue stumbled in saying it aloud, "Burn-Burn-olff." It hung heavily in his ears as did the other names he had heard among the homesteaders: Gjerdrum, Bjornsterne, Dronfjeld, Kjaempedal; syllables strange with the echo of places steep with crags or quiet with the misty peace of valleys.

Norskie names, Mr. Edgely called them. Johnny remembered how Mr. Edgely had hooted once when Torsten Torgrimson, the hired man at the Peisers', had stood wide-eyed over a colt's taking a two-rail gate without touching a hoof. Torsten had shouted, *"Den jomper fens, den jomper fens."* And it was Mr. Edgely who had poked fun when he drove into Mr. Muri's yard to buy hay and Mr. Muri, in his best English, had assured him in neighborly fashion, "Jah, sure, I have hay. De prise is four dollers, *naar* he take it *paa* the sloo."

Mr. Edgely laughed all the way home. "There he was, that old Norskie. 'naar-ing' and 'paa-ing' like a brat," he told Uncle Herm at the store, roaring his mirth.

Uncle Herm cackled a little, friendly to one who lived near by. There was sourness, however, in the way he growled on the road home, "That Yankee, he laughs at *our* names, like that, too, when he visits other folks." Not that Uncle Herm regarded Mr. Edgely with anything but neighborliness. He would continue to exchange seed or a season of haying with him. But here he spoke out of something deeper than any neighborliness; something that had no beginning in his memory but broke from bone depth and innate stirrings and the slow accumulation of the folk mind.

"Burn-olff, it must be." Johnny spoke the name slowly.

"No, no." Uncle Herm jingled a handful of the spikes, their four angles flashing back the sun in slants of quick, white flame. "You say it just like Banker Ford in Mary's Hill. It's Brynjolf, not Burnolf. No wonder Tjöstöl Skjelle changed his name to Chester Shelley. People don't say names right, nor spell them, either. Moses, the time we had with ours!"

"Uncle Augustus's name on the gravestone—" Johnny pulled at a sliver as if he were arranging a matter in his thought—"it's spelled different now, ain't it?"

Uncle Herm nodded. "The postmaster had it one way and the banker another and the assessor couldn't spell it at all. It was Bharwolf and Bearwolf and Beerwolff, and the Almighty's corruption couldn't get it straight." Uncle Herm tweaked his mustache. "Well, I had enough of that after a while. I went to Banker Ford and the courthouse and I said, 'Now, here; my name's Barewolf from this minute on. Maybe you can get that right for once.'"

"Nothing more to it than that?" Johnny was eager.

"Well, if it's a matter of law, maybe you need some court hocus-pocus But there's lots of folks I know that's got no more to stand on, for a name, than their own say-so. I 'member one feller, a Noreegion, I guess he was. Hell, I don't know; maybe he was a Swede. Anyway, his name was Aas but he didn't keep it. He said he wasn't going to have some damn-fool clerk make a slip and put an *a* and two *s*'s in his name. So he switched it to Blackstone. He had a Yankee neighbor by that name; thicker'n waterbugs they were." Uncle Herm chortled, pocketing the spikes, and picked up the ax. "I guess that popple there's as good as the next."

Johnny waited a moment, his jaw determined. "Was my pa a bad man, Uncle Herm?" He spoke so matter-of-factly (though a throb hurt in his temple) that he caught Uncle Herm off balance.

"Bull Schwartz?" Uncle Herm answered before he thought. "He was my best——" He stopped so abruptly he nearly bit into the last word. He put the ax aside. "Now, boy, what——"

"Aunt Phrena told me." Johnny's tone was flat. "All bad she says he was."

"Now, Johnny." Uncle Herm tried to see his way. He fished out the spikes. "Women get foolisher ideas than the milkmaid about the hired man." He asked softly, "She told you?"

Johnny nodded. His fingernails whittled on the *f* of Brynjolf. The telling was slow, full of ragged patches of silence, bitter as yarrow.

Uncle Herm slipped the spikes into his pocket again. They jingled against those already there. He didn't look at Johnny. "It was so easy to promise *her*," he said. "As long as you were a little shaver, it didn't seem to matter. But now——" His eye jumped from Johnny's anklebone to his black hair. "Like a weed," he finished his thought. "Many times I wanted to speak. I could see the questions settin' on your tongue, only you didn't have the nerve. And me?" He shrugged. "Guess me and Phrena, we're pretty bum kinfolk to you."

He disregarded Johnny's quick protesting hand. "It's so. But you was her sister's kid. She got me to promise I'd let her handle you. She hated Schwartz so. And I—well, Moses Almighty, I—I liked her; still do. Oh, she's fat and crybaby and all but her heart's sound as oak and she's—well——" He dug a spike from his pocket helplessly. "Maybe I pitied her once and never got over it. I don't know. Anyway, that Albert Schwartz, he hurt her the way no man should hurt a woman. Pretended he was in love with her; for a joke. She believed him. He had such a way with women. When she showed how she felt, he just laughed at her. Called her Fatty at a party once and drank a toast: 'Here's to your fat annies!' He did."

Johnny kept his eyes on the ground. Uncle Herm sighed as he jabbed a spike into the autumn-warm earth. He hunched down on a log. "I wanted to hit him for that. The only time I ever wanted to put my hand on him. Phrena was so—well, so broke up. And there was your ma, too. She was unmarried then, so young and pretty and—and fluffy like a head of beer and——" He broke his dream of a thwarted love. "Anyway, Schwartz married her and I married Phrena. Afterward Schwartz was sorry about Phrena and tried to make up to her. But Phrena handled him like a can of poison. Me, I can't keep a grudge; me and him shook hands over a schooner of beer. But I never could get over the way he treated your ma— later on, that is." After a pause he said softly, "The way you look sometimes, it's her all over again."

"And the girl, the other girl?" Johnny's voice monotoned.

"Na ya, Johnny." Uncle Herm pulled at the spike distressfully. Bits of earth clung to it, obscuring the sun reflections. "Seems like Schwartz was always in some girl's skirts. That other one, she married again, after your pa was——" He glanced up quickly, knowing what Aunt Phrena would say to such talk. "Albert Schwartz wouldn't fit into Pastor Steuber's Sunday school maybe. But a kinder-hearted man never heezed up a keg of beer. Wasn't a man in the brewery wouldn't have sweat blood for him." With the hammer he drove the spike strongly into the wood of the log. "Johnny, you mustn't sour yourself. There's no need to hide your face. It's always so. A pa and a ma start you out. But you got to keep going by yourself."

There was quiet. A falling leaf crackled among the twigs. The broken box slipped from Johnny's hands. He let it lie where it fell. Uncle Herm rose awkwardly. "Well, that heifer's going to light out for Dakota, if we don't fix the fence."

They worked slowly. And the thoughts that lay between the blow of a hammer and its echo in Norton's woods were no more bitter than the berries of the Solomon's-seal hanging its purple bells under the curving arch of its stem. They finished. As they came back, Johnny picked up the box where it had fallen. As if clinching the nail of an idea firmly in his mind, he stuck into his pocket the panel with the name "Brynjolf" seared in the wood.

10

The Pastor opened school after his stacks, smaller this year, were threshed and the grain was heaped in his hen coop of a granary. Johnny went back to the Catechism with more eagerness in his legs than he thought possible. A book before his nose blurred the sharp edge of memory. There was relief in knowing that this was his last year at the church school. Next term he'd be in District School, if he went at all. Few boys did after confirmation; fewer after their fifteenth birthday. Heinie Beerwagon wasn't going this year but was hiring out to Uncle Herm and the rig. Johnny had a quick lift of spirit at the thought of District School. Perhaps it was the heady ferment of autumn, the yellow of leaves, that made him think of Lilice's hair. He was sure by now she'd forgotten him. He hadn't her.

He avoided Aunt Phrena when he could and was self-assertive when he couldn't. She regarded him with fretful impatience as if what had been said or done was justified and daring him to contradict her. She was less friendly with the Marchens even at church. She remained so until one afternoon when she ran out of sugar and went herself to borrow some, a spleeny tilt to her head. She returned, sugared with neighborliness though Mr. Marchen still plagued her grimly and enjoyed it.

That fall the walking preacher gathered his flock at the Edgelys' again, and, for all his grunts, Uncle Herm carted her over when he could, returning each time to swear he had his gullet full of the kind of dishwater and slops Brother Erdman poured out. Usually Kurt drove. In spite of her proddings Johnny refused to go, saying he had a man-sized chunk of the Catechism still to pile in his head. From his words, Kurt was neither glad nor sorry, much to Aunt Phrena's grief.

Aunt Phrena however swayed with recollected ecstasy. "Such sweet promises in his sermons! It would do you good to hear them, Johnny. What a glorious morning it will be when we meet our loved ones gathered over the river!" She almost intoned the words, her gaze far away and heaven bound, as if she were already choosing her angelic comrades. (And would there be one with a cap stuck jauntily on the side of his head?) "The Pastor himself could learn much from Brother Erdman."

The Pastor, an ear in everybody's house, and outraged over the meetings at the Edgelys', was quick to learn about this straying into alien corn. He wailed over the pulpit about the chosen ones who stiff-neckedly whored with the false gods of Canaan and Baal. (Johnny wondered how you whored with a stiff neck, but let it go, sure that the Pastor knew what he was preaching about.) These, his chosen ones, the Pastor complained. What did they do? Having wallowed in the pitch and filth, they returned unrepentant to the fold, "like dogs when they have no other place to go." Anger bristled his beard.

The congregation, awakened to delight, went home, each one rejoicing that somebody had been singed by the fire of wrath. "Didn't the Pastor scold nicely today, though?" Mrs. Tetzell twinkled at Mrs. Peiser as they gathered their wraps.

Aunt Phrena attended the Pockerbrush church regularly, patient with the Pastor. "He will see the grace one day, poor man." She attended Mr. Erdman's services at the Edgelys' just as regularly. Alongside the Pastor's crustiness she laid the crumbs, sugary with warrants from Heaven, which she picked up at the meetings. She went both to the log church and to the revivals with unembarrassed equanimity. On Sunday forenoons all the Barewolfs went to hear the Pastor. On Wednesday and Sunday evenings Kurt drove Aunt Phrena to attend Mr. Erdman's sermons.

On her and Uncle Herm the Pastor frowned especially. These thresher people were a stubborn folk. Once he exhorted Uncle Herm, "Bruder Barewolf, your spouse attends these meetings outside the church. That is contrary to the will and ordinance of God."

Uncle Herm answered mildly, "You tell her that yourself, Herr Pastor. You got more words to spare than I have. She's sick and stayed home today, but she'll be here next Sunday."

The Pastor strategically hurled his arrows from the pulpit, however, not quite certain that the armor of his shield would repel Aunt Phrena's moist stubbornness. Perhaps it was because she gave generously of her eggs and garden truck and Uncle Herm's wood and cash, and came to warm a larger portion of the basswood pews than any two women there that he crimped his lips over what he'd like to say and remained watchfully silent.

All that winter Johnny was plagued by the Articles and driven into the corners of bafflement by the horns of "justification." He still mixed up the prophet Micah with the angel Michael and once put the Medes and the Persians with Peter and Paul. But he had questions and answers packed solidly in the drawers of his mind.

That spring Sophie's baby was born; an easy birth, though Clymy ran out to the hen house at Sophie's first cry, Mr. Marchen told. In a moment between the Sixth Commandment and its exposition, Johnny wondered mildly about her strong arms and that twisted turnip of a Clymy. Warm-skinned at his thoughts, he hastily dug at the words of the explanation.

He trudged off through the slush of spring, muttering the books of the Bible, "Habakkuk, Zephaniah, Haggai," in rhythm with his plodding steps. He nailed the prophets and the rules fast in his memory with a jolt of his heel, envious of Kurt. For Kurt cackled names and happenings in long strings with such ease that Johnny was sullen.

Before confirmation Sophie's baby was named. Under the Pastor's freshly trimmed beard it achieved that rebirth by which flesh is renounced and spirit released, all according to institutional rite and writ, not by immersion or dubious sprinkling but by proper pouring on of water. Johnny watched Sophie nurse the baby after services. He watched with a nameless sort of feeling in him. This sucking, kicking morsel was flesh of Sophie's flesh; yet the tiny face was the face of Clymy. Clymy and this girl—a quiver tightened in his legs.

But when the Pastor shook the reins in departure over his ponies and the wine was sweet in small glasses, Johnny was mirthful over Sophie's complaining. "Men have all the good times," she mourned. "If a woman has a little fun, she has to suffer half a year for it. Can you imagine a man with a belly big as a bran sack and dragging it around for weeks? Unless he's got a beer gut, of course." Clymy never heard her. He hopped at her heels, proud and delighted and more than a little puzzled, as if biology and he had met by accident and he wasn't quite sure whether he was progenitor or appendage. Johnny grinned at his small important cough.

Before he knew it, so does day crowd upon the shinbone of day, Johnny was confirmed and had button shoes with tips so pointedly narrow that they puffed his chest with arrogance though they galled his toes with anguish. More than once at church he rubbed the leather frantically to ease a pinched spot on a joint and longed for home and the blessedly cooling moment when the shoes were slipped off and the bones relaxed with flesh and blood, and he could hang the buttonhook clinkingly on the nail.

Dread of the confirmation rite unsettled his sleep sometimes so that he woke to find himself shouting, "I don't know, Herr Pastor. Don't ask me," and Kurt shaking him: "Wake up, Johnny, can't you? And quit banging my nose with your fists."

The confirmation day itself was for him prickly with excitement and a kind of fear. The spring sun was hot and the blood pounded in his ears. But he forgot panic, his shoes pinched so. He marched down the aisle with the rest, walking as stiffly and delicately as if he were treading on eggs and rotten ones at that. Those shoes were like iron fists squeezing his toes into sharp knots of ache. Even at rest he winced. He was thinking of cool creek water for his burning feet, not the Catechism, when the Pastor asked about original sin, and so he tripped over the question and pitched head-long into error. How Uncle Herm would feel, he was ashamed to think. The others didn't matter.

Questions bounced from the altar where the Pastor stood; answers flowed along the curve of the half circle of chairs where the confirmands sat glued with sticky importance and moist apprehension, Kurt at one end and Snoose in the middle and he at the end. He only smiled wanly when the Pastor asked Mosey Fritz: "Do you renounce the Devil and all his works and all his ways?" Mosey, frightened and uncertain over the meaning of "renounce," not knowing how to answer, finally shouted, "No." When the Pastor rephrased the question, a glitter in his eye, Mosey yelped in cornered frenzy, "No—er, yes; I don't know; ask Papa." The benches screeked as the congregation moved and rustled, trying to hide glee underneath a proper Sunday decorum, although Heinie Beerwagon almost ended the ceremonies by bellowing his loud, "Haw, haw, haw!" The Pastor's icy "The services will continue when these unseemly disturbances are quieted" brought gravity back to the benches.

On another Sunday Johnny would have savored the fun in this; now he tried to wiggle a toe out of its agony. But when he knelt awkward with pain at the altar and the communion wine was on his lips, he forgot ache and confusion in the sudden trembling that shook him, this wine a seal and promise to something beyond him to understand. His hand shook and the Pastor's dark gown swam in a black haze and the hymn book slipped from his unsteady fingers.

Later, when the Marchens and the Nussbaums and the Schadels came to share the confirmation spareribs and cabbage and the glasses of dandelion cordial Aunt Phrena poured, the communion wine lingered on his tongue, less like a taste and more like an odor rich and strange and dark with portent of indescribables. For a miserable, hurtful moment, raked deep with silent loneliness, he longed for his mother and for her smile here with him where the apple-tree buds on the twig were no bigger than baby ears and pink-red as roses; where all the spring's rejoicing rode in waves of plum-blossom fragrance strongly on a mild wind. Her smile faded oddly before the notion of another—a smile pulled back by a dimple, honey-colored hair mixed with apple buds. . . .

He shook himself for a fool. The way Aunt Phrena would scold over such folly; thinking about folks like the Roses who weren't even properly received by the church, much less members of the elect. It was bad enough to have him attend District School in the fall where all manner of heathen came together and the Rose girl, too. Johnny had a queer stir in his blood at the idea of meeting her again. Why, he'd see her by the hour; that is, if he attended.

All that confirmation day Uncle Herm hid chortles behind his mustache, and acted as if he could have pitched a hundred loads of manure in an afternoon. With a glance at Aunt Phrena and Kurt, he bridled his ela-tion. He shook hands with Johnny before the services for encouragement, and after for grinning pride. His finger raised in caution against Aunt Phrena's finding out, or Kurt's, he slipped a silver dollar into Johnny's pocket. "Better hang on to it; keepsake, or something. Not many left, the way the gover'ment is squeezing silver." He behaved as though he had a partner now.

Aunt Phrena bustled among the guests with ladles and forks and bowls. Whenever Johnny came within reach, patience touched her lips. She said plainly it was no credit to him that she was happy; he could make her joy endless, if he wanted to. Kurt was solemnly dignified, the certificate in his hand, a warrant for his taking on the manners of the aged, his heaviness accentuated by a tight, black suit. He talked with the Nussbaum boys and the grownups that day more than with Snoose and Johnny.

The Dunkels had been invited, but Mr. Dunkel, with a glance at his wife, shook his head. "We come on another day," he said, clucking his horses into step cheerfully. Johnny knew they wouldn't. What pillar of strength was this, he wondered, by which Mr. Dunkel could laugh and joke and put the grub hoe and the breaking plow to the widening of his acres, when his little Gretel was dust and grass and violets by now, and his wife slipping into a land grotesque with shadows and twisted mem-ories?

He ambled past the apple tree beside Snoose, both of them hushed by the consciousness, however vague, that this day had significance beyond new suits and button shoes, they couldn't have told why. Something had been mixed this day with their blood and bone and breath, something which had little to do with the round of seasons, the planting of kernels and the cutting of stalks, but was forever, like the curved zenith and the inescapable sleeping stir in the heart of seed. Perhaps it was in this that Mr. Dunkel sought valiancy under sorrow.

Snoose pulled down a twig with apple buds half open, filling his nose with the sunny smell. Out of nowhere he said, "I'd like to get me a Jacob's ladder to heaven and fool around with the angels."

Johnny let this foolishness go by, answering jovially, "Lots of real girls around here you can monkey with. Em'ly Musser, for instance. You got plenty time for angels later on."

"Real girls?" Snoose caught him up quickly. "Like Lilice, eh? You don't forget her, do ya? Johnny, you're as thin and easy to see through as rain." He went on swiftly before Johnny could utter his blissful protests, "Gramma says every feller's got a guardian angel that follers him along. I'd like to take mine swimming in the creek."

Johnny stopped abruptly. "Angels in the creek?" He gasped over the sacrilege.

"Why not?" Snoose chuckled. "Guess they can swim. I wonder how an angel looks with his feathers wet—like our old rooster in the rain, tail dragging?" He left Johnny open-mouthed. "There's Kurt yelling. Let's see what he wants."

The folks rattled away at choretime. Johnny was unbashfully hearty in receiving their hands ("Good luck and see you soon"). Beside him Uncle Herm was a slouch of happiness against the door. Aunt Phrena, divided between pride and aloofness, waved her apron. When they had gone Johnny climbed the stairs and gratefully squeezed out of his shoes into the roomy coolness of pants and the freedom of bare feet, and went to the quietness of pastures for the cows.

Not even Old Man Geppert could remember an autumn as fiercely blazing in dark, ominous red and wild canary yellow as this one, when Johnny was nearing sixteen. It was as if the year's end would make up in beauty what it had neglected in yield, for this season as in the two just past, crops had been short on the stem and meager in the head. Uncle Herm crouched impatiently over his account book. But there was balm in the odor of leaf and drying twig mixed with smoke. Unburdened of some things if cumbered with others, Johnny ran freer than he could ever remember, despite the dark chokecherry-colored shadows that sometimes came. When light rains fell like a hand sprinkle of tiny drops, the smell of woods damp and meadow wet was like wine in his nose and he felt like dropping pitchfork and running with the fox on the ridges.

He helped Uncle Herm thresh occasionally instead. Twice now this season he had cut bands (it was always Uncle Herm's rig to him, no matter how much of it Mr. Schadel and Alb Hukelpoke claimed as their share). Mostly in the evenings after school or at the week's end, he stayed at home helping Kurt dig potatoes or harvest corn with the hand sickle, and dreamed of Lilice at school. He plugged the mouse holes in the granary with strips of tin and sewed patches on the ripped grain sacks.

On Saturdays he plowed. Ribbon by black ribbon he laid the underside of earth bare to heaven, the handles throwing him aside when the share hit rock, so that a naked foot he thrust out in order to brace himself caved the edge of the furrow down, and earth clung to his ankles. Often his bare flesh knocked against jagged granite and he swore with enthusiasm, stopping to nurse the ache and wondering whether Aunt Phrena's advice about wearing boots wasn't good after all. More than cockle and wild rose with stubble were tipped under his moldboard, however.

Under his work ran the tantalizing memory of his confirmation day. He couldn't forget it, as though willy-nilly he had been thrust forward into the years and wasn't sure how it had happened. With a shock that stopped him behind the walking plow and made him call, "Whoa, there," to the horses, he saw that he was sixteen—or nearly so. He was not far from black whiskers and a man, though his whiskers were still mild and kittenish. Why, at seventeen, Willie Geppert married and crawled into bed with a girl. At eighteen he had a kid——

Johnny's brain flip-flopped in confusion. It took three rounds of the early fall plowing he was doing to steady him.

He was attending District School, indifferently interested in what Mrs. Sperry had to offer but keenly alive to Lilice two seats ahead of him. He could stop going to school after his sixteenth birthday. Most boys flung aside the speller and the geography book long before that. Lornas Tetzell wasn't returning although Mosey Fritz still struggled to get out of the Fifth Reader. Snoose planned to go until Christmas. Kurt was going. He would, the whole term, older than anyone there but agreeable to Aunt Phrena's urgings.

"You go, Kurt, even if they haven't a *Vater Unser* at the public school. You're confirmed now and Mrs. Sperry's a God-fearing woman. Somebody's got to do the figuring in this family." Johnny didn't doubt whom she meant. Kurt himself stated, "I figure on finishing that Seventh Reader."

Because Uncle Herm insisted, "You go too, Johnny. Learning never gave anybody the colic," Johnny went. He wasn't sure he'd stay the term through. Uncle Herm needed him, he could see that.

Gatha and Em'ly Musser were there and the rest, all under Mrs. Sperry's darting eye and her huge bobbing bustle. Not that Johnny cared about them (except Snoose). Not as long as she was there. And there she was, Lilice in the next row and two seats ahead, so disturbingly near that the curve of her cheek got into his pencil and one day the coast line of Europe which he was trying to draw became unexpectedly smooth and regular, except for a dimple somewhere on the shore of Holland.

Often as he plowed in these fall days, he remembered the first day of that term so happily he could have danced in the stubble at the recollection. He had seen her the moment he opened the door. She hadn't as much as glanced at him at first. But at recess she had left her desk and flowed to him. He was sure she hadn't walked. And there was a glow on her shoulder he was sure came from her hair. She was willowy, about his age and tall enough to come level with his ear. Her eyes nearly closed when she smiled.

"You're Johnny." He was savagely happy she hadn't put "Schwartz" between her full red lips and hoped he'd never hear the low softness of her voice jangled with that syllable. "I remember you. You came to our fire." As though the flames and the brief sanctuary of his winter coat were still in her mind, she said simply, "Thank you, Johnny." He understood without knowing exactly why. He could only bob dumbly. Why did his teeth cling together as if they were stuck in taffy candy?

"Where're you going to sit? My name is Lilice." She spoke it as her mother had, that night of the conflagration—Lileesa.

He mumbled he didn't know what, seeing her name on the spelling book—Lilice Rose. He almost fell into a seat, Heinie Beerwagon's old one two seats back of hers. He settled down. He would have fought anyone disputing his claim to a seat so near hers. At that it was fool's luck and no credit to him, his getting this place, he admitted later, irate with himself.

The boys ragged him at dinner but he only wrestled them instead of fighting. He had charity even for Mosey Fritz whose eyes were by no means friendly. But all the Moseys in Pockerbrush could not have aroused his ire that dinnertime. In the following days he actually put perkiness into his recitations, he who had promised himself to lazy through the last of the months of school remaining to him. It was more for the light he saw in Lilice's eyes, however, than for the grade Mrs. Sperry put in her record book. At that, he sickened on dates in history and capitals in geography.

But Lilice chose him for partner in pump-pump-pull-away on Monday; he "skipped-to-mallew" with her on Tuesday; she rowed "four in a boat" with him on Thursday; and once in run-sheep-run the two got separated from the rest of the hunters and were lost for half an hour. The whole group searched until they were found walking along a path, the game forgotten and deep in talk that was mostly silence.

Snoose tickled him all the way home that afternoon. They wrestled in the woods, scuffling among the leaves and grabbing at each other's bodies, breathless with bull-calf struggle, their hands boyishly exploratory, their young manhood aroused and sweet to them as warm, late-October hazelnuts.

He ached to carry Lilice's lunch bucket home as Snoose did Em'ly Musser's sometimes. But Em'ly lived beyond the Marchens. Lilice—he fretted and fumed over this—went east to cross the bridge and he lived west and their paths homeward carried them apart instead of together. Often as he peered at her covertly and she was quiet, he was distressed by what seemed a kind of shadow on her face.

On other days he joined Snoose and Mosey in plaguing Mrs. Sperry. Once the boys, Johnny among them, chewed brown paper into juicy, tobaccolike wads and put them on the bustle while she bent over a copybook. The cuds rode like little brown ducks as she minced among the seats. At her sudden movement they fell soggily. The boys hung heads over their desks, beet-red with breath and laughter squeezed in. She was furious. "Who," she demanded, her eyes darting like a wren's, "who among you masticates tobacco?" She made the boys, all of them, tarred with the same pitch as they undoubtedly were, clean the floor. The girls were innocent, she shrilled; no lady would lend a hand to an act so heinous.

Johnny was ready to slop a dripping lump in a drawer open in her desk, when he saw Lilice shaking her curls at him. The fun fell out of the prank. He flung the mess into the wastebasket and she dimpled at him. . . .

At the recollection his grasp on the handles loosened unguardedly and the plow jumped; a crook marred the unswerving furrows. He didn't mind, smiling over the "giddaps" to the team.

Across the fields the pasture woods were kindling. Basswood leaves were lemon yellow, the edges eaten brown by the rust of the year. The black haws in the pasture (Uncle Herm called them "black horse") ran to red leaves and coal-jetty fruit, meaty and glistening. Now and again he left the plow and the horses panting while he crawled over the fence for a handful. His white teeth were darkly speckled when he returned. Mostly, when the team or his own legs demanded a space for rest, he leaned against the handles or hunched on the furrow edge, whistling softly impatient twirls and trills while he poked at the thoughts in his head and the earth caked between his toes.

A restlessness plagued him when the hum of a threshing machine disturbed the calm of the year's dying and lumber wagons rattled over the hills in the cool morning stillness. When the wind was right, the distant drone and the yells troubled him so that he hardly had the patience to bring the elm tree across the field into his sight—a guide for uncrooked furrows. The whine of cylinder, the *slip-slap-slip* of the belts, the *riddle-raddle* of the gears—these began to hum a kind of melody in him when he cut the bands—a melody that curiously got muddled with the sound of Lilice's voice.

He was lengthening in his trousers, slender and looking taller than he really was; eyes black and in excitement winking fast as a popple leaf in a low wind; teeth milky white against the red of lips; hair that was black and insisted on rolling into curly tumbles in spite of the water and the exasperation with which he plastered it down. "Don't want these old bull curls on my head!" he exclaimed peevishly, jabbing the comb against the waves. Some of his vehemence (though not all) came from the blemished fruit of thinking, Curly black hair—that's what Aunt Phrena said.

He was quick as a weasel and had more strength in the lumps of muscle thickening on his bones than anyone believed; so Kurt found more than once. There was lightness in his heels but already the pull of stubbornness about his lips. He'd yell at the team, "Devil grab it by the hind legs, get moving there!" to shorten the rounds. This inching along was too slow for the stew beginning to boil in his veins. "Feller staggers behind the plow the day long and what's to show?" he fretted, talking to Snoose. "Takes eternity to lay a field over." He still walked unshod, as Snoose did and other boys, though Kurt didn't. Boots and shoes were a luxury for winter's pinch, now that prices were sagging toward the nadir and expenses soaring to heaven.

For him, change dragged over the hills on a poky nag, slow as rust but as inevitable. The difference a year made was hardly perceptible. Oak and pine and hedgy underbrush still crowded shadows into the dooryards, though farms were bulging out of the clearings rod by rod. Each season grub hoe and breaking plow lessened the number of stumps in a field. Stones were "burned" into submission. Johnny liked the crackling sound when cold water struck the heated rock and pieces split off with sharp jagged edges.

The roads were mostly cow paths, the logs in the corduroy musting away, leaf and needle, into swamp rot. Here and there a "grade" of dirt was rounded off; new wood was laid to bolster the wagon trails in the boggy places. In the worst weather it was worth a wheel or a singletree to go to Mary's Hill. Wolves howled over the lake from early frost to late April;

sometimes in desperate chase, they barked and yipped in the middle of July.

The hen house wanted paper on its roof and the rail fences became so rotted and sagged by a burden of snow and brittle age that a squirrel's weight joggled them and they collapsed. Timber by timber they were replaced with greener lengths or forgotten in shining wire that snagged tree and post together.

Uncle Herm still scattered his wheat by hand, striding over the field. Morning and night, Aunt Phrena patiently skimmed the milk in the pans when the coolness of the cellar brought the cream in floating islands to the top. There was talk of a contraption known as a "cream separator." Mr. Schadel had seen one at the fair in Fergus; a thingamajig undoubtedly spawned by the Devil. How else could metal and tin pour cream from one spout and milk from another? Guffawing, Uncle Herm said the next thing you knew, some smart aleck would rig up the cow so that a farmer needn't do more than stand by and shosh her; cream would leak out of one set of teats and milk out of another.

Uncle Herm had bought a harvester the year before. On this machine an elevator carried the straw over the bull wheel and dropped it on a platform where Mr. Marchen or Torsten Torgrimson bound it. Sometimes Kurt or Johnny crouched there, hands roughened with the stalks they were binding with hemp cord and their backs twisted with as many knots as the twine they were using. They'd try to be deaf when Young Matthew Dornhover got a self-binder and shouted derisively at his neighbors still enduring sore kidneys and callused fingers over hand binding. Excited at how much more work could be accomplished with how little sweat, Johnny was full of needles of impatience to get one. For once Kurt was on his side, however much Uncle Herm exclaimed that the crops were as thin as his pocketbook and Aunt Phrena sniffed wetly that people who didn't have anything were always wanting something better than their neighbors.

In the years before, under the blade of the cradle, fields had always been left as unmarked and close-shaven as a meadow. Now however bull-wheel tracks, narrow ribbons of bent-over stubbles, divided the acres into strips. Cradles hung in the sheds, the dust on their handles tracked by the whiskery mice. Mr. Dunkel's did. It had ever since his house became packed with loneliness and he bought his first reaper. Now he was getting a binder. No longer did Mrs. Dunkel gather fistfuls of straw for a cord to tie the sheaves. Iron hands bound the straw.

Any day now Uncle Herm would sell his oxen and a patience as sturdy as oaks would leave the barn. Johnny felt a twinge, wondering how it would be not to hear Bully's rumbling low at feeding time. Mr. Dunkel still kept oxen. "Ain't going to let some nag driver sell my bullies for wagon grease. Not me. I'll pasture 'em first. If they live and I live, they'll die mine."

Henry Splies, the blacksmith from Mary's Hill, who built a shop near the church and the store, said gleefully he was tickled that folks were buying frisky teams, now that oxen were getting scarce. Horses ran away easier than a yoke of steers and so completely did they smash wagons and buggies that Mr. Splies's account book fattened and he could sooth the Pastor's thunders about laboring on the Sabbath with a gentle increase of the yearly contribution.

Horses were the real hustlers, Johnny decided. He had to grant that when a plow hauled by oxen struck a stone, little damage was done; but when a plow drawn by horses banged into rock, pieces of the singletree flew one way and the driver the other. But a high-stepping pair of blacks, or a span of grays like that which the whisky drummer at Mary's Hill had— with them hitched to the new buggy he saw advertised in the paper, Devil! but couldn't a feller sweep up to a shindandy on Saturday nights and hand his girl down, a girl like—— He lost a step behind the plow and stumbled. His grip on the curved wood was hard. "Giddap, there!" he shouted.

No matter how hard he tried, some things refused obstinately to be smoothed down but stuck sticklike up in his cogitations the way the springy wolfberry bushes did in the new plowing. There was that in Kurt, for instance, which rubbed him raw at times; a twistiness that left him undecided and empty-handed. Johnny remembered the red-spotted calf with an irritation not yet gone to ashes. Some day he'd explode over the lofty fashion Kurt strode across the yard with a calf, or stood beside a bull, square-footed and heavy, as if what he had a fist on, he'd keep.

This fall more than ever Kurt was jumpy, now indifferently friendly, again stolidly resentful, as if he knew or sensed the slow struggle that went on behind his back, and out of loyalty sided with Aunt Phrena. A hint of what grumpled in Kurt's brain, a dull resentment, perhaps more, blazed forth in wooden fury one afternoon when they swam in the creek.

And Aunt Phrena herself. She still dropped the kernel of a hint: the cloth of her brother Zacharias was equal to redemption if Johnny but accepted it. She was persistent, unaware how barren the soil was that rejected the seed. "You got the Devil right in you," she'd said again only a day ago. "You'll go straight to Hell."

How did you watch yourself against brimstone, Johnny wondered. How did Kurt? Or Aunt Phrena herself, for that matter? Why single him out? Did folks who had devils make good preachers? Or did the preacher school knock the Devil from you? Suspicion grew, a burdocky, rough-edged growth: What she really wants is to get rid of me. He wondered what hope she had feathered in Kurt. If it was the farm, Kurt could have it. I'm going out and hustle for myself before long.

But there was a more ominous roll in her words when he thought of a dark shadow that slid in his mind. Devil in you. Suppose it wasn't a satan of fire (like the Pastor's) but one of flesh? You could reject a demon of flame but what about a devil of bone laid in your bone and blood in your blood and the fault not yours? All right then, if it's coming out in me, let it. I won't stop it. He flung a clod truculently. And if anything gets in my way, I'll smash it. Kurt can have the place and choke on it. As long as *she* says I got a devil, I'd like to spite her.

He shivered at other times, bracing himself against the throw of the plow and recalling the Pastor's fiery prophecies and Aunt Phrena's gloomy forebodings. He encouraged himself: You wait. I'll get me a thrashing rig and then I'll show them. Vague and formless were the "them" but menacing nonetheless. I'll make them crawl to me. Aunt Phrena'll get mad then. And Lilice—— Lilice, all the crinkly friendliness of her. What would she say if she knew that he was soaked in—oh, he didn't know in what vinegar of badness?

"Giddap, Devil take you!" he shouted at the horses. "Never get the plowing down, loafing this way." He plowed so that the sweat ran.

11

The Monday before his birthday, a morning of skies so deep that the arch of the zenith hung close enough overhead, it seemed, to grab a handful of blue, he kicked up sand in the road beside Snoose, walking to school, his toeprints clear, the big one a separate smudge, the little ones a crowded row. "What Aunt Phrena'll say, I don't know and I don't care," he told Snoose. "I want a birthday party, too, for once in my life, and she ought to let me have it." He saw Kurt, a dozen rods ahead of him, walking with the Schadel boys. Kurt's boots were shining with the polish of the stoveblack brush he'd given them. "He's had two parties."

Snoose shifted the books under his arm. "Might as well say it." His gray eyes were warm as the October sun. "Me and Sophie—we figured on giving you a surprise party. But since you plan——"

"Snoose," Johnny interrupted him, his face halfway between joy and disbelief. "A surprise party like Jackie had last year? Oh, I never had one— never." The handle of his lunch bucket rattled, so eager he was.

Snoose looked away hastily at the joy lighting up something like loneliness in Johnny's eyes and said disconnectedly, "Your aunt's had her dander up and we didn't dare ask. But Sophie got her nerve again. She went to find out this afternoon."

"I'm going to ask Lilice." It slipped from his tongue before he thought. Half defensively his grin widened.

Snoose chuckled and banged his bucket against Johnny's rump. The sandwiches inside rustled and the bottle of coffee clacked and gurgled. "You cakewalker, you got it bad, ain't you?"

Johnny was too excited to pay attention. "I'll ask her at recess. You think she will?" he questioned as if Snoose's "yes" would help to make up her mind. Then he was cast down. "If she won't—well, I might as well have a funeral as a birthday party."

"She'll go with you." With a grin Snoose saw brightness growing on Johnny's face like a lantern with the wick turning up. "I'm asking Em'ly to be my partner, if she comes, and she will."

They plodded on, both silent, this laying bare of hearts suddenly too sensitive with intimacy for them. They lengthened their steps and soon were with Kurt and the Schadel boys.

When he came to ask her at recess, Lilice was talking with Kurt, all flutters and smiles, Kurt like a sponge soaked in her gaiety. He bent toward her in so friendly a fashion that Johnny's arm went rigid. Johnny heard her say, "Shoes," and saw her glance at his bare feet and laugh, putting her hand to her lips. Hammer-struck, he rooted where he stood, her laugh wild in his brain, the red in his face dying to gray. Funny, was it? he gritted.

He looked down and saw his toes stiffly spread, the end of each whitened a little about the nail from the way he stood, poised and tensed. He saw dust powdering the slant of a foot. There was the splash of mud he'd got in poking with a toe at a beetle on a puddle edge. There was a bunching of scar meat on an arch, red and ugly, where a spike had gouged to the bone and the wound had healed raggedly. Heavily his gaze followed a crack between pine boards of the floor—a crack that ran between a pair of boots and a pair of shoes, the one polished, the other daintily narrow. This one had side buttons and was gayly shifting, its wearer vivacious.

He felt choked, his collar tight. He saw Lilice turn toward him, her look a beckon. Miserably, he tried to cover one bare foot with the other. Then he swung away, his Adam's apple all at once so large and hard that he could hardly swallow. Wordlessly, he slunk off. He joined the ballgame but the bat had a crook in it and the ball wasn't where it should have been, no matter how savagely he swung. At last he threw the club down. There was no fun in the nip game either; the sticks were clumsy as fence posts. And his dinner tasted wormy and mouse-tracked.

Kurt swept by, jaunty and with tail feathers high. Johnny grabbed him. "What did you tell Lilice about me?" His tone was deep and direct.

"When?" Kurt tried evasion.

"At recess. And don't try to wiggle out of it. You know what I mean." Johnny's fingers began to curl, fight hardening his muscles.

Kurt shrugged. "Oh we—nothing much. Lilice was saying—well, about your bare feet." Kurt's dark brows heightened. "After all, big feller like you." He bent and flicked a scrap of wood from the toe of a boot.

The fight drained from Johnny's arms. "Oh," he muttered. Her friendly beckon, that blurred away. He remembered her laugh only. But the laughter was like burlap on a sore place. He glared at Kurt and bounced away. He shouldered into the ante-high-over game but moved so dispiritedly that the boys were disgusted and told him so.

Finally, digging his hands in his pockets as though dragging out a decision, he strode in search of Lilice, his tongue white-hot with barbs, spurred by one notion: he had been hurt and he was going to hurt someone else, he didn't care much whom. He found her in the woodshed entry where the coats hung and the lunch baskets were rowed against a wall. She was hanging up a jacket that had fallen—his own, if he'd had any sense in the blaze that shook him.

"So you don't like my bare feet?" he burst at her, his voice brusque and unreasonable, though with more than a quaver in it. He stuck a foot pugnaciously toward her. She drew back. "Well, skin's as good as leather any day. Think shoes make the lady, huh?" Sorrow welled into him the moment he had spoken but it could not bring back his words.

Her gaze was startled for a moment. Then surprise at his behavior changed to frostiness. "Why, you can dance bare in a snowbank, if you want to," she flung at him. "I don't care." Her eyes gathered a flash of anger. "You're a nasty stuck-up, aren't you?" She bustled off, flinging over her shoulder, "I never said a word against your old bare feet." She added enlighteningly, "You're horrid, that's what you are," and slammed the schoolroom door in his face.

He picked at a splinter of basswood, hoping the door would open. It didn't; it hid Lilice at her desk, angry tears smudging the lines of Kingsley's *Water Babies* in the Seventh Reader. He sighed and was so peakish the remainder of the day, Lilice's face like a lamp squarely turned from him and all shadowy, that Mrs. Sperry advised him after the last class, "Inform your aunt that you require a mild dose of paregoric."

He might as well take it; it wouldn't be any more unpleasant than his thoughts. On the path home, Snoose was as tongue-tied as he, knowing with the animal instinct of youth what trouble had fallen. Only at the gate near the Marchen house where they separated did Snoose say, "I won't have Em'ly for my partner either. She can be alone, this time. Or eat supper with someone else."

Johnny heard the faint underbreath of woe in his willingness. "Don't be a bull's hind leg." He was blunt, though the shove he gave Snoose was one of gratitude. "You better 'scort her around, or I'll do it myself." He pretended carelessness but failed, and slouched homeward. Snoose watched him go with a sigh.

At home Johnny found that the party had been settled down to the last cooky. Sophie had been there and had wheedled Aunt Phrena into good humor by praising her fifty-year-old recipe for sour-emptyings bread.

Aunt Phrena couldn't help being snippy to him: "S'pose it is so: a person can't become a year older now without a birthday doings." She lifted a spoon and inquired suspiciously, "You planning to ask the Roses?" As if he were intending to invite a skunk.

"Why not, if I want to?" he flung at her. "It's my party."

"S'pose so," she agreed dourly. "It's little I have to say in my own house." She began to twist her apron, a sign of coming tears he couldn't mistake. He said hastily, "Well, they ain't coming." Let this mollify her, if it would. Whether it did or not, she baked apple pies that spilled juice and deliciousness prodigally around the edges, pepper on her tongue but sweetness in her baking.

Two afternoons later Johnny slammed an armful of sticks on the pile they were gathering. Snoose, over with him after school, dropped his load. "That's enough for kindlin'," Johnny said. But Kurt gathered more pieces. The weather was still so untouched by frost or autumn chill that the robins were deceived into lengthening their stay in this second spring, unnatural and out of season. Up from the south drifted the hum of the threshing rig, busy at Mr. Schadel's.

An eye on the sticks, Johnny said low to himself in a mutter, "If she didn't bawl so much and wet the wood——"

He shrugged. But Kurt heard and turned in his slow determined way. "What did you say about Ma?"

"Nothing that matters." Johnny spoke evenly. A kind of tenseness stretched between them. Then he caught Snoose's arm. "Let's take a run to the crick. I got to be clean for the party Friday night."

"It's not the swim. It's the rig you want to see," Kurt told him bluntly. "You'll go by the clearing, I know you will." When Johnny nodded stubbornly, Kurt added, "Ma said to get plenty of wood, with the thrashers coming tomorrow or the next day."

"There's plenty." Johnny kicked the pile. "Come on." He itched, ready to fling off shirt and pants. "Sun's still high, a long ways."

"Uncle Herm—he had a row with Old Dresser over the grain tally." Kurt piled arguments as Alb Hukelpoke did cordwood, a piece at a time and that with patience. "If he gets mad——"

"He won't hurt none." Johnny fidgeted. "Ready? I'll race ya, Snoose." They tore down the cow path in a rush, Johnny careless whether Kurt followed or not. Deaf as corner posts to whatever warnings about evening chores buzzed in the back of their heads, they ran, the air warm in their faces. Kurt puffed behind.

They climbed the ridge eastward, breaking like divers from the depths of hazel and plum brush to the sun and the cleared space near the top. Stumps still told of oak and elm that had fallen under ax and crosscut saw for the barns and lean-tos in the widening clearings below. Johnny stopped beside Snoose near an ironwood tree. Kurt called to them to wait.

Below them the creek was lost in woods except where a bend of water kneed itself into Uncle Herm's clearing, larger by many acres now, and took the late sun on its ripples. Beyond, hidden in trees to the southwest, was the church with no white spire to tower beside the evergreen in the graveyard as they had in Mary's Hill. Beyond that were the level places with few trees they called the "prairies."

Over west lay Mr. Schadel's field. Near the creek was the rig, looking more like a toy than anything else at this height, the circle of horses clouded in dust and the driver a dark figure scarcely seen. "That's Alb Hukelpoke. Sheetin' Judas, but he can lay down the lines!" Johnny teetered excitedly. The straw carrier was like an arm slanting up from a body. Men were tardy in their movements on stack and straw pile but faster on the side where the grain teams waited. Once a wagon, slow with the weight of sacks, crawled buglike away, the driver riding.

"That's your pa, Snoose," Kurt said. "I can tell by the black horse."

Snoose answered, "He'd better whip him up. He's lazin' again."

The wagon crept toward a grove that hid the granary and the shop and Mr. Schadel's other buildings. Before it vanished, another wagon, hitched to a yoke of oxen, dragged into sight. A man like a small dark peg walked beside them. Slowly horses and oxen came together; met; and for a moment at this interval of space were mingled in a gray patch of movement. Then they drew apart.

"We got two less stacks this year than last," Snoose said. "We get littler and littler every season." A haze of dust and distance grew redder. Faintly over the treetops came the sudden shouts of men and the bellow of an ox, dirt in his throat and wanting water.

"Old Jeremiah's getting dry," Kurt observed, patting a sore place on his finger gently. "That break in his beller is getting kinda hoarse."

"I guess so," Snoose agreed. "Dunkel had better water 'em. 'Fore he knows it, his bull team's going to head for the sloo hole, wagon and all."

"They're a darn good span, though," Johnny said defensively. Then he added, "Mr. Dunkel hasn't changed much. But Mrs. Dunkel—I wonder how he stands it."

They nodded, heavy with neighbor sadness, their gaze on the distant field and on the stacks of grain that were like small beehives with the tops sliced off and growing wider as they grew shorter. Johnny squeezed his sight to make out whether Uncle Herm's tall form were standing above the feeder where a separator man should stand, but the dust smoked heavily around the front of the machine and hid it.

"They're not near a quarter done." Johnny chewed on a twig. "Betcha if I drove the power you'd see the bundles fly." He bragged so that Kurt looked at him.

"They'll finish if they don't break down," Snoose said. He chuckled in his queer gurgling fashion, tickled by laughter fingers hidden behind his gray-stone-under-water eyes: a secret mirth that tantalized Johnny into friendliness but drove Kurt to moody exasperation. "With the thrashers at your place, you won't see your Lilice for a couple days, Johnny," Snoose went on. He was in a strange teasing mood.

"If Johnny wants Lilice to——" began Kurt when Johnny half yelled, the shadows rushing blackly, "I'm not talking to her. She's not my Lilice. Shut up, both of you."

They nudged their toes in the leaves. Silence spread again. Snoose offered all at once, "Want to see my lickin'? I got it again." They crowded close while he pulled his shirt and drew it curtainwise upward. Kurt was wooden but Johnny goggled over the slantwise crisscrosses, red and angry still, marking the slender back, and the purplish spot like an indelible thumb press at one end of each stripe where the tip of the rawhide had clawed at the flesh.

"Gee-gods sakes," Johnny gasped. "That's black-and-bluer than Heinie Beerwagon's lickin', by a long shot. Your pa—he lays it on, don't he?"

"I guess." Snoose spoke flatly, as if it didn't matter, half proud with honor. "He caught me slicing a punkin." He couldn't hide the edge of bitter hate.

"No more'n that?" Johnny pulled the shirt down.

"I'll get even with him—some day." Snoose stuffed his shirt in. "And plenty, I guess." His gray eyes clouded.

Johnny mulled on this for a moment of twig-chewing. Getting even. Waiting maybe half a lifetime to square things up. And what if they didn't square up finally? The days wasted and the strength spent. Like the hours Uncle Herm could count, nettle-burned with Aunt Phrena's nagging. The balance was heavy there, one-sided and hanging low.

Snoose brushed away a leaf. "Sun's getting down. Not much time left for a swim."

They were gone in a crackle of sticks down the long slant and out over a tree-and-grassy pasture. Johnny ran ahead, fingers at his buttons, his shirt flying to tangle in a willow bush even before his heels came to a stop beside the place where the water was deep. Snoose crowded behind, and after him, Kurt.

The creek hurried over shallow stretches noisily with gurgling, sucking sounds and slowed to smooth and almost moveless silence in places where the water ran ear-deep. And in the calm eddies behind elbows of rock, patches of chaff and straw dust from the threshing upstream turned wheel-like, endlessly in motion but arriving nowhere, until the ice of winter stopped them for a season in a cold web of stillness.

A wiggle of his hips and Johnny stepped clear of his pants as if glad to be naked. From nose to belly button he was as brown as the light molasses bread Aunt Phrena made, his ribs lean as split-willow hoops Uncle Herm used to tighten weather-dry barrels. But his muscles were lumpy with hard growing strength. He rocked on his toes and giggled at Kurt turtle-crawling from his overalls; yelled "Whee-ip" to Snoose, careless if anyone heard, and stuck his belly into the wind before he tested a foot in the ripples.

Kurt hunched behind his overalls a moment, pulling at preacher's lice in a seam, as if half scared to be caught bare. He dropped his britches suddenly, called, "Git your shirt off, Snoose," and streaked in clumsily, spray lacing shoulder-high and wide at each jump. For no reason he gave Johnny a shove and stood white-skinned and hip-over in brown creek water, his hands slapping at the vanishing bubbles.

Johnny came up, spitting a mouthful of the creek, glowering deeper with each choking cough, half his forehead plowed into the wrinkles of beginning anger, half smooth. "No more sense than a woodchuck," he yelled and made for Kurt. But Kurt plunged into the water, heavy as a muskrat. Johnny was fast behind. Snoose, his clothes off at last, stepped in and saw minnows like fingers of dark shadow scattering from the deep hole where the water boiled and foam burst up and where one twisting body was pale and the other only a shade darker than the creek itself.

Kurt broke water first, standing half blinded by trickles and gasping.

What happened then happened as quick as the swing of a porcupine's tail. Johnny, nearer Kurt than he knew, shot up as logs do under the spillway in Hoffman's dam when the river freshens in spring—shot up, his head cracking straight under Kurt's chin. Kurt half fell, hand grabbing his jaw. He stumbled for the bank. Water rippled around Johnny's calves as he slowly followed, taking this too as something he had started.

Kurt danced about, his mouth streaming redder with each scared gulp. He caught up his shirt and stuffed it against his lips so that his yells were muffled. "My tongue, my tongue—I bit it off."

Johnny held out his wet brown hands as if wanting to help, shivering knees and ribs, as though the pain he saw on Kurt's face raked through him, belly and shoulders. Then his lips hardened with a "don't-give-a-damn-if-I-do" sort of look. Kurt bawled, "Snoose, Snoose, my tongue——"

Snoose grabbed him, though his legs were twisty and as unsafe as hazel sticks. "Hold still, and quit slobbering." His tone was sharp with fright.

Kurt snapped from him. His body screwed up like a clock spring with pain. "Blockhead!" he tried to shout at Johnny, his voice heavy with the weight of hurt, all that grumbled in his brain rushing out in a blaze of agony. "Ma's right. A troublemaker, you are, always. You got the Devil right in you. You oughta be horsehided if Uncle Herm wasn't such a—such a peahen." He spat scorn with the blood in his mouth. "You'd better be a preacher after all, as Ma says, and fast, or you'll go straight to hell—that's what you'll do." He was shrill when he wasn't slavering.

Johnny trembled, his lips pinched but rebellion in his eyes. He watched Snoose trying to bring quiet. "Stand still, Kurt, and let me see," Snoose ordered.

"Oh, Snoose, I bit it—I felt my teeth go through."

"Shut up and open your mouth."

Johnny waited, shaking all his nakedness, but the gladness in Snoose's laugh ("A hole snipped in there, all right; but your tongue's as long as ever") did not thaw the cold weakness in his flesh, all his young and prickly years wanting to yell, "It wasn't my fault. Why lay this on me?" A numbness locked his teeth, the word unuttered and left to dam. Some-day—Johnny felt this as he did the first chill fretting the air with a presage of icy winter—someday he'd have it out with Kurt once and for all, the gates breaking and the flood roaring. But not this moment nor the next while Kurt pulled at his buttons sullenly, shame cooling his outburst, and Snoose crouched beside him.

Then Snoose saw the red welt like a whip stroke where Johnny clawed at his naked shoulder. He arose, sorrow in the bend of his white body, and took shirt and pants to him, wordless as a bone. Johnny swung aside as if he didn't care, snatching the clothes. But Snoose saw how twisted his face was—lonely as if he hadn't a hole he could crawl into.

12

They came up the path to the barn, late by an hour, to find the cows mooing at the barn. Aunt Phrena, fussing with the milk buckets, was short with them. "I'll bring the strainer cloth." She was ready to scold but didn't, noticing Snoose, and let her moist china-blue eyes say for her how hard she had to work, she who had once taught school and played the organ in the church in Fergus, and wasn't it a beggar's pity that a neighbor woman like Mrs. Marchen would let her boy drag others off swimming when thrashers were practically in the yard and work piled kitchen-high? But you wouldn't catch her talking, not before neighbors.

She answered politely, however, when Snoose, eyes down at what was plain on her face, said eagerly, "I'll help with milkin', Mis' Barewolf."

She replied tearily, "That's mighty helpful of you, Charley." She uttered "Charley" with a dreadful sort of emphasis, eying Johnny meaningfully. "Snoose—ach, what a name!" she had said more than once.

But Johnny walked as if he had a tickle in his toes. He was glad that Snoose, milk pail in hand, was here to soften the helpless rebellion that rode him, especially when he saw Kurt poking at the bitten tongue. He struck the two tin cups on the milk stand and let the afternoon's frettings slip away with the sloo grass he shoved from the mow.

He grabbed Snoose by the shoulders; lifted him an inch or so; exclaimed, "I'll let you strip the old heifer. She's easy as mud to milk. Never kicked yet." He added, "Sure your pa won't come along home?" and was satisfied with Snoose's "They'll be thrashing till after dark. Bill's home." With un-necessary loudness so that Aunt Phrena would be sure to hear, Johnny offered, "I'll go help you finish your milking after a while."

With milking done Johnny and Kurt lifted brimming cups and drank. Snoose refused: "Warm milk; it makes my stomach queasy." The three went to the watering trough to slosh the cups clean.

"Uncle Herm tells fortunes by the foam," Johnny said. "You take a hunk of foam and some water and shake it together in the cup. If the foam sticks to the side, it's money. He used to do it, only with beer, in the old days. Kurt gets slugs of it. I never."

Snoose drew back as though something cold had touched him when Johnny and Kurt, each shaking a cup, held for a moment a tin of milk froth swirling on water.

"Oh, Kurt's got money again." Johnny spilled the water pettishly. "The side is slippery with it. And I got none." He looked up. "Go ahead, Snoose. You try it." He was eager. This brought Snoose closer to him for a moment and longer.

Snoose hesitated before he hastily dipped up the foam. Johnny watched him and then bent over the half-full cup. Instinctively he exclaimed, "Look now; a crooked half-moon. That's bad luck. Worse'n finding a toad the first thing on Sunday morning." A pucker came to his forehead when he saw Snoose staring at the cup as if hypnotized.

Snoose said in husky voice as though someone had shut his throat and he had little air, "Gramma said I never would live long."

Solemn as if for the moment he were ten years old again and playing "bury the dead," Johnny cried, "Here, Snoose, give it to me," and splashed the water to the ground. Swiftly he spat on the wet place and made an X in the puddle with the spit in the center. "That'll take the cross off it," he prophesied earnestly. Then he laughed in a kind of confusion, the number of his years suddenly deriding this kid folly. "Least, that's what Uncle Herm says. I don't believe it any more." But he eyed the moist black spot in the dry earth soberly as though it were just as well not to take any chances, not when this might ward off the evil of earth and sky. But Snoose was strangely thoughtful the remainder of the evening.

Johnny thought about it afterward when his swinging legs had carried him along the path back home. The pucker became a worry wrinkle above his eyes as he remembered how Snoose had stared at the cup in his hand. It was Snoose's saying that bothered him, the queer tone: "Gramma always said——" For a lengthy time he stood in the dust, disturbed by something he couldn't put his hand on. Then because he was tired and tomorrow was coming with threshers and more work than two hands could do, he growled, " 'Gramma says——' Oh, Devil grab it by the hind legs," and went inside, forgetting this new disquiet laid over gladness.

13

By the Friday night of the birthday, he was heroically morose. For all he cared, Aunt Phrena's juicy pies might as well have been stewed in yarrow. The moon running silver on the autumn-fired trees was no more than a smoky lantern. The stacks remained unopened, for the rig had broken down and the threshers were still eating Mr. Schadel's meat and potatoes. "Getting fat on it, too, I'll bet," Mr. Peiser grunted.

Johnny said hello glumly to the Marchens. They walked over, Sophie stepping carefully with the baby and Clymy behind her, carrying the diaper bag. The Peisers drove over and the Nussbaum boys rode. Gatha

Blumen came with her brother, caroling sweetly as she jumped from the buggy, "Happy birthday, Johnny, and a million more!"

He answered in mumbles, thinking, Not a birthday more, if they're like this. Why do girls have to spoil everything? Snoose did have Em'ly for partner, after all. Johnny nodded to him with what he was sure was a "go-ahead-and-have-a-rip-of-a-time" sort of expression. It was more like a hen drooping with the pip.

To Johnny's wonderment, ready as he was to be ruffled, Kurt, blooming in a new silk tie, acted queerly subdued. When a Peiser girl reached hands to him and wanted him to be leader with her in the "last couple out" game, he protested, "This is Johnny's party. You ought to let him lead off."

Johnny bugged in astonishment. This was like Kurt, though: calm indifference one moment, dull flickers of resentment the next. He had grumbled loudly about his hurt. But at school he'd been so proud of the hole in his tongue he'd exhibited it loftily. He'd let superiority mix with his smile until Johnny growled spitefully, "Aw, charge a three-cent nickel for the side show."

But this night Kurt had little to say. Johnny never guessed that he had Lilice's firm "No" buzzing in his ears, for he'd gone to ask her himself, and took her refusal in his own fashion. If time shaped people's minds, he had plenty of it to wait.

Johnny joined the game, leaden-ankled, until Uncle Herm, with a shout and a flourish of the faucet, rolled a keg with shoves of his foot from the granary. Aunt Phrena's nose grew longer perceptibly over the tapping and the first foamy rush but she remained quiet when the cups and glasses frothed on the rim and on the lip.

"Well, boy!" Uncle Herm was hearty. "Confirmation past and now a birthday. A man pretty soon. I had a job in a brewery when I was sixteen. *Prosit!*"

Johnny lifted the glass. He had sipped brew in years before; he drank now as one in the circle of men. The foam tickled his nose, and the malty taste, cool and slightly bitter, was tangy. He needed no urging for a second. When it lifted his spirits somewhat, though he belched, he recklessly reached for a third. He grew bold; yelled, "Devil grab and away with it!" at nothing in particular. He caught Gatha about the waist and, in spite of her delighted screams, whirled her in the "four in the boat" game.

He tried to kiss a Peiser girl in raw-headed nerve and in plain sight of the circle; which so impressed the Nussbaum boys that one of them, with a beckoning side twist of his head, called him behind the machine shed and uncorked a bottle. "Take a swipe there, feller. Say, you could heat a girl up in no time."

Johnny tipped the bottle. Fire flamed over his tongue. He wanted to strangle over the red-hot splash gurgling in his throat but this new man-nishness in him, stiff and heedless, wouldn't let him. He swallowed bee's stings and ant bites; gasped, "Wheeyew," and returned the bottle. The warmth under his belt, rising in waves of confidence, ran into his legs and to the tips of his fingers. He listened with sharpened ears and roared jovially, dizzily uncertain in his delight, when Arty Nussbaum said, "That little limb of a Peiser girl—wouldn't mind dangling her tits myself, I wouldn't." He wanted to whoop and dance; vowed he would go to a shindandy the next Saturday. They ought to have a hell of a time to-gether, he and Arty. Uncle Herm's chortles were an encouragement and Aunt Phrena's disapproval a goad to recklessness. He slapped Snoose on the shoulder and once pushed him closer to Em'ly, yelling, "Have a good time, kids," as if he were an old man and the goose feather down on his cheek were whiskers frosted with age.

But he ate his birthday pie and coffee alone, bitterly sorry for himself, vengefully hoping that Lilice had the colic. He refused Gatha's beseech-ings although he guessed she was hungry to sit at his knees. There were vinegar in his pie and gall in his coffee. His hand unsteadily spilled coffee among the cookies on his plate. Sadly he contemplated his birthday. Alone, and nobody caring. Tears rubbed his lids—tears of dolorousness released in beer. He looked in vain for Snoose.

Suddenly he put the dishes aside and stumbled toward the barn, wanting desperately to cry. He came past the chicken coop where the haystack was a loaf of silver gray in the night. His feet were cushioned in sloo grass, himself in shadow.

There they were, the moon splashing over them, unmindful of the earth, those two, Snoose and Em'ly, leaning against a side of timothy, their heads close together, Snoose curling a lock of her hair on a finger.

"Know what I'd like to do?" Johnny heard him say. "I'd like to un-tangle a twist of moonlight and mix it with your hair." He saw Em'ly put a hand on Snoose's cheek for a moment in caress, a low laugh throbbing.

Pain that was stirred by loneliness and not by whisky giddiness gripped him so that tears started again, tears coldly sober. He went away, his steps all at once steady, as if he'd made up his mind.

Before he dived under the covers that night, late as it was, he dragged his boots from under the bed and polished them with fierce rubbings.

He was thorny as a prickly ash on the next Monday. He wanted to say, "Forgive me, Lilice," but the iron in him bent slowly. It was more her fault than his anyway, he decided stubbornly. At recess, however, he rounded a corner of the woodshed and bumped into a group of girls.

Lilice was there, standing alone, the Fleischer girls and Betsy Lorimer regarding her with pursed lips and sneers. He had run into a pause between words. It required no second sight to see that the air quivered between them. Tears blurred Lilice's eyes. The shadow was on her face again. A crushedness about her mouth made him want to rush up and slap the Fleischers. Before he could utter a syllable, held by astonishment, the girls ran off with a triumph on their faces that couldn't be mistaken. With broken entreaty, but wordless, Lilice looked at him, as if begging him for something; then turned and ran, too.

He stared in baffled annoyance. What critters girls were, anyway; about as predictable as colts in a pasture! But tears—Lilice crying—he wished he knew what those Fleischer brats had done to torment her. Stubbornness dissolved. The bell rang.

During the next period he plotted savagely to strangle the Fleischers—at least, drown them, Lilice bowed her head so dejectedly. At noon he came eagerly toward her. She was the last to leave the schoolroom. With imploring in his eyes, he said, "We're going to play 'four in a boat.' Will you—will you be my partner?" His smile was all white teeth and his legs jiggled. "Please." Slowly the syllable in a whisper dragged like a clog from him. "Please." He was empty of further word, this one squeezed through his lips.

She took his eagerness in one square look which he couldn't dodge; a gaze hard yet fair. What started out to be a haughty denial fluttered into friendliness, as if she knew he had apology in his pocket but sewed away and inaccessible, and she took his running to her as a kind of penitence for rudeness and therefore acceptable. More than that, in his humbleness she saw a kind of understanding of what he had seen beside the woodshed. "Of course I will, Johnny." Her voice was low. He swallowed gulpily.

When he glanced at his feet with a great batting of lashes, she twinkled with merriment. "I declare," she said. "Boots. You needn't have." As if he'd asked the question, she told him, "I said to Kurt the other day I was sure you'd smash a toe, going without shoes like that. You wouldn't listen, or I'd have told you." She ended somewhat plaintively, putting blame on him gently. In imagination, then and there, he pounded himself to jelly.

"Lilice," he whispered, not sure that she heard, "you're—you're—oh, I don't know," and caught her arm. He shouted grandly, "Everybody ready?"

When the rest swept along, Snoose reminded him with a chuckle, "We are, when you are."

Never had he remembered "four in a boat" (a stupid game otherwise and kids' truck) so full of rippling sweetness and the solid meat of fun. While they waited for Gatha to decide whether they ought to play "fruit basket upset" next or "last couple out" (minutes linked with the blood beating in his temple), Johnny said, "I'm going bandcutting again. Uncle Herm says maybe pretty soon I can feed." Brag pranced in his jubilation. He didn't notice how Lilice's smile slipped away into a cloud.

"You mean you'll work right close in front of the cylinder teeth?" she asked as if she'd never thought of this before.

"Yep. Herky Morrison got his glove caught last year," he answered thoughtlessly. "He was darned near dragged into the teeth." He rubbed his hands gleefully, the feel of bladed straw already on his flesh. "By Judas, if I ever feed, I'll make those bandcutters sweat."

"I hate them." She spoke softly but her vehemence startled him. "The powers and threshers and all." There was a shadow on her face. He thought of her father, helpless on a stone doorstep.

"Why, Lilice, it's as safe as a baby's cradle," he joked her. "You stand on the separator and feel the cylinder hum in your toes and the shakers rattle your jaws—Judas, you get goose-pimples, I tell you."

"And broken bones, too," she retorted flatly. "Father—" he saw her shiver—"he sits there, day after day and——" She worried a bit of lace on her collar.

"Well, I—accidents happen, but——" He began to stutter.

Gatha shouted, "Let's couple up for needle's eye!" Breathlessly, she begged, "You be my partner, Johnny? Lilice can——"

The bell rang. He relaxed in thankful relief. "Got to run, now," he said, including both in one sweeping nod. The two girls locked eyes in a quick stare before they followed.

At noon he went arm in arm with Snoose to the sun side of the schoolhouse, dinner bucket swinging. There was mirth in the hog-larded bread and laughter in the meat, although he lamented to Snoose, "Why did me and her fight, anyway? I wish the party were tonight."

He flexed the toes of his boots gingerly, longing for that well-being he felt when his feet were bare in mud and earth and sun. Rather wistfully he scratched a place where his flesh itched under cover. "S'pose a feller can't be a kid and go barefooted all his life," he observed with reverent sadness.

Thereafter he cramped his feet into shoe leather and endured the blisters that cracked open the skin between his toes. He achieved decency at last if not liberty. His boots had a polish that bettered Kurt's. He sensed a higher respect for himself in Lilice's glances. He was warmly gratified when even Aunt Phrena admitted, albeit grudgingly, "You'll be a man yet, if you wait long enough."

14

Before the days spilled into November, Johnny was cutting bands again. He stood knee-deep in the straw that slipped between his body and the cutters' table, the geography book closed and its worded leaves hidden, Lilice a lazy comfortable weight in his mind. Soon now Uncle Herm would thresh at her father's place. It would be the first time, for Old Man Rose usually waited for Bory Tetzell's outfit late in the season. But this year Uncle Herm insisted, "No sense letting him sit with a couple of stacks. A neighbor's a neighbor. I don't care what else he is."

Alb agreed and Mr. Schadel gave in, though Mr. Nussbaum glowered: "The Pastor's right about harvesting among the members and not the outsiders."

When rain misted over the valleys, however, and stacks were slants of silver on the wet side and the threshing stopped, he returned to school, reluctance in his gait. Gently malicious, Aunt Phrena, neither dissuading nor encouraging him, said merely, a dour kind of satisfaction in her tone, "Ach, ya, Johnny, he *knows* what he wants. Pieces of school and pieces of thrashing, they fit together." Uncle Herm tugged his whiskers but let the rig and little else catch his attention.

His head so full of threshing that a *rumble-s'rum* confused the arithmetic problem, Johnny wiggled in his seat not far back from where Lilice bent over her geography. The chapter in physiology—the organs of the abdomen—was full of the odor of haymows and horse barns. He was miles behind in classwork. He'd leave the geography class studying in Vermont and come back to find them somewhere near Minneapolis. Once Mrs. Sperry said sharply, "Threshing indubitably calluses the five wits, does it not, John?" The whole school laughed, Mosey Fritz the loudest, though none understood Mrs. Sperry's words. They enjoyed deeply the red on Johnny's face.

One day in arithmetic she sent Kurt to the board. He wove ciphers together in such dizzy columns that Johnny sweat. The show-off! That's for me, Johnny thought. His lips twisted. It irked him to know that Kurt was rods and away ahead of him in being able to say clearly what a page of words finally added up to—agility that would be forever stranger to him.

It was pleasanter to think about Snoose and how together they would go threshing next fall. Lornas Tetzell was bragging that his brother Bory was getting a steam rig and would smoke the power threshers right out of the hills. Mosey Fritz sided venomously with Lornas: "That ought to cook the starch thin in somebody's pot." But he said this when he was on the north side of the schoolhouse and knew Johnny was on the south side, or not there at all.

Uncle Herm and Mr. Schadel laughed at the news. "Wait till he gets stuck in the swamps. He'll need all the teams in Pockerbrush to haul him out."

Johnny heard this with a kind of excitement uncurling inside him. Most of all, it was pleasant to think with sleepy undertones about Lilice bent over her geography book.

One day, for good and all, he left the schoolhouse for the threshing rig and without much regret. Uncle Herm had said with a sidewise glance, "Na ya, Johnny, the cutter quit and I'm shorthanded again. Want to come?"

"Course," Johnny answered. "I made me a new cutter knife." He showed Uncle Herm the mower section he'd fastened slotwise into a handle of wood. Thereafter the stick-knife stayed in his pocket. He sharpened the cutter on the whetstone and was ready. Next week he would be at Lilice's house. It was kind of a song.

But there were days of tiredness when he would have accepted a hundred schools and ten Pastors for one afternoon free of the cutter's knife. Or so he thought. Hour after hour he hacked at the bundles that fell before him. Mornings were frosty now and he shivered; noons warm and he sweat; evenings dank with the feel of cold. When the weather changed with mid-November frigidness, chill winds like currycombs dragged over his face. The draft over the separator, always contrary, billowed dust from the machine about his eyes. He wiped sweat that salted his eyes until they burned flame-edged at each wink.

There was almost urgency in the hope that in the next minute Mr. Schadel would take Herky's place and for a slow breath or two, the cylinder, its teeth blinding with the sun in them, would spin vainly. Then he could unsling his tendons and sinews and let slackness like wine flow into the aches of his body. He yearned for a blanket even on stone and for utter forgetfulness in sleep. He'd mutter savagely, "Could just as well loaf at school as this."

He'd wait for lunchtime with a sharpness of longing that stretched seconds into hours. In a kind of wildness he'd twist toward the house, as if his entreaty would hasten the opening of a door or hurry the women at their cooking. The sight of Mrs. Fleischer's wrinkled cheeks or Mrs. Schimmel's shady bonnet was as sweet as the sandwiches and cookies. For when the women came, puffing a little and shooing children and chickens from their paths, the machines stopped and he could slump down and nibble relief with his bread. That ten-minute space was as precious as the water he gurgled recklessly.

When a box got hot and bubbled oil and the rig halted, he half crouched in his place, watching Heinie and the pitchers crawl about on the stacks, their forks beside them; watching the strawstackers clear a standing space for their feet and scratch chaff from their necks. Sometimes he brushed away the straw in front of him and revealed the wood of the table. It was chipped with knife slashings and roughened with the carvings of initials, crude bodies of naked women and rows of tally-box numbers computing somebody's run of grain. On one board a stud topped a mare; on another a knothole and a carving suggested bluntly a satyrlike penetration: the whittled longings of the inexperienced and the unsatisfied. The table where Jackie stood was smooth. Mr. Schadel had turned the boards. But underneath cobwebs wove girdles on a gallery of nakedness.

When Uncle Herm called, "Hey, Johnny. Crawl under that darn straw rake once and tighten the bur; she's loose again," he moved sluggishly. Afterward his fingernails would leave white trails on his skin where he scratched the grease. His wrists and the upper edges of his hands were powdered with dust. At first he blew it away in puffs; now he let it gather layer by layer listlessly, a part of his skin itself at last. Sometimes he'd boss the old, slow-legged accordion player. "A little more muscle there, Anders Stramff. This ain't a waltz you're playing. Get the bundles over on the table so's Herky can reach 'em."

Anders would laugh, good nature in his face, and lean to say, "You come next Saturday to the granary dance at Blumens'. By Gott, I'll make you sweat, too." Johnny nodded.

Before day ended, weariness meshed him in a web of pain. Cramps knotted the muscles of his legs until he wanted to yell, and his feet, bloodless under the pressure of standing hours in one spot, felt like clods of lead. He had to stomp vigorously to send the blood singing in his toes. During such hours he tasted envy bitter as snakeroot, his head full of Snoose and Lilice easy in their seats at school while here he crawled tired as a dog. Miserably he'd creep into the haymow. But sleep dropped stonelike on him before he could sigh deeply and he lay insensible the night long.

For all the twinges in his joints, however, he wouldn't have given a straw for a desk at school, except that he missed Snoose. When Aunt Phrena finally said that he could at least finish the year with Kurt, he protested loudly.

The hum of the thresher was a melody beginning to ripple in his blood.

"Keep 'er humming at an even pitch," Herky would say, feeding the hungry teeth tirelessly until his motions were a part of Johnny's dreams, disturbing his sleep. "Keep 'er going. Not too high, not too low, but middlin'. A middlin' hum." And soon Johnny came to sense that slowly undulating, even-murmured *rum*-ulation which was a sign of threshing cleanly done, of a cylinder expertly fed. The flows of loosely shaken straw must be steady and scattered the width of the concaves. "You hear it?" Herky would bend toward him. "Purrin' like a he-cat." Johnny's head would bob, and he was sure that he could have put on Herky's gloves and satisfied the roaring appetite of the machine.

To this both Alb and Herky would undoubtedly have agreed. But not Mr. Schadel or Mr. Nussbaum. When Mr. Schadel stood back of the feeder head, watching the crew, crustiness in his gaze, or Mr. Nussbaum dourly shoved his bulk across a stack, they put Johnny on trial. Young sprout with notions, they seemed to say. Watch yourself. Johnny's fingers tightened on the knife handle.

He came to know the bowels of the separator as he knew his own ribs. During a breakdown he'd crawl into its dim, crowded belly, his nose full of a smell like that of a mouse nest—the odor of crushed straw and stringy twine, oil and tar and the dust of weeds. Hammer or wrench clutched in his fist, he'd lie on his back, helping to mend a shaker or a sieve or unclog a plugged-up straw rake. Corner and crevice became as familiar as the seam at the bottom of his pocket. He poked a finger into every oil hole.

Once in a while after dark had put a stop to fork and wagon, somebody tapped a keg of beer. The crew gulped the foamy drink like water, thirst in them like a dry sponge. Johnny liked the gentle headiness that spread a balm upon the soreness of the day. In the haymow Old Anders, perched on a rolled-up blanket, often tweedled a waltz from the white teeth of his accordion, filling the haymow to the rafters with sway-and-surge until a couple of pitchers, excited into longing for softness in their arms, would shamble awkwardly in dance, their steps ruffling the hay and raising a thin dust. And through the music would come the *m-m-ma-aw* of a hungry calf or the snort of a horse, and overhead the flutter of sparrows confused by the lanternlight. With the waltz circling in his head, Johnny would remember his mother, not sadly any more but dreamily, and the red ribbon, its brightness beginning to dim, and Lilice, sweetly though not imperatively.

In the middle of the week they wheeled into the Rose yard where a straw-covered shed stood not far from the black ruins of the lightning-struck barn. Johnny had been more than a little stirred at the idea of cutting bands in Lilice's yard until he remembered that she'd be at school. Besides, the Rose stacks numbered only a setting and a half. With good luck they would be finished and on their way to Peisers' before dark. He'd probably catch no more than a glimpse of her. He wondered about the elder Roses and how it would be eating at the table where her mother, the unbaptized, served potatoes and meat, and where her father dangled his helpless legs. Mr. Schadel, oiling the separator, pretended he didn't care but Mr. Nussbaum was so disturbed, helping to stake the power down, that Alb Hukelpoke jeered, "Look at Arnold, once! Judas, he acts as if he'd put his finger in cow manure, coming here to thrash."

"If I had my way, Rose could knock out his grain with a club." Mr. Nussbaum was curt. "People who stay away from God's Word and don't join the church——" He flung a hard-eyed look at the house.

"Sheetin' Judas, you think you'll get a better place in Kingdom Come because you belong to the Pockerbrush church?" Alb was jovial.

"I got a better chance, by jippers!" Mr. Nussbaum pounded conviction into a stake.

"I wonder." Uncle Herm's voice was quiet. "Those who think themselves safe in the fold—I wonder. Maybe a lot of folks are fooling themselves."

"You made a nice piece of money on that wood deal with him, didn't ya, Arnold?" Alb cut in jibingly, adjusting a chain. "Rose's money suited you all right, didn't it?"

"That's got nothin' to do with it," Mr. Nussbaum blustered. "We had some business——"

Uncle Herm interrupted him. "Here's a man got a year's work in a setting of grain. It ain't my business to say if he's holy enough to thrash for, or bad enough to leave alone. I'll thrash him, if he believes in the Devil."

Mr. Nussbaum was shocked. "The Pastor would like to hear that."

"Maybe he would." Uncle Herm picked up a grease box, unperturbed. "But Rose's grain won't thrash any harder than the Pastor's."

"Freethinker, that's the way you talk, Herman Barewolf," growled Mr. Nussbaum, anger in his words. "In the congregation I came from, they fixed people who didn't belong. Weren't you taught in Catechism that the unbeliever must be cast out?"

"Surely was," replied Uncle Herm earnestly. "But I'll let somebody else do the casting out."

"And you expect the church to bury you when you——" Mr. Nussbaum was beginning furiously when Uncle Herm broke in, "Seems to me I heard something about a feller that's without sin can throw the first stone."

Alb chuckled at Mr. Nussbaum's glowers. Mr. Peiser said, "That tallies with my ideas to a T."

But Mr. Dunkel said surprisingly, "You're both a little off the track. It's not what the Pastor says and it's not what you fellers say. It's what you believe—that's what clinches the nail."

Johnny was warmly grateful to Uncle Herm but wondered whether there wasn't solid meat in what Mr. Nussbaum said. How many times hadn't the Pastor thundered that the unbeliever had no part of grace? He puzzled over Mr. Dunkel's saying.

"I'll thrash Rose's stacks, Arnold. Do what you want," Uncle Herm ended. "It's neighborly. If God wants to kick me downstairs for that— well, I don't mind being kicked."

All morning Johnny watched Old Mr. Rose direct the threshing from his seat on the porch—oats in this bin, wheat in that, the straw pile north of the barn—as if his pain-bleared eyes were birds and flew about the place, and distance held no chains for his flapping bones. Adam the son (Johnny remembered his grief over the burned pony) ran here and sweat there. He was three years older than Kurt, a heavy-shouldered, docile boy, who had left school years before to put his futile strength in the place where his father had stood. Already a kind of slump lay on him, not only on shoulder but on brow, the wrinkles of forty plowing up a forehead not yet twenty and tiredness crow-tracking the corners of his eyes. Johnny liked him, as much for himself as for the hint of Lilice's smile on his lips.

Of her mother he saw no more than a blue dress near the pump. The brightness of water gushing from the spout was a silver glitter against the blue cloth. Mrs. Peiser, over helping her, brought out the lunch. There was a stone jar of juniperade, cool and the color of dark wild currants. Nowhere else had throats been washed so sweetly. Though Mr. Nussbaum tapped his pipe scornfully, Johnny and Alb and Uncle Herm with large helpings lowered the level of coolness swiftly. Once he saw Mrs. Rose gathering an armful of wood at the pile. She was a tall, big-boned woman, large of bosom and gray of hair. Moments later a puff of dark smoke plumed from the chimney. His tongue moistened in spite of dryness and his stomach rolled—dinner was beginning to bubble in the pot.

He was washing at the tin dish under the trees, his cheeks running suds and his hands groping for a towel, when a voice hearty with roundness said, "That's wet as a dishrag. Here's a dry one." He felt the stiffness of new-washed cloth against his neck. A soap-clean smell came to his nostrils. A swipe at his face and through moisture-webbed eyes he looked into that square direct gaze he remembered seeing at the Edgelys'. He hadn't recalled that her skin was as clear as it was, though a kind of weariness lay like a shadow on it.

"So you're Herman Barewolf's Johnny," she said, gathering the soiled towels and hanging up clean ones. Johnny thought of the cloths he'd put his nose into at other places. At most farms there were two towels for the threshing gang, sometimes three, streaked with grime and almost dripping with other men's leavings by the time he picked one up. And those at the Fleischers'—he wasn't squeamish about dirt but he had held his breath and shut his eyes, the towel, burlappy and rough, was so stiff with a week's wiping and one corner so brownish where Mr. Fleischer had sopped tobacco spit from his mouth. He hastily brushed his nose to forget.

"Lilice tells me you're good friends," Mrs. Rose continued, the tiredness in her face lifting.

He twirled a plug of towel end into his ear desperately, cheeks as red as if he'd scrubbed them, before he burst out, "Wish I could draw the way she does. It's—it's as real as a picture."

"You like drawings and music and such things?" She paused in her work, her regard steady.

He didn't try to dodge. "I—I don't know." He swallowed, finding words sticking in his throat; yet he found talking to Lilice's mother someway pleasant, only he wished he did know more about drawing and pictures than the illustrations in the *Prairie Farmer* and more about music than hymn tunes and waltzes and polkas. "Don't know much about them," he admitted honestly. Then to cover ignorance, he said in sober haste, "I like pictures about thrashing rigs and such."

"Yes; oh, yes." A shadow deepened in her voice. "You like machinery. I've heard about that, too." She turned to go.

I've said the wrong thing again, Johnny thought in panic. The sadness on Mrs. Rose's face—that was like the shadow on Lilice's face that day in school.

Over her shoulder Mrs. Rose said, "Lilice plays; pretty well, I say. If you'd like, maybe she'd play for you."

Afterward the memory of that day and night in the house of the unbaptized oiled the sharp edges of many a weariness into smoothness. There was the dinner with a salad which Mr. Nussbaum poked at with his fork but refused to eat and which Alb Hukelpoke ate with his pie, thinking it was a new kind of pudding. . . . Old Man Rose, dried up and wizened except for his dreadful hawk eyes, carried to the table by Adam but cutting his own meat into hunks with a heavy knife . . . the room cool with flowered curtains, and the piano in a smaller room beyond with music on the rack, the word "Chopin" in large, red, blossom-embroidered letters on a cover, and near by a tall case of books . . . the fine white cloth (most tables had red-checkered or oiled stuff) which Uncle Herm, with a wild look at his dusty, grease-soaked sleeves, regarded with alarm until he drew out his large blue handkerchief and spread it solemnly under his plate. He grinned when Mrs. Rose laughed, "Put it back, Mr. Barewolf. My scrubboard won't hurt this a bit." . . . Late afternoon and Lilice standing for a moment in the path, her hair merging with the yellow of the leaves, and her hand lifting for an instant before she vanished indoors . . . Jackie leering at him and cupping his hands as if to cover breasts . . . Lilice running to the barn later, a basket on her arm, and Jackie bending toward him to shout in a lull of work, "Go after her, Johnny! She's hunting eggs. A lot can happen while you're egg-hunting in a horse manger." With any other girl's name he would have found delight and shot back an answer in kind. But Lilice's—he wasn't sure why he drew back, not liking this, irritation rubbing him someway.

What lay pleasantest in his mind in those autumn days was that night and Lilice's playing. Half of the rig stayed in the yard after all. Uncle Herm and Mr. Schadel drove to the blacksmith shop to repair a wheel on the power that had broken as they started to move out. The rest of the crew and the separator drove away for Mr. Peiser's. Johnny remained with Jackie. Around midnight, Uncle Herm figured, they'd have the wheel fixed and be ready to haul the power over.

It was after dark and he and Jackie were helping Adam gather the grain spilled at the feeder head. The lantern stained the kernels a waterish red. Suddenly the piano flung its notes into the silence and the night paused to listen. Softly the music wove over the yard, a song that had in it the loneliness of the unbefriended, of empty chairs and emptier pillows on the bed.

"You hear that?" Adam's voice held pride.

"S-sh." Johnny let the kernels fall.

"She's playing for you, Johnny, eh?" Jackie nudged him. "Maybe she wants you to——"

"Oh, shut your teeth," Johnny snapped impatiently and left Jackie's mouth and the sack open by tossing away a handful of grain and plowing into the dark. . . .

He sat on the porch. The bright window framing Lilice at the piano darkened the night. The piano raced in a reckless, defiant mood and then sank into plaintiveness like that which cried in Old Anders' accordion on nights when he had too many beers and memories of the past beat like wings against the doors of the present. Her head bowed over the keys, as though she were listening. He felt the point of an oat kernel sharp between his fingers and brushed it away, unthinkingly, the music bringing back the voice of his mother singing. Her song was faded now as an old picture but sweet as the first flower in spring. Lilice's hands moved. The melody leaned on the dark.

"Like it?" He jumped. The darkness banged with the two words. Then he saw Mr. Rose blackly in a corner. Without waiting for an answer, Mr. Rose went on, "It's something after a hot day. I got ears if I ain't got legs. That makes up for some things. Not always, though." He spoke as if to himself. "No, doesn't make up for much. Pain ain't the worst a feller faces. Not when God is against ya." His chair screeched. "Go in, young feller, if you want to."

Johnny could hardly mutter, "Thank you, Mr. Rose," as he slipped past, glad to get away. He entered.

Not until her hands lifted from the last echoing chord did Lilice turn to him. The dying sound was a weight on his heart. "I saw you come," she said as if she'd expected him. He saw the red letters of "Chopin" as she arranged the music. "You don't shuffle your feet. Adam always does." The lamp was bright in her hair.

"Play that again, will you?" He spoke abruptly, almost as though in command. Mrs. Rose, overhearing while she shelved her glasses, regarded him with knitted brows.

Lilice shook her head. "I can't, tonight. I'm all rumpled up inside me." There was a woebegoneness about her, head lowered and fingers knotted, that reminded him of her teary eyes that recesstime at school. He wanted to banish with a loud chuckle what troubled her, or else dash into the yard and forget this in the company of Jackie and Adam.

Mrs. Rose stood in the door. "Why don't you run for a bucket of water, Punkin?" she said. "I'll make a fresh pitcher of juniperade."

Lilice started to go. Johnny was quickly at her heels. "I'll help. I'm pretty good at pumping water."

Then from the porch came the sound of a fall, a heavy helpless sound, and a groan. Lilice caught his arm with a low cry. "It's Father. He's tried to get to the stone step again. He says stone is good for him." It was as if she found release in speaking. She would have run but Mrs. Rose's firm tones stopped her. "Nothing you can do, Lilice, except not cry. You know that. Get the water. I'll tend to him."

Through the kitchen and out they went together, this between them, holding them wordless. Halfway to the well they could see the porch and Old Man Rose (it came to Johnny with a jolt that he wasn't older than Uncle Herm). But Old Man Rose was gathered in his wife's strong arms.

For an instant the lighted door was blackened by their silhouette, husband and wife, she carrying him, his legs dangling, his body shapeless against her breast. Then they were gone.

Under the hiccupy squeal of the pump and the later splash of water, he said eagerly, to hide the shivers running in him, "I like that name— Punkin. Bet your ma thought of it."

"She's got a garden full of punkins," she said tonelessly, as if her tongue were miles behind what her brain was thinking.

Off to the east, rising moon radiance burned behind a hill. All at once a kind of tenderness for her swept over him and he wanted to tell her what would soothe her grief. But speech was frozen as water in the spout in winter. Finally, all he could say was, "You play like—oh, I don't know. It makes me want to dance, only I couldn't. Not when you play like that." Even while he spoke he wondered what his words really meant. The pail ran brimming and he spilled it out.

"I'll pump a second bucket," he offered lamely; "it'll be colder." He flinched as icy drops, flung back, struck his hot cheeks. He wished he could see her face. What could he say that would make talking easier? He asked casually, though his ears ached for her reply, "You going to Blumens' Saturday night—to the dance?"

"You're going, I s'pose?" she countered unexpectedly.

"Me? Oh, I don't know. Maybe," he fumbled. "Gatha Blumen goes to dances and I thought maybe you——" He pumped vigorously, sure that he had blundered again.

"I know Gatha goes. But she belongs——" She let the words hang in the noise of the pump before she said, "I think Mama's right. A girl has plenty of time for dancing—after she's seventeen." There were pauses between the last three words.

"Oh, sure, sure," he agreed quickly, disappointed. "No sense in a young one's going——" He trailed off miserably and wished that Snoose were here. Water splashed at the rim. The moon lifted a curved red back. In its pale copperiness he saw that she was crying. "Lilice, I didn't—what did I——" He wanted to stop pumping but, in a sudden fright, dared not.

"Nothing you did, Johnny." He hardly heard her voice. Then she put a hand on his. He almost stopped pumping.

"I'd do anything, if *he* didn't suffer so much," she choked. "Pain, that's all he knows, morning and night. Sometimes when I'm running to the barn, I just slow to a walk. With him tied down like that, I don't run much any more. I feel that it's my fault he suffers so much."

"Your fault?" He was horrified. "Why, that's crazy. How could it be your fault?"

"I don't know." Her hand lifted forlornly, then settled back on his. He stopped pumping. She said as if this couldn't be kept back, "He slipped from the platform and got into the wheels of the power. That was a year before we came up here." She told this, an old story matter-of-factly related, yet with a sadness that quivered with bitter intensity. "They took off his feet. He just sits, banging his chair to pieces when the pain comes." Her voice was a low moan. She was silent a moment.

He wished ardently that he could grab the pail and run, but stood, warmth holding him, a warmth on the top of his hand where hers lay. After a while she asked strangely, "Nobody ever makes fun of you, do they?" Her fingers on his knuckles trembled. "Or calls you——" She couldn't go on. With quick anger he thought of the triumphant jeering faces of the running Fleischer girls.

"Calls me what?" he insisted.

"You never feel sorry about anything, do you?" He was so baffled into silence by her words, that she almost laughed—a muffled, throaty sound that was spare of happiness. "I'm gabbling like a magpie. Come, pail's full." As they went houseward, side by side, the moon threw their shadows faintly ahead of them.

15

They were threshing at the Peisers' on Saturday. All afternoon the crew talked about the dance at the Blumens'. "I'm gonna have one dance in my granary before I put my wheat in," said Mr. Blumen stoutly. "You bring the crowd and I'll furnish the beer." He was a loose-bellied man, Gatha's father, with a face that was red and always a little moist with sweat, as if juices boiling inside him were gently oozing out.

The crew put extra speed into the forks, though Anders quit early, to Johnny's disgust. "I must rub me some sheep's fat into mine fingers," he told Uncle Herm; "otherwise tonight I can't play." He left after lunch. The crew was shorthanded. Uncle Herm dug in his whiskers.

Johnny glowered at the empty place on the stack and the fewer bundles that fell on his table. "Somebody needs to be boss around here," he muttered, throwing his knife at a board. The blade stuck deep in wood. Alb chortled, "Well, go a little slower and the fun lasts a little longer." Nobody else objected; threshing and dancing, after all, were neighborhood affairs.

Johnny would have gone to the dance if Uncle Herm had. But Uncle Herm shook his head. "Old badger like me—after a week's thrashin' I like my bed and plenty of cornhusks in the tick." They both thought of Aunt

Phrena. Both would go to church tomorrow. No decent thresher handled a pitchfork on the Sabbath; no rig ran.

Jackie could hardly wait to wash or eat. "Boy, am I gonna get tooted to the gills tonight!" he bragged.

Herky, almost fresh in a new-washed shirt, said, "Hope some bastard messes with me. I'm spoilin' for a little trouble." His bony knuckles were pointed.

Johnny saw them go with a pang of disappointment. The lantern he held wobbled over the broken straw-carrier slat Uncle Herm was repairing.

Uncle Herm sneaked a glance at him. "When you're seventeen or eighteen she won't try to stop you," he mumbled, as if he were twining a thought of his into Johnny's and finishing it.

"Long time." Johnny sagged over the lantern. Uncle Herm pounded a rivet sharply.

Monday morning was dry and gray and bleary, but no more so than most of the members of the crew. They were still caught in the webs of Saturday night and the dance. Only Anders was cheerful in a baggy sort of way. The others looked as if they'd had what Heinie Beerwagon called a "hell-bear of a time." Johnny was divided between wanting to laugh and feeling envious, they boasted so and hinted with a lifted brow or a kept-back phrase, tantalizing with hidden meaning.

Jackie was greenish. Alb had stomach trouble—belly-worry, he called it. Uncle Herm had to dose him with blackberry brandy now and again. Even so he hung on his whip. The teams, sensing that the iron was out of his curses, jiggled slack-traced around the circle. Mr. Nussbaum grumbled that it wasn't that Alb was sick; all he wanted was the blackberry brandy. The cylinder, lacking momentum, slogged and howled in its teeth until Mr. Schadel swore.

Herky was sickest of all. His arms were wooden and his feeding irregular so that the separator chugged and clogged and the cylinder whined shrilly one moment and growled hoarsely the next. Johnny watched him anxiously. More than one head of grain went through the shakers untouched and the tailings elevator ran full. Uncle Herm, examining a fistful of stems still heavy with wheat, shook his head. He wanted to finish Peiser by noon of the next day, the weather holding dry and the dust whipping where the horses trod.

Mr. Peiser began to damn things fluently. "Drinking's ya all right. But when a man takes a whole Sunday to sober up and then can't hardly stand on his feet—well, what can you do?"

Mr. Nussbaum watched from the granary with a narrow twist of his lips. "Hukelpoke spoils a man's horses the way he handles them, that's what he does," he said to Mr. Peiser, who came by with a shovel. "And I ain't going to have my sorrels spoiled."

"Grain in the straw pile again," Mr. Peiser grumbled. "Feller sweats a whole year planting and harvesting and the damn thrashers pile the grain with the chaff." In irritation, he forgot that at other farms he had been a thresher, too. But today he was the farmer and these stacks his, and that made a difference.

Forenoon lunch was a lack-appetite meal. Herky slumped on the ground, content with a teaspoon of Hoffman's drops in sugar. Jackie was still pukish and when Mrs. Peiser offered him a cheese sandwich, he grabbed his middle and ran vomiting behind the stacks. Mr. Nussbaum muttered about the horses again so that Alb Hukelpoke, easier in his stomach after a fourth dose of blackberry but hiding it, flung the last of his coffee into the grass. "Sheetin' Judas, handle the lines yourself, then! Or you want me to break in somebody else for the job?" Alb looked straight at Johnny and a queer expression grew on his face.

"No, no," protested Mr. Nussbaum in great haste. "You drive, you drive."

After lunch threshing was no better. The cylinder grunted. At the machine Mr. Schadel glared at Herky. "Sure as hell, Monday morning is the shirttail of Sunday," he growled and disappeared behind the separator. Herky was glassy-eyed now; sweat trickled from his yellowish-tinged face; his arms moved like a tired-out swimmer's. Johnny was worried into vigilance.

All at once Herky sagged over the table and fell against Johnny's shoulder. "Can't make it," he gasped. "My guts is afire." He stepped down, collapsing on the pole.

Before he knew what he did, Johnny got around the table and stood firmly in Herky's place. The cylinder began to raise a whine. He must choke that mounting shrillness. Beside him, Jackie goggled, sickness momentarily forgotten, his mouth opening in surprise. Old Anders gaped in a moon-round amazement. For a second the rest of the pitchers stood, their forks poised.

Johnny tossed the knife on the cutters' table, yelling, "Get in there and cut, Anders," his voice carrying strongly. Anders hesitated and then came. Jackie slipped his blade through a band. Johnny stood before the blur of those flying teeth, hungry for straw or stem or human bone. He hardly breathed and his belly was tight. "Bundles! bundles!" he shouted.

Afterward Uncle Herm used to say (though Aunt Phrena wouldn't listen), "Bull wheels of Moses, there was Herky on the ground, a fist in his stomach, and the separator goin' wild! And that little stinker stepped into Herky's place and laid the straw down as nice as a hoptoad. Old Schadel coulda chewed weeds when he saw. 'Gott in Himmel,' he says, 'he'll crowd the concaves and smash everything to hell!' He cooled off, the machine was running so smooth. After a while he got Bachmann out of the straw pile to feed. But that Johnny, he held her down by the tail, all right, while he was feeding."

It was no longer than the time it takes to pitch half a load of bundles before Bachmann came. Johnny took up the knife in the bandcutter's place again. But for that interval, light on his toes, his whole body swaying to the rhythm of his curving arms, a glow on his face not yet hidden by dirt, he laid bundles of heads as if in sacrifice before the snarl of this demanding god; and like deity, the hunger of its insistence never once was satisfied. And in that interval, while Alb whooped his approval and Old Anders cut bands in awe-struck obedience and Mr. Nussbaum was sour, he knew (as if he hadn't known before) and Mr. Schadel knew and the rest, that one of these days he'd take his stand beside Herky; beside any one. Each slash he made the rest of that forenoon was whetted with satisfaction.

At dinnertime, the crew was reserved except to mutter, "Darn little legscrew, he didn't do so bad." Their silence told more than their grunts. Anders said proudly, "You kept the cylinders humming, Johnny." Jackie had a mild attack of jealousy, although he was free with his wonder.

But Mr. Nussbaum mumbled over his sauerkraut, "Next thing he'll want to drive the horses on the power. Little tails get such big notions." Johnny's teeth bit into a hunk of bread sharply.

"Not a bad idea." Alb gingerly helped himself to the milk soup with cinnamon which Mrs. Peiser made for his roiled stomach. "Not bad a-tall. Sheetin' Judas, he can swing a team around on an Indian penny and not a hoof'll touch the war bonnet Old Longacre's daughter is wearing!" Mr. Nussbaum slopped cream in bleak disagreement, in no hurry to argue with Alb's pepperiness.

Dinner over, they went back to work. Between Hoffman's drops and blackberry schnapps, Herky managed to stiffen his back enough to return to the feeder's platform. But Alb's long body slumped. The soup was no help to his intestines, he said gloomily. "It's gonna begin streakin' through me like water," he prophesied darkly. "You fellers be ready with a handful of straw, if I get the runs and light out for the bushes." He haw-hawed weakly.

But the gleam in his eye was stronger than his stomach. When Johnny helped him hitch up the teams, he said, "No, young feller, ain't nothing you can do, unless you want to shoot an old 'coon like me that don't know better'n to get pickled in beer." His glance followed Johnny, leading the horses to water; there was a glow in it. "Guess this is as good a time as any to show Nussbaum who's boss. I'm gonna like this play-sick."

At afternoon lunch when Mrs. Peiser brought sandwiches, molasses cake and cookies to the yard in a clothesbasket, Alb couldn't nibble a bite, he said, though his look was hungry.

Johnny wolfed the bread and meat. "You sweat a lot, don't you?" asked Mr. Dunkel. When Johnny nodded, he added, "That gets the thrasher's belly out of you." The crew bunched around the basket. Mr. Dunkel let a thread-waisted yellow wasp feed on the jelly that clung to a fingernail. It buzzed hungrily, drunk on plum jelly, crawling over his horny flesh. Then it made off awkwardly in autumn spurts of flight, short and unwieldy.

Crouching over his knees, Alb said provocatively, "That damn sorrel of yours is up to his tricks again, Nussbaum. Acts like he's pulling the whole rig, as long as I got my eye on him. Soon as he gets behind my back, the bastard lazes in the tugs and hardly moves. I'll step him up yet, though." Mr. Nussbaum didn't know whether to be pleased or annoyed.

Mrs. Peiser waved her apron to shoo the flies off the cake. "They surely love to suck that m'lasses."

Uncle Herm gulped the strong steaming black coffee. "Hot weather in fall and hot coffee for lunch. That sweats a feller's underpants wet." He helped himself to a sandwich before he declared to Mr. Schadel, "That left shakerbox is hot again. Moses Almighty, is she sizzling!"

"Know it, the bitch." Mr. Schadel absently licked jelly from a finger that was smeary with grease and got both in his mouth. He spat loudly, his lips drawn back like a calf's with the taste of oil. "*Himmel Donnerwetter!*" he howled, snatching a handkerchief from a pocket and rubbing his tongue. "If that don't taste like horse muck, I wonder what does." The circle laughed, Mrs. Peiser joining primly though her daughters with heartiness. Mr. Schadel went on, "That box got to have new packing tonight. You got a piece of leather laying around, Peiser? I used the last strip this morning."

"I saw an end hanging in the granary," offered Mr. Nussbaum, and Peiser nodded.

"Come along, then. I need it." Mr. Schadel shook the coffee grounds in the grass and put away his cup. "You fellers start up when you're through eating." He arose with a grunt. "Hukelpoke there is green enough to paint from."

Said Mr. Dunkel out of the wisdom of much driving, "No trick now to handle four teams on the power. Let me tell you, though, 'taint long ago

there was more oxen than horses. Then we hooked up a couple of steers
with a span or two of horses. Whoop-Jinny-and-fall-down, the trouble we
used to have!" His plump face creased with memory.

"Sure." Alb pulled slightingly at a stem of shepherd's-purse. "Oxen
goes best in a straight line. But the teams used to go so fast in the circle,
the oxen got dizzy. Half the time you had to stop to get the blind staggers
out of their legs."

"My bullies never did." Mr. Dunkel tapped his cup defensively. "Course,
we didn't go so fast," he admitted grudgingly, loath to leave as much as a
slur on his animals.

"Sheets, no!" Alb muttered and ended the argument with a pea-green
grin and a plaintively hypocritical "Ah, Judas, my belly!"

With the last sandwich chewed and sloshed down with a wash of coffee
and Mrs. Peiser putting the tablecloth back over what was left in the basket,
the crew trudged back once more to places where their boots had moved
before, the pitchers to the stacks, the grain men to the wagons, the straw
men to the straw pile, Herky with Johnny and Jackie to the feeder. "Last
leg of the day," Johnny exulted.

Alb woggled to the nearest team and leaned against a sweep pole, one
eye wide in the direction of the granary. "Johnny," he called in a weak
voice. When Johnny came, he moaned, rubbing his stomach, "Guess my
balance wheel is clean out of kilter." He looked up quickly. "You drive."

"Me?" Johnny stepped back as if struck by a poleax.

"Take 'em easy but let 'em know you're boss. That's all there is to it."

"Oh, gosh, Alb." He was in a rush of doubt. "I'd like to try but——"

"Hop up, then."

Alb's confidence in him was like a hand on his shoulder but he fumbled,
"I dunno, I— Mr. Nussbaum, he's purty particular about his team and——"
Blood pounded in his ears.

"Judas Proost, I'm driver here! Never mind Nussbaum." Alb moved
irritably. "Besides, I'd like to show him what's what around here."

At the separator men began to glance inquiringly toward the power.

"Well, I——" Johnny began and suddenly straightened. "Sure, I will."
Breath hardened his belly. The kingpin of the rig——

"That's the sausage. I'll help you get started." Alb shouted, "Anders, you
can cut bands for a spell."

Johnny handsprung to a sweep pole and mounted the power. A tingle
prickled his toes as he put his feet on the platform where the grease tub
stood and where Alb's shoe leather had worn the wood smooth with
shuffling, whip in hand. The whole crew turned to watch, the pitchers

making inclines as they hung on their forks. Anders Stramff lifted the cutter's knife in wonderment. Jackie wore a "now-this-beats-all" expression. The straw men on the pile were hidden to their suspender ends in the loose straw. Mr. Dunkel stood with a steady gaze among the grain men. Johnny felt their eyes like so many flung bolts bouncing against his senses.

He picked up the bull whip, the breath stinging his nostrils, his lips pinched tightly and half his forehead crawling with wrinkles. Here he stood on a small square platform, the power and its snarl of gears under his feet, around him the four teams hooked to the four sweep poles, each span tied to the pole ahead of it. Not a strap of leather did he have to swing between himself and a horse, by which he could have gee-ed or hawed the animal. Voice and whip were his reins; the round of the circle and long practice the guides.

For a space of panic Johnny hesitated, sweat moistening his armpits. Suddenly he bellowed, "Jeru-u-u-sal'm, lay into the leather there!" His fingers tightened on the whip. What laughter would babble from the separator if not a hoof stirred, not a wheel turned! But the horses knew this voice that had brought them cans of feed and buckets of water and scratched away the tiny black flies that swarmed in their ears. Before Alb could catch a bridle to start the circle moving, two teams lunged forward, his and Mr. Schadel's. Mr. Nussbaum's sorrels and Mr. Peiser's blacks stepped uncertainly. The sweep, turned by the other teams, knocked at their heels. The gears and the couplers of the tumbling rods revolved unsteadily, clattered dully and jerked; stopped, started again. Cog protested bangily against cog; the tumbling bucks wobbled.

"I'll smash something, sure as poppin'," Johnny gasped in a sort of fear. Alb watched him, feeling that he was going to be really sick. At the separator somebody told Uncle Herm. Men had questions in their regard. Johnny felt tightness pulling at him like hands. Desperately he yelled, "Gee-up, there!" at the Nussbaum horses. The whip in his hand uncoiled and licked out like a snake's tongue, exploded in a pistol shot of sound. At once traces jingled into tautness, the gears hitched but whirred faster, more smoothly, the "knuckles" merged their separate *ken-nock-a-ken-nock-as* into a steady clatter. "Come on, now!"

Under his yells, less strident now, softer and more coaxing, the teams went into a pace that sent a smile over Alb's lips. Johnny flicked a glance at him. The tightness relaxed at Alb's vigorous approval.

With the whip and a long yell he touched the speed up a step faster. He felt gear and cog vibrating under his soles; heard the sucking slutching noise of grease. A kind of smoothness ran in the iron. Herky waved to him and motioned the pitchers to work. Jackie and Anders were ready with the blades. Johnny saw them bend their muscles. Bundles twisted on the fork, landed on the tables, moved under Herky's elbows. When the straw met the brush of the cylinders, Johnny felt the slight slowing of the gears, as if a brake had been applied and a weight were holding back pinion and wheel. He shouted again and velvety smoothness flowed like oil. He could see straw pushing up the slant of the carrier. The spout at the end of the tailings elevator streamed with chaff and unthreshed heads of grain and straw. They were brought back to the cylinder for a second gnash of steel, since they had escaped the first.

Suddenly Johnny laughed, a long laugh with face upturned and white teeth shining, the furrows above his eye uncrawling. Nerve and sinew unthreaded. He stood, free and easy beside the whip. Even then, this first time his legs spread commandingly over the wheeling iron, he was blindly aware of something in his hands (not tangible as leather is or fork-handle oak), something that was more potent than whip or club or bulging shoulders.

He didn't know why but in a swift moment he sensed every muscle in his body firm with a queer elation that was sweet as bread to hungry teeth, as good as the honey-colored thought of Lilice—almost. Power— power which spun iron and lifted shakers, which ripped the coffined life of wheat from its husk and poured grain from the spout into the buckets in the tally box. Power which was deaf to any thought about the sweat of a pitcher heaving the bundles correctly; about a feeder offering stems to the cylinder or the grain men pulling the heaped bucket past the tally arm in the register box. "I'm the boss," he exulted. Crushed into forgetfulness were Aunt Phrena's horny-hided words and the wormwoody questions he jabbed into his own flesh. "They're going to come crawlin' to me. I'll show *her*." Power—and it lay under his hand, at the touch of a whip, in a bark from his throat.

As he was to do many times thereafter, he lifted a heel on the grease tub. The smell of horse wet and manure trod into the earth was pungently rich, an aroma suggesting fertility and strength and the endless cycle of kernel to manure, to earth, to blade, to kernel: the immutable mutations of cellular destiny. Jubilantly he returned Jackie's hand wave and raised the whip to salute Alb—Alb who behaved as if he wanted another schnapps now. One by one the teams passed around him over the box concealing the first length of the tumbling rod. Dust strung away from the circle like a mist cloud hanging over a meadow.

Then Mr. Nussbaum and Mr. Schadel tore over the grass of the yard, Mr. Schadel slapping a piece of leather, Mr. Nussbaum beelining for his team. Johnny saw them as figures running in a far-off valley. Even if bull wheel or pinion had been silent, he wouldn't have heard their shouts. He was ear-stopped now. Uncle Herm stood near the feeder, wrench in hand. Mr. Dunkel poised a sack.

"Hold the teams back, by jippers, hold 'em back!" yelled Mr. Nussbaum. Then he ran squarely into Alb.

Alb thrust him aside roughly, seeing what he meant to do. "If you grab a bridle of your team, Arnold, by Judas, you dicker with me. I started him off."

"Who told you to let a little hind-end like him drive my team?" Mr. Nussbaum began to foam.

"Sheetin' Judas Proost, I'm driving this power!" Alb began blazing. "If I say Johnny takes my place, that settles it."

"Why you always siding with that kid for?" asked Mr. Nussbaum, furiously truculent.

"I'm siding with nobody," roared Alb, his lips whitening. "But I'm not standing in a feller's way when he wants a chance to show what he can do." Suddenly he thrust his lean face near Mr. Nussbaum. "You've been eggin' me long enough, Arnold Nussbaum. I'm belly-sick of your horse muck."

All at once they were striking at each other; then they were rolling on the ground. There was a snarl of cloth as a shirt ripped. A horse shied from a leg swiftly upflung. But Johnny drove, all his strength set on keeping power and separator evenly droning. This struggle between neighbors was oddly at distance from him.

Uncle Herm and Mr. Dunkel pulled them apart. There was a scratch on Mr. Nussbaum's cheek. Alb rubbed the blood splotching his chin and shouted, "You put a hand on a bridle and, by God, you unhook your spavin-legged, double-crosseyed crow's meat and go home. You can knock out your wheat with a hammer and a floursack, all I care. I ain't thrashin' for you."

Mr. Schadel joined them. What he and Uncle Herm said to them Johnny never knew; cared about less. But their anger simmered to glares. Perhaps Mr. Nussbaum realized that his stacks, as yet unthreshed, were weathering darkly by the day. Both knew how the neighbors regarded those who split a threshing ring. Mr. Nussbaum flung away, his ire by no means softened at the sight of Mr. Schadel reluctantly admiring Johnny standing, chin high, on the power.

Johnny's long yells were more like pieces of song—songs that were part of the steady note of the separator, of the low *riddle-raddle* of gears slushy with grease, the song of the thresher.

It was dusk when the sweeps halted at last. Johnny stepped down. A glint of fading red from the afterglow struck brightly over his knee on a place worn shiny on a chain. For a moment a tinge of crimson hung about his shoulders. The snort of a horse was a crash of sound near him. Dark figures gathered about the separator and a batlike shape crouched on the feeder head. There was a moment when stillness lay heavy as a blanket over the yard.

Then across the hills rushed a sound queer in their ears. It was high-pitched and like two notes on an organ played together, clear and somehow pleasant, as if it might break into melody any moment. Something like it they heard in winter when the sawmills ran, but that was hoarse and guttural. This was a long spear of shrillness hurtling over ridge and valley, rousing up the echoes.

"It's Bory Tetzell," Johnny was the first to break the stillness that followed. "The whistle on his steam engine."

"Aw, no," Mr. Dunkel scoffed from darkness, his voice plain but himself unseen. "How could he get over from Loon Lake?"

"It's him." Johnny slapped his dusty jacket excitedly. "It's the bull-traction engine. Lornas says with that engine Bory in a day can thrash again as much as with horses."

"Lornas can ride a bull's tail, too." Uncle Herm's tone was disparaging in shadow.

"And Bory'll get stuck in the swamps twice as often as with horses." Mr. Schadel spoke out of the dusk wherein he was working. "Oh, I guess we'll still be chasing horses around the power when Tetzell's engine is back in the woods with the sawmills. That's the only place for a steam engine."

"Yah, that I think, too." Anders Stramff joined the general notion.

They returned to their jobs, this momentary disturbance not troubling them as much as a twist in a belt or a slat broken on the strawstacker. They had conquered this day though they were tired. Let tomorrow bristle with its own Bory Tetzells and new steam engines.

Johnny began unhitching, his head lifted as though he were listening. The sound was gone but a kind of echo lingered in his ears.

Long after Jackie snored and the crew moved restlessly in sleep, Johnny tossed uneasily, drowsiness elusive. There were crowding in his mind the troubling hours of that afternoon. The whip was in his hand again, the horses passing, teams in review, a piece of straw whirling in a yellow blur around a tumbling rod, the might of wheels grinding. Too much in tumult for repose, he slipped into his clothes at last, crept downstairs and out. Even the smell of manure was stale at this hour.

A hazy moon burned copper-yellow on the barn side. The separator was a black mass of shadow, the power octopuslike with its long arms stretched out, silent and lifeless now. He crossed the yard with long strides. Once his toe caught a neckyoke carelessly flung near a pole; he stumbled. The Peiser dog grumpled from his house but took a friend's smell in his nostrils and trotted over. His nose was wet in Johnny's hand.

Johnny climbed to the platform and sat on the grease tub, scarcely noticing the coldness of the barrel top chilling his flesh. The moon laid bronze on his tanned face. He shivered, more with excitement than with the night cold, the rig alive again with belted wheel and fanning sweep and the clutter of rods, men putting their muscle energy on fork or bundle or sack. Mingled with the suspiration of the dark which is like a sigh out of midnight, he fancied he heard, far away in another valley (it may have been in another age), his mother singing,

"Johnny behind the rocking chair."

But the words tangled with the clash of gears, became lost . . . and the moon's yellow was like hair, honey-hued hair that waved and danced and changed to stems and beards and heads of grain . . . wheat in waving miles bending over the ridges, over the prairies and into Dakota beyond, as Uncle Herm had spoken once long ago. And rising like sharp points of cloud, a whistle-screech tore through the fabric of moon and shadow.

He shook himself. The night was rock-still, as if it had ears and were listening. Faintly rose the rush of water over rock in the creek; faded. He stood up, his shadow grotesque on a sweep pole. Then he bent swiftly. He pulled off his shoes and stockings and jumped into the trodden circle. Dust, cold as the flour Aunt Phrena brought downstairs in January from the winter-icy attic, exploded over his bare toes and ankles. Slowly he padded where that afternoon the horses had plodded, the dog at his side; and the moon yellowed the dust that puffed up so that he had gold at his heels. Once around. He stopped. Before him lay the tracks of his bare feet plain in the carroty-colored light; even the toes were as distinct as the cushion marks of a wolf in winter snow. Kid's foot, he said to himself; kid's truck. A kind of sadness was in his saying. *And Time spun the cylinder and grain fell from the head.* The hourglass tipped, and the boy in him paused reluctantly and ran out: the season of growing weather slowed to the season of hardening kernels.

He shivered again. "Devil grab such a fool!" he muttered. He climbed back on the platform and, blowing the powdery dust away, jerked his shoes over his feet. He stood straight and firm beside the whip he caught up. "All right then," he half whispered harshly, "if it's *him* that's in me." His shadow was pointed as a black spear. The lash of the whip curled limply. But the dog put tail between its legs and slunk off, whining. For the length of time it takes a shadow to move a hand's width across a board, Johnny stood there, jaw clamped. What was past, was behind his heels; what before, ahead of his toes,

Part 3

THE SEASON OF
HARDENING KERNELS

H E WAS seventeen the Sunday Bory Tetzell drove past the Marchen gate and he saw the "bull engine" and caught for the first time the queer mingled odor of steam and coal smoke and hot grease. It clung in his nostrils.

That was another short-crop year. "Three in a row now." Uncle Herm was grim. "Don't know what we'll have to thrash this fall except cockle seed and bull thistle. Bory Tetzell's going to thrash his neighbors and go right out to the flats. No money thrashing here. Ain't much here."

For weeks the sun dawned in lemon and set in crimson with a stretch of unscratched milky blue between. "The Lord's blue," Mr. Dunkel called it but Alb Hukelpoke said his potatoes needed rain. The fields lay weather-dried and sun-parched. A stone dropped in a short-stemmed wheat patch sent a cloud of black dust exploding upward. The creek ran itself almost out of sight among the rocks. Minnows, trapped in the pools, settled vainly at the bottom, dark swarms of them rooting at the merciless stone. When they lay on their sides, silver lined the shallows. Johnny caught bucketfuls and let them swirl away in the deeper channels toward the river. He had plenty left over for bait. And above him, flipping his tail on a dying limb, the belted kingfisher waited, sleek and fat, and rattled his bill in the thirsty land.

Juneberries, blue-skinned and growing juicier with each day's squeezing drought, ripened in such clusters that their slender branches were arches of purple fruit. Bird droppings were indigo on fence posts and rails. "It is always so." Aunt Phrena nodded emphatically. "A drought year is a June-berry year. The Lord always saves something from the fire, as Brother Erdman says." She was incensed, however, when the birds, flying over her Monday wash, left grape-colored stains on her white sheets. "Shoo, you long-legged beasts!" she puffed, waving an arm of Uncle Herm's shirt at the robins, the grackles and the catbirds that idled, Juneberry-full, in the basswood trees. "Why the Lord made birds nasty so that I have to do my washing twice, I don't know," she fretted, hurrying the clothes inside.

In the upper pastures the hazel leaves began to fold and dry. As if sun and searing winds were minor plagues and not enough, grasshoppers milled over the fields; the wheat stalks bent under the destroying weight. In the corn patches the noise of their chewing on the leaves was like paper crackling, until Johnny was sure not a spear of green would remain.

To the south on the "prairies," folks were dragging "hopper dozers" across their fields—troughs of tin, the insides of which were smeared with sticky tar or oil. From a rack just behind the trough they hung a canvas to force the pests down. Bushels and baskets of them, their wings webbing with gluey death, the grasshoppers fell. They were scraped out in piles and burned. Fires stank with their roasting bodies, a new Gehenna. But clouds more, alive and hungry for green, drifted from acre to acre. Where they lay their hunger down, only the brown earth remained.

Unimpressed, Mr. Dunkel snorted, "You should have seen them in seventy-six. You had to tie the bottom of your pants shut, or those hopping devils would crawl into your underwear. What they really liked was onions. Whoop-Jinny-and-fall-down, they ate the onions out of the ground and left the holes; and the chickens ate the 'hoppers and we couldn't eat eggs or chickens, they tasted so of onion and grasshopper juice." Johnny was glad that up here in the ridges, less of the evil on wings came flying, though no one escaped ravage entirely.

Rains when they swept over the hills were gossamer-thin—"mosquito drizzle," Uncle Herm said. "One drop for every forty acres. You can't grow wheat on that." There was envy almost in knowing that west of Mary's Hill and in scattered dribbles over the Valley, showers fell in puddles and the grain lifted a rich head. "That's where the thrashers will hike for, this fall," Uncle Herm maintained, worry like a kind of dust on his face. "Bory Tetzell's going to knock out his neighbors' stacks and then off to the flats. He's trying to get Norton's job, this year. Norton's given up using his own rig."

Most of Norton's fields, moistened by a slanting shower or two, were better than the lean acres of his neighbors, better than Uncle Herm's. Aunt Phrena sighed martyrlike. Johnny remarked to Snoose not without malice, "Wonder how she squares *that* up with the Book," and regarded the dark woods over the creek—Norton's.

By the time they reached the hills, the clouds were not much wetter than wrung-out towels. More than once that summer as the fields shriveled toward the harvest, Johnny wondered whether this was what the Pastor meant, what Aunt Phrena gabbled about—the year of the locust and of bitter bread.

He grumbled over the hay he was raking for the barn, impatient and restless, now that school days were past, the final book closed for him and

the future like a hedge of prickly ash before him. School was ended for
Lilice also, he knew. She was at home with soft hands for her father and
the curses he hurled from his bed. Sucked as dry with pain as the fields
were with drought, he lay at last as flat as a man can and still go unburied.
Only when Lilice's fingers twinkled over the keys and the piano mourned
in the lower octaves did he sigh and let woolgathering release the hard
ropes of ache.

Johnny had seen her at the Edgely granary "raising" after corn-planting
time, and felt a pang at the tremble of her lip as she greeted him. When
he asked, "Your pa?" she shook her curls. "I shouldn't have come. Mother
said I ought, though. She's pretty well tuckered out herself. If he gets
worse while I'm away, it—I'd—I'd feel that I was to blame."

"Why do you take it that way, the blame, always?" he questioned
brusquely. "No sense in that. Your ma, she——"

"Don't say a word about her, please, Johnny." Her voice was low but
there was such hard insistence in it that he was silenced. "She's the one
that holds us together. Without her, I'd—we'd——" She turned away
abruptly.

"Lilice, I'm——" He floundered. "It's always wrong, what I say. Always."

He hung his head so miserably that she moved as if to put a hand on his
sleeve but didn't; only said gently, "No, Johnny. What you say is right.
You make me feel that it's right. But I'm—I'm so mixed up inside me."

She went back to a pile of studding where Adam, her brother, was
talking with Lena Haber. He and Lena were "going steady," the neighbors
said. Johnny watched her go, distress tugging at him. "I'd like to waltz a
smile on her face," he told himself. "That's what I'd like to do."

He remembered his words as he stabbed the pitchfork into the sod one
day. "Waltz her. Slim chance I've got." He saw Aunt Phrena coming
into the meadow, lunch basket in hand. "Slim chance. Feller can't go
anywhere, dance nor nothing, *she's* always in your britches." Heinie Beerwagon was attending the shindandies; Lornas said he'd as soon miss a meal
as a dance. Gatha Blumen was going, and without her folks at that, the
neighbors cackled. But Mrs. Blumen said she wasn't afraid, her children
had been brought up on the Catechism and the Book and knew which was
their right hand and which their left. She didn't mind if Gatha went to
the neighborhood dances where people she knew gathered. The Pastor had
other ideas.

Johnny and Kurt went only under the protection of Aunt Phrena and
Uncle Herm although Aunt Phrena admitted that Kurt was growing so
lunky he could probably go by himself. By her tone, she meant that

Johnny couldn't. Which made him vow, "I'm going, the first chance I get." In spite of Sophie's instruction he had never led a girl in the dance.

Lilice stayed at home and for that he was selfishly glad. She was stuck under her mother's thumb, Mrs. Peiser said. No use in the young bucks going over to ask her; her father was so grim, they hadn't enough courage to screw up. Good! thought Johnny but to himself. The notion of Lilice waltzing in the arms of Arty Nussbaum or Lornas Tetzell filled him with an uneasiness he couldn't explain.

It was more than the heat and the scanty wind-ruffled cocks of sloo grass that brought the grumbles from him. He poked at the hay. "Just like last year—thin as a broncho's hide and stiff as wire. It is going to be like this always? You pitch hay into the barn in July and pitch it down in December; you pitch it into the cows one day and pitch it out of the barn the next, all manure, and haul it to the field. It's——"

"Can you think of a better way to make the fields rich?" Kurt interrupted him. Over her lunch basket, Aunt Phrena wheezed near by.

"Rich for the weeds, yes. We keep hustling all right," Johnny granted. "But where do we get to?"

Aunt Phrena, listening while she opened the basket, said grimly, "Where you want to get to—a feather bed? Man was made to work."

Uncle Herm flung his fork aside and wiped sweat before he sat near the lunch basket. "We could be worse off. In the big towns folks are kicked from their jobs; hundreds marching around the country looking for work. Banks are going broke, too."

Kurt twisted his lip in slyness. "Maybe you want to start on your own, huh, Johnny?"

"Maybe." Johnny was vague, avoiding the pin point of detail but suspicious at the question. There were fewer stacks in the meadow that year and less hay in the mow than Johnny could ever remember.

Then one day the bank at Loon Lake closed its doors. Farmers drove into town, buggy whips in their fists but tightness in their throats. At first they thought the cashier had run away with the money. He hadn't, they found, although, white-faced and trembling, he had sweat in explanation. The farmers returned to their acres. They looked at ashy earth and pitiless sky and found no answer.

And a sort of fear crept over the hills, fear of unfilled bins and pockets empty of silver and want stalking the heel. Some folks packed their duds and moved to Fergus and even to St. Paul, there to sweat under the lever and the wheel. The Roses were heels over in debt; how much longer Norton would carry them, nobody knew.

Even Mr. Marchen, losing some of his levity, shook his head over his mortgages. "Liable to lose the place yet, kids," he told his family. He had to think about Sophie, bellying with child again and birthing near, and about her husband. There was the house on the eighty almost ready for them in the fall. But there might not be a housewarming for them. "Clymy's like a guinea rooster," Mr. Marchen said dispassionately. "He's all right to have run around in the hen coop but cripes, he's no man."

At the store and the blacksmith shop and in the gatherings after the services at church, Johnny heard the neighbors in harsh complainings over the "Crime of 1873" and "goldbug conspiracy" and "fifty-cent dollars." He made neither head nor tail of it, although nobody needed to tell him that times were hard and money scarce.

Kurt chattered airily about cheap silver and expensive gold, until Johnny told him he'd know more about it if he had some. Aunt Phrena, assured of sustenance by other means than economics, said folks ought to be thankful if they had pickles and sowbelly: grumbling never did fill a lunch pail.

Once Alb Hukelpoke slapped two coins on the blackened wood of Mr. Jimpson's counter, a liberty-head nickel and an Indian-head penny. "'Silver coinage free!'" he scoffed. "They'd beat us out of our last whisker, those money men in Washington." He tapped the penny scornfully. "They used to make us believe that she was an Indian, that girl there. First Americans, free people. Horse balls. White she was and Old Longacre's daughter. He was a politician or an engraver, or something that Washington pays big money to. Sheetin' Judas!"

Warmly Alb lifted the "liberty head." "A nickel, they say, but no 'cents' on the back—no sense in the head, either." He scratched his cheek ruefully. "This nickel cost me five dollars, about ten years ago. I thought I was gettin' a five-dollar gold piece. It's about the same size, but it's nothing but gilt over nickel. Copperplatin', Banker Ford calls it. Five dollars shot for a nickel. And that's about the way with them Washington money men."

Uncle Herm drooped into the house one day in July, worry creased in his eyes. Heat rushed in with him. "Bull wheels of Moses, this'd dry a calf's pizzle!" Johnny grew thirsty at the way Uncle Herm swallowed a dipper of water. "Be lucky if we can fix the busted things on the thrasher this year. Can't think of buying new stuff. Money costs twelve, fifteen percent to rent."

"Trouble, trouble in everyone's mouth!" Aunt Phrena was doleful over the Book.

"Norton's been purty good about it."

"Huh." Kurt spoke up. "Foreclosed on the Baumans, didn't he?"

"Oh, sure." Uncle Herm sagged. "But Norton's pinched too. Can't blame him too much if he——"

"—if he forecloses on the Barewolfs—" Johnny could have finished Uncle Herm's sentence. He listened with a prickle of apprehension. This he had heard before: debt and crop failure and animal loss. But never had it come as close as his own shirt; never had it threatened to crawl inside, as now.

"It is the day of the Beast, as Brother Erdman says," Aunt Phrena predicted gloomily. "Judgment is just around the corner and them that's touched pitch—well, they better repent in a hurry." Without haste she probed Johnny with a look. Now that she'd given up the preacher school, she hovered like a hawk over the notion of keeping him in the white innocence of a "good young man." So she said. As if making certain of two roads to heaven, she prayed at Brother Erdman's meetings as faithfully as she did at the Pastor's Sunday services, to the Pastor's growing ire.

Johnny left the house. Heat burned in the fields. A robin, clinging dispiritedly to a rail on a fence, was slack-winged and open-mouthed.

Snoose met him in the path. Sweat buds shone on his forehead. What he said scattered for Johnny an afternoon of fishing, and sharpened the uneasiness that had come with Uncle Herm's complaining. "I'm scared we got to leave our place," Snoose told him.

"Leave? You mean move away?" Johnny felt that somebody had poked him hard in the ribs.

"Pa and Ma went to Mary's Hill. I don't know what they'll be able to do about the mortgages. Ma bawled this morning."

Johnny picked to pieces the green sack of a hazel nut, half-formed and juicy, the kernel small and white. Snoose gone and the place next door empty; worse: strangers setting their truck in the places where he and Snoose had wrestled and laughed boyhood into youthfulness.

"Clymy needs machinery," Snoose said wearily. "Sophie's ready to have another kid. They can't have both, I guess." Snoose slivered a twig. "I—you heard——" He hesitated, then said miserably, "Adam Rose went by this morning. He says they'll prob'ly leave this fall."

The hazelnut slipped in Johnny's hand. "The Roses too." His tone was flat. Fragments of green fell over his loosening fingers.

Snoose nodded. They sat still, oppressed by more than the heat. A jay mewed hungrily from a pine.

Johnny burst out, "Where will you go, Snoose?" Under his cry was the question, "Where will the Roses go—Lilice?"

"Don't know. Set up farming in a gopher hole, maybe." Snoose's chuckle had wryness in it.

Johnny moved angrily. For an instant he wanted to shout, "Don't you know any better? No time to play foolish." Then his anger melted iciclelike in a warmth of shame. Why, he'd put Snoose's troubles inside his shirt, any day. He said hollowly without looking up, "Don't know who's going swimming with me, Snoose, if you go away."

Snoose rolled over on his stomach. "I get scared sometimes, trying to figure how we're going to get along."

Johnny broke a minute of hot silence with a sudden "Let's go thrashing this fall, Snoose; me and you. Pitching bundles on the flats. I get to feeling every potato I eat is one less for *her* plate." Meaning Aunt Phrena. He kicked at the cracked earth impatiently.

"I know." Snoose agreed. "But thrashing—— The flats are dry as——"

"Not west of Mary's Hill. A stretch there got rain. I'd like to see Bory's steam engine. He was pretty foxy, going up in the Valley after thrashing last fall. Never came near here; and then moving into the lumber camps for the winter. Made heaps of money, Lornas says."

Johnny was ready to throw cap and pants into a bundle but Snoose was shy of this unknown prospect. He'd wait and see, he said, knowing that he'd follow Johnny.

2

It was raspberry-picking season when he met Lilice and Mrs. Rose in Norton's woods. By that time Mr. Marchen's spluttery signature on a new mortgage at the bank permitted him and his family to lay their bodies against the sharp fang of necessity for another year. But the Roses were in debt to Isaac Norton and Norton would wait and consider the harvest before he drew the purse strings on his debtors.

Johnny was in the hollow opposite Norton's woods mending a length of broken fence. "About time you fixed it," Kurt had grumbled only the night before. "Twice now the bull's been across the crick. Lucky the heifers keep him close by. If he gets into the woods, you can hunt him yourself."

The coolness of the hollow brought the sweat running. Johnny hammered fast, uneasiness in every stroke. Matt Dornhover had his pasture fenced with wire and Uncle Herm had thought next year to string barbs through this shade. But now, rails would have to do.

Over the creek Norton's woods loomed somberly. A peewee's lonely cry troubled its murky depths. He put a shoulder against a basswood for a moment of rest. The creek had almost run itself out of rushing sound, so little water ran. He slapped a mosquito without rancor and saw a yellow lady's slipper bobbing where the sun spangled a brush pile with flecks of light. Snoose would have hunched over it, had he been there, poking into the brown-ribbed shoe with a twig to dislodge a bee. Johnny's lip curled with a feeling he couldn't suppress. That was past forever and on yesterday's page.

Then he heard a clear voice, a woman's, calling, "Lileesa." Lilice. His blood bounced. Mrs. Rose—like that night at the fire. They must be in the raspberry clearing which bordered a swampy elbow of the creek. With the hammer bulging his pocket and the nails jingling, he stepped from rock to dark rock, leaving no more trace than a mink. Butterflies in a yellow swirl flickered over a mossy patch. They beat the air without sound.

He crashed through the sumacs that bordered a tree-scattered clearing. Raspberry stalks, arched in red berries, grew here, tapping the seepage of the swamp.

There was Mrs. Rose, sunbonnet pushing above the leafy clumps. She waved when she saw him. As he floundered ahead the long rough stems clawed at him and almost dragged the hammer from his pocket. Waist-high hung the heavy red fruit of the raspberry, scarlet as Lilice's lips—he stumbled over a root. He picked a handful and crowded them into his mouth. They had a sweeter taste when he saw the pinkness of Lilice's bonnet poke through the green of sumacs.

"Got your bucket?" she called. The basket she lifted was brimful of friendliness if only quarterful of berries. He had a queer breathlessness in his lungs as if he'd been running.

Mrs. Rose pulled a curled leaf from her bonnet and straightened up. "My, but I've got a crick in my back!" There was a worn look on her face. She said wanly, "For a while, I thought sure Mr. Norton had come to see what had broken into his woods."

"Ma was scared he was going to bring the sheriff," Lilice giggled. Johnny crinkled over the sunshine in the shadow of her bonnet. She went on, "They're just going to waste, these berries, nobody picking them. So why not us? Besides—" she caught a berry with a pucker of seriousness—"this year our cellar shelves are going to be empty enough."

Johnny agreed so somberly that he asked, "Got another bucket?"

Mrs. Rose brought one, saying, "It's not the sheriff, Punkin." She sorted twigs from the berries. "I know they're going to waste. But we should have asked Mr. Norton. That's only fair."

Johnny frowned. "A man with money enough to start fire with, if he wants to—I don't think he'll miss a berry or two."

"Or even three." Lilice was disdainful. "Besides, it's only a mess of berries. Nothing important to come rushing mad about."

"What you do in little things, you'll probably do in big, my mother used to say." Mrs. Rose's fingers twinkled among the leaves.

"Old bloodsucker, that's what Norton is." Bucket between his knees, Johnny grabbed a spray. The leaves swished as if shaken by a young tempest. Berries dropped, as many flying wide as plopping in. "We owe him." He spoke bluntly. "Lots. The thrashing rig's in the bargain."

Mrs. Rose leveled a glance at him. "That's where it hurts you, doesn't it?" she asked softly. She went on, "We haven't settled with him either. He was a great help when we first came. Gave us a start. He's not so black as you make out, Johnny. These hard times, he's lost money himself."

Johnny wanted to ask, "Is he putting you off the place?" but grumbled instead, "He charges twice over to make up for it. I wouldn't go nearer him than a skunk." He smashed a beetle he caught sucking a leaf.

Mrs. Rose's look deepened. "Maybe. Nobody likes a lender, I guess. And a debt—that's the stepsister of hate. My mother used to say that, too." There was a kind of mischief in her tone that reminded him of Lilice at school. "The more you do for people, the less they'll thank you for." In a swift moment Johnny wished he knew out of the memory of what bitterness she spoke.

He was limber in his fingers, helping them fill basket and bucket. After a while Lilice drifted into an alcove of the clearing. He saw the bonnet sink among the bushes. The heat swirled into his throat. Berries, thick before, thinned to a despicable few. They must be plentifuler elsewhere.

He blundered through the thickets toward the corner until he found the bonnet near, pointing straight at him. Blindly he walked into the brushing end of a limb that arched down, and ducked at the boniness of wood against his temple. With an impatient toss, he shook his hair back.

"Don't!" Lilice said, her voice creamy. "I like it that way."

"Like? What did I——" He stopped in bewilderment.

"Your hair. It's—it's full of waves; curly, almost."

"Well, gee-gods!" he began disgustedly, hand flung to his head, ready to slap the unruliness into place.

"Let it alone, now!" she ordered crisply, but so pleasantly that, in pungent bliss, he obeyed her command and went to his knees before a bush burning with the fire of berries.

She was only the thickness of the raspberry clump away, her hands busy, a ring with a stone flinging blue stilettos of light through the stalks. If he leaned forward and reached far, he could touch her. Once as she shifted position, he saw the ankle she thrust among the leaves. Like drops of blood, a dozen berries fell from a shaken spray into the green creeping ivy.

He heard her say, "She's pretty, too. No wonder she's the belle of the party."

Winking to clear befuddlement from his sight, he asked, "Who?"

"Gatha Blumen. You needn't pretend you didn't listen." Gone was the imperiousness of a moment before. "Of course, she's native here. Everybody knows her. Nobody'll ever have cause to blame her for anything." Her plaintiveness was almost a whimper.

At the sound he jerked forward. His longing broke restraint and tumbled headlong into entreaty. "Lilice, if I get to go, will you be my partner at a dance?" He held his breath, frightened at his rashness.

Even with the bush between them he sensed the quick joy that almost exploded into "Yes" but instead moderated into the cautious reserve of "Well, I don't know; maybe I——"

He slanted back, content. "You wait," he insisted, "One of these days I'll drive over and get you in a buggy."

"Maybe you will." She laughed teasingly. "And maybe I'll set the dog on you."

"I'll risk that," he caroled, dizzy with boldness.

She arose quickly. "I'll think about it," she conceded primly from the depths of her bonnet. But her hasty steps were almost flight to the circle of safety where her mother stooped over the picking.

The afternoon sun gathered shadows about them before Lilice flicked a berry into her basket. "That's my last," she said. She licked her juice-running fingers.

Mrs. Rose agreed wearily. Lines of tiredness were etched on her forehead. "You come over and we'll have raspberry pie—with cream," she told Johnny. There was thanks in her heartiness.

Lilice hid in her bonnet. Helplessly he implored an invitation from her but she remained provokingly silent. He watched them go and cuddled what satisfaction he could get from the twinkle he was sure he saw in the shadowiness that hid her eyes. A cicada began his metallic litany, a dream phantasm of hot noon, but stopped with a *tick-tick-tick*, his heat song cooled at the tip of evening. Johnny settled the hammer in his pocket and headed for home.

That night after he washed the smell of cow and horse from his fingers, he got the comb and, standing before the mirror, spent so much time poking at his hair and winnowing it into shiny rolls, his fingers hooked under the locks, that Kurt looked up from his farm paper. "Thought you didn't like bull curls?"

For a moment the comb poised over a twist of black hair. Then Johnny said evenly, "I don't much. But as long as I've got them——" He shrugged indifferently. With a final pat he put the comb away. Thereafter his head was a maze of unruliness. But Aunt Phrena stopped her sewing long enough to lift her nose, as if in this tonsorial care she scented mischief.

3

With the cutting finished (the shocks in the field heartbreakingly few), Uncle Herm got the rig into shape at Mr. Schadel's, though with more than one headshake and fierce clawing of whiskers. Threshing began, a lean beggarly job. In the wagons more sacks were empty than full. The level of grain in the bins was at ebbtide. And while the year's meager leavings began to trickle from the spout, Sophie moaned and sweated another child into a world already clamorous with sorrow. Clymy looked like a rabbit stricken with hawk fear.

Snoose was cutting bands now. Johnny tended the power at times, exchanging the whip with Alb, though this didn't happen often. After the day Alb got his heel caught in the gears Johnny drove more regularly. Alb had his shoe torn off by the cogs. He limped for days, unable to bear the strain of standing in one place, and complained that his anklebone had been cracked. While he humped about the power, ready with advice, Johnny handled the lines.

And in that time the folks in their round of talk began to say that Herman Barewolf's Johnny drove the power with such an even steadiness (the cylinder tethered to an unchanging hum) that he must have had an eye on every bundle and an ear for every kernel rattling over the sieves. Never, so Mr. Dunkel averred, had so little grain been found in the straw piles.

"Cripes, that Johnny, he purty near saved what little crop we raised!" contended Mr. Marchen. He slapped Johnny so violently that his teeth banged together.

And this good opinion spread in the congregation until Norton heaved his bulk into his pew one Sunday and stared long and unblinkingly at Johnny. He nodded at his own conclusions. "That Johnny of yours," he told Uncle Herm with a thickset grin, "he's a hustler, all right. I like 'em that way." Uncle Herm nearly bit his tongue keeping this praise from Johnny, but for reasons of his own, he did.

Few of the neighbors disagreed with Norton. Mr. Nussbaum did. "By jippers," he demurred, "you forget the feeder. It's the man at the feeder— he's the one that saves the grain. And Herky did it this year." The neighbors shrugged him down. Always there was this unanswered question among them, a spark for the smolders of argument: who was more important on the rig, the feeder or the driver? But this year, with short stems and small bundles and the grain all heads (what there was of it), the feeder had an easy job.

Herky admitted that. Mr. Marchen said stoutly, "Why a kid *couldn't ya* clog the cylinder with that thin stuff." And so even Herky sided with the neighbors against Mr. Nussbaum.

Uncle Herm glowed, but Johnny himself was unimpressed. He was too full of snaky thoughts these days—days when he avoided Uncle Herm's gratification with a kind of shame, knowing what he was about to do. He might as well strike Uncle Herm across the face. "Where does it come from—what I'm going to do?" he'd think wretchedly. "Does it come from—from *him* again?" He refused to face an answer.

In those days too the neighbors began to say among themselves quietly that Barewolf's Johnny was a tough one for a boy—well, a young man, then—of his age. A hard worker and a hard driver, yes, but without pity for a tired back or a weary muscle. "The way he dragged Old Bachmann over the coals!" Mr. Peiser related to his wife in scandalized reprobation. "And for no more reason than that Bachmann took a rest and let his side of the machine run empty for a while. You'd think Bachmann cut a hame strap or something. Johnny certainly called him down. But he finished the stacks faster than Alb Hukelpoke could. That's the main thing, I guess."

Brush fires smoked in the hills, starting no one knew how. Peat bogs reeked with hidden flame until the air was like a weight on the lungs. The valleys dimmed in the blue-gray haze. The sun was bronzy at midday and bloody at dusk. Far up north whole townships, pine and oak and cabin in the patches, were ablaze and folks, terror clamping a hand on their thumping hearts, fled before the roll of a fire-shot avalanche. Many fell. These they found blackened under ash along with deer and porcupine and squirrel, whole families, so the stories ran.

On a warm Sunday the neighbors gathered at the Marchens' to baptize Sophie's baby. "That's her second," disapproved Aunt Phrena.

"Clymy's not doing so bad," grinned Uncle Herm. "Don't the Bible say that a feller should be fruitful and multiply?"

"Well," sniffed Aunt Phrena, "they needn't be in such a hurry to keep His word." She was annoyed when Kurt guffawed.

In the Marchen yard folks gabbled over chinch bugs and the dear cost of coal oil to lift the darkness of the night. They gaped at the Marchen cousin, a machine-shop man from Fergus, visiting here. They shook their heads over Mr. Dunkel. That man. Troubles or no, his whistle over the farm rang strongly. Folks wondered where he got his inner strength, for Mrs. Dunkel sat listless as a dog some days and on others wept forlornly, searching in the attic with calls for Gretel. Mrs. Peiser went to borrow eggs once and found Mr. Dunkel scrubbing the floor, she gossiped. When the neighbors talked with him, he sometimes said, "The Lord will never give me more than I can handle."

Snoose drew Johnny aside, his gray eyes sparkling, his hands tugging at his pants. "Got a surprise for you, Johnny. It's more for your *insides* than your outsides." He chuckled in his strange way, his gaze on the porch where Em'ly Musser and Gatha Blumen sat under the grapevines.

"Insides?" puzzled Johnny.

"Wait and see," was all Snoose would say.

Old Anders was there, itchy for the accordion, but lamenting, "Gettin' old, I am; can't play much any more."

"Aw, now, Anders," Alb expostulated, "lots of tunes you ain't played yet."

But Anders sighed. "Purty near thrashed out, Alb. It's the ants that bother me—ants crawling in my eyes when I'm dead and I can't scratch 'em out." He was doleful among his years, his lost youth revived today in Sophie's baby; but tomorrow he'd remember his people away in Minneapolis—his folks who would one day call him back, he always said. So far they hadn't.

The Pastor was there, hackles spiny in complaint over the way Brother Erdman was getting a meetinghouse built despite the leanness of men's pocketbooks, while *he* had to bow before the Lord in a log church. His frosty regard did not miss Aunt Phrena and Uncle Herm. Later he stared, heavy-lidded with outrage, as Lilice and Mrs. Rose drove into the yard.

Snoose tickled Johnny's ribs. "My surprise. I knew they were coming. Mrs. Rose didn't want to at first, but Adam said he'd stay with the old man. Sophie invited them."

Johnny warmed with gratitude. What a feller that Snoose was! And Lilice, how sweet she was; how she had twinkled that afternoon in the raspberry patch, he remembered. He put his hand to his hair, freshly twisted into a tangle of waves.

But he was almost shy in giving his hellos, she was so prim and aloof in a dress of starchy white with lace at the sleeves, the dimple sedately pulling at her smile. Her mother, erect on the seat, was dressed in gray the color of a mourning dove's throat. "Thank you, Johnny," she said in her quiet way that had a hint of liveliness in it. She put the lines in his hands. "Flixie is a little skittish but I know I can trust you boys to take care of her. Come on, Lilice."

They rustled toward the house. Lilice remained at the porch with the other girls. Mrs. Rose entered the door. In the house, Aunt Phrena surveyed her and Lilice with the dignity of one who is invulnerably sanctified.

Johnny and Snoose hurried back to the yard to find the girls already corralling the boys in the circle of "four in a boat." Gatha called to them, "Hurry up, you poky ones, if you want a partner," and languished for Johnny in a brownish dress that he thought dowdy beside simple white.

He joined the game, frisky as a puppy for friendliness. Remembering the afternoon in the berry patch, he was sure of Lilice's smile. But he found that she was different now, different from that day as hot is from cold, and soon he was bruised with hurt. She eluded him; was as evasive as a shadow; froze him with a curt refusal, thawed him with a reviving acceptance; lilted in the swingy song,

> "Choose your partners, don't delay,
> We don't care what the old folks say,"

her voice above the others, clear as a redbird's. She followed the steps in a lively fashion.

He went cold when she rested in the arms of a Nussbaum boy.

> "Eight in a boat and it won't go round,"

she sang as if the shadows at home had been brushed aside and for this moment she nibbled recklessly the sweetroot of joy, tangy and like wine in her veins. She swayed near him dreamily:

> "Bow to the pretty one that you have found,"

and looked squarely at him. He simmered radiantly, the ice gone. Brown, that's what they were, her eyes. He wondered why he'd never thought brown was a pretty color.

She was his partner in the next set. Gatha flounced her skirts. He grew so boisterous that he pushed against Snoose who was asking Em'ly. But Lilice, prancing through "the drunken sailor," left Johnny for Kurt with such merriness that he felt slapped. She shook back her shimmering hair until Gatha, biting her lip savagely, tried the charm of sophistication. Gatha cooed airily in a pause between games, "What a time we had at the dance last night! Lornas Tetzell was there. He and Mosey Fritz are thrashing with Bory." She batted her eyes. "How that Lornas can rye waltz. He just floats." She clasped her hands.

But Lilice stole Gatha's unbashfulness and hinted with sly boldness that they ought to go to the creek in couples to hunt shells. When several boys pushed forward, Johnny not far behind, she decided swiftly that her ankle was tired and they'd better play "last couple out."

Before the boys could recover from her shifting mood, Gatha cut in swiftly, venom hidden in her virtue, "Well, maybe Lilice could go to the creek with the boys. I couldn't." She lifted a spiteful shoulder. "A church girl has to be *so* careful——" She giggled playfully. "Let's do as Lilice says: play 'last couple out.'" They began scattering.

But Johnny saw how Lilice put her hand to her lips as if Gatha's words had been fists striking her. The shadow he remembered seeing at school lay heavy on her face. He glared at Gatha and stepped quickly to Lilice's side. Melting tenderness for her and anger at Gatha encouraged such temerity that he caught her hand in a violent grasp, insisting almost roughly, "Be my partner, Lilice!"

As though his offer were further hurt, she ripped her hand out of his, her mood variable as a dust devil in a field. "I've been twice already." Her chin was up. "Thanks just the same."

"Oh!" His arm dropped, her tone a dash of chill water to his eagerness. "Is there a limit, then?"

"What did you expect?" she snapped. Seeing how ruffled he was and enjoying it, she goaded him by smiling up at Kurt. "My, but he is stubborn, that Johnny, isn't he?"

"You should see him on the thrasher then," jibed Kurt. "Like a rooster on a manure pile, the way he throws his hands at the cylinder."

Her eyes unshuttered in a jerk of what might have been fear. "Oh, he'll get——" she began impetuously, and stopped, as if betrayed into words before she knew, and not liking it. "He is stubborn as a wheelbarrow," she said without much definiteness, slipping her arm through Kurt's for the next game.

With anger and misery shaken together, Johnny was sullen. He wanted to cup his palms on her shoulder rounds and rattle her head about, but, more than that, he was eaten with desire for her friendliness and her smile. Words plugged his throat.

Suddenly he put a splint of straightness in his back and grinned widely if ruefully. He grabbed Gatha and paraded with her, tail high, his voice swaggering, "Can't slow the circle down, can we, Gatha? Put a feather in your heels, there, and come steppin'!" There was such eagerness in the curve of Gatha's arm as she went with him that Lilice, observing, let her hand in Kurt's go slack.

With mirth and fervor they lost breath in the games. And in a small room in the house, the Pastor sat in a circle of men, discoursing profoundly on the woman taken in adultery. After the second round of dandelion wine, his profundity grew with the flush that crept from his beard into the clear area of his cheeks. "Ah, yes, the divine forgiveness of Jesus here is—it is indeed exemplary," he was saying when he looked up. Mrs. Rose with Mrs. Peiser entered the room. "Na ya," he broke off shortly. "The world is full of unrepentant Magdalenes."

Abruptly he left his chair and strode away. The circle sat in uneasy silence. It stared at Mrs. Rose. With proud erectness she regarded the Pastor's stiff departing back. But she put a lacy handkerchief to her lips to hide their weary trembling. Outside on the porch the Pastor settled into talk with Mr. Marchen.

In the yard the games lifted in merriment. And nobody but Snoose was bothered that Johnny seemed to be elbow in elbow with somebody else when he galloped past Lilice; that Lilice was either just leaving a partner or swinging with a new one when she tripped past Johnny, and that in the "allemande," they touched each other's hands as if with the leaves of the poison sumac. Snoose saw them with a kind of woe, but pursued Em'ly now in, now out of shadow.

The trees were stretching their darkness farther by the minute when Sophie crossed the yard to say, "There's something to drink and cookies on the porch." Before the boys had time to select the girls, she proposed, "Let's make this 'Ladies' Choice.'"

The boys dropped back, defeated. Johnny sagged behind Snoose, hoping Gatha would choose anyone but himself. She wouldn't, he realized, and wished that he and Snoose with cool wet glasses and pastries crumbling in their palms could sneak into the lilac bushes as they had many times before, and quench their thirst with drink and their inquisitiveness with desultory talk. But Snoose, palpitating over Em'ly who was encouraging him, had no eyes for Johnny. He was leading Em'ly off to the grapevines. Sophie called to Gatha.

Johnny sighed and scratched his ear dolefully, prepared for Gatha's warble, "You can't say no to me, can you, Johnny?" He wondered fiercely if Kurt were Lilice's choice, but kept his head determinedly away from her. Notions like dark birds flashed through his brain.

And so it was that he blinked when Lilice's throaty voice drove warmly through his ire. "May I have the pleasure——" she was beginning primly but the hint of mockery failed.

She stood at his side. In spite of himself he turned to her. Her brown eyes asked more than an invitation. "I'd be glad if you'd have a cooky with me, Johnny." Her voice was low.

He wanted to snarl, "I got a limit on my partners, too," but there was a sort of ruefulness in the way she looked down that made him swing to her more eagerly than he knew. Not that she begged as much as a finger of his favor, except that given as freely as earth gushes forth in springs of coolness. He could see that.

In a wash of gladness, he smiled, taking what was offered now without the crooked pins of questions stuck into his acceptance. Together they walked toward the porch. And seeing them, Gatha left Sophie. With a quick clench of fist, she tapped the arm of a Schadel boy and followed them, talking brightly.

On the way Lilice asked, bothered by a thought she couldn't avoid, "Kurt said Hukelpoke got his foot caught in the gears." She shivered. "Was it— was it bad?"

"Aw, Kurt's jaw claps like a fanning mill." Johnny shrugged, blind to the yearning in her, blind to everything but this captive joy, his for this moment. "Nothing wrong with Alb except a limp."

Her lips puckered as though she looked on worry again—worry like an unkenneled dog that had crept over the hills and was snuffing here at her heels.

The porch and the steps and the ground before the house were dotted with folks in chairs and on blocks of wood and on the grass, islands of expanding egos, their bodies' weight flattening blade and stem. Mr. Marchen sat cross-legged on a step. The Pastor's head pendulumed as he rocked in his chair.

Johnny found a spot for Lilice near Snoose and Em'ly under the grape leaves, yellowing in autumn.

From the doorway Aunt Phrena saw them. Her pale blue eyes darkened as if she'd stepped on a toad. "Ach, now this!" she murmured. "Poor sister! You'd think *he* spites me on purpose." It wasn't only of Johnny she was thinking. Her fist on the doorjamb tightened with purpose.

Cookies crumpled between teeth and were swallowed with dashes of Juneberry juice fragrant with mint leaves—Mrs. Rose's idea. She and Mrs. Blumen trotted about with pitchers cooled in a woods spring.

The Pastor regarded them dourly. He was exegetical over the necessity of keeping the fold pure and of one strain, and the danger of contamination from the black-fleeced interlopers. Folks listened. They swallowed his ideas and their refreshments together, and were unperturbed. Their nearness to the earth, the all-embracing, unrejecting earth, a nearness beyond the Pastor to understand, blunted his homiletics.

Then Mrs. Rose paused at his chair to refill his tumbler. Quickly he put a broad flabby hand over the rim. With raspy emphasis but without a break in his discourse he went on as though she weren't standing there, or were beneath his notice. For an instant she waited; hesitated; then with quiet dignity went and tipped the pitcher over Mr. Marchen's glass.

A few moments of talk later, Mrs. Blumen, seeing his glass empty, offered the Pastor more. At once he broke his dialectics and chirruped with friendliness, deliberately audible, "Yes, thank you, Mrs. Blumen. Just a good drop more, please. It is always a pleasure to see a Christian woman over her household tasks." Dark crimson bubbled over the green leaves as she poured.

A kind of silence spread over the group. Folks gathered their curiosity in one stare. Mrs. Blumen twittered, self-conscious giggles rippling her bulk, "Oh, Pastor, so kind of you! At our house we *always* say grace before meals." The Pastor bleakly approved.

Mrs. Rose stopped sharply. The way she lifted her chin reminded Johnny of Lilice. The ladle in the pitcher clinked, abruptly loud, metal against resonant glass. Mr. Marchen, choking an exclamation, uncrossed his legs. Beside Johnny, Lilice's head drooped flowerlike and then was flung back, a bent-over stem released from tension.

With a motion so calm no liquid splashed, Mrs. Rose advanced toward the Pastor, one hand free and outstretched, the other burdened with the pitcher, a kind of gray suppliant before the altar of his grimness. "My offering was poor, I know, *Mister* Steuber." She poised for a second over the affront to his title, scarcely noticing that he straightened in his chair. A rustle went through the people. "I guess you call my hands the hands of an unbeliever, don't you?" she continued. "But they've starched and ironed and washed; whose more? And they've been folded in prayer, too. You won't believe that, but they have; over sickness and——" Her voice faltered. Lilice set her glass down so close to Johnny's that the two touched with an icy tinkling. Mrs. Rose steadied herself. "Over sickness and crippled bones. They've had tears on them."

"A woman's word," the Pastor started quoting sententiously, "should be heard in the kitchen. The blessed Apostle says, 'Let your women keep silence in——' "

But she halted the phrases on his lips imperiously. "You judge us only because our name is not in your church book. That's right, isn't it?"

"That is not true," the Pastor half shouted, stung to the ignominy of defending himself against this woman.

He tried to go on but she overwhelmed him with her intensity. "You examine things well on the outside, Pastor Steuber, but what about the inside?" she insisted.

The Pastor rose augustly. "By their fruit you shall know them," he pronounced with awful composure. "Righteous folk show the harvest of their faith by yearning for the church and——"

"We belonged once," Mrs. Rose interrupted him as though he were a neighbor talking about the price of oats. "The God they preached about there——" Her voice became uncertain before his black tallness and the memories that came rushing. "There was no mercy in Him. Pitiless as a stone." The pitcher wavered in her hand. There was anguish in Lilice's eyes as she turned to Johnny.

"You defy God with such rebelliousness." The Pastor was kindly triumphant. "Yet you expect——"

"Mister Steuber." The pitcher klinked. "But a little while ago you spoke about casting the first stone." Suddenly she swayed, solidness going to pieces in her, and reached out a hand as if for strength. There was none except the cold lip of the pitcher.

Lilice came to her feet quickly. Johnny, as if impelled, cried, "Stay here, Lilice!" but she pulled away, crying softly, "Don't Johnny!" She ran to her mother.

But Mrs. Rose gathered herself. Quietly she said, "I am glad you can afford to throw the stones, Pastor."

What argument garnered from chapter and verse the Pastor had ready; what Mr. Marchen wanted to say, rising from the step, wrath on his face; what Johnny thought to do, seeing Lilice take her mother's arm and help her to the door—whatever their intentions, a harsh screech scattered them like leaves before a gust. It tore its two-tone way into their ears, jerking them around where they stood or sat or leaned. Johnny moved so precipitately the glass tipped and left the leaves green in the tumbler, a rill of fruit juice trailing crookedly over the grimy pine boards. The late afternoon woods rang and reechoed harshly with the scream of the engine.

Somebody yelled, "There. It's coming down the road." Everyone crowded to the fence that kept the road out of the Marchens' yard.

"It's the steamer," Johnny cried and ran to the gate. All else, even Lilice, was for that moment, squeezed from his mind. Snoose came at his heels, deserting Em'ly. They stood there, Johnny's slenderness toughening with muscle. He was taller than Snoose by an ear. There was excitement in the lean of their bodies.

Down the road came a churn of dust and the iron sound of wheels crunching and snapping on rock and sand. Scarcely heard in the metallic clamor was the clopping of horses' hoofs. Around a hazel-heavy bend rolled the "bull" engine hauled by a team of satin blacks, their nostrils flaring at the pull of the tugs, their hames polished and their harness rings gleaming. The boiler, a long black barrel with a box slung under one end, was mounted on four wheels. The firebox hung between the rear bull drivers. These huge wheels crunched against the stones and spun pebbles from their edges. The smokestack at the front of the boiler thrust up like a long black pipe.

As the rig moved along, a bushy, black-dog's tail of smoke billowed rearward over the two-wheeled fuel tender with its pile of cordwood, its barrels of water and its box of coal; over the tool chest propped half open with a wrench handle. A length of tubing crawled out of a barrel and wormed snakily into the belly of the engine.

Folks pushed and elbowed, gawping at this huge ebony shape that wheeled along their chicken-tracked roads. They stared at the gauges and pet cocks and the governor with its balls balanced on springs like three worlds on curving axes. They drew back from the hiss that was like a barnyard of mate-hungry ganders. A wisp of steam curled about the whistle shell.

Johnny shifted a foot, his blood as heated as if with a fever. Then his nose tilted, full of the bitter smell of hot oil and smoke and steam. "Oh, Snoose," he breathed softly, "if I could get my hands on those levers——"

Bory Tetzell stood on the rear platform, the throttle a black stick at his shoulder. On a seat just in front of the flywheel sat Makin Boone, feet braced against the iron foot piece for balance, driving the team with taut lines. In the fuel tender rode Lornas Tetzell and Mosey Fritz, Lornas with a smear of coal dirt on his nose. Mosey waved to no one in particular, yelling in chesty importance, "We tried her out today. You fellers still poking your nags?" Behind them the separator man with another team hauled the thresher.

"Have to thrash a lot of bundles to pay for a hunk of iron like that," Uncle Herm observed. "No wonder Bory kept out of sight last fall and went out to the flats."

The Pastor growled, "Profaning the Sabbath with their stinking machine."

Bory Tetzell let a scrawly grin show his tobacco-yellow teeth. He was a burly, slow-moving man with a mean look. A scar on his cheek, ripped there by a flying piece of broken wheel, pulled his face sidewise into the stiffness of a grimace. A rough-tongued man, the neighbors said: hard on his men, his horses and his women. With great bull-like playfulness, as if he knew this were unnecessary but that here was laughter for a joke, he jerked the door of the firebox open, letting red streamers of flame flicker on the black barrels; snapped up a stick of pine and shoved it into the opening. With a blue handkerchief he slapped the dust from his oily fingers:

this was Sunday and he must be clean for the company. All at once he yanked at the whistle pull. Instantly the air was split wide by the jagged edge of the blast.

Some of the kids jumped like struck colts. A little girl screamed and burrowed into her mother's apron. Her mother, holding her close, scuttled behind the broad shoulders of her husband. Most folks cringed a bit, if they didn't hop in their boots. The whistle bellowed rawly in their ears. Used as they were by now to the raucous throat of the engine, Bory's team skittered a trifle. Makin drew them up with a backward lunge.

The whistle stopped but the sound fled over the trees, Bory's hoarse laughter roaring after it like a heavy tail to a light-feathered kite.

The rig passed along. Even when the willows like a curtain drew between it and the yard, and the last noise of metal clanking on stone was losing itself in the distant bushes, the folks gazed long after the sound and the smoke sailing over the elms. A part of their woody lives had been marred by the jutting iron of this experience. It would widen with years. They would carry it with them all their lives.

"Bull wheels of Moses!" Uncle Herm's exclamation was loud in the stillness of their wonder. "Betcha a feller could thrash till the steers got home with *that*. It's like the engine I run in the brewery, only on wheels." The Pastor frowned.

"It's crazy, that's what it is." Mr. Schadel was emphatic. "If the horses run away with that mess of iron and you tip over, you're gonna have an explosion; blow everything square to—" he paused, the black of the Pastor's coat in his eye, and finished mildly—"to little pieces, that's what you will."

A gabble of opinion ran along the fence. The Pastor shook his head prophetically. "Worshipers of Baal and Ashtoreth," he muttered. "Of man's folly there is no end."

Johnny's eyes were hard and black with excitement. "I've made up my mind." He was barely audible. "Snoose, Snoose, wouldn't it be *something* to thrash with that rig?"

Catching his enthusiasm, Snoose answered heartily, "I wouldn't have to harness *all* the horses, every morning, thrashing time."

But the Marchens' cousin, the machine-shop man from Fergus, dismissed their wonder with a derogatory "That old tub? You should see the new styles. They don't need horses any more. Why, the new engines pull themselves."

The folks tittered and nudged each other in disbelief and Mr. Schadel grumbled, "Funny how a little dandelion wine runs to some fellers' heads."

Just then there was a rattle of wheels. Mrs. Rose and Lilice, waving to Sophie and the Marchens but chillily indifferent to the remainder of the company, whipped past them and down the road.

She went and hooked up the team, Johnny thought; she and Lilice, all by themselves. He was dejected and regretful, now that the engine was gone. Mournfully he gazed after the vanishing buggy.

Suddenly Mr. Schadel shouted, "Look it, once." He ran through the gate. Near the edge of the road beyond the newly printed bull-wheel tracks where it had fallen from the firebox, a coal of wood smoldered briskly in coils of blue smoke. Catching a spray of dry grass, flame leaped up hungrily under a blow of air. Mr. Schadel stomped the red tongues back into dust. "Dropping fire, like that. I wouldn't have one of those critters on my place. Fine thing, if that had landed in a stubble field or somebody's meadow." A finger of blue smoke wavered in the dust and died.

4

In those next weeks after the baptizing at the Marchens', Johnny, bitten by the ants of impatience and soured by the slow gall of his own thoughts, was fretful around the thresher and grumpy at home. Aunt Phrena, thinking to uproot whatever of Lilice was growing in his mind, suggested, subtle as a monkey wrench, "That Gatha Blumen, she's a nice Christian girl. You don't see much of her, do you?"

Johnny's fingers ground white half-moons in the red of his palms. It was on his tongue to shout, "Everything I want you're against. Lilice is my business. Keep your nose out." Instead he grouched from the room, leaving her frown-faced and picking at the Book.

Even at the rig Johnny was irritated. Less and less did the creak of gears in the power and the ear-hurting clatter of knuckles in the tumbling rods perch a song on his lips. In his mind the steam engine ran with the quietness of brooks.

His whip crackled over the horses until Mr. Nussbaum fired up in protest. But even he was silenced by Johnny's shrug and his frigid "Do you want to get thrashed now, or next Christmas?"

He'd shout, "Hurry up, there, you bundle slingers!"—as if he owned the machine, Heinie Beerwagon said—and he'd sink the stakes for the power with easy violent swings of the maul. His body was hardening with the iron of young manhood. The muscles of his arms tightened his shirt when he heaved a sack of grain into a wagon or hoisted a wheel into place. He and Heinie wrestled sometimes. Now it was Heinie whose bulk yielded with a grunted "Got plenty; leave me up."

By turns he was loud-tongued and huffily reticent. Tiredness ached in his feet from long hours of standing on the platform. Dirt itched in his nose. By the half day dust smoked from the trodden round of the circle and hung bridle-high. It was so thick that horses without legs seemed to float in an ashy cloud. His sneeze was a small echo of the horses' snorts.

At noon the dust stretched away on the wind poles like a curtain but in the quiet of sunset it rose about him like the circular gray well of a tower, himself in the center. The long straight red of the sun flushed it crimson and the pink of the hedge-rose; dusk faded it to satin pearl. From the center boomed his voice. From the wall sounded the jingle of harness and the rubbling snorts of the teams. So Snoose saw it often.

But through the hazy wall Johnny beheld only a wash of fire and now and again a bloody orb and afterward a dun obscurity hiding separator and all. Horses moved around like dim, mouse-colored phantoms.

Sometimes the stink of horse wet and manure stirred with earth choked him so that when Alb came to take his place, he jumped into fresh air like a diver and pumped his lungs greedily. The acridness stayed on his tongue, however, and mixed with the supper's potatoes and meat.

He made fun of Old Man Dresser and the little piles of grain stacked by his three daughters, Amaria, Seligkind and Gretelein. These heaps near the settings contained their sheaves, gathered head by fallen head in the bull-wheel tracks behind the harvester and in the corners where the horses trod the standing wheat. "Save a little for mine girls," the old man always said when Uncle Herm threshed these piles separately.

" 'Save a little for mine girls,' " Johnny mimicked him sourly.

"It's a favor for the old duffer," Uncle Herm chortled mollifyingly. "We have to slow up a little, maybe, resetting; or the pitchers have to carry the bundles a long way. But he's a good neighbor. He'd give his Sunday wooden shoe to help out."

"He can keep his wooden shoe," Johnny fidgeted. "He saves a peck of grain for his girls and we waste half a day, waiting."

"We got time when we ain't got nothing else," Alb reminded him, but Johnny was bearish. He waited peevishly through the half hours and sometimes the hours while the rig was being reset. Uncle Herm maneuvered the separator between the stacks with one team. Alb Hukelpoke tried to draw the power into line with another. While they shouted and squinted their sight, the crew idled on slouching legs. Heinie whittled a "B" on his fork handle. The rest of the teams stood slack in their harnesses, the teamsters in negligent talk.

Alb liked to "line 'er up." With time and sweat and shouts of "C'mon, now!" and "Back 'er up, there, boys!" he brought the power and the separator into that position where the "couplers" joining the tumbling rods ran easily and made the least racket. "Two times you diddle at it," Alb was fond of saying. "The third time she goes." Often, however, it was the fourth and the fifth. It was a part of threshing, though, accepted with indifference.

But Johnny watched, kicking a tuft of grass impatiently and grumbling, "We could thrash half a setting, the time it takes to set and reset. Horses are so slow. And all those men cooling their butts." More than once Uncle Herm tugged at his whiskers over a covert glance at him. And Snoose blinked sadly, wondering whether this misery was girlsickness alone.

With unanticipated agreement Kurt said one day, "Johnny's not far wrong about wasting time. We spend half a day in moving and resetting. I read somewhere, these traction engines—they can turn around on a three-cent nickel."

Johnny answered briefly, "Reading about it—that won't help Hukel-poke line up the rig."

What rumpled him into short temper was plain the Friday evening he said to Snoose, "I'm quitting tomorrow." They had wiped the crumbs of Mrs. Schimmel's pie from their lips and were walking toward the haymow. "You want to come?"

"Johnny!" Snoose turned sidewise and almost tripped. "In the middle of a thrashing run?"

"Bory Tetzell got the Norton job, Jimmy Nussbaum told me," Johnny muttered raggedly.

"Tetzell!" Darkness hid the disbelief that shocked Snoose. For this he hadn't bargained.

"He's leaving for the flats Monday. Three of his pitchers quit. I'm going with him, even if you're not."

"But Bory——"

"He's a stinker, sure. Lornas and Mosey Fritz are working for him. They're no better. But I'll pitch bundles for anybody gives me a day's wages." Johnny's voice was uneven with recklessness. "I've got to be my own boss, Snoose. I can't here, with—with *her*."

"I know." Snoose tried to juggle the pieces of his confusion into order. "I was thinking about the thrashing rig and—and——"

"Uncle Herm." With bitter emphasis Johnny helped him out. "Go ahead and blame me, Snoose. You can't say worse things than I've said to myself a thousand times, these nights." There was almost hopelessness in the way he sagged momentarily against Snoose's shoulder.

"Not blaming you." Snoose linked his arm in Johnny's. At the touch, Johnny's elbow crooked solidly about Snoose's, as if the warmth of comradeship were sweeter than he knew. Snoose went on, "It's just that he depends on you so much. And Alb says you're getting to be the best driver around here; a good feeder, too. The rig's going to go to pieces if you——"

"Don't be a bull's hind leg." Johnny dropped Snoose's arm, knowing better where he stood than Snoose imagined. "Uncle Herm—he's been so good and——" The syllables failed huskily on his tongue. "I feel so damn mean and skunky I could——"

"Seems like he'll feel you're stepping on him," Snoose persisted, "if you——" He paused, not sure how to continue.

There was a silence that appeared to take a flinty shape. When he spoke Johnny's voice steadied with harshness. "Well, let him. I'm leaving. If I have to step on somebody to get ahead, I'll do it, even if it's—even if——" But he couldn't say "Uncle Herm."

They neared the barn. Snoose asked quietly, "Monday?"

"Bright and early. The job'll take a good while. Norton's got half in stacks, half in shocks."

"I'll have my duds ready."

Johnny gripped Snoose's arm in a fierce grip. They climbed into the haymow.

5

For a long time Uncle Herm sat quietly folding a pleat in his Sunday trousers, as if he wanted to savor all the bitter tang of Johnny's words, the misery in Johnny's hung-low countenance. "Na ya, boy." He sighed deeply. "I left my folks too, and a good job for this Pockerbrush country."

Johnny looked up. The gentleness in Uncle Herm (no anger at all) filled him. The rings of his throat tightened and shame swept over him, shame that the tears would show, big as he was. He twisted his knuckles into white knobs. The Sunday afternoon was bright with calm.

Uncle Herm continued, "Can't blame you for wanting to get a job of your own. Me and Phrena, we ain't been much as kinfolks to——"

"Hit me with a club, Uncle Herm, but don't say that," Johnny cried, breaking the tightness in his throat. "Whatever I've needed you've given me, when—when——" When you could, Uncle Herm, was in his mind; when Aunt Phrena let you; but he couldn't utter the thought, knowing how Uncle Herm felt about her.

As if he understood, Uncle Herm said, "It's like the calf deal all over again, ain't it?" Johnny nodded dumbly, the tightness and the shame gripping him again.

"That's what I thought. What is it now?" Uncle Herm's question was half sad, half quizzical. "Is it a farm you want to get for me with your wages, or a team of horses, or maybe—" slyness pointed his mouth—"a new thrasher?"

Johnny's head bobbed vigorously. Shamefacedness left him with Uncle Herm's understanding. His eyes grew blacker in excitement; words broke from him. "Don't you see, Uncle Herm? I'll get me wages and save, and you keep on thrashing and we'll get a bigger rig maybe next year. And we'll thrash heck out of the hills and——"

Uncle Herm rasped a frog in his throat. "Guess I'm gettin' old," he said and stopped pleating his trousers.

Johnny drooped his shoulders again. "If it's Bory—because I'm going to pitch for him——"

"Well," Uncle Herm conceded, "ain't much good anyone's ever said about him."

"No, but he got the Norton job and that strip of thrashing west in the Valley. It's the largest run anybody's got around here." Johnny's eagerness didn't hide the calculation in his words.

"And the most wages," Uncle Herm said dryly. "That's what you're really aiming at, huh? Well, sure." He began fiddling with the pleat again. "No, it's not exactly Bory Tetzell. It's—well, it's——" He hunted for expression.

Johnny finished it in his own thought: It's leaving *me* in the lurch, Johnny, and going with a man who'd like to burn me out, that's what it is. Johnny kicked at the dried earth. Aloud he said, "I know he's a stinker——"

"It's not that," Uncle Herm interrupted. "You can work for the worst stinker, if you're happy over what you're getting."

"I know what I'm getting." Johnny straightened up, confidence reasserting itself. His manner grew determined. "And I'm going to get it."

"Ya, Johnny." Uncle Herm sounded tired and worn. "Ya, Johnny, I'm afraid you are."

6

Perhaps it was Kurt who told Aunt Phrena; perhaps Uncle Herm. She was waiting for Johnny when he came for the milk buckets that Sunday evening. He braced his shoulders, knowing that she would scold; dreaded her rebuke.

She set the buckets on the table. As if to provoke him, she said bluntly, "It ain't good enough for you any more, our rig, is it?" Never before had she acknowledged the thresher except with scorn.

"I've talked with Uncle Herm. I'm packing tonight," he answered with such finality that she put the drying cloth down.

"So. This is what it comes to, all my promises to your ma. That trash from Loon Lake."

"Who else pays such good wages?" He faced her calmly. "I don't have to live with Tetzell."

"Our place is too small for you, then. You want a bigger pasture. That's it. A Christian home, now—that is too strict, so?" He stood near the table, his face set, looking upon her with an indifference that startled her into momentary silence. As if defeated her hands loosed their hold on the cloth.

He heard her clamor but it made little sense to him. Then she was saying almost pitiably, "Much have I forgiven you, Johnny. Some day, maybe, you'll say the same for me." She twisted the cloth. "Stay, Johnny!" she pleaded. In surprise he banged the pails together. "For your ma's sake, stay! How can I sleep, you with that thrasher who never darkened the door of a church in his life? Johnny, I promised your ma," she wailed.

He saw her with destructive clearness then—a huge, bundly sag of flesh huddled at the end of the table. Where he had expected a starchy bolt of resistance, he found only a queer sort of hollowness, as though he'd pushed against a sack and experienced not the unyielding press of grain but vacancy instead, flabby and weightless.

For a moment he was puzzled and strangely lost, not yet realizing how surely youth had closed and barred the door upon him and how his young manhood had begun to clear a wider arc of understanding. Though he guessed vaguely what acrid portions of stubbornness and bristly pride she had swallowed to beg this of him, he was not moved, the ice in him as unmelted as glass in the sun. "Can't be pinned to apron strings all my life," he said clearly.

"When I get to heaven, what can I tell your ma, you in bad company?" she quavered.

"Bad company?" He nearly laughed.

"There are plenty of girls here—" she tried an oblique tack—"who read their Catechisms and go——"

"Plenty of girls but not Lilice Rose," he interrupted her bitterly.

She hurried on, "Always you are against the good sweet things, just like——" Her pause quivered with unsaid words.

"Just like Schwartz," he said without anger but with a forlornness that slacked the hold his fingers had on the bucket handles. "I shan't forget. I've eaten it with my meat and potatoes these years."

"I saw you and that Rose girl at the Marchens'. You could just as well visit with some other girls, Gatha or Prudence Fleischer or——"

"You can save your talk," he said dully. "If I'm bad, like my pa, I'm not good for Gatha either. But it's not Gatha you're thinking about. It's Lilice you don't like. Why?"

"Don't mix what don't belong together."

"She belongs as much as anybody." In a wave of rashness goaded by her persistence, he cried, "She's my girl. And nobody's going to stop me, neither."

Aunt Phrena half rose, seeing with deadly clearness where this would lead. Her chair scraped on the floor. "No, no, Johnny. Hear me, it is the truth. The tears of those who play in the house of the unbaptized and the unchurched—they are burning, burning tears."

He gathered the buckets as if she'd spoken about the weather. "If you got an extra clean shirt, I'll pack it with my duds." He left the house.

Aunt Phrena caught at the chair, then sank back. Quietly she plucked at the whiskers of thread sticking up where the cloth was torn.

Between house and barn Johnny idled to a stop in the path. Warmly the sharp points of stars pricked the dark south where Lilice lived. The echo of his words, "She's my girl," sent a freshet of dizziness over him. "Did I really say that?" he gulped. Under the echo, however, squirmed Aunt Phrena's unuttered accusation: ". . . like Schwartz." Like Schwartz. Like *him*. Running after girls. Wanting them. Bad boys did that. Bad . . .

His forehead crinkled but he couldn't hold back the longing for Lilice that rose in him like a dull tugging pain. He would have set the buckets down then and there and legged it dog-fashion over the creek and through Norton's woods for a visit with—well, with Adam at the Rose farm beyond. He would have (he was sure) if Monday morning weren't demandingly near and, with it, the bull engine and Bory Tetzell and the job on the flats.

"Wait till winter comes," he decided. "Lilice, I'll make tracks in your snowbank, see if I don't." And contenting himself with anticipation, that delusion which for most folk is more actual than realization, he rattled the buckets to the barn.

And at the Rose house over the creek and beyond the Norton woods, Lilice came downstairs, her Sunday dress rustling and an air of Cologne water about her. Excitement livened the tiredness in her eyes. She leaned almost remorsefully against her mother. "It doesn't seem fair, you here alone. If something happens——"

"Brothers don't ask sisters to go to parties very often," Mrs. Rose shushed her. "Hurry now, Punkin, before Adam changes his mind. Besides, it's many a long night I've sat up alone—" she nodded in the direction of the bedroom—"when he was at the machine." She patted Lilice's arm. "Say hello to Mrs. Morrison. It'll be a nice party."

A moan came faintly through a closed door.

And while Lilice was riding to the Morrisons' with Adam and Lena, thinking, I wonder whether he'll be there, Johnny stood before the mirror after chores, comb in hand, lifting and patting his hair into black valleys and hills.

Kurt said over his farm paper, "You might as well stay here with the rig. Don't see that you're doing any better, going with Bory." He tried to appear indifferent.

Johnny caught his inner envy and was glad. "When I'm fired," he snapped, "I'll come begging you for a job."

Silently, his back to them, Uncle Herm puttered over a harness.

"Sleeping in straw piles and what not!" Aunt Phrena remonstrated. "Don't you know night air is bad for the lungs? I wouldn't open a window for one sniff. My Uncle Siegfried died of lung fever."

"Makes a man tough," said Johnny loftily and went upstairs. He packed his bundle; rummaged among his things and tossed aside what he'd outgrown, as one does who starts on a journey so distant he may not come this way again.

He found the red ribbon that had been tied about the neck of the doll with the china head. With its faded scarlet curled in a palm, he sat on the bed. How dingy it was! The threads were soiled and the luster gone. Try as he might, he couldn't bring back the smile of the china face (smudged into forgetfulness the memory of his mother's smile; dark and shoulder-near the name and presence of his father). He poked at the ribbon with a thumb; rose quickly. "Fooling around," he growled. "Got lots to do yet." He flung the ribbon on a pile of castoff garments in a corner. It made a dull coil on a worn-out jacket there in the shadows.

With ungentle fingers he rummaged among his stuff. He found the panel with "Brynjolf" scorched brownly on it but this he put away as something he'd want another time. After a while he pitched a tattered shirt into the corner. Its ragged folds swept over the pile, over the shabby, unwanted jacket, over the frayed edges of the red ribbon.

7

Bory Tetzell spat out a chewed straw and jabbed at his scar with a little finger. "Two of Barewolf's gang." He surveyed them with a squinty glance, his Monday morning temper uncertain. "What makes you think I'd hire you kids?"

Snoose pulled at Johnny's arm. "I told you he wouldn't," he muttered, aware of Lornas and Mosey near by. "Let's go back to our rig."

But Johnny pushed him aside. He shouldered past Mosey Fritz. "Sure, we're from Barewolf's gang." He faced Bory doggedly to hide his qualms. "And Herman Barewolf's gang, they're hard workers. You don't have to like Uncle Herm to know that. A feller that's handled thrashing all over the country the way you have——" He let his white grin add to his praise. "Besides, you pay more," he said directly. "And I need the money." ("I," Johnny said, not "we," Snoose noticed.)

Bory chewed this information with another stalk. He grinned. The scar seemed to open nakedly so that his face was a mask with a lower edge ripped aside raggedly. "You don't let the wind blow under your heels, do you, kid? All right. If Barewolf don't want you, I'll take you on trial. Throw your bundle in the tender. We start at noon." He flung over his shoulder, "Remember this. I trust nobody. If I catch you monkeyin', I'll kick you hind-end before, and then fire ya." His promise was stamped with a grimace.

Mosey swapped glances with Lornas. His eyes slitted. There were old scores to be settled. On this threshing run they'd be sweet in the paying.

On that Monday afternoon Johnny and Snoose rode the separator into the west and into the Valley, and put the hills behind them for a space. Folks were soon grumbling, "That Barewolf's Johnny. Leaving his uncle and the rig like that, after all that's been done for him. Ach, what are kids coming to?" Of Kurt they said, "You can depend on him. Steady as time."

But Lilice, hearing that Johnny had gone to work on Tetzell's machine, listened to her father's moans and shut the sickroom door swiftly, shivering. She remembered the Barewolf rig in the yard and Johnny at a cutter's table. He had stood near the dust of the cylinder—near enough to put a finger on the blurred teeth of death. Now he was going out to the flats with that reckless, drunken Tetzell outfit——

Well, what of it? What's he to you? she demanded of her anxiety. I guess he doesn't care much about me or he'd stay here and—— She caught up a broom, realizing how silly the notion was. I don't care. He's not going to make me feel bad. I won't think about him. Ma's right. If he wants to go threshing and get hurt, let him. I won't think about him. Won't even think of his name, she resolved energetically.

All that afternoon she crowded "Johnny" away with broom and dust cloth. Once she moved swiftly to the piano and swept into a wild hysterical *tarantelle* until loud thumps came from the bedroom. But she couldn't brush away the thought of wavy black hair and a white grin that was not far from laughter. The machine was like a jagged fragment in her mind.

8

Tetzell's rig moved over the last long hog-back of a hill. Johnny and Snoose rode the separator. The separator man handled the lines. Ahead of them Makin Boone, the fireman, drove the team which hauled the engine, cold and dead now, its fires black ash. Bory was on the tender with Mosey and Lornas. Behind them a wagon brought the feeder and the rest of the crew. Last of all came the water man with his barrels.

They saw the Valley floor spreading away miles from where they were, a table-evenness of land that faded from the sight and merged into the vague, skim-milk, washed-out blue of the horizon. Here and there were groves of trees, the rough-edged markers of a farm. So vastly far these reaches stretched away that a shack or a cloud hurt the eye with a sense of physical interruption. It was as if the beholder had stumbled over a rock and were momentarily swerved from his path.

Johnny never forgot the feeling of quick smothering uneasiness that ran over him at the sight of the Valley: this flatness, this space, this land without recognizable division, this sky, cloud-tracked but unblemished by the smallest wing of bird, this void—it rose up with the wall of the horizon, higher, higher, zenith-high and seemed to bend down and lean upon his head and shoulders with a weight that made his breath come thick and sent him twisting round to look behind him where the hills lifted ridge and slope. In their rugged folds lay security. He huddled under the collar of his jacket.

But Snoose jumped to his feet in excitement and pointed. "Look Johnny. God's dancing floor." He swayed to hold his balance on the unsteady top of the separator. "I've always wondered what its bigness would be like." He was queerly stirred.

"Sit down before you fall into the bigness." Disgustedly, Johnny grabbed Snoose's jacket end. "I'm not going to drag you up."

In this area where showers had fallen, there were fields of wheat and shocks without end—shocks that were large and bulky near by but which shortened and grew smaller in the distance until they were like dots and specks, and then like pin points under the far sky and finally were only the illusion of iotas.

"Judas, what a lot of pitching to do out there," Johnny observed mournfully, rubbing his callused palms, daunted by the miles of wheat.

"You think this is something?" the separator man queried. "Huh. You ought to see the big farms over west and up north. Thousands of acres belonging to one man. Takes a day to pull a furrow from one end of his place to the other. In good years they use three or four machines on one farm. It takes weeks to thrash one place. Big machines, too, not little coffee grinders like this one. In good years, that is. Looks like the big farms are burnt out too this year."

They began descending the hill. Johnny tried to shrug off a queer uneasiness. But all he could think of was an immensity like a chasm, himself on the edge, into which he might tumble. It was to bother his sleep.

They were to thresh here on these Valley acres for days—until the rainy afternoon Bory's fist cracked into Johnny's face. And not once in that time did Johnny escape the harsh awareness of all the longitudes of distance, unbroken, undefiled. But Snoose seemed to spread feathers of enjoyment and take vastness in one flight.

"I'd like to pull me a mountain into the middle of the prairie," he said one day when he was loading bundles and near enough to Johnny to speak. "I'd sit on the top of that mountain and shoot me a couple of spit balls. I bet I'd hit a flea sticking his head out of a crack in the hills."

"Snoose, for God's sake." Johnny waved his fork disparagingly. They had finished a run of stacks by that time and were hauling bundles from the field. "Shock thrashing," they called it. Soon now they would be going to Norton's farm. "I can't figure how you like these damn flats. It's so—well, so lonesome here. Not a house in miles. And roads. They're not even decent cow paths."

"What you want roads for?" Snoose demanded. "Roads never take you straight where you want to go anyway. They always go around." He chuckled, his gray eyes lost in teasing, but serious, too. "Not a fence in sight, Johnny. You can go where the wind goes and not a twig to hinder you. I like it here. It's open. God don't have to rub a tree out of His eye to see."

"Aw, Snoose, keep your pants up or you'll drain into the river." Johnny was ready to be annoyed. "I'll stick to the roads. You go cutting across the fields, you might get lost." Snoose's grin over a shock was monkeyish.

Two days later they were threshing for a farmer named Ash. Johnny and Snoose each drove a bundle team. So did Mosey and Lornas. Bory saw to that. "You hire my pitchers to drive your bundle wagons," he told the farmers bluntly, "or I'll pull out." Which was surly bluffing, as everyone but Bory knew.

Ordinarily, farmers depended on the stream of migratory workers that flowed riverlike through Mary's Hill and the Valley towns each fall. From southern plain and undulating prairie they came, these seasonal laborers, trampers of the road, following the trail of wheat and the clink of silver from Texas through Kansas and the Dakotas. Like grasshopper swarms they settled into the Valley and remained until the fields were bare. Once the shocks were threshed and the straw heaped into piles or scattered over the stubbles, they trekked into Canada, or, feeling the chill of the winter's first flake melting on their cheeks, turned and wandered back south into the sun.

Usually, with promises of top wages, savory cooking and a bed soft as a maiden's dream, farmers had little trouble in diverting from the roads such workers as they needed. Nevertheless, a thresher would seldom find a farm oversupplied with help. For one reason or another, there was a hauler lacking on a bundle wagon or a sacker on a grain team.

Many times the owners of small farms complained bitterly that they sought for men in vain. "I've hunted high and low," one would tell another. "By roadway and crossing. The big farmers hired all the shockers. Us little fellers, we get what Paddy shot at." If the year were one of meager yield, the stream of workers dried to trickles, the men heading for areas where rain had fallen and the crops offered better pay. Some folks said that the migrants were only one step behind the showers.

This year what labor there was ran barefoot seeking jobs and the landowners were more finicky. When they could, they hired the regular crews of threshing rigs that pulled into the flats. These, they said, were more dependable than bird-of-passage help. For that reason rather than his truculence, the farmers listened to Bory and agreed to hire his men.

And so on this Ash farm, eight bundle wagons swayed and lurched over the field trails, bringing the loads of shocks to the bandcutters' tables. Wherever the haulers worked in the fields, heaving the weighted forks, the rig was in their sight, so flat the land was, and the *chug-a-chug* of the engine and the cylinder hum were in their hearing.

Johnny glanced up the wall of butt ends on his wagon one afternoon and smirked a little over the neat way he'd packed the tiers of bundles and built his load. Alb Hukelpoke used to say that you could always tell a good thrasher by the way he stacked his wagon or "set" his machine. Bory was just a little off in both, Johnny was certain. He himself was more than proud of his own work.

Over the stubbles the whistle screeched, two shorts, two longs, two shorts, darts and lances of shrill command: "Bundles, bundles! Hurry up with what you've got! Hurry up!" He saw the bursts of steam, the short white jabs, the longer cloudy thrusts, jut into the air before the sound broke into his ears. "Get a hustle on you, Jackson! You're late again," he said aloud, half in commiseration for Jackson, half in pride that his own load was ready. Usually when he drove up to take his turn at the tables he'd find that he was early and had time to spare—time for minutes at the engine and talk with Makin Boone, the fireman.

He called, leaning on his fork, "Guess I've piled up 'bout enough, Snoose."

"I'll pitch on an extry shock or two." Snoose, not far away, giddapped the team. "Keep that smart Mosey Fritz's mouth shut. He's always braggin' how much he hauls."

"I'm going to stuff his trap, one of these days." Johnny climbed his load. "Whoa, there, boys," he soothed the horses. Near the top he said, "You can carry what Mosey hauls in your shirttail." The team stamped. "I'm going in, Snoose. You got plenty, too. First thing, you'll hit your head on a piece of sky." The team started moving. "Watch that rough spot near the rig, or you'll tip over, Snoose."

From the top of the load Johnny turned almost eagerly to the smudge and the dust that hung in the air forty acres away. There was the separator as he'd always remembered it, with its long strawstacker slanting up and dabs of straw floating gently to the heap below. The teams—"bucking" teams they were called—dragged the straw away before it swelled into a yellow pile under the stacker. Even the way the bucking teams scurried over the stubbles, pushing the straw in front of a "bucker" bar between them, and scattered the load as they trotted over the acres—even this was common as grits to him. What gave him a queer bump was the engine. Gone was the round of horses circling the power. Instead there was the bull engine puffing its dark billows upward, a lash of steam whipping above the steam chest. Between separator and engine wavered a belt, a thin thread at this distance. Gone too were the tumbling bucks and the box over which Mr. Nussbaum's sorrels hesitated to pass. Not lengths of tumbling rods but a long endless strip of canvas carried motion to the separator now. He almost sighed over memory. Yet at home Uncle Herm's rig still used horsepower and tumbling rods.

With Snoose following he drove across the field. The sound of threshing grew as he approached the machine. It gave him an odd feeling, this swell of iron clash. He guided his load into place. Ahead of him stood a rack still half full of bundles, the pitcher at work.

Got time for a breather, he thought, seeing Snoose draw up on the opposite side of the machine. He slid from the load and went to the engine, waving at Makin Boone. "What did you say reg'lated the governor—a valve stem?" he asked as he came.

Afterward, remembering the sweat and the dust and Bory's anger,

Johnny was sure it was the rosy warmth of the firebox and the thin-faced, lanky friendliness of Makin Boone, the fireman, that kept him from jabbing his fork into the prairie stubble and quitting; Makin and the engine. Between loads and during the minutes of a breakdown, he slouched in the straw heap not far from a bull wheel, his ears open to the plunge of the piston and the *hizz-soo—hizz-soo* of steam like a breath sharply drawn and swiftly expelled against the teeth. He helped the waterman at the pump and felt the throb of the hose under his foot as sloo water gurgled hollowly along the low-slung tubing and into the boiler. Unquenchably thirsty with the sweat of iron and flame and steam, the engine swallowed barrel after barrel. Johnny scratched his head over its long draughts. He put a finger on the gauge which measured with a pencil of bluish water the thirst or the surfeit of its belly.

He listened to Makin's saying, "Me, I'm like those gulls flyin' over there. One month I'm in Texas and 'nother in Kansas and then I'm here. Quit when I feel like it. I don't wait for my dung to cool."

Johnny hunched his shoulders the way Makin did. He poked into boxes and twisted pet cocks into wheezes of live steam, until Makin said, "You must figure on runnin' one o' these things, the way you monkey around."

Johnny wiped a smear of grease on his pants. Then he said slowly and firmly, "I aim to." He glanced up at the levers and wondered how it would feel, the iron of control in his hands—a push on the throttle, the sharp, imperative snort of the exhaust, the startled blur of the flywheel rushing into motion. Not jerkily, as Bory did it, but with easy tries and gently. So he'd do it, he decided.

Makin looked at him. "Guess you will, at that." He pushed at a forkful of straw. "Want to try firin' a while? Keep your eye on that smokestack and don't let 'er blacken."

Without a word Johnny grabbed the fork. There was a queer tingle in his blood as he poked the first heap of straw into the mouth of the fire chute and saw how with each chug at the smokestack, the straw was sucked jerkily inward. Eagerly he swept the tines into the pile for another forkful. At his look, Makin grinned understandingly.

But when Tetzell strode toward the engine, Johnny dropped the fork. No use in getting Bory more riled than he usually was.

Something a teamster said about Bory stuck in Johnny's mind. The teamster had told a bandcutter: "Funny how Tetzell got Norton's job. It's a big job, you know. Bub Weiser from south of Mary's Hill was s'posed to have it. Norton promised him. And then one night somebody caught Bub back of the Chicago Emporium over in Mary's Hill; beat all hell out of him. Bub's still laid up. He never drug his rig out of the yard; never oiled

a boxing this fall. Wasn't it lucky for Tetzell that Bub had—an accident?"
Johnny regarded Tetzell's burly shoulders with the beginning of a kind
of hate.

Sometimes, sitting on the platform and letting the lazy *chug-a-chug* of
the engine get under the beat of his blood, Johnny felt his muscles,
tensed after seven hours of pitching, gently, easefully softening, relaxing in
motion with the rhythm of live steam and iron. It was as if a living hand
were cradling away the tug of weariness.

"How did you get to know so much about engines?" he asked Makin one
day. "Your—your pa learn you?"

"Pa? Hell, no!" A curl of flame crept out under the door of the fire
chute. Makin slapped it into black ash with a bare hand. "Never had pa
nor ma. Me, I'm a doorstep kid. But I've been most places and done most
things since then. Ran away from the foundlin's' home."

"But your name——"

"That." Makin rubbed the fire-scorched handle of the fork. "Saw 'Boone'
in a book I read once; liked it and took it. I made up the other. I'm me
alone and nobody else, and I made up my own name—seeing my pa didn't
think enough of me to give me his."

Johnny's hand thumped down. A knuckle hit iron and the skin reddened. Thoughtfully he sucked the finger.

On many mornings thereafter, no matter how much Snoose groaned,
"What you want up so early?" and sank back, Johnny arose with Makin's
sputtery lantern. The two set off to "fire up" before Johnny fed his
team and Snoose's.

They'd trudge across the fields, the lantern glow pale on the stubbles
crispy with frost, the night wind so raw in their throats no amount of
buttoning jacket or coat protected them. They'd find the engine a hulk of
coldness.

"Kid, you must have an awful hankering for this. You could be sleepin'
'nother half hour," Makin said once. His fingers were stiff with chill-
numbness. He dropped two matches before the third bit its stubby pointed
flame into the kindling straw. A pigtail of an icicle crooked from a pet
cock.

"I have. I aim to get somewhere where I'm my own boss." Johnny's
breath made a wet spot on chill metal. "I've got a heap of grubbing to do,
before I get there." In the east dawn was no more than the glimmer of a
candle flame behind a door just opening.

Those were the effulgent minutes after all. Most of his days were
lengths of heaving strain, the flash of fork tines, now into the bundle at his

feet, now out of the bundle over his head . . . minutes of lolling on the load in the nest his body crowded out among the sheaves, waiting his turn at the cutter's table . . . shivering in morning chill, uncomfortably moist in noon heat, trembling in evening cold . . . waiting for the unhitching hour and time for talk with Makin or tussle with Snoose or a pitcher, litheness not yet contracted into inelasticity . . . grinning when Mosey Fritz turned a corner too sharply and smashed a wagon: Mosey's fox face pointed with desire to fling back laugh for laugh and hesitating; "Just let him try!" dared Johnny . . . Snoose opposite him, his bundle partner, talking more and more about Em'ly Musser: "I'd swim a river to see her, Johnny" . . . Lilice's face in the blur of the flywheel: would he swim a river to see Lilice? Bitterly he reproached himself: Maybe she's mad after what happened at the Marchens'; won't look at me. When I get home, Lilice, when I get home—— Hum of his voice, hum of the separator . . .

There were the moments when he jumped up from drowsing reverie to find the rack ahead of him empty. His turn now. "G'up, there," he yelled. He clutched the lines wildly to hold his balance. Bundles twisted under his feet. Butt ends brushed a cutter's table as he drove into place. The cutter's eyes were white marbles in a gray face.

Then the unloading, tier by tier carefully. He could do it in his sleep. First a tier on one side, then a tier on the opposite; otherwise the rack would sag on the heavy side and tip the wagon over. Keep an eye on the band where the fork strikes fanglike: eye follows the arc of the bundle. The slight tug as the straw slides from the smooth tines to the table. The island of elbowroom in the tumble of bundles. Bundles, bundles. Yells, "Whoa, there, damn you!" as the horses, restive with the wheels so near them, move impatiently. Bundles, bundles. One more bundle and there are the floor boards, the bottom of the rack. The last row of bundles, heigho, heighee, how quickly they vanish, once your feet are steady on firm underpinnings! Up go the last. Then "G'up, there!" and away you rattle, let the next man pitch in his own sweat awhile. Coolness of wind on hot chest and belly. Ruddle of wheels against the bony arches of your feet, jarring your teeth, lower against upper. Out into the fields again. Over and over. But in those moments between the first sheaf and the last, how much of youth (the prairie-searching eye, the peak-leveling mind) is left under the fork: youth, that lubricant of toil, of life, of slow mill-grinding time. Over and over. Day after day. From farm to farm . . .

Almost every night Johnny would look over the flat lands and see the horizon inflamed with the red of burning straw. There were hedges of crimson where the chaff and stems lay scattered in the stubble. There were scarlet towers where huge piles shot flame high into the night. It was a strange, a weird sight, a bizarre kind of ritual under the sky, the ritual of man's improvidence. Those fires leaping out there, smoky and baleful— they might have been stellar torches flung to earth, smoldering to extinction in a foreign, terrestrial sphere.

One time they entered a yard where the barn was small and the house of sod smaller. They slept in a straw pile that night, buttoning on what extra jackets and shirts they had. Shaking with cold Snoose burrowed closer to Johnny. Chaff rubbed against his ears. In a kind of brother warmth, sleepy body against sleepy body, they twitched away cold during the long hours until daybreak. They had breakfast by turns in the small house. But it was a solid breakfast that belied the humple-cornered shack and drove out the chill. "Devil!" exclaimed Johnny, gulping his hot coffee. "I nearly shivered myself into a sweat last night."

And once at another farm a teamster, strapping his horses into a cloud of dust, rumbled up where Johnny pitched. The teamster yelled, "Whoa!" and his horses snorted in the gray haze that swept ahead of him. "God-almighty, I'm not eatin' in that house," he said, drawing back his lip in disgust. "I went to the pump for a drink and there was Old Lady What-ever-her-name-is; never did hear it. But there she was, washing the weevils off a hunk of cheese. I seen it. Crawly vermin."

That night at supper he and Johnny and Snoose and Makin drank the coffee but scarcely soiled a knife or fork on the thin, soupy hash they got. They slipped bread under the table and into their pockets and abruptly scraped the chairs from the dirty cloth and their untouched plates.

"Devil grab it!" Johnny held his stomach, thinking of Aunt Phrena's meat and potatoes and the raspberries Lilice picked, as they hurried to the engine. "That butter—it wasn't even decent axle grease."

"Some people's meals—lummy," Makin said. "You can't get your teeth through the gravy. Where'd you find the chicken nests, Jackson?"

They had boiled eggs and bread without butter for a meal that night— eggs stolen from the nest by the wily teamster and boiled in an old can, in water steaming from the engine. They sucked every clinging fragment of yolk and crumb from their fingers, their bellies still flat with the hungry clamor of muscle and blood.

"I'm that empty," mourned Snoose, "I could eat the shells."

And once in a homesteader's barn, rats held squeaking carnival and hung the crew on a peg of sleeplessness through heavy winking hours. Makin said, "They're fighting the snakes. I saw a couple wiggling into the hay."

"Snakes?" The men scattered, most of them to the straw pile, Makin, Snoose and Johnny with them. The separator man crawled into the belly of his machine. But the waterman stayed where he was: he'd been bitten by things lower than rats and snakes, he said.

And always the whistle, the nerve-rubbing whistle (Bory with a long whiplike tongue lashing over the fields to the uttermost acre), shrieking their legs into sweatier effort. *Toot-toot, toot-toot, too-ot, too-ot, toot-toot:* hurry up with what you've got; hurry up! Time and again on long hauls men were late. They shouted at their teams, knowing how the crew would snicker. "What did you do out there—lay eggs?"

Once a trace broke and Johnny drove in to find himself three turns behind and Bory glowering. Always the whistle. Often he'd hear the long, snaky water call drag across the flats to the ponds and see the waterman whip his team into hurry. Or there'd be jumpy, impatient *dit-dit-dit-dit-dit's:* sacks, sacks, sacks. He'd stop to squint at the grainmen riding a dust cloud toward the machine. Morning and night he jerked to work at the whistle's bark: *toot-toot,* start up! At quitting time his ears became stony with the rush of steam and the shrill monotone hanging like a roof of sound overhead.

The crew threshed by day and found what rest it could in straw or hay at night, or on the open prairie. Hate glittered like a blade sometimes. A teamster settled an argument one morning by grabbing a neck yoke. With a jingle of rings he smashed a bundle hauler's arm. Johnny heard the bone crack like a pipe stem. Snoose shuddered, milk-faced.

The crew "greased out" a Dago one night and slapped their thighs as the swarthy-skinned, scrabby-whiskered man scuttled into the dark, his clothes oil-soaked and grease-smeared. "Guess that settles the wop talk nobody but him understands," the men exulted, justice executed.

And one noon Johnny found Snoose in the haymow, shoulders furiously hunched over what was lying on the floor. The air was strong with the stink of human muck. "All over my new jacket!" raged Snoose. "No dog did that. My jacket was hanging on the nail there. Somebody——"

"Mosey Fritz," Johnny said positively. "I'll bet a three-cent nickel." His expression brought Snoose to his side.

"You can't be sure." Snoose pushed the jacket with a toe. Disgust wrinkled his nostrils.

"Maybe not. I wouldn't trust Lornas but he's not that dirty. Nobody else here got anything against you." Johnny glowered. "It's not really you, Snoose. It's me. Mosey don't dare knock into me, so he spites you, the two-toed rat."

"I'm not scared of Mosey," Snoose answered resolutely.

"Course not. But he's a manury sneak." Johnny paused; then said, "Give it to me, Snoose."

He washed the jacket at the watering trough behind the barn, ready to welcome inquiry with short words, especially Mosey's or Lornas'. But no one saw him.

When he met Mosey later he calmly butted against him. Mosey spun and half fell. "What the devil!" he blustered, regaining his equilibrium. "What do you——"

"You want to try shoving me?" Johnny asked, the words froggy and hoarse with desire to put hands on Mosey. "Or shall I take *your* jacket off and sit on it?" His fists were hard knots of bone.

Mosey's mouth wiggled. His bluster oozed away. "I—I don't—I ain't lookin' for trouble. Besides, I'm in a hurry. Got to watch my team." He slunk off among the bundle wagons.

Two days later after lunch Mosey cornered Snoose. Johnny came on them as Mosey was teasing, "Don't you wash a-tall, Snoose?" His pudginess was squashy with derision.

"Maybe I don't dirty myself," Snoose snapped hotly.

"You don't say." Mosey sniffed daintily. "Seems there's a funny smell around here right now."

Charging in, Johnny struck and jolted patches of white light through Mosey's head. Mosey tumbled backward. A startled realization sagged his jaw. His shoulders hugged the earth.

Johnny stood over him. "That's a sample, Mosey. What's got a funny smell?"

"I—I don't know. I was just funnin'." Mosey tried to crawl turtlewise away.

"Funnin', were ya, Mosey?" Johnny yanked him to his feet. "Not smellin'?"

"No, no." Mosey bobbed his head violently. "Snoose don't smell. Honest. I didn't mean——"

"What's the ruckus, fellers?" Lornas stepped from behind a rack.

Something in his swagger reminded Johnny forcefully of Bory. He thought, The sneak, he stood there, listening to every word. Aloud he said grimly, "If you want another smell, Mosey, just hang around. Go ahead, you dirty pants-wetter."

Mosey took three fast steps toward the safety of Lornas' side. He halted there, gaining courage from the pitchfork in Lornas' fist.

"Any special trouble here?" Lornas was casual.

"Nope." Johnny stood ready. "What I said to Mosey, that's for anybody that wants to pick it up."

"Oh?" Lornas moved the pitchfork and measured glances with Johnny. Then his eyes shifted. He changed his mind. He prodded Mosey, snickering, "Looks like you need a face wash. What did you do, run your face into a fence post?" Deliberately he swaggered off, tight as a coiled spring. Mosey trotted after him.

"You shouldn't have done that, Johnny," Snoose asserted. "I can handle myself, especially with Mosey."

"Sure you can," admitted Johnny. "If I was dead sure Mosey smucked your jacket, I'd settle with him in a minute. With Lornas, too."

"And get Bory riled in the bargain." Snoose shook his head. "That Lornas, he don't say much, but he's worse than Mosey. Ten times worse."

Some days when rancor hung over the crew like thunderheads (the separator man rowing with straw piler over a spilled can of oil, a feeder bandaging his cut fingers and threatening to castrate a clumsy-handed bandcutter), the air sang like a fiddlestring with the tenseness of waiting for the quarrel to explode.

Over these lashing outbreaks, as if he loved them, Bory purred, fingers clawlike. "Hee, hee, how you like it, kids?" he snickered at Johnny and Snoose. "A few heads cracked, that's what I like to see. It makes a good crew. You can't be a thrasher until you've cracked a head or broken an arm, or been under the wheel." His lips became moist with his thought.

"Under the wheel?" Snoose asked unluckily. "You mean fall under the bull wheel?"

"No, kid." Bory's eyes became as mean as a boar pig's in heat. "No, this wheel won't kill ya, just make a man of ya." He guffawed wetly. The scar pulled and jumped like a strip of fresh red beef flipping. He slapped Lornas knowingly. Mosey looked around, wiggling with anticipation, now that he could depend on the security of numbers.

Bory said, "Maybe we'll make a thrasher out of some of you yet this fall." He flicked a glance over Snoose's slenderness, a hard-muscled, deceptive slenderness.

9

They finished at one place, hooked a team to the engine, hooked a team to the separator, giddapped the rig to another. They threshed at the Ampers', the Scogginses', the Slocombes'—Johnny couldn't remember which farmer was which. "Just slowpokin' along. Not much better than it was at Uncle Herm's," he grumbled.

"We thrash faster," Snoose insisted.

"Sure. But we waste almost as much time. Bory's no better than Alb Hukelpoke when it comes to handling the team and lining up the engine. He gives me a gut-ache."

They finished at the Slocombes', neighbors to Norton, one morning. Over the prairies Johnny could see the red elevators of Mary's Hill rise from a fold in the ridge. That afternoon they hauled the machine onto Norton's place. Half of his farm was rolling land, half was valley bottom, flat as an ironing board. The greater part of his fields was empty of shocks, the grain safely in the stack.

Johnny and Snoose were riding with the waterman when they drove into the yard. "Four Oaks Farm" Norton called his place. He was proud of the gnarled old trees that flung shade over his doorstep. Three were almost leafless now. The fourth was dead from lightning stroke, the bole splintered and weathered gray. But Norton wouldn't have it cut.

The house sent Snoose into a dreamy mood. It was large, too large for one man and his wife. There were towers bulgy as Norton himself and sharp dormers and squares of window long as a bed sheet, bordered with yellow and blue panes.

"No wonder Norton's important," Johnny said. "A place like this—anybody living here would feel that he was boss."

"I'll bet there's a ghost in those towers," Snoose fancied; "maybe a couple of spooky lovers."

"More likely rats." Johnny gawped around. "What a passel of buildings!"

Except for the cow and horse barns, Norton called his buildings "houses"—the pig house, the hen house, the sheep house, the hands' house. So Johnny learned later. The hands' house where his four hired men bedded and kept their truck was a white, clapboard box of a place not far from the oaks. (When they trooped in that night, they found two lanterns brightening the large cluttered room and shining on the harnesses and farm gear overhead. A faint smell of leather oil hung between the walls. The four hired men would sleep in the main house during the threshing. Makin shouted, "Lummy, bunks! And pillows! Crawl in, you bundle stiffs; take your pants off first and don't grease the blankets.")

Norton was waiting for the rig. He was a large man, big of belly and bulging of neck, with a nose that was bulblike but eyes that were watery in mildness, hiding the raven's gleam and the hawk's stare. Oversized and stumplike he stood planted in his yard. Upon this rich and influential landowner Johnny gazed with hungry curiosity but little friendliness.

Norton gave directions. Bory began to set the machine and line up the engine. He shrieked profanities at the horses.

"Wonder how many tries he'll make this time," Johnny said louder than he intended. "He took six at the Slocombes' and then the belt flew off twice. Worse than Alb Hukelpoke."

"Don't think much of him, do you?" A smooth voice slid over Johnny's shoulder. Johnny whipped about. Norton stood there. His smile was watery.

"He'll pass." Johnny was noncommittal.

Norton laughed. The sound was unexpectedly mirthful. "Bory's a purty good thrasher. Of course, he's the kingpin this year. Some rigs never even steamed up."

"You got a good crop," Johnny conceded, meeting him halfway, thinking, I'd like to get my hands on the mortgage you hold against Uncle Herm, you bloodsucker.

"I had rain." Norton modestly claimed his kinship with the elements. His thick fingers tangled in a heavy watch chain. "Maybe next year'll be wet and we'll all have crops."

"Up our way some folks lost their farms. I guess even Uncle Herm has to scratch to keep ahead of—of the sher'ff." Johnny couldn't hold back the words. The thought was very near his tongue, "What about the Roses?" but he couldn't ask. Snoose folded a straw carefully.

"Them that lost their farms is mostly loafers." Norton's bulk was placid. "A man would be a fool to lose a hard worker. Never lost a penny on your uncle yet. Don't expect to." He untangled a finger from the chain. "I give every man a chance."

As Norton walked toward the barn, Snoose said, "He could help a feller a lot. I'd hate to have him against me, though." Thinking of the winter nights Uncle Herm had spent over the figuring of this debt, Johnny agreed but sourly.

At the fifth try, Bory "lined her up." Shock threshing at the Norton's began. Johnny hung near the warmth of the engine and Makin's talk, his eye on the throttle.

Then in the middle of a forenoon just as Johnny flung the last bundle on the cutter's table, Uncle Herm drove up. Even his whisker ends seemed to frizzle with gladness when he thumped Johnny's shoulder. "These flats agree with ya, boy?"

"I wouldn't give one square foot of hills for a whole section of this." Johnny waved at the prairies vehemently.

Uncle Herm smiled. "Broke me the damn bull-wheel cap. I had to wait in town. Thought I'd skitter over and see if Bory's old teakettle puts motion in the separator."

"It's got power and to spare, except in heavy stuff." Johnny climbed into the rack again. "In a good year, there's money rollin' on these prairies. Look at Norton's shocks." He grabbed the lines. "I'll get behind if I don't get along. G'up, there!" As he rattled away he saw Norton coming to shake hands with Uncle Herm. But Bory, near the water wagon and flipping a piece of rawhide, stayed where he was.

Johnny drove into the field, a tingle leaping in his blood. The touch of Uncle Herm was a kind of medicine in his veins. He looked eastward. There were the hills, the hills of Pockerbrush, closer now, Uncle Herm's heartiness drawing them a sweet hand's space nearer. And Lilice was brought nearer, too. Lilice . . . A snatch of song bubbled from him, one he'd heard Makin baritoning over the hissing pet cocks:

> "She baked her bread and she baked it well
> And she baked it harder'n the hubs of hell."

Lilice, sweeter in distance than in nearness, the red of her lips. "Whoo-ip!" he yelled. The horses switched from a trot to a gallop. "I'm going home one of these Saturdays and take in a dance," he promised himself. Lilice, Lilice . . .

When he returned, teetering on his full load, Uncle Herm had gone— Uncle Herm who had talked with Norton and had watched the engine awhile; who had watched Johnny pitching in the field a long while before he flicked his horses lightly and drove away.

The next morning during an interval of waiting for his turn to unload at the bandcutter's table, Johnny fired the engine, one eye wary for Tetzell, though he wasn't exactly sure why. He enjoyed a sense of victory in knowing that he was learning the firing job and getting the "feel" of the engine, throttle and valve. But he was apprehensive, too, for Bory, unpredictable of temper at best, might come pouncing at any moment and bellow him back to the wagon. More than once Bory had caught him with Makin's fork in his hand while Makin loafed near by. At such times Johnny felt the muscles in his arm go tight. With a thin smirk Bory had observed the way Johnny relinquished the fork. Beyond a squinty disapproval, however, Bory said little, as though waiting for a moment when his roaring anger would be most impressive.

This morning Bory came from the granary, ugliness in his short steps. The scar twitched. Norton was with him. They had disagreed about the measuring of the grain. Bory found Johnny pulling the empty fork from the fire chute and Makin idle behind the water wagon. Truculently he stood near the bull wheel. "So that's why the old bitch pops off all the time this morning. A green hand firing again." He glared at Johnny. "I thought I hired you to pitch bundles."

"My load is waiting. Jackson is ahead of me." Johnny's fingers on the handle were taut. "I'd like to get the hang of firing, if you don't care." He grinned with stiff amiability, more at Norton than at Bory.

Bory grunted, "Get back to your lousy pitchfork!" He bellowed, "Makin, where the hell are you? Tend to your firin', or dust your heels down the road." With the scar a raw grimace, he slammed the toolbox and strode away.

Johnny's fingers relaxed. There was sweat in the palm of his hand.

Norton stood a moment, weighing Johnny like a bag of silver before he asked, "Been firin' long?"

"Nope. Not long. But I'm getting to handle her." Johnny put the fork down. "Makin learned me."

"Seems to me—" Norton was judicial—"the engine didn't pop off more than ordinary."

"Course it didn't." Makin returned to the firing. "And nobody but a muck eater like Tetzell would say so."

When he stopped to talk with Makin thereafter, Johnny was poised with vigilance. Two days later a strap broke on the harness and he came running to borrow Makin's knife to make a splice. Norton was there, leaning against the tender. Smoke boiled from the stack, darkening as it mixed with air. As he ran Johnny thought, A spark in the straw pile and the Devil himself couldn't stop the burning.

Norton was saying to Makin, "You ever fire a traction engine?"

"Sure." Makin leisurely clawed together a forkful of straw. "Over west and down south. They use 'em mostly for plowing. Pull like a son-of-a-whistle. The steer wheel is——"

"Makin, I busted a strap," Johnny interrupted him. "Let me have your——" There was a noisy clattering at the separator. Iron hammered iron, and broken ends banged. Wild shouts came spinning through the dust.

As if he'd been pricked into knowing what to do and without thinking, Johnny was on the platform. The levers in his hands slowed the engine swiftly and smoothly. The racket clumpered into silence.

His knees all water and gravy with weakness, Johnny stepped down. He felt foolish and guilty, as though Aunt Phrena would come presently and scorch him with sniffling blame. "Devil take it!" he muttered. "Makin, I don't know why I did that. I heard the yells and I just——"

Bory waddled up fast. "I need the concave wrench. You stopped her just in time, Makin. A stone got in the teeth and——"

"I didn't stop her." Makin helped him find the wrench. "It was Johnny there."

"The hell you say!" Bory halted to twist his scar. His glance was never less friendly. "Still monkeying around, huh?" He tramped off, clutching the heavy wrench.

Norton was about to follow him but stepped back to say, "You never miss a trick, do you, boy?" Johnny warmed to a kind of friendliness in his tone as if in this respect he and Norton understood one another.

10

Bory was thick-lipped with satisfaction over the stack threshing. "I like to thrash out of settings. This shock thrashing. Damn me, it's no good, leaving your wheat in the field to color out," he told Norton. "Wheat in the stack gets you a better grist of flour any day."

"Stacking takes time," Norton argued. "And it costs money."

Listening over a cup of coffee, Johnny decided that Bory was right. At stack threshing a thresher had his thumb on bundle and sack, pitcher and grainman. Threshing from the shock with teams and wagons scattered over forty acres, that was different. Then a thresher had only the whistle to hurry the pitchers and keep the bandcutters busy. To be sure, shock threshing did mean less resetting, less moving about, if the straw buckers did their job. And you could knock out two farms in the shock to one in the stack. But stack threshing—— Finally, he couldn't make up his mind which would bring in the most cash with the least trouble.

For the stack threshing Norton hired extra men. Most of his own help came down with "thrasher's stomach." In their beds they grabbed at their bellies and groaned. The new men were transients of the many that passed through Mary's Hill. This year as every other, they had come, following the tide of harvest, meager as it was: tramps and teachers, demi-hoboes and divinity students, factory workers empty of pocketbook and emigrants with the gutturals of foreign lands on their tongues, peasants and nobility. The jetsam of irresolution they were, a rootless migratory drift like the chaff of threshing on the waters of a creek.

Of the four who accepted hire, two were of the kind Uncle Herm would have sicked the dog upon, Johnny was sure. They arrived during a noon period. They were bearded, trap-lipped, stony-eyed wearers of ragged shirts and cracked shoes. Their faces quickened at the sight of food, a woman and silver in a palm. Within an hour's pitching Bory, sorting out the straws of kinship, called them jovially by their first names.

The other two were of a different stamp. One was plump and jolly, with the red apple of youth in his cheeks, and no older than Johnny.

Good nature was in him like a fire so that Johnny and Snoose exchanged names with him before he could tumble his bag upon a bunk in the hands' house. He was a divinity student.

But the last man was a man with a pointed brownish beard; a husky man who made no more of his weighty bundle than a bag of air. He was a longish length of bone and muscle put together in large pieces; big-handed and straight-backed as if what he carried were balanced on his head. Silenski, he said his name was. When he stepped down from the wagon, he stumbled and fell. He was up again catlike, so tranquil of face, his chuckle soft, that nobody in the crew laughed over his saying, "Ta eart'—she is hard like a fool's heart." His r's rattled in the deep well of his throat.

In his unpredictable way, Snoose said, "That man—you know, he looks clear and clean—just like Ma's lamp when she's got the soot cleaned out of the chimney." But Johnny shut his ears to such a fancy.

One glance that first night at the plump, apple-cheeked boy where he lay reading a small Bible, and Bory yelped, "A parson—a kid psalm-singer gettin' his text! What you going to preach on?" There was a meaty jocu-larity in his manner. On his bunk Silenski of the pointed beard tapped his lip with a long finger on which a ring twinkled—a ring with a crest on it. From his bed Johnny noticed that the crest was of gold. Above him Snoose rustled to the edge of the mattress and looked down.

"I'm not a parson yet." The divinity student smiled plumply. "I have a tremendous amount of studying to do. Just now, I'm rereading Ecclesi-astes through the Red River Valley," he added sociably.

"Ecclesiastes." Silenski sat up. "T'at is of a perfection," he said softly.

"We could get you a trough of water, s'posin' you want to baptize any-one." Bory roared guffaws of self-appreciation. Silenski looked at him.

The student drew back. "It takes more than a watering trough to bap-tize," he announced crisply if somewhat sententiously. "You know your business. I'm trying to know mine. It's a free country."

"I know some verses, too," the separator man offered. He began intoning solemnly, rolling a heavy emphasis upon the rhymes:

> " 'Here we are at Paddy's table,
> Lean as the homesteader's heifer Mabel;
> A bowl of soup, a pot of 'taters
> For all the plates and all the eaters.
> Yesterday there were six of us,
> Today there are four of us;
> Eatin' is lean for two of us.
> Thank God, there ain't no more of us!'

Is that Peter or Paul?" he asked, mockery sticking through his ponderous gravity.

Lornas snickered like a fox. Bory held his stomach, the scar purpling with his hilarity. Johnny grinned, not sure what else to do. But Snoose worried a hangnail unsmilingly. Silenski gazed on the laughter with a puzzled frown. The student bit his fat lip.

"Read us a piece," Makin proposed. His glance at the rest plainly said, "Here's where we have some fun with the kid." From fist to fist he tossed an iron spike as long as his hand and as square as the small dice which two pitchers were throwing on a board. "I ain't been in church lately; not in twenty years."

But Bory snarled authoritatively, "He can keep his damn preachin' to himself. I'm not——"

"Let ta boy read." Silenski spoke quietly but his voice rang. "I like ta Scriptures. T'ey hurt nobody." For a moment Bory was snaffled into speechlessness over this trampling on his authority.

The student hesitated. "Go ahead, boy," Silenski encouraged him. "Read somet'ing. What you like."

The student smiled at Johnny and Snoose and shrugged his shoulders as though he'd meet folly with folly and end the farce with the least amount of squabble. "I was thinking that everybody wants to be master nowadays and sit in the high places," he began, youthful seriousness bland on his plump cheeks. "People are like the wedding guest in the parable. Nobody wants the lowest seat. But the words say, 'When thou art bidden, go and sit down in the lowest room; that when he that bade thee cometh, he may say unto thee, Friend, go up higher: then shalt thou have worship in the presence of them that sit——'"

Over the student's reading, not breaking but rather swelling the youthful sonority of voice, flowed Silenski's meditated syllables, liquid in their gentle insistence, one stream unhurriedly twining with another: "'And ta Master said: Be not concerned at want of place; be concerned t'at t'ou stand t'yself.'" His soft voice filled the aisle between the beds and was lost among the harnesses under the ceiling.

The student lowered his book. Above Johnny's head the mattress whispered as Snoose moved. Johnny crabbed his brows. The men watched Bory.

Silenski went on, "'Sorrow not at being unknown, but seek to be wort'y of note.' Ye-as." He finished with a twist of his ring.

"Damn me, another preacher!" Bory haunched around. "What you don't find traveling under a pair of britches these days."

Paying no heed to him, the student was asking Silenski, "What passage is that? Proverbs or——"

"Ha, no. It is not in your book, my boy." Silenski leaned forward and picked up the spike Makin had thrown aside. "A great teacher of ta East said it. He was one you call a heat'en." His lips moved quizzically. "Read more, my boy."

Feeling authority slide from him, Bory said virulently, "I'm hitting the bunk and I want the lanterns out. This is what you can expect from scum like preachers. I wouldn't have one dead in my crew."

"Read, boy!" Tetzell might as well have been a suckling for all the attention Silenski gave him. " 'For whosoever exalted himself——' "

Bory rolled to his feet and strode to Silenski's bunk. "Look—ee here. My name is Bory Tetzell. I'm the boss around here, and when I say——"

"Bory Tetzell, ye-as." Silenski regarded him with the fatigue of one examining a tiresomely ubiquitous specimen. "It is your name, ye-as; but it is not you. You are legion."

"God damn it, I'm Tetzell!" Bory roared and crouched to strike.

Makin slipped his feet into his bunk as if to get out of danger's sweep. The dicers threw and froze in their places. The little dice rolled on the board, poised on their edges, fell—and lay still. Johnny drew himself together. The student closed his book.

But Silenski's beard pointed steadily at Bory. Only his shoulders straightened. His fists closed lightly about the two ends of the spike, his thumbs apexed against the center of the iron. "Why do you spit at Heaven?" he asked unruffled. "Heaven—she does not mind." His hands jerked to his breast in a sudden rustling snap. No spasm of strength marred the peace of his thin face. "Ta spit—she fall back on you." One hand unclenched. The spike lay in the palm, bent into the curve of a horseshoe. A fleck of metal twinkled. A small indentation at the base of a little finger lost its whiteness and reddened slowly. "Poof!" Silenski made a mouth apologetically.

Bory goggled. His pig eyes widened. There was a moist sound as he slobbered over his breath. Silenski flipped the spike on the bed beside Johnny, his hand as unshaken as if he'd lifted a thumb-and-forefinger of snuff, aristocratic, delicately aromaed.

Bory's stiffness collapsed. He slouched out of the hands' house.

"You care to read more, no?" Silenski sighed regretfully.

"No." The student shoved the book under his pillow.

"It's a pity." Silenski began to unbutton his shirt.

Makin poked at the bent spike. "Lummy, but you must be a stout one!"

"No. It is not ta muscle." Silenski shook an empty sleeve of his shirt in denial. "It is ta—how shall I say it?—ta whisper of ta mind. Poof! Like t'at." He spread his hands with a gesture Johnny thought queer and foreign.

Makin laughed. "I got to sleep on that one."

Johnny handled the U-shaped iron with the curiosity of one who suspects a trick. Later Snoose hefted it. Thoughtfully he hung it on a nail near his head. After a while somebody blew the lanterns.

11

Clouds slid in from the southwest. One morning the window near Johnny's bunk was blind with streaking rain.

Makin stirred, sat up and murmured, "Rain. Music, music, that's what it is. Fiddles and mouth organs. Nobody but a fireman can tell how sweet it sounds. Don't wake me for breakfast; don't wake me for a hundred weeks." The blankets rustled over his head.

"You boys might as well go home," Norton told Johnny and Snoose after breakfast. There was a feel of snow in the wind. "If she dries over Sunday, we'll thrash next week. Give your uncle my best."

They caught a ride to Mary's Hill, eagerness in their hurry. Not until the long crooked back of the first ridge humped up behind him and shut the rolling, empty miles of flatness away did Johnny draw a long breath. "Judas!" He sighed deeply. "It's good to see something that's so close by you don't have to stretch your eyeballs to find it." Snoose only half agreed.

From Mary's Hill they partly walked, partly rode to the store at the church crossing. With every hill and slant of valley, deeper grew Johnny's sense of putting aside an uneasy weight, of burrowing into the lap of security. A kind of warmth grew in him, hastening his steps. "Ah, Judas, I hope I'm buried here!" he said fervently. "Not just yet though, not for a long time, yet," he added hastily.

They followed the path they'd tramped so often on the road to Catechism at the parochial school. As they shuffled along, Johnny said what he had several times before: "They're good workers, Silenski and that Bible student. But to read the Bible for fun and like it—I can't figure that."

"Well, if a feller's going to be a preacher," suggested Snoose.

"Silenski's not," Johnny interrupted. "He'd just as soon read the Bible though."

"Not the Bible only," Snoose declared. "He read to me one day—remember when the elevator clogged? I climbed his load and he had a little blue book. It was about a river. What he read was——" He paused and gazed off over the hills, unable to tell in words what he had heard.

But Johnny said, "I can think of one good story—Goliath."

"Some stories, though," Snoose confided; "they come back to me. David and—what was his name? Jonathan. And Jacob on the ladder."

"All I remember is a headache." Johnny kicked a stone.

He left Snoose in the Marchen yard. As he turned to go, Jackie came from the barn to query, "Going to the dance tonight? Peiser's tapping a keg. They finished his barley couple days ago. Wetting the barley, he calls his shindandy."

Lilice, will you be there? flashed like a quick, bright bird through Johnny's brain. He asked, "You going, Snoose?"

"Guess not. Think I'll maul the pillow early. I'm gonna see Em'ly tomorrow."

Johnny swung from him. "Sure I'll go, Jack." The promise was spoken before his mind decided, so eager he was. It was as meat for hunger to be home. Uncle Herm must have finished with threshing by now, and Kurt with plowing. But Lilice . . .

On the path home he stopped, however, aware of a nagging queerness he'd noticed the moment he'd seen the church and the store and the Marchen farm, and all the places that were familiar as his little toe. It was as if he gazed upon the valley from a woods path new and strange to him, and he saw its length as one with the wind of distance in his eyes and the dust of unfamiliar roads in his nostrils.

"It's not been very long I've been away," he muttered. Not long, counted in weeks, no. But measured in hours and minutes, it was a hundred years at least, he thought. There was the ridge with the cleared space, once the beginning and the end of his world. And there the huddle of buildings which was Uncle Herm's farmstead. How well-timbered and roomy they had always appeared to him. Solid and foursquared to the valley he'd left them so short a time ago. How small and shrunken they were now because of this strangeness in him. They were like the oversized winter gloves he'd stored away one spring and found shriveled to scantiness in the fall, too tight for use.

Devil, but Uncle Herm surely needs a new barn, he decided. Oh, grab it! He struck off at a trot. I'm home. I'm going to a dance. Lilice . . .

The feeling persisted though it was almost blotted away by Uncle Herm's chortling welcome, "Good to see you, boy. You got the straw out of your ears yet?" and Kurt's flickering interest.

Though he was ready to be suspicious, even Aunt Phrena seemed less dismal. (Or did she only appear so? he speculated.) "You sit right down," she said, banging the coffeepot almost cheerfully onto the flame. "About time you got some Christian food into your stomach. There's clean shirt and pants on your bed."

Regarding her judiciously, he wondered that he'd ever cringed before her. Even when he said at supper, "There's a dance at Peisers'. Thought I'd go with Jackie," and braced himself for onslaught, Aunt Phrena merely nodded as though she expected no less than this.

She grumbled, unable to resist a sermon, "Folks can be yet so tired but they'll run and dance their legs off." She added, "Kurt's going. And that nice Gatha Blumen—she'll be there."

Almost laughing himself into feeling kindly toward her, he went to the mirror with a comb and rooted new tumbling waves into his hair.

Anders Stramff had already tweedled a crowd of couples into a waltz when he and Jackie arrived at the Peisers'. There was whooping in the corners with heavy bull stamps of boots. He grinned at the welcomes the folks gave him. "Hey, there!" "If it ain't the thrasher! How's the flats?" "Got yourself a pocket of money yet?"

"You bet. We got a hell of a big run out there," he answered. Importance swaggered in his hips. "Figure on maybe trying Canada."

He wove through the crowd, on the lookout for Alb (so he told himself), the music tapping in his toes even before Mr. Peiser offered him beer. "Na, Johnny. Home in the rain, huh?" Johnny nodded and swigged two glasses in a row, to Mr. Peiser's admiring, "You got a reg'lar thrasher's throat." Johnny hitched his belt complacently. After that, he wished— oh, he didn't know what, but she wasn't here. He wished he'd gone to see her.

He was jovial over his refusal to try a second shot from Herky Morrison's bottle. "Just had a splurt," he said, shouldering away.

Alb Hukelpoke sailed by, humpling in the waltz with a neighbor girl, a glass of beer waving in a free hand. He yelled, "Hello, Ma," as he passed his wife sitting on a bench, small and plump, a square hat pinned firmly with a long glass-topped hatpin. A sprinkle of beer fell at her feet. Already his eyes were webbed with vagueness.

When he saw Johnny, he staggered from his partner's arms, bellowing, "Well, sheetin' Juu—das!" and pounded Johnny's chest. Anders Stramff swung the accordion in greeting.

Heinie Beerwagon pawed at Johnny with a thick-tongued "Got a tonky of a story, Johnny. Listen," but Johnny shook free and lost Heinie in a thicket of shoulders.

Then a hand pulled him into a space under a lantern and he heard

Gatha's trill. "Johnn-ee! Why, Johnny the thrasher! I asked your aunt about you in church only last Sunday."

He stared at her. Gatha at school (how long ago, long ago); Gatha at ordinary parties, hair primly drawn to the sides and back, and braided into stiff tails, plain in a grayish dress—that was one thing. But Gatha in a dress that was gathered at the belt, her boyishness almost hidden by and yet suggested in the puffy waist and the folds of the sweeping skirt—that was something else.

"Where in Judas did you get the doodads?" he asked in a mellow mood.

"These?" Her hand toyed with a wave of cloth. "Oh, me and Ma—we tucked it together." She stepped so close that she juggled against him. "Dance with me," she coaxed prettily.

"Aw, I can't." He was suddenly all shuffling legs again.

"Sophie says you dance smooth as satin."

"My satin got a rip, then." He laughed boisterously. "Besides," he added weakly, his body almost swaying to the tune, "pitchin' gets a feller out of practice."

"Bet you're afraid to try." She dared him. There was a coyness about the lift of her chin that bothered him.

"Afraid?" He let his voice slide up. "Takes more'n you to scare me." In a wave of courage that was partly beer and partly a surge of music he caught her about the waist in youthful roughness and swung her onto the floor, exactly as he would have done at school in the "skip-to-mallew" game, or as he would have pulled Snoose into a sprawl-legged, shambling square-dance hop. "That's what I do to people who say I'm afraid."

She squealed and settled into his arms. He joggled into the polka, light on his feet after a couple of false steps, and wondered why this dancing with Gatha wasn't quite the same as swinging her in a game at school, although she was as kittenish as ever. He thought, Why, she's all but grown up. He was puzzled over the queer feeling that grew in him when on the crowded floor she pushed against him and he felt her body nudged against his. Otherwise it was like—well, like dancing with Snoose, boy-fashion, he decided. If Lilice were here . . .

Bold with rhythm and music and sweat, he danced with a Musser girl—Em'ly's sister—and asked one of the Habers for the next two-step. Thereafter, the first tweedle of the accordion and Anders' slow "Waltz next," or "Get your partners for 'birdie in the cage,'" sent him skipping, all tiredness forgotten. By the time he'd flowed into half a dozen sets, he heard girls ask one another in voices low enough for him to hear plainly, "Have you danced with that Johnny? You got something coming, if you ain't. The way he barrels you around his legs."

The flush on his cheeks brightened. His shoulders held the press of soft hands and his arms were eager for the curve of women's waists. No, this certainly was not like dancing with Snoose; he was sure of that. If Lilice were here, if Lilice . . .

And there she was. "I'm having a dream," he said to himself. But there she was, coming in at the door. For a moment of blood rushing outward until he felt dizzy, he saw only her, Lilice with the cherry-red lips and the smile buttoned back with a dimple; Lilice with her hair brushed up and peaked in a Psyche knot and her slightness hidden in a dress that was thin-waisted and had ruffles at the shoulders and swished about her ankles. Grown-up like Gatha, but not kittenish: the pliancy of willows in her walk, a quiet dignity sobering her face as though sorrow had already stripped the tinsel from the hollowness of joy.

He realized that he was moving toward her and stopped. Beside her—— He sucked in his breath as if somebody had jabbed him in the ribs. Something like a dipper of cold water jerked his spine back. Beside her was a man . . . a boy . . . anyway, a male—Jimmy Morrison, Herky's brother, a boy who reminded Johnny of Snoose, slender-hipped as Johnny himself; brown hair and a gay laugh.

Jimmy touched her, and Johnny's arm jerked up as if he'd been yanked by a puppet's string. They moved into the dance, Lilice's lips curving redly in words to Jimmy, Jimmy all eyes down for her——

Johnny shut them away blindly. In the waltz whirl, a couple shoved him aside. Woodenly he stumbled from their path. Aunt Phrena—the notion came unbidden—that's why she was so happy. She knew Lilice was going with Jimmy Morrison. Everybody knows but me. He tasted this bitterness with a kind of relish and slunk into a corner; and how dark the corner was when all the lantern brightness gathered on honey-colored hair near a head of brown! Desperately he considered Herky Morrison and the sharp forgetfulness of his bottle—and shook his head.

Alb and Anders lurched upon him there, Alb's arm in comforting in-ebriation about Anders' shoulder, Anders free to grieve over his folks in Minneapolis, now that Heinrich Muehlbank had taken over the accordion.

"Aw sheets, Anders! Nobody's forgetting you." Alb wobbled on his feet. "Best damn 'cordion player—*hic*—in the hills; ain't he, Johnny?"

Johnny nodded dumbly. These old men—what did they know about a lean young sorrow, tender as a vine, that burned with nettle heat in the mind, flamed in the heart? Lilice dancing and his arms empty . . .

"All these years they've forgotten me. Left me alone." Anders wouldn't leave his memories. "But me they'll call. If I'm dead and buried, me they'll bring home to Grandpa's graveyard. We're all buried there."

Another time Johnny would have been mirthful inwardly, they were so drunkenly sober and solicitous one of the other, a sagging reed propping a sagging reed. Tonight he wanted to tell them, "Go away and howl in your own corners. I got my own troubles." He lost Lilice in the swaying crowd.

"It's the ants." Anders poked at his face. "When they bury me—it's the ants crawling into my eyes and I can't pick them out. Promise me, Alb, and you, Johnny." Anders aimed a crooking finger at Johnny's chest, missed, and almost fell. "When my folks they call me, promise you'll take me up and send me home. Promise." He hiccuped sadly.

"Sure, sure, Anders," Johnny put him off, hastily edging sidewise. "Me and Alb—we'll do anything you say." He escaped, thinking, Poor old coot. No folks either. He searched for Lilice. There she was, two-stepping with Kurt.

At the end of that dance he gave in. I've—I've got to dance with her, he thought desperately. Somewhere deep in his head, however, furious scorn echoed: Are you going to be fool enough to go and beg, when she's been monkeying around with another feller? Somewhere nearer, he answered himself: Oh Judas, yes! I'll beg her—beg her anything. I'm buckling under.

He pushed himself forward. At her side he said softly, "You couldn't refuse a neighbor, could you?" He tried to be playful but his lips were stiff with hurt.

"Why, Johnny!" she exclaimed brightly, brushing him with a glance she made as casual as if he'd been a rafter and she were passing by. But she looked down quickly at the handkerchief twisting in fingers that began to tremble; and so she hid what he yearned to see. "This dance?" she questioned seriously. "Well, I promised—no, it's the next one I promised to—" she hesitated—"to Jimmy."

"Sure, sure," he assented with heartiness thin as honeycomb ice over waters dark and tumbling in the rapids. "Sure. But this one——" So many words thickening his throat, the heart running ahead of the tongue—and not a syllable to drop into the crowded, noisy silence; Lilice twisting the lace, Johnny biting his lips, waiting for music.

The melody flung out its tangling ribbons, weaving them together.

> "Waltz me around and around, my darling,
>   Over and over again,"

sobbed the accordion. And Lilice was in his arms. She hadn't settled there as Gatha had, but was poised lightly, as swamp silver might, there one breath, gone the next.

Between them silence had the voice of clamor. His lips were a hand's space from hers—but it was like miles he dared not traverse. His knees were like rusty hinges. Lead weighted his ankles so that he stumbled. In a momentary dizziness he felt her fingers tighten on his arm.

"I'm sorry." She was flustered. "My clumsy feet. Did I step——"

"Oh, Punkin!" he burst out before he knew. He didn't notice how that name shook her. Oh, step all over me, he thought; trample me down with hobnails, you don't hurt me. But when you look at Jimmy, it's like a red-hot jackknife in me. "You're so light——"

"Don't call me Punkin," she cried fiercely. "It's hard enough to——"

"To——" He paused on her word.

Not to think of you, she almost said but continued quickly, "—to get rid of a nickname."

"It's such a nice name," he protested inanely. Oh, keep talking, Punkin. It's sweeter than accordion music. "I thought about you, lots of times at night on the prairies. We thrashed——"

She missed a step and grew rigid so that he pushed against her gently. "I don't want to hear about it." Vehemence filled her tone. "Not one word."

"But Lilice!" he tried to say. "All I meant was——"

"Can't you talk about anything else?" she cried bitterly, unreasonably, her unfairness a cloak behind which she hid an ardor she attempted desperately to suppress; an emotion that brought at once sweetness and shame. "No, no. The first thing you say is threshing. Well, I don't think much of threshers." She struggled fiercely to keep tears away. "Not much."

He felt her breaking from his clasp; felt coolness where had been her body warmth. He stood empty-armed. He tried to follow her but dancers bumped him, came between, tossed him aside. Dully he saw her talking with Lena Haber and Adam. Yes, and there was Jimmy going to her, and she was nodding to him.

"I'm gonna get drunk," he decided wildly. "God damn awful drunk." But this hurt was deeper than any whisky-burn could alleviate. Wordlessly he passed through the crowd; paid no attention to Jackie, who was staggering and asking Mrs. Peiser for a cup of coffee, bragging proudly, "I damn near puked my guts out."

In the yard the cold air stung Johnny's nostrils. Uncertainly he hobbled among the buggies and wagons. "Around and around again," the waltz hummed with sadness. Back there were the dancers, the shuffle and the laughter. But not for him. "I don't think much of threshers. . . ." The nettle prick of haunting words stung hotly in his skull so that he shuddered. "I don't think . . ."

Slowly he set off for home. The music thinned to a plaintive echo with each step he took along the road. He topped a hill. "Waltz me around, my darling." He wasn't sure whether he heard music or mockery on the night wind.

And back at the Peisers' the accordion saddened beneath Anders' fingers and Lilice pretended not to look for Johnny. When somebody said, "I guess he's gone home; I haven't seen him anywhere," she stopped looking intently and put away the lace handkerchief. "Let's go home," she told Jimmy. "I'm tired."

"But it's still early."

"Please. I've—I've got a headache."

Over the hills Johnny plodded like one not yet awaked from drowsiness. Once he let the stars prick their brightness into his eyes. But their sharp points splintered and broke and finally blurred. He slumped and swore cleansingly at the earth.

12

With a drying Sunday to encourage them (though Uncle Herm was dubious), Johnny and Snoose returned to Norton's on Monday. They opened the hands' house door while the hired men were still picking dinner out of their teeth.

Snoose asked, "Going to thrash this afternoon?"

Johnny remained glum and silent, so reticent that Snoose rammed his fingers moodily into his jacket. On the way over all his efforts to poke a grin out of Johnny ended in grunts or muteness gloomier than before. What happened at the dance Snoose didn't learn until days later and by that time the news was as mildewed as old bacon rind. But Em'ly Musser told him about the Morrison boy.

The divinity student sat near a window, the book on a slanted knee.

"It's still damp and gonna be damper," Makin answered them, swinging jauntily from his bunk. His clothes were ready to be bundled. "The way she's cloudin', looks like she's gonna leak again. And if she does, I'm pulling out. To hell with Bory! He can do his own damn fixing around the engine."

"What's he want fixed now?" Johnny tossed his bundle on the bed. Snoose climbed into a bunk.

"Anything that rattles, I guess." Makin leaned bawdily against a bunk post. "You fellers been diddlin' over Saturday? I got me a little tart myself. I'm going back for more. Lummy, let 'er rain."

Johnny listened, scornfully deliberate, but Snoose wore a shamefacedness that was slightly pink. Glancing at the divinity student, Makin grimaced and caught at his belly. With hunched shoulders he rumbled in a coarse baritone:

> "At the bar, at the bar,
>   Where I bought my first cigar—
>   All you boys, listen now, to what I say.
>
> "Gin and rum, gin and rum,
>   Pretty girls to whisper, 'Come'—
>   The nickels and the dimes rolled away.
>
> "Then upstairs, then upstairs,
>   Oh, she took me unawares—
>   A dollar, it rolls farther, so they say.
>
> "But by chance, yes by chance,
>   There I ripped my Sunday pants—
>   Now I have to wear them every day."

He laughed raucously. With an unblinking gaze the student mixed the verses with Matthew and Paul.

Snoose thumped to the floor abruptly. "Let's go find Norton; see what he says." Johnny followed in no hurry. As they crossed the yard, Snoose said, "That Makin, he ought to take his mind for a swim."

No thrashing: Norton confirmed Makin's opinion. But they could hang around. Bory planned to grease the engine and talked about cleaning the flues, once he got back; he might need help, if he got back sober. They'd get their board anyhow, Norton promised. Then he said, "Watch you don't cross Bory today. He's ornery when he's got a bottle." Snoose regarded Johnny with something like fearfulness.

They puttered about. After a while they passed the barnyard where the rig stood, and wandered toward the river, not far away across a pasture lot. Snoose wanted to say, "Jimmy's taken Lilice to dances only a couple of times, Em'ly says," but the way Johnny kicked a disk of drying cow dung forbade speech.

With each step Johnny heard a mocking echo, "I don't think much of threshers. . . ." All at once he wished that Mosey Fritz were here; he'd like to pitch into somebody. But he couldn't deny the bitter truth of self-accusation: Why didn't I ask her long ago? Jimmy's younger than me, even . . . no claim on her . . . you never took her and he did . . . why didn't you? Wanting to lay blame on shoulders other than his own, he enjoyed the luxury of thinking, Aunt Phrena. It's her fault. She never let me go to parties. Always yelling "No." . . .

The path bent around a cottonwood near the water. Its massive base hid Silenski until they were almost upon him.

"Hah, Sneese," he hailed, waving a book he'd been reading. "Ah, w'at I'm saying. Sneese—such a *spitzkopf* as I am. It is Snoose, ye-as. And Johnnee." He kept a finger between the pages. His beard was freshly trimmed and his shirt white against the dark of the battered coat.

"Sit down, sit down." Snoose lounged on the grass. Somewhat uncertainly, Johnny sat on a rock. He saw that the leather of the book held a stamped golden crest—a crest like the one on Silenski's ring.

Snoose asked, "Is it about the river you're reading again?"

"Hah, you remember." Pleasure brightened Silenski's thin cheek. "Ye-as, ta river—ta river, she is like wisdom; she flow and flow. Ta man he jump in, ta river no care. Ta man he jump out, ta river no care. Ta man, he make ta choice."

Johnny scratched the rock, fidgeting. Snoose tensed a little, leaning forward, as one listening for shackles to snap and fall.

Opening the finger-held place, Silenski began to read softly and as if to himself, as indifferent as the river to whoever heard him. He read with a throatiness that spoke of a country of dark waters and marshlands and shaggy conifers by the sea. The reading made little sense to Johnny, scorched as he was with the nagging image of Jimmy bending over Lilice, Jimmy drawing tenderness from her lips. . . . He hitched his pants irritably and searched the ripples for excuse to hurry away. What was it that made Snoose look so—well, so hungry as he listened, Johnny wondered.

Now and again a sentence or two of the reading unsnarled in his mind; stuck there. ". . . and Death said: 'The good is one thing, the pleasant another; these two chain a man. . . . Yea, the wise prefers the good to the pleasant, but the fool chooses the pleasant through greed and avarice. . . . A man who is free from desires . . . though sitting still, he walks far . . . but he who is not tranquil, and subdued, or whose mind is not at rest, he can never obtain . . .' "

Silenski broke off and said gently to Snoose, "What is it, *bübchen*—a barley beard in ta eye?"

Snoose nodded, head lowered and beyond words.

Johnny began, "Whatever in the world, Snoose—" but Silenski swung the point of his beard like a spear upon him. "You never get a barley beard in your eye, Johnnee, no?"

"Barley——" Johnny began to simmer: was Silenski making fun of him? "Course I don't. I——"

"Hah, ye-as." Silenski closed the book. "Sometimes—sometimes it is good to get a barley beard in ta eye."

Johnny sprang up impatiently. "Come on, Snoose," he ordered roughly. "Bory's prob'ly back and needs us." He marched off huffily. Snoose hesitated, one hand at his face. Silenski was tapping his lips over his book. There was a kind of longing in Snoose's face. He turned and followed Johnny.

Lornas and Mosey with Bory were crawling about the separator. They were like—like dirty mud turtles: the thought brightened Snoose's mood as they came along.

Bory had the red of whisky swelling his eyes and truculence like a hide upon him. With a tumble of cuss words he bellowed, "You two, there; help Jake with those new leathers in the pump!" He licked his upper lip when he saw Snoose.

With Jake the waterman they went to work among the barrels.

By midafternoon with more clouds and a chill in the air, Bory finished at the separator and came to the engine. The two pitchers, his cronies now, followed him. As he passed Snoose, Bory's lip crooked speculatively. He brought the pails of grease, the flue cleaners and the fire hoes. Lornas and Mosey joined to help. The clang of firebox door and the rattle of chain, link over link, broke on the dull, lowering air. Johnny bent over the washer he was cutting from a piece of leather.

After a while Bory called, "Hook yourself to a grease bucket, Snoose, and grease the flywheel gear, will ya?"

With a wry face, a face that said, "Why don't he pick you, Johnny? Ain't much I know about his old engine," Snoose obeyed. For a moment he stood beside the bull wheel, or driver, as Bory called the large rear wheels. The rim came to Snoose's shoulder, Johnny noticed. Above it and to one side was the flywheel, the belt mark shiny on its face. A narrow space separated the two wheels. Snoose climbed the driver spokes, the bucket swinging.

"You'll have to kinda get between the driver and the flywheel," Bory told him. "That's the best way. Otherwise you can't reach anything." He walked away. Mosey and Lornas heard him. Suddenly their faces went foxlike with expectation.

Johnny crabbed his brows, not sure why he felt a prickle along his spine. He watched Snoose.

Snoose stood on the top of the driver. Balancing himself with the upraised bucket, he hesitated, disturbed. Then he slid into the space between the two wheels, his heels on the cleats. He leaned forward. The gear was under his hand. The flywheel was against his chest.

Quick as a weasel Bory swung around. In two strides he was back. He caught Snoose's ankles and jerked him down between the driver and the flywheel. There Snoose was pinioned, flat on his back on the rim of the driver. Like a huge bar the flywheel kept him from twisting over. Within Bory's reach his legs and lower body hung on the round of the driver like a victim on a torture wheel.

"Got you under the wheel, you little squirter," Bory shouted. "I'll make a man of ya."

Before Johnny could move, Bory's hands were at Snoose's waist. There was the rip and rustle of tearing cloth. With a numbness that was cold in him, Johnny saw Snoose's pants and underwear torn to the knees, tag ends flapping; saw Snoose's body white against the black of boiler and the oil of gears. Mosey and Lornas waited alertly on their feet.

Bory bent down and scooped a handful of grease from a pail. Vigorously he slopped it across Snoose's flesh, thigh and groin. "Betcha I'll make a man of ya." His lips were wet and the scar jerked.

A red haze fogged Johnny's sight. All in one move he was on his feet, in his hand a wooden pump handle. Headlong he plunged toward Bory.

But Lornas was there and leaped. Mosey and the two pitchers flung themselves forward. Lornas caught the handle; Mosey butted against Johnny's shoulder. Johnny fell, Mosey and a pitcher on top of him. Far away he heard Snoose's shamed whimpering.

Desperately Johnny rolled half sidewise: his fist shot up. He felt his knuckle bark Mosey's face. Lornas drew back a foot and kicked. Johnny moaned sharply. A hammer knocked breath and sense into a moment of dizzy pain. He heard Snoose again and struggled partly up. They held him tightly with knee and arm. Bory laughed stickily in pleasure.

As if he were spitting out a nasty taste, Johnny began screaming filth upon Bory: every dirty name and surname his tongue remembered and his fury originated. He spattered them over Bory, a dung heap of vituperation, the bowels of anathema.

Bory was undeterred by mere words. Not until Snoose slumped back pale and exhausted did he let him go. Then he lumbered toward Johnny. His hands were claws in oil and dirt. He stood in front of Johnny. The scar twitched.

And only Snoose saw Norton there, or thought he saw him dimly. Norton started forward, catching them all in a sweep of his head. He halted, as though he were standing before a table whereon lay at his right a heap of silver and at his left a pile of chaff. Wheeling, he hurried to his house.

"Calling me names, were you, Schwartzie? You potsucker!" Bory braced himself. "I'll loosen your teeth, Schwartzie." Calmly his fist struck Johnny's jaw. Not full strength but jarringly, as though he wanted to extract the uttermost farthing of pain with the least amount of deadly bodily harm. Again and again.

Blood rilled over Johnny's lips. Stickiness was on his tongue. A tooth loosened. Mosey's leering face tipped over suddenly and then righted itself crookedly. Lornas' foxy grin was clear one instant and gone shutterlike the next. Dusk began swirling between Johnny and the scar, the scar that jerked before every blow landed . . . jerked . . . jerked. . . .

"Pour water over him." Satisfied, Bory returned to his flue cleaning. "Next feller that opens his gab, gets the same," he threatened, the fire hoe swinging in his hand. Seeing Johnny wobbling on the ground, he yelled, "Now get to hell out of here, Schwartz, or I'll kick ya so you can't walk a-tall."

It was Snoose and the waterman who helped Johnny to his feet—Snoose holding the tatters of pants and underwear about him to hide the grease and the dirt and the purplish bruises where his flesh had struggled against iron. Together they went to the hands' house.

Deaf to Makin's "What in the great god Tophet——" Johnny dragged himself to his bunk.

"Bory," the waterman answered Makin. "He got rough."

Snoose gathered his bundle. "Come on, Johnny," he said. "We're going home."

"Home," Johnny muttered, his lips flabby with puffiness. "Snoose, I——"

"Come on," Snoose cried. "Right now. A dog ain't kicked around the way a feller is, out here." At the tremble in Snoose's voice, the dizziness in Johnny's head cleared.

"Think you can make it?" The waterman was solicitous. "Don't know whether Norton's got a team he'd let you——"

"Damn right we'll make it." Johnny was hoarsely grim. "Devil grab all, we'll make it. I'd puke over any help I got here now."

The divinity student, disturbed by the locust noise of earth, hurried forward but had no words of comfort. Silently he helped them. Once Johnny grabbed a bunk post to keep the floor from slamming up into his face.

Together they set out—sneaking away, Johnny mourned. Sneaking. But the word hurt like a weight in his head and he stopped trying to make sense of anything. At first each carried his own bundle. After a while Snoose carried both of them tied together. They followed a road that looped near the river. Johnny wove in the track sometimes. Now and again a tree leaned to an angle that made his stomach sick and changed his ankles to mush. Sometimes the Pockerbrush hills seemed to rush toward him with a roar; he had to catch at something or fall backward. His tooth ached. It moved at the push of his tongue. More than once he stumbled and would have sunk knees to earth if Snoose hadn't put an arm about him.

As they neared rippling water Johnny slumped to the ground. "I'm done," he groaned. "I'm all in." On the borrowed strength of Snoose he crept to the river's edge.

A bitter hour, this—the eating of gall and pain. Not the honeycomb of praise, the accolade of neighbor grace: "Cripes, that Johnny, he's a thrasher on the flats and Lilice is his girl." No. No. The blistered pods of wormwood, the muffled back-turned jeer, that was his portion: "Greased out. Fired. Hee, hee, hee. And he got a lickin' to boot. And Lilice is keeping company with a regular feller." Yes, that was his portion, a bowlful and running over. But the lave of coolness and Snoose's arm over his shoulder brought something like firmness to his stomach and solidness to his legs.

It was then that he saw the tears on Snoose's cheeks. Not boy's tears but man's tears, brimful of helpless fury and humiliation. Between the rags and torn patches he saw the white skin marred with the purple of bruises where it wasn't dirty with grease. The gray eyes of Snoose—how often had they reminded him of gray marbles under water. They were only stones now—stones with pieces chipped and hacked out of them. And shame grew in Johnny—shame so deep the red of it never left his heart nor tinted his cheeks but lay a crimson tide under his skin. He felt choked. "Always of myself I'm thinking." Remorse wormed in his mind. "Myself, myself. Always."

"Don't feel so bad," he tried to comfort Snoose. "A little water and scrubbing and you'll be washed clean again."

But Snoose burst out through the hands that covered his face, "I feel so dirty, so dirty inside me, I'll never wash clean again. Never."

As if he were moving numbly in a dream, Johnny drew his handkerchief from his pocket. He pulled aside the rags and tatters, and wiping the grease and dirt from Snoose's body, knew a comradeship so close to him that a breath would have toppled restraint.

It was momentary, short-lived as a snowflake in spring. Hatred, cold bitter hatred, came and rooted blindly hog-fashion. Revenge twisted a crimson rag before his sight, hiding even Snoose in what seemed like a smoky glare. Through his swollen lips he let out hate with the blind hog's grunt, "Wait, Bory Tetzell; you wait. Some day, if there is a God, some day I'll break you, body and bone."

Snoose got into clean pants. Johnny flung the rags into the water. Rainbow rings of oil circled from them, rose-colored and yellow. But the tints were broken by the river's waves.

Together they set off. In the crusting earth each left his track—the one steadying with purpose, violent, heel-hard; the other lagging, shuffle-gaited, as if a blow had been struck and an inner fane demolished. Rain began to fall.

13

For a week there wasn't so much as a slit of blue in the clouds. Between intervals of downpour, drizzle-mist by the half day curtained the hills. Puddles spread in the yard as talk about Johnny and Snoose in the neighborhood. It widened rapidly, hurried by Bory's swaggering in a saloon one day in Mary's Hill. "Damn me, I knocked that Schwartzie's teeth clear back of his ears." The neighbors heard and cackled. Before the week ended, exaggeration set in and bloated the tale.

Once they started, rains streamed over the ridges. They seemed in haste to soak the last dry corners they'd neglected these months, and promised green in the blade and yellow in the ear next season. "Looks like a long-crop year, all right," Uncle Herm prophesied.

Johnny shrugged for answer and grumbled off. Uncle Herm regarded him anxiously and wished the liniment he used in the barn were as healing on a soreness of spirit as it was on the sprains and stifles of his horses.

By the hour Johnny brooded darkly over his work. He was short-tempered and moody. The cuts on his lips and the purplish swellings on his cheeks knit up and vanished but the bruise in his memory festered and smarted as if poison sumac, freshly gathered, were laid on daily. At supper sometimes or at dinner, when hunger nudged in his belly, he remembered the scar and the jolts against his head. But he remembered far more vividly the derisive faces of the crew, full of contempt for him. And his appetite would fail. Even the sympathy he recalled in Makin's voice, in the divinity student's— even this he was sure was tinged with the kind of pity that set his teeth edgewise. Now the neighbors were gabbling.

And Lilice. He hardly dared consider what she'd think (and therefore kept repeating what he hoped she wouldn't say). Certainly she'd flaunt him with laughter now. She'd be with Jimmy, dancing with Jimmy, waltz after waltz. . . . He'd shove his plate aside, gulp what coffee remained in his cup and go outdoors, or up to his room to probe vacancy with a dull stare.

On Sundays he'd help Uncle Herm or Kurt hitch the team but refused to step into the buggy for church. He merely grunted when Aunt Phrena recommended the sweetness of Mr. Erdman's "precious promise" sermons. She had soothed the ache in his flesh with arnica but rubbed his inner bruises raw with her scoldings. "Ach, that thrasherman. Horsehiding's too good for him." He knew she hadn't included in her blame what she really meant: "Well, that's what you wanted, Johnny. Running with the heathen like that. Na, I told you so." Satisfied, she went to church. She heard the Pastor's sermons and was solemn over condemnation and doom; attended Mr. Erdman's services and wept over grace.

"What I'm looking for, I won't find in church," Johnny told himself. "If I could get my hands on Mosey, or Lornas—or anybody." He caught up a milk stool in a quick grasp. Almost desperately he wanted to pitch into a fight or get pig-staggering drunk or do whatever rashness would remove from him the stigma of humiliation and raise once more his beaten self-esteem in the sight of the valley, of Lilice, of his own self.

"If I could take Lilice to dance, just once!" he yearned. That would be a small kernel of satisfaction. But he couldn't bear the notion of her amused refusal. Her words returned to hurt him.

He avoided Snoose sometimes without being sure why, and kept out of the neighbors' ways. Between chores he tramped miles through the hollows of woods and along the shoulders of hills. The solitude of a ravine, soothing his pain like an ointment formerly, was now as clamorous with his own tumult as the leafless boughs overhead were, loud in a tangle of clacking wind-swept bones.

Scornfully he reminded himself of his braggy, "I'll go to the flats, Uncle Herm. I'll save. You thrash here. We'll get a new thrasher. . . ." The echo of those words swung like a taunt through his brain. A new thresher. How could he get a new thresher? Oh, if he could, if he could only set foot on a new rig, he'd thresh so that sparks would fly from the smokestack, and the dust from the separator would choke any man who dared to say a word. Anyone who . . .

He grunted. No sense to such notions. None. He stood behind a tree, just as he and Snoose used to do, and spied on the squirrels, still intent on the leftovers of the acorn harvest. But there was no comfort in watching the frisky animals. With savage accuracy he flung rocks and sticks and smiled grimly to see them whisk from sight for their lives.

There was some balm in Uncle Herm's outraged, "We got a law in this here Pockerbrush country. And a good jail in Mary's Hill for scrappers. I'm gonna talk to the sher'ff."

There was a little comfort, too, in Kurt's sympathy. For Kurt was about ready to agree with Heinie Beerwagon that they ought to gather the valley boys and pound Tetzell's face into fresh beefsteak, inch by inch for the frying pan. They ought to, not so much for the sake of Barewolf's Johnny as on general principles. No one like Bory was going to boss the valley boys.

But to all these heroics, which were half serious, half bravado, Johnny replied only, "That'll make people gab more. They talk too much now. I'll heal. And I'll settle Bory's slops in my own way."

At this threat Aunt Phrena took flight in winged alarm. "Not another spite match; like the cradling. Ach, Johnny, no, no! Your poor ma——" He plugged his ears with resolution.

How the neighbors gabbled when Mr. Marchen caught Bory one day and demanded the wages Snoose had earned! "By cripes, I made him fork over," Mr. Marchen bragged afterward. ("It was more for himself than for me," Snoose told Johnny.)

The neighbors huzzaed, "Why don't Johnny get his money, too? Is he scared of Bory, maybe?" Bory had threatened, "Just let young Schwartzie come and try to collect. I'll smash what teeth he's got left."

But neighborhood opinion was getting hot, not so much over the mauling which Johnny had received as over the swaggering ways of Tetzell. And Tetzell knew it. When Uncle Herm met Bory in Mary's Hill, therefore, Bory, remembering jobs he might want to solicit next fall, paid without a grumble or a bluster. That same day he took his engine up north to the lumber camps for the winter. Lornas and Mosey went with him.

At supper that night Uncle Herm put the money on Johnny's plate. But Johnny scooped it up and rattled it back into Uncle Herm's palm. "I wish Bory would have choked on that," he muttered hoarsely. "You keep it. I don't want it now."

"Ach, you take it, Johnny," Aunt Phrena said firmly, sure that some kind of justice had been executed here. "You sweat enough for it."

"Some things," Kurt observed muffledly through a mouthful of bread he was chewing, "some things come pretty high-priced."

As if he understood Uncle Herm slowly pocketed the money. "Some things you can't even put a price tag to," he said, his eyes suddenly keen. "It ain't the money, huh, boy?"

"No." Johnny ladled the gravy morosely. "Not by a long shot. It's a hell of a lot more than that." He mashed his potatoes hard at Aunt Phrena's disapproving brows.

By the time Lilice heard it, the story had Bory using a club and Johnny beaten to the fine consistency of plum butter and not far from his death's hour. Adam heard several versions before he brought the news to her. "I guess he's pretty badly cut up. Mrs. Peiser told me his teeth were so loose, he could spit them out."

"Oh, no, Adam! Not his teeth!" she cried impulsively. The bucket she was carrying slipped in her grasp and water splashed on her toes. "Oh, no!" She wiggled her feet to shake the wet off.

That evening she distractedly put a pinch of saleratus and two table-spoons of salt in the flapjacks she was making. Adam sputtered but Mrs. Rose laid down a fork quietly. With the pouring of the syrup came a faint moan through a closed door.

That Saturday Jimmy Morrison went to a dance alone, bewildered and faintly resentful. Lilice's "No, Jimmy, not tonight" was inexplicable to him. She almost called him back. Instead she let the door click firmly.

Winter scattered the feathers of cold over the ridges. The day of the first snow Uncle Herm, busily nailing cold out of the hen house, said, "Jump on Betsy and ride to the store. I gotta have me some more nails. And ask Jimpson how much the roofing is a roll."

Johnny entered the store in a flurry of haste, his bristles out to snap words with anyone. He bumped into Lilice so hard, he almost knocked her to the floor. Absorbed in mentally counting her change and glancing back at Mr. Jimpson, she hadn't seen him and was half spun around by his humping shoulder. Packages flew. He put out a hand to keep her on her feet.

When she saw him, gladness she couldn't hide trembled on her lips. "Oh, Johnny, your face isn't cut after all," she cried fervently as if in relief from a bothering worry. "I'm so—I mean—they said——" She gasped in reddening confusion.

Warmth like a spring wind drifted into his face. The cold lump in his chest began to melt. There was a kind of singing in his ears. "Lilice, does it—does it really matter?" He wanted her to tell him. The song in his ears stopped to hear her.

"Oh, yes," she breathed, and hastily tried to check her words.

He would have bundled her in his arms then, laughter exploding the tenseness in him. But she bent away to gather up the packages, saying quickly, "Of course it matters. I hate to think of any of my friends getting hurt. I can't stand it. Last week when—" she paused; then said deliberately, though there was a tremor in her voice—"when Jimmy cut his finger it—well, it's so messy," she finished jumbledly, suddenly finding she couldn't say what she wanted to.

His ardor was nipped by a chill but he couldn't help asking eagerly; "Next Saturday night—let me come for you. There's a dance at the Blumens'——"

"Oh, my. Saturday's a long way off." She evaded him in a breathless flurry. "I'll have to run. Mr. Whiteland's giving me a ride." He looked so forlorn and dispirited that she paused and tried to say with calm indifference, "If I'm there, I'll save a waltz or two. That is, if I'm there." The door clicked her away.

Addledly he stood there, trying to gather himself, aware that a gray afternoon was rifted with bright promise. Or was he only fooling himself? "Ya, it is a snowy day," he answered Mr. Jimpson mechanically. Now what was it Uncle Herm wanted him to buy, anyway?

Over the unwrapping of packages, Lilice bubbled, "There ought to be a law against it. The way people make things worse than they are. He isn't hurt at all."

Her step was so full of hopping that Mrs. Rose, storing away the dried apples and salt, paused with a hand on a shelf. "You mean Old Mr. Fleischer?" she questioned with a twinkle. "I didn't know he had been hurt."

"I didn't say Mr. Fleischer." Lilice's cheek grew hot. "In fact, I didn't mention any names."

"I know." Mrs. Rose unscrewed a jar. "You like that Johnny, don't you?"

"Well, I——" Lilice's fingers tangled a free string into a knot. "He's just one of the neighbor boys but I guess he's nice." She tried to speak lightly as if of something casual. "We've really never been together much. Anyway, Jimmy has a nicer smile I guess."

She was so informatively reticent that Mrs. Rose smiled and asked gently, "It makes you mighty glad when Johnny is near you, doesn't it?"

Before she could answer, a voice, muffled yet strident in its human agony, lifted beyond the door that was shut. "It's the pillows that upset him now," said Mrs. Rose.

Silently they stood there a moment, Mrs. Rose at the shelves. Lilice was near the table. Her breath caught in a sob. "Can you go right on liking a person—when you're scared of what will happen if you do go on liking—him?" Her fingers rattled against the package. "I hope I never see Johnny again."

"Lilice." Mrs. Rose came to her. "I'm not the one to answer that." She

put an arm about her. "When he—" she glanced at the closed doors—
"worked in the sawmill, I used to sit up and wait, hour after hour. I could
hear the saws." Her voice grew unsteady. "I'd fall asleep praying that
when I opened my eyes, nothing would be changed, everything would still
be the same. Finally it wasn't the same."

"But a threshing machine isn't——"

There was so much hope in Lilice's tone that Mrs. Rose's arm tightened.
"We always find reasons," she said. "But we have to live with ourselves
as well as with others. It's a terrible thing to have to live with fear and
worry by the hour—even a small worry."

"Yes, Mother." Lilice's voice was dull with acceptance.

"Sometimes, Punkin," Mrs. Rose sighed, "it is best to say no to your
heart, once and for all."

The paper in Lilice's hands crackled noisily.

14

Never had he remembered a Saturday that dawdled so in coming.
"Course *she* won't be there," he prophesied bleakly. On Thursday, to
prove his disbelief, he bought in Mary's Hill a gray-checkered cap, its
squares arrogantly unsubdued, which struck his mood. It was a cap so
belligerently styled even a gentle nature felt impelled to knock it off. He
wanted it that way.

Before he left Uncle Herm's kitchen that Saturday night, he fitted it
at a "touch-it-if-you-want-to-start-trouble" angle on his wavy black hair.
He stepped back from the mirror; tilted the cap with grim satisfaction.

When she came in and saw him, Aunt Phrena cried as if to a risen
shadow, "Ach, Johnny, how you scared me! You look like——" She
sank into a chair, hunted to earth by the remorseless past.

"Like my pa, eh?" Johnny tipped the visor defiantly. "Sure. And why
not? I'm of his blood. You told me that often enough."

She drooped awhile there, after he'd gone, before she got the Precious
Comfort Book. But all her searching ended in a kind of tired silence, the
quest in the opened leaves unprofitable.

Only for a moment did Johnny slow his pace before Snoose's gate. Then
he shrugged. This was not for Snoose. This was between himself and
whatever shadowed destiny lay before him. He followed the road to the
three-cornered crossing where the Nussbaum boys and Heinie and Jackie
Marchen waited. And joining them, he wallowed in girl talk, piquant in
raciness as pepper, and grew hard of breath over leaping desire and vicar-
ious daring. His body swayed to the unholy ditties he paeaned. It never

occurred to him that he would have sulked at home if Lilice's half promise
hadn't brought him forth to brave the neighbors—brave them with a smile
or a fist, he didn't care which. This, he was sure, he was doing of his own
accord and with his own courage.

Joviality crowded between the walls of the Blumen house. In a whirl of
red-cheeked frenzy, Johnny whooped and stamped in the polkas and
roared with the caller in "birdie in the cage." He squeezed Gatha into
shrill delight. Her eyes grew languorous until she noticed that though his
body was near, his mind was at the door looking outward. Delight icicled
into annoyance.

He waltzed with the lilt of hope undeferred, one eye raised whenever a
newcomer entered the room. The wine of recklessness shone on his lips.
Even in quiet his fists were partly curved as if he expected someone to
challenge him and was ready for quarrel. If Lornas were only here, or
Mosey Fritz. But they were in the lumber camps.

Jimmy Morrison arrived. Johnny crooked his elbow, his clenched hand
against his side. When he saw that Jimmy was alone, his fingers loosened
and he peered at him. That Jimmy, he certainly looked sicker'n a bull calf
tonight. What was there about him reminiscent of Snoose?

He saw Snoose arrive with the Mussers and had no more than a nod for
him. He saw how Em'ly sparkled and was piqued to notice how Snoose's
gray eyes over her were hooded with the blind boy's mask, heedless of
earth. Snoose's nod was as absent as Johnny's was short.

Under schooners of beer and truculent boldness Johnny slapped Job
Krumlich's face for asking about threshing on the flats, but he relaxed his
elbows under the mollifying easiness of the Nussbaums. His cap was a
dare, pert as a fledgling rooster. He grew loud with Heinrich Muehlbank's
limber waltzes (for Anders Stramff no longer sobbed over the accordion but
stayed with the Hukelpokes—"aus ge-played," he mourned—and nursed
his aching knuckles, twingy with rheumatism, near Alb's fire).

Then Lilice was there. She had come with Adam and Lena Haber (not
with Jimmy, not with him). Johnny shed raucousness like loose feathers,
his tongue and body stilled into quietness as one finding a hushed valley
during storm. Slowly he nudged the perky cap into sedateness on the top
of his head. Without knowing how, his gaze unintercepted by the passing
couples, he moved toward her.

She saw him coming. I've made up my mind, she thought. I'll be nice to
him and that's all. He can have two dances. Two, I said. And if he gets
rough, I'll—I'll slap him. She gloated a little over her firmness.

She smiled with metallic brightness at him now; smiled brightly at
Jimmy, at Kurt and Snoose, at everyone.

Careless of the folks about him, Johnny begged, "This waltz?" before she had slipped off a wrap. Begged for hope, a special revelation.

"Certainly you may." She was proud of her level impartiality. "I promised." He was deaf to all but her consent. She accepted his hand; so he thought.

(And in that waltz Snoose, holding Em'ly as though she were a dream in vibrant flesh, forgot the mockery of earth; Gatha remembered it and bungled in the rhythm; and from a corner Jimmy wondered why in hell he ever came.)

Johnny almost missed the first steps. His arm about her seemed wooden. Her shoulder was dizzy-near. The scent of Cologne water was like the clean odor of rose petals. "I don't want to wake up," he murmured to himself, his cap shapeless and no longer perky, his black eyes veiled, all senses shaken, a ribbon of forgetfulness beginning to unwind.

He whirled her up a hill of waltzes, down a curvy vale of polkas, over a ridge of tripping schottisches, until she seemed to be spinning even when they stood waiting between dances; until lanternlight and grinning faces and shadows on the ceiling ran blurring together. Two dances, three, five (why remember?). Until she gasped like one who struggles for more than breath after exertion; until the shadows between the lanterns thickened.

Then like a thunder spark she seemed to hear her father's sharp agony swallowed in a roar as of wheels. Blindly she tore away. "No, Johnny; not the next one," she quavered. "I—I mustn't."

"Oh, Lilice!" He didn't know how hoarsely low his voice was. "Lilice, Lilice!" His strength towered against her. Her eyes widened. She almost rushed from him.

As if ecstasy (the ecstasy of blood) had been snatched away, he let anger, eyeless anger, swift and unreasoning, fill him, the male beast thwarted. He saw her choose Kurt in "ladies choice." Grumbling, he disdained further dance, wallflowered near the musicians, the melodies flowing past his unmindful ears as a stream past a rock.

Gatha came snuggling to him there. She purred her annoyances. They made little meaning then, although they would later. She was saying, "I don't see why she comes." Disparagingly she considered Lilice two-stepping with Snoose. "Nobody in our set invites her."

Absently he said, "I'm here. I wasn't invited either."

"Course you're always welcome." She giggled and pressed closer to him. "This wasn't exactly an invitation party. It's the queerest thing. Some people are so fresh, always pushing in."

"Let's dance," he said abruptly, and shoved the cap into a belligerent tilt. She swished into his arms.

Lilice saw them and looked quickly away. How can he? she asked the
sag in her heart. The mean thing. How can he? Just now we were so——
Oh, it's mean. She apologized aloud, "I'm sorry; I'm clumsy tonight." She
thought, Of course. Gatha. Naturally he ran right over to her. They were
confirmed together, I guess. . . . Church people . . . She wouldn't mind a
dozen threshing machines. . . . With a kind of strangle in her throat she
said, "Yes," and went into Heinie Beerwagon's pawing clutch.

She refused Jimmy's offer to ride home in his buggy and went with
Adam, whimpering into a clenched fist with hard unintelligible woman
logic, "This is the way it is, then. I'd like to slap his mouth, the smarty;
and hers too."

With Lilice gone Johnny was restlessly slack-legged. He resisted Heinie's
offer to "kill" a bottle. Finally he drove Gatha to a sleepless bed by saying
good night fervently outside the door. In a moment of intolerable loneliness, he hugged her fiercely. He dropped his hands so quickly she almost
fell. He rushed away, to stumble on home alone, the company of the
Nussbaums and Jackie suddenly more than he could bear.

He envied Snoose with a harsh angry resentment—Snoose driving with
the Mussers, Em'ly near him. Snoose, the dreamy, spinning his meshes of
silver fancies. To Johnny sometimes they were folly and sometimes they
were an echo of longings he sensed deep within himself—echo of haunting
beauty beyond a hill.

Did Snoose feel about Em'ly as he felt about Lilice? Wanting a girl till
it hurt. He wondered how it would feel, her smile curving under his lips.
And with that thought crept another on slinking feet. Did *he*—is this the
way *he* felt about girls, his father, in the years that belonged to Aunt
Phrena and Uncle Herm and now some way belonged to him too? A
kind of shame rode him with spiny rowels. He almost despised his flesh.
But longing was greater than contempt this night. Over and over he muttered, "She's going with me to a dance, one of these nights. And Devil grab
anyone who tries to stop me!" He slung the checkered cap spitefully on a
nail.

15

Snow piled to the second rail of the fences that season. Uncle Herm
chortled, "Yep, kids, it's gonna be a long-crop year," and marked his account
books with a more careful pencil than ever. With Johnny troubling his
cogitations, he had long talks with Banker Ford and once with Norton.
Clymy and Sophie were finally established, bed and cupboard and bag-

gage, in the new house on the eighty. (So Mrs. Marchen told Aunt Phrena.) Its walls were log but the roof was sawed lumber. Kicking at the snow he piled against the foundation, Clymy set his thin rabbit face and determined to cover the logs with boards next year.

"That Sophie!" marveled Aunt Phrena. "Ach, such a woman! Bundles up her kids and all and drives over to visit the Roses. What she sees in that woman——" She stirred puzzlement into her cake batter.

During that winter Brother Erdman left the meetinghouse empty for a month. The fervor of the Lord's spirit had exhausted him, he said, and he must replenish the wells of zeal in conference with his brethren in Minneapolis. While he remained away, Aunt Phrena, deprived of his assurances, watched the state of the world in uneasy apprehension, not sure it would last until he returned.

Thaws came with shifting, unpredictable weather. Rain laid crystal over the drifts so that winter birds, picking at the ice-locked seeds, thinned to the rib bone and died. The partridges that at dusk slanted down and vanished into the snow-heaped brush piles for the night remained there, smothered by the glass door sealing their tombs in the dark. Pawing wolf and fox dug them out. Feathers scattered in the underbrush.

They found one the afternoon Snoose helped him haul the summer's firewood. Johnny pointed a mittened hand. They saw a cock under a snowy pile, its neb lifted frantically against the clear pane of ice that barred his way. But the jewel of his eye was glazed white and frost clothed his tongue.

"Just look!" Snoose tapped the brittle sheet pityingly. "He could see the sun, he was so near to freedom."

"So near," Johnny repeated, fiercely restive, "so near and froze to death after all. He never made it. No, he never——" In a sort of fury, he raised a heel. His heavy overshoes crashed down. Ice splintered and brush crackled. The partridge rolled into the sun. "Now he's free," cried Johnny.

"Free!" echoed Snoose. "Free!" Stiff in crackly debris the feathered body lay, its toes still curved in fight against the quilting death. For a moment Johnny regarded it soberly. Then he turned away. "The owls will get it tonight," he said and plowed into the underbrush.

He left his tracks in the drifts going to dances that winter. With rough amiability he pushed into the crowds, searching for Lilice. She seldom came. Under the cold snapping the nails in the rafters, Mr. Rose grew worse; the human warmth began to ebb. When she did come, each time with Adam and Lena, she accepted his dances sparingly, as though she'd erected bar and gate against him (against herself too) and meant to keep this side of them. She smiled as lightly on Jimmy Morrison as she did on Johnny.

Before long the checkered cap was an indicator of his mood. With Lilice away, it perched cockily on his head; with her in his arms, it flagged limply, not far from decorum.

When she waltzed with him, properly aloof (so she thought) but melting at the edges in spite of herself, Jimmy gloomed from a corner. When she danced with Jimmy, there was Johnny glaring from a wall, jealousy snapping like an ember. But when she danced with somebody else (and mostly she did), both drooped in the corners glowering. The interloper trod on the hot coals of their antagonism. (And in the secluded places, oblivious of human storm, Snoose and Em'ly drifted into that solitude where touch is understanding.)

In a short time it was common talk among the neighbors that Lilice Rose was "going" with Barewolf's Johnny—that is, when he could pry her away from Jimmy Morrison. Aunt Phrena heard about it at church. "Did you know, Phrena?" Mrs. Peiser tattled. "Johnny and that Lilice Rose? They practically hug each other in the square dances." Talk buzzed over the pews before and after the Pastor's sermon on "Slander Not Thy Neighbor."

After church Aunt Phrena shot Gatha a spiteful gleam. "Ach, that girl! She could get Johnny, if she wanted to. A little spunk instead of cabbage, that's what she needs in her backbone. I wish she'd fix the porridge of that Rose girl." At home she played with the notion of marching into the Rose house and giving that Lilice a piece of her mind—a good strong piece.

What Mrs. Rose wasn't told she guessed. "Well, Lilice," she said one afternoon, sprinkling clothes, "so you have two beaus. Most girls seem to have trouble enough with one."

"I haven't even one." Lilice shook out the cloth she was ironing and lifted the sadiron from the stove, her cheeks rosy. "I think Jimmy's mad at me. And I can't help it if Johnny asks me. Why, Mother, I can't just turn my back on him. I don't encourage him. Really. In the ladies' choices last time, I didn't ask him once."

"And in the gentlemen's choices you never refused him once, either, I s'pose." Mrs. Rose nodded. "Well, I'm not going to start now being a mother who makes up her children's minds for them, and then spends the rest of her days hearing them blame her and feeling sorry for herself. Not me."

Watching the rivalry, folks guffawed benignly, titillated by the heady spirits of young love.

One winter's night Johnny and Kurt begged the team and sled of Uncle

Herm and, for all of Aunt Phrena's sniffling distrust, took Jackie and the Nussbaum boys with them. It was late that night when Johnny said, "Kurt, look. You can go home with Snoose. I'm—I'm figuring on giving Lilice a ride home."

"Well, I don't know." Kurt was unresponsive. "We came here share and share."

With more patience than he had known Johnny pleaded, "Kurt, just this once, do we have to argue?"

Kurt shrugged. "Take the sled then. Mind you, it's my turn next."

But when Johnny asked Lilice, she protested, "No, I couldn't go with you. Adam will——"

"Adam!" Johnny mocked. "When he's got Lena, he don't know you're here."

"Well, I——" She moved uncertainly, snared by his nearness, wanting to go but determined to hold him away. "If Jimmy could go with us and——"

"Jimmy! For Judas' sakes, Lilice, I——"

"Don't get mad. I half promised him." She fluttered anxiously. "No, I didn't really give my word—not to anybody. I——"

In the end, with half a triumph better than none, Johnny and the Morrison boy both rode in the sled. He sat on one side, Jimmy on the other, Lilice in the shadowy box between them. Nobody spoke. The snorts of the team were trumpet-loud in the moonlit silence. Beside the sled ran its shadow, quieter than the pads of weasel.

Silence stretched painfully until it seemed to groan. After a mile of clopping hoofs, Lilice observed without much confidence, "It's nice, sled-riding, isn't it?"

"Peachy," said young Morrison. "Surely is," said Johnny. Both were grumpy. Their words came together, struck like the curled horns of billy goats bumping. The night stillness that followed creaked with ludicrousness they couldn't escape. In a moment of wanting to laugh, Johnny decided sanely, Nothing wrong with Jimmy, really, if he'd keep away from Lilice.

He forgot his common sense an instant later when Jimmy proposed, "Come with me next Saturday, Lilice. I can get the sled, too." Johnny yanked the horses roughly.

But Lilice nipped all budding expectation. "I'll probably not go at all, Jimmy. Father's—Mother needs me."

When they *clip-clopped* into the Rose yard, a window was pale with lamplight. They knew what it meant. Late and yellow lamplight, the sign of country waiting, of bodies stricken, man and animal, of death at the window.

"No, don't come in." Lilice hurried from the sled. "It's—it's all right. Good night, both of you." Her steps creaked on the smooth glittery path to the house. A door opened yellow upon the night, closed darkly.

A quarter mile down the road, Johnny leaned forward. "I've had my fill of this, Morrison," he said fiercely. "You're under my feet wherever Lilice is. And it's going to end damn quick."

Jimmy fired up. There were blows, his slenderness against Johnny's stiff muscles, hardened under the fork these months.

Johnny left him half buried in snow and drove on, muttering, "You can cool off there and walk home." Before he'd gone a mile, he jerked the team to a stop. Moon on the drifts was white over acres of fields but he saw a small dark huddle in the snow, a body willowy as Snoose's and a mouth that was black in the moonlight—a bloody mouth. "Oh, Devil grab it!" he mumbled and swung the team around.

He came on Jimmy staggering down the road. "Get in!" he ordered harshly.

"You can't bluff me." The Morrison boy plodded on.

"Get in, or I'll drag you in!" Johnny helped him. "No sense in your walking home. Here's a handkerchief."

Jimmy wiped his lips. "If you think you're favoring me by——"

"Oh, shut your trap!" Johnny yelped.

He drove eight miles out of his way that night. With numb toes and shivering ribs, the team tired, he returned home at last. Before he left the barn, he climbed into the cold mow and poked down forkfuls of minty hay for the horses. Tomorrow Aunt Phrena would say with patience that was as irritating as a wet suspender, "Na, ya. Johnny. Fighting. You like to make our name a stink word among the neighbors, don't you?" Tonight he was too tired to think. Slowly he clumped the path to the house.

Anders Stramff died that winter and was buried in the graveyard of the tiny Pockerbrush Reformed Church in Mary's Hill—the "rooster" church, folks called it, pointing derisively at the metal cock on the weather vane. "In that church they'll bury anyone, heathen and Hottentot," the Pastor fumed. He showed by text and Bible verse why Anders could not lie under the evergreen in the yard near the log church.

"Good thing the rooster church is closing down," Mr. Nussbaum said. "No wonder they got so few people going there, when they bury folks that ain't even members of the church."

"It's true," Aunt Phrena told Johnny. "Ach, my! There is no place in holy ground to bury outsiders."

Johnny shivered. He remembered the Alberts boy lying in a corner of his father's field, laid there with a Bible verse read over him by Old Mr. Alberts himself but with neither church rite nor congregational assent. With a dull ache Johnny thought of the Roses. Outsiders.

However, Mr. Dunkel put the Pastor in a rage by observing mildly, "Ya, I s'pose on Judgment Day you can expect angels to fly up from the Pockerbrush church by the dozens. But over in the 'rooster' congregation and in Erdman's meetinghouse, you'll find nothing but devils." (Mr. Dunkel's wife sat listless in her rocker these days. Sometimes he locked the door sadly upon her.)

And Sophie Marchen Humber said after services once, "Funny how God made up His mind about the Pockerbrush church." But Mr. Nussbaum answered dourly that the Devil always had a longer tongue than Christian folk.

Recalling how neighbors hung over Anders at the parties and dances, forgetting daily agony in the rhythm of his tunes, Johnny thought bitterly, "He was good enough for them then; now they spit on him and listen to Heinrich Muehlbank." He was filled with pity at Alb Hukelpoke's saying, "Poor old duffer! He'd lay there, waitin' for his folks in Minn'apolis. All he could think about was the ants getting into his eyes."

Near spring Old Man Rose died at last; breathed heavily on a curse that bubbled vainly at his lips, and sagged to death.

"Her pa at death's door and she, that Lilice, at the dance, flinging around. Ach, such people!" cackled Aunt Phrena, her triumphant look at Johnny saying without words, "Huh. And you keeping company with such folks."

"But he was sick a long time," slowly objected Uncle Herm. "The girl can't just sit and wait; young folks at her age."

"Christian folks and church members," proclaimed Aunt Phrena, "they are sober-minded and prepared for the last call." She waved a soup spoon adamantly. "Wonder who'll bury him? Steuber won't, nor Erdman. And the rooster church is closing."

Kurt outraged her by suggesting, "You'd think Steuber and Erdman were gods and had the say over heaven, instead of a quarter acre of graveyard."

"You learned better than to say that," she sniffled. "It is in consecrated ground we must be laid."

"Does it matter?" Kurt asked. "The man's dead."

Aunt Phrena was doleful over the soup. She said no more to Johnny about the Roses nor mentioned Lilice. She waited for this vinegary truth to soak in.

For a sick while Johnny, nagged by the thought of the Alberts boy in unhallowed ground, wondered where they would put Lilice's father. But he forgot that in thinking about Lilice herself. He was haunted by the whiteness that had crept over her face when the Haber boy brought the news. They had been waltzing, her cheek so close to his that he felt her warmth. Then a Haber boy, frightened into shivering, caught her arm.

"Where's Adam?" he cried loudly. "You must go home. Something awful's happened. Your pa——" He gulped. "I came by there, and your ma——"

"Oh, Johnny." She swayed against him. "She's alone there. I was afraid it would happen this way."

In his longing, Johnny put a finger on her cheek as if a touch would erase the sorrow there. But she drew back quickly, almost proudly. "I'll go with you, Lilice," he offered, but she refused. "No, Johnny. You mustn't."

She gazed pitifully at the circle of folks, the music dead, the flesh numb. Her eyes were beaten down by the shower of missiled glances, some crinkled with understanding, some indifferent, all curious. As if she were aware, however dimly, of what he couldn't see as yet, as though she knew instinctively that death at last was dragging into plain sight all she had shut her eyes against, she said, "Please don't. We'll have to do this for ourselves."

Johnny had a strange feeling that she stood alone there and that a space of distance froze like water in cold December between them, barring him away from her.

He followed her to the door. She turned and whispered, "Good-by, Johnny. I wish we——" She was gone. A chill wind blew into his face.

In the days that came after, he began to see with ever-sharpening clarity what she meant. What he had known long before but had thrust back into the outer night of his consciousness was now taking shape and bulging forward into undeniable reality. It's crazy, he said to himself time and again. Crazy. Lilice an outsider. A wild plant and alien to cultivated grain and therefore fit only to be pulled and thrown aside. Unbaptized, unconfirmed, unchurched, yes, unburiable. Furiously he counted off the evils on the four tines of his fork.

Crazy as a lunatic, he decided. But there it was. Not that folks would have spoken right out in public how they felt about the Roses. Nobody objected to their help in a stretch of road building or refused their aid in a night-long vigil over a sickbed. The way Mrs. Rose had watched over the Peisers' youngest when Mrs. Peiser lay worn out at last and Mr. Peiser had driven for the doctor. The way Lilice had spent a week helping out when the Schimmels were down with the lung sickness. They were just neighbors then, necessity's kinfolk.

It was different in other matters. He could see that. For instance, in the circle of the elect, there was the lofty matter of lower and higher criticism of neighborhood talk, text and opinion. He couldn't help noticing that a distinction was drawn, fine as thread but firm as rock, on such matters as who was seen in whose company, who was invited to what wedding or basket "social" or confirmation, who was "going" with whom, and what could marry what.

"Who does the inviting around here?" he questioned the milk stool fiercely. "Why, members of Pastor Steuber's congregation and Erdman's meetinghouse. Laugh all you want to," he told himself sober-mindedly, "there it is."

Sadly he remembered that, by accident or by design, the Roses were usually the last to be threshed and then grudgingly—so it seemed to him—at the very end of the run. That is, except when Uncle Herm had pulled his rig into their yard. Even Uncle Herm met squabbles.

"By God!" Johnny kicked a bucket the length of the barn. "If I had a rig, I'd thrash her first of all." He had a moment of deep triumph.

A cow mooed from the stall where the oxen had stood. He was prodded into chill actuality. He picked up a fork as though to defend himself against doubt. Neighborhood talk. Neighborhood judgment. All that hard opinion formulated into the semblance of doctrine and dogma. Did a person really dare flout it and still remain in one piece, in good grace and respected reputation?

But there was Lilice. Lilice of the red lips, the sadness entangled in the button of her dimple, the sweet trick she had of lifting her hand as if she'd touch his ear and send the blood starting but dropping her fingers with a quick gesture instead . . . Lilice.

"Oh, Devil!" he gasped uncertainly. The fork slipped in his hands. He leaned heavily against the manger.

So quietly that gabbling tongues for once were far outrun, Old Mr. Rose was buried at the rooster church. Only the family and Lena Haber and surprisingly Sophie and Clymy stood in the thawing snow where the earth gaped like a wound. The mound was a day old before Johnny heard. His pillow was sleepless against his cheek that night.

This last committal rite the minister performed. Then he locked the door of the little church. There was nothing left for him to do there. His flock had vanished; the pews were empty. He packed his wife and kids and the Bible, and went to Fergus.

Spring blew over the hills and rooted in the hazels. Soon yellow-hearted flowers of the bleeding stem spilled their faint fragrance on the wind. Lilice gathered the flowers anxiously but they left her untouched, worried as she was about her mother. Mrs. Rose was more ill than well now. The release from the bondage of her husband's sickbed, the reprieve from the years of crippled limbs were almost too great to bear, as the healing sun is too bright for one long accustomed to prison darkness.

Lilice put the flowers in a vase and fluffed the pillows into comfort. "You lie and rest," she commanded. "The bloodroots are prettiest now." Quietly she took the house and the chickens upon her shoulders. "Rest now."

"For a day or two, yes." Mrs. Rose sighed. "I'm glad summer is nearly here." Her gaze on Lilice was soft.

Sophie came to visit one day, babies and all. "I was all out of prunes," she boomed. "And I was at the store and decided, well, I'd just run over and sit awhile with Mrs. Rose." She held her youngest on her lap.

It was while the teacups were steaming and Lilice had gone from the room that Mrs. Rose said almost pleadingly, "Poor Lilice! She works like two women. Her father's death——"

"Huh. Her father's burial, you mean," interrupted Sophie bluntly. "Two churches and not a spot of ground here for him. The people in this neighborhood! How they can come to church every Sunday and look so pious—watch out, Buttel—" she broke off hastily—"you'll spill the cup."

"They don't really mean it," Mrs. Rose said calmly. "But Lilice is sure that——"

"It's Johnny, ain't it?" Sophie interrupted impatiently. "What's he done now?"

"I guess nothing he can help." Mrs. Rose hesitated. "Ah, Sophie, what does one learn from tears after all? I don't know." She let the tea cool. "Lilice begs me to sell the farm and move to Fergus to live. But Adam—— well, there's Lena Haber. And he really likes this place. I don't know. Lilice doesn't get much sympathy from him. All she can think about is that Johnny is a member of the congregation and she's—she's——"

"Huh." Sophie set her cup down and began buttoning the baby's coat. "If Johnny listens to that, he ought to be horsewhipped." She pulled her eldest nearer her knee. "What a lot of bother men are! They have everything their own way. Johnny's got a good heart," she went on. "But he's a man and all men are stinkers. You'd think the Lord could find a better way to breed up people than by having men underfoot."

The bloodroots faded. Lilice picked the last of them, nagged by the thought, I s'pose Gatha's his partner at the dances now. Naturally he ran right over to her. I wanted my way and now I've got it. Oh, Johnny. Lilice sighed. She would have quiet now. No more wheels. Beautiful quiet. If only the snowy petals of the bloodroots weren't like a white grin sparkling down at her.

More than once Johnny stopped his spring's work to stand, looking southward. Scrupulously, however, he observed Pockerbrush respect for grief, enunciated by Aunt Phrena and in all likelihood agreed to solemnly by the neighbors. "Ach, ya," she had declared more than once; "a house of mourning: no visitors for two months. And the family: no parties or dances for a year."

Johnny kicked the earth clods stubbornly. "If I go, there'll be talk. Long-nosed priers."

About the time violets tinged the grass in the meadow, Snoose appeared on an evening of clouds so feathery crimson the throats of hummingbirds might have been scattered in the sky. His gray eyes were dream-lost. He lagged across the yard rather than walked.

"Stepping on your own feet tonight, Snoose," Johnny ribbed him.

"Come on!" Snoose dug his hands deep in his pockets. "I got something to tell you."

On the pasture road Snoose picked up a rock and sent it rustling into the new leaves. He jabbed Johnny's arm with a fist and burst out suddenly, "Em'ly—she's promised to marry me." His sad face glowed like a flame brightly in mist. "Oh, Johnny, fetch me a rope and I'll lasso you a star."

Hammer-struck, Johnny blinked. His fingers came to Snoose's shoulders. For a moment he stared, the bit-and-auger of envy sinking in. His hands gripped Snoose's bones in a joy that was leavened with yearning. "Snoose, Snoose!" he cried and was so close to salt under his lids that he flung into wrestling with him. They fell to the ground together, as boyishly they had years before.

"I'm not married yet," Snoose gasped, sitting up. "Won't be for a couple of years. I'm going to hire out this summer. Looks like a good year. Em'ly will wait for me."

Snoose married and Em'ly near him. All that next week the reflection was a torment to Johnny, his own arms empty. Unrest flooded him. Somewhere in that week he made up his mind. He wanted Lilice and he wanted her imperatively.

If Snoose can, I can, he decided grimly. I'm going over to Lilice's, proper or not. What he'd say, he didn't know. But the thought set his hands to sweating. A hammer tapped muffledly under his breastbone.

Where he'd keep a wife didn't bother him then, any more than it did Snoose or a dozen other young men in the hills. He might have echoed what Young Matt Dornhover had told the father of his girl: "I've got me two hands, an ax and a grub hoe. I'm willing and I'm not sick. There's land ready to clear, and wood for a house. I ain't run out of sweat yet."

Many in these ridges had started that way; some with less. If Lilice were with him, close to him as his own skin, closer, he could hold up his head and defy anybody in the community. So he dreamed.

Grain sprouted bushily as if this year earth, rested after a long sleep of drought, were pricking seed and stem with vigor. "Tillering," Uncle Herm said. "Did you ever see such tillerin'?" he rejoiced, curling a finger around the whiskery shoots radiating from a stem. (Mr. Dunkel called it "stooling.") He clawed at his chin, leaving a smear of earth, and regarded the restless way Johnny left a half circle of shoe marks printed in the moist soil. "Bull wheels of Moses, we're in for a real harvest, barring hail or storm!" he chortled. Then he said casually, "Think you can fire a steam engine this fall?"

Buried in a drift of his own uneasiness, Johnny heard his words but not his meaning. He muttered, "Who'd hire me, after—after last fall?"

"I'm aimin' to." Uncle Herm couldn't hide the mischief in his voice. "Course I am. You can handle the firing. Guess I haven't forgotten how to run an engine."

Johnny looked up, hope like pain cascading over him. It seemed to him that sweetness grew in the lush spring green. He knelt beside Uncle Herm. His young fingers caught and circled about Uncle Herm's bony hand stuck with earth and full of bushy tender sprouts—shoots of the year's promise. Tomorrow and all the seasons beyond rushed about him with so great a noise he almost choked. "Uncle Herm, you mean it—you really mean it?"

"Nothing settled yet." Uncle Herm changed to serious planning. "I've talked with Norton a little. If he rents us the money, all right. Otherwise— well, it won't be so easy. Machine companies—they're leary of risking anything these days."

"And Aunt Phrena?" Johnny sorted out another obstacle as though he meant to count even the worst.

"Phrena, ya." Uncle Herm rose wearily. "Well, you leave her to me. I'll tell her. She knows a good bargain."

"Then we'll do it," Johnny cried exultantly. All at once he was sure of himself again. Why, it was clear as the sky after storm. He'd have a threshing rig and he'd marry Lilice, and even Bory Tetzell would have to take a back seat. "We'll do it, Uncle Herm. You and I. And they'll come crawling to us." His lips tightened into a hard, scarlike line. There was no salt under his lids in this joy. "We'll have the finest rig in the hills." (Finer than Bory's; yes, Bory with his pounding fists and his bull engine.)

Under Johnny's crushing fingers a clod of dirt pulverized; the dust scattered with a breeze. "They'll crawl to me, whoever they are," he muttered. Let the neighbors talk, if they wanted to. He didn't notice the sadness that crept over Uncle Herm's lean jaw. He heard himself jubilating inwardly, Lilice, Lilice, I'm coming to get you. Now you'll listen to me. You got to.

In spite of Uncle Herm's persuasion, Aunt Phrena fretted her doubling chins with scoldings. "Ach ya, all these years, debts, debts, debts! And now more to worry us sleepless!"

"There's money in wheat, lots of it," insisted Uncle Herm. "If we get a decent crop——"

"If," she snorted. "Always it is 'if.'"

But in this matter Kurt took Johnny's side. "With luck, we ought to pay back Norton in three, four years. The old debt, too. And be free for once. You should read about the big farms up northwest, the money they're making."

"Big farms!" grumbled Aunt Phrena distrustfully. "Big and broke! They are going to pieces. It says so in the papers."

"In bad years, yes," Johnny interposed. "But these bad years—they can't keep up forever."

Only half convinced, she mumbled into silence, Kurt's approval carrying more weight than Uncle Herm's predictions or Johnny's eagerness.

With the infant summer in his steps, Johnny took the buggy down to the creek. He unhitched the team, took off his shoes, pulled his trousers over his knees. Bare flesh twitched away from the touch of cool earth, warming now but holding the chill of January winds. Stepping lightly as a cat, he rolled the buggy into the brown water. "Ooooo," he gasped as he splashed in deep. Ripples sucked at the hubs. He scrubbed wheel and shaft into sun sparkles. As the trickles foamed from spoke to spoke, he mourned happily over an improvisation:

> "Oh my darling 'Lice Gray,
> They have taken you away,
> And I'll never see
> My darling any more
> Till Saturday night. . . ."

For all that the skies were the gray of a dirty curtain the Saturday evening he drove into the Rose yard, his whistle matched the robin's treetop carol. The tune ran out of him when from the porch Mrs. Rose said, "No, she's not home. Mother Haber is sick and the little girl ailing. Lilice's spending the night there. I sent some herb tea."

"Oh, ya." He eyed the point of his shoe glumly. In a tide of baffled impatience, he wished he'd brought his checkered cap after all.

Mrs. Rose twinkled at him. "I haven't seen you in a long time, Johnny. Come and sit awhile. I don't move from this rocker. Lilice and Adam are getting as common as dandelions to me, so I need a new face to talk to."

"We've been pretty busy." He evaded direct answer but moved not a muscle to step down. "Spring's work, and now summer on us."

She nodded at him. "Dressed up for the dance, I see. Even a stickpin." She drew her rocker nearer the wall. "How much do you like Lilice?" she asked abruptly.

"Well, I——" He nearly dropped the lines. Earnestly he gathered them into a tight knot. "I'd wear my fingers into blisters for her. Anytime. Ever since that night at the fire. I'll never forget how she cried over the pony."

"Little punkinhead!" Regret tinged her voice. "She's had tears in her life—more than her share, I guess." She saw him fiddling impatiently with the lines. "Come down and talk awhile," she coaxed.

"Thanks, no. As long as Lilice's not——" He stopped in confusion. Mrs. Rose hid her smile. "I guess I'll peg along," he ventured uncomfortably.

"Of course if there's a dance, you'll have to go, even without a partner."

He was not prepared for her quick thrust and answered with a simmer of belligerency, "Why not? Saturday night comes only once a week."

"And you don't want to spoil your fun on any account." Her laugh had an edge of seriousness. "Come and sit. Maybe you should know this. Lilice will never tell you, but I will. I think you'd like to hear it."

Halfheartedly, he tied the horses and came to perch in a chair as uneasily as a swallow on a ledge; as if he had little time, and would she hurry?

But Mrs. Rose settled herself quietly as though they were old neighbors. "Tears she's had enough, I know that." There was so much sadness in her speaking that he hitched unhappily. "The sorrows that come to us, I wonder how much blame is ours, how much is nobody's fault?" She smoothed a wrinkle in her lap. "I've never whipped Lilice in my life. But I couldn't save her from tears. My babies came late. We married late, as fashion goes, Hans and I. He worked in a sawmill. I used to worry dreadfully for fear he'd fall into the teeth. I guess Lilice sucked fear with her milk from me."

The chair creaked as he looked up startled. Even in wildest speculation, he couldn't imagine such talk in Aunt Phrena's mouth. He listened wide-eared now.

"All Lilice can remember about her father is crutches. She couldn't even sit in his lap without bumping against the wood. And I remember once—" Mrs. Rose drew a long breath—"she brought him a birthday gift, a handkerchief she'd stitched. She could hardly stand still, giving it to him, watching to see how happy he'd be. And the pain came on him, a terrible spasm. He threw out his arms the way he would when the pain came, and struck her—struck her in the face." Her head bowed. "We had a terrible time quieting her that night. And for what he'd done Hans felt so bad. He cried—you have no idea."

Her voice was so low he could hardly hear it. A horse stamped clop-pingly. He felt a tight longing for Lilice grow. If she'd run up that path now, if——

"I've tried to bring my children up as decently as I knew how. I think they know right and wrong as well as most do. But there is human right and wrong, and there's what the law says is right and wrong. I don't know. They seem awfully far apart sometimes. I read somewhere that taken together they are the pivot of a human equation as well as a moral law. I like that. Course, we don't belong to a church." She spoke flatly. Her glance at him was sidelong. "We're—outside."

She let the word hang in a silence he could almost hear. Outside. Like a keen-whetted knife it swung between them, between him and Lilice, too.

"When I think about Mr. Steuber and his preaching, all law, no mercy, the flame and the whirlwind; and Mr. Erdman groveling before his God like—like an animal that slides along——" Her hand moved impatiently over the arm of the rocker. "No. No, take away dignity and self-respect and you haven't much left."

He shifted about as though sitting on broken clamshells. Don't talk about preachers and law and stuff, he thought vehemently. Tell me about Lilice.

"Would you like a cooky?" She broke his thought so suddenly he jumped. Her smile was as motherly as though he were a twelve-year-old and there on a visit. "Lilice made a jar today."

Over the munching he waited for her to speak. "If I could," she went on, "I'd spare Lilice one single sleepless night. I s'pose it's foolish to talk about it. She'll fall in love with someone. I won't be asked about that." She gazed at him as squarely as she had at the Edgelys', the first night he'd seen her: a look he couldn't dodge. "I want her to be happy. She's had enough of broken bones. Don't you think she deserves better than wheels— wheels that crippled her father? I'd send her away to live if I could. But I can't." She broke a cooky in half. "All that too, I s'pose, is beyond my hands, one way or another."

Soberly he arose. Wheels that crippled her father. . . . The syllables grated. Without a word he climbed into the buggy. She saw him go. Before he slapped the lines down, he called, "Tell Lilice I'll be back. Soon." He grinned wryly. "Guess I'll stop at Snoose's for a while—if he's home. Too warm for dancing anyway." The wheels shimmered as he drove off.

Thoughtfully, Mrs. Rose piled the cookies in a trembling heap.

The anemones were like stars caught in a bright twinkle and dropped in the grass. Lilice twined several about her fingers as she sat beside the empty lunch basket. In the meadow hay was drying in its own warm, sweet odor. Adam had just clattered away on the mower, sighing in huge belly-contentment over the bread-and-meat sandwiches.

She sighed too, but happily, full of Johnny in her mother's talk about his visit. "Tell Lilice I'll be back." The brown in her eyes deepened. "Not to Gatha," she trembled, gathering the flowers. "Not to her. To me. Oh, Johnny!" She remembered his arm about her with a kind of pain in her breasts.

She gathered the blossoms. To live in Fergus! How she had happened on the notion, she wasn't sure, unless it came with Kory Mercer and the talk about the sale of his farm on the following week. Kory was going to sell out and go to live in Mary's Hill, and for no other reason than that his wife had got tired of feeding chickens and slopping hogs and milking cows. He had promised to get a hired man and build her a new house. But she decided that a mildewed cottage in Mary's Hill was worth two new houses with pigs and cows in Pockerbrush.

Lilice was thinking about Kory and his wife when the notion came. If we could go to Fergus! she thought without defining "we," though she wasn't thinking about her mother or Adam. A house in Fergus . . . a bank clerk makes good money . . . or a clerk in a grocer's like Lena's brother . . . a house of our own . . .

She snapped a flower at the stem, tumbled those she'd gathered into the basket and wandered meditatively homeward. "The meadow's full of windflowers," she told her mother. She brought water and a vase and began arranging the blossoms. Mrs. Rose leaned back.

After a while Lilice asked softly, "When Father was in the sawmills, did you—did you ever ask him——" She twisted several stems together. "Would he have taken other work if you'd asked him?" She bent over the vase.

"Poor little Punkin!" Mrs. Rose spoke half to herself, though she watched Lilice keenly. "It is many an eye you'll cry red over the strangeness of a man, for all the good it will do you." She sat forward. "I begged him, Punkin. Many times. But when a man makes up his mind, he makes up a woman's too. Unless she hates him. That's what my mother always used to say. I've heard it said that when a woman crooks her finger, a man will come running. Well, it's mighty few men I've seen running. But a woman——"

"I'll never run." Lilice tore leaves away fiercely. "Never," she added softly. The broken pieces of green whirled and rocked to the floor. Dismally she clung to the image of a cottage in Fergus, of roses, of a grocer's clerk with black hair and a bright smile.

They drove out to Norton's one day. Uncle Herm jovially la-la-la-ed a ditty over the lines. "Corn's surely shootin' up." He jiggled a thumb at a gray-brown field that quiltlike was knotted with the green twists of young corn leaves.

Johnny wagged his head approvingly. Until they arrived at Mary's Hill he'd had little to say, his excitement at this trip marred by an undercurrent of half-resentful uneasiness. All that past week he had muddled over his visit with Mrs. Rose. Time and again her words returned to disturb him: ". . . she deserves better now . . . wheels that crippled her father . . ." He asked himself at last belligerently, "Was it my fault Old Man Rose got caught in the gears? What's it all to me? No wheel is going to hurt me. Wonder if I'll ever see the day old women don't row about something."

But when the machine shop and a distant glitter of sun-reflecting black paint and polish came into his sight, he pointed as eagerly as a ten-year-old. "Lookit; there's one of the new engines. Judas, what drivers! I'd like to get my hands on that steering wheel."

"We'll take a turn past the shop, coming back." Uncle Herm giddapped the horses. Johnny twisted in the seat, looking behind him.

After a while of driving, Uncle Herm said casually, "Seems like Kurt would rather plow and haul manure this fall than go thrashing."

"He's welcome to it." Johnny shrugged indifferently, glad Kurt wasn't going to be bossing around.

"Well, sure," Uncle Herm agreed. "So it's between me and you." He slapped the lines. "I thought you'd like to sign the papers, too," he said earnestly, as if he'd snare Johnny forever to his side with a rope of obligation. "Once you get your John Hancock down, you'll feel you got a piece of the world by the tail."

Johnny nodded, unraveling a thought in his mind. Schwartz on the paper. "Schwartzie." The sound hung like a shadow back of his ears.

Uncle Herm was saying, "I asked Kurt first." He glanced slyly at Johnny. "Seeing as how he's her—— You know how it is," he finished hastily. Johnny nodded. Uncle Herm and Aunt Phrena. No hours of nagging, no years of growing old, could change his regard for her, it seemed. A queer tug came at Johnny's heart.

Uncle Herm went on, "No, Kurt didn't cotton to the notion. He thinks there's too much wheat raised. It peters the soil out. After a while, it won't grow anything a-tall. Bull wheels of Moses!" he chortled. "That's a crazy notion. Ground is ground. It'll last as long as we will."

Johnny, letting the future roll over him in sweet triumphant waves, scarcely heard him. He was going to fire a steam engine in the fall. Brushed out of sight were Mrs. Rose and the Saturday night he'd talked with her; gone almost Lilice herself. There was one gnarled and wide-fanged obstruction—the sound of Schwartz.

Carefully Norton let the fox behind his watery eyes search the face of Uncle Herm (solid, weather-worn, honest-chinned Uncle Herm) before his gaze leaped suddenly upon Johnny's eagerness. He noticed the tense stubbornness, the easy white grin. Then the mask cracked to let a fleshy appreciation through. "You pay your interest, Herman Barewolf. You and the Roses and a few others. About the only ones that do."

"Maybe; but Moses, it's only by scratching the shirttail," said Uncle Herm, rue in the pleasure of his accomplishment.

"It's by the tail that you swing the animal." Norton screeched open a drawer. "Guess I've got everything ready." He rustled papers onto the top of the desk.

Johnny let the held-back air in his lungs blow softly over his teeth. It struck his tongue coolly. Soon it would be done. A couple of pen scratches, the crackle of documents passing from hand to hand—and the new rig would roll into the Barewolf yard, say, late in summer: a traction engine and a new separator. Soon now his name would be black on white paper. Johnny Schwartz. Johnny . . . The past wriggled snakily through his mind. Johnny . . . For the rest of his life there would be that name which had never once brought a smile to his lips, only the haunting echo of something that made him cringe aside . . .

Uncle Herm leaned forward, a hand sliding along a knee. But Johnny pushed against the chair back until the narrow bar was an edge of strain across his shoulder blades. He saw the clumsy penholder move in Norton's fist. Suddenly the steel at the farther end seemed to be tearing ragged letters into his mind. All the shadow-hung years at Uncle Herm's house, the days of Aunt Phrena's toothed suspicions, the nights sleepless with bitter dreams haunted by whispers that lay foglike over the valleys of his thought

—all these rushed up like something cold and icy out of the years. They spoke in his voice.

Norton's ink-rusted pen was sputtering something on a line when Johnny said, "If my name is to be there, write it Johnny Black." His words came slowly as one who speaks after much thought, carefully, deliberately. "Johnny Black."

Uncle Herm let his hand slip past his knee. The crackling of paper ceased. Norton looked up. There was a queer silence.

"Black?" Norton pulled a flabby lip. "But ain't Schwartz——"

"Schwartz, yes," Johnny spoke without rancor but his knuckles whitened. "It means 'black.' It's always been so for me. I might as well keep it."

"But, Johnny." Uncle Herm peered at him, aware dimly out of what deep springs this muddy water welled. "Your pa's name—Schwartz is a good solid name. You——"

"Nothing wrong with Schwartz," Norton interrupted, measuring Johnny, head and foot, as if for a new suit.

"It's not yours. You don't have to wear it," Johnny told him, a thickness coming over his tongue. He couldn't say, "It has to do with *him* and something that comes into my throat when I hear the word." A fingernail bit into the flesh of his palm. "Schwartzie." His voice rose bitterly. "As long as I can remember plain, I've heard 'Schwartzie' from people. 'Little Schwartzie.' Nobody stood behind me when I tried to shut their mouths."

"Na ya, Johnny." Gray moth wings of tiredness left Uncle Herm's face old all at once and sad beyond the possession of a thresher to erase. "If changing your name will help——"

"My name *is* changed," Johnny insisted. "I've changed it now. This minute."

"Well, how shall I put it down?" Norton moved impatiently.

"Write it the way I want it, or don't write at all." Johnny snapped into vehemence. "From now on I'm Johnny Black. Not Schwartz. Never Schwartz again." As though he had slammed forever a door upon a dark figure in a passage that led into the past.

Norton looked to Uncle Herm for confirmation. Uncle Herm nodded as if he were giving away a part of him more precious than he knew.

There was a long quiet scratched deeply by the cat claws of the pen. At last with a sigh that wheezed from the fullness of his paunch, Norton blew gustily on the paper. "I made one for you, Johnny; a separate one. You can sign."

Johnny tilted the bulky pen and hunched over the paper; ink ran along the line blackly. The letters in the unfamiliar name blurred, and the breath clogged his throat. The pen slipped from his fingers. Johnny Black. He stared at the thick scrawl, at the *l* leaning heavily on the *a*. A fierce sort of joy shook his hands at this which he had made with his own flesh, as much a part of himself now as his arm was, or his leg.

Norton's voice seemed far away. "If you make a go of this, we'll see about thrashin' my place. I promised Bory Tetzell——"

Later those words would return to whip him like a lash. But on the ride home he could think only of the paper crimpling in his pocket and the inky name thereon. Uncle Herm's stoniness bothered him a little. But he was too busy over the echo of his own pride: "I am Johnny Black—from now on."

"I still think he's a bloodsucker." Johnny slid the paper into Snoose's hand. It was a warm afternoon that next Sunday. A bee landed on a white clover blossom. The stem bent.

"Well, Norton's never been well known for being generous," Snoose admitted. There were dirt calluses on his hands—hard, horny skin from the Peiser fork and the Peiser fields. "It's coming your way, Johnny." He searched the paper raptly. "Now you got it. A steam engine rolling along on its own power. Why, you could practically crawl up Jenny's Peak with it, and blow your whistle from the top, Johnny." He chuckled softly. "Norton certainly smelled a bargain, didn't he?"

"He'd grab the last goose a feller had on the place, if he'd get the interest that way." Johnny punched a toe into the soil. "Well, maybe a feller's got to do business that way, to keep the poorhouse over the hill."

"Johnny Black." Snoose's fingers crinkled the paper. He ran a thumb under the name. "I'm tickled, Johnny. Not because of the name so much. No. It's making up your mind to—well, to kick aside what you've got, and get yourself something new and shiny. That's what I care about."

"Uncle Herm took me to the bank and the courthouse." Johnny grinned with complacent modesty. "I guess it's settled."

"Half the time folks'll be calling you Schwartz." Snoose chuckled.

"I know. Maybe it'll be worse than before. Talk, talk."

"They'll get used to it. Folks get used to anything, if they hear it often enough."

"Oh, Snoose!" In a moment of uncertainty mixed with fear, Johnny caught at Snoose's knee. "Maybe it's true. Maybe I'm black—black inside." But the uneasiness vanished in the sunniness of Snoose's deep laughter and in the surge of his own confidence. "I'm glad I changed my name. I don't know how to say it, but—" his eyes were half cloud, half glitter—"I feel that—well—" he struggled—"I feel I can take a deep breath now."

Snoose waved his hand in dreamy agreement. "It's like wings, Johnny," he said in his own way. "You can fly high now. But you can fall, too; fall far like a hawk gone crazy with the sun."

"It'll take some pushing to make me fall." Johnny gouged out a heel-depth of ground. "I've got my two feet planted."

Snoose didn't hear him. "Names are just on the outside, though," he said. "They change like the shape of Sophie's hat. Our name used to have two dots above the *a*. Gramma said it meant fairy story or something like that. But we lost the dots. They were too much trouble to make, Pa said."

"You're chokeful of fairy stories all right." Johnny ruffled him bluntly. "As far as I can see, you can't thrash a setting of wheat with a fairy story." Before he left, he asked teasingly as if he'd just then remembered it, "Think you'd like a job tanking this fall, Snoose?"

"I wondered when you'd ask." Snoose arose. "I've been sitting on thistles the last half hour, waiting. Just try and keep me away."

The neighbors had their say. "Ya, his old German name ain't good enough for Johnny Schwartz. Has to have something special." Mrs. Peiser couldn't gather her skirts fast enough to rush over to the Roses'. "Well, Lilice, what do you think of that? Changing his name to Johnny Black."

"Why, I—" she regarded Mrs. Peiser's gossip a moment—"I think it's a beautiful name." Afterward, she remained in deep thought.

The Pastor bemoaned such behavior in a fourthly of a sermon. However, Mr. Edgely told Johnny, "Black, that's a good, hard sensible name."

When Aunt Phrena heard about the name-changing, a queer satisfied gleam shot into her eyes, as if this were the beginning of settlement of accounts past due. She had so little to say that Johnny watched her suspiciously. Not that she regarded the new name with anything but disfavor; and when the neighbors began to talk, she grew restive. Finally one evening she let him know how she felt about it.

"Black." She gave the pepper shaker an extra twist over the soup pot. "Ach, couldn't it be a good German name like Hageldorf or Kesselbaum? But no; it must be Yankee." Her tone was as biting as the pepper in the shaker. "You 'shamed to be a German? Want to run after the Edgelys', na?"

"That's got nothing to do with it." Impatiently Johnny flung his jacket on a hook behind the door. "Didn't even know it was Yankee. What do I know about the old country that you talk about? Never been there." He brought a chair from a corner. "Even Uncle Herm wasn't born there."

"Na." Aunt Phrena finished stirring the soup. "And so you can afford to laugh at it?"

"I wasn't born there, no." Uncle Herm sat at the table. "But my folks were. They brought me up strictly in the old-country ways. I'm not ashamed of them. What I say and think—I guess that's old country speaking in me, even if I never wet my feet in old-country dew." Aunt Phrena began ladling the soup. Johnny sat down.

Kurt drew up a chair. "It's old country all right," he said. "But it's mixed up with the new things right here in Pockerbrush."

"Maybe," Uncle Herm went on, almost mournful over the spoon he lifted. "Old things are good enough for me. But Johnny there—I guess what I say goes into one ear and out the other."

Johnny sensed with a pang the hidden ire that smoldered in Uncle Herm's voice. He cried desperately, "I'm not making fun of the old country. How could I be ashamed of you, Uncle Herm? That wasn't why I wanted to change——" Suddenly he couldn't go on to say "Schwartz." As if cornered he muttered, "I don't know why you're all against me like this."

"The good old things are laughed at in this country." Aunt Phrena handed the bread around. "Look at that Mr. Edgely. How he laughs at the *pumpernickel* and the *schwat suer* and the harvest festival and the *Missionsfest* at the church. He laughs at good German names too, like Bierwagon and Oeltrug and Silbernagel." She speared a slice meaningfully. "Nowadays it must be Yankee, or it is worthless. American, Mr. Edgely calls it."

"All I know for sure is Pockerbrush here." Johnny dipped his bread stubbornly into the soup. "It's a good piece of Minnesota; a good piece of America, too, I guess. It's good enough for me. I'm satisfied. I never lost anything in the old country."

"That still doesn't help you any." Kurt helped himself to more soup. "We've got old-country blood in us. Only a blockhead forgets that. But like Mr. Muri says——"

"That Noreegian." Aunt Phrena swished with her spoon.

"Don't care if he is Norwegian." Kurt stirred tranquilly. "He's in the same boat with us. Like he says, the old must make the new stronger and richer. You can't do that by throwing it away. You can't throw your grandpa aside and forget him. Of course there's no sense in listening to grandpa all the time either."

"Noreegians!" Aunt Phrena sipped noisily. "Call themselves Johnson today and Anderson tomorrow."

"I don't blame them." Johnny swallowed his bread and returned her look defiantly. "I've had my bellyful of Schwartz, too."

"What's all the yelling about?" Kurt asked Aunt Phrena. His level voice grew warm. "It's not the first name that's been changed around here." Suddenly Johnny found himself on Kurt's side against Aunt Phrena and Uncle Herm. "Look at Tjöstöl Skjelle and Mr. Weisslandt," Kurt went on. "If Johnny wants a new one——" He shrugged.

Uncle Herm shoved his plate back. "Schwartz was my friend," he cried in swift and bitter anger, his ire riding to the surface. "His boy talking like that about his pa. Go ahead, spit in your own well, if you think the water will be any fresher." He left the table. The door slammed behind him.

Kurt continued eating, his fork and spoon peaceful, as one who has done much work and expects that his daily bread and potatoes will lie sweetly on his stomach. But Johnny wondered whether there ever would be sweetness in bread again, no matter how much hunger prodded his belly.

Thereafter, Uncle Herm never failed to call him Black, Johnny Black. Scrupulously so. Until Johnny felt the implied blame in his carefulness. Not until the new rig came and they were at the Pastor's, ready to start the new season, did the bristly hedges between them fall away. Then it was that Uncle Herm cried heartily, "Well, Johnny Black, my fireman, here she goes." He grinned broadly; clapped Johnny's shoulder and stepped to the platform to handle the throttle. With the fork in his hand, Johnny bent over the fire chute to hide in his face what he didn't want even Uncle Herm to see.

But that was long afterward, when distraction itself, clawed and toothed, tore in Johnny's skull. In the days following the soup supper and Uncle Herm's slamming from the table, he shut eye and ear to what he saw and heard; to the tired silence fretting Uncle Herm; to Aunt Phrena's grumbling; to Kurt's indifference. He thrust them away behind the glitter of a new threshing rig, sharp-darted and blinding. And hour by hour his thought brightened with desire: "Lilice, Lilice, now I'll never listen to your 'no.'"

17

Sometimes, looking upon the engine that fall, upon the red star in its flywheel and the hawk-on-the-shield design raised boldly in iron relief on its fire door, Johnny wondered whether anyone could be at once so happy and so wretched as he was these days, and still move and have his being among his kind!

Here was the new threshing rig and he a fireman. For this he had counted tomorrows and tomorrows. From all the weary days of sweat on the flats (and days before that), he had looked to this shouting hour when with pride in his arches he'd swing to the platform and handle the throttle. Now that hour had arrived, was present. He was fireman in earnest (and engineer in practice, Uncle Herm said). And where was his pride, where his jubilation? Devil, if there were mirth anywhere, he'd like to borrow a wagonful.

Yet in moments when the *chug-a-chug* of engine and the soft breathing of fire in the box murmured of smooth, iron-under-velvet power, power that drove a straw carrier and cylinder with an oily might, he'd feel all his young manhood rise to strangle breath in his throat. He could have wept with laughter, with the strength his fingers tied in smudgy ribbons about the fork handle, with the bulge of elation lifting his ribs, if he could have forgotten Lilice awhile—Lilice and her tears, spring-water-clear drops cutting her face into wrinkles of hurt and grief; if her face hadn't come remindingly from the blur of a wheel or her tears in a clinging tit of moisture under a pet cock. When they did, gladness congealed lumplike in his chest; the honey horn of joy was dribbled with bittersweet so that he was scant of patience. With the restlessness of a cat he was ready to move from farm to farm.

The morning they were to move from the Barewolf yard to the church and the Pastor's settings, he grumbled, "Why can't we start here, at our place? Every fall, the Sunday before thrashing begins, the Pastor scolds about the thrashers. And then, sure enough, every fall, we begin the run with his little horse piles." They were beginning at the church acreage as usual. Mr. Whiteland was renting it then, and he belonged in Uncle Herm's run.

"Well, Pastor's got to have his little day," Uncle Herm answered mildly. "The church is a place maybe we better not forget. We got baptized there and we'll be buried there." ("Not all of us," Johnny thought grimly, remembering Old Mr. Rose.) "It's sorta the center of things, or ought to be." Uncle Herm rubbed his nose. Johnny banged his fork against the firebox.

They moved to the Pastor's, Uncle Herm still leaving a crooked track in the road. He never quite mastered the swing of the steering wheel; hadn't since the very first day when, in Mary's Hill, he had tried to hook the engine to the separator. He had started backing the engine toward the pole of the separator which Johnny was holding up ready to be fastened to a clevis under the platform of the engine. Something broke the steadiness of Uncle Herm then. He swung the wheel, white-faced and staring. Helplessly he saw the engine under him backing into a grain tank; heard the crash; heard Johnny's yell. Then, panic-frozen, he realized that the engine was heading rear end first toward the bank of the river. If a machinist, standing near, hadn't jumped on the platform and caught the levers, the Red Star would have stopped its wheels on the river bottom.

Johnny rushed up from the separator. "Whatever happened?" he gasped, more frightened than Uncle Herm. "I'm shaking so, it's a wonder my bottoms hold together."

"Moses Almighty!" gulped Uncle Herm, pale to his whiskers. "Guess I got the wrong lever."

By the time they started at the Pastor's, however, Uncle Herm steered with more confidence. Though occasionally he still wove from road edge to road edge, he found he had trouble only when he "lined up" the engine with the separator. Aware of this and hiding whatever pride he had, he urged Johnny to take the wheel. In the weeks of that fall he let Johnny exercise a squinting eye and a calculating hand. He'd jump from the platform, saying hastily, "Twist her tail, Johnny! Get her straight on the cylinder wheel!"

With a self-assurance that quaked at times, Johnny shifted a hand quickly from throttle to steering wheel. The engine chugging a lusty freedom, he brought the belt slapping into a swaying tightness between the two machines.

Once the neighbors heard about the thresher, they tethered their gossip on the news and fattened it. "Well, I want to know. Those Barewolfs, they're getting pretty uppish, a steam engine and a new separator; even a new water tank. Cripes! And that Johnny, him that wants to call himself Black. Well, some people certainly think their spit don't smell."

The Pastor added a grumbling bass to the chorus. He wasn't at all certain (he said) that Herman Barewolf was safely within scriptural behest by using the violence of steam and fire to thresh grain, since man undoubtedly was meant to use flesh, his own and his animals', to harvest his grain. Surely all history, Biblical and secular, proved this. "Worshipers of Baal and Ashtoreth!" he mumbled. But this was after his own settings were in a straw pile and his grain safely in the bin.

When he heard about the thresher, Alb Hukelpoke left work and his wife and hustled over to say loudly, "Sheetin' Judas!" and grab Uncle Herm's arm. "You can't keep me out of thrashin' dust, Herm Barewolf. If you're gonna handle the engine, let me run the separator. Me, I'm damned

good at finding oil holes—or any other kind of holes." So it was settled.
Heinie Beerwagon offered to come. So did the Nussbaum boys. Mr.
Dunkel agreed: said he had to get thrashing done in a hurry now. With his
wife so bad and all, he couldn't leave the place for long. And their consent
was honey and wine to Johnny's heart. If only Lilice, Lilice with anger
tearing at her lips . . .

He aroused Snoose one Sunday from a reverie of grain rippling upon a
hill, thick and wind-troubled as a girl's hair—Em'ly's hair. For this afternoon Snoose was at home and no longer Mr. Peiser's hired man. But he
was so full of Em'ly, he only stared when Johnny told him, "Well, the
tank job is yours."

He murmured out of dreaminess, "Johnny, did you ever notice? Em'ly's
eyelashes—they curl up like the fringes of the honeysuckle." He blinked
into awareness and muttered, "Job?"

Johnny had a moment of sorrowful envy. Snoose and Em'ly. Like the
acorn and the cup these two had grown together, firmly and quietly. No
harsh sliver of disagreement roughened the sweet texture of their intimacy.
Lilice and me, Johnny thought soberly; seems like all we ever do is have
words. And she's so darned sweet.

Then he shrugged the cloud aside with a noisy "You're going to be my
tankee, Snoose," as if that settled it. "We got a tank with a pump. Water-
hauling is going to be really easy this year. No more water barrels to fill."
And so Snoose became part of the crew.

But Mr. Schadel said grudgingly, "No hair off my backsides if Herm
Barewolf wants to bury himself in debt. Let him go ahead. Ya, ya, if
I can't have my horses working alongside me, I'll quit thrashing. I ain't
gonna have no snortin' straw-burner settin' fire to my rig, no sir-ee." Then
he added with a little malice, "That Johnny—let him tootle on his whistle,
smart like he thinks he is and changing his name. Wait till that heavy
engine breaks through the bridges and falls hind end up in the creeks.
That's when my horses will have to pull him out. I'll thrash circles around
him yet."

A few of the neighbors agreed with him, not yet recognizing, as he
did not, the shrieking sound of doom trembling in the air. Out of respect
for long custom, they asked Mr. Schadel to thresh their stacks. But most
of the folks, relying more on faith in Uncle Herm than in the efficacy of
the new straw-burning rig, agreed to give the engine a trial. "Let the old
steam kettle come! We'll have the teams and the horsepower ready, in case
she blows up."

Johnny heard about their talk. His fork stabbed into the straw heap.
They had finished at the Pastor's, moved to the Schimmels', chugged to

other neighbors'. As they passed the District School (Johnny wondered whether his initials still remained beside Snoose's on the desk they had shared), Mrs. Sperry and the scholars tumbled from the schoolhouse. That is, the scholars shrieked happily away from the history lesson. Mrs. Sperry followed more sedately. She was grayer now, Johnny saw, and her bustle was more subdued. On her face in wrinkled threads of weariness were marked the care and patience she had lavished on these children and those that had come before these.

The kids bunched on the road edge, tensed with the fearful importance of this moment. Barewolf's steam rig was passing by. They were so wide of eyes Snoose said, "They're going to need pincers to shut 'em again." Johnny peered at them from a greasy countenance. There was an ache in him, half of loneliness, half of resentment, at their fresh, untried bewilderment, so full of eager potentials, bound as it was now by astonishment at the threshing rig. He reached forward and yanked the whistle cord.

They jumped. Some of them hid behind stumps in the schoolyard. One ran inside, waving his arms. One boy leaped high in a sort of frenzy, shouting, "Let 'er tootle, Johnny!" Even Mrs. Sperry was decorously startled. But a little girl sank down and cried bitterly. In her wrenched face Johnny saw Lilice's again. Shame swept him. He dropped the cord and wished he might jump down and, with his arms about her, laugh her into smiles again. But Mrs. Sperry gathered her up. The schoolhouse slipped away among the bushes that hedged the road.

Where the rig dusted among the stacks and the engine smoked in the yard, the folks came together, their remarks slipping out easily with their spittles, clear or stained with the brown of tobacco twists.

"Look once," Mr. Nussbaum pointed dourly. "Traction engine they call it. But the machine companies don't trust their own contraption. They ain't sure it'll pull itself. Look there. They got a place there in front for the pole and the eveners to hook horses on, just in case the old devil can't pull itself from the spot. And by cripes, they got a seat over the right front wheel for the driver, just like Bory Tetzell's. Na ya, when they get stuck—" he bobbed his head in the direction of Uncle Herm and Johnny— "they'll make good use of it."

That evening Johnny brought a wrench. With vicious twists he unscrewed the burs and the fastenings, and pitched the driver's seat into the bushes. "If I sink to my ears in mud, I don't want to see it on the engine," he told Uncle Herm and Snoose.

They did get stuck. Now and again, in spite of Johnny's protests, they hitched teams to the front axle. However, with a little planning, with pries and heavings, with corduroys over the wettest places, with mild expletives from Uncle Herm and curses from Johnny, they managed to pass through the swamps and over the trembling bridges (though timber and abutment creaked) without more than a heavy expenditure of neighborhood prophecy and some loss of time.

To be sure, they avoided swamp roads and bridges when they could. The rains were moderate this autumn. They came too sparingly for this to be called a wet year. "Wait till it slops down," the neighbors warned agreeably, "and the roads get so soupy you can drop a wrench right through a graded road and it'll never stop till it hits China, then you'll see." Johnny grunted wrathfully.

He was even more scornful when they came to Old Man Dresser's and he saw again the little grain heaps near the settings—the piles of hand-tied sheaves built there by Amaria, Seligkind and Gretelein. Old Man Dresser was a frugal man, the neighbors said, and his daughters saved him money. They sweat like hired men in the fields; at night, tired into snorting, they slept with their virginities, inert as clods.

The old man used to set the clock ahead in the morning and back at night—to get a quarter hour more work out of them; or so the gossip ran. With bent spines and grubbing fingers they gathered the heads and bound the sheaves and piled them into little stacks. These the old man had threshed separately. "Save a little grain for mine girls," he'd tell the threshers. Superlatively honest, he sacked this grain and set it apart.

Once the girls managed to gather five dollars in a harvest. "Hoopla!" they chanted to the neighbors. "We don't have to ask Pa for any money this year. Now we can get *bummels* for our hats." With this money their only allowance, the girls clutched hungrily at the meager beauty of a ribbon for a waist or an ornament for a hat—a scabby freedom, thin in a profitable year, thinner in a season of drought.

" 'Save a little for mine girls,' " mocked Johnny. "It wastes a lot of time."

"We always done it," said Uncle Herm. "Some things, you do them so often, you feel lost when you don't."

"Wastes time just the same," Johnny persisted. But when the face of Amaria came to his mind, sad and worn, he hung his head, thinking of Lilice and how stricken she had been, her mouth trembling as though he'd struck her.

Sometimes he left his fork and paced a hundred steps away. He turned to look upon the rig. There was the engine with its jaunty plume of smoke and Snoose on the water tank, the pitchers on the stacks and the separator breathing dust at mouth and tail. He should have been jubilant. A yell or a whoop shouldn't have been far off. But he remained silent, the joy

THE SEASON OF HARDENING KERNELS 299

locked in the ice that had frozen with Lilice's reproaches and her hapless cry, "All you think of is the rig, night and morning." Slowly he turned to the fork and the pile of straw he was stuffing into the engine's belly. "Wonder why it is," he muttered gloomily one time. "No matter how red my apple looks, there's always a worm in it."

They came to Alb's place on a windy day and had a small fire. Sparks from the engine winked into straw near the stacks. They brightened into flame. A pitcher saw the smoke. There was a wild yelling and a wilder waving of forks and gunny sacks and more danger to human limb and life than anything else.

"That coulda been a bad one," Mr. Nussbaum gloomed afterward.

"Aw sheets!" Alb minimized the matter. "You need a little fire under the tails of them pitchers, or they'd never move their shanks."

They moved the rig among the buildings in Mr. Dunkel's yard. The *chug-a-chug* of the engine, tossed from wallside to wallside, was loud and confined as they went between the barn and the granary. Once beyond the buildings it escaped and diminished into field and pasture.

As they neared the house, the door was flung wide and Mrs. Dunkel came running, white-eyed and staring, pale as a weathered clamshell. She waved a broom at the engine. "You can't have her," she screamed. "You can't take my baby, you devil. Get out of here!" She gathered rocks and flung them. One landed clanking on the boiler; one shot past Uncle Herm; one clunked against the auxiliary tank beside Johnny. With more stones she came forward. Her gray hair tumbled wispily. She rushed up as if to wrestle the iron wheels with her bare flesh. Johnny saw that tears half blinded her. He grew sick with pity. Uncle Herm slowed the engine.

Then Mr. Dunkel was there. Firmly he coaxed her back into the house. She followed docilely, the storm spent and her grief distracted. Mr. Dunkel himself made cold-meat sandwiches and coffee for the threshers that lunchtime. He carried it out to the yard himself and was cheerful over the ragged hunks of bread he cut, and the bitter brew. "You'll get better vittles tonight, boys," he promised the crew. "I got some womenfolks coming. For lunch, a slip of bread and meat, I thought I'd do it myself." As they munched there in the yard, the crew heard a thin wailing from the eaves and knew how Mrs. Dunkel cried behind the locked door under the rooftree.

Only at suppertime when more leisure was needed to cook the meat and prepare the gravy did Mr. Dunkel permit Mrs. Fleischer and Mrs. Peiser to come and set his table and meddle with his pantry. The crew trooped in and sat down to eat. With the buttering of bread and the passing of the coffee, they heard thumping noises overhead. But Mr.

Dunkel settled himself hospitably at the table and saw to the heaping of the plates; or called, "There's more bread under the cutting board, Mrs. Peiser, if you'll slice some. We're just now empty."

Hungry as he was, Johnny blunted his appetite more with memory than with meat and potatoes. Before Mrs. Peiser brought the pie in, he left the table and slouched into the darkness that hid the engine. He sat on the platform, a red crack of light from the firebox a crimson scar across his nose and cheek. The still-hot iron warmed one shoulder; the night chilled the other.

"Poor old Dunkel!" he muttered. He thought about that afternoon and Mrs. Dunkel, the rocks in her hands and the pitiful grief that blinded her eyes. And all the hurt of another afternoon surged back and caught at his throat, the summer afternoon he'd gone to the Roses, to tell Lilice about the threshing rig.

He had whistled over the way and found her in the garden picking peas. The sun was a hot belt laid across his neck. There were butterflies in the cabbages. But he rejected earth and sky and saw only her. Every sinew rang like tightened wires at the sight of her. She straightened up with peapods in her hands. As if another walked in his place, moved in his shirt and pants, and not he at all, he took her in his arms. "Lilice," he whispered, "let me hold you tight, you have no idea how tight!"

At first she protested, her hands, full of pods, lifted against his chest. But he yearned, "Lilice, let me, let me!" She yielded her stiffness. Something for which she had been searching a long time, lonely and afraid, had come to her with his arms about her, safely and with love.

The pods scattered and fell over his arms except one in her fingers which she held before his eyes. With laughter too deep to bubble on the tongue, he saw her finger tips grow firm and whiten a little on the pod ends. In an unsteady instant he longed to have a part of his own flesh between her fingers—the lobe of his ear, the end of his nose, a twist of hair. . . .

She split the pod and held the kernels against his lips. Don't let anything spoil this minute, my sweetheart, she sighed to herself. This minute and all the years that swung hingelike upon it, a house with roses in a city . . . You've come to me. Nothing can take you now, she thought, pressing against him. Nothing can take you. . . .

His teeth caught the pea kernels; nibbled her fingers. He leaned his head to push them aside. As if she'd asked a question, he whispered, his lips close to hers, "Lilice, Punkin, marry me! Don't be afraid ever! Don't listen to what anybody says! Love me!" Words tumbled in a froth of eagerness. "I'll get a farm and build you a house. We'll have a big place. Lilice, you know I'd blister my fingers working for you. You know that."

He bent nearer; spoke the breath of syllables rather than words. "Uncle Herm bought a thrashing machine and I'm half owner." Before his insistence the tangle of her fingers went down. He felt her lips quiver under his; yield to his demand.

Tardily his last words made sense. Her lips moved as though a silver sharpness had been thrust quick-deep; relaxed in that sightless ecstasy which is close kin to oblivion; then lifted firmly, imploringly against his (Oh, honey of the grapevine, drop your poison, drop your bane).

It may have been aeons later that his hands on her cheeks felt the hot moistness of tears; her tears. He drew back. Out of an ecstasy that was like one where eyes are hung with the curtains of sleep, he saw crystal drops break her smile into wrinkled grief. . . .

A handful of chaff fell. His body moved sluggishly on the engine platform. In a kind of pain he swayed, now into, now out of the crack of firelight. He remembered how she stood there crying, "It was so hot today. I was wishing it were spring again and cool. But it's all winter now. I'll never plant roses——" Her voice roughened into a sob. She couldn't say "Roses on a white cottage far away."

Long afterward he would remember how she broke from his lips and his arms and stood there that day, then groped blindly along the path. "Oh, Johnny, when will you think of me for once—just me?" The sorrow in her tone was like hard anger.

"Think of you?" he cried bitterly. "When don't I think of you?" He followed her, calling her name, all his longing in the way he caught her arm.

She swung on him fiercely, anger blazing through the wet of her lashes, a vehement sun through misty rain. "Don't you touch me, Johnny Black!" she cried. "All you think of, all you live for, is machines. Well, I want something more than an engine in my house."

He tried to pull her toward him. With a swift movement as though she grasped at anything to hurt him, she bent and ripped up a pea vine and slashed the green whip across his face. Light as gossamer it would have been at another time, striking in the mirth of love play. If it had been a leaded blacksnake, scarring his flesh, he could not have been stunned into greater immobility. He froze there. Dully he watched her run to the house. The door banged. . . .

The fire in the engine flickered. Iron snapped with the heat cooling. "Think of you?" he repeated mournfully. He covered his face with a mask of hands, too sick to care whether the fires in the engine were banked for the night or not.

A lash of flame whipped between the spaces of two fingers. He felt the redness bounce on his eyeball and away. It struck again. His nose moved into wrinklings; itched with the remembrance of green leaves brushing it. With something like a groan he rubbed his hands across his face and slid off the platform. He grabbed up the fork to get something hard in his hands. "Lilice, Lilice," was on his lips but his chin tensed. His fingers went rigid. In a wild surge of rebellion he muttered, "All right then. Devil take her and all her kind! There are other birds in the bushes, and by God, I'll find them!"

In the haymow afterward he listened to the song that was being yanked roughly into melody by Heinie and a Nussbaum boy. He even accepted a swallow of Arty's bottle, and grinned when Alb warned him, "Don't you do it, Johnny, unless you want to wrap a piece of liquid barbwire around your guts. Sheetin' Judas!" He watched Snoose sitting in the lanternlight reverie-gathering ("Em'ly, let's hang kisses in our house like pictures on the wall"). Sullenly he joined in a line or two:

> "I was thrashing in the Valley,
> Oh, the Valley fair to see,
> When the farmer's pretty daughter,
> She fell in love with me.
> She told me that she loved me;
> She took me by the hand
> And sweetly told her mother
> That she loved a thrasherman.
> 'Oh my daughter, oh my daughter,
> You will kill me grieving sore
> To fall in love with a thrasherman
> You never saw before.'
>   'Well Ma, I don't give a damn for that.
> You do the best you can.
> For I'm bound to thrash in Dakotaland
> With my roving thrasherman.' "

And over the ridges at the Rose place, Adam Rose bent above the wash-dish that night. Through the soapsuds he said, "In February sometime. That's when Lena wants it." Silently Lilice hung a clean towel.

"The first wedding in my family," exclaimed Mrs. Rose. "I'm entitled to a good cry, I guess. Don't expect it, though." She sighed and plucked a thread in the shawl about her shoulders—a woolen shawl for the chill weakness that lay on her bones and would not be warmed away. The pillow crackled against her ear as she moved her head. How Lilice did like a smooth and starchy piece of cloth, pillow or shirttail, she thought, and let her hand slip to the chair arm.

Adam wiped his face. He said no more. There was little to say. After the wedding Lena of the sharp peering eyes would bring her boxes, her dresses, her cherished bottles of ilang-ilang perfume and Florida water (those essentials for "any lady's boudoir cosmetique," said the advertisement of the Emporium in Mary's Hill) and mix her clothes with Adam's.

Lena's a good girl even if she is a little sharp, Mrs. Rose told herself. But three women in the house . . . There was a coolness on her shoulders at the thought; she wished Lilice would brew a pot of tea.

But Lilice was thinking, Day after day, I'll hear them. They'll be cooing and cuddling. And I—— She fled to her room and the sanctuary of tears and prayed that salt would rub away from the page of her mind the print of black hair and the strength of his arms on her shoulders and the warm taste of his lips. . . .

Sometimes in that season of threshing Johnny moved like one whose feet know to the least pebble a well-trod path and follow it, but whose head is far from the motion of walking. Mechanically his bones and sinews obeyed the imperative demands of the engine. Gather the forkful of straw from the pile beside the driver, shove it into the firebox, keep your eye on the water gauge, don't let the smoke turn white, the old bitch is eating up steam again, whistle for water: *woot, wooot, wooot* ("Grab it, Snoose's been gone half an hour; wonder what he found in the creek this time— another scooter?"), too many ashes, fire don't draw, rake 'em out under the wheels, don't think of her, don't think of her . . .

"Devil grab it, I won't." The tines clanged against the firebox. But her face remained in a steam wisp, her voice in the purr of greased wheels.

Bone-weary he plunged into sleep, a broken smile (her smile) riding the sound of *chug-a-chug* into oblivion. Uncalled by Uncle Herm or Alb, he stirred in the dark of mornings and slid up the far wells of sleep, summoned clock-punctual by an iron watchman guarding depths deeper than marrow. Morning after morning he woke to a dull awareness that four thirty without red dawn had come. Yawning in the dark and tiredly resisting the fun of slipping a cold hand inside Snoose's drowsy-warm shirt, he left the nest of his and Snoose's body heat and shivered into outer clothes. After lighting the lantern, he climbed from the haymow, or, on those rare occasions when the crew slept in a house, clumped downstairs before the farmer stopped his snoring.

He set off for the engine. On those mornings when ridge and valley chilled with autumn, the raw dawn needled him with cold so that he stooped against it as against a wind, though not a twig stirred. Sometimes a dog whuffled commiseratingly from a resting place under a porch as the small patch of light and shadow wavered across the yard; but the rooster on his perch was still head-on-a-side for a second sleep.

Many times the rig was in the yard itself or near by, and the distance he had to walk short. But as they threshed westward and approached the Valley, it was often set far in a field, a walk across a forty or a sixty. Once from a knoll coyotes lifted their explosive barks which they drew into thin howlings against the early day, disturbed by this lonely lantern winking across the fields. In spite of himself he felt the hair on his neck bristle, the ancient sign of resistance to attack. His hand on the lantern handle tightened. After sunup he could see his tracks, a dark meandering trail in the frosted stubbles.

Stone-dead the engine hulked, goat's beards of ice catching the lantern-light and glittering redly from the pet cocks. Only in its deepest belly did a hint of yesterday's white-hot turmoil remain. The splutter of a match was a raw sound in the still unlighted day. In the firebox it was a diminutive crackle, far from the roar of vitality that soon would shake wheel and toolbox.

With a shielding hand Johnny thrust the flame into the cavern of the firebox. When sometimes it fluttered and died, darkness like walls fell from the corners. He could almost feel a black weight like soot on his stretched-out hands. Even with smoke blooming from the stack—more guessed at than seen—there was the slow coaxing of the flame and the gathering warmth. "Until she gets five, ten pounds of steam in her, the old bitch don't breathe at all; she just smolders," Makin Boone used to say. Time and again Johnny swung the lantern up against the steam gauge, peering at its oil-dirtied glass to see whether power were beginning to leap and pry within the shell of iron and show its liveliness clocklike under glass. "Damn old slowpoke!" he muttered and envied Snoose still lying, arm curled over head, in sleep.

Reluctantly the hand of the gauge climbed the degree marks. When it perched upon ten, he turned on the "blower" and heard the first strangling gurgles of steam in the stack forcing a draft. Through the vents in the firebox door he saw the upright flames bend, rise and then lean like grass under wind toward the rear wall and the flues. "She's heatin' up now," he mumbled. The water glass returned crimson slivers of the lantern when he lifted the light to see the water level. The gurgle in the stack became a purr, a throaty rattling, a gentle roar, swallowing other sound. Damn funny! he cogitated. You can coax a ton of iron like this into life but, Devil grab it, you can't do a thing with a woman!

He shut the blower down for a moment. There was a quick silence marred only by crackles and a faint hiss. He turned the blower up and heard a metallic rushing noise of steam. He stabbed a poker viciously into the unresisting fire. By the time Uncle Herm and Alb trudged along, coats pulled close to their chests, steam was high in the gauge, the engine hissingly alive, cog and piston ready, and day was turning early lemon into late rose. They all returned to the farmer's house for breakfast.

They threshed at Mr. Haber's across the creek from the Musser place. Down where the water ran deep and wide Snoose pumped silver splashes. Water fell through a square opening into the empty tank. It hit the bottom with hollow, metallic noisiness, grew quieter as it rose. Snoose pulled and pushed the handle. The hose stiffened with each intake stroke; relaxed; stiffened. In a shallow place in the water he had placed a bucket. It lay on its side. Little water circles whirled over it. Into the bucket he had thrust the hose end, shielding the wire-protected snout from mud and sand.

Snoose whistled "Emmalina." He gazed over the water at the house of Em'ly so ardently that he left off pumping. The hose sagged limply. Soon minnows began to poke into the shadowy inside of the pail. Twice in the afternoon Johnny's warning *too-ot, too-ot, too-ot* jerked him into pumping furiously. Coiling the hose and gathering up the bucket in a hurry, he trotted the team and came up, traces jingling, water thrusting a misty head through the opening and breaking into silver sloshes over top and sides.

That night on the creek bank Snoose rolled up his pants and with an oak limb paddled a basswood log across the water. He let the starlight pale in Em'ly's nearness. He returned just before Johnny waked but his chuckles were eager that day and he was livelier than anybody.

Mr. Musser himself told about it, tossing a handful of chaff up at Snoose on his tank. Johnny didn't hide his grin when he found out. Later he wrestled Snoose into the straw pile; pummeled him and grabbed at his legs until Snoose yelped, "Hey, you want to wreck me for life?" But in sober afterthought, Johnny grew silent. Snoose's gay chuckles tortured his reflections with drops bitter and mouth-twisting as gall: Em'ly in Snoose's arms, his fingers cupped about her chin; those whispers that bring warmth to the skin and a faster breath in the throat—he shook his head to displace a burden. This darkly running imagination drove rancor into his musings.

"For others, such stuff; never for me, no!" As one whose finger ends return again and again to a scabby wound, to find relief in pain, he brought back to his mind that hot afternoon in summer, Lilice in the garden, Lilice breaking from his lips and arms. . . .

They moved the rig to Clymy Humber's place where Clymy, less runty someway now, was proud. He had a right to be. His farm was well started, the first crop of his field garnered and the third crop of his strength growing in Sophie's body.

Sophie came to the engine, water pail in her fist, all smiles to see Johnny. "Well, if it ain't that fightin' Johnny. I never catch sight of you any more," she welcomed him. "You men, you can go where you please, but a woman—she stays where she's put."

"That's not what I hear tell," Johnny twitted her. "They say Clymy's buggy turns in at a lot of farms hereabouts, and Clymy has to walk if he wants to go anywhere."

"Seems like folks know my business better'n their own." Sophie remained unperturbed. "I'm no tattletale. But some things I hear need to be talked about." She glanced at the engine. Snoose hadn't yet arrived with the tank. Uncle Herm was busy with Alb, both digging holes to level off the separator. Pitchers and strawmen knotted into groups, untied and scattered.

She set the pail on the engine platform. "I got something to say to you." She drew him aside. "You can get mad at me for talking, if you want to. But I stuck up for you when you were hardly old enough to button the front of your pants. So listen." Her manner was brusque. "Lilice Rose drove over yesterday."

"Lilice?" His eyes flashed wide with hope, clouded again.

"Her ma ain't none too well." Sophie smoothed a wrinkle in a sleeve. "A nice young thing, Lilice. Why did you fight with her?"

"I? Fight?" He stepped back in outraged bewilderment. "Why, I never——"

"She began to cry, the poor critter. Right there in my kitchen. She's got to cry someplace. She can't worry her mother with fretting." Sophie almost glared at him. "I got the whole story out of her. You men! Hearts you got as big as beer barrels and brains the size of hazelnuts!"

"Judas Priest!" yelped Johnny, pin-stuck by her words, her blame whipping his ire with a lash of nettles. "She wouldn't listen to me. I still don't know for sure what she jumped at me for, and then ran into the house. What did she——"

"Don't climb out of your britches." Seeing the angry glint in his eye, she patted his arm. "I didn't mean to stomp all over your feelings, Johnny. But that poor thing! Something's hurt her terrible. Looks to me like she's been scared all her life; still is."

"Women's truck." Johnny kicked the earth violently, pricked by a thorny memory. "She wasn't scared to snap at me."

"Of course not," exclaimed Sophie triumphantly. "And that proves it.

She got mad at you because she prob'ly cried her pillow wet the night before."

"She's seen the last of me, that's for sure." Johnny tugged at his jacket sleeve. "Guess that's what she wanted anyway," he added angrily mournful.

"Blockheaded as an ox." Sophie shook her head at him. "You men! No wonder God long ago gave up His job walking here on earth. He lost so much patience with you critters, He had to give up. Only a woman can get along with a bullheaded man, and then only halfway."

She left him abruptly; gathered up her pail and marched toward the house. He went back to his firing, more ruffled than ever. "Feller that can understand what a woman's talking about ought to be elected president," he growled. "It's hell all around."

Not once during that autumn had he put on his best suit to appear at a neighborhood party or dance. On Sundays he slept at home more times than he went to doze under the Pastor's sermons. Persistently he shut his ears to Heinie's persuasive "They're picking up the slivers at the Schimmels' Saturday night. Get into your knee britches and come along."

"Aw, what's the use?" he had answered morosely. "Seventeen hours a day around the engine—that's enough for me. I guess I can get along without having a skirt wrapped around my knees for an extra hour or so." Even the invitation in Arty Nussbaum's bottle didn't bring him on the floor. At home Aunt Phrena preened a guarded satisfaction though she was crisp at his neglect of the Sabbath.

But on the Friday after his talk with Sophie, Heinie said, "You're gonna forget how to sashay, if you don't come along to a shindandy pretty soon. Arnold Nussbaum is having a granary dance Saturday night. That cousin of the Fleischers—the one that's visiting this fall—she'll be there. She's one that'll heat your grease."

Johnny hesitated. Then in a sullen mood, "All right," he said. "Feller catches hell if he does and he catches hell if he don't. I might as well go."

Once more he let two step and polka limber his legs into smoothness. Not only on Saturday nights but sometimes in midweek he forgot fireman's cramp, and walked or rode to the dances, sometimes a mile away, sometimes ten. He'd come to fire up the engine in the morning, red-eyed without a wink of sleep, the dance like a drug in his joints, slowing his step to a crawl and turning day into a kind of fog through which he crept, weary-limbed and dead to thought.

He met the new girl, the cousin of the Fleischers. Tillie Schwingend was her name. He hung greedily over her friendliness, second-best though it was. In his present mood, it was richer than the lean fare he was sure he was starving on, these days. He responded to her glitter heatedly, thinking with acrid self-pity, "Nobody else gives a damn anyway. I'm goin' to have me a little fun."

She was a small bundle of arms and legs, intoxicatingly light, with lips that were wetly red ("Rouge de Théâtre," Em'ly Musser whispered to Snoose in shocked delight). She had blondish hair ("That ain't natural," Gatha told Johnny maliciously; "she's blondined it"). Genuine or not, Johnny liked her brittle tininess of appearance and of voice, and the way she squeezed the muscle of his arm the first time they met. He responded avidly to the unreticent almost childish promise in her shrill "Why, where have they been hiding you? Bet you can kick the ceiling like a Norwegian."

Laughing headily, Johnny danced with her and fell into boisterous hilarity. Thereafter he salved more than one dull ache in her company.

(Aunt Phrena fretted again over the stories she heard. Lilice was told—with brisk elaboration. She remained silent and brewed her mother's tea with a bitter longing no sugar could sweeten.)

On dance nights Johnny scraped the grease away under his fingernails; washed until his skin was apple-red. He tilted the checkered cap at a perky angle once more. One evening during a two-day wet spell, he spent a slow twenty minutes with comb and water, almost spitefully rolling waves into his hair.

"Hog troughs!" Aunt Phrena said scornfully. "People who run to dances every night—they are as much trouble to themselves as girls with their spit curls."

He flung the comb down noisily. If nobody else did, at least Tillie exclaimed over his curly hair. That night in growing defiance he sipped of Arty's bottle; waltzed Gatha into a frenzy; answered Heinie's slippery tales with ones as slippery; and hugged Tillie fiercely.

"What you monkey around with her for?" Alb asked the next morning. "She's just a kid."

"A kid? Her?" Annoyed, Johnny assumed an air of knowing what he really didn't know. "Say, she's all right."

"Nothing but a little bundle of wild oats," Alb told him.

"Well, even a wild-oat bundle is all tied up in bands," Johnny replied with what he thought was rakish boldness. "I aim to do a little bandcutting in that territory myself."

"Suit yourself." Alb walked away without saying what Johnny knew he meant to say.

During a short spell of Indian summer Johnny went to a dance at the Peisers'. After the space of cold weather just past, the air even at night had a soft, caressing quality which with the smell of moist leaves and smoky meadows brought a yearning for the touch of wind and a wild sweep from a hill-top. The frost shackles of winter, lately so threateningly near, were flung aside for a moment; the summerlike hours were the sweeter for being under doom.

Tillie was waiting for him that night. "Come on, you old firebox tender," she giggled at him, careless of the listening folks around her. "Come on. I've got a new wiggle for the rye waltz."

A queer sadness plagued him as Tillie snuggled close. He thrust it out of mind. After a second dance he joined Arty for a "nip"; took such a hefty swig that Arty protested, "Hey, don't kill it at one throw!"

"Couldn't help it," Johnny answered. "Here," and for all of Arty's unwillingness, pushed silver into his palm.

He went back to Tillie and poked at her ribbons; grew warm with desire over this heady armful. His hand slid over her shoulders, coaxingly, purposefully, possessively, until the alarm that fluttered her lashes dimmed to dreamy subduedness, acquiescence, willingness. Once a question seemed to uncurl wormlike in a remote corner of his brain: Is this the way *he* felt, any girl in *his* arms, wanting to rid himself of fire under the skin?

Heedlessly, he put his head close to Tillie's shoulder. With a wildness that crumpled thought (that trampled with hob-nails crudely over a sorrowful reminder, Lilice, Lilice), he whispered, "It's nice out. Let's—let's walk for a while." His voice and hands were insistent. Almost blindly she got her cloak. They went under the stars. . . .

It was Heinie who pulled Snoose into a corner. "Didja see him, that Johnny? Cripes, but that feller's got it. Went for a walk with that Schwingend tit. Arty Nussbaum said awhile back that Johnny talked about flattening some bushes. . . ."

Chilled as if with a December wind, Snoose broke away. "Johnny, Johnny!" he grieved. "Don't start a fire you can't put out." He was so disconsolate Em'ly asked, "What ails you? You're shaking. You cold?"

He answered softly, "It's nothing. A piece of the earth just hit me, that's all."

The next day, his face twisted with the lascivious curiosity of the inexperienced and the unsatisfied, Arty pried at Johnny's recalcitrance for a glimpse of that knowledge which would confirm his own febrile imagination. "Well, didja find something in the bushes, Johnny?"

Johnny snorted but said nothing. At last, however, seeing how eager Arty was, he broke his close-mouthedness and bragged, "There's bushes there will never grow again."

Arty's lips screwed up in delight. With hearty embellishment he told the rest of the pitchers. Johnny was a hero in the crew during that forenoon.

But he avoided Snoose and was busy elsewhere when Snoose came near. Just before starting-up time, however, Snoose and Alb found him alone on the sunny side of the engine, punching holes into the sod with a stick. Alb was whittling at a piece of pine slab.

Johnny glanced at them. He couldn't escape Snoose's direct and un-flinching look—a look filled with a strange pleading. Johnny's cheeks stained a dull red. "I know what you're thinking, Snoose," he said quietly; "it's been on your face all forenoon." He shook his head, crestfallen. "I was mad, all right; madder'n hell. And I wanted to, I guess. But you're right, Alb. She's nothing but a crazy little kid. She pants and acts up, but that's all." He scratched his forehead, covering his eyes. "She began bawling and—well—" he laughed ruefully, as if his manhood had been ques-tioned—"I wanted to, but hell—" He shook his head, discomfited, and arose.

Alb clicked the blade of his knife understandingly, as though aware how far the feet of wild desire outran performance. "That's the way it goes. A woman bawls and a feller buttons up his pants. We talk a lot but we're never as bad as we'd like to be."

With the gray in his eyes lighted, Snoose chuckled, following Johnny back to the tender. He linked his arm in Johnny's for a moment. "You needn't tell me," he said softly. "It really wasn't Tillie's bawling that stood in your way. It was Lilice, wasn't it?"

Johnny picked up the fork, nodding, his tongue heavy with loneliness and shame and hurt, wishing suddenly he were nine again and could cry the way children cry, chest-deep and cleansingly.

18

The accident happened near a week's end. With the horse tied at the hitching post and the stone jars from the buggy in her arms, Lilice had entered the store and set the butter on the counter. Before she could search for her list of groceries, she heard Mr. Jimpson say to a neighbor who was getting his mail, "Ya, the Barewolf rig. 'Bout an hour ago or so. They took him home. He fell from the engine, or got throwed, I don't know rightly which. He's hurt bad. His back's broken, Henry Whiteland thinks."

Johnny! Lilice's hands came together and knotted. Johnny! The counter tipped in the sudden dizziness that swept over her. She put out a hand to keep the jars from sliding. Johnny, don't be hurt . . . I knew this would happen . . . don't you dare faint, she prodded herself. The cold gray stone steadied her. "Hurt and maybe dead and I haven't told him I——"

She almost ran to the door and out, forgetting butter and groceries in a stinging rush of fear. The halter rope tangled in her hands. I'm going, I can't help it. I mustn't think. Don't, don't let him be hurt!

After a century or two of frenzied jerking the rope came untied. Stumbling, she climbed into the buggy. "Giddap!" she faltered and brought the lines strapping down. "Oh, Flixie, run, run, run!"

With a weight that sagged more between his shoulders than on his heart, Johnny left the bedroom, knowing what he would do. Behind him he left agony on Uncle Herm's lips, drawn parchment thin, and the pain that racked grunts from him . . . Aunt Phrena's trembling mouth over the drops of medicine she counted into a glass of water . . . Kurt's heavy lids blinking . . . Mr. Peiser's grim silence . . . Alb's shaken cheerfulness. He shivered.

He was only underfoot anyway, he decided. His mind was strangely impatient at the realization that the rig remained idle at the Whitelands', the crew aimless. Somebody must pull the cord and whistle them into motion. Not for a broken bone or a severed muscle did the harvest stop; for that matter, neither did the swing of days, the slow pace of shadow under the sun, the growing strength of earth. The wheels must turn, the cylinder (like the threshing floor of Time) must hull the kernel from the husk, whether good or bad, whether meager or plump, whether few or many.

He left the kitchen, trying to bring clear the awful moments of that day. (Afterward even Uncle Herm couldn't remember how it happened. "I climbed up, for some reason, and was going to step on the driver," he recalled. "That's all I know." "Sure," Alb figured out. "He slipped and the flywheel threw him.") They had finished a setting. Uncle Herm had brought the rig almost to a stop. He had moved the engine forward. The belt clapped like hands in its slackness. Johnny was at the straw heap, gathering a last forkful.

Then he heard a wild yell and the sound of something heavy thudding to earth. He ran, and there, beyond the driver, lay Uncle Herm, limp as a torn vine, his shoulders moving, his hands pulling at his sides. His voice was broken, "My back—I can't—I can't feel my legs. . . ."

Johnny stepped outside. In the yard the team on the spring wagon still drooped from that frantic run. Half-pityingly but firmly, Johnny muttered, "It's tough, old boys, but you got to run back to the machine again. Alb has to come, too. Kurt can stay with Aunt Phrena until the doctor comes. Peiser, too."

He was pacing restlessly when a rattle of wheels bounced round the corner and there was a buggy swinging toward him. Before breath fluttered into words, Lilice was running over the grass, crying, "It wasn't you, it wasn't you, oh my dearest!"

His arms bound her to the laughter on his lips, to the throbbing in his heart. An untamed rush like flame swept over him. "I'm all right, Punkin; don't cry!" he whispered. There was no tangle of fingers to hide her lips now. Some part of those weeviled days before was squared up in that white moment of touching lips.

Even if he'd known he wouldn't have cared that from a window Aunt Phrena saw them and her fingers on the teakettle handle tightened. He kept saying over and over, disavowing his own senses. "I don't believe it. I can't believe you're here, Punkin."

He heard greedily her despairing "I'm scared, Johnny; scared when you're away, but scareder yet when—when I think you'll never come back to——"

"I'm always coming back." He lifted her chin. "Don't be scared; don't, Punkin! From now on I'm taking care of you. Next spring we'll be married. I'll get a farm and build, and we'll have a place of our own."

"Next spring," she mourned, and glanced at the house where Uncle Herm lay.

"We'll have enough money. Nobody around here thrashes the way we do." His fingers on her shoulders tensed.

"The thresher," she murmured, huddling closer in his arms.

When he'd finished telling about the accident, he said, "Alb's coming soon. I've got to go, Lilice. The job's standing still. I told Snoose to keep up steam."

"Not now!" Lilice put her hands to her cheeks, wide-eyed. "Not back to the machine when your uncle——"

"Why not?" The idea surprised Johnny. "I can't help him. Besides, he'd want me to. The rig is waiting. I can't stop thrashing. There's still a run of jobs to do. Jim Meisner, up north of Mary's Hill—he's got a run of shocks. He's been asking for me, they tell me." Enthusiasm flushed him into forgetting all but tomorrow and what he'd do.

"Johnny!" she begged, empty of words to say what was fear-laden in her heart.

But his fervor brushed aside her pleading. "Nobody's going to beat me at thrashing, Punkin. I'm going to be the biggest thrasher in Pockerbrush. You wait. I'll build you a house as big as Norton's—bigger than his." His black eyes snapped. "Don't you see? It's coming from the thrasher."

"Yes, the thresher," she sighed.

When Johnny would have led her inside the house, she pulled back. "No, it's better not to. Your aunt——" She lowered her gaze.

His fingers pressed her flesh arrogantly. "Well, she might as well get used to it. She'll see you often."

"Please, Johnny!" she whispered. "I'll visit your uncle another time. Tell him to get well—for me."

"I'll tell him more than that, Punkin." He bent to kiss her. "I'll tell him about us." As they walked to the buggy she clung to his arm.

She was halfway home when she remembered that Mr. Jimpson must be puzzled over the jars of butter on his counter. Turning around, she drove back, not quite sure whether this day were one for mirth or the dark garments of sorrow.

The rest of that season Johnny rushed from engine to separator, from Snoose and the tank wagon to Alb and the grain spout, as though he were a dozen people, as though with bone and muscle he'd flail the heads of a ridge of stacks in a morning; heap bin and granary rafter-high with the clean kernels of wheat and oats; and exorcise winter and the first tumbling flake with a talisman of pitchfork and grease can.

He took the throttle as if the handle were made for his grasp, disregarding the fact that folks railed at him. "That Johnny Schwartz, or Black, or whatever he calls himself! A young squirter like that! What does he think he is, running a rig by himself? Don't care about his uncle. Fine thrashin' he'll do, his uncle flat in bed. I wouldn't let him move into my thistle patch."

He hired Marty Borman as fireman: a stooped and scraggy man who had been with Bory Tetzell one year (and hated him) and up in the lumber camps years before that.

He cajoled the men into working; grinned with hard whiteness or swore against their inertia. He stretched tendon and thew; cursed when his sinews failed after salty hours, early and late. Alb and Snoose and Heinie Beerwagon stuck burlike at his side, Alb snorting, "Sheetin' Judas, that young feller Johnny—he's a damn good thrasher!" Without their persuasion Johnny would have found the run, or what was left of it, stumbly with obstruction. The men themselves couldn't help viewing him with a grouchy sort of admiration, however. Night after night, they'd be snoring before he blew the lantern and settled into dumb sleep; he was the first to strike a match in the early hours and shake the fireman into wakefulness. They resented his driving will but approved the way each job was feathered with speed.

The neighbors themselves began to perk their ears up over what they heard. "I can't believe it. Thrashed Whiteland's brother in a day and a half. Last year they had the machine three days. Na, that young Johnny Black, he that was Schwartz—too bad his uncle is down in bed. The boy is finishing up Barewolf's run as if Herm were there himself to boss him."

To be sure, Johnny outraged Mr. Whiteland by breaking into the season's run and thrashing the Roses before he pulled on to the farm of Mr. Whiteland's son-in-law.

"You promised to thrash Henry next, or your uncle did," Mr. Whiteland puffed angrily. "And now you——"

"The Roses' place comes before Henry's." Johnny smeared grease into a cup, undisturbed. "Why should I pass them?"

"They're not in the run this year." Mr. Whiteland began to lose patience. "Next year, if you——"

"Every fall they wait until last," Johnny replied determinedly. "Nobody seems to care if snow falls in their stacks."

"It was agreed that Henry comes next," shouted Mr. Whiteland. "If Herman Barewolf were here——"

"I'm running this rig." Johnny began to simmer. "I promised to thrash Henry, and I will. I guess he can stand it, being a day or so late. Even then he'll be finished quicker'n if he had Bory Tetzell's rig."

Remembering how green his stacks were in some years before Tetzell or Barewolf got to them, and how early the threshing was this year (comparatively speaking, for snow hung no more than a day or so away), Mr. Whiteland relinquished the argument.

The neighbors rocked with glee. "That Johnny Black—ya, Johnny Black is his name—he certainly took Whiteland down a peg or two."

With only a slight rash of complaining the crew accepted the break in a run, though all knew why, and never failed to twit Johnny about it. With heavy jocularity Heinie said, "You might as well pull over to Muri's place and thrash the Noreegians too."

"Why not?" Johnny regarded him seriously. "I wish I'd have thought of that sooner."

"Cripes, you don't mean it!" gasped Heinie. "This rig ain't never——"

"Next year, that's worth thinking about." Johnny left Heinie rubbing his forehead.

And so with a queer pull at his throat muscles, Johnny steered the Red Star into *her* yard. The wheel tracks in the road were never straighter, though they always had been straighter than Uncle Herm's. He was as vigilant as ever over the way the engine was lined up with the separator but he did pay more heed to the house and the hope that he'd see Lilice than he did to the steering wheel.

Let the pitchers gawp, he went to the house for drinks of water. A jug beaded with coolness sat near the engine and the well wasn't more than a step away. "It's fresher in the house," he grinned at Snoose. Not even a clogged sieve and dusty delay ruffled the happiness of sampling a cooky new-drawn from the oven.

It was a bright space in the uneven flow of days that autumn. But he didn't know how often Lilice parted the curtain and let the engine in through a narrow width of glass—the engine that purred quietly out there, rocking gently in its brutal power, its shiny surfaces jagged with broken pieces of reflected sun.

Once, attracted flylike to the honeycomb of this novelty, Norton came. He poked his hand into the chaff of the tailings; let a palmful of wheat cascade through the air; nodded. Johnny wanted to ask, "How about thrashing your crop next fall?" but Norton left quickly with a short "Keeping her going, huh, Johnny?"

Now and again Kurt, weary of plowing and of piling stones into heaps, came to help an afternoon or so at the grain spout or the feeding tables. He'd return home each night, bringing again in the morning such news of Uncle Herm as Johnny, home on Saturday evenings and Sundays (or parts of them) could see for himself: Uncle Herm settling loglike into a marsh of pain.

Uncle Herm would let a joke crawl over his lips when he saw Johnny. From much experience he'd warn, "You watch out for that sieve now, or it'll clog on you. And that front shaker arm—it needs a new boxing." Never once did he doubt that Johnny could handle the rig. His confidence tided Johnny over many a crooked hour. But yearning roughened the pause between their words. Such longing to be up and round the machine, wrench in hand, sharpened in Uncle Herm's eyes that Johnny could scarcely keep still in his chair.

In spite of Uncle Herm and the hours of the rig, never had he known such lightness of heel, such ease of elbow swing, such promise in the rose-becoming-lemon of the dusk. Lilice, Lilice. Weary as he was sometimes, he tapped strength from an inner reservoir. Often he drove the shoulder-bruised tank team home. He hitched it to the buggy. Aunt Phrena might as well have saved her sour comments for all the concern he paid. While she muttered, thinking, That Rose nit. I wonder——he went to the Roses to lose himself in a starlit hour of Lilice's hair against his chin and Lilice's murmurs against his shoulder, the reins tied to the whipsocket and the buggy and the team quiet on a hilltop. When he held her close after a black day of breakdown and delay, brightness like warmth spread through him.

He talked about longer runs then and the promise of the next year. Lilice listened, shuttering out time with his voice, and tried not to think of Uncle Herm. She sucked this moment dry against the arid places of tomorrow. Sometimes they were both stilled, the night and their nearness to each other sufficient, nor whispered on the moon.

The next day the sound and the dust of wheel and shaker solidified these moments into the rosy timber of dreams: . . . it's got to be a big place, a good house for her . . . next spring or summer . . . she's my girl, my girl, my girl . . . Whirl, whirl, whirl . . .

They went to dances and lost themselves in the mazy rounds of waltz and polka. When she danced with Snoose or Heinie or anybody else, he wasted time in wolfish stares, as if her partner had vile designs and any second he'd charge into the circle and carry her away. He answered questions without making sense. When politeness, if not gallantry, forced other girls into his arms, including Gatha, he strode into a waltz as if he were steering a plow, and gingerly held his partner away. He avoided the imploring in Gatha's eyes; pretended his cuff needed attention when she twittered at him. Tillie had gone back to Fergus. She had fluttered through his memory like a brazen leaf of autumn, admired in its graceful arching, forgotten once lost sight of among the wet and cloggy bushes.

But when Lilice came, he held her tightly, his muscles firm, so that she whispered, "Not so close, Johnny. I can't breathe."

"I'll breathe for you." He hugged her. "You think this is close? You ought to see how tight I *could* really hold you."

His feet found the rhythm of hers so smoothly that they slipped over the floor as one. "A dance with you like this, Punkin, and I can keep my legs working for another week," he said. "You're always so—so—oh, I don't know," he stumbled. "I get hot and sweaty but you're cool—cool like the hide of a watermelon."

Once after a dance when the buggy strayed to a standstill on a ridge she said pensively, "Gatha was pretty tonight. She has all the boys around her." There was trouble in her voice—had been all evening, he remembered.

"Well—" he shrugged warily—"she didn't have me."

Lilice drew her hand from his exploring fingers as if his warmth made more difficult what bothered her. "Johnny, you go to church Sundays, don't you?"

"Such a question, Punkin!" He groped for her hand. "Sure I do, when I get around to it." She eluded his touch.

"And—and go to Lord's Supper regularly?"

"I—I guess so. Easter and Christmas anyway. Never miss Easter. Always during the holidays. And whenever the Pastor announces a Lord's Supper Sunday and I got time to go." He laughed, uneasily aware of the direction of her probing but refusing to acknowledge it.

"The boys and girls at the dance tonight—they go regularly too?" she questioned, not with doubt in her mind but with that faltering hope by which the assurances of others justify our own uncertainties. The buggy moved by spoke-widths forward; the teeth of the horses cropping the leafless hazels were loud.

"Most of them do. Heinie Beerwagon usually has a good story to tell during the absolution." He moved restlessly. "Look, Punkin, if you are worrying——"

"It's nothing." She turned to him quickly, shutting away a nagging thought. Her voice was suddenly gay. Her fingers crawled into the warm tunnels of his fists quickly as though pursued by a phantom in the dark. But there was a wistfulness in her tone that he would recall later and try to forget as now he tried to avoid what was becoming too large to ignore.

Once on a Sunday afternoon of walking, she wrote with a stick in the dust of the road, "Mr. and Mrs. Johnny Black." There was a quick light in her eyes. "Why did you change your name?" she asked casually.

He caught the stick from her hands to hide how taken aback he was. "Oh, no reason." He couldn't tell her then. "I—I needed a new one."

"Changing a person's name—" she paused, as though the age-old rite of possession, the hard earth and one's name as title to it, an urge remote as the first breath, stirred in her—"Mother says it's like pulling stakes and starting over."

"Then you don't like it," he said, ready to be hurt with disappointment.

"No, it's not that. I——" She gave up what had puzzled her. "No, I like it. Johnny Black. It'll wear. I never could say 'Schwartz' without hissing like a gander." They both laughed as over a new plaything in which there was hidden a joke.

As the season drifted into the rain and sleet of the last threshing days, he spent evenings nibbling cookies with her and sipping tea under the lamp where Mrs. Rose poked at the loops of yarn on her knitting needle and Adam near the fire warmed the day's knots out of his bones. Tea he'd never known on Aunt Phrena's table. He wasn't sure he liked it. But to see Lilice over pot and plate filled him with hominess so deep that the wryness of his first taste was sweetened as with sugar. He would have nibbled worm-wood root contentedly.

Afterward he might coax her into playing. Usually she demurred, "I'm all out of practice." When she did let her fingers sink among the keys, the somberness of minor chords, heart-tautening, falling into mournfulness, sang into the room more often than the bright triumph of the major. He never understood what she played, nor that a tremulous phrase might have its own meaning. He only felt steeped in contentment—the well-being that came over him when the surge-and-throb of the engine rhythmically soothed his muscles into relaxing.

More and more Mrs. Rose kept to her chair and her shawl. With a glance as sharp as her needles she observed them. So they've decided, she thought once, half-sadly. I guess we never learn from the troubles of other folks; we learn only from our troubles; and then—then it's too late, too late. Nothing is gleaned from yesterday's grief. Each must suffer and weep before he knows that he is crying yesterday's tears.

Aloud she said gently one night, "Perhaps your Aunt Phrena wouldn't mind having a cooky with me some afternoon."

Johnny's cup rattled on the saucer. "Sure. Of course she'll come," he asserted. He was far from confident, thinking, I've got *her* to face yet. I don't care. Nothing she can do will change me. He sipped the tea.

At home Uncle Herm stared at the bottles left at his bedside by doctor and neighbor—red stuff guaranteed to kill pain wherever it lurked, head or toe; green stuff warranted to loosen the rock scales in a teakettle and rout pain in one swallow. There were plasters and the ingredients of poultices. Mr. Peiser brought a bottle of something he swore would bring a man leaping full-blooded and hale from his pillow. His grandfather had compounded it and he himself had tried it on his cat's distemper. For two days the cat had run about the yard like mad; but it had recovered, except that, from that day forth, its tail stayed as crooked as an auger.

"Bull wheels of Moses!" Uncle Herm fretted. "That stuff would burn the inside of a slop barrel. So much truck and so little help." His eyes lit up behind his shaggy brows like a lamp through hazel twigs when Johnny clumped down beside the bed. "I can smell you, Johnny," he'd say in greeting. "Oil and smoke and straw dust. It's a good smell." His fingers wheedled their way through his whiskers. "How's the rig coming?"

"Finishing next week," Johnny could tell him at last. How many times, almost baffled by the intricacies of concave adjustment, of sieve arrangement, hadn't he wished with sweaty heartiness for Uncle Herm beside him, to hand him advice with a screw driver or a wrench? "I see you got a bottle of new stuff."

"All this fuss," Uncle Herm trumpeted. "I'll be up and kicking in a week or so. Seems to me my knee is better today." But there was something pale about him that vaguely bothered Johnny. Uncle Herm mended slowly, if at all.

As he sat there smothering disquiet, Johnny was conscious that Aunt Phrena walked on tiptoes of anger, waiting to pounce on him. Only last week she had begun firmly, "Neighbors talking about you at the dances—you and that——"

He had shouted at her, "Let them talk. I've got a job to do." As he sat by Uncle Herm's bed he was suddenly aware that it was one thing to have the crew rib-tickle and joke him friendlywise at the rig, and another to have the valley gabble its gossip about him and Lilice. He cringed a little in spite of himself and sneaked away when Aunt Phrena went into the woodshed.

Uncle Herm was alone. How quiet it was, the room empty of Johnny's clumping shoes. He sagged on his pillow, eagerness dimming, his fingers relaxing into mournful indolence. There was left for him table and chair, the Fergus paper; and from the kitchen, a soft kettle-bubble quiet, and now and again the heavy tread of Aunt Phrena.

19

That season of threshing ended in snow with the gold of oat dust shining in a drift. At the last farm place wheat kernels arched in flight from the cylinder and like a handful of flung shot vanished into holes in a wind-chiseled snowbank.

One day Johnny brought the rig home. Only Marty Borman, the fireman, and Snoose came with him. After the last cleanup the crew had scattered as the chaff that blew from the straw carrier. A lip of ice hung from the pump spout. Snoose huddled in his heavy dogskin coat. The bones of charred wood and blackened planks near the pump told how often Snoose had built a fire to thaw out the piston and release the water from a knot of cold.

The wheels crunched through the snow in the yard with a thin, squealing iron sound. As yet there was no shed for the rig. Johnny drew it beside the granary and let the steamy bowels of the engine gurgle and complain into coolness, into winter's pale frigidity.

Snoose and Borman went home. Johnny raked the ashes. The sooty pile hissed deep into the crusted snow. Kinks of burned straw, black and flaky, light as gossamer, streamed away under a wind and stained a wagon-length of snow. For the first time a threshing rig, engine and separator, stood winterlong in the Barewolf yard. Uncle Herm heard it come, twisting on his pillow. But his window looked toward the north; he couldn't see it from his bed.

Now it was Johnny who hunched over a slate and a pile of duns. He brought them to Uncle Herm one evening. Together they mumbled over the figures of addition and subtraction, mainly subtraction. With quick uplifts of chins they regarded the remainder.

"Better'n I thought." Uncle Herm snuggled his shoulders more comfortably against the pillow; the cloth whispered. His legs were stumpy and helpless as cobs of wood under the quilt. "I guess you s'prised the neighbors."

"We've got them crawling," Johnny said with more vindictiveness than he realized. "Next year we'll get a bigger run. We ought to hire a crew, too. I'm sick to puking about this exchanging job for job."

Uncle Herm peered up at him sorrowfully. "Johnny, Johnny! Always you think folks are against you. You always have, from little shaver up." There was pity in his voice. "You're wrong, Johnny. Nobody's against you. Taking them all in all, folks are purty generally on our side."

"Sure they are." Johnny stacked the bills. Irony sharpened his agreement. "Sure they are. They're on my side as long as I stand over them with a club. Otherwise you'd see how fast they'd trample me down—me or anyone else, I guess." He held the papers fast with a thumb. "This year the harvest was good. Nobody kicks. Let there be a failure next year and you'll see how fast a thrasher gets it in the neck." He gathered the remainders of last year's struggle—the duns, the pencil, the slate—and arose.

From his pillow Uncle Herm looked at Johnny. It seemed to him that a kind of mist rolled between them. "Your ma," he quavered, ashamed of weakness but hurrying on. "She was gentle. She trusted everybody. You trust nobody."

"She trusted everybody," Johnny repeated mockingly. "She trusted my pa, too. Did that keep her from bawling her heart out?" Moodily his eyes went to the square of window black with night. But inside him he had a notion to sink beside Uncle Herm's shoulder and weep into the pillow, "I'm sorry, Uncle Herm; I'm sorry." He stiffened. Without looking at Uncle Herm he said woodenly, "I'm satisfied this way." He put the papers aside.

In the kitchen Aunt Phrena, her flappy cheeks red from steamy water, cleaned the sopping feathers from a chicken. When he came she prodded his mood with a cheerful "Sunday the Blumens are coming along for dinner after church. Ach, I hope this old rooster won't be too tough." She hummed "Nearer my God to Thee," a hymn of good nature.

He didn't answer her. Gatha again, he thought without compunction for her. "I've a mind to go hunting with Snoose." Her satisfaction was so bubbly that he paused before he went upstairs. She's made up her mind about something, he concluded. It's more than Gatha, too.

Adam and Lena decided on the last of April for the wedding. "He says when, but she made up his mind," Lilice told Johnny. "He really wanted it in February. He has least work to do then. But she wanted April."

They would be married at the Habers'. Mr. Erdman would speak the binding words. Johnny was excited, all this talk about veils and a wedding cake and a dance in the barn—if the weather warmed—somehow close and important to him.

When I get married, he spun a web of fancy for himself, it'll be in a church, not at any house. And there'd be flowers on the altar and Em'ly Musser playing something on the organ and Snoose would be his best man and Lilice . . . Lilice beside him in a dress white as a water-lily petal. At the notion he felt a prickle in his hair, delightful as a reverie; and was deaf to a faintly clamorous, What church? There's the Pastor.

Over the wedding plans Lilice bloomed with the color of the honey-suckle in her cheeks. "Em'ly Musser is going to play the organ. I hope she'll watch that C-sharp key. The reeds are dead. I'm going to wear gray, Johnny," she added softly. "Pearl gray."

"Whatever you wear, there'll be no prettier bridesmaid than you," Johnny said, fervently moist. They were going to the basket social that night.

"Mother's tucking it." Lilice fumbled pensively at a button on his coat. "Maybe I oughtn't go with you this evening," she said quietly all at once, as if this were not a new idea but one she'd mulled over in secret hours. "Maybe I ought to stay home."

"Not go?" He caught her hand quickly. "You said you made a basket and——"

"I did make one." With the forefinger and thumb of her other hand she pinched his knuckles gently. "Gatha would know whether to go or not, wouldn't she?"

He moved impatiently. "We got to hurry, or——"

"Would she let a boy, say a boy from Mary's Hill, somebody from—well, a different congregation—would she let him escort her to the social tonight?"

"Oh, Punkin!" He was instantly evasive, wary of those mazes in which his own thought had wearily run corners and circles. "I guess she wouldn't mind who it was, as long as it wore pants." He giggled hollowly over his joke.

She looked at him a moment; then said, "I'll get the basket." Her chin was lifted in determination to forget whatever buzzed warningly in her mind. "It's got a paper rose. Mind you watch for it. That awful Shierhauer boy nearly got it last time. I made taffy candy, the kind you like."

On the road back home he felt her silence like a shawl between them. The jingle of harness and the occasional screeping shriek of iron runner on gravel in the snow whetted the edge of stillness. "You've hardly opened your mouth tonight," he said at last, almost diffidently. "You let me eat all the candy, too." Overhead the dome of midnight was spiked with patterns of glistening silver heads. "Left your tongue at home, huh?"

For an instant she leaned against him. Her breath softly drawn was the sibilance of a snowflake against his ear. She said quietly, "I didn't want to tell you, but it's been troubling me for weeks."

He braced himself, sure that what was coming wasn't good. She went on, "Your aunt came to see me, a week or so before Christmas." She spoke so calmly that for a while he was surprised into gladness.

"She did?" he echoed. So Aunt Phrena was beginning to thaw. "Never told me about it."

"She didn't come to have a cup of tea." At the quiver in her tone, his incipient delight poised and sank. "No, Johnny. The first thing she said was, 'You don't know very much, do you, Lilice Rose? Or you'd be ashamed of yourself.' I'll never forget how she——" Her head rested on his shoulder.

Misery cold and damp slid over him—misery too deep for anger then. His arm about her tightened.

"She didn't come to the front door but stood in the shed. She wanted to talk with Mother, too, I guess. But I—Johnny, I got so mad I could have bit her." Through his coat he felt her muscles stiffen. "Mother had one of her weak spells and was sleeping. I couldn't let your aunt upset her, when all she wanted was to scold. Oh, she was ready to finish me off, right there in the woodshed."

All he could say was a helpless "Punkin, Punkin!" His lips were beginning to harden with rage.

She went on mournfully, "You better start scolding me, Johnny. I shut the kitchen door on her. She was stirring up such a rumpus——"

"Scold you?" He brought the lines down with a snarled "Giddap, there, you devils!" The horses quickened a lagging gait. "Scold you for something I'd like to do myself? No." He burst out, "Why can't people let us alone? All my life, Aunt Phrena's been butting into my business."

Lilice was not far from crying. "I didn't let her say much. What she said sticks in my mind, though. Johnny, she said if I was a girl decently brought up in the church, I wouldn't behave this way. I guess I slammed the door then," she murmured unhappily. "Maybe she's right. Maybe I'm bad for you, a good member——" She began to sniffle.

"If she's right," Johnny blazed, "I hope I'm always wrong. Listen, Punkin." He bent toward her earnestly. "She's never going to meddle with us again. Never. We'll get married and move to a place where it won't matter what she thinks." But he didn't say, "This spring we'll be married." He didn't even mention summer.

"Johnny," she begged but he wouldn't listen. The words she meant to say, "Johnny, when, when?" were shaken into dizziness, into forgetfulness of arm and lip against her. And in her nearness he could forget too. Let the bony-shanked worry-nag be lashed into oblivion. He had Lilice (though he hadn't found a place to start farming). He had Lilice and tonight and the new threshing rig. But Aunt Phrena he kept in his mind like a toadstool growing in the dark.

It was the next day that wrath sparked from him like a struck flint. They were at dinner. Aunt Phrena dished the pork hot from the stove. She dropped a share on Kurt's plate. The grease spattered. She moved as if to give Johnny his portion. Instead she forked several slabs at her place. They tumbled near the fried potatoes. Then she scraped what remained onto Johnny's plate. A trivial matter, common as a weekday and one he'd scarcely have noticed ordinarily. But not today, not this moment, hitched tandemwise as it was to what had gone before.

As though the fat sizzling on the cold plate ignited ire, he suddenly rattled spoon and dish with a hard fist hitting the table. "Butting into my business!" he shouted. "Going over to the Roses and raising Cain! You keep out. I'll tend to my own affairs."

Kurt poised a bite of pork staring at him. But Aunt Phrena set the frying pan on the stove. "Na, then, is it not my business, my sister's own son forsaking the good Christian ways? Johnny!" She came to the table. There was so much entreaty in her voice that she was almost solemn. "If I am sour on your tongue, don't think about me. Think about your ma. Ach, would she want you to——"

"What's there to think about?" he interrupted heedlessly. "It's not much I remember about Ma. And what I did know, is just about gone. She might as well be a stranger."

"Ach, Johnny, to say such things!" Aunt Phrena caught at a chair in something like horror. "Your ma hearing you in heaven. Is that what you learned in confirmation, forgetting your folks and running after heathen and Hottentots?"

He picked up a spoon carefully as if the cool weight were a guard against what blew his eyes into flame. "How long am I going to hear you tell me that I run after heathen and——"

"You do. Swill and husks, that's what you like, not decent Christian ways. It is Schwartz all over again," she shrilled, the tears ready to fall but checked by anger.

The spoon clattered to the table. Dumbly he looked at her. All at once he was aware that this bitter denunciation did not stem entirely from dislike of Lilice but from a dark pattern wrought before the seed of his identity had been sown—Schwartz and the wasted years of the past spilling their rattly kernels into the present, into his present and Lilice's. It was this that shrilled in her voice.

In a quick flash of understanding he said, as Snoose might have, softly, "You liked him a lot, didn't you, Aunt Phrena?"

As if she'd been struck she gasped, "Liked him?" Purple tinged her cheeks. "I hated him," she cried vehemently. Stricken with dismay at the echo of her words, her hand trembled at her lips. "Ach, no. Hate him I don't. I am a Christian woman. God will—He will reward Albert Schwartz in His own way." It came to Johnny then how deep must have been her love for this man that in these years so much hatred could have trickled and been gathered rill by rill, a reservoir of venom at which to drink. "But you, Johnny. Like pa, like boy, I always said. You follow——"

"I follow my own way and nobody else's," he answered flatly. "There's no sense in trying to remember what I never learned. I'm taking care of myself. I'm me myself and I've got nothing to do with what my folks were." He settled down to eat, scarcely knowing whether food or ashes were between his teeth.

Aunt Phrena gazed upon him as though such evil (like henbane) ought to be uprooted with blade and hook. Kurt buttered his bread and blew at his coffee unperturbed.

Johnny would have packed his belongings and set out to work for Mr. Schimmel who was asking for help, now that spring was approaching. But Uncle Herm pleaded, "Don't go, Johnny. Don't! I've got to have somebody here, or I'll stay in this bed till they carry me out."

"There's Aunt Phrena," he wanted to say but didn't, feeling a sinking weight in his chest at the sight of the bony knob of Uncle Herm's Adam's apple, thinning by the day with pain and chafing inactivity; or so it seemed.

Against his own bitter protests he saw that Uncle Herm wouldn't have the strength to leave this bed by the time spring's work came around. He and Kurt would have to plant the fields this year. But more—and this enkindled a sort of fear—would Uncle Herm be well enough by summer, middle summer, to gather the neighbors into the threshing circle, the big threshing circle Johnny had planned for this season and had bragged about?

Seldom was the circle made up from year to year of the same folks. For one reason or another several might drop from the run this year and be added another. This might happen because of the tardiness of a season, the damp or the drought of an autumn, the necessity for cashing in early on the harvest's yield in order to meet the demands of a creditor. Or this might happen because of neighborhood disagreements, disputes between thresher and farmer, dislike by members of the circle for members of the crew. Out near Mary's Hill a farmer had left his accustomed circle because his daughter married a man who hated the owner of the threshing rig. Johnny had seen this happen over and over.

His good record last season would speak for him. But with Uncle Herm gone as his shoulder prop and stay, would the neighbors (the sweat started at this), would they come back to be bossed by a young man not yet old enough to have more than feather whiskers on his chin?

Never had he been more uncertain than this night, looking down upon Uncle Herm. Maybe he'd have to sell the rig . . . there was the spring's work . . . there was the promise he knew he'd give Uncle Herm: the promise to stay . . . and there was Lilice. I can't tell her we'll be married this spring, or this summer . . . she can't stay with Aunt Phrena . . . wait, wait until fall; Uncle Herm will be better then and things will look different. . . .

"All right, I'll stay then," he assured Uncle Herm.

Uncle Herm tried to thank him. There was more urgent pleading in his shrunken jowls and in the tremulous fingers than in his voice.

"You'll be up and around by spring," Johnny encouraged him. "Just you get a sniff of that pussy-willow weather and nobody'll keep you under the quilt." Johnny was far from believing this himself. He stayed on Uncle Herm's farm. And the shadows in the corners of that house grew no lighter.

The Barewolfs were invited to the wedding only because Adam insisted. He remembered that this year his stacks hadn't greened with sprouting and with waiting. But of course Uncle Herm couldn't go. It took half a day's strength and much grunting, he said, just to find a cooler spot for his tired ribs. "Wouldn't I be limber in a polka, though?" He grinned slowly. All the ointments and plasters, all the poking and probing which the doctor from Mary's Hill did, all came to no more than a slow wasting of flesh that winter, and a hesitant opinion: "There's a twist in his back. Can't say for sure how long it will last." The doctor had driven away. He was a new one, named Young Doctor Wilson. Old Doc Huber was dead and buried.

By the end of March Uncle Herm was no better than before Christmas; worse, Johnny was sure, a flicker of alarm sliding down his spine. With Uncle Herm in the bedroom, Aunt Phrena couldn't go to the wedding, even if she wanted to, and she didn't. She wasn't sure Erdman was proper in marrying this couple.

Em'ly Musser didn't play the wedding hymn after all. She was practicing sturdily the afternoon the Pastor came. What he told her he gathered into a sermon with a text, a fourthly and a fifthly for the next Sunday's worship. "It is not seemly, my brethren," he proclaimed, "that one of our members should partake of the unclean rites of the worldlings, and so touch the fleshpots of the whore of Babylon." Gravity like a cushion softened his trumpetings. "Be ye separate, saith the Lord." His face turned weather-vane-fashion under the gusts of his solemnity and pointed at the Barewolfs—or so Aunt Phrena said. "The sacred cup shall be withheld from everyone who will not so do."

"That was meant for us," Aunt Phrena was certain. "Ach, the poor man! But grace will come to him, too, by and by."

Johnny squirmed at the church and at home. How much, he wondered, how much of the Pastor's sermon comes from the Book and how much from wanting to have his own way, and nobody disputing him?

With a sour grimace Adam reported at home, "Well, Em'ly Musser can't play. The Pastor forbids it and the Mussers are good church members."

Lilice put a hand to her cheek. For a moment she stood there, the future growing like an inching worm into the present. Then she rumpled the sleeve of her dress. She laughed shortly. But the print of three finger tips remained momentarily white on her cheek.

At the Habers' on the days before the wedding, house and granary (they would have a granary dance), pantry and sitting room awaited the nuptial pair and the wedding guests. The tables were lengthened. From the center hanging lamp in the sitting room to the four corners strips of twisted paper showed now pink, now white. Over the wedding cake would hang a white paper bell. The granary was cleaned to the last mousehole, the last cobweb swept down. Concerned over tracked and dirtied floors, Mrs. Haber hoped the warm weather, now drying the puddles, would continue.

Two days before the wedding the thaws of April froze in a blizzard of howling snow. A couple of Uncle Herm's calves were caught in its sudden blast and marooned in a pasture ravine. After an hour's staggering search,

Johnny and Kurt found them. With ropes they dragged the terrified, hunched-together animals homeward. The calves struggled mightily. One threw Kurt against the side of a stump. He fell; came up again at once, but limped. "Hit my ankle," he groaned.

They brought the calves home. The chill prickles of snow melted on their cheeks and foreheads. Afterward Johnny stepped from the barn door and headed for the house. It was like putting his hand against the leaning wall of the storm.

Kurt followed him. "Can't see the chicken coop from here," he yelled. In the house, he grumbled, "Damn little ungrateful beast! He certainly swung my foot against that stump." Gingerly he kneaded the swollen ankle.

Johnny slapped his mittens against a knee. A shower of wind-driven snow fell from them. "What a duster!" he said. The valley was clogged with drifts.

In the Haber house, Lena crumpled the bridal veil to her breast and wept. Her mother scolded. In the Rose house Adam gloomed, "If this keeps up, I'll have to get married in a snowbank."

But Lilice baked more cookies. "It storms one day and clears the next. That's the valley weather," she comforted him. "We might as well be prepared."

By the next afternoon the clouds broke. The neighbors began to burrow and plow their way free again, despite the cold. The weather moderated, however. The wedding day, though cloudy, was warm enough to steam the southern roofs, and cool enough to hint of snow. By noon the Habers' drifted yard was black with sleds and cutters.

Johnny drove over in a sled with sideboards above the box. On the straw in the bottom he piled robes and blankets. The horses would need coverings; the teams would be haltered outside, for the Habers were short of barn space. He drove alone after all, leaving Kurt to rub his ankle beside the stove.

The wedding was like a fragrance in his mind, a queer ferment in his blood. As the horses wallowed sometimes belly-deep through drifts, he kept seeing Lena and Adam together, these two bound by the mysterious significance of this day. He whistled a quivering delight to a nuthatch that *yank-yank-ed* exploratorily zigzag fashion on an elm tree.

The folks greeted him with shouts, "Well, Johnny, how's your uncle?" "Devil of a storm, eh, Johnny? So late, too." "Didja have to shovel any? We did."

He saw Lilice in the kitchen, aproned for the tables, when he came in with the wedding present under his arm. He'd never seen the red in her cheeks so velvet, so like the tint of petals on a stem, as if in her mind, too, were glowing the flame of this day. A queer trembling made his hands shake.

Mrs. Rose was there, serene in her woolen shawl, though the spider webs of fragileness were pale on her face.

"How can you take it so calmlike?" Mrs. Fleischer wanted to know. "Your son marrying and everything. I bawled myself sick when Willie married. And Mrs. Haber. I just borrowed her my last handkerchief."

Johnny went back to the yard, his toes dancing light. The Marchens were there but Snoose wasn't. For this he had a momentary loneliness. Since Em'ly wasn't to play, none of the Mussers came. "Without Em'ly I wouldn't have any fun," Snoose had said. The Blumens weren't there nor the Nussbaums excepting Arty who came with Heinie and the Beerwagons. In fact (Johnny took this in with a rebellious pang), more guests drove in from Loon Lake and Mary's Hill than came over neighborwise from those nearest in ridge and valley. He shrugged finally.

He had a humpy moment when in the granary he found Lornas Tetzell and Mosey Fritz. Mosey gave him one glance, gulped and dissolved among the shoulders of the folks. But Lornas, hard-eyed and deliberate, strode over. He smiled thinly. "Hullo, Johnny—" he hesitated—"Johnny Black. Heard you thrashed like an old-timer last fall."

Heinie Beerwagon and several in the noisy crowd saw him. They watched attentively. Johnny's lips were frosty. He balanced springily, his elbows rigid with fight. "I guess so." He spoke evenly. "It wouldn't be hard to beat a bull engine, though." There was a broad invitation to trouble in his measured tones.

Lornas drew together, his eyes slitting. But when he saw Heinie Beerwagon and Arty Nussbaum sharp-featured over their glasses of beer, he lifted his shoulders negligently and forced a grin. "Guess you're right at that. No bad feelings, Johnny."

"Nope." Johnny looked at Lornas' proffered hand as if it were something on a manure fork. "No bad feelings, Lornas. No good feelings either. You just keep out of my road, that's all."

Lornas flushed. For an instant glance struck glance as flint does steel. Then Lornas shifted. He shrugged away.

Johnny felt queerly buoyant, this triumph adding pungency to the ferment in his veins—a pungency that had nothing to do with the glass of wine Mr. Haber offered him.

All that afternoon, wherever he went he seemed to see Adam and Lena. His eyes followed them as a ripple the wind. There was between those two an electric anticipation that quickened in him yearnings he wouldn't have put into words. When Mr. Erdman had pronounced the final "Amen" and the bridal couple were rescued from the kissing and the hand-shaking, Johnny saw how steadily, how alertly Adam gazed on Lena, blind to all else, a look vibrant with the future; how a downsweep of Lena's eyes brought Adam's sudden, impetuous step forward.

A girl at Johnny's side whispered to another, "If a man ever looks at me like that, I'll—I'll go through the floor." As though he wasn't sure of himself Johnny swung away, almost fearful of the headiness that arose like waves of drink, warm and desirable in his flesh.

But when he saw Lilice the yearning quivered into greater intensity. After supper he caught her arm almost possessively as she hurried with plates and knives. "Do you have to wash dishes?" He grimaced at the left-overs. "A bridesmaid and all? They're going to start dancing pretty soon. Can't you sneak out?"

"I don't know." She wavered uncertainly, avoiding his probing glances. "You'd think nobody had a brain left, the way they run around here. The pantry's a mess. And the kitchen——" She waved the plates. "Poor Mrs. Haber—I got the hartshorn bottle twice for her." When his fingers tickled at her elbow, she jerked away. "Don't, Johnny. I haven't time. These dishes can't stand around gathering crusts." She went into the kitchen reluctantly.

Darkness settled blackly for the night. He hung near the door waiting. Lamplight yellowed rectangles on the new snow; sectioned them with black bars. Horses snorted somewhere, patiently awaiting the morning hours and the end of their owners' mirth. Overhead a star flung a lance of silver through breaking clouds, and dodged out of sight. With evening, cold drifted down, hard and biting. From the granary came the tentative *tum-tum-ta* of a tuning fiddle and an upsweep of accordion notes. Mr. Muehlbank and the players poised on the verge of the wedding waltz. (Not Anders Stramff now; not Old Anders afraid of the ants.)

The door opened. She stepped from the yellow of lamplight into the dark with a swish of ruffle and fold and a cool garden smell of Cologne water. He was deaf to the chat and the laughter of Margie Haber and the rest of the girls. At Lilice's side he whispered, "The first dance, Lilice; and the second, too."

"Well, I—maybe I'm——" she began, but he insisted, "All of them, Lilice."

"Not all, Johnny. Just most of them," she said firmly. But she softened the compromise with a hand slipped into his for such a hasty moment that the touch was gone before he closed his fingers. The lantern-yellow through the windows of the granary flooded his face. His grin was wide.

The body heat of the crowd rather than the stove in the corner near the players warmed the granary. At first the windows were partly frosted and white; soon they melted into night blackness. Lena and Adam began the dance with the wedding waltz. While they circled the floor three times, the couples waited, clapping their hands. But Johnny, Lilice near him, restlessly moved his feet and swayed his body, swinging his arms as if he were in the allemande-left of the square dance. Too itchy with impatience to wait, he stomped his heels. He pulled Lilice to him and half-circled her protests with preliminary steps.

She drew back. "Everybody's watching us." She tried to smooth down fluster and annoyance. "Everybody."

"Do you think I care?" he demanded softly, urgently. "They'd give anything to be in my shoes." Her eyes closed in swift pity for him—the unfathomable, almost instinctive pity of woman for the sightless, unreasoning importunity of man. The other couples joined in the waltz and saved her an answer. She came into his arms dreamy-lidded as buds nodding in spring.

The rest of that evening was as run together as the stains in Aunt Phrena's fruit masher. A haziness lay about him so that the floor seemed to go uphill slightly and his feet climbed it. The sooty lanterns bobbed and wove in a feverish blur, like candles seen through the lashes of nearly closed eyes. Only Lilice was real, his arms full of her softness, her red lips near, a summer-rain cool freshness close to his chin.

He waltzed her so sprightly that twinkles glimmered from her, he polkaed her into breathless giggles. He kicked his feet in the corners and stamped his heels in the swing-your-partners. Not for many dances did she escape him; not once did she refuse him. His arm was so firm that the shortness of her breath came from more than the square-dance steps.

The moon peeked through an eastern windowpane. During a pause Lena told them, "Your ma's gone home with Old Mr. Whiteland, Lilice. She's a little tired. She says you're not to bother, she'll get along." They scarcely heard her. Lilice shook herself as if earth spun far away and any sound was an intrusion. Johnny swept her into the next dance. Once his head came down until a ruffle on her shoulder tickled his nose. She struggled a moment as though against the dizziness of his arms, but failed.

The moon climbed the rooftree of heaven. Once Heinie Beerwagon offered him a glass, and beer from a ladle. He shook his head, drunk on more than the vine contained, or the sprouted barley. Before it pitched low out of sight, the moon was penny-bronze at a western window. Through ribbons of music and laughter he saw her eyes and accepted what he saw. They were the liquid brown of ripe, sun-warmed hazelnuts. Water welled under his tongue; he swallowed gulpily. He couldn't keep his lips off her curls. He longed to put them on her smile. His eyes closed.

Once her fingers for a butterfly instant tugged at the lobe of his ear. "Punkin, Punkin," he murmured hoarsely into her hair. "I get live steam popping in my chest when you do that." At his insistence her hand on his shoulder pushed against him. She bent back like a flower on its stem and lay against the curve of his arm, her face all rose petals and perfume and velvet in his dizzied skull. "Let's go home," he whispered. For a poised instant she hesitated. Then she went for her wraps.

Like one aware of sleepwalking he said his good-bys and hitched the team. His breath was pale smoke in the lantern glow. Gently he tucked Lilice under the robes. His shouted "Giddap" echoed in the clear, frost-particled air. The sled jingled down the road.

Afterward he remembered (though not who first suggested it) how with laughter he had flung blankets across the double box above her head ("A tent like Indians," he exulted) and crawled down beside her, guiding the horses through the space between the endgate and the blanket above. From this cave of darkness they could see the horses, darker moving shapes against the night.

"It's cozy, like your kitchen," he said and burrowed deeply under the blankets, into scented warmth. "Or like rabbits' fur." He held the lines twisted in his left hand.

A bump of the sled—or was it his own nudging?—and her head was on his shoulder. "Punkin," he whispered. His eyes closed in a drowsiness more alert and sharp than midday wakefulness. The lines slipped from his fingers. The ends dragged across the blankets; hung waveringly on the endgate. The horses slowed, shuffled at their own gait.

There was the darkness of the blanket canopy then and the silence— silence given a voice in the alphabet of finger and thumb, in the vocabulary of touch. The *clip-clop* of hoofs thinned in the snow to a faraway sound. After a while the horses swayed from the road into a meadow. They stopped to browse at a haystack. The lines slipped over the endgate and fell curling into the snow. The night was like one holding breath, finger on lip, to listen.

Once Lilice's voice arose in a stifled cry, as if the fierce and dreadful shape of tomorrow were thrusting sicklewise into her mind. But he hushed her with murmurings that held no reason for the ear but for the heart, sound outrunning sense. She sighed and accepted pain as if it were a benison.

He felt the wet of her tears on his cheek. But he was past caring for tears then—for tears or a whisper or a cry. A mad swirl flung him numb and beaten into spaces where reason and volition are as the gropings of the blind. Resistlessly it lifted him and flung him down again, surge and sway, in a motion as old as the tempestuous pull-and-push of the Cambrian sea upon the ancient egg cell, or as new as the to-and-fro movement of the threshing engine, vehement under the violence of throbbing steam. It cast him into awareness at last, spent and weathered as one cudgeled by the wind and the hail.

20

Sometimes in the months of that summer and fall, Johnny wondered how the red fan of dawn could unfold so calmly, the day rise, the afternoon set, the night erase hill and valley from the eye, all with the quiet strength of hope that will not be denied, when under his skin there was a rush-and-tear, a dreadful crowding of hour against hour until his skull ached; when he had a feeling that he was being hurled tongueless and afraid toward an end as final and inevitable as the hand's width of earth whereon a leaf falls at last to rot; when the opiate of sleep, heavy as chains, brought meager solace for the uneasy dreams that curved his fingers into the pillow.

Even that spring had been a queer mixture of thaw and frost, anemone and rank weed, of mirth rubbing under his ribs and bleak anxiety tightening in his chest, of Lilice and Uncle Herm, the two, running side by side, honey and vinegar, as, near the barn, roily water and clear ran together in the same April stream.

That spring he and not Uncle Herm scattered the kernels from an outflung hand. An uneven job, he had to admit; Kurt would have cast with a steadier hand. But Kurt dragged the kernels under the ground, while he finished the seeding. In the house Uncle Herm wasted to bone and loosened sinew under the quilts. The way he slumped there, hollow-cheeked and silent, regarding the space between his bed and the door as if therein he measured all his future, sent Johnny racketing from his chair and out, shaken by what he dared not face.

The last snows had scarcely dried and left the marks of winter's dust upon the thresher before, anticipating autumn, he was ready to fire the engine. In spare moments he fussed over a boxing or crawled into the separator until one evening Kurt drawled, "I'll bring you a quilt, if you figure on bedding on the sieves tonight."

When Snoose came to borrow seed corn for Mr. Peiser, Johnny said, "You better get your knees limbered up. The beards are going to fly this fall. You watch us thrash." To himself he prayed, Oh, let Uncle Herm get well!

Snoose chuckled, too busy with a mesh of fancies to bother about an iron clang. "Honestly, Johnny, one of these days you're going to have smoke curling out of your ears."

With every crossing of the yard from house to barn or hen coop, Johnny looked upon the engine beside the granary. When disquiet irked him like a sliver of barley beard in the eye, he let smokestack and cylinder fill his sight with healing. They were cold and dead now, but he went to the fields, brisk with knowing how alive they'd be with sough-and-hiss and chug-a-chug in the fall, in threshing time. It was as good to think about the engine and tomorrow as it was to bring Lilice sweet to mind.

In that bloodroot season, after the sun had opened the pockets of winter, she was like the fragrance of violets to him. Over the plowing and the harrowing he'd bring back that Saturday after the wedding, when he'd gone to see her. Memory burned in his flesh. How diffidently, how solemn almost with fright he had trudged across the fields to the Rose house! Where he stepped, thaw water stood in the heelprints.

Over and over a notion came to plague him, wrestle as he might to put it away from him. He—he, his pa, must have felt like this. He had played with his girls too. But he took his fun and laughed about it. . . . The ground was smeary under Johnny's feet as he walked along. . . . I couldn't make fun of Lilice. Never.

Ahead of him the Rose chimney smoked above the trees. He squared his shoulders. I am not ashamed, he told himself stolidly. It is a man's way. In all these ridges, he wondered what man could honestly say, "About this, or such stuff, I knew nothing before I came to wife."

Damn few, of that I'm sure, he answered his own question, kicking the slush in front of his toes. But of this he was aware also: What man would admit indiscretion of one kind or another, except drunkenly or bawdily or in vaunting pride? For indiscretion triumphantly whispered behind hands, undetected, is that fillip which among his cronies adds at least an inch to the stature of a man. But indiscretion found out, laid in the open, the object of public scorn—that is something else. For at this, outraged manhood and womanhood, espeeially outraged womanhood, screams for the lash of castigation, of social ignominy. (The private shrills of women are publicly justified by men, or the race would have vanished ages past.)

I'll make it up to Lilice, every bit of it, he told himself again. I'm not ashamed. It was true, his black eyes held Snoose's or Uncle Herm's or a neighbor's as steadily, as openly as before. Yet he wouldn't have revealed this to Snoose, close as they were. He guarded an inner rectitude in secrecy.

Nor would he have blurted this out to Arty Nussbaum, except perhaps in the last dregs of the bottle. Arty's slipperiness over girls, however, put a wry twist on his mouth these days.

Lilice hid her gaze for a moment as if flesh accused her, when in greeting he had looked at her squarely. Then she took his hand frankly. "Come and see the presents Adam and Lena got." She pulled him along, eager as a boy with a slingshot. A kind of relief sang in his laughter. They had stumbled in a rock pile, to be sure, but were only skin-bruised. Now, untouched though wiser (as they supposed), they clutched a measure of security. "Punkin," he had murmured back of her ear, "when we get a roof of our own, when we're . . ."

They settled nothing. There was the spring's work (he argued with himself); there was the threshing ring to gather up, once Uncle Herm was able to hobble about; there was his word to Uncle Herm; there wasn't a farm place he could think of just now, fit for Lilice to start housekeeping in; there was Aunt Phrena. He might bring a dog home but he'd never bring Lilice into Aunt Phrena's kitchen. (And there was the evil sweaty moment he'd have to spend with the Pastor. But this he thrust from his calculations . . . for this time, at least.)

Then the spring's work was finished—finished for all that a man could do. The rest lay with the earth and the sky and the tilt of the season. The day he found the wheat field lifted and cracked into tiny openings and the white of stems changing to the green of the first blade, he thought, Let it be a good year, and waited avidly for the sturdy "tillering" to sweep up like young grass. The gray of harrowed fields vanished in a flood of green that welled from the root, thick and rich and succulent, and washed over the knolls.

When he came upon the white lances of the corn prying up the small trap doors of earth, he sank to his knees and balled a fistful of soil. Leaning forward, gently he laid a pointed stem bare to sun and sky. "The seed—it is growing. It is swelling and breaking through." He hunched there between the rows at the end of the piece, quiet as the earth in his hand, the body of this earth. When he arose and went, there were kneeprints in the loose soil as if he'd been kneeling on the edge of a dark prayer rug.

That spring there were some laughter and much harsh talk in the valley over the news that Bory Tetzell at last had got himself a wife. "A damn shame, though," the folks gossiped. "A man of forty hitching himself to a slip of a thing like Regina Fleischer and she not more than seventeen, eighteen."

They had been married, not by the Pastor nor by Mr. Erdman, but by the justice of the peace in Mary's Hill. "And that ain't much of a wedding,"

Mr. Nussbaum observed sourly. "By cripes, 'bout all it's good for is to let them sleep together legal!"

"Ach, the poor thing!" sighed Aunt Phrena. "What she won't find out, living with such a man. She won't dare show her face in church again." Remembering the scar and the hairy blackness of Tetzell's arms and chest, Johnny felt his stomach move. The memory of hate like a sickle curved out of the past.

There was talk too that Lornas Tetzell was visiting at the Blumens' and that Gatha was seen in Mary's Hill with him. "They say he goes there real often," Mrs. Peiser told Aunt Phrena.

Johnny and Lilice talked about their wedding but settled nothing more than to agree, "Just before thrashing; that would be a good time."

She listened to him, the shadow of trouble on her face. Once she set him squirming. "You want to be married in the Pockerbrush church, don't you?" she asked.

"Huh? Well, I——" He tried an offhand manner. "Oh, I don't know. As long as I can call you my wife, what difference——"

She wasn't to be put off by playfulness. "If you had your say, though," she prodded him.

He moved uneasily. "Well, it's the place where I was confirmed and all. Uncle Herm and I go there; at least before he got hurt. Aunt Phrena thinks Erdman——" He stopped miserably.

"Johnny- how can you stand it?" she burst out at last. "I still remember the Dunkel funeral. Poor Mrs. Dunkel screaming and the congregation getting hysterical. And Mr. Steuber—why, I think that man enjoyed himself that day. And then at the Marchens'; what he said to my mother——"

"I know, Punkin; I know. We've said this before." Johnny twisted about. "I can't say I like to hear Old Steuber pounding the altar with his fists. But you can sort out what's important, and shut your ears to the rest. You can't take him seriously all the time. He'd have spoiled my life long ago, if I'd——"

"What's the good of going, then?" she flashed. "And how do you know what's important?"

"Now, you know better than that." He squirmed, not sure how to answer her, wondering what he'd say if she probed further. She didn't, seeing his confusion.

He said, "Uncle Herm helped build that church and that's where I—— Well," he stumbled; "it's my—my——"

"I know. Your church, after all." She spoke softly. "It really means that much to you, for all that you laugh at it." There was in her voice the wistful quality of one meeting a barrier of stone and beginning to realize its height. "And you think the Pastor will marry us when I don't even belong——"

He saw her lips trembling. What he had been afraid to admit, then, had been a crooked spike in her own thought. "Oh, Lilice. I don't—I——" he stammered. Then he cried in a low tense voice, "He's got to, I don't care what happens. He's got to, if I have to carry Uncle Herm to the parsonage and——" He paused and kissed the tremble on her mouth. "Don't worry, Punkin. I'm going to talk with him." He didn't say he'd rather eat thistles.

With an eye on the engine Johnny wondered how he'd begin to unsnarl plans for the fall's threshing. Dared he hitch up the team and boldly make the rounds, asking for jobs, as Uncle Herm did sometimes? But of course Uncle Herm did it, not to start a run, but to complete it. . . .

Mr. Schadel wasn't going to turn a wheel this year, he heard. The horsepower thresher would stand beside the blacksmith shop, rusting into uselessness. . . . Well, that meant more open jobs. If I could only get Norton's run, I wouldn't give a kick of my left foot for all the stacks in these hills, he dreamed. Oh, I s'pose I'd thrash them. Folks around here are all right. But they'd have to jump to my whistle, Devil grab it!

Uncle Herm settled the matter one summer's night. "You might as well know it," he said gruffly. Johnny sat down wearily. "It is not soon I'll get out of this bed." Uncle Herm moved on the pillow. "If there's any thrashing to do this fall, you'll have to do it."

Johnny nodded dumbly. This too he had to face now.

"Bull wheels of Moses!" Uncle Herm's voice quavered in a wrath that left the sweat shining on his forehead. "To lie here——" The pale eyes sinking into the bone until there seemed only a helpless glimmer under the lids—Johnny didn't know where to look. Perhaps it was this, perhaps the desire to unburden a little of his own weight, that made him tell Uncle Herm, "Around thrashing time, I'm going to get married to Lilice Rose."

The troubled look that etched a frown above Uncle Herm's brows faded. He smiled. Time and again Johnny would recall and squeeze strength from the hearty assurance of that smile, unsteady as it was. "I'm glad you told me, boy. What I hear tell of her, the Rose girl is fine; a hard worker, knows her place."

"But not a church member." Johnny spoke harshly what had to be said.

"No," Uncle Herm agreed. "No. The Pastor would say she is outside our pastures. But I've had time to wonder. Whose pasture is it? The Pastor's? Maybe it covers more territory than he thinks; more people, too." The quilt on his chest seemed almost too heavy for his breath. "You marry for love, Johnny; not for duty. You hear that."

"But the Pastor," Johnny pursued grimly.

"Ya, the Pastor," echoed Uncle Herm. "He is hard, Johnny, but he has a heart, too. You speak to him. Or let him come here." And that was about all that could be said.

"I'll see him the first free afternoon comes along." Johnny nursed a tiny flame of hope.

Uncle Herm put out his hand. "You marry for love, Johnny; for love. I married out of——" He shut his eyes then. Johnny remembered the blue threads on the closed lids.

But he was further encouraged the day he met Alb Hukelpoke at the store. "You figuring on hittin' the road alone this year, thrashin'?" Alb asked.

"Figuring on it," Johnny answered with a sturdiness he was far from feeling. "If you kinda help me, Alb."

"Aw, sheets, sure I will." Alb slapped Johnny's shoulder. "Shouldn't be hard to get the old run together, even if your uncle ain't around. Folks got a pretty high opinion of you, thrashin' like you did last year." Johnny preened himself, Alb's praise oil to his roughened ego.

Snoose waded through the puddles of a rainy Sunday to find him in the barn, currying the team and humming. Corn was almost knee-high then. The fields, touched with the golden hint of ripening beneath the summer green, whispered drowsily under rain that fell lazy as mist.

Snoose's chuckle simmered with a delight he couldn't keep to himself, in spite of the tag ends of indifferent remarks he drawled. Johnny hardly failed to notice this but said nothing. Finished with currying, he banged the comb against a studding. Dust exploded from the wood. The thick choking odor of dried horse sweat and hair tickled the nose as keenly as a straw. "You got Peiser's corn all hoed?" Johnny flung the comb into a box on the wall.

With a grimace Snoose flipped a thumb across a palm, leathery with gray-white calluses. "I could slide down Jenny's Peak on my hands and never feel a sliver."

"Kurt says the corn in the hollow comes to his belt." Johnny hitched his trousers. "We'll be cutting grain in a week or two. Next week I'm going to take Alb with me and get the thrashing runs lined up. It's about time." He tugged importantly at a horse's hair wedged in the rough bark of a post. "I'm going to ask Norton, too. Won't be any skin off my backsides to try. The feller that gets Norton's job gets practically what he wants." Snoose nodded absently.

They talked about bread-and-milk matters—things that were on the edge of what they would talk seriously about later on. . . . Sophie was going to throw away her washboard and get one of those new washing machines to wash the babies' diapers. "If Clymy wants kids, he'll have to help clean 'em," she said firmly. . . . Alb Hukelpoke was going to buy a stone for Anders Stramff's grave. The machine-shop man in Mary's Hill talked about buying the "rooster" church and setting it up somewhere as a seed-and-feed store. "Poor old duffer of an Anders," Alb had told a circle of men before services at the church one Sunday. "Judas, how we clapped when he played the waltz. But nobody gives a damn how many gopher holes are in his grave." . . . Lornas Tetzell had a new top buggy and took Gatha Blumen to a stage play in Mary's Hill. The godless theater—wait till the Pastor's nostrils caught the odor of this iniquity. . . .

"Well, out with the cat," Johnny said abruptly. "You asked Em'ly and she's set the date. That's what you wanted to tell me, wasn't it?"

Snoose chuckled without surprise. "I'm on my way. She halfway set a date. When she finally decides——" The knuckles of his linked hands whitened under a quick pressure. "You know, Johnny, if somebody told me, 'Feller, you can have the moon or Em'ly, take your pick,' I'd say, 'Mister, you can keep the moon.'"

Watching him, Johnny felt a sudden loneliness, as if for all his muscled trying, something were escaping him, something which like sleep or hunger, came without striving, something like a tang or a flavor in meat and drink, without which the ingredients were flat and unpalatable. But he shrugged this feeling off when Snoose cried, "Let's make it double, Johnny. We've always been together. Let's be so when we get married."

"How you know Lilice'll have me?" Johnny grinned with that perversity which delights in hearing what it already knows.

"If you don't know by now that she'd live in a barn with you, you'll never find out." Reproach edged Snoose's jesting.

Johnny agreed heartily, ready to dream tomorrow's joys above yesterday's reality. "Let's, Snoose. A double wedding. That would be something."

"Two cakes on the table, the two of us leading the wedding dance." Snoose opened his mouth as though more air than he could hold were in his lungs. "With two of Torsten Torgrimson's *Huldrekall* to wish us luck."

"And two kegs of beer on the dancing floor," Johnny cried giddily, already holding the handle of a schooner. "What a night that'll be! Mind you get back to the tank, pumping water, the morning after," he broke off jocosely, "or I'll fire you. I'm depending on you this fall."

"'Never depend on a woman with her first kid,'" Snoose mimicked Alb Hukelpoke. "'Or a man in his wedding bed.' If I'm going to get married, you'd better hunt yourself another tankee." They both laughed. Had

Johnny been watching, though, he might have seen that Snoose was more than half serious.

Before Snoose went home Johnny said, "I'm going visiting tonight. Come over early and we'll take a swim before we go."

"I can stand one," Snoose agreed.

The clouds misted away to patchy skies. A sun burned redly among the blue and craggy thunderheads, promising more wet in the night. He finished the chores.

They went to the creek, their Sunday best on their arms. Snoose unbuttoned his clothes and nakedly stirred a toe in a ripple. His slender body was knotting with muscles but there was a lean beauty here which reminded Johnny of a mink running.

Shoes and stockings off, Johnny removed his shirt first and then his pants. He kept his underwear on and whooped into the water.

"How come you're not swimming bare?" Snoose asked, rubbing his nakedness.

"Oh, I dunno." Johnny twitched a shoulder. "You never know who comes snooping." Snoose saw how the red of more than swimming rushed into Johnny's face.

Drops still on his chest, Johnny ducked out of his wet garment and into clean clothes. His body glistened, white and untanned. They finished dressing. In spite of threatening weather Johnny wore his newest trousers.

Clear as a redbird's note he whistled over the hills and across the creek to Lilice's house. The afterglow spread lemon and robin's-egg blue and water-grass green on the slant of the western sky. Happiness rippled in his stride.

He stumbled back in the dark pocket of midnight. The whistle was hushed on his parted lips. They were dry with his hard breath except when rain in sharp gusts like flung hand-sprinkles moistened them. If there had been a moon earlier that night he had forgotten. Now and again a snake tongue of lightning flickered and illuminated the swollen folds of thunderclouds.

But all he heard in the wind's roar was Lilice's despairing moan, "Johnny, what shall we do now? I'm scared . . . scared." Sometimes he wasn't sure he was splashing through the puddles of this road but was back there in the ledgy pasture, in the dryness under a lip of rock where he and Lilice had gone, so vividly did he feel her despair in the terrified way she sought the refuge of his arms. "I didn't want to tell you, Johnny. But I'm scared."

In that moment he had hardly been able to answer her for the dread

like a dash of April water, icy with winter in its drops, that had crept over
him, chilling his lips, his throat, his body so that her hair against his cheek
was summer-warm. His teeth would have chattered if he hadn't braced
himself against shivering. "Hush, Punkin!" he managed. "Don't say any
more. I'm—I'm all in a snaggle."

But there was no hushing her now, the worry spoken, the nagging revealed. "It's Lena I'm scared of. She's so prying." She snuggled against
him. "I love you so, Johnny," she murmured. "Don't hate me."

"Hate you?" His tightening arms were a promise. "I'd have to hate
myself a lot more first."

"That I should bring this to you," she mourned.

He wouldn't listen. His ear rubbed against her curls. "There is nothing
to cry about," he said determinedly, the chill gone. "Nothing. Tomorrow
or the next day I'll see the Pastor. He'll remember that Uncle Herm is a
congregation member. Then we can plan everything." He spoke calmly
as if that settled the matter; settled it easily. Her fingers touched his chin.

"You haven't seen the Norton house, have you?" He felt her hair brush
his throat as she shook her head. It warmed him into dreaming away what
ought to have been questioned and answered. "That's the kind of place
I'm going to build for you. For you and——"

"Johnny!" She brought him back to the wind's bluster and the first rain-
drops and her own slow words. "Johnny, in these nights, what your aunt
said comes back to me. No, no, listen!" she insisted when he would have
interrupted. "Listen. Maybe she's right. If I had been properly brought
up, would this—this have happened to——" She pressed her face against
him. The words failed.

"What difference does it make?" he whispered. "Let's not talk about it.
I was brought up, what you call properly, and I . . . if you're to be
blamed——" He couldn't go on.

"It isn't the same." There was agony in the way she drew apart from
him. "You're a man. Don't you see?" He could hardly hear her low
words. "Johnny, if Gatha . . . this wouldn't have——"

He almost laughed. "Punkin, are you jealous of Gatha?"

"Oh, Johnny, you don't understand," she cried desolately. "Gatha's a
properly brought up girl who——"

"And she goes to church," mocked Johnny. "You little Punkinhead.
Why, I've got enough church in me for both of us." He tried to soothe her
into mirthfulness. Momentarily comforted, she felt safe from the lances of
thought.

But the somberness of wind and the thickening night, darkened even
more by the lightning's distant red flash, gathered round them. They ran

for the house. As they stood for a moment in the lee of the barn, she began to cry bitterly against his shoulder, "I'm scared, Johnny . . . scared. . . ."

All the way home that cry hurt in his ears. As he splashed through the puddles he heard it above the thunder rumble and the roar of the wind. It linked itself with the promise he'd made: "Tomorrow the Pastor . . ."

As it turned out he didn't go to the log church the next day after all. At noon Alb came driving to talk about the threshing run. The weather was still murky. "Well, Johnny," Alb said, "thrashing's not far off and harvest no farther'n you can swing a cat by the tail. We got to get lined up before Tetzell or somebody else sneaks in ahead of us."

Johnny nodded, glad that Hukelpoke had come and the Pastor could be remembered tomorrow.

"Now, the way I figure it," Alb began, "a small circle, one we can depend on, year after year——"

"Nope." Johnny pitched the notion into discard. "No money in that. We got a good machine. We need a big run. You know, Alb—" he squinted—"this year I'm going to ask Mr. Muri in."

"But, Johnny!" Alb clawed at his pants in astonishment. "A Noreegion? We've always sort of kept the thrashing circle amongst ourselves and——"

"Time we got new grain in the circle then." Johnny was flatly·stubborn.

"Sheetin' Judas, Johnny, they work diff'rent, them Noreegians!" Alb said dubiously. "They with their coffee four, five times a day. And——"

"You think their coffee is any worse than our beer?" Johnny grunted. He didn't mind seeing Alb wince. "Mr. Peiser used to hire Torsten Torgrimson. So did others. Nobody minded."

"That's diff'rent," Alb replied sociably. "Torsten's a hired man."

"He's a Norwegian first; and a good man, too. He pitches as many bundles as Heinie Beerwagon. No, Alb. Mr. Muri goes in."

Alb nodded, if reluctantly.

"So does that Swede—what's his name?" Johnny continued. "Mr. Berling. And what about the Eyetalian that just moved in—Giannini, or whatever his name is? Let's get him in, too." Johnny laughed, gay in this minute of forgetting the clamor at the edge of his thought.

"Sure." Alb gave in a bit sourly. "Get 'em all in. Kitten, cat and tom. Mr. Edgely, too. Yankee and Dutchman and Norskie. It's a good mixture."

"Why not?" demanded Johnny. "Their wheat's as good as the next feller's. So is their pocketbook. I aim to get me every damn farmer into the circle from the Diemer Hills to Loon Lake." He added thoughtfully, "It's Norton's job I really want."

"Norton's?" Alb struck a fist against a palm. "Sheetin' Judas, boy! You aim high. You'll get yourself in trouble with Bory Tetzell if——"

"My rig will thrash rings around his. He's got nothing to crow about."

"Guess you're right at that," Alb mumbled, persuaded against his will by Johnny's hard determination. "You thrash the way you did last fall, doing an honest job and keeping your good name—" the words clanged into Johnny's head—"keeping your good name among the farmers, and you're going to be like bull after cow—nothing's going to stop you." Alb went home, his doubt sparkled with wonder.

But Johnny remained as if rooted where Alb had left him. Keep your good name. Keep . . . It echoed dully with each beat of his heart. If it became known . . . if the Pastor found out . . . the lash of gossip driving the news over hill and valley . . . Sweat budded on his forehead. If Alb, whom the Pastor regarded as a doubtful tendril in the vineyard and capable of God knew what profligacy—if he could say this warningly, what would Mr. Schadel say? Or Mr. Dunkel or the other members? And these were the folks who harvested the acres of grain and chose whom they wished as thresher. If they found out . . .

He'd have to marry Lilice at once, tomorrow or the next day. The Pastor must . . . Ah yes, the Pastor; the Pastor with his sharp beard and his long fingers. If he refused . . .

Moisture dampened the shirt under his arms. No, not yet. He'd not see the Pastor yet. Not until he and Alb had gathered the farmers into a pattern of threshing jobs. I'll get a big run, he soothed his alarm. I've got to get it; the biggest yet. That'll keep people's mouths shut. And I'll thrash so fast, nobody'll dare open his gab, no matter what they think. A thin barrier against the prickles of tomorrow.

Alb in the buggy beside him, he hustled among the farmers. In the fields grain was taking the yellowish hue of ripeness. With Uncle Herm's name as a persuader, with Alb's jocularity to clinch the argument, sometimes with a loud hilarity and swigs of bottles, he discovered how heartening was a landowner's "Sure, we'll try you again, Johnny. You did good work last year"; and this despite the qualification usually attached: "Your uncle, best damn thrasher in these parts. If you do half as well as he did——"

Sometimes, noticing this man's laughter and that man's confidence, he wondered, drawing behind a thicket of reserve, Would you shake my hand, would you invite me to dinner—if you knew. . . . Or would you sick the dog on me? . . . Or were these only the night birds of worry, darkly feathered in his own brooding and coming home to roost?

On rides between farms they traced out the pattern of activity: the number of stacks on this road, the shortest space between this farm and that, the best routes by which to avoid boggy swamp grades and rickety wooden bridges. By the end of the next week he brought a spot of red to Uncle Herm's pale cheeks by reading a list of names. It was long enough to keep him busy for a while. "And there'll be more. Some only half promised. Others will let me know soon." Johnny leaned forward excitedly. He tapped the paper. "But these—these are small jobs really. I can do most of them in a day or more; some in less."

"It is good, Johnny," Uncle Herm said raspily. "But you hafta look out for some of them fellers. Take Peiser, for instance. He's honest, but he'll beat you out of a half-bushel of wheat, if he can. And Schimmel; he'll bellyache about short weight, no matter what you do. Bull wheels of Moses, the rows we used to have with him!" A shadow came into his eyes— the shadow of such longing that Johnny abruptly pocketed the list. Soon now the thresher would whir disturbingly on the air, the whistle would demand shrilly, "Hurry with the sacks, with the water! Start up!" But Uncle Herm—would he stand as Johnny remembered him, one foot on the feeder head, his body leaning forward in expectant alertness?

He left Uncle Herm for the kitchen and a drink of water. Aunt Phrena peered at him over her patching. Between them was the sullen vigilance of dog and woodchuck, an acceptance of what could not be avoided. With the promise of the Comfort Book in her hand, she waited on grace for him, too.

Kurt sat over a heap of pamphlets he'd got from the Agricultural College in St. Paul. In the past year he had subscribed to the *Stock, Farm and Home* and in that paper had read what he could about farmer's "institutes." He wished he could attend one.

"What you want there?" jibed Mr. Marchen. "Listen to a college perfesser who don't know which end of a cow gives milk?"

Farmer's "traveling schools" these institutes were called; one had been held in Fergus the year before. "By jippers, ain't no schoolma'am going to tell me how to pitch manure," Mr. Nussbaum asserted stoutly.

Kurt talked about the experiment stations in the Valley. "They're trying wheat that won't rust, don't matter what the weather is," he reported.

But Mr. Peiser said, "Ya, they plant a spear here and a spear there, I'm told. A grasshopper eats it before harvest, and what does that prove?"

Kurt lifted his shoulders tranquilly and bent over his pamphlets.

To all his studies Johnny said, "If the wheat grows, keep your hands off and let it. Of course," he added dubiously, "if you can get a grain that gives you a better yield, maybe it's worth bothering with." About this, however, he was doubtful. Kurt only surveyed him thoughtfully and a little scornfully.

This night Aunt Phrena peered at Johnny while he lifted the dipper. Kurt merely turned a page. But in his room Uncle Herm lay very still. Softly he repeated the names Johnny had read—names of neighbors returning to a run he'd probably never see. He heard the tin rattle and the splash as Johnny pitched the dipper back into the pail. His nostrils thinned. Tears in hot streams rilled over his cheeks. He tried to wipe them but his bony hand slid helplessly past an ear and lay on the pillow. He let the tears run, hot salt scorching not his skin but deep into his heart.

In that harvest season Johnny often wished there were somewhere a cool and lonely place where he could shut his eyes and his mind and leave nag and fret behind as in the creek water he left the sweat and grime of cutting grain and shocking, the hauling of bundles to the stack. The endless stretching of nerves until his skin seemed to crackle . . .

There was the Pastor. Him he'd see before very long. Ardently he wished for that hour when he could say, "I've been, and that's over."

There was Alb objecting, "But we always start at the Pastor's; have for years."

"Not this year," Johnny said stubbornly. "The rig is here on this place. Why go elsewhere first and then come back?"

"Well," temporized Alb, "don't know. But Steuber can make it gol-darned mean for a feller, if he's crossed."

Johnny put a wrench down carefully. Tomorrow or the next day he'd have to make his peace with the Pastor. Maybe it might be just as well not to poke up a hornet's nest. Next year—"No," he snapped, catching up the wrench. "No. The rig begins the thrashing here." Where the thresher was concerned, nobody would boss him. "Let him rail, if he wants to."

There was Lilice, terrified at the future, twisting her fingers as though she longed breathlessly for a gold band and the consolation of murmured "I do's" to ward off the grim shadows of fear and uncertainty. "You didn't come Saturday. I walked the floor until my ankles ached."

"I told you." The fists in the pocket of his coat trembled with intensity while he tried to hush her. "Me and Alb were getting more jobs. We didn't get back until two in the morning, Saturday. We were trying to land Norton's job."

"I'm scared." She didn't tell him how, in dreams, the thresher roared and she seemed to hear her father yelling and Uncle Herm screaming. She put his hand against her cheek. "That Lena—you have no idea how she looks at me."

It was the Pastor who drove a spike of desperation into Johnny's skull. In those afternoons just before threshing, Johnny sometimes felt that he ought to hold his breath in fear of what the next hammer stroke, the next turn of a screw in his hand might bring. Often between the unstitching of a belt and its retying, he wondered that his skull held together the frenzied jumble, the dull ache of despair. . . .

He went to see the Pastor. For a minute that dropped its hard weight like an hour, he sat in the stiff, slippery leather chair of the study while the Pastor regarded him dourly over the tent ribs his fingers made above his nose and beard. Johnny wiggled his hands, fumbling with his hat which slid over his knees. The study was spare and unyielding: a heavy desk, a severe chair, a window facing north draped in somber cloth, a floor unsoftened with carpet or rug, walls disciplined into sternness by mottoes and pictures of iron-jawed church fathers. At his desk the Pastor waited, his singleness of purpose reinforced by the leather backs of homilies and commentaries at his side—cases of them. A yardstick laid across a shelf would have touched the spine of every volume there.

Johnny twisted in the hard chair. His nervous ribbling fingers poked at his hat, his hat which he, as an acceptable member of the Pockerbrush church, had laid aside respectfully in the presence of reverence. The Pastor took his leisure. Remembering Johnny's rebelliousness as a confirm-and, the stories he'd heard about him since, he meditated over this fidgety behavior. At last he lowered his hands. "So. This was to be expected," he pronounced. "A family that considers steam engines more highly than the honest labor of hands; where the housefather is a church member, true, but a stiff-necked, unrepentant one, lax in the decorum of his household. For his spouse worships with the heathen and his foster sons run in the pasture of Ashtoreth. A house divided——"

"All I asked——" Johnny's voice broke. He cleared his throat raggedly. The Pastor's eyes flicked over him. "All I want," Johnny insisted, "all I want is that you marry us—tomorrow or Sunday. But soon."

"So?" The Pastor's question slid up from bass to alto with quickening interest. "So hasty? The mills of God grind slowly. We must not be hasty." He was quiet for an inquisitional moment, his beard moving with his thin smile. He watched Johnny's fingers worrying a fribbly spot in the hatbrim. He said nothing for a moment. Before this he had known how efficacious are silence and time as correctors of the conscience.

"Na, Bruder Schwartz—ach, Black.'" He noticed how Johnny went rigid at the syllable. His tone softened ominously. "You are aware that this girl, this Rose maiden—she is not one of us." He paid no attention to Johnny's quick stiffening. "She belongs to the unregenerate, the heart still unsanctified——" He turned abruptly. "She will join the church?"

"Why, yes, yes. I—I guess so." Johnny mumbled, off guard. This he had not asked Lilice, had taken for granted. But the question, coming so directly, sent him floundering. His fingers dug at the hatbrim. "She can join, can't she?" Eagerness brightened his query.

"Na, certainly, certainly." There was unction in the Pastor's voice. His eyes gleamed. With a thumb he patted his finger ends as if he were recording the tales he'd heard about Johnny—the dances, the rowdiness, the drinking, the brawls; these and the inattentive Sunday yawns, the holy services ignored, perhaps other matters. . . . "Certainly she may," he continued. "When a knowledge of the truth has come to her heart, when she is reborn in the spirit, when she has acknowledged all of her sins——" He let silence pass a judgment. Johnny's hand clinched over the hat. The Pastor noted it. "She will be instructed this fall and winter. Next spring you can marry her, perhaps——"

"Next spring!" Johnny interrupted hollowly, the future tightening his lips. "No."

"Next spring, I should think." The Pastor lifted his hand in the alert position of a cat that finally has the smell of a cornered mouse firmly in its nostrils.

"No!" Johnny cried in a kind of anguish, speaking before he thought. "Then it's too——" He stopped, frozen.

"Too——?" The Pastor hovered over the word. "Too what, Bruder Black? Too—late?" Then he pounced. His hand fell on the desk in a slapping bang. "What are you trying to hide, you stupid sheepshead?"

"I? Hide—I——" Johnny stammered. For all his trying he couldn't stop the dull brick red that flowed over his cheeks, his forehead, his ears.

Furiously the Pastor rushed on: "Do you dare hide some unspeakable iniquity by coming here and——"

"No!" Johnny sprang to his feet. Anger drained the red from his countenance. Grayish white patches grew on his cheeks. "Herr Pastor, I asked only that you give——"

"Unchurched and iniquitous!" the Pastor boomed. "Nobody enters this church until he or she repents—" his voice grated—"repents in sackcloth and ashes. A girl like that who——"

"Sackcloth—why, you don't even know her." Anger mounted in Johnny's tone. All at once his awe of the Pastor fell away in flakes. "You stand there and condemn her. You like to think the worst, don't you, Herr Pastor?

Well go ahead, then; do!" In cold anger he jammed the hat on his head; stood disrespectfully covered before his Pastor. "Go ahead then, think the worst, and the Devil grab it!"

Before the Pastor understood, Johnny had shut the door behind him and was gone. Incredulous, shocked at this flagrant insult to his dignity and position, the Pastor sank back in his chair and tented his fingers over his beard. For a long time he stared at the commentaries of the church fathers.

Johnny tramped home, following the path where, springs before, he and Snoose had gone to and from the church. But no fragrance of those Aprils in anemone and violet, far away, came to him now. Instead he knew a hot and sweaty tumult in bone and nerve. There was wild wrath first. But on the heels of anger dragged despair. On the periphery of his awareness like a throbbing pain were the repeated syllables, What now? What now? . . . Why did I come to see the Pastor? I knew this would happen, deep inside me. And how I hoped it wouldn't! Oh, Judas, what am I going to tell Lilice?

He didn't know. He didn't know. If she said, "There's Mr. Erd- man——" But he hadn't the courage to go as far as that.

Only one thing mattered, he decided. He must get a large threshing ring, bigger and better than anyone in the hills had ever seen. . . . That'll shut their mouths. Oh God, I wish we'd begin thrashing tomorrow. . . . Not to think, not to think, hiding all behind the cogs of wheel and the bright flash of cylinder teeth.

At home he found Snoose waiting for him near the separator. "You're just the feller I want to see," Johnny hailed him, shutting away the Pastor and this last hour in the immediacy of a task that wanted doing. "I'm buy- ing a new team for the tank wagon. Fleischer's young blacks. You know them. Prancers from 'way back, if I ever saw any. You can clip along at a pretty rate." Snoose would probably jump out of his pants when he heard this—so Johnny had told himself more than once.

But Snoose was lackadaisical. "That's fine, Johnny." His interest was far away. "I'm on a holiday. Not even thinking about work this after- noon."

"Holiday?" Johnny was irked by his indifference. He squinted at the color on Snoose's sandy cheeks, the gray-stone eyes dreamy-lidded. "You've made up your minds, then, you and Em'ly?" he said gruffly.

"Mine was made up long ago. What a time I had with *her*." Ruefully Snoose shoved his cap above his ear. "We're going to move onto the Trenne place. Remember? North of Mary's Hill. Pa Musser found it for us. We——"

"You're going to do a little tanking first," Johnny said bluntly. He picked up the oilcan. "I got this team especially for you."

"That's what I came to tell you. You better catch me on the run." Snoose moved uneasily. "Em'ly wants the wedding early next month. So do I."

"That's the middle of thrashing," Johnny objected. "I——"

"It's a good time. Red leaves and grape smell. The echoes over the hill are clearest then." Snoose slid into reverie again.

"Oh, Devil grab it, Snoose!" Johnny burst out impatiently. "We ought to be ready to move out to the flats by that time. Maybe we'll have Norton's job by then. We just can't——"

"You said a double wedding." Snoose only half heard him. "What could be better, Johnny?"

"Oh!" Oil spilled over his hand from the can. He let it dribble. "Well, I don't——"

"Em'ly's planning to fill the church with red leaves, and hang bittersweet on the lamps. Frost ought to open them by then. And I know a patch of gentian."

With bitterness that was like an ache, Johnny stood there. Here was Snoose planning a wedding as though it were a jaunt in the woods, happy over gentians and the scarlet of the bittersweet cup. Red leaves in the church! he thought miserably. "And we haven't even a doghouse to be married in."

He couldn't meet Snoose's gaze. He patted the oil on the back of his hand aimlessly; saw the hair rise and lean in the oil like bent grass in a stream; and suddenly felt old and worn as if his youth had wilted into experience before it had attained a blossom. Snoose with his gabble about echoes over the ridges—kids' gabble, that's what it was. Wouldn't that feller ever leave the nonsense of dreams and put his feet down squarely on the rich earth of reality, of work, of getting ahead in the world?

Almost with scorn Johnny demanded sharply, "What's the tearing hurry? You waited this long, you can wait till winter." He added thoughtlessly what was to be a joke, "Or do you have to get married?" And wished he'd bitten his tongue rather than uttered the words. For him to joke . . .

Snoose blinked his eyes as if clearing them of the last cobweb. His gaze was level. "I'm not as big a man as you are, Johnny—in muscles, anyway. But I'm man enough to hold onto my body."

The shame in Johnny's heart should have glowed upon his cheeks like a blown ember. But wrath shadowed it. The Pastor and all that had happened came in a rising ire that sapped the color from his skin and left him pale; anger against Snoose, anger he couldn't hold back. I'm not going to get mad at him, he thought; I'm not. But his breathing was heavy. "So you want to quit?" he said aloud.

"I'll stick with you for a while," Snoose promised. "But I told you before to find another tankee. You know that." The afternoon light was almost golden on his lashes. "I'm tired of grease and oil and chaff in your neck and sleeping in straw piles. I want to smell autumn burning—and a clean pillow."

"All right then," Johnny half shouted. "So let it be then. I'm depending on you. But I'm not getting married next month—maybe never." Furiously he strode away, muttering under his breath, "I'm not mad at him. I'm not. Damn it all, he makes *me* so mad . . . kiddish . . . in short pants yet. Next thing he'll play dolls."

He was too disturbed that night to ask Uncle Herm about the adjustment of the sieves for barley.

"You look kinda peaked," Uncle Herm observed. "Everything all right?"

"Oh, sure, sure." Johnny evaded him.

"Dunkel was saying this afternoon that Bory Tetzell figures strongly on Norton's job. He figures on getting a cent more a bushel too." Uncle Herm sighed. "I've thrashed years and settled for what a man could pay, not for something that would fill up my pocketbook. But times change." The chair creaked as Johnny shifted. Uncle Herm asked, "You're sure nothing's wrong?"

Johnny avoided answer. "Bright and early Monday morning we start."

"You've made up your mind?" Uncle Herm fumbled on the pillow. "Starting here the way you planned? The Pastor won't like it." But he saw that Johnny was in no mood for arguing. He gazed dully at his swinging back.

After supper Johnny noticed the hole in the brim of his hat. He stared at it, this mark his fingers had made there in the Pastor's study. "Devil——" he muttered and flung it from him. He never wore it again.

Quietly then as if he'd decided what he'd do but not yet how, he told Aunt Phrena and Kurt, "Next month sometime, I'm going to marry Lilice Rose." He let the words drops slowly. The lamplight was tinged crimson with the red flowers in the shade. But he couldn't talk about the Pastor and that afternoon. Aunt Phrena hesitated over the paging in the Precious Comfort Book.

Kurt raised his brows above the account book on which he was penciling and grunted. "It didn't take a prophet to foretell that." He made a cipher neatly. Aunt Phrena glared at him.

"I know it is in thrashing time," Johnny said woodenly. "It is no use to argue. I've set my mind on it."

The pages in Aunt Phrena's fingers swished with rapid turning; stopped. She looked at him in a kind of horror. She'd done her best and failed; she had opened the gates to flowery pastures for him and he'd chosen the path to a dark swamp. "Na, marry her then. But don't promise Erdman half a pig as Adam Rose did. You won't get it here." She clapped the book shut. Fury echoed in the popping sound. "Marry her, but not in this house will I live with her." Tears streaked past her nose. The door of the bedroom creaked behind her sobbing.

Kurt fixed a digit, her storminess indifferent to him. "You needn't ask Steuber," he said with more friendliness than Johnny had ever seen in him.

"I know." Tiredly Johnny rubbed his forehead. "Don't tell this, Kurt. I did ask him. It was bitter words he gave me."

"What else did you expect? It is the bone and blood of his thinking. He can't change." Kurt didn't look up from the account book. "There is Erdman then, or the justice of the peace." Implacably his pencil hunted on a trail of integers.

"Oh, Kurt!" Johnny buried his head in the crook of an elbow. All the years of his boyhood under the Pastor, under Aunt Phrena, rushed to his mind: the towering condemnations, the half-understood terrors, the dreadful question of "from whence" and "where to," for which, instead of meditative contemplation, there was the shaken fist of doom, intimidating the brave questing spirit and whipping it into groveling, abject, uncomprehending animal fear . . . disobedience . . . damned to hell-fire . . . for Lilice . . . for him. . . . He had scoffed gently, condescendingly at this. With growing pains and settling young manhood he'd grown above this, he was sure; in anger and frustration he had rejected it as beyond him to understand and so invalid. But now the hawk of doubt pursued his thought relentlessly through the many rabbit warrens of uncertainty. . . . "Kurt, if it is true, as the Pastor says—" his voice was muffled—"we're lost if we don't——" He couldn't say more.

"That—" Kurt pointed a decimal precisely—"is what each of us will have to find out."

Johnny arose, a sag in his shoulder. It was as if suddenly he was a stranger at this table, in this chair. He moved toward the stairs. As he passed the bedroom door, he thought he heard a moan come forth, a man sound squeezed from agony. He hesitated; thrust fists into his pockets and slowly went upstairs.

He was busy at the separator next day. Over the repairing of a boxing he groaned, "What shall I tell Lilice? What?"

He was shaping a piece of tin when Alb Hukelpoke drove up. "Don't ask me where I've been the last two days," Alb greeted him but didn't unhitch his team.

"Didn't think to ask you." Johnny put the shears aside.

"Well, I was in Mary's Hill. Sheetin' Judas, what a tagle I've been in!" From his pocket he brought a letter. He tapped it quizzically. "Ya can never tell when the prodigal goes home, as the Pastor says. Johnny, Anders is going home at last."

"Anders? Huh?" Johnny almost dropped the piece of tin.

"Just as he used to say. 'Member? They've called him, even from the grave."

Johnny's eyes bugged.

Alb was solemn. "His sister's died," he explained. "The last of the family. In her will she wants Anders buried in the family graveyard." He folded the paper. "Poor old duffer! He didn't know how fast he'd be forgotten. You'd think he had a few friends, after all his accordion playing. But no. I asked Schadel to help me, and Nussbaum, too. But they say Anders rots as well in the rooster church as he will in Minn'ap'lis."

He put the letter away and leaned forward. Johnny drew back from what he sensed was coming. "You got to help me," Alb begged. "This afternoon——"

"I? With all the work I——"

"Anders thought a lot of you," Alb hastened on. "While he was sick, I 'member him saying, 'That Johnny feller, he's one you can depend on.'"

"Alb, we're going to be thrashing next Monday. I've got my backsides sore, hurrying the work. This afternoon I've got to see Peiser about an extra grain team. Alb, I can't do it." Johnny whittled at the tin.

"He was such a lonely old duffer. I just thought——" Alb pulled at his jaw. "Well, guess I'll have to do it myself. Old duffer, I can't go back on him."

Exasperation almost exploded from Johnny. But there were the worry furrows in Alb's brow. He thought of Uncle Herm's tired, web-marked face. Lonely and alone. He tossed the tin to the ground. Would the dead never molder without reaching a grisly hand to clutch at his shoulder? The dead, shadowless but determined, standing in the path of the quick. "All right, Alb," he said harshly. "Devil grab it to hell, if one more thing happens between now and Monday, I'm going to smash something!"

All the way over to Mary's Hill Johnny fumed, "Why I said I'd come, when I've got all that work——"

"I know." Alb was sympathetic. "I know you're in a cat's rush to get started. So am I. But you'll sleep better, knowing you done this for Anders. Ain't much he'll ever ask for again."

Johnny was silent. Alb dragged a bottle from his pocket. "You're gonna need a stiff gut for this, boy." The whisky jiggled as he offered it. Johnny shook his head. Alb helped himself.

In the churchyard they waded through grass ankle-high. Between them they carried a large box. The moss of desertion greened the stone steps. Crumpled of tail and head where rocks from skilled boy hands had struck, the rooster on the weather vane contemplated God's small acre with a desolate mien. In the graveyard weeds and blue vervain flourished rankly.

After Alb had gurgled deeply at the bottle, they set to work. Grudgingly the sod made way for air and sun. "Poor old duffer!" Alb grunted. "He was always scairt the ants would get in his eyes. Now he ain't got any eyes to speak of. Once you're dead . . ." The spades bit deeper.

When what had been Anders was only an offense strong on the clean air, Alb jabbed the spade into sod and reached for his pocket. (Where now was the accordion music sweet under the yellow of lanterns?) Alb said, "Have a snort?"

Johnny neither saw nor heard him. All at once with a sharpness of detail that choked him, as a nightmare of falling does, he saw Uncle Herm here, Uncle Herm who had kindness inches deep in the wrinkles on his face, the scrabble of whiskers into which his fingers strayed . . . Uncle Herm a huddle of earth-gnawed bones. . . . Was this the reward of the unrepentant, those lost from the fold, as the Pastor had said . . . lost as he would be and Lilice . . . Lilice? . . .

He shivered. Horror trembled on his tongue's end. In a kind of mist he saw Alb raise the bottle in salutation; dimly heard him say, "Well, Anders, my boy, here's to your first resurrection!" He gripped the spade against what howled triumphantly in his ears. Words rattled in his throat but none came. Dully he poked at the clay on the metal.

21

Threshing started at the Barewolfs' before dryness obliterated the fulgent green and red of Monday morning's dew. All the forenoon long Uncle

Herm twisted sidewise on the pillow, straining shoulder and neck toward the window at the head of his bed, eager to see more than the ceiling and the folds of the curtain. By the half hour the sound of engine and separator, and the noise of men in the yard tugged at his ears.

He squirmed with chest and pushed with elbows. "Oh, Moses, just once!" he prayed. Sweat came and he grunted. But hip and thigh and leg, for all their usefulness, might as well have been plaster, or the bones of another body. After a while he lay very still and let rumble and clatter mock him with its nearness: steady hum of wheel and gear . . . grind of cylinder . . . easy chugging of the engine, now running effortlessly, now gathering piston and valve into strident explosive *chug-a-chugs* over a feederful of damp bundles . . . snarl of the cylinder and then the quick, licking noise of eccentric and belt as the machine ran free again . . . faraway yells of the teamsters at the grain spout and the nearer "Back up there, damn you!" at the granary . . . once the passing of a wagon so close to the window the wheels seemed to grind on the sill . . . Aunt Phrena's heavy tread in the kitchen and the sizzle of fryings, bubble of cookings . . . Mrs. Marchen's voice as she came later to help. . . .

Once Johnny came in, face spotted diseaselike with oil, in his hand a dipper of water leaking coolness from its sides. "Wheat's going pretty good," he reported.

"Na, that's nice." Uncle Herm swallowed weakly. Finally he spoke what had been bothering him. "Don't know what the Pastor will think, Johnny, you starting here. We always began with his stacks. It seemed the right thing. We——"

"Don't care." Johnny took a long drink before he said flatly, "Pastor gets his grain knocked out like the rest, when his turn comes, not before."

He left Uncle Herm uneasy on the pillow; crossed the kitchen, indifferent to Aunt Phrena's grim disapproval. How the church must have buzzed yesterday. "Na, for once the Pastor didn't get his way. . . . Betcha somebody'll catch a blistering from the pulpit one of these Sundays. . . . That Johnny Black . . ." He hadn't been at services. By today the ridges were gabbling. Let them. He clamped his jaw and hurried out to the engine to see that Snoose had the water level up.

He stopped at the tank wagon and patted the fidgety horses. Black as the skin of ripe haws they were, his new team, shaking their bridles, keeping Snoose watchful with their determined pull at the bit. Johnny's eyes snapped darkly at them, as if he recognized in their impatient stampings some of his own restlessness these days, rebellion against the jagged iron of curb and snaffle. Even Alb Hukelpoke admitted the team was the fastest in the outfit. With them horses, Snoose shouldn't have to skin his elbows keeping water in the old bitch's belly; so Heinie Beerwagon opined.

Snoose was busy at the pump. Johnny glanced at him. Instinctively he wanted to grab at Snoose's ankles and yell, "Snoose, you old water-pusher you!" It would have been a gesture toward his kinship with Snoose. But not now, not now.

He was ruffled and commanding of speech, or moodily silent, whenever Snoose was near, as if he found it hard to accept Snoose's serene indifference to anything but Em'ly's curls and the Trenne place north of Mary's Hill. "Mooniness," Johnny called it. Once when Snoose let a siphoning hose slip out of the auxiliary tank and water spilled in the dust, Johnny yelled, "Damn it, Snoose, quit dreaming and tend to your business!"

Snoose jerked up. He returned Johnny's anger with steady calmness and picked up the hose. Thereafter, when he wasn't occupied at the tank, he'd climb on the separator beside Alb, or shout jokes with Heinie, or chew kernels of wheat at the grain wagons. Johnny's mouth tightened.

By the week's end Uncle Herm's straw pile lay acres behind. The coal of Johnny's engine was heaped on so many of the farms in the season's run that folks, meeting at the blacksmith shop and the store, exchanged wonder with their chews of tobacco and wads of gossip. "Thrashing so fast, the grain's all going into the straw pile, that's what it is. . . . They say the wheat's so cracked the elevator won't even take it. . . . But I heard different. . . . Jippers, though, if he keeps this up, we'll be through thrashing before the rains set in!"

Folks came in wagon and buggy to sit in the yards and watch the pitchers swing the bundles and the grainmen hurry their loads. But most of all they kept their faces toward the engine, the blur of the flywheel, the white bush of steam above the chest. With shrugs or muttered admiration they saw Johnny stand like a dark figure of impatience over the steering wheel or stride purposefully toward the separator. They jumped when the scream of the whistle, shrill and piercing as needles against the eardrum, sent horses rearing in their harnesses and teamsters yelling, "Whoa, damn your mangy hide!"

Johnny avoided them when he could and was short and prickly when he couldn't. If you knew—he glowered at their curiosity—what wouldn't you say? And he tried not to think of Alb's thorny "Keep your reputation clear"; tried not to think of Lilice and the night he'd told her about the Pastor.

He had dreaded that meeting. But with that queer sensitiveness by which a woman becomes aware intuitively of what a man gropes toward by experience, Lilice glanced at him, at the way his brow tangled in frowns, and said quickly, "Well, you still live in Pockerbrush, don't you?" The button of her dimple moved with her smile. "Maybe you'd like a handful of sugar plums? There are some below the hill."

She brought a bowl. He followed without being sure why. Out of hearing distance of the house, she said quietly, "The Pastor told you what would happen if you married me." At his misery she slipped an arm into his.

"If Uncle Herm were up and around——" He left off abruptly. "Sugar plums won't be ripe for a week yet."

"I know. I had a fight with Lena today."

"You—oh, Lilice," he groaned, "what next?"

"She says she's going to have a baby. She bragged about it." After a moment she continued, "I guess there's not much she doesn't know."

There was silence for a space of walking—silence that had their own thoughts clamoring within it. In a near-by field white rocks were like the ghosts of a boneyard. "I know what you're thinking," he said at last. "It's what I've been sleepless over the last nights: that Mr. Erdman would marry us."

"You don't like him," Lilice said flatly. "Nor the meetinghouse."

"Oh, Lilice, I don't know." He swung aside fiercely. "It's not him so much. But that slop religion—bawling and throwing yourself on the floor. I'd never feel properly married. Might as well go to the justice of peace like Bory Tetzell did," he muttered grimly. "And that's no wedding at all."

At the hopelessness that began to draw at her lips, he cried, "I didn't mean that, Punkin. I'll do anything for you." They huddled together. And out of the rocky field trooped the ghosts of the future, mocking him— phantoms of shame, sly-eyed with gossip, loose-lipped as old mares . . . phantoms smoky with judgments: "Thou shalt not . . . depart, ye cursed, into everlasting flame!" . . . phantoms of derision: "Hee, hee, hee, think you're the big cheese, don't you? Think they can't thrash without you, eh? Norton's job . . . Norton's job . . . Norton's job, hee, hee, hee . . ."

Together they stared at the plum hedge and saw not the acorn-shaped fruit already yellowing with autumn sweetness; they saw the gnarled and twisted elbows of limbs and the long spines that stuck needlewise from the wood. . . .

This is the last straw, he thought, the last drop that spills the glass.

In the next week a man from north of Mary's Hill drove up. "I got a farm on the flats. I can get you a string of jobs, if you finish here in a couple of weeks. Can you do it?"

Johnny peered at him, tight-lipped, grim. "I think so," he said quietly and hurried the crew a little.

A day later men from the flats came. "We got a run of shocks and stacks. It's yours if you can move out in a couple, three weeks, maybe."

"Let you know in a few days," Johnny promised. And his hand on the whistle cord was hard with purpose.

That evening the machine-shop man in Mary's Hill rode out to see him about a new drive belt—a gandy belt, he called it. The sun was no more than a bundle's width above the western ridges. He brought news that sent the blood through Johnny's temples in short, painful spurts. Bory Tetzell had squabbled with Norton, rowed with him, the machine-shop man reported. Bory was asking a cent more per bushel of grain. Norton was balking, said he'd get another rig. And Bory was ranting that he'd tear the guts out of anybody who dared accept Norton's job.

"Tear out guts, will he?" Heinie Beerwagon flexed his arms. "Maybe he will on his crew. He'd better keep his snoot away from this rig. I got a nice fork tine I'd like to twist into him."

On Saturday nights Tetzell pounded the bar in Jacklin's saloon; and once in plain sight of the customers in the Emporium, he quarreled with his young wife and slapped her. "That poor little one!" folks sympathized. "Those Fleischers, marrying her to a brute like that!"

"Devil!" breathed Johnny, his skin prickling with excitement. I know it, he thought; sure as I stand here. There's nobody else. Norton will ask me. I know it. But face to face with what had egged him with desire these months, he hesitated, temporizing. Maybe I shouldn't, with all the jobs I've got ahead of me. . . . And there's Lilice . . . It's a big place, Norton's . . . I've got to take it, if he asks me. It's what I've waited for. . . . If Uncle Herm were only back on his legs! . . . He banged fist against fist violently.

But when he thought of Bory for a moment, his teeth came together. The smoldering embers of hate, banked in the ashes of waiting, revived now and began to smoke under the fan of expectancy. "The bastard!" he muttered, remembering Bory's knotty fingers slapping against his mouth; remembering the filth on Snoose's body. "The dirty bastard!"

Such enmity, however, was swept over (though not forgotten) in a rush of feeling about Norton, Norton, the pivot of his hope and his doubt. If I could get his job, I could face anybody and—anything, he decided. But he wavered. Restively he followed alongside the slapping belt to the separator.

On this evening the sun with redness but with little warmth was tinging the remaining stacks with rich crimson. He saw the farmer's boy climbing the bulge of a stack, searching for eggs. Only a moment before, a hen, disturbed when a pitcher tossed a fork up the stackside, had cackled into a burst of outraged wings from a nest near the top.

Now the boy waved an egg into the sunset. With a shout that was lost in the clatter of the separator, Johnny ran, leaped up and caught at the straw of the butts. He pulled himself up. The pitchers snatched an instant from their work to notice him indifferently. The straw pilers were too tired to shrug their shoulders. No one saw a strange jubilant intensity flush his cheeks (except Snoose who sat on a grain wagon—Snoose who stirred and then settled back. "It's not time yet, Johnny," he said softly).

The farmer's boy laughed wildly at this adventure with the engineer high on the side, almost the pinnacle of the stack. Johnny helped him gather the eggs. Then he climbed to the top and stood there, his body dark above the topmost cap bundles.

The sun cleared a thunderhead. In the sudden brightness, Johnny's black hair, his lifted face, his shirt and greasy trousers were soaked with a dark crimson like that of the red oaks in the valley. Below him the dust over the separator billowed in smoky waves in which Alb's oil-smeared cap was as sooty as a coal. Sun ran liquid red on the polished tines of the forks. The grainmen hoisted the bags on the farther side. And back at the straw-carrier the pilers were looking hopefully at each other: "Quitting time pretty soon?"

Beyond the twisting drive belt was the engine, plumed with a bent feather of smoke and steamy with wisps from the pop-off. Over west in the bloody sun the valley was cherry red misted with purple grape. Beyond the hills lay Norton's and the flats. "It's yours, if you take it." The words of the men returned to him. He shivered. This valley, now, this farm whereon his engine chugged—from the tip of the stack, it was like a small world there below, fiery with evening, lush with the richness of harvest. "It is yours, if . . ."

It was time to unhitch the teams for dinner and bring the engine to a stop. Already the pitchers were stabbing their forks down. Above the diminishing squeal of tin against iron from the separator there came a harsh clatter of wheels.

A spring wagon almost bounced into the yard. Rims and spokes blurred with dust, rubbled into silence. A raspy voice bellowed, "Whoa, there, you bitches!"

Out of the wagon sprang Bory Tetzell. With him were Lornas and Mosey Fritz and three lean-jawed men from his crew. Heinie Beerwagon, wiping the sweat from his neck, saw them first and quickly jammed the handkerchief into his pocket. He thumbed another pitcher's ribs; waved at

Alb and pointed. Leisurely he slid from the stack and picked up a neck yoke.

There was ugliness on Bory's face, ugliness that moved under the heavy whiskers. Only the scar was naked—naked and twitching in the stubble of hair. Mosey, pudgy as ever, walked as if he'd lost his heels and trod on pointed stones. Lornas advanced with caution in his movements, his face fox-sly.

Johnny was near the engine when they came. He stiffened when he saw them; his eyes hardened, guessing why Bory was here. Suddenly he was light on his feet as gossamer down.

Bory strode up truculently. "What the hell you mean, breaking up my run?" he demanded, sweeping his arms as though he'd brush Johnny and the Red Star into a ditch the next second. "Think you'll get Norton's run, eh? Why, I'll bust you into so many pieces, you'll——"

"Will you?" Johnny stepped close to him. Between them lay an elbow length of hate. "I'll have something to say about that. I'm not asking you whether I can take Norton's job."

Hands curved and arms crooked, tall as Bory himself, Johnny waited, the muscles of his arms tight against the cloth of his shirt. There was no need for explanation; no need to say Norton hadn't asked him. This was something to square between himself and Bory, beyond a setting of grain or a run of jobs.

Disconcerted, surprised for a moment into hesitancy, Bory hulked there. Remembering the kid at Norton's, the kid he'd knuckled into bloodiness, he had confidently anticipated cringing, slack-limbed fright. Wasn't he Bory Tetzell? But there was little cringing here, only a thorny edge of defiance, eyes that were pitch-black with the dark fire of hate. There was no more fear in them than in marbles. But beyond hate there was contempt, undisguised scorn that Bory couldn't avoid.

They searched each other as if their eyes were measuring sticks. Bory's men crowded in. Mosey's hand slid down and found the knife in his pocket.

It was Lornas, wary as a fox, who yelled, "Watch yourself, there, Bory!" and nudged Mosey's elbow warningly.

Bory's glance shifted with the quickness of a snake's tongue. He took in what Johnny couldn't see: the neck yoke in Heinie Beerwagon's grasp, the long wrench in Alb's fingers, the crew alert to spring forward.

"If you start something, Bory," Heinie was saying gently, "be damned sure you can finish it." He hefted the neck yoke as easily as a willow stick. The iron circles clanged as they fell against the metal hasps. Steam hissed angrily about the piston.

"Don't need your help, Heinie," Johnny snapped, tensing for fight, blind to everything but the red scar jerking in the whiskered face in front of him. "Me and Bory—there's an old account between us hasn't been paid."

But Bory, experienced in the ways of losing knuckle skin, had mixed in enough of threshers' squabbles to know when he was outnumbered. Without a word he spun around, almost knocking Mosey aside; he returned to the buggy. With suspicious backward looks, Mosey and the men followed. But Lornas walked at Bory's side.

Whip in hand Bory called gruffly, "Keep away from Norton's, Johnny——" He paused and then continued deliberately, "Schwartz. You got a big crew back of you now. But I'll meet you sometime—alone."

The lash crackled; harness jingled as the team shouldered forward. Dust and a bend in the road took the buggy out of sight.

"The bastard!" Johnny's exclamation mixed with the hiss of steam. He swallowed; the crackly sound of throat cartilage was loud in his ears. "The dirty, unwashed bastard! I'll show him. Why, nothing'll stop me now. Nothing."

On that day was spilled into Johnny's blood an urgency that lashed him forward without mercy, without hope almost, with disregard for Lilice even, so that when her red lips came to haunt him, he tried to erase memory with a steady squint at the steam gauge, or a busy inspection of chaff in the tailings elevator or cockleshells in the grain spout.

He hurried the men into pitching while the cold of dawn still whitened the grass. Sweaty-browed he cursed because the space between sunup and sundown was short as an inchingworm. He yelled the crew into sweating by the yellow of lanterns candle-pointing the dark. When Heinie demurred, he blasphemed him into submission; when pitchers, working on the basis of neighborly exchange of help, threatened to quit and break the run, he wheedled them grimly back to the forks. He swore at Alb and called Snoose names. If a hotbox delayed the cylinder for one moment, the crew leaned back to acknowledge the profanity sparkling through the air.

"Brimstone," Heinie opined one day. "You can almost smell it. In two minutes that Johnny loses about five Sundays of religion."

Balefully the whistle screeched over the ridges: "Sacks, sacks!" and the grainmen hastened; "Water, water!" and Snoose broke a dream of Em'ly to scratch up bucket and hose, and strap the blacks into a trot; "Bundles, bundles!" until the neighbors sighed, "Not even the pitchers sweat enough for him now."

He took one look at the three piles of grain in Old Man Dresser's yard— the three piles gathered achefully by the three daughters, Gretelein, Seligkind and Amaria; three heaps of grain that meant a ribbon on a hat and lace on a sleeve and beauty for lackluster souls. One sour glance Johnny gave them and ordered, "Thrash 'em like any other! Dump that grain with the rest!"

When Old Man Dresser murmured querulously, "Save something for mine girls," Johnny growled, "I can't waste time on a quart of wheat. If you want your stacks thrashed, I'll thrash 'em; if not, I'll pull out."

And Gretelein, Seligkind and Amaria, peering from a window, turned and saw in one another's faces the weeviling of the year's harvest, the dusk of their lives, bleak as the bareness of a frosted tree. "Now Pa'll take all of it; now we'll have to ask him for money; there'll be none for us." None for a ribbon . . . a lace . . . a ruffle. Almost with hatred they clumped back to their pots and kettles, deprived even of that which they scarcely had.

The crew would have stabbed their forks into the bundles and quit before another shovelful of wheat had spouted into the sack, if a grudging respect had not held them—respect for bullish tenacity and strength apparently inexhaustible, for all that it was tapped by the hour, the keg overturned but never emptied. "Aw sheets, what can you do with such a feller?" Alb wanted to know in quizzical despair. Heinie agreed.

Let a shaker arm break, Johnny was first to burrow into the dust and chaff of the separator. If the boiler needed fixing during an afternoon of drizzle weather, he crawled dourly into the firebox, hot as it still was with the remainder of the forenoon's roar and flame; he'd come out, hair plastered blackly with sweat, red as a steamed beet of arms and face.

If the engine sank rim out of sight in a swamp road, Johnny shouted aside the offer to hitch a team to the axles: "To hell with that! Get some timbers and chop down some tamaracks. We'll pry her out," and was first to put the lever of his back against the sucking mud, letting the fireman handle the steering wheel.

Sometimes, though, he half-raised fist to the zenith and muttered, "Stop me, will ya? Devil grab it!" as though he had a private wrangle with God. The crew grumbled but stayed.

But in intervals of weariness so deep that slumber was almost a heaviness upon the marrow, Johnny slumped head in elbow against the steering wheel or toolbox, too drawn of vigor to care that the fireman noted him or that the crew observed him. Sometimes in a wreath of steam from a pet cock he'd see Lilice and long tiredly for her arms as one in a far country for the sweetness of home. But he remained where he was. She waited for him only a township away, if one numbered ridges. But she was miles from him, if one counted the determination that came with having Norton's shocks in his eye.

At night in eerie sleep he'd hear her cry, "Johnny, what will we do now?" and wake to groan; or from a dream of her cheek against his lips he'd rock into awareness, mumbling drowsily, "Lilice, wait for me!"

He neglected her until she fled to the sanctuary of tears in her room; until Mrs. Rose pleated worry into the folds of her sewing; until Lena pared her scrutiny into even greater sharpness. (Lilice putting her fingernail on the months in the almanac.)

He'd almost groan into a clenched fist, "Lilice, what am I doing to you?" But he'd shrink from reproach and nourish the torture of doubt. "If Norton doesn't give me the job—if they find out—laugh, that's what they will, from Jenny's Peak to Mary's Hill." The hand on his forehead would grow hot and he'd long for a sponge of coolness to temper the roil in his skull. At last one morning while he was filling an oil cup, he tamped grease firmly into the cap, his mind made up. "Let it be so then. The justice of peace won't ask questions I can't answer." Even this decision brought little relief, however.

In all this confusion of straw and chaff and kernels of grain, Snoose wrapped tranquillity like a blanket about him. Though Johnny's whistle made him scramble more than once, he refused to break one bubble of his reveries over Em'ly. For all that Johnny scowled and the crew titteringly ribbed him, he let his gray-stone eyes take in distance as if it were timber and rock, and out of it he would build gable and window, wall and rooftree wide as the cupola of heaven. "Thrashing will keep; Em'ly won't," he told Johnny once when he was behind in work.

He merely chuckled when Johnny rumbled back, "Thrashing won't keep, not in my rig."

At Mr. Musser's Snoose was about as useful as a pitchfork with a broken handle, Alb snorted. He idled at the pump, looking about for Em'ly. He hung at the kitchen door where Em'ly, darting birdlike in and out, fed him crisp and new-baked butter cookies. The crew laughed and twitched at his trousers.

Heinie observed, "Good thing for Snoose those blacks are the fastest around here, or we'd prob'ly have to spit in the boiler to keep the water up."

But Johnny pried Snoose away with a sour, "Want to hook the hose to the teakettle, Snoose? Next thing you know, we'll be wasting time waiting for you. Stop snoosin' around."

When they threshed at Mr. Haber's, across the creek from the Musser place, Snoose paddled through the water, autumn-cold as it was, to sit with Em'ly and make of silence a burning conversation under early starlight. The Haber boys were searching in the bankside willows for a strayed heifer. They caught sight of Snoose in midstream, swimming easy as a muskrat. The pale afterglow on the water was broken into ripples about his shoulders as he swam, his head turned back to see how the hollowed length of basswood log, into which he'd piled his clothes, was following him. It did. At the end of a piece of twine he'd filched from Mr. Haber, it followed him doglike behind. He climbed ashore, his body white in the growing dusk, and slowly pulled the log in. One stocking was gone; the trousers were wet to the knees but his shirt and shoes were dry. In the exhilarating warmth of clothes over skin damp but briskly red from the cold water, he tied his shoestrings. The last the Haber boys saw of him, he was loping toward the Mussers', singing, "I Had Fifteen Dollars in My Inside Pocket."

The Habers told the story with variations the next day. The crew guffawed but more gently than usual. They laughed in understanding rather than in derision, as if in Snoose each saw, almost enviously, something of the wild, coltish and unbridled imagination that once was his own but which was now safely haltered and stabled, a gelding of lost achievements.

Johnny grinned in spite of himself. For once he said little about Snoose's droopiness that afternoon. But his mirth was brief. He chewed over the bitter reminder that Snoose would have a church to marry Em'ly, and the colored leaves of autumn. For Lilice there'd be a quick buggy trip to Mary's Hill and the justice of the peace. Folks would laugh; they always did over that which was none of theirs. But they'd laugh *with* Snoose walking dog-blind into love; they'd laugh *at* Johnny hiding love like a wound. And that made all the difference. When he thought of the Pastor, anger boiled.

Then Norton actually came, and came to say, "Ain't going to be bullied into paying a cent more; not by Tetzell, at least. Can you thrash for me in a couple of weeks? I got mostly stacks this year. You'll need a crew that'll stick."

Johnny lowered his head grimly. Nothing is going to stop me. Nothing, he thought. "I'll make it, or there'll be hell to pay," he told Norton. And with the blacksnake of his energy drove team and teamster until the neighbors wondered how long he'd last.

He startled them by threshing on Sunday, which, as everyone with a hair of sense on his head knew, was not far from cursing God to His face. They all remembered the story Old Man Fleischer was fond of telling—the story of Kasper Hofman, a neighbor in the early days, a churchless man and rimful of iniquity, who insisted upon cradling on Sunday. When a storm arose, threatening to sprinkle his wheat, and thunder rampaged in the valleys, he shook his fist at the clouds and profaned the Sabbath air. And then it happened. A long curling twist of God's wrath, red as a heated poker, felled him with a roar. When his wife and children came, there he was, changed to solid stone, muscle and finger and bone, all coal-black rock, the sickle stuck in his heart. So fast was it embedded that no one had the strength to move it. He was buried with the blade in his heart, iron and stone together. He was buried in his own pasture. Though sod had long since flattened the mound, Old Man Fleischer could take you to the very spot.

"Laugh, if it's funny to you," Aunt Phrena told Kurt. "I won't stay on this place if Johnny ever thrashes on Sunday here." The Pastor, beard twitching, got down his handbook and the homiletics for a sermon on the evils of blasphemy on the Sabbath.

Johnny bluntly told the crew over the meat and gravy of a dinner meal, "We're behind, that's all there is to it. Until we finish this run, we'll thrash every Sunday from now on."

The buttered bread Alb was dousing in his coffee slipped from his fingers into the cup. It floated raggedly, brown and flecked with golden disks. The strawmen growled over their potatoes. Said Mr. Peiser, aghast, "We got Lord's Supper at church next Sunday. I can't come." Trouble salted the cabbage at the table.

Johnny speared a piece of meat firmly. "Glad you're speaking up. This exchange of work—it's all right for small jobs and neighbors. It won't do for me. Just when we get rolling smoothly, Peiser's got to go to church, Fleischer has to fix fence and Schimmel gets a bellyache. You all go home and to hell with the rig. No siree!" Johnny gulped coffee stubbornly. "From now on, I'm hiring a crew. I'll pay five cents more than any thrasher in the hills. You go where the rig goes and you work when I say so, or you get fired. If you want orders, ask me, and nobody else. I'm doing the thrashing around here."

Bob Fleischer and Mr. Bachmann quit that hour and the Nussbaum boys wanted to. "Not going to be bossed by a kid that can't shave decent yet," Mr. Bachmann growled. "He's not a kid exactly," he amended his statement quickly. "He's not twenty-one yet, though." But most of the men agreed with Johnny and stayed. The Nussbaum boys finally grumbled themselves into acceptance.

Thereafter the crewmen regarded Johnny's dark face with something like awe. The valley jiggled with excitement. "Did you hear? His own crew and he works them rib-hungry. The man is crazy. A shower was coming up and he thrashed till eleven o'clock at Whiteland's; wanted to go on, but Whiteland cooled him off. Crazier than a peahen, that's what he is."

And Old Man Fleischer told how he stood on a hill one evening at dusk and looked down into Mr. Schimmel's yard where the engine troubled the air with a witch's tail of sparks. He swore he saw two red devils at the whistle cord and all hell flowing from the smokestack. "The smell," he vowed; "it was straight from the Pit."

Johnny smiled grimly when he heard about this talk. "I've got them," he'd think. "Got 'em crawling to me." But the exultation left him like a boy grown old before his time, sad and weary long before growing wise. "Oh, Lilice, Lilice . . ."

Sometimes the grainmen and the pitchers and Snoose from his tank wagon peered at the engine in the late dusk—the engine with scarlet in its throat, the glare of fire under its belly and the flicker of drawn flame wavering on the water barrel or the toolbox. And above the drivers they'd see Johnny crouching darkly at the steering wheel. The weird yellowish eye of a lantern hung from a support rod at his side and spread an unholy nimbus about his shoulders. His body swayed with the rhythm of the engine but his flesh and bone were taut. They knew that, standing where he was, he was no farther away than their own ribs, so ready was he with curved fingers to reach for throttle or whistle pull: "Bundles, bundles! Water! Sacks, sacks!"

Among the crew animosity, leavened with caution, piled like straw at the end of the carrier: anger flashed like a whetted blade, a blade sheathed in sullenness. But hour by hour the cylinder had its greedy fill of stem and fecund head (the strength of summer's sun, the resistless warmth of earth); the straw heaped up; the grain spout belched its kernels into the sack. Stacks vanished, whole settings of them. Straw piles grew. And Johnny threshed . . . threshed. . . .

22

They arrived at Mr. Jobel's in the ridges on a Wednesday. His place lay six miles north and east of Mary's Hill—a ragged section, gullied with ravines and jutted with the sharp, upthrust knees of morainic peaks. It wasn't easy country for the rig. The engine drew deep breaths and flung them out in slow tumbling rushes of smoke as it lugged the separator over the steep narrow roadways—"cow paths," Alb called them. It was hardest for Snoose and the water team. Most of the sloos were dry now. He hauled the water from an oozy pool in the tamarack swamp a mile and a half away.

"Damn glad we're not far from the end of the run," Johnny said to the fireman. "I'm going to finish by Saturday or bust a flue. Monday we move out to the flats. And I wish to Judas Proust Snoose would grease up his hind end and get that water here. We're down to burning again." He rushed to the platform. Savagely the whistle cracked over the hills.

A minute later, Snoose swung the blacks up on the trot. Water splashed from the tank. "I whipped 'em up," he explained, hitching back on the lines. "It's a long pull to the swamp hole."

"That team is fast enough to bring the tank here, if you'd limber yourself." Johnny glowered at him. "I don't want to have to stop the rig on account of you, Snoose. Not too much time left between now and Monday. We move to the flats then."

The water when it came was roily and lifeless from stagnation, hardly fit for use. The engine "foamed," the pipes hiccuped and threatened to clog, and the hand of the steam gauge pointed uncertainly. More and more the separator jerked and grunted as though spitefully glad to find its steamy master weak and diarrheic this day.

Johnny found Mr. Jobel and ordered two rain barrels hauled to the engine. They would store a small amount of emergency water and so hold off delay for a short time, if that became necessary. "Don't depend on the barrels, though," Johnny warned Snoose. "They won't keep us going long."

That evening he drove into the Rose yard. In the twilight his face was streaked with sweat and grease. Hearing the wheels Lilice broke off talk with Mrs. Rose and Adam and rushed outside.

He drew her up on the buggy seat. "Lilice, Punkin," he said in a quiet fashion, "be ready next Sunday night. We'll see the justice at Mary's Hill."

Blindly she caught at his shoulder. She hid her face against his oily shirt. "Oh, Johnny. You're sure——"

"I've got to hurry back. We broke a casting. Splies at the blacksmith shop is fixing it."

"You're sure about this?" she persisted.

"I don't know," he answered tiredly. "I only know what must be done."

"Oh, Johnny, if you should feel sorry about this later, I——"

"Sorry?" He left a smear of grease when he leaned his cheek against hers. "As long as I've got you, I'll never be sorry." To himself he was saying, It is done now; whatever happens, it is done. As he rattled away he looked weary and as one who has made a hard bargain but isn't sure how much he has lost.

That next afternoon before lunch Snoose was late with the water again. The whistle shrieked commandingly through the draws and coulees, ragged and short-winded with Johnny's impatience. Snoose heard it half a mile from the tamarack swamp. But all his hurry against distance and the drag of rocky slants, all his strapping of the team, all of Johnny's fretting, all of man's fretting, for that matter—what are these to Time? What are these to the finger's length of miles between the Here and the There—Time, the misnamed, unraveling its blind sequentials, ripping the sheaf and husking the core in the inevitable Today, scorning man's Tomorrows which *will be* but never *are*. Snoose yelled, "Giddap, there!" and yelled against the swing of Pleiades, the tilt of Saturn, the sweep of Mars his red, malignant way.

Johnny prowled about the engine as if seeking a loose nut or an empty oil cup he could rage at. The extra barrels emptied to dregs. The auxiliary tank gurgled and went dry. With a malevolent curse he glanced at the sagging water glass. Then reluctantly he stopped the machine, every grate and shudder of the slowing mechanisms a thorn scratching his flesh. He waited. The engine hissed.

With the team on the run, Snoose wheeled the tank wagon into the yard. "I got stuck in the mud," he gasped, driving beside the engine. "I tried a new place and——"

In a fury of unreasoning, unthinking rage, Johnny stormed, "Mooning again. Devil grab it, get that hose unlimbered! It's not enough to have breakdowns. You have to be late with the water."

"Johnny, I drove as——" Snoose was beginning but Johnny bellowed, "Get that water going and shut up!" Suddenly, as if Snoose's slenderness, stubborn as Johnny's own, for all its pliancy, were more than an eye could hold and retain its untroubled depths, Johnny swung away and left. Quickly he walked to the separator. There, perched on the edge of a grain box, he thrust his hands into the cool flow of wheat. But there was no coolness here. Now and again he flicked a cockleshell from among the kernels and spitefully pitched it away. The stacks were already a quarter down but he was too irritated to notice. This quarreling with Snoose, his friend . . .

After a while the box swayed and Snoose bobbed up on the opposite side. The kernels in Johnny's fist snapped away. "What the Devil!" he barked. "Can't quit monkeying around the separator, can you? Stick to your tank!"

Snoose returned Johnny's smoldering gaze tranquilly, frankly, as if to say that "mooniness" held a firmer basis than "earthiness"; he knew when to wag a tongue and when not.

Johnny lifted from his seat as though touched by a hot match. His lips pursed. Anger like a currycomb raked over him. If it were anybody but Snoose . . . He jumped from the box. With short, jerky steps he returned to the engine. At the tank wagon he touched a horse's nose for a cool moment. As he rounded the driver, he saw Snoose, water bucket in his hand, climbing the side of the stack to the thirsty pitchers above him.

The fireman clanked at the front fire door, raking coals. Johnny glanced at the tank. He heard a sound of water and stopped as if ax-struck. His heels dug into the grass. On the ground lay the end of the hose, fallen there after it had slipped out of the barrel. The rest of the hose curled up into the wagon tank. It was siphoning its roily contents into a spreading pool. Water gurgled at the hose end, bubble-flecked. Earth suckled greedily as at a nipple.

Something clanged in his skull like iron banging against iron. Brightness snapped, whether outside himself or inside, he couldn't be sure. Red anger hung on his lids like frost and blinded him. "Devil grab it all to hell!" His voice was almost a scream. He flung the hose at the tank. Water squirted fanwise. He started for the separator, rage against Snoose burning in him.

Dimly he heard a wild yell—a pitcher's yell. And what he saw froze through his rage to halter momentarily tendon and muscle. All the dust of cylinder and straw rack seemed to shake into his sight for an instant, so that what happened moved hazily: Snoose on the ground, broken, kicking, trying to rise and falling limply, one hand lifted and already streaming redly . . . the belt still flopping above him as if relieved of a weight it had just tossed carelessly aside . . . Alb yelling . . . men crawling and sliding down the stacks so recklessly they brought their pitchforks with them . . . Snoose flopping grotesquely there like a bundle of old clothes, limply animate. . . .

In hours of desperate reproach afterward Johnny wasn't clear how a leg moved or a finger crooked. Through anger that was like a fume he sensed that he was running to the engine, that he was driving steam against momentum, bringing wheel and cog to a squealing standstill; that there was a cry within him far behind the crags of anger, warm as blood, warm as comrade's blood—"Not Snoose!" Snoose, close to him as a shirt; closer; near as his own skin. "Not Snoose!" But a crimson fan winnowed his anger; the boy cry grew fainter. . . . He rushed forward . . . heard cries: "Fell back . . . fell into the belt . . . hit the feeding table . . . ribs caved in. . . ."

He shouted, "What the hell's the trouble now?"

"Quick, Johnny." Somebody grabbed his arm. "Your team. He's got to get to a doctor fast. Your horses——"

"What?" he demanded. "Unhook my——"

"He's bleeding bad. Our teams are slow. If he don't get to a doctor fast, he might——"

With a frenzied swing Johnny jerked away. Suddenly as if from a far height he looked down on the partly threshed setting of grain, the gold of its kernels showing through the dross of straw; looked down on Snoose—

Snoose, eyes half-closed, his lips trying to say what his heart no longer could . . . lying there on the autumn-cropped grass. . . .

Alb jostled his arm. "Quick, quick, boy!" Johnny blinked. All at once, it seemed that there were two of him, one crying lonely as a child, "Snoose, Snoose," the other stiffening into cold deliberate purpose under the clamor of the all that had gone before, the years of the weevil, the empty years, the dry-husk years crying for the kernel, the years of Schwartz and the loneliness, and now the sweet respite of the thresher. . . .

Then he was shouting, "No. My team stays hooked."

"Johnny, if he don't get——"

"No. I've got thrashing to do." Almost blindly he glared at them. "Hook up a grain team, there. And Arty Nussbaum—you get on the tank wagon." He swayed as if drunk.

"Johnny——"

"My team stays on the tank wagon. Get your own." And seeing them stare, he shouted, "Bundles. There's thrashing to do. What the hell are you waiting for?"

Through a kind of fog that might have been the dust of chaff and stem and kernel husk, he ran to the engine. He heard someone yelling, "Bundles, bundles," without realizing for an instant that it was himself. His hands were on the whistle pull before the steam hissed against the pistons, before a cog moved. "Start up, start up!" shrieked the whistle. The wheels began to turn. Dust fell. The cylinder brightened with motion.

There was a great roaring in his ears. Any minute now, the seams of his skull would split. Dully from his position he saw Mr. Jobel driving and a spring buggy move past, a dark box like a coffin . . . in it the white face of Snoose, a hand lifted. Was it his own voice, or was it another's, Snoose's voice, faint as a boy's calling his cows home at dusk, "Johnny, Johnny, don't blame yourself; don't . . . "? The hand fell. "Em'ly . . ." (That must be Snoose calling, he thought helplessly.) "Em'ly, the echoes over the hill . . ."

In desperation he jerked the whistle. "Bundles, bundles . . . hurry, hurry." *And Time, the great cylinder, whirled and snarled into the meat of bundles; and the kernels fell.*

The spring buggy moved out of sight. Somewhere he was sure he heard a sobbing, as though for someone who would never return. But there were no tears on his cheeks. His face, pale as the steam that curled from a pet cock at his feet, was flint and granite set toward the black smokestack and the separator beyond.

Part 4

THE SEASON OF
GRAIN IN THE HARVEST:
THE EAR AND THE HUSK

1

THAT winter the Johnny Blacks lived on the small place Mr. Whiteland's son had farmed for two years but had deserted for a job in Fergus. The house was of log though wintertight in roof and floor. It was like a rectangular box partitioned into a small bedroom and a larger room which was kitchen and parlor, with a loft overhead. Lilice had four openings to anywhere—a trap door in the ceiling near a wall ladder, another in the floor cellarward, a bedroom door and an outside door into the yard and the clearing and the road north that led to the Rose farm and home.

Here they brought such odds and ends of pots and ticks and crockery, his truck and hers, as Mrs. Rose provided and Uncle Herm let them have of the upstairs clutter (though Aunt Phrena gave each piece as one counting heartbeats and fearing the last). It hardly made a wagonload.

What else they needed to keep bone comfortable and stomach eased Johnny bought at the store sale, for Mr. Jimpson, feeling rickety with the "misery" in his joints, decided to quit selling molasses and eight-penny nails and "essence of coffee." "No money in it anyway," he complained. "Everybody got a team and buggy now'days, and lickety-long they drive to Mary's Hill for the stuff they buy. Used to be when they had oxen or they had to walk, they came to my store. Not now. Now they can't get to places fast enough." One day he put counter and shelf and box up for sale, and the post office went to Mr. Whiteland's house until it was moved to Toffman's store north of the District School.

What they didn't find at Mr. Jimpson's sale Johnny bought in Mary's Hill. And so in the bedroom they had a new bed covered with Mrs. Rose's star-pattern quilt. They had a chair from Aunt Phrena's upstairs that banged with a loose rung when anyone sat in it. A new stove glittered near the cupboard shelves on one side of the larger room—the kitchen end, Lilice called it. There was a plumply stuffed, green-and-gray-fabricked couch near a table and a small rack of books on the other side—the parlor end, she said. (Lilice read in the volumes occasionally; Johnny scarcely thumbed the pages.)

They could afford this much, at least, Johnny told her. It had been a profitable year. Even the neighbors admitted that. "Cripes, that Johnny must have salted a mite of money away in the bank. Look at the runs he thrashed here in the hills and then all those jobs out on the flats and north of Mary's Hill. . . . And Norton's, too, don't forget. Jippers, who'da thought Barewolf's Johnny would get such a big job? Bory Tetzell nearly cracked a flue; says he's after Johnny's hide and he'll tan it yet. . . . Lornas cooled him down this year, I hear tell. . . ."

"Well, Johnny didn't finish sooner than anyone else," objected Mr. Nussbaum. "He ended in snow just like Tetzell or Barewolf used to."

"Sure, but look how many more bushels he knocked out for the farmers; more'n Tetzell and that new rig—what's his name?—put together. . . . Big year for Johnny, yep." They gossiped at church. "But that was last year. Who'll want to hire him to thrash for them this year?" they wanted to know with a quick glance at the cemetery.

By Christmas Johnny and Lilice had been settled, the cobwebs swished from the corners, the mouse smell gone, and the last spider driven into patient hiding. Mrs. Rose spent the holiday with them. Though Lilice and Johnny strayed into patches of silence neither disturbed, and let the tea cool and the fire snap while Mrs. Rose talked, there was cheer in the way they joined her in two or three thin carols (the rig safely dead-cold beside the slab-board barn, the season of crashing wheels and the hurt of iron to flesh over now for a season of forgetting). But then Johnny remembered other Christmases and other evenings at the Marchens' and stopped. His throat was rough as a sieve. It hurt, he said.

Though it was early in that December when they carted their things to the log house, it hadn't been until back there in mid-November that Johnny decided to take the place and had asked Mr. Whiteland. After muddling through many hours of chaff and steam Johnny told Lilice about the plan. He couldn't tell her that sometimes (while the engine rhythmically throbbed into the flesh of his thigh as he leaned against a driver), sometimes he wondered about setting up a house for himself: the nailing of a bracket to a wall, the painting of a floor, the putting of a field to plow and the prosiness of a shirt wet from an afternoon's grunting over the plow handles. From these he edged aside a little. Not that he couldn't do them, or wouldn't. "I'm not afraid to work," he assured himself, rubbing his calluses. "For Lilice I'd grub a hundred acres."

And so he would. Duty-bound he'd sweat over the stumps, or any job, for that matter. But he'd never do this from choice, not while the rig invited him to put a hand on the steering wheel. Give him the rig, the flash of sun on a flywheel, the *slip-slap* of belts, the mist that floated with smoke from the stack when the wind was right (sweat from the iron belly of the engine) and he'd put liveliness into the crook of an elbow, and shoulder and hip against the biggest setting of stacks in Pockerbrush, and laugh. The engine was different from plow or house. It was alive, some way. It was a throbbing, almost breathing entity of steel and iron, warm and sweaty as he was often warm and sweaty. However, had anyone accused him, he would have denied this with a heat not far from cherry red. Nevertheless he made a bargain with Mr. Whiteland. For the next year the place would be his.

When he told her (she was still at home then) Lilice said, "A roof of our own and nobody to care if the dog runs in." She sighed deeply as in relief, and wound on her finger the wedding ring, still so new there was no mark on her flesh.

"It's not much," he said, somehow embarrassed, "but I'm not asking you to stay there more'n this year. I'll see to that."

She kissed him. At his sudden broken "Oh, Lilice, if I didn't have to remember—" she coaxed, "Hush now, my dearest. You look all tired out. When we get home, our home, I'll put you to bed for a week. You'll just sleep." She touched the tip of his nose—and hid worry, that remote cousin of fear which in its nagging is remote only in kinship; worry that projected itself from the gables of yesterday, shadowlike into this hour; worry over Aunt Phrena's dire words; worry . . .

Earlier still in that autumn (in the first part of November and the middle part of October after the accident), he had threshed on the flats. The rig left a trail of straw behind it. But even when he had miles between himself and the hills, he felt (as if he'd been there) the shock and the sorrow that stirred the valley as a rising wind does, fluttering angrily opinion and comment like rags on a bough.

"Lets that poor boy lay there, and his own good team hooked to the tank wagon. Old Jobel's nags, they're good but no pacers. . . . Crazy, thrashing-crazy, that's what he is. . . . Seems like a nice man. . . . Oh, I don't know; wild, he is; wild as the devil. . . . Well, get him away from a steam engine, he seems like a sensible person. But with the throttle in his fist, he's a hard one. . . .

"Killed that boy just like he'd stood over him with an ax . . . terrible, terrible. . . . The boy *was* hurt pretty bad. . . . Horsewhip him off the place, by jippers, if I had my way. . . . Such a nice feller, that Marchen boy. Jobel says all the way to town, the kid kept saying, 'Ain't your fault, Johnny; it's the engine. Ain't your fault.' Out of his head then. But when Jobel got in sight of Mary's Hill, well, the boy turned his face aside and . . . awful, ain't it, though? Ya . . .

"That poor little Musser girl, Em'ly; she just bawls and bawls; wearing herself thin as a shingle. . . . Old Musser says he'll take a flail to his stacks before he'll thrash with Barewolf's rig again. . . . And poor Mrs. Marchen— did you hear that Phrena Barewolf went right over and took care of her? Ya . . . Well, Young Doctor Wilson says the Marchen boy was all busted inside. Doc says even if he'd been right there at the rig, he couldn't have done a thing. Internal hem'rage, or whatever lingo the doc calls it when they bleed to death inside . . . awful, awful . . . Yep, couldn't have saved him . . . terrible . . . 'ain't your fault' . . . awful . . . the engine . . . Johnny Black . . ."

When the news came to Aunt Phrena, she let the supper plate she was washing slip back into the water. "Ach, in my graying hairs, I hear it again," she murmured. "Somebody dead and Schwartz mixed up in it." She brought the Book but found little comfort in it that night. Tears spotted the pages. Where they fell the paper drew together and bulged like a small scab.

The next day she shook the folds of her dress straight and went over to comfort Mrs. Marchen. Sophie was there with her children. But it was Aunt Phrena who bound Mrs. Marchen's sleeves with ribbons of dark material and hung a veil black as night about her hat. And it was she herself who pulled from the oven the bread that was baking and saved it from crusting to the hardness of bone.

Mr. Marchen glowered at her, anger in his limp. But Sophie put a firm hand on his shoulder. "It is hard now, Pa. But a grudge—he that carries it, he's the one that gets hurt most of all."

Kurt said to Uncle Herm, "Now that it's done with, there's no sense in talking about blame. Doctor Wilson says the fastest team couldn't have saved Charley." (Now that his ears were stopped with silence and earth smothered his breath, and no crack of the sunset he loved squeezed through under his lids, now they called him "Charley" respectfully, not "Snoose.")

Uncle Herm rubbed an ear on the pillow. "Nothing you can do about bad luck," he said tiredly. He peered at the quilts about his knees. "Nothing, except wonder why it comes. It's too bad this had to happen to Johnny. Too bad."

But Lilice, a dead weight growing in her breast, clamored inwardly, "Please, God, don't let me hear about it; don't let me think," and ran to the ampleness of her mother's lap. There she wept as one who knows at last that the hounds of fear are unleashed and howling in pursuit.

"Lilice, it isn't Johnny." Mrs. Rose tried to comfort her.

"No; but it's worse this way," she choked. "They were such friends. Brothers couldn't have been closer."

"Punkin, it is more than that, you crying this way." She raised Lilice's chin and through the tears searched Lilice's eyes. "So you think you can hide secrets from me? Adding trouble onto trouble for yourself. Or do you want Lena to find out and tell me first?"

"Oh, Mother, I'm——" Crouching at Mrs. Rose's knee, she let sorrow dash like flood waves over her heart. . . .

The day before the funeral, those of the crew that were neighbors or acquaintances of the Marchens, grim-mouthed and grumbling, had decided what they'd do. "We don't work tomorrow. Even if he ain't going to the burying, some of us got respect for the dead. We're going." They were threshing at the Livermores', just south of Norton's Four Oaks Farm. A quarter of a mile east lay the Valley shore. There the river curled among rounding hills on which trees grew sparsely, and through draws in which were hidden meadows and small farmsteads.

When the crew came to him, Johnny said calmly, "All right. I'm not holding you back." He spoke gruffly. "Livermore here thinks we can get help for tomorrow. Go, if you feel so about it."

"Damn right we do!" one of the Nussbaum boys growled. The crew turned away. Alb and Heinie teetered on their heels, doubtful what to do next.

As he stepped from the platform Johnny stumbled. He caught at the edge of the toolbox for balance. How he'd lined up the rig that day, he wasn't sure. Long after the belt had ceased its flopping slaps, he had stood, the throttle in his fist, staring at, but not seeing, the straw pushing up the incline of the carrier. The *chug-a-chug* of the engine, echoing so stoutly among the ridges, was pressed down and weak now, a feeble coughing in the immensity of the Valley. He hardly noticed the smeary cloud brushes thickening into solid banks and threatening autumn rains.

"The way that Johnny feller looks," muttered Alb uneasily, "'tain't good for him out here alone."

"I know it." Heinie's broad features softened. "Tough on him." Alb agreed. But neither uttered what the crew was saying.

That afternoon rains sprinkled field and yard, and the matter was settled. Those of the crew that were going bundled up and got ready to return to the hills.

Alb found Johnny poking among the rubbish of the toolbox. "Better come along anyways, Johnny," he wheedled gently. "This ain't easy to face, but running away won't——"

"I'm not running away," Johnny flared. "My job is thrashing. I'm doing it."

"Sure, sure, Johnny." Alb sighed gustily. "Judas, I didn't mean to ruffle ya! I jest thought——"

"It's no use asking me." Johnny huddled down on the platform. "It's not the Pastor so much, nor the churchful of people. It's—it's like Anders Stramff out there alone in the——" He bent his head over the tools. Alb shuffled his feet; wordless at last he joined the others. . . .

It drizzled the afternoon they buried Snoose. Under a canvas stretched over the tender, Johnny watched a tit of moisture grow on the end of a straw, break and fall; grow, break and fall. Here he was alone with the rig on this Valley farm. What remained of his crew was in Mary's Hill. Mr. Livermore and his family were there too. The yard was empty. Long strides of distance separated him from the ridges. But his mind was back there, shrinking from the winding sheets of grief that hung over the log church; from Aunt Phrena's "Ach ya, rain or snow in the open grave, it is a sign that another burial will take place in the congregation soon"; from the figures shuffling under the evergreen tree in the graveyard. Back there was the bitter necessity of giving back to earth what was forever deserted of life. His hand rustled on the canvas.

In the middle of the afternoon the rain stopped. Wind began to break the clouds. Moodily he tramped about the sodden engine. Droplets of water gathering on smeary governor balls or pistonhead glittered in the hot wet sun. Once he thought he heard a bell tolling. But it was only a piece of tin banging hollowly on the separator. He gazed at the near-by hills, small and gopher-pilelike though they were, as if in those folds lay security he could put his hands on, and hold to.

The Livermores returned in time for chores. At supper Mr. Livermore invited him in. "You might as well eat with us. There's a bed upstairs. Guess you haven't slept on a pillow for a good long while. It's going to thunder for sure tonight."

Johnny mumbled his thanks. A wild restlessness dug spurlike at him so that he could hardly wait for the rice-with-raisins Mrs. Livermore brought to end the meal. He went outside. Lightning flickered in the dark southwest. He lighted a lantern and returned to the rig.

He puttered about. He pried off the cover of a grease tub and put it back again. Slouching to the separator, he poked woodenly among the sieves; handled a wrench and laid it down, not sure what it was. In a moment of gazing eastward he thought he saw the curving line of the hilltops. Longing filled him.

He stood for a moment, then blew the flame of the lantern and strode into the darkness. Lightning jumped brightly on the horizon back of him. He crossed the fields. Soon he was conscious of ground rising under his toes. He climbed the first knoll back. Only once did he glance over his shoulder at the window lights of the Livermore house and a single candle point farther westward lost in the Valley. Then he followed sloping ground into a ravine. Shoulders of hills, dark with protective shadow, rose about him. He felt guarded and safe, yet despairingly alone, as if he'd come home to familiar things and found the house empty and the family gone. Tiredness rolled over him like a wheel. He longed to bury his face in grass, in Lilice's lap, in utter forgetfulness.

Lightning stuck a red fork across a cloud. In its flash he saw in the long ravine a distant house, trees scattered on the slants, and a haystack. Thunder grumbled distantly. It might rain again after all, he thought.

In a sheltered place he sank down heavily, as though his pockets were filled with iron. Crooked lances of fire jabbed the darkness, now here, now there. Over him a tree leaned out. He put his hands on the ground. Sod under his fingers . . . sod . . . sod like that which humped up brokenly in the cemetery . . .

"Echoes over the hills," he seemed to hear Snoose say. And all that had grown like a deadly tetter about him in those past months, all the senseless ire, the animosities, all fell flakelike away and left him naked before the blaze of an awfulness that stunned him. Norton's job was his now, would be his as long as he and Norton agreed, yes; but Snoose . . . How many times today, yesterday, the afternoon before, hadn't he looked up at the tank wagon, a grumpy hail on his lips, and had swallowed quickly at seeing Arty bent over the pump handle!

In a rush of desperate mournfulness, childishly cowering before truth, he yearned to slide backward into time: one moment with Snoose again, walking side by side with him over the pasture road, swimming with him, bubbles-over-shoulder in the creek. . . .

Like an animal mortally hurt and seeking respite before death in the solace of grass, he flung himself face downward, his head in the crook of an elbow. "Snoose, Snoose, forgive me!" His fingers curled about grass and fisted. "I couldn't think of anything but the rig and Norton's job. If there is forgiveness, forgive me. . . ." His body shook.

A roar overhead and the storm broke. It crashed over the hills in fire and fury but in no rain. Ropes of lightning swung and twisted crazily across slants of purple sky. There were sudden bursts of flame. White-edged fire ripped the livid grape-purple folds of the sagging night. Roar on roar pounded the sense flat and numb and helpless. (Was it outside him, filling the ravine from rim to rim, or inside him, this turmoil crushing him to the sod?) Cascades of reddish light fell, showers of blurring rose and diamond-white. Bluish arrows stabbed the eyes into blindness.

Rivers of brightness flooded the ravine with fierce, unbearable intensity. The house sprang violently out of the night's black skirts. In the swiftness of a flash, there was the strange whiteness of a gable, the jetty thrust of a chimney, the unalleviated sharpness of a rooftree, windows wild-eyed and crimson with reflected fire. (But no rain . . .no wetness under the lids, only the fire of salt unwept like a barley beard drawn piercingly across the eyeball.)

There was the peculiar way a spurt of lightning wrenched the perspective, made the familiar unfamiliar, bent the lines of the perpendicular so that a barn leaned wildly, a house bulged its walls, a dead tree swayed, wild wind humming in its lifeless branches, a haystack slid down a slope of meadow, hills shouldered up incredibly higher than their wont against a sky startled into whiteness.

Hills jarred with the sky's wrath, rain hurled itself into spatters, crash after crash hammered into the ravine, filling it with tumult . . . tumult like that which cracked and flared in Johnny's head so that, oblivious of thunder without, wracked to earth by eruptive inner weather, he lay, face hidden, wetness on his cheeks, one hand fisted in grass, his body twisting. "Snoose, my friend, my friend Snoose . . ."

2

Of the crew that went home, only Alb and Heinie, Arty and a strawman returned. Enough was enough, they said, and the neighbors agreed. Grimly Johnny hired other pitchers and other bandcutters in Mary's Hill, or where he could find them. His crew was less of Pockerbrush the rest of the year and more of the Valley and the foreign parts beyond. Observing his new crew on the stacks and in front of the cylinder, he wondered whether this was to be his portion, a stranger on his own home paths.

He and Lilice were married the next Sunday. Johnny borrowed a top buggy from Norton. In the drab, unlighted sitting room of the justice of the peace, cluttered with unmatched chairs, a table, a couch and a desk heaped with papers, letters and documents, they joined hands. (No red leaves and crimson bittersweet kernels in the church, no echoes over the hill.) The ring slipped over her knuckle and settled into place. With a birdlike gesture, Lilice lifted his hand and put her lips against the ring on his finger. "I feel—almost safe now," she murmured, sheathed with hope against the jut of danger. Almost . . .

He hugged her in the gladness of one who is unashamed. Afterward they drove to the Rose farm and blunted the spikiness of Lena's inspection by announcing, "We're married. Don't we look it?" Johnny added like a boy come on a visit and not sure of his welcome, "I'd like to stay the night."

In sad understanding, Mrs. Rose nodded, her eyes full of tears. When she shook his hand she whispered, "Don't mind me, Johnny. But I thought it would be different—for Lilice."

His head lowered to hide his face. His hand tightened over hers. He had nothing to say to her. And so began the acceptance of what had to be accepted, wail or jubilation, the smile covering the secret hurt.

Later the door of Lilice's room shut behind them. On a table was a vase of downy gentian, its velvet-blue saw-toothed petals tinged with the color of the lamp. But its freshness was rusted and spotted brown, as if a blight had eaten at it. They were alone with themselves, alone with a shadow that would not leave the room.

Next morning with the sun he returned to the rig. The round of bundles continued. It would, week after week. He told Alb, "I got married last night," and bought a keg of beer for the crew.

To hide his surprise Alb retorted, "Aw sheets, you didn't fool me none." He buried nose and mouth into the foamy head on the glass. "Ah me, I wish I had two bellies for a pony of beer. But you can't drink more than one bellyful at a time, can ya? Hell of a note." Johnny waved a glass in agreement. Tickled along the backbone with the beer, Alb chortled, "Well, how does it feel, having a missis to get the ice off your bed, huh, Johnny?" The crew guffawed over their drink. Arty and Heinie recounted all they'd ever heard about wedding nights. Johnny touched mugs with them but there was the staleness of flat brew on his tongue. His mirth was short and brittle.

Back in the ridges there was a fever of tittle-tattle, of "H'm" and "What do you s'pose?" It was the more pleasant because at first it was unsatisfied. "Justice of the peace," said Mr. Haber. "Just like Bory Tetzell."

"Well, it may be legal but, by jippers, it ain't right," grumbled Mr. Nussbaum. "A member of the congregation behaving so. He's a member, but that's about all, that Johnny Black. No churchgoer."

"Nope," said Mr. Haber. "I don't know what we're coming to, kids acting the way they do. Lookit that Gatha Blumen. Running around with a loafer like that Tetzell boy, Lornas. Bet she never learned that from the Pastor at confirmation school. That Lornas. There's a lout for you."

"Well, whoop-Jinny-and-fall-down!" Mr. Dunkel burst out once, listening until he was ready to explode. "That Johnny now. Folks have gotten married outside the Pockerbrush church before, and I can't see they took any harm from it. At least they don't fight and quarrel any more than those married by the Pastor."

"Don't look right, though," objected Mr. Nussbaum. "A wedding needs a preacher, someway."

There was more gossip that fall, though of a minor sort. To the grief and wailing of Aunt Phrena and Mrs. Edgely and a flock of other ladies, Mr. Erdman announced that he needed a rest and was going away. He had exhausted the pinnacles of emotional valor again and must hurry away south, there to gather new spiritual resources. He would send a brother to labor against their backsliding. As it turned out, the meetinghouse remained unheated all that winter and far into the next years. Aunt Phrena looked for his return almost with the fervor of one expecting the second coming.

Out on the Valley floor Johnny tooted for sacks. As week after week drew autumn nearer winter, he had a puckered satisfaction in jotting figures into his black leather account book, figures that would make Uncle Herm's thin face shine. Even Aunt Phrena couldn't deny the sums that eased away the year's obligations.

The last job finished and the separator clean, Johnny pulled the rig to the empty Whiteland yard and left it near the granary. He raked out the ashes and drained the pipes and called it a year. Soon he'd bring Lilice here; soon now her face at the window would greet him as he came in from the barn. In Mary's Hill he bought a stove, a gesture toward domesticity, and hauled it out to his place—his place he could say now. He pushed it into a dusty corner of the house. It was glittery but cold, waiting for the kindling and the flame.

He came home to Lilice and found the Rose house bedeviled with the hooked, protective jealousy of two pregnant women. Adam escaped to the barn whenever squabbles heated the conversation. There was scorn in Lena's appraisal of Lilice, of Lilice's clumsiness, of Lilice's selfishness. Lena herself was sewing baby clothes now, threading the needle and making stitches from the superior height of one who is completely justified by rite and ceremony. She tossed her head, clearly maintaining, "Really, how you can look *decent* people in the face——" Before her all but speaking disdain, Lilice wilted. Mrs. Rose's look pleaded with Johnny.

On the second night he said firmly, "Tomorrow we move to our place. We'll stop at Uncle Herm's. There's my things to pick up."

The next morning in a raw wind they set off. A meager pile of belongings bumped in the wagon box, Lilice's mostly. Snow hung bitingly in the air. On the way to Uncle Herm's, Lilice said, "I'll stay in the yard and mind the team. You go inside."

"Nope. Too cold for you." He patted her mittened hand. "Aunt Phrena's done the worst she can do to you," he said confidently, not knowing yet what was the worst. "She'll never bother you again. You're my wife and you go where I go."

Kurt welcomed them with gruff friendliness. His bushy brows, thick and long for one not yet far past his majority, drew together compassionately as he looked at Lilice. But Aunt Phrena wasted no more than one glance. She left the dough she was rolling on the cooky board and waddled into the sitting room, closing the door behind her, the folds of all her chins stiff at this outrage.

Lilice held herself rigid but there was sorrow on her lips. Silently Uncle Herm held out his thinning hands to them. The glint of moisture was in his eyes. "Bull wheels of Moses, you look so good and fresh, you two. You smell like outside." His bony Adam's apple jerked. "In this place, I've got nothing but the stink of bottles."

Impulsively Lilice bent and kissed his cheek. Uncle Herm kept holding her hand. "With you, madel, I think Johnny is safe," he said quietly. "That is, unless he's a fool."

Johnny grinned at him. "I know when I'm well off."

While she sat with Uncle Herm, Johnny went upstairs to gather his shirts and pants and the buttonhook. He bundled them up. Into a box he put his loose truck. He was holding a pair of stockings in one hand when the fingers of the other, scrabbling in the drawer, touched something rough. He picked it up. It was a small panel of cedarwood with the name "Brynjolf" scorched in dark letters on it. Letting the stockings slip into the box, he stood there, holding the panel, his eyes clouding. "Brynjolf," he said. Absently his thumbnail followed the smoky B. A foreign name. Like Silenski's. How long ago that had been! Long not in years but in experience, that experience which stretches a moment into a decade and makes of a year no more than a moment. "Brynjolf." That was past too. So many things, button-bright in youth, had been rusted in the tarnish of perception.

Slowly putting the panel aside, he finished packing. He brought his things downstairs, the panel thrust into a jacket pocket. As he passed a window he saw Kurt at the barn. The warmth of the kitchen touched his face. Aunt Phrena had the oven hot for the cookies. He opened the stove. Into the flames he poked the cedarwood panel. Hastily he shut the lid upon the first fierce crackles eating at "Brynjolf."

Uncle Herm's voice rose. "Upstairs, Johnny," he called, "you'll find a chair you can have. It's got a rung loose but it'll do for a starter."

Lilice came and stood in the bedroom doorway. Johnny put a foot on the staircase. As though Uncle Herm's voice had brought her out, Aunt Phrena opened the door of the sitting room. Her face was as one who has struggled with flesh as well as with spirit. "There's a bowl-and-pitcher set upstairs too. It's Herm's. You might as well take that," she offered unexpectedly. There was no generosity in her tone, only a prickly sense of duty. "And there's a water pitcher and a set of glasses. They're mine. And that lamp with the roses on the shade. I won't have it said I didn't give something to the wedding."

Johnny's foot scraped on the stair. He watched Aunt Phrena in a puzzled way. But when Lilice would have thanked her, Aunt Phrena snapped, "I don't want a word from you. I know my duty and I do it. So." Restraint broken, she let flow all the bitterness she had harbored and brooded over these months of seeing Johnny not only escape her but bring to her rooftree the dark crows of suspicion and gossip. She cried, her voise rising, "Na, you two sparrows, you." She almost spat the words. "You think you can trample upon the ways of God, don't you? Live as you please. To think one day I should see my sister's son—poor dear dove—her son marrying outside the church. But you—" she glared at Lilice—"what else can one expect of you? If you had any church in you——"

"That's enough," Johnny shouted, going to Lilice. "You can't help it, can you, Aunt Phrena? Spoiling the very day we go to our home."

"I spoil?" she shrilled. "Na, and what can you say about yourself? Souring my life. All the Pastor learned you——"

"I'm not a kid any more." He put his arm about Lilice.

"Johnny, I——" Lilice turned to him, a trapped kind of look in her eyes.

"Don't let her scare you," he said. "She and her church—they both scold."

"If she's right," breathed Lilice. Her hands were clenched together. A finger pressed the wedding ring as if it were a talisman against calamity.

Goaded by his words, Aunt Phrena cried, "Ach, you are all Schwartz and not my sister's son, no matter what you call yourself. Wicked in blood and bone——"

"Lilice, come," Johnny said. "This is not for us to listen to. We have work to do at our place."

They gathered their possessions, even those Aunt Phrena offered. "I've sweat enough to earn what I get," Johnny muttered grimly. They were ready to go when they heard Uncle Herm call feebly, "Lilice." She hesitated. Johnny said, "I'll take the boxes to the wagon."

Lilice crossed the kitchen to the bedroom. For all the attention she paid her, Aunt Phrena might as well have been a stool. She found Uncle Herm picking tiredly at a cotton twist in the quilt.

"Don't hold it against Phrena," he begged in a raspy voice. "Don't, Lilice. She means well. There has been much trouble in her life."

"Don't worry, Uncle Herm." Lilice put a hand on his shoulder.

"Too bad, too bad." Lilice saw how his eyes crinkled with the effort to hold back the tears. "This I thought should be spared you. But no." His headshake was the slightest movement. "Johnny is a good boy."

"I'll watch over him." Lilice drew the quilt about his shoulder. "Don't you worry." She leaned over him and said as earnestly as though this were a promise sealed with an oath, "Uncle Herm, I love him so much it hurts. I'd go through the darkest night to be with him. There's no road too long."

Uncle Herm could only look at her, dumbly plucking at the quilt.

When Lilice came to the kitchen Aunt Phrena stood near the table. Perhaps it was the calm, proud manner in which Lilice shut the door of the bedroom; perhaps it was that queer antagonism which a woman recognizes and hates in another; perhaps it was something else jerking in her barbwise that made Aunt Phrena scream, "You shameless!" and pour upon Lilice the rage that shook her lips.

Her back as stiff as a cane pole, head high, Lilice went out. But the words pounded into her ears before the door shut behind her: "There is a mark set on those who are children of iniquity—a foul and loathsome blot. What is done in secret shall be made plain as day. You wait, you——"

The clicking door silenced the rest. For a wintry, snowflaked moment Lilice was certain her legs would bend and buckle like frozen stalks under the weight that grew in her heart. She stumbled toward the wagon. His loading finished, Johnny helped her up. They *clip-clopped* from Uncle Herm's yard.

Silence bristled like a hedge between them, a thorny hedge from which dark birds croaked at her: ". . . done in secret . . . plain as day . . . You wait . . ."

At last he said miserably, "Well, say it, if you want to. Say you're sorry you married me and——" His voice dragged into mumbles.

After a while of wheels crunching in the frozen road dust she answered, "Because of what she said? In some ways, Johnny, you are such a fool." She slipped her arm through his and pushed fingers into his hand fisted about the lines. "I'll never be sorry. Nothing can make me want to lose one hour of you, unless it be my own fault. The best I've known has been with you." (The best we know and the worst lies with those who are skin-close to us.)

Dumb with gratitude he grinned wanly at her. "Punkin, two girls like you in the world would be too much."

In falling snow they arrived at the Whiteland place and crossed the yard. It was an apron-sized piece of long-grassed autumn sod. Through a white curtain they saw the faded red of the separator, the dark hulk of the engine, both silently turning gray. Lilice hunched down when she saw them and looked toward the house quickly. As the wheels turned, slabs of pressed snow clung momentarily to the rims and fell flapping back. The points of horseshoes cut through the thin snow on the ground and were blackly distinct in the wagon track.

They carried their belongings into the house. Together they unhitched the team and walked side by side through the slanting reeds of snow, their shoulders in intimate touch. They shut out weather (though no worry) behind them with the closing door.

Johnny set up the stove and started a fire. That night they ate supper from the jars and packages Mrs. Rose had put up for them. Lilice sat in Uncle Herm's chair (the one with the loose rung) and Johnny sprawled on a pile of bedding. The air was rank with mouse smell, unleavened this past summer by anything except the odor of decay. There should have been laughter buttering the sandwiches here, and mirth as condiment for the beans. Instead there was mostly silence. Their nearness to each other was a sweet protection they did not query, behind which they found refuge, however temporary, from doubt, from weevily reflection, from all the mousing tomorrows that crept back of time's wainscoting.

After much yawning, they heaped the ticks and quilting into a couch on the floor. Lilice curled in a nest of blankets. Beside her Johnny unlaced his shoes. Their own home and they together and alone. But how different from what they had both dreamed of. They lay down side by side at last. Over the quilts flickers from the stove quivered, lighting the upthrust of Johnny's knee, crimsoning Lilice's hair for an instant. His hand touched her cheek.

For the quietness of minutes they lay awake, each afraid lest a stirring rouse the other. Mice squeaked in bursts of running in the loft, a dozen of them seemed to fall over their own skimming heels. They rustled where papers were scattered in a corner. Carefully Johnny groped for a shoe and found it. He hurled it at a bulge of scampering. The shoe banged against a wall and thudded back grotesquely. There was a shocked, stretched-out incredulous silence. After a while came a tentative scurry; then a hush that seemed to have questions in it; finally a mild querying squeak.

Johnny and Lilice held their breaths. Why the brittly, surcharged feeling that crowded in them was smashed then and there, instantly, completely, neither knew. But suddenly they were laughing, choked, gasping, in almost hysterical mirth that had no beginning but was. They rolled and shook in the middle of the mouse-quiet until at last they huddled together, her cheek in the palm of his hand, her fingers at his temple, both slack-nerved and cleanly warm for this while, the tight chain lengthened, the fetters relaxed.

The next day Johnny said yes and no when Lilice agreed or disagreed to put this here and that there. In the afternoon he bought bed, cupboard and supplies at Mr. Jimpson's. On the following day he would go to Mary's Hill. In the nice chin-cupped-in-hand discussions on the arrangement of this chair and that couch, in the companionship of wearing down the sharp corners of strangeness into the familiarity of home, there was time for little else than the necessities of the now.

That winter Johnny rented a wood lot on the farm. He cut and hauled cordwood. He drove a lean bargain with the machine-shop man for a seeder, a plow, a harrow: the farm tools he needed. Once he brought home a dozen hens and two roosters and penned them in a jog in the barn. No sooner were they released than there were the scattered feathers of rooster fights blowing over the snow.

In the log house Lilice baked and stitched and added a teaspoonful of coal oil to the water when she cleaned the windows. Pepper or salt shaker in her fingers (or a nutmeg, a stick of cinnamon, the buds of cloves), she'd stand over pot or kettle, head on a side, gravely deciding how much or how little of each would strike the fancy of Johnny's taste. She felt life growing firmly in her flesh.

They could laugh at Lilice's pride in the stove and the stone-hard biscuits she baked the first time she tried the oven. The stove was black and shiny. It glittered with raised nickel-plated trimmings. On one end was a reservoir where water was kept warm from the heat in the firebox. Projecting from the stovepipe at the back were shelves, one on each side of the pipe, for the coffee can and the teapot. Above these a warming shelf. "If this winter gets any colder, Judas, I'm going to crawl up there myself," Johnny teased her one day.

But there were evenings when the laughter thinned to the creak of a chair and the sputter of flame. Then the shadows of the past mixed with the darkness in the corners, and the lamp on the table could not drive away what stood guestlike though uninvited at their table.

One night he prowled restlessly from window to stove. Lilice stitched, rocking in the chair, disturbed but waiting. In quick torment he stood at her side, crying, "A man could go crazy sometimes, thinking, thinking." He shut out sight and hearing in her lap then. "He was my friend, my best friend." The words came hoarsely. "On the flats there, I kept looking at the tank wagon, getting ready to yell, 'Snoose.' There'd be Arty Nussbaum pumping away. It's—it's . . . Seems like the best part of me is gone."

"Don't, Johnny; don't. If Snoose were here, I think he'd understand." She hushed him without hushing herself. Make me understand about the threshing rig, too, Johnny. Over the life she felt stirring within her, she heard the echo of harshness. "Done in secret . . . plain as day . . ." She pushed it out of her mind. But it returned.

At the Marchens' (they were told) Mr. Marchen brooded. Sophie came to scold, "What has happened has happened, and there's an end to it. How long do you think a person must chew his own gall?"

For weeks the path between the Marchens' and the Barewolfs' had remained inches deep in snow, untracked except by rabbit, dog or wolf. One day, however, Mr. Marchen dragged his limp through the drifts. He shook the snow off in Aunt Phrena's kitchen. He spent an afternoon with Uncle Herm, discoursing exhaustively on aches and sprains and the damnable susceptibility of folks to trouble and sin and all hell's corruption. Neither said a word about Johnny; both understood. Mr. Marchen was crabbily polite to Aunt Phrena, just as he always had been.

And one day Sophie drove to the Whiteland place in the cutter. Johnny and Lilice greeted her uncertainly, in spite of Lilice's invitation, "Do take your things off."

But Sophie bustled into the room. "I've left my kids to home," she said heartily. The cold of the afternoon came in with her like an odor. "Clymy's nursing a cut foot. His ax slipped. Such a clumsy man. He can see to the kids for a while. It's little enough a man knows about a woman's work."

"It's so—Devil grab it, it's good to see you again!" Johnny hung her coat away. His exclamation was brimful of such fervor that tears stung Sophie's eyes. He didn't see them but Lilice did. Quickly she came to shake hands with Sophie.

Don't be a big goose knuckle now, Sophie said to herself fiercely. Aloud she boomed, "Well, how does married life suit you? Does it still pinch like a new shoe?" Her chuckle noisy, she exclaimed over the stove ("That shiny stuff, it looks nice, but you'll get a backache, polishing it"). She examined the couch, the table, the bed. ("Still both on one side, eh? You wait till he begins to warm his cold feet on your back, you'll shove him over.")

Lilice made coffee—Sophie detested tea and said so. They had cookies. Afterward, with a rough handshake for them both, she put on her coat.

Nothing more was said. Much had been uttered. As she gathered up the lines, Sophie took in the threshing rig with a sudden tightening of her lips.

Johnny watched her go. There was such lightness in his heels that his shoeprints in the snow were short and quick. "Judas, but that Sophie—" he said, entering the kitchen, "—what a woman she is." Lilice nodded, clearing away the dishes.

When he went to do chores, a whistle curled over his puckered mouth, the first in months. He slapped the black team's rumps with a peremptory "Whoa there, boys! What a woman."

Over her dishes Lilice was thinking, Sophie takes it hard. But there is no grudge in her. I don't see how she can be so—so solid and good. Insistently a thought beat in her mind like a pulse. Above the fire crackling spitefully she heard Aunt Phrena's harsh "You shameless. No church in you . . . what else can you expect?" A dish clattered against a dish. Is that it? When you belong, are you—different? Is that why Sophie——

At the Mussers' Em'ly played the organ again. Sometimes, however, when the C-sharp key sounded, wheezy and almost dead in the reeds, she'd drop arms on the keys and her head on her arms. The discords moaned, sighing away at last for want of breath.

At the Barewolfs' Uncle Herm at night saw on the windowpane the frost gardens flourish whitely. Then, blighted with the summer warmth in the room, they turned black, wilting as cucumber beds did in autumn. Kurt laid the plans for the farm beside his pamphlets and the *Farm, Stock and Home*. Aunt Phrena grumbled that the new preacher, Mr. Erdman's substitute, was certainly slow in coming; slow in hurrying the spirit back to the empty meetinghouse. No sweet promises.

At the Blumens' Gatha hid an almanac in the folds of her dress. In her room she counted the months, panic drawing at her eyes.

3

The baby was born early in February, a thin puling length of rib-marked crying. It had so mournful and sickly a face that the gladness in Johnny's heart constricted. It was a hard birth. Mrs. Rose had come in the morning but after a sidewise look at her thin, blue-veined hands and her humped-forward shoulders, Johnny harnessed the team.

In a wild gallop he drove to the Humber place. "Will you come?" he asked Sophie politely, though he opened the door without knocking. "It is her time, Lilice's."

Sophie caught the pleading under his diffidence. Untying her apron strings, "Clymy," she called from the doorway. "Clymy! Clymee!" When her husband stamped in from the barn she was gathering her things. "There's cold meat in the stone jar and potatoes to fry in the cupboard. And there's bread. You and the kids can stand it until tomorrow. I'll take Baby." She bundled herself and the child. "I'm ready," she told Johnny.

On the ride back Johnny said, "If anything happens to her, I'll——" He slapped the lines down harder.

Sophie laughed at him. "You men. You're spunky enough in bed, full of candy sweetness. But you're flappy as a rag when it's birthing time. That's when a woman might as well be alone. A man just gets in the way."

He grinned wryly. On another occasion he would have doubled with mirth.

All that afternoon and evening he was ready at a jump to whip the team toward Mary's Hill for Young Doctor Wilson. The blacks stood harnessed. Sophie heated water and warmed flannels in the oven, and chattered. Mrs. Rose teetered in the rocker. Johnny wanted to swear at this woman calmness.

By midnight Sophie was sitting before the stove, washing the baby and relating, "Ya, my second was like that, too. Not much hair for months." Mrs. Rose drowsed.

Trembling in every muscle, Johnny sat beside a pale and flaccid-cheeked Lilice. There was such a wan, lost-boy longing in his face that she picked together strength to smile at him. "Shall I move over? You look as though you needed a good night's sleep."

Sophie brought the baby. "There's your son, Johnny." She put the bundle gently beside Lilice.

Eagerly for all her tiredness, Lilice's gaze like hands drifted over the baby's features as though she were searching for something and was relieved when she couldn't find it.

Later, while Mrs. Rose slept in her chair and Lilice lay with closed eyes, Sophie broke the quiet of kettle purr and fire crackle to say in a low tone, bluntly, "You got a pretty sick boy there, Johnny. If he were mine, I'd have him baptized—just in case something happens."

"Bap——" Johnny stirred as if to snatch his son from the bed where he nestled beside Lilice. "If he's that sick——"

"Hang onto your oxen," Sophie calmed him. "No use letting them run away. Your boy will be all right, Johnny. But I've had my kids baptized inside a day or so for less than this. Them little fellers are so tender, you——"

"Ask the Pastor?" Johnny picked up a sliver of kindling and broke it across. "Sophie, that day when I asked him to marry us, I was a kid again and in school, the way he acted. He was ready to lick me, if he dared. All

I remember is 'Don't.' Not one word have I heard from him that makes me glad to be alive. Uncle Herm says the Pastor has a heart somewhere. I haven't noticed it."

"Strict he is," admitted Sophie. "But you can't let that stop you from having your boy baptized, Johnny," she added in alarm.

"We'll see." He flung the pieces of wood in the box, evading her query. "The little feller will get along. He's got you to help him. We'll call him Ernst, unless Lilice minds.

Neither saw that Lilice lay wide awake, listening.

Adam tied his horses in the yard the next afternoon, thirsty for news. Lena was expecting their baby any day now, he announced perkily. "And how is the little Black bugger?" he asked. He leaned forward to poke a finger into the small clenched fist.

Several mornings after, Kurt brought helloes and *"mach's gut"* from Uncle Herm. He kept to himself Aunt Phrena's sour "Weak and puny, the baby, so? Well, living like that, what else could *she* expect?"

The neighbors weren't sure whether Johnny's son was cause for jest or acid blame. "Not married so awful long, them two," Mr. Nussbaum observed dourly.

"Well, that Johnny feller—" Alb answered, "with him everything goes like his thrashing. He gets things done in a hurry." .

"Kinda sick, his kid is," Mr. Peiser said. "But what can you do?"

Remembering their own first-born and the tremors that shook them, the neighbors softened a little the harshness they had stored up against Johnny. Not all of them, but many.

Through February and half of March the baby drew its breath stickily and with whimperings. More than one night Lilice and Johnny burned the lamp and fired the stove into the gray of morning. Lena's baby came, a boy so plump and barrel-chested Adam reported his first cry was more like a laugh than anything else. "You ought to see how he grabs for my chin. He's got a fist the size of a small apple." Adam wiggled in pride.

Johnny nodded, a shortness in his replies. Lilice, glad for Adam's sake, was asking inwardly, "Why? Why? Do these things really happen? Or are we all dreaming and will wake presently?"

The baby died one evening; cried chokingly and waved its hands, one tiny fist closing like the petals of a flower tightly. Johnny drove wildly for Sophie, bringing her fresh from a pan of dishes. He turned the team around and lashed them in showers of snow over the road to Mary's Hill and Young Doctor Wilson. There was nothing hands could do, or bottles in a black bag, no; nor prayers, for that matter. So Johnny saw.

Lilice sat crumpled in a chair, her hands folded over the wedding ring as though whatever petitions she had lifted upward were falling back to her, stricken as white birds are, riddled by the shot of the hunter. Johnny was gray of mouth and cheek. Both crept like phantoms, heavy-footed, from house to barn and from barn to house, from bedroom to kitchen to bedroom where the baby lay.

Clymy arrived in the bright morning sun to take Sophie back. The icicles along the eaves were stilettos of frosty fire. Before she departed, Sophie, coat on and fascinator closely wrapped, said, "Johnny, now there is no help for it. You must go to the minister."

Fiercely he broke his restless pacing. "I'd run through barbwire rather. What can he do except add more . . . ?" His hands fell to his sides.

"Then you must take the shovel yourself," she told him bluntly, misunderstanding him. "Dig a grave in the pasture. We'll stop at Uncle Herm's."

"Pasture?" he mumbled, staring at her, a kind of horror growing on his lips. A grave in the pasture. Like the Alberts' boy. He shuddered, turning toward the window, shaken into uncertainty by that before which animosity is clown's play and anger the resort of children. He saw the Humber sled draw across the window and disappear.

The afternoon had almost slid westward when the door opened and Aunt Phrena shoved her largeness across the threshold. Outside Kurt was tying up the horses. At the way Lilice shrank back momentarily and Johnny stiffened pugnaciously, Aunt Phrena said, "There is no time for black looks and evil speaking. Ach ya, you want to drive me out of here. I know that. But the bread must be baked for this, and the floor scrubbed, no matter how sharp the scolding is."

Johnny would have denied her this compassion if Lilice hadn't been so huddled and broken; if he weren't too numb to care; if neighborhood opinion about rejecting a hand offered in calamity weren't so fiery. "Stay then," he muttered and went outside, avoiding what Lilice could not avoid.

For that afternoon there were short phrases between the two women. Aunt Phrena said no more than was necessary for the use of pot or pan. She baked and cleaned. Once she spoke up to coax Lilice into bed with a vinegary cloth across her forehead.

Though both Johnny and Lilice felt her presence like burdocks in a shirt, they were resentfully glad for her acidly calm strength. In this trouble it smoothed away drudgery that would have lain heavily on hearts already sagging with burden. Aunt Phrena gave her help freely if ungraciously, expecting nothing in return. When Lilice asked hesitantly, "If you—would like a cup of tea," she answered crustily, "I'll make my own coffee. This is not done for your sake. Ach, I know my duty." They were glad when Kurt came to get her.

Lena couldn't come. The baby was cuter than a bug's ear, Adam confessed lamely, "but Lena's afraid he might take cold. There's so much sickness about."

Before noon of the next day Johnny walked to the church. He found the Pastor in the barn, forking manure into a heap. Through the open door the Pastor saw him shuffling along the path. "Na, ya," the Pastor muttered. "When death strikes, they know where the church is. Otherwise——"

Grimly Johnny said, "Herr Pastor, my son is dead. I ask you—there is that to be done——" He couldn't say, "Will you bury my flesh?"

The Pastor put his fork aside. "Whoa, my ponies," he commanded his nervously stepping team. "Na, Bruder Black," he began with professionally consolatory comfort. "The Lord has dealt you a heavy blow. His ways may be mysterious but they are just. Come to the house; we will talk. We must be patient, not rebellious——"

"How long can a man suffer and be patient?" Johnny burst out before he knew. He checked himself, his face stony. "Herr Pastor—" he spoke slowly; the words rasped in his throat—"I asked you, will you bury my son, or must I carry him to the field and dig his grave myself?"

The stricken look on the young face (like a spring plant wilting in a frigid season) and the clamped jaw halted the Pastor's barby solace. "Come in, my son," he invited gently. He added strangely in a voice softer than Johnny had ever heard it, "Who may know how long suffering must—— I lost a son, too, years back there." (At another time Johnny would have marveled at this; now he was too racked to heed another's sorrows.) As if regretting he'd spoken, the Pastor lifted his beard to a fierce angle. "A pastor is the shepherd of his flock," he uttered sententiously, pulpitwise. "I will not deny you what help my office and my conscience offer. Bruder Black, if you will step into——"

Johnny heard him with the outer senses only. "Between us there is no need to speak more," he said. "I have yet to see Alb Hukelpoke about digging——" Touching his cap, he swung on his heel and strode away.

From the barn door the Pastor observed the dimming figure. "Na," he muttered. "How many stripes, and how hardly must they fall, Johnny Black, before you bend your stiff-necked back?"

And so, let lamentations hang upon the logs of the house where they might and the wild hands clasp in grief, another scar broke the white space in the clearing under the evergreen tree. The mound was heaped, but not until the tears were started freshly three times, and the eyes ached with the dryness of salt. Three services to bury the dead. First there were tears spilled in Johnny's house and handkerchiefs moistened; then there were watery eyes at the church; finally, there were tears during the longish committal service in the graveyard, the folks shifting in the freezing cold. For in this Pockerbrush church the treble wringing out of grief was a salutary rite esteemed by pastor and congregation alike. Let a man number his days; regard seriously the brevity of grass that is cut in the noon sun and withereth before the cooling dusk. Let him consider life unfrivolously, to the last vinegary drop.

Johnny moved like one not yet awakened to reality, his arm in Lilice's slack and dead. Only once did he shrink at the touch of stinging, raw-nerved pain. He nearly stumbled over a clod breaking from a drift on a recent grave, and knew that underneath the webbing frost and the lifeless root lay what remained of Snoose's mortal laughter, his comrade chuckle, his friendliness. . . .

As they turned away toward the evergreen and the entrance to this acre of God's ire, both were stooped as with bundles not of their lading. Mr. Marchen humped up to them. He caught Johnny's hand. "Na, Johnny," he said, "now we both have a grave in the churchyard." He hesitated, patted Lilice's shoulder, continued, "It has been bothering me a long time, Johnny," and without explaining himself, stalked away. Johnny knew what he meant.

Aunt Phrena went home to the comfort of the Book, vaguely triumphant. "Na, always I say it: Those that are outside, they bring trouble with them." From this she drew what satisfaction she could.

Johnny and Lilice went back to their house, wondering that so small a weight of flesh and blood, once removed, could leave behind so vast an emptiness. Why? Many times he probed his experience for answer. Why did this happen to Lilice and me? For punishment? Was it perhaps dreadfully true after all, what the Pastor had said: "The sins of the fathers . . ." Or was this *him* again, reaching from the past? . . . He tossed the notions with the manure he pitched. "I'll not believe that," he muttered. But the notions persisted.

"Why?" he asked Mrs. Rose one evening when he saw Lilice folding a tiny shirt. He stood beside her while she put the garment away in a box. "Why did it have to come to us? Was it because we—we——" He sat down. His hands at his knees gripped solidly together.

"Who can say?" Mrs. Rose pulled her shawl closely. "Letting yourselves run wild like that, no sense left in your heads—that's no credit to either of you. If I had my way, Johnny—" her voice thinned to harshness—"being a mother and my daughter precious, I'd tear your hair out." She smiled grimly, a grimness whose source was humiliation and pain and resentment at the upheaval of established decorum, but tempered with pity. "You didn't use much sense there. It is something you and Lilice will have to settle between you. But as for punishment—" her shoulders rested against the chair back—"it would be a queer world if punishment came to a child every time the elders misbehaved."

"It's a queer world anyway," Johnny said like a youngster puzzled at a sum in addition that wouldn't come right. "There's Uncle Herm dying on his back., Your man was like that, too. What good is suffering to anybody? What use? All Uncle Herm wants is an oilcan in his hand and a chance to putter around a separator. If that's too much to ask——"

"They say suffering makes you a better person, a more understanding soul. I wonder." Mrs. Rose bent forward and drew a finger across Lilice's cheek. "I wonder very much. I guess all we can do is to be still *inside*. It is the best, I s'pose, and not the worst that happens to us at last."

"The best!" Johnny echoed bitterly. He was thinking. Be still inside. Where did I hear that before? Giving it up, he said, "Is this a sample of the best that——"

" 'It is a terrible thing to fall into the hands of the living God,' " Lilice interrupted them suddenly. "That's what the Pastor said today. It would be awful if he were right. Dreadful punishment waiting for us and those we love, and . . . and Ernst not baptized . . ."

She stared blankly at the stove, as though what she saw there unsteadied her. Fire through the chinks in the top of the stove flickered redly across her forehead and cheeks. She screwed the ring on her finger circlewise. Mrs. Rose swayed forward, backward. Johnny slumped in his chair.

Long after Mrs. Rose began to snore her thin fretful snore, Lilice lay awake. When Johnny stirred on the pillow she whispered his name. She felt his hand grope toward her ear. "Punkin," he answered.

"The night Baby was born, I heard you and Sophie talking." She hesitated, then went on: "You wanted him baptized in the church, didn't you? It would have meant much to you."

The rustling on the pillow ceased. He didn't answer.

She continued: "I can see that. In spite of everything, that's what you wanted, no matter how angry you are at the Pastor. That's it, isn't——"

"Punkin, hush." She heard the stubble of his whiskers catch in the cloth. He said, "The more I see of church, the less use I got for it."

In a voice so quiet at first her meaning escaped him, she said, "I stand in the way, don't I? If I belonged——"

There was a rush of air as he flung up the quilts. "For God's sakes, Lilice, I can't stand it, hearing you say such——"

"It's true. If I belonged——"

"Nothing to keep me away from church," he interrupted her. "I was confirmed there."

"Nothing except——"

"Don't you say it, Punkin," he said vehemently, half-aloud. "When you want to go, we'll go. If you don't, we won't, and that settles it. I don't care one way or another. But this is surely so: Where you aren't welcome, I'm not either; no, nor our kids." His cheek scraped closer until he could kiss her. "I'll not hear another word about it."

The clock whanged an hour triumphantly. A coal snapped.

"Punkin——"

"Johnny, I love you so."

Mrs. Rose stayed on into spring and summer. She couldn't go now, she said, Lilice drooped so. The real reason was Lena, for Lena enjoyed setting a table for two more than she did for three—except for company, of course. And Mrs. Rose knew that only too well.

Johnny was glad to have her stay. It warmed him somehow to find her rocking near the stove when he came in from work outside, his nostrils frosty. There was comfort (comfort for Lilice, he thought) in knowing that her voice thawed the chill that hung under the ceiling.

He was thinking about her the afternoon he ransacked the toolbox for a handful of nails. In his search he uncovered a spike bent until it was nearly U-shaped. "Silenski!" he exclaimed. "What Mrs. Rose said the other night. That's where I heard it before." Silenski, Silenski reading something about a free man . . . a free man, though he sits still, he walks far . . . a free man.

He pitched the spike back. How was a man to be free, how was he to be still in his mind, all this hell breaking? "Oh, Devil grab it!"

With her mother in the house Lilice began to flower again, a faded kind of blooming these spring days. The Humbers drove over, a heartiness huge as her body in Sophie's chuckle. Clymy was diminutive beside her, when you noticed it. You seldom did. There was a perkiness about Clymy that made even Mr. Nussbaum grunt, "By jippers, for a pea-sized one, he ain't such a bad man." The Humber buggy came often, the children screaming noisily. The oldest was tall for his nearly eight years. "Long-legged bugger." Sophie would pull at a lock of his hair. "Think of it. Next year he goes to school."

With the trillium's white promise, laughter, subdued perhaps, but cleansing as soap in a dusty crevice, rang in Johnny's house. He and Lilice rode with the Humbers to Mary's Hill sometimes. Once they joined them in a picnic. "Good to breathe fresh air again, all that winter closeness in your lungs." Sophie stretched voluptuously.

Lilice poked a twig sharply into Johnny's ribs. When he lunged at her she cried, "It was an ant."

"I know it, and I've got her." She didn't resist him. There was this much to think back on happily. Only now and again, when she happened on a ribbon or a knitted cap did she draw aside from a weevily thought: Don't let it come; don't let the harvest come with threshing! . . .

For all the mirth that curled over his lips when Lilice was near, Johnny began the spring's work with disturbance in the way he slung a bag of grain into the seeder box. Summer not far off (nearer on the calendar) and the threshing jobs again. But this year, with folks remembering last autumn, this year . . .

For a time he was sure he'd never toot another whistle in the hills except defiantly to say he didn't give a damn for any job there. Once he told Alb Hukelpoke, "Guess I'm like a skunk in the neighborhood. Might as well sell the rig."

"Aw sheets, what you talking about?" Alb ran a thumb against his whiskers. "You licked? Hell. A man worth the salt on his potatoes is three-quarters cat. Kick him any which way, he always lands on his feet. You'll have *some* thrashing to do, wait and see."

Some thrashing. Johnny's mouth tightened. Sure, little hen piles. The leavings of—of Bory Tetzell, maybe. No, thank you. If he couldn't have a big run, he'd have none. I'll go out on the flats. The farmers here, they can thrash their manure piles themselves, if that's what they like. . . . I've got Norton's job anyway. . . . He clung to the notion. It was like a bar against the future.

But one forenoon Mr. Marchen came by. "Na, Johnny," he called, "how's the corn?"

"Sprouting." Johnny went to shake hands. So much was uttered without voice in the firm clasp of fingers that Mr. Marchen could say, "There has been much twaddle this winter about hate and settling scores. I want to tell you this, Johnny. You can thrash my place any time this fall—if you want to."

If he wanted to—— Johnny watched Mr. Marchen rattle away. If he wanted to—— Why, these hills, these hills were his province over which the smoke of his steamer waved like a banner. You could make money on the flats. But the hills, the hills . . .

With the spring changes he found neighborhood opinion, ice-fast in winter, thawing somewhat. "Ya, that Johnny Black, he got troubles piled like cordwood all right. . . . Losing his kid like that. . . . Terrible thing, though, about that Marchen boy; but I guess accidents happen around a thrashing rig. . . . Accidents—I should say so, somebody's always getting hurt around them. . . . Black's a good thrasher if he weren't so uppity. . . . Hard luck, his little feller dying. . . . I kinda think I'll have him thrash my stacks this year again. . . . Ya, guess so, too. . . ."

Not all the folks melted. There were plenty who said, "Serves that Johnny Black right. Acts like he owns the country."

There was discontent regarding other matters also. "Looks like Pastor Steuber is getting old and soft," Mr. Nussbaum growled to Mr. Dunkel once. "Burying that Johnny's kid, just like it was all regular."

"Well, Johnny's a member," defended Mr. Dunkel. "He's got some rights."

"Rights!" snarled Mr. Nussbaum. "Ten years ago the Pastor would have put his foot down and said no." He tamped his pipe vigorously. "By jippers, we need a new preacher, a good strict one."

"Whoop-Jinny!" exploded Mr. Dunkel. "Didn't you learn in Catechism that in case of trouble, a member can baptize his own kids? Bury 'em, for that matter. And marry, too. I 'member my old pastor told me if a boy and a girl got sweet on each other, and he said, 'I'd like to marry you,' and she said, 'I'll take you for my husband,' and they meant it, they were married in the sight of heaven. No matter what folks said. All the church does is make it public."

"Freethinker!" shouted Mr. Nussbaum, dropping hot tobacco embers on his fingers. "Ouch, there! You want to make it still easier for young squirts to get together. It's fellers like you, Wilhelm Dunkel. That's why the church and the country are going to the dogs."

And so, while many held their grudges against Johnny, many others came to the log house to write their names in the account book. It was as if in death a sacrifice had been made to valley gods. The folks were appeased. Looking at each familiar name scrawled blackly, Johnny felt the growing season rise within him. The stalks and stems of confidence he'd given up for dead were beginning to green again, to slit the old bark with new shoots of hope. He whistled as he greased up the wrenches. During evenings or when rain made fields soggy, he tinkered at the separator.

Lilice put the cradle in the loft. She avoided the sight of the rig. "I wish winter were here; winter and spring." But Johnny whistled "After the Ball" and prepared for autumn. Now and again, after he'd seen Mr. Marchen or heard about Em'ly Musser, a pang would twist in his flesh, the sun clouding, and he'd cringe before memory. He never visited the

Marchen place. Hastily he'd 'dig at his work, his mind alive with a cry,
What shall a man do with a wrong he has done? Let it sour him forever?

That summer the valley hugged scandal, bare-bosomed scandal, to itself,
first with outrage and then with satisfaction. One night at a dance, Gatha
Blumen quarreled with Lornas Tetzell, entreating him "to do something
about it." Plenty of windy ears heard it. By lamplight, not far from dawn
(so the folks imagined it, tongue over lip), Gatha peered at herself in the
mirror and drew from a hidden place an almanac. In the morning she came
downstairs after her father was safely cutting grass in the sloo. She rushed
to Mrs. Blumen's ampleness, nearly smothered confession, hands over her
face. "Ma, I'm sick, I'm sick. I'm going to have a baby."

On Sundays there was at the church a lusty hubbub that delighted the
folks much more than the Pastor's sermons did. Mr. Blumen stormed. He
threatened he was cleaning his shotgun, a muzzle-loader but deadly. Noisily
he shouted he was getting the sher'ff to arrest the scoundrel, whoever
mother's son he was.

Mrs. Blumen scarcely peeked from the shield of her apron, she lamented
so. "I don't believe it's true. Not my daughter. I brought my kids up on
the Catechism. We all say grace before meals, and everything," she told
Mrs. Peiser, and flung up her apron, howling. Gatha was locked in her
room, "on bread and water," Mrs. Peiser chattered.

There was a busy pointing of fingers and a hasty retreat to virtue among
the boys of the congregation. "The unregenerate sprigs!" thundered the
Pastor. Lornas settled matters. He brought easy breath to more than one
unmustached stripling by disappearing from the hills one night and vanishing Dakota-ward.

In a week, however, having no relish for being hunted, he returned—"to
spit in their teeth," he said. Once more uneasiness prickled among the
boys. There were heads close together and earnest conversations in the
gallery on Sundays. Lornas protested his innocence loudly and denied all
charges, his tongue slippery, his actions foxlike.

Promptly Mr. Blumen, the sheriff and the law swooped upon Lornas.
Before he knew where his wits were, he was hustled off to jail. "There!"
roared Mr. Blumen, dusting his hands in satisfaction, his act a kind of
propitiation to violated chastity. "There! That'll hold that young stud."

Mr. Blumen was so confident he insisted on a trial. The Tetzells hired
a lawyer from Fergus, a "slick one," Bory trumpeted. "Why, I'll mortgage
my rig all over again, if that'll lick Old Man Blumen."

There was much examining and cross-examining at the trial. Lornas
flung a net of accusation. Into it fell several trembling nineteen-year-olds

and a man of twenty-five. They had been interrupted in their haymaking. Frightened, with shirts not entirely buttoned, they were hurried before the judge.

Under that fine sense of jurisprudence by which lawyers demonstrate the efficacy of loopholes for escape rather than the sanctity of justice, Gatha was confronted with testimony. Badgered into confusion by "yes" and "no," she finally admitted there had been "other boys." (Where is the evidence that convicts the chemistry of a glance, the catalytic force of touch, a finger on an arm and lips curved provocatively?)

In the flurry of countercharges and denials, the case was finally dismissed. Gatha went home with her folks. ("I hope her pa has a horsewhip ready for her," said Aunt Phrena.)

Aunt Phrena was outraged. Such behavior. She longed for the assurances of the meetinghouse. But no Brother Erdman appeared with the chariots of promise. "You s'pose he's gone for good?" Kurt asked. She glanced at him angrily, disdaining to meddle with prophecy.

Gatha's baby arrived, a girl. The Blumens gave it their name, Mary Blumen. (At Thanksgiving time, Gatha came to church tentatively, a little fearfully. Seeing no howling judgment rise with fisted stones from the congregation, finding no more than a crusty look or two flung at her and the baby, she began to attend regularly. Beyond a certain embarrassment in Mrs. Blumen and the Pastor's hovering pause before the word "harlot," the matter was dropped. Who casts the first stone . . .)

By harvesttime Lornas stepped from the jail, a sort of tarnished hero, his behavior slier than ever. He even came to church, insisting, "Nothing's proved against me."

After service one Sunday Aunt Phrena noticed him swaggering in a circle of admirers. She stopped. Her lips twisted as if her tongue had come upon a curdled savor. She gripped her hymnbook. If it had been a stone, she would have hurled it.

All the way home she guarded herself against a sardonic amusement widening Kurt's heavy mouth. When he said as they drove into the yard, "Looks as if Gatha's kid will have to hunt up a father," she snapped, "Fix your own dinner, you who are so smart." Angrily she puffed toward the house.

Lena Rose shrilled waspishly that Gatha ought to be run out of the country. Johnny told Lilice, "I'll bet you a flock of your pancakes against a Bland dollar that Lornas is the one after all. He's a weasel, he is. Some day me and him'll tangle."

Lilice said only, "I'm sorry, awfully sorry for Gatha." Gatha, who belonged, she who was a member—— Lilice furrowed her brows trying to find in this affair some triumph for herself. Whatever she found gave little solace though much pity. With the realization that autumn would bring whistle screeches, she thought, I don't understand it. I don't. . . .

4

That season, though the yields of grain were fair, Johnny's runs were small. With the queer braiding together of fact and gossip into pigtails of doubt, some folks hedged and some balked, deciding to wait for Tetzell after all, or some other rig that might come through. "That Johnny Black's rig—it ain't the only rig in the country." Which was nearly true. Besides Tetzell's outfit, there was another, Bluber's, starting up in the south townships. And there were those who passed through annually.

Johnny guessed that this was a kind of tribute the folks were exacting from him. Not all had been forgotten. Outwardly Johnny accepted this, working his fingers into calluses. Many a farmer's thorny comment he turned aside with a laugh that was loud in his teeth, but far from his heart and ribs. Inwardly he simmered, swearing to himself, "This is the last time I'll ask you, Fleischer. From now on you'll come to me, Mercer."

Alb was with him again, vigilant as hawk over kicking gopher whenever a box ran hot or a sieve clogged, or too much chaff became mixed with the grain. His hands were becoming so grimy that "In January, by Judas, I peel like an old sausage," he told Johnny.

Heinie was feeding this year, shoving the bundles into the cylinder teeth, marriage thick in his brain. Jackie Marchen offered to drive the tank wagon but Johnny refused. "You can do it all right," he mollified Jackie. "I can't let you, though; I just can't." Jackie went into the stacks as pitcher. Even then Johnny avoided the haw-side settings where Jackie's blue shirt was plain against the fresh bronze of the opened stacks. A Haber boy, one Johnny knew by name and sight, giddapped the team and pumped the water. Marty Borman stood at the firebox and swore when the engine foamed and the injector failed to work.

And so Johnny's rig dusted over the hills again. Never was he so careful as that season, never so cautious, for all that he drove the men with as harsh a tongue as ever. Behind him like the smoke of his engine floated neighborhood approval: "Damn good man . . . thrashes clean and thrashes fast . . . Cripes, I'm gonna plant me more wheat next spring; the way he thrashes, I'm making a little extra money this year. . . . Sure, there's money in wheat, if your grain don't spoil, waiting for a thrasher; it's getting thrashed early that's important. . . ."

"Well, I don't know about that." Mr. Dunkel spoke up at Toffman's store one day. He tapped his pipe on his heel; ran a straw through the stem; sniffed it with a wrinkling nose. "Whoop-Jinny, that pipe of mine sure needs a change of diapers!" He cleaned it, continuing his objection, "Don't know about wheat. I'm planting me a patch of rye this fall, and some oats and barley next spring. I'm adding some good cows to my herd. There's money in a good heifer—more reliable than wheat." He lighted his pipe. His cheeks sucked in with each pull of air. "Ah," he sighed contentedly. "Breathing easy as a baby. Nope." He spat. "Gotta mix wheat-growing with livestock and other grain, boys."

The neighbors tittered, the dollar marks of wheat in their minds. Kurt agreed with Mr. Dunkel. "Wilhelm's got the right idea. You got to farm less and do a better job," he insisted, tapping a pile of agricultural pamphlets. "Full-blooded stock and disease-resistant strains of grain——"

From farm to farm Johnny heard the neighbors laughing at both of them. "That Kurt Barewolf, he thinks he's gonna farm by reading a book. . . . Ya, he'll find the manure don't fly out of the horse-barn window. . . . And that Dunkel. He's gonna get a bull with papers—pedigrees, he calls them. Whoever heard of a bull with a baptismal certificate? Hee, hee, hee. I guess the old steer will do the business whether's he's full-blooded or scrub. . . ."

"Whoop-Jinny-and-fall-down!" rumbled Mr. Dunkel. "You fellers got cold mush where you ought to have brains. Take Schadel's cows. Good scrub stuff. They give pails of milk when they're fresh and the grass is green in the pasture. But that lasts anyways no more'n a couple of months. Then the cows go dry and Schadel sits there and strips and squeezes, trying to get an extra drop. But the cow's dry. That's what she'll be the rest of the year, dry as a bailed-out well, and eating high-priced feed. No siree. I want a cow that'll milk say nine, ten months of the year."

"Hee-hee," snickered the neighbors. "He don't want a cow. He wants a milk bag. . . . No cow'll milk three-quarters of a year; wear her out. . . . Kurt Barewolf says they got cows around St. Paul that do. . . . Kurt, he better fix his north fence before his heifers get into my cornfield again. . . . Dunkel's calves ought to have a preacher so the baptism papers come out all right. . . ."

Johnny laughed with them. "The more wheat you fellers raise, the more I'll thrash," he said more than once. "And the more I thrash, the more you can figger on having in the bank. That's simple as one-two-three."

He couldn't make up his mind about Mr. Dunkel. How anyone could talk about improved strains of cattle and diversified farming while his wife remained at home, mad as a colt that had eaten snakeweed, was beyond his

THE EAR AND THE HUSK

understanding. Or so he said. Yet no one in the neighborhood did he regard with greater admiration. "That Dunkel, he makes a little go a long way."

The rig, moving over the hills, linked farm to farm with a belt of bull-wheel tracks in sand, in mud, in solid earth. Pulling the separator from place to place was often more nightmare than reality. When the rains sluiced down, there were holes in the roads the size of a cow. Some roads were little more than two wheel tracks among stumps and stones. Others were so steep they were gullied and rutted if you so much as spat on them, Alb was sure. And roads in the swamps were so trembly the peat bogs shivered and a warbler's nest rocked gently far out on a tamarack limb.

Sometimes Johnny wiped sweat and grease in sighing relief when he finally brought the engine into a farmer's yard, the separator at its tail. "Judas, I thought we were goners for sure! That grade across the sloo—the water's ten feet there, at least."

The bridges troubled him more. Those over ditches were log platforms so dry-rotted and wet-decayed, so broken with holes, they were open traps for a horse's leg or a man's foot. Those over creeks were spans of logs and planks that swayed to a man's stride. They sent more than one team rearing in panic. Those over larger streams or dry washes—there was one called Drywash Bridge—were frameworks of iron and log and plank, loose-jointed and rattly, so that a wagon rumbled over them like thunder, and gravel and dirt showered into the water or the rocky bed below.

Only a few of the bridges would bear the weight of a threshing rig and these were often miles apart. He was at Mr. Haber's and wanted to pull the rig to Mr. Schimmel's, just downstream and across the creek. There was a bridge there but Mr. Schimmel warned, "Can't cross the bridge. By Gott, I nearly broke through with a load of wheat."

"How you think I'll get to your place—fly?" Johnny demanded, irritation overriding him.

"Go around. That's the only way."

"All that long road? I'm damned if I will." But he did. He moved three miles north, crossed a span of logs, haunted by a presentiment that any moment he'd be crashing through into the water. Then he moved three miles back, although the two farms were so neighborly, you could practically throw a wrench from one yard to the other, Heinie Beerwagon said.

Alb came to Johnny one morning, disturbed into frowning. They were ready to move. "That bridge at Toffman's Ford," he said. "Sheetin' Judas, she wiggles like an old maid's nose when she smells a man."

"Well, we got to cross there." Johnny swung the steering wheel. Smoke shot upward as he touched the throttle, unfolded rosettelike. "I'm not going another five miles out of my way. Got the cables, Alb? And the planks?"

"Yep," Alb shouted and they started. They came to the Ford. Alb tried dissuasion again. "Look, Johnny," he warned: "you're running this rig, but that bridge ain't safe."

"Get those planks down, Alb."

"Johnny, you'll break your neck some day. If you'd think of——"

"I'm thinking of my job," Johnny answered grimly. "I've got thrashing to do. No bridge is going to stand in my way."

They approached the bridge cautiously, engine, tender, separator. They uncoupled the separator from the tender. Then, like an old badger reconnoitering a suspicious odor, the engine with the tender crept forward alone. Alb banged the planks ahead of the wheels. There was a creak of timbers, then the cracking of planks, the groaning of stringers, sudden "plumps" as stones fell into the stream, a hollow echoing as the *chug-a-chug* of the exhaust struck the sounding board of the water and bounced back. At one moment there was a menacing lurch as the wheels bore on an infirm spot. The fireman stood ready to jump. Johnny caressed the levers, his fisted knuckles white, his lips bloodless with pressure. . . .

Then the engine was across. Marty Borman leaped to the ground, cursing in deep relief. Johnny wiped sweat. Alb came running.

They snaked a cable back over the bridge. With it they drew the separator across. Alb piled the planks into the tender again.

"Devil take these bridges!" Johnny helped recouple separator to engine. "I'd rather thrash a manure pile three times over than cross a bridge once."

That fall Johnny told Mr. Peiser, "You fellers got to get the town board to fix them bridges. My rig hasn't learned to swim. It's not a mushrat yet."

Mr. Peiser promised. However, folks said, "Oh, them bridges ain't so bad. You put some planking on them and they'll hold up awhile." Nothing was done.

Down south, so the story ran, Bluber had tried to cross a bridge and lost his nerve. Before the engine was a quarter of the distance across, before as much as a stringer creaked, he had jumped from the platform and run ahead. On the farther side he waited, beckoning and coaxing, "Come on, Betsy; come straight ahead, you old son of a frozen horse tail."

Tetzell had a small fire during a job that fall. Not much damage done. "Just careless. That's what happens when you get to be Papa," Alb remarked sagely.

Heinie joined Mr. Schimmel's haw-haw. "He's surely proud of that kid of his'n, Bory is. By Gott, he brags he'll make a thrasher of him," Mr. Schimmel said.

"Tetzell ain't doing so bad for a man of his age," Heinie admitted from the lofty strength of young manhood.

"Well, Heinie—" Alb cast a disparaging glance at him—"the older the buck, the stiffer the horn, they say."

"That's what they say," mourned Mr. Schimmel. "But I dunno. Me, I'm past fifty and seems like I ain't fit for more than drainage."

Johnny listened and thought of Bory's son, healthy and strapping; of Gatha's little girl, adopted by the Blumens, a hardy youngster. The muscles in his jaw corded. He said nothing while the crew belittled Tetzell's fire.

But over near Mary's Hill a rig was burnt to the four truck wheels. Not a bundle of the farmer's setting of eight stacks was saved and a barn near by roared into flame, a whole year's sweat billowing upward in smoke. Some folks were grumbling, "Damned old chimneys, that's what those steam engines are. They drop sparks into a man's stacks and burn him out."

"I told you that long ago." Mr. Schadel was dismally triumphant.

Roads and bridges and fires, these were only a few of the burdocks in a thrasher's pants, Johnny thought. His hand on the throttle was steady.

Cold and rain sank early upon the ridges that year. Before long stacks began to green with the sprouted kernel where they weren't black with weathering. No longer did Jackie and the pitchers find the circled layers in the stack easy to handle. With intertwining growth and the matting process of damp, some of the bundles were sewn together so firmly that a pitcher had to wrestle with each one, it seemed, and tear it bodily from its moorings. What landed on the feeder's table in front of Heinie was hardly wheat or oat stems but whitish, moldy strings of decay. The smell of "rot-burnt" grain and wet straw was foul in the nostrils. Time and again the grain clogged in the spout. Moist chaff stopped the tailings elevator. Up on the straw pile the strawmen poked at the clotted trash that moved up the slant of the stacker. "Cripes, that's mucky stuff! We're just pitchin' manure from one pile to the other."

At the log house Lilice fed the chickens and piled cucumbers and cabbages in the garden. With Mrs. Rose to shorten the days in talk (though nights were long in a bed she couldn't warm alone), she put the garden up for winter, thinking, "If Ma weren't here, I'd—I'd—I don't know what I'd do." She put busyness as a guard against the hum of threshers floating up a valley. She numbered the days and named the places where Johnny might be. Now he's at the Schimmels' . . . now he's threshing the Peisers' . . . tomorrow the Muris' . . . oh, don't let anything happen to you, my dearest!

5

Change like a hooded animal crept over the hills, now stumbling into something like haste, now standing in the fearful hesitancy of the blind, without movement at all. Or so it seemed to Johnny in those first six years of his married life.

Some things remained constant as the break-up of ice in spring. Folks planted grain and harvested it in the season's roll. So they had done since the first most ancient spread hand scratched the seed into the earth; so they were doing now, though iron drill-fingers disturbed the clods these days. They went to shindandies on Saturday nights and attended church on Sunday mornings, piously trying to forget the night's frivolity in the morning's seriousness. They saw death thrust a funereal holiday into the crusty labor of the midweek and sighed that the days of man were numbered indeed.

They gazed on new love, the young with anticipation, the old with envy, and renewed faith in themselves and in the future with the hope they saw in the marriage rite, with the upspring of hilarity they found in the wedding dance. This untried couple would build that Tomorrow which youth dreamed of and which maturity regarded distrustfully and relinquished sadly, having become wise in execution.

Other things (looked at between the hours of cutting winter wood, of grubbing new land in fall or spring, of threshing in autumn) moved slowly into different shapes and forms. Farms like oaks might take a small piece of eternity to grow in size but they did inevitably. Thinking about larger thrashing runs, Johnny saw with a sparkle how the fields crowded furrow by furrow into the woods, yesterday's pasture becoming tomorrow's wheat patch. Fields used to be fenced in and the woods left free, there was so much of them, Alb observed once; but now the fields were left unfenced and the pasture woods were surrounded with barbed metal shining in the gooseberry bushes.

Before anybody could say how it happened, everybody was threshing with steam rigs, it seemed. Engines and separators were getting bigger and clumsier and more expensive. Few horse-power threshers remained, except perhaps up north and in the newer settlements. Mr. Schadel's stood near his shop. Turkeys roosted on it. Instead of grease their droppings filled the cogs of the bull wheels. One year, in a pet of anger against what he called "them gol-danged straw-burners and the high prices the thrashers charge," he oiled the power and the separator, and threshed his own stacks. But so many folks came to laugh and titter and poke curiously at the gears ("Like they never seen a horse-power before," fumed Mr. Schadel) that he pulled it huffily back to the south side of the shop again. There its wheels gradually settled into the sod.

One year Mr. Dunkel, still refusing to sell them, pastured his oxen. Before long they were white bones in a raspberry patch. "I said if they lived and I lived, they'd die mine," he used to tell Johnny. "And whoop-Jinny-and-fall-down, they died mine!" The ox yoke joined the cradle under the rooftree of the machine shed. Both were webbed now with the dust of winters and the slow flame of rust. Mice left their toe prints on the wood.

The oxshoes, of which Mr. Dunkel used to have so many, became lost in the clutter of old boxes or lay rusting in the grass. Once when he threshed at Mr. Dunkel's, Johnny saw an oxshoe in a corner of the granary. He picked it up. With the old iron in his palm, he thought of Uncle Herm and Black Billy; of a span of oxen shuffling across the yard, leaving in the damp ground near the barn the marks of newly shod hoofs. He could almost see the curved prints, the five dots of the nailheads in each shoe, the gougings of the four sharp lugs, one at each end of a shoe and set at angles, one to another. How much rain had washed over the hills since then, bitter rain and sweet, how much snow had drifted, to rub away forever even the last hoof-mark of the oxen!

Horses were neighing everywhere now and whinnying loudly in their traces, their only rival steam. In the papers there were accounts of automobiles. Some dreamers, intoxicated on the wine of prognostication, said the day would come when horses would be as forgotten as the oxen now were.

But these things, horseless carriages and mad prophecies, belonged to the faraway East. That was the region where sin coiled in the dollar sign, and bright lights (electric lights in many places) hooded the pious with darkness, as the Pastor had so clearly indicated more than once. You saw farther in the pure radiance of a coal-oil lamp. In the valley, however, such heresies were as foolish as the notion of abolishing the annual mission festival at the church.

True, the folks who used to come to services in lumber wagons or on foot now came in buggies or in spring wagons. The rich ones (like Mr. Norton) even spanked along in surreys with lamps in front and fringes on the top. In years past when folks untied their horses after the services and giddapped from the churchyard, there had been a great thunder, a banging of wagon boxes and bolsters and heavy iron tires. Now there was the softer *riddle-raddle-riddle* of lighter wheels, the wiffling noise of vibrating spokes, a genteel sound, and the *slip-slap-slip* of buggy harnesses. Some folks, however, still came in wagons; more than one member walked to church.

Once Mr. Marchen, jocular over a sermon, flourished his whip on the way home from church and galloped past Mr. Nussbaum, who, with Sabbath dignity, was sternly reining in his sorrel span. Outraged over such neighborly affront, Mr. Nussbaum shouted, "By jippers, if he thinks his blacks can run, I'll show him." With Mrs. Marchen squealing (so Jackie told Johnny gleefully afterward) and with the Nussbaum women holding crablike to their seats, the two men raced halfway home, dust flying and hoofs spurting pebbles. Other drivers, seeing the wildness and the incredibly reckless speed of the two racers, wheeled hastily out of the road or into the brush to let them past.

"Gol-dang fools!" yelled Mr. Schadel, waving a fist. "There ought to be a law against such fast driving."

Blacker words were flung after the racers as the folks rearranged their coats and skirts and peace of mind, and climbed back into the road. The Pastor's sermon was hardly remembered that day. But the very next Sunday the Pastor grimly revealed the wiles of Satan in this new age of speed.

The congregation was growing too. A new church was being built. For a long time it had been only talk. Many folks, living on the east side of the township and beyond, had grumbled at sending their children to confirmation school over six or seven miles of snow-drifted or spring-muddy roads. They had objected to driving that distance themselves, Sunday after Sunday, especially when folks on the west side, where the church stood, could practically spit in the graveyard from their own farms, Old Mr. Mercer growled. "I work my team six days a week, and on Sundays I have to chase them seven miles to church. No wonder they're a barrel of bones. We ought to have the church in the center of the township."

The Pastor reminded him acidly that nobody hesitated to drive or even walk seven or eight miles to a barn dance or a house party; yes, and that after a long day's sweat in the fields or in threshing. Folks went to shin-dandies, no matter if mud or snowbanks reached the armpits.

Then too, folks were becoming more prosperous. Times were no longer tougher than bull's meat, as Alb Hukelpoke said. Crops had been good. There was almost merriment at the jingle of silver in a pocketbook. They could afford to erect a new altar unto the Lord.

After much higgling and haggling, the new church was built not far from the old. It was erected in the cementing amity of harangues and squabbles and a couple of fist fights over just where God's altar ought to stand. But folks were proud of the new white structure with the green tower and the spiraling steeple, the gallery inside and the arched windows, even if the seats were still rough board and hard to sit on. The anteroom at the entrance served as a schoolhouse.

These things came on so gradually, Johnny hardly thought of them as change and therefore accepted them unprotestingly. Seldom indeed was he aware, except dimly and in disturbance, how manifoldly and in what subtle ways Time had shifted the perspective. About other things he was blindly doubting.

There was all this talk about diversified farming and one thing and another. There was Mr. Dunkel (like Kurt) filling his mouth and the neighbors' ears with notions about new methods of conservation.

"It might be purty smart to plant hay and sell it, just like wheat or oats," Mr. Dunkel proposed once. "And I don't see why we can't start up a farmers' club, the way they do in other townships. Then when you fellers want to arger about farming methods, we'll get together and bust a nail keg or two."

One autumn day (the rig was at Mr. Peiser's then) Mr. Dunkel, Johnny and Kurt were riding a lumber wagon from the granary to the field. The wagon jolted in and out of dead furrows and shallow ditches. Mr. Dunkel said, "Rough bitch, this land of Peiser's." They hit a bump that made their teeth bite together.

A grin crooked Johnny's red lips. "Your pants holding up, Kurt?"

To steady himself, Kurt grabbed at the sideboards. "There ought to be some way to stop these washouts. All that good dirt washing into the sloos."

"Plow 'em shut," Johnny said shortly, ready to argue. "How else? Only way I ever heard of, and the easiest."

"Maybe." Kurt was slow to give in. "But we've done that all these years, and look at it."

"Sure." Mr. Dunkel pulled at the lines. "We plow 'em shut in fall and the rains next spring wash them all out again. The ditches grow deeper."

"Well, what you going to do?" demanded Johnny. "Stick your backsides into the ditch and stop spring rains?"

"Mr. Muri piled rocks one year," Kurt began.

"Judas, his plow must have been dull as a board," hooted Johnny.

"Ya, see, that's what a farmers' club is for," insisted Mr. Dunkel. "There you can talk over such stuff."

"It's worth sitting on and thinking about," Kurt said as they drove up near the machine. The wagon stopped.

"You fellers go right on sitting and thinking until the green grass sprouts from your butts." Johnny swung a leg over the box and climbed down. "I've got thrashing to do." Nevertheless, he was vaguely disquieted. There was an independency in Kurt and Mr. Dunkel that broke the smooth roll of custom and gently shook the fabric of accustomed ways.

These matters troubled him when he had time to think about them. But that was seldom. Usually, there was too much work to be done on his acres and on his rig to worry about that which couldn't be halted any more than

a falling drop, or changed any more than the shining forth of the rainbow.
Nine months of the year he was shoulder-deep in labor as preparation for
the three months of threshing in the fall. And there was Lilice.

He grinned crookedly sometimes, thinking about her. In spite of the
deadly wear of custom and habit, he delighted in her. When her lashes
fluttered and half hid her eyes in that certain way he'd come to recognize
and yearn for, when she reached out to touch him but didn't, he was stirred
in the flesh as much as ever. The blood in his veins seemed to pause for a
step and then (as though a knot were untied and a bag spilled of its fullness), it tumbled through his body in a run of heartbeats. Water oozed
under his tongue. The sinews tugged queerly in his thigh. During the
threshing season he drove home as eagerly as if it were Saturday night and
he taking her to a dance for the first time.

"She's—Judas, she's some woman!" he thought, driving back to the rig
in the morning. "There ain't no one like her. But she's more than that, too.
She gets ahold of my *insides*. I can talk with her. Better than with any one
one except——" (But he couldn't say Snoose. He rubbed the name from
his mind by thinking of Lilice.)

He first noticed the strangeness in Lilice the summer Robin was born. He
walked into the kitchen one day when Robin was a month old to find her
fix-eyed and staring. The baby in her lap kicked lustily all his naked limbs.
The washrag was crumpled in a tight fist. "Johnny, Johnny," she cried,
her voice squeezed into a whisper. She let the washrag slip into the basin
on the chair beside her. "Look." Her finger trembled over but did not touch
a faint discoloration near the baby's eye. A drop of water fell on the little
one's cheek.

"Nothing much to see," he answered, poking a thumb at the baby's chin.
"That little bugger takes to water like——"

"It's a scar," Lilice said breathlessly. "A mark."

"Oh, sure," he said calmly. "Lots of people have 'em. Arty Nussbaum's
got a reddish mark on his cheek—a birthmark. And 'member that funny
little hollow in Em'ly Musser's——" Em'ly Musser. He stopped. Em'ly
Musser, the sad-mouthed, the woebegone, who was marrying Jimmy Morrison that summer—Jimmy of the brown hair, whose slenderness reminded
Johnny more and more of——

"Oh!" Lilice cried as though entwined in his thought. She clapped a
hand to her cheek. "Oh, Johnny!"

"Whatever's the trouble?" He gathered himself, easy once more, his lips
widening in a stiff grin. "A mark like that's the commonest thing in the
world."

She picked up the washrag mechanically. Water wrinkles circled from her fingers. "I don't know what came over me," she said then, a faint redness sweeping into the paleness of her cheeks. "Such a dreadful feeling, as if I couldn't breathe and got dizzy. Such a silly." The dimple unbuttoned in the suggestion of a smile.

"You're a queer duck, Punkin." He bent and let his cheek touch her temple. He couldn't express his relief. "Punkin," he whispered. The baby kicked at the washrag dribbling water on his belly.

The discoloration, whatever it was, vanished in a week or so. Lilice never spoke of it again. The baby grew and Lilice bloomed until she looked like the girl who used to dance in his arms, Johnny declared. A great lightness of spirit filled him then. But he remembered that day. He remembered how she studied him covertly, crow's-feet crinkling at her eyes. He remembered how she moon-gazed over her sewing, staring at the lamp by the minutes together until Robin's cry shook her from abstraction.

When he was ready to leave for the threshing runs that year, she held him, whimpering, "Johnny, be careful, be careful."

"You silly," he said, half angry at her insistence. "Can't you get over this foolishness? I'm as safe on that rig as I am here in the yard."

"How can you say that?" she murmured. "Last year Bluber's separator man fell off the separator and got hurt. And then Tetzell's fireman got burned." No need to remember Uncle Herm or Snoose.

"Sure, the blockhead. What else can you expect of Tetzell's fireman?" Johnny shrugged. "Got drunk one night and crawled to the engine to get warm. He fell against the firebox, he was so pig-eyed. Nobody gets drunk on my rig, not while a wheel is turning, anyway."

He left her. Lilice went back to the cradle. Both held the same thought: there were two lying flat and long, one under a wool-stitched quilt, one under a spread of grass roots.

6

Uncle Herm died that early autumn. He struggled with the knots of pain until his breath failed. As though glad to escape at last this clutter of bones, he hardly more than slumped back and lay still. There was a time when Johnny would have sworn the earth's axis would screech to a stop, should any harm come to Uncle Herm: the stars prick a cold dark heaven forever, if it happened at night; the shadow of day freeze where it fell, if it happened under the sun. Uncle Herm with kindness inches deep in the wrinkles of his face—there must be something wrong with a universe that no longer had a place for him.

But it did happen and no star fell; no, not even the feather of a sparrow whirled to earth because a man gave his bone and flesh to the roots of grass and dandelions.

Robin was a month and a half old the afternoon Kurt had come to get Johnny. "He's asking for you. He's mighty bad." There was on Kurt's face neither indifference nor compassion, only a stolid understanding. "I think this time it's——" He lifted a shoulder.

Johnny was threshing at Torgrimson's new farm that day. With a quiet "Watch things a little, will ya, Alb?" and instructions to Marty Borman, the fireman, he went with Kurt.

Aunt Phrena took his hand almost gratefully when Johnny arrived. He felt a pang at the gray in her hair, but thought, "Well, it's little wonder." She flung up the apron to sop tears.

Uncle Herm opened his eyes so slowly it was as though his lids were heavy curtains and drew up laboriously. After a moment of questioning search, he quavered, "Na, Johnny, it is better than pills to see you."

"How are you today?" Johnny swallowed over his question. Such foolishness.

What was meant for a smile barely moved Uncle Herm's lips. "Like yesterday, like yesterday," he murmured. "I'd like to see your little feller, Johnny. Robin. It's a nice name." He appeared to sleep with wide open eyes so that Johnny called almost fearfully, "Uncle Herm. Uncle Herm, are you—is there anything I can get?"

A moment of wandering back, and Uncle Herm said, "Na, Johnny, one of these days I'll know what we all want to know. Maybe I'll see your ma."

With thickness frogging his throat, Johnny asked, "Shall I get the Pastor, Uncle Herm? Kurt's got the team still hooked up." This would not continue the breath longer, he knew, but it would be eminently proper.

"Pastor?" quavered Uncle Herm. "He was here last week. I told him to baptize your boy. He smells of brimstone." As though the past that hung shadowlike over his mind lifted and let memory in, he tried to speak out, and failed. Sweat started on his forehead. Johnny sat stricken.

At last Uncle Herm broke the silence on his mouth. "Johnny, Johnny, I thought—I thought I had so much time left for thrashing, so much time left. Where has it run to? Where . . ."

He died that night, while over the hills in Johnny's house Robin slumbered and puffed the air of tomorrow's promise in and out, in and out of his lungs and while Johnny tried to make the bread and potatoes of Lilice's meal savory on his tongue.

"Suffering all these months." Lilice brought the gravy.

"I can stand anything but that." Johnny's mouth went crooked. He held back the tears. "Twisted like a hopvine——"

"Hush," Lilice said as though he were Robin. She came to lean against him. He turned his chair sidewise and held her on his lap. The gravy jellied in the bowl.

The next day, in spite of Johnny's demurrings, she went to help Aunt Phrena. A queer almost appreciative look came into Aunt Phrena's eyes. She understood. They were even. A day's exchange of baking and sweeping in the black hours of sorrow had been duly given, duly accepted. That much was settled.

Threshing continued while for a decorous space Uncle Herm lay in his house. Faintly over the fields drifted the song of the separator. But his ears were stopped forever against the rattle of wheel and shaker. In the kitchen Aunt Phrena tiptoed heavily.

On the day before the funeral, Johnny threshed at Mr. Muri's. He was in a tearing hurry, in order to begin at Mr. Unsinn's the following morning. In spite of himself, irritation at the delay prickled in him. "Devil," he grumbled. "Always something to upset a feller's plans." Then he lifted the chisel he was carrying and flung it violently. It clattered against the wheels of the tank wagon. That evening he told the crew, "No thrashing tomorrow."

"Ya shure, by t'under," agreed Mr. Muri. The men nodded.

In the darkness he rode home, his thoughts sadly on Uncle Herm. Hell of a twisted world . . . There's Uncle Herm. He liked my ma. And there's Aunt Phrena. She got sweet on my pa. Judas. My pa marries Uncle Herm's sweetheart and my ma marries Aunt Phrena's beau. There's a riddle for you. And not one of them, not one, got enough happiness to fill a half-pint can, except maybe Uncle Herm.

He felt almost sorry for Aunt Phrena, he wasn't sure why. Plenty of gall in her teeth, he decided. But Uncle Herm—by what alchemy had he transmuted pain and futile regret into patience and quiet laughter at the world? In a way Uncle Herm was like Mr. Dunkel. For Mr. Dunkel was alone now, serenely blind to the sympathy of his neighbors. His wife brooded behind the iron gates of the asylum in Fergus. Sometimes she screamed. But he whistled sprightly as a redbird.

Them two fellers, Johnny thought. The rest of us bawl but they got a smile ready. For them, what's past is past.

As he unharnessed the team (the windows in the house shining with home and Lilice), a notion stung in his head: Tomorrow the funeral and no thrashing. This much I can do for Uncle Herm. But I could not do it for Snoose. Not for Snoose. The harness grew heavier in his grasp.

They buried Uncle Herm the next day. And no sparrow fell, no star. The Pastor used the text: "For all our days are passed away in thy wrath: we spend our years as a tale that is told . . . teach us to number our days that we may apply our hearts unto wisdom." Psalm 90:9-12.

Over the grave Aunt Phrena planted purple Easter lilies and a peony bush. She raised a headstone after a proper interval. On it she had struck: "Herman Barewolf." Below it: "In God there is hope." In a row of graves not far away was another head marker. This one was of iron with a plaque on the cross. On it was a name in faded gold letters: "Augustus Bhaerwulff." Not many folks remembered that the two men were brothers.

7

Kurt began farming Uncle Herm's place as his own. He drove Aunt Phrena to weeping protests by spending more time on experimental plots, trying this strain of wheat and that of oats, than on all the other acres put together. "Ach, Kurt, the neighbors, they make fun of you," she quavered. That his crops were as good as the neighbors', better sometimes, hardly excused him.

"Listen." Kurt paged in the bulletin he'd just received. "If I could find a way to reduce smut in oats, Nussbaum and Marchen would be the first to come running for seed. And they'd brag about the bushels they got per acre, without any credit to me." He continued his experiments.

Since neither Kurt nor Aunt Phrena objected, Johnny took the rig as his own. There was a warm glow in his cheeks the day he settled the payments and so cut whatever strings bound him to Uncle Herm's farm. That same day he went to see Mr. Nussbaum, the treasurer of the church. There was more than a little malice in his grin when he offered the bills.

"You coulda knocked me over with a darning egg," Mr. Nussbaum exclaimed later. "Up and paid his church dues, two years back and the next year, too. Wonder why he don't come to church oftener. Course, that wife of his——"

The Pastor told Mr. Nussbaum, "Na, a lazybones of a churchgoer, that Johnny Black." But he permitted the dues to be entered in the treasurer's book. As far as ink on a page in the congregational record went, Johnny remained a member of the Pockerbrush church, properly and duly certified. He had very little intention of attending services, except when he felt like it.

"I'm just about all paid up," Johnny said to Lilice that night. "I guess we won't have to eat bacon rind after all." He flipped his bankbook. "You know what, Lilice?" He bent and kissed her. "The way things are going, I'm gonna get me another rig in a year or two. The new rigs have got a thingamajig on them, a self-feeder that will thrash so fast the bandcutters will be left in the dust. Poor old Heinie will like that. He won't have to get his knuckles cut up any more. Specially now that he's got the Muri girl on his mind. Judas, a German marrying a Norwegian. Wonder what his kids'll be like, half Norskie, half Dutchman."

(He didn't tell her how at first he'd scoffed at self-feeders when Kurt indicated their advantages. Nor that he pondered lengthily whether the new separator ought to be equipped with them or not. But when he was convinced that he could save time and make money, he opined he might try them.)

"Two rigs?" questioned Lilice, as if that multiplied twice whatever shadows she hid in the wells of her eyes.

"With the self-feeder," Johnny went on, "I can get rid of three men at a throw—two bandcutters and a feeder man. That's so much hard money in my pocket. I can cut the price under Tetzell or Bluber, if I want to. I don't. But I can still make ends meet and lap over a little." There was such a steely twinkle pointing his glance that Lilice looked away and put a hand to her cheek.

That winter they moved to the Krumlich farm and were neighbors to the Morrisons. Herky was in Canada now. Jimmy ran the place.

The Krumlich farm was a hundred and twenty, much of it in wood and pasture, but rich in loamy fields. The moment he learned it could be had for renting, Johnny went to see Mr. Krumlich. The deal was made, though Mr. Krumlich asked, "Why don't you get yourself a piece of woodland and grub it? Then you can build, and you got a place to call your own."

"Oh, maybe." Johnny grinned easily. "I'm getting along. I don't mind cutting the wood. But I'll let somebody else do the grubbing of the stumps."

After the log building, the Krumlich house was so roomy Lilice rattled around in emptiness. She sang loudly, not only to hush Robin but to fill the four downstairs rooms with the noise of occupancy. There were a kitchen, a sitting room, two bedrooms. Upstairs the two rooms were as bleak with rafters and square-headed nails as the one at Uncle Herm's. Mrs. Rose slept downstairs.

The baby thrived like the burdocks near the barn. He had a way of kicking up his legs, covers or no, that brought Lilice running to scold him ecstatically and hide his plumpness caressingly under warmth. Sometimes she'd come wet-handed from the dishpan, just to see how he'd thrust a fist up at her, or lie in that calm repose, the quiet that suggests in a child endless mobility. His breath fluttered in his nose.

Sometimes she'd think, Ernst. I wonder what he'd look like . . . like me or Johnny? He'd be big, maybe as big as Adam's boy. Adam's boy—my, he's large and handsome! Gets his looks from Adam, not from Lena. Of course, he's big for his age . . . nearly four years . . . nothing wrong with him. As if to reassure herself, she'd go quickly to the cradle and peek at Robin. Sometimes she'd undress him with quick, fumbling hands, searching the soft body breathlessly. No, no. She'd laugh at herself, gathering the squirming arms and legs to her breast.

They had him baptized Robin Charley that winter. ("Let's call his middle name Charley," Johnny had said out of a woebegone mood. He couldn't look at her. She had thought of her father's name, but there was so much pleading in Johnny's voice that she consented. She put her hand into his.) With Alb Hukelpoke and Sophie Humber as sponsors, they went to the Pastor's house on a Sunday. Lilice, nervously twisting a handkerchief, one eye on the baby, said nothing. Johnny waited for an opportunity to bristle.

The Pastor looked so grim Alb Hukelpoke nearly swallowed his wad of Indian Twist. Sophie held the baby. She flustered the Pastor by regarding his stiffness with indifference, almost as though saying, "Well, my goodness, you men, you, can't you hurry up?"

Frowning darkly the Pastor picked up the Catechism as if he questioned their right on sacred ground. He said dourly, "Na, you're a lazybones of churchgoer, Johnny Black."

("Steuber was mad, all right," Alb reported at home. "But he came around.")

After the service the Pastor announced, "Na, Johnny Black, it is necessary that I talk about this son of yours. He——"

"There will be time enough for that," Johnny interrupted bluntly without waiting for the Pastor to finish. "On another day." He took the baby and led the way to the door. The others followed.

For a long while the Pastor regarded their departing backs, so angry his beard bristled and he forgot about the baptismal fee. "Such people." It wasn't until later that he found the bill lying on his desk. It was as large as the best members of the congregation could offer. A mite larger, he admitted.

At home Lilice took the baby as if in relief. "I'm glad you are safe, my dear," she said softly.

Johnny's eyes widened. It was on his tongue's-end to ask, "Safe? What do you mean, Leesa?" But the queer look on her face halted him. Her brows were gathered into a knot, her gaze pointed in a stare. He felt again the nudge of this strangeness growing in Lilice. Uneasiness disturbed him, but he shrugged it away.

8

That spring Brother Erdman returned, round of cheek and brimming spirit full, his zeal replenished in his long absence. Mrs. Edgely baked a pan of cookies, his special favorites, to welcome him. Soon afterward he felt the spirit shake him so profoundly that he invited the neighbors to the meetinghouse—"For a special ingathering," he announced. "The very stones of this house cry to the poor broken, weeping soul, 'Come in, come in, my beloved, and wash away your ills in my comfort.' Put everything on God's broad shoulders. Care not for tomorrow, not even for bread. The Lord will provide." Aunt Phrena hastily attended the service.

The very next Sunday Pastor Steuber lined his sermon with scorn that was fiery. Like another Elijah he shouted, "Cry unto your god, you Baal-worshipers. 'Baal, Baal.' He answers you nothing? Mayhap he sleeps. Cry again. Startle him from his slumbers with your sinful hymns. Remember how the priests of the heathen temple were destroyed, you defilers of the eternal God."

His congregation buzzed. Many folks conversed in low, serious tones. "I wouldn't set foot in that meetinghouse. . . . By jippers, it's asking for a stroke of lightning."

"It could be," Mr. Dunkel agreed mildly. "It depends on who gets struck." But Aunt Phrena was sure that the Kingdom was immeasurably more secure, now that Brother Erdman proffered his sweet promises again.

That spring after a light snow, Adam's little boy was killed. Adam was hooking a skittish pair of young horses to a stoneboat. He was attaching the last trace when one of the horses stepped nervously and kicked. In sudden rage he caught the lines and brought them slapping across the horse's rump. The team leaped ahead; the lines were torn from his hands. The horses galloped across the yard. Then Adam saw the boy playing in the snow, dragging the sled behind him. He tried to yell but there was a band on his tongue; he gurgled. The horse ran forward. He heard a shrill, small scream. . . .

For a while, a short while, the little boy's hands still gently patted the snow on his sled. There was that much to see. But as Adam gathered him up, the little hands went limp.

Jackie Marchen brought the news to the Black house, riding over in a hurry. Pale and breathless, Lilice cried, "Lena, you poor thing, you poor thing!" Johnny held Robin closer. Mrs. Rose wept.

After a while Lilice made up her mind. "I'm going over, Johnny. I'll stay a couple of days."

"And leave me? Lilice, it's bad enough——"

"Mother'll stay here. I'll take Robin. It won't be long."

"I don't see why you have to go," Johnny grumbled. "Lena didn't come when——"

"Johnny, I'm not exchanging a run of threshing with anybody," she reproached him.

"I didn't mean that." He kissed the baby repentantly. "I hate to have you gone even for a day."

"And Adam? You think his boy will be back in a day?" She went into the bedroom. "He was such a strong, big boy." Her voice came muffledly.

Without further word he harnessed the team.

In the Rose house they found Lena hysterically upbraiding Adam. "It's all your fault. You always got to have him around you. He never stayed in the house. Always outside with you. It's all your fault."

"Oh, Lena, don't." Mrs. Rose tried to console her. "Don't. It only makes things worse."

Adam sat near the stove, his face numbly in his hands. "I told him not to play in the yard while I harnessed the team. I told him," he muttered over and over. "I scolded him. I scolded him. And now——"

In sudden desperate terror Lilice clutched Robin to her, this second-born, as though she saw the dark hags of fate, those haters of laughter and the grin of happiness, about to snatch with bony fingers even this remainder of a meager joy.

"This is more than a man can stand," Johnny burst out. "I'll drive over in the morning to see you, Lilice." With Mrs. Rose at his side he stumbled into the spring dusk.

Brother Erdman came to weep comfortingly with Lena. Adam went to the barn. Almost frantically, seeking balm for inner hurt, Lena went to the meetings, dragging the reluctant Adam with her. Prostrate she beat the pine floor beyond the railing with her fists, begging for consolation. Adam sat down to many a meal his own hands cooked after work in the fields.

One day Mrs. Rose decided to go home.

"But why ever?" Lilice protested.

"Poor Lena. That girl's gone all to kindling. Adam needs me." She gathered her bundles and returned to Adam and Lena, and the numb chill that hung from the ceiling. Now and again, she joined them in attending Erdman's services. "For Lena's sake," she confided to Lilice. "Really, though, I'm getting old. That smart Erdman and his smooth manners. It's pleasant to hear him although I know he is more than halfway fooling me. It's a sign of age, I'm sure."

In those early summer days after her mother had gone and the wool shawl was no longer draped over the rocking chair, Lilice shrank before the realization that this autumn for the first time she must face the threshing season and Johnny's absence alone—alone with the baby. More than once she hugged Robin fiercely so that he cried out. All tenderness, she hushed him then, her fingers straying without thought to his temple. It remained fair and unblemished.

Sophie visited less often. "It's too far to drive," she complained. "Whiteland's was far, but this is worse, this Krumlich place. Hide yourselves like pocket gophers." When she did come she remained in the thought like good news and on the tongue like a piquant savor. "Clymy is going to buy that forty next to ours. Times aren't so bad now," she chattered. "Last Saturday we danced at the Meiers'. That Mrs. Meier—such clothes! She made her husband jealous. Just like a man . . . Clymy got a little too much *kümmel schnapps*. I had to drive home. Ya, these men . . . next Saturday it's at the Peisers'."

She rattled on, filling Lilice with a vague longing. "We never have fun any more," she yearned. "Trouble, trouble, morning and night, it seems."

"Ya, I know," commiserated Sophie. "Why don't you come Saturday? They got a new caller for the square dances. The way he jigs when he calls!"

Long after she had gone Lilice let unease nag her. At last the longing crystallized into determination. She put the baby into his cradle and went into the bedroom. "Death and trouble," she murmured. (Death to the kernel, death to the sprout, death to the greening blade.) From a closet she brought her dresses and flung them on the bed. "I don't care. We don't have to bury ourselves." The dresses certainly needed tidying: a frill drooping here, a cuff wrinkled there, a pleat as dull-edged as a lath.

"Johnny," she said at supper over his favorite dish of herring and milkgravied potatoes, "we haven't been to a dance for years, it seems. Sophie goes. She sets her kids in a corner and dances till poor Clymy's tired as a horse. Couldn't we go for once?"

"Judas, Punkin!" He speared another piece of herring. "It's a long time I've waited to hear you say that." Happily he poked a fork in her direction. "Peiser is going to have a dance Saturday night. Let's go to town tomorrow and buy out the Emporium."

"Sophie was telling me about a waist they got on sale." Her smile bloomed.

"Sale," he scoffed. But his eyes snapped blackness with excitement. "You get yourself a dress and some doodads that will make their whistles pop. I need some shirts myself. Good stiff fronts. And don't you ever get me another of those linen collars. I'd just as soon wear a band saw. If you do, I'll make you wear it yourself." There was haste in the way they flung themselves into the forgetfulness of gaiety.

On Saturday night at the Peisers' then, the Johnny Blacks, their Robin cooing in Sophie's arms, danced the first waltz of the evening in a cloud of stares and scarcely muffled "Ahs." Flustered more than he cared to show, Johnny struggled with the newness of his suit, a "Fancy Colored Mummy Effect Silk Mixed Worsted Round Cut Sack Suit" (so the Emporium described it) with pale green and pale blue squares ("Each square is half an inch in diameter," the clerk had whispered ecstatically). These squares formed checks with black centers. It was the Emporium's most colorful. He looked down proudly on Lilice, though the movement nearly choked him, the celluloid collar was so tight and the stiff-bosomed shirt so like a piece of tin crowding up his chest.

His eyes were black with fun and with desire, she saw. There was a certain hard crinkle of his eyes she'd come to recognize, and a downsweep of his lashes, slow and deliberate, which seemed to tickle over her skin until a delicious panic rushed through her breasts. She hoped her skirts were billowing out as she wanted them to.

She was still in a flutter over Mrs. Peiser's upraised hands and jealous exclamations. It wasn't every woman in Pockerbrush who could wear a box-plaited shirtwaist with puffy sleeves and a flare skirt ("with thirteen gores," uttered Mrs. Fleischer piercingly), a frivolous belt and a collar that gave stateliness to her neck.

There were mutterers in the corners, shielding their whispers with curved palms. "Them Blacks; a mighty jumpy couple . . . she with her brother's child hardly cold yet. . . . Well, his uncle ain't been buried so awfully long. . . . You'd think he'd have some shame, that Marchen boy dead on his conscience. . . ."

They never heard the whisperers. " 'Waltz me around and around,' " hummed Johnny, hugging her. " 'Member, Punkin? Gosh, you're—you're as pretty as when you danced the schottische, years ago."

"I can still dance and you know it." She bobbed her chin at him. "Better than that Haber girl you danced three times with tonight."

"What!" he gasped, genuinely astonished. "That little chit?"

"You couldn't put a needle between your head and hers," she told him. "Do you have to dance with your head so close——"

"You little devil. Wait till I get you home." He breathed deeply.

Thereafter it was common as dandelions to see the Black and the Humber buggies in a night-dark yard where a dance flickered yellowly in the windows of a barn or a granary or a house. They polkaed and square-danced, whirled themselves dizzy.

While Sophie danced, light in her ankles for all her size, Lilice minded the Humber brood. While Lilice waltzed or two-stepped, Sophie cooed over Robin's head. Clymy and Johnny, however, dodged a sobbing infant or a sleepy four-year-old whenever they could and happily swung in the corners—until Sophie grumbled, "Them menfolks. We women take turns watching the kids. But the men, they run off with the neighbors' girls, the lizards."

"Not Johnny," Lilice beamed at her. "Why, he was really mad when I picked Heinie in the ladies' choice. I guess that Muri girl didn't like me either. Ah, well." She shrugged.

When she was in another's arms, for all that it was dancing, Johnny was amazed at himself for being irritated. He couldn't help it. She's so damned—oh, I don't know, he thought. Once after Arty Nussbaum had waltzed twice in a row with her, Johnny tapped Arty's shoulder.

"This is where I cut in," he insisted shortly. He swung Lilice into the rhythm. "What do you mean, dancing all night with that feller?" he demanded more roughly than he knew.

"All night? Twice." She tantalized him with a smile. "Johnny Black, that's the nicest compliment I ever——"

"Compliment?" he growled, not yet mollified. "You behave yourself, or I'll compliment you where you won't like it."

She laughed at him, her finger tips nibbling at his ear.

On nights such as those, flushed and tempestuous with the evening's whirl, spinning with company and laughter and (on Johnny's part) a glass of schnapps or two, they'd come home and go chattering to bed. As if winning a reprieve from an inner disturbance, she'd let Johnny have his way, her fingers tangled in his wavy hair. But even in her yielding, there would come now and again a nameless dread (in ecstasy there is also oblivion). She'd find herself straining against Johnny's impetuous demand, the hard intimacy of his embrace. Lost in the recklessness of flesh, Johnny'd feel her slight reserve with a hint of irritation coming to his ardor. But his clasp remained unrelaxed.

And one night, in drowsy wakefulness, too excited to sleep, they lay a long hour, each listening to the other's breathing. She's a hard sleeper, he thought. Judas, if I could sleep like that; sleep like Robin, nothing to bother me . . . nothing to bother me . . .

She thought, He's so dead to the world, I could reach over and tickle him, and he'd never move. The way he breathes when he sleeps: such a long time between two breaths. I get scared. Suppose he didn't breathe again; suppose I lost him. Why do I think of such crazy things?

She moved restlessly, sighing. His ear scraped over the pillow. She felt his lips quivering like a boy's brokenly against her cheek. "Punkin, I wish I were a kid again, and me and *him* together. I'd make it all so different."

He wasn't sure whether it was crying or laughing that squeezed his throat when her tears itched along his nose. Night stretched its blackness away beyond the bed, beyond the ceiling, beyond the rafters of the world. They lay quietly as though listening, eyes wide in the unsleepy dark.

9

In July the Pastor thumped the pulpit in the old church for the last time and moved God and the Scriptures into the new. Before long, the congregation would celebrate the mission festival service and dedicate this monument to the Lord's plenteous grace and mercy. The building was white inside and out, but, Mr. Dunkel thoughtfully observed after a couple of sermons, the thunder and the brimstone hadn't improved in flavor.

To the celebration they would invite members of sister congregations at Loon Lake and Mary's Hill and Fergus. That is, the Pastor would. They would have joint services in the forenoon and more in the afternoon. Folks would bring their dinners.

In the afternoon a student serving his internship down in Fergus would speak. Gabriel Ewig, they said his name was. A queer kind of person, Mrs. Peiser said her sister in Mary's Hill told her. And her sister had it straight from a cousin in Fergus who knew a man that had heard him preach. He was full of notions and odd ones, at that. His preachings (like black sheep) strayed far from those pathways beside the troubled waters which Pastor Steuber had made familiar to his congregation. Or so the story ran.

Johnny and Lilice heard about the festival. "I s'pose a feller ought to go to church once a year." He stretched and yawned. "A *missionsfest* is as good as Easter or Christmas."

Lilice was very quiet a moment before she said, "Why don't we go then?"

"Oh, I don't know." Johnny relaxed. "I really ought to take a look at the canvas on the stacker. I've got my hands so full all week, Sunday's about the only time——"

On Sunday morning, however, Sophie and Clymy drove up. "Well, I never!" Sophie bustled into the kitchen. "Eating breakfast and the sun four hours high! Lazier than bull calves, you two."

Clymy, shooing his three kids ahead of him and carrying the fourth, stepped lightly over the threshold. He kept a stern fatherly eye on them. Johnny couldn't help noticing that the rabbity attitude was mostly gone, now that Clymy's acres were widening, his crops improving and his brood of children growing. There should have been a ludicrousness about the way he squared his little chin against the world but there wasn't. That chin was too pugnaciously alert.

"Come in, come in," said Johnny, getting chairs for them. "Sit and have a slug of coffee."

"We got up so late," confessed Lilice, bringing more cups and saucers. "Johnny is the hardest thing to get out of bed on Sunday mornings."

"Ya, them men." Sophie tucked back a stray curl. "They'd keep a woman in bed with them till the chickens scratched at the door—unless it was to make fire, of course." She poured coffee into a saucer. Before she blew on it, she said, "Listen, now. There's a *missionsfest* at the church. Get your duds on and come with us. Student Ewig is going to preach. They say he talks right back to the ministers and they don't like him. I'd like to hear that."

Johnny demurred, enumerating his work as excuse. Lilice spent a moment in emptying her cup, as though coming to a decision. Her finger tightened on the handle. She said gently, "There's a fresh shirt in the drawer, Johnny; a collar, too. I'll have to get some sandwiches ready. But it won't take me a second to clear this up."

With the Humbers they went to the festival on this hot day. Johnny grumbled that a man couldn't call his soul his own, the womenfolks made up their minds and his too.

When they arrived the hitching posts in the churchyard, three rows of them, were lassoed and tangled with the ropes and straps of horses tied there. Every place was taken. With many other folks who arrived too late for a post, Clymy unhitched his team under the trees south of the church. Some folks stopped their wagons and buggies in the cleared space beyond the graveyard. At first Clymy had guided the horses in that direction. But Johnny hastily said, "No. Over there. Under those elms. That's a nice shady spot."

At a prod from Sophie, Clymy said, "Oh, sure."

They drove into the coolness. Johnny helped unhook the team. Soon the horses were munching hay. The bag of oats and the dinner baskets were placed under a tree. Lilice worried, "I hope nothing gets at them," and Sophie comforted her. "Nothing here to harm, except ants, and they'll get in anyway."

They joined the twos and threes and half-dozens that were forming on the way to services. Aunt Phrena was there. She nodded distantly, her three chins folded together like Anders Stramff's accordion. She used to say, "That Rose thing, Johnny's wife," when she was forced to speak of Lilice. Today she held her tongue; in fact, there was about her a reserved courtesy not far from friendly.

Kurt stopped to ask Johnny, "You really figure on getting that self-feeder, or are you just diddling with the idea?" But Johnny, in no hurry to provoke neighborhood opinion, charily evaded direct answer.

Of the morning service Johnny remembered little. Pastor Steuber himself was in the pulpit. "He's getting along in age, too," Johnny said to himself, noticing the salt-and-pepper of years sprinkling the dark hair and beard. In spite of the partly opened windows, the odor of paint and new lumber seemed to hang from the dazzling, latest-styled chandelier (five coal-oil lamps in a circle) that dangled from the ceiling on a long chain.

Johnny's eyes shadowed with the sleepy drone of the Pastor's Sabbath anger. Long time since I attended a regular service, he drowsed. Not much change, though. He watched a bluebottle fly crawl on the floor at his feet. It entered a patch of sun, its wings shaggy with sunburst, then it dimmed into shadow.

It was a wink or two before a shout from the pulpit dragged him into awareness. The Pastor was warning, "Not one fleck, not one jot must soil the white purity of these new walls, white as the purity of the Lord. Keep ye clean!" he cried at the congregation. He glared at the gallery where several of the young fry were telling Saturday night stories and tittering. Silence fell. He continued, "If you are afflicted, even as the heathen are; if trouble weighs you down, if calamity howls at you, you alone are responsible. There are punishments from God for sin. Repent ye! Turn to God's word before it is too late, or you must hear the awful condemnation, 'Depart from me, ye evil ones!' Repent!"

Under his shoutings Lilice's head sank lower and lower. Sin. Evil. Lust of eye and the flesh. Whited sepulchers. Could she ever stand here with Johnny as a member? Every act, every thought-flicker importuned of the heart and the mind by laws older than the Medes and the Persians, without which the race and the individual could not survive—all these were muddled, sullied in the Pastor's denunciations. No different, no different, she thought, remembering her mother and that day at the Marchens'.

No wonder Johnny stayed at home on Sundays. She pulled at a coarse thread in her gloves, this way, that way, the rat's nest of the past scattered about her, littering her mind with that which she longed to forget.

The last amen and the click of Mr. Dunkel's teeth snapping off a yawn came together. Outdoors the air freshened Johnny. Lilice, holding Robin, was as subdued as a partridge hen but Sophie, hungry with the smell of dinner in her nose, bubbled with talk. "Na, it's a new church but an old sermon. He scolded nicely, didn't he, Johnny?" Johnny agreed.

How could they be so unconcerned? Lilice puzzled. The Pastor had just now practically condemned all of them to perdition. Yet here they were, hungry for dinner. Didn't the Pastor mean it? Or didn't the congregation worry about divine punishment? I don't understand it, Lilice thought.

As they headed for the refreshment stand at the rear of the church, Sophie grabbed Lilice's arm. "That must be him there—Ewig," she whispered hoarsely.

They all hesitated in their stepping, observing this man in the unpretentious gray-black suit (not the frock coat they always saw the Pastor in), who walked with Norton. He might have been a businessman like Mr. Jimpson or Banker Ford. He was so unministerial in appearance that, earlier, Mr. Fleischer mistook him for the new clerk in the machine shop who had come with the Mary's Hill flock. Bustling up to Mr. Ewig he had asked, "Say, how in hell do those new self-feeders work, they got on thrashers now?"

Smiling, Mr. Ewig replied, "As I understand it, they've been experimenting with them for several years and they seem to be satisfactory. I——"

Then Mr. Norton hurried up, nudging Mr. Fleischer's ribs. "Pastor Ewig, this is Mr. Fleischer," he said in a somewhat sepulchral manner as befitted the occasion. "One of our good members."

"I have already met Mr. Fleischer," twinkled Gabriel Ewig—at which Mr. Fleischer choked on his tobacco spittle, bugged his eyes like a catfish and tottered away. "Mein Gott, the man is a minister." The self-feeders were wiped from his mind. The story buzzed over the lunch baskets that noon.

As they neared the stand, Sophie said, "They say Ewig used to farm. The call came late but when it did, he dropped everything, sold his farm, left his wife with his folks and went to preacher school."

"I wonder what he'll preach about this afternoon. Will he be like the Pastor?" breathed Lilice softly, as though wishing she hadn't come.

"Folks say he don't preach the way he's s'posed to. Don't wear black clothes all the time either." Sophie shook her head. "And he talks common as ordinary folk."

Johnny said, "I thought he looked kinda old to be a student." He estimated Gabriel Ewig with a backward glance. "I thought he'd be a young one." (Suddenly he saw the apple-cheeked divinity student in Norton's bunkhouse and Silenski and heard dimly on echo of rippling water. . . . "And Death said, A man who is free . . . though sitting still . . . he walks far . . ." A river bank and Snoose.) Silently he took Robin from Lilice's arms.

Against the rear wall of the church had been built the "lemonade" stand. It was a tentlike structure of canvas supported by poles. Under it was a counter of rough planks. Behind the counter were tables on which cooled jars of lemonade, milky with the whitish flakes of broken lemon cells and slightly tinged by the color of yellow rinds. But in the July heat it was the lumps of ice, thick with coolness to set the saliva running, that brought out pocketbooks and silver clinking on the oak counter.

Kids begged, "Pa, kin I have a nickel?" and Pas complained, "A nickel? I just gave you three cents. God sakes, the way kids spend money these days!"

There were packages of candy and a box of oranges. A stem of bananas hung from a crosspiece. Behind the counter, Mr. Peiser and Mr. Schadel in white aprons took on a terrifying if somewhat embarrassed importance, and dealt out gumdrops and peppermints with the shrewd gravity of Banker Ford computing the percents of stocks and bonds.

Johnny bought lemonade though Sophie protested, "For the whole bunch of us? You shouldn't have." Stirred by such generosity Clymy dug up his pocketbook and banged down the money for a dozen bananas. ("Wasters," muttered Mr. Nussbaum, buying himself a couple of cigars but offering a smoke to no one. "A belly hungry for sweet stuff—by jippers, that's what makes a man poor in no time.")

"It isn't often we see bananas." Lilice nibbled at the creamy flesh. She smiled at the crestfallen little Sophus Humber, Sophie's oldest, ten years or thereabouts; for when a neighbor boy said to him, "Let's get us a banana," Sophus who had never seen one before had answered, "Them things? I don't like yellow pickles."

"Course you didn't know," Lilice consoled his red face.

The smell of banana mixed with the smoke of before-dinner pipes. Mr. Schimmel complained bitterly, "I come across that bridge over the dry wash. There was a rotten plank. By Gott, my bay horse fell through and busted his leg right off. I had to shoot him."

Johnny broke into this talk. "If I go through and smash my rig, you fellers on the town board, you'll hear from me."

Folks gathered in discussion or hastened to their vehicles for the lunch baskets. One of Clymy's boys gurgled through a mouthful of chewed banana, "Kin I have some candy?"

"I should say not!" Sophie exclaimed indignantly. "The idea! I worked over potato salad and sandwiches, getting a big dinner, and you kids stuff yourselves with candy. Not a lick more. Clymy, we're waiting for you." She interrupted Clymy's talk with a neighbor about a newfangled way to stack straw—a wind stacker. "Let's get dinner off our minds and into our stomachs," she said. "The kids will get a belly-ache, all that sweet stuff."

They sauntered back to the team, exchanging "Helloes" and "My, it's hot, ain't it?" with the neighbors, who, in the shade of trees or an angle of the church, were already deep in the cooky-redolence of basket and hamper. A horse, one of Clymy's, raised his head and whinnied. "Wants his oats," Clymy said. "He knows when it's dinner, don't ya, boy?" He brought the bag and dumped the feed into boxes. The horses nosed the grain eagerly.

Johnny pushed the scattered hay together. "Now we can eat, too," he said.

While Lilice unpacked the baskets, guarding the sleepy Robin with one eye, Sophie spread the cloth and threatened her kids with a spoon. "The next feller that sticks a finger in the cooky box, he gets a couple of slaps behind," she scolded. "Buttle, you stay off that tablecloth."

They laid the plates and saucers. Johnny squatted down near Robin. "Judas, that Norton, he gets so fat, every time I see him his pants are stretched farther." He snapped at an ant that ran up the quilt toward Robin's face. "Get away, you bugger. Ya, I hear Norton's making money heel over ankles. He's got stocks in God knows how many oil wells and gold mines."

"So I hear." Clymy reached for a plate.

Sophie opened the sandwich box. "Clymy, he don't care for 'em," she admitted. "But I'm partial to them. That's rose there, and those nasturtium."

"Flower petals in the sandwiches!" marveled Lilice. "Sophie, if you aren't the smart one."

"I butter the bread good and thick and put the petals between the slices," Sophie explained proudly. "Then I leave 'em to draw through over night."

Clymy wouldn't touch them. "I'll take my sandwiches plain."

Johnny bit into one, tested and sniffed as if scented bread were unpleasantly new in his nostrils. "Oh, they ain't so bad," he pronounced judicially. "Rather have my flowers in the garden than in my bread and butter though."

"Ya, them men," Sophie grumbled. "A woman can half kill herself, getting things nice for them, and they turn up their noses."

After dinner, sighing prodigiously, Johnny and Clymy wandered off to the next wagon to chat with Mr. Peiser. Lilice and Sophie packed the dishes and the leftovers. "If I ever see Clymy offer to stay and help with the dishes, I'm gonna get sick and call it a day," Sophie grumbled. "Don't you kids go far," she called warningly to her boys. "We're going back right quick now." Over the scraping of potato salad into a square of paper, she said abruptly to Lilice, "Why don't you join the church here?"

Lilice hesitated, knowing how this was meant. "Sophie, I don't know. The Pastor stands against everything that seems good inside me. When I think of his sermons and what he did to my mother——" She paused. "I don't know. I'm scared of all the terrible things he preaches about. And Johnny hates the meetinghouse. He won't go there. So. And I hate to have Robin grow up afraid all the time, the way Johnny says he was."

"You mustn't take it so serious," Sophie answered comfortably.

"But if you don't take it seriously and the Pastor doesn't mean what he says——" Lilice spread her hands futilely. "I don't know, but I wouldn't care about it."

"I see how you feel." Sophie nodded. They finished with the packing.

When the men returned they all went back to the church. And in the gathering crowd Lilice saw Gatha Blumen tripping along. At her side was her little girl, four-year-old roguishness in frills and prettiness. There was no shame in Gatha's cheek (Lilice saw); no humiliation shadowing her giggle, nor the corner-wise manner in which her eyes flirted with Arty Nussbaum or the unmarried men or Lornas Tetzell—most of all with Lornas Tetzell.

How can she? Lilice wondered almost in envy. I wouldn't dare show my face, I'd be so ashamed. . . . She belongs, that's why. Yes. That's it. And so she has forgiveness. . . . The notion flashed brightly, faded. Lilice twisted the wedding ring as though this were her only grasp on solid respectability.

With dinner over, the folks squandered a nickel or so more on the lemonade stand. ("Squander, that is what it is," the Pastor had said; "and the mission need is so great.") Most of them, however, remembered that there would be a second passing of the collection plate that afternoon—"for the poor, naked heathen in Africa, crying for the gospel," the Pastor had intoned. They found seats early, therefore.

Lilice sat on the women's side with Sophie. She hardly dared lift her eyes to the pulpit and the black cross on the white cloth.

After a quick searching glance Johnny saw Mr. Tellerman, new in the ridges that year and as yet unbespoken for in the threshing runs. Johnny hesitated, thinking, I shouldn't . . . he'll have to ask me first. Nevertheless he slouched into a seat beside Mr. Tellerman, who nodded vigorously.

At Johnny's grin he sidled over. "I meant to talk to you anyway," he whispered, churchliness making his voice hollow. "You got your runs all filled up?"

"Well—" Johnny consulted his toe severely—"pretty near full, all right."

"Oh." Mr. Tellerman drew back disappointed. "I thought maybe——"

"Course," offered Johnny, "maybe we could squeeze you in."

"Could ya?" Mr. Tellerman brightened. "Everybody says you do such a good job, and quick, that I——"

"Tell ya what," Johnny whispered hurriedly, seeing the curtains of the Pastor's cubicle waving, a sign of impending worship. "You come over next week and I'll see how things stand."

Mr. Tellerman leaned back, content, pious again, now that mammon had been satisfied. Johnny cleared his throat. They both faced the altar, seriousness drawing their countenances into stern fixity, though Johnny relaxed over the thought, Well, that's another job on the list. I certainly didn't ask for it, either.

The services began. Student Ewig preached. What they heard that afternoon left the folks neither impressed nor yet unaffected. The things Student Ewig said about missions they had heard before. Used as they were to ringing periods smoking with divine inspiration, they found his mild but firm delivery curiously flat. Besides, he spoke as if he were on a hill and alone with each member and this sermon were an ordinary talk between them about God and salvation and the duty of man. There was no more waving of arms or rasping of tensed vocal cords here than over an agreement between two neighbors about the exchange of a day's threshing. No shouting, no quavers of emotion, no simulation of tears, no prostrations, no violence. In his black gown he looked curiously patient and kind. Was it sorrow that brought the slight droop to his shoulders? Bitter meditation and study that gentleness to his eyes?

Lilice gazed at him absorbedly, listening as though a hand were put out toward her and she had but to grasp it to secure—what? And his eyes: they were as steady and warm as a firm clasp of the hand, inviting her—— She drew back. No, it couldn't be for me.

Some of the things Ewig said startled the benches and brought quiet to the gallery. "It has been said from this pulpit, 'Keep the purity of this church.' Yes, keep it, but keep it no more and no less than you keep the purity of your inner selves. We as pastors and those who go into the mission field, let us consider how *we* keep this purity inviolate. It is conceivable that as much defilement may come from this pulpit as from those pews. . . .

"The spirit of God works from within. No one was ever corrected into virtue, but accepted. If you are bringing a gift to this mission work because of outer compulsion, because an order, no matter whose, has demanded it of you, take back your gift. It has nothing more to do with *you*. It is straw and chaff; the kernel is without life, the sheaf worthless and fit only for bedding. . . .

"We won a war not long ago. Neither politicians nor newspapers allow us to forget the victory. If God sends war and pestilence in order that nations be humbled into seeing their evil ways, then we have outwitted Him. Never have we been more aggressive, more expansive, more ambitious. The war has accelerated research and discovery to such a degree that life two decades ago, one decade even, seems nearly as remote and unbelievable as the Crusades. If our prophets are only fifty percent correct, it is conceivable that folks in these pews may see automobiles crowding the horses from the roads, airplanes outstripping birds, electricity powering machines even on remote farms. . . .

"Wars will be seen, not as scourges of God, but as errors of men; plagues and pestilences not as visitations of God but the ravages of animal parasites, controllable as the dread yellow fever now is, by the efforts of men. . . .

"Man must understand the laws of God in Nature. Is not the spiritual world governed by understandable laws? . . .

"One of our leading theologians says, 'Today art, industry, invention, government—all these are captives marching in Christ's triumphant procession up the hill of fame. . . .'

"It is inner peace a man seeks, a quiet walking in his soul. . . ."

("Though he sits, he walks far. . . ." The thought fluttered idly on the edges of Johnny's awareness.)

Everybody turned to see how the Pastor was taking this. His beard seemed to bristle with the starchiness of anger and his neck was rigid as a stovepipe. He sat, his back stiff in the seat.

"Whoop-Jinny!" exclaimed Mr. Dunkel afterward. "He told 'em, that Ewig did. The Pastor caught it in the gizzard, just like the congregation." Most folks relished this as they did spice pickles.

On the whole they liked the sermon. "Judas, it's about the first preaching I've heard where I didn't feel singed," Alb Hukelpoke said. They couldn't agree with Mr. Nussbaum's ringing "Freethinker, that's what he is. Jippers, the Devil don't have a better friend than a freethinker." As for Ewig's prophecies—well, they weren't any crazier than the stuff you read in the papers.

After services, as the two servants of God stepped from the church door, folks divided respectfully and opened a path for them, walled by half-turned backs and shoulders, furtive with listening ears. That the two men were in heated argument folks saw by the way the Pastor thumped his hymnal against his palm.

"It is written in the Old Testament—" he was saying when Ewig vehemently interrupted him. "Do you mean to say that a document, full of tradition and legend, written for a partly Oriental people, popularized during a crisis some six hundred years before Christ, is to be regarded literally as a guide for us in this our land in the year——"

The Pastor twitched Ewig's gown sharply. Folks were screwing around toward them, ears swinging wide as granary doors to hear two pastors disputing and disagreeing. With quick regard for secular decorum, the Pastor said, "We will talk more fittingly in my house. Come. Such grievous errors! I can show you by text and verse——"

They went away. Folks clacked one to another. "That feller's going to have a tough time getting through preacher school, I'll bet," said Kurt. "They'll probably salt him away in some hole-in-a-corner church and let him spoil there."

After services the Humbers returned to the Black house. Johnny liked the student preacher and said so.

"I'm glad." Lilice squeezed his arm. "He made me feel—well, I don't know. I could ask him to help me, if I got into trouble," she added almost to herself.

"Anyway, he don't beller," conceded Sophie. She yawned comfortably. "Ya, it's nice going to *missionsfest*. The sermons give you new ideas. And then all them heathen taken care of."

She and Clymy and the boys drove away home after a while. Johnny and Lilice waved good-by. As he slipped off his new shoes and dragged the old ones from under the bed, Johnny wrinkled his brow. "You know, Lilice, I can still taste that rose stuff from those darn sandwiches."

10

That autumn, before a wagon moved in the threshing runs, Lilice realized with a dread she couldn't put into words that she was pregnant again. "Why is it I'm so shaky this time?" She pressed her hands to her sides. "Whatever happens, let me be strong enough to bear it. Johnny, Johnny, I hope it's a girl."

That autumn Johnny put the Red Star into Marty Borman's care with Heinie as separator man, and himself drove a new engine and a new separator into the fields. "Let somebody else do the feeding for once," he encouraged Heinie. "You got your share of knuckles cut and broken."

Heinie, blown like a pouter with self-confidence, agreed, now that he was married and dripping-full of the Muri girl's love. That autumn two Black rigs moved on the roads.

Though he belittled it, Johnny was savagely proud of the new Buffalo Head, its heavy drivers, twice as wide as the Red Star's and taller than the tallest wagon wheel; of its heavy weight pressing the cleats deep into grass or roadbed; of the new injector, even when it didn't work, which was half the time; of the shaggy buffalo head embossed on the fire door at the front of the engine; of the whole handful of new gadgets he fingered under Alb's chortling delight.

Alb himself was so important over the separator he could hardly keep his brichin' up, Heinie said. Johnny listened, grinning while Alb exclaimed learnedly over the concaves and the latest in cylinder teeth, the improved grates, the straw rakes with their notched division strips and serrated projections. "They're just like the fins of a damned old fish," Alb said. "They'll shake the hell out of the straw. I don't see how a kernel of wheat can get into the straw pile." The stacker was of the newest design. It easily folded half the length of its carrier back over the separator, like a worm bending its tail rearward over the rest of its body.

"Darn good stacker," Johnny conceded. But the stackmen in the straw pile spat chaff and stem ends. "It's just as dirty as before. There ain't no harder job in thrashing than sweating in the straw," they groaned. "When you sneeze, it's pure dirt."

Kurt had talked about a wind stacker lately. Somebody had invented one. With it you blew the straw into a pile with a blower instead of dropping it at the end of the carrier and heaping it by hand. But the strawmen laughed. "The machine men will improve everything else before they get to us. We're forgotten in the chaff."

It was the self-feeder that provoked wonder and a good deal of ire among the neighbors. "Every year it gets worse," declared Mr. Schadel. "More kernels in the straw pile."

"Course," agreed Mr. Nussbaum. "By jippers, a machine can't feed bundles as evenly as a man can by hand. Every time the separator clogs a whole mess of heads never get touched by the cylinder, and out into the straw pile goes the wheat." Some of the farmers grumpily said they were going to quit the run, if Black put too many newfangled gadgets on his rig.

Serenely Johnny got ready to thresh the grain at his place. He hadn't been nearly so cocksure the day he and Alb were in Mary's Hill and, over a schooner of beer, heard Fritz Mueller, an old thresher from the flats, bawl out, "Self-feeders? Wouldn't have 'em. I tried one. The damn bundles went in so fast, all I heard was a *r-r-rooomp*, and the separator damn near stopped. The belts began to smoke and there I was, clogged up. I lost half a concave of teeth and burned three new belts. To hell with self-feeders!"

Hastily Johnny dragged Alb from the saloon. "We got to see about this," he muttered. From Alb there was lowering doubt and a dubious spitting of tobacco.

Even when the machine-shop man gave the self-feeder a trial before their eyes and Johnny saw it work "slicker'n a bug's ear," as Alb admitted, he was tempted to agree with Alb's profound saying, "You can't trust a salesman. The bastard's got a devil's nest of tricks to fool a feller."

Not until he and Alb tested it privately on a pile of bundles at home did Johnny let out a whoop of confidence. He was ready to believe Kurt's prediction now: "It's the best investment you can make. It'll pay for itself in one season. They've been used down south a lot." Never once did he mention Kurt's advice, however.

This year he'd hired more boys from the ridges than ever before. He let older men and kids pack the straw piles neat and high. It was a hand-picked crew, if he ever saw one. You could lay a bet on their muscles and their clannish loyalty, despite an elbow or two of Satan among them.

The morning he started the threshing at his place, the "elbows" came out. It had rained the night before. By ten o'clock, however, the stacks were dry enough to open. Several farmers, who had rattled over in their wagons, were already gawping at the separator, its red-trimmed-with-green sides radiant in the sun, its self-feeder sticking out a pugnacious jaw above the front wheels. Even before he caught at the whistle cord to signal the start of the year's run (a long, ear-grinding blast followed by a "Toot, toot, start up") he saw by their side smirks one to another that several of the crew planned to give the self-feeder a trial, all right. If they could, they'd clog the machine, choke the cylinder with straw.

Well, let them. He was ready. For a moment he let the rig idle in belt and wheel and shaker. He couldn't help grinning at the self-feeder. How it jutted there at the front of the separator, a stack bulging on each side of it! Like the underjaw of a pickerel or some other mad fish it was. There was the carrier belt moving up the gentle incline toward the knives, the rows of sharp pins stuck in the cleats sparkling as they caught the sun. There was the wild pawing of metal arms at the end of the carrier, each one sharp with a sickle blade. These arms moved on a crankshaft and were controlled by a governor.

He saw Alb standing (as Uncle Herm used to stand . . . Uncle Herm), one foot on the feeder head. Waving at him, Johnny pulled the throttle. The wheels began to clank and turn faster. "Sling the bundles in steady," he had ordered the pitchers. "Leave a space like a man's hat between them."

For a space of minutes while Alb stood as if on guard, the pitchers obeyed, innocent as boys passing a watermelon patch. The tops of the first stacks were sliced off layer by layer. Suddenly the pitchers began throwing the bundles faster. The spaces closed up. The cylinder began to boom and *chug-g-g.*

Lifting a fist, the index finger projecting, Alb made a circlewise motion. "Speed 'er up. Let 'er have the ginger."

Johnny opened the throttle a notch. As though gathering breath against attack, the engine seemed to pause, then barked a ferocious *chuga-a-a-chug* and sent wheel and cylinder humming into a higher key. Bundles flew faster under the jollity of the pitchers. Johnny pulled the lever again. The engine snorted. In a kind of rage it whirled the cylinder faster. Shaker and shaker arm rattled furiously. The grunting and booming diminished although they did not entirely cease. The men pitched as if they'd choke the gullet of the thresher with a stack at a forkful. But the machine ran eagerly now, for all that wheat by the peck ran over the sieves, kernels by the handful remained in the ear, grain scattered into the straw pile.

Let a couple bushels go by, Johnny thought grimly. Pitch until the sweat runs down your tails, you young devils. I'll show you who's boss here.

At any other farm he couldn't have done this. He could here on his own place. The pitchforks lunged. Bundles flew. The pawing knives flashed. But the machine swallowed what was given it with no more than a louder grunt or two. Before long, breathless and panting, a pitcher halted his swift pace, wiped sweat, looked disgustedly around, and jabbed his fork down in surrender. The rest followed his action. The feverish exertion moderated to a steady lift-and-swing-out, swing-back-and-thrust-into-bundle, lift-and-swing-out: a pattern of rhythm they could continue by the hour. Not again, except under rare stimulation, would they spill their strength so prodigally. Something like authority had been established, authority they could brag about.

Before lunchtime that afternoon, Johnny banged the screen door and entered the kitchen. Sophie was there, setting a large basket on the table. She had come during the forenoon. "Na, I don't want to hear one word," she had answered Lilice's protests. "You ain't as light on your feet as you think you are." She peered frankly at Lilice's thickening body.

Now she watched Johnny drink at the pail. "You got a sponge in your belly," she said.

"Those pitchers out there look hungrier than wolves." Johnny peeked over the rim of the water dipper. It was as close and hot in the kitchen as it was in the yard. "Lunch about ready?"

Lilice brought a loaf to the table.

Sophie sharpened a knife. "It'll be ready as fast as fingers and fire can make it," she snapped. The *chug-a-chug* of the engine mingled with the rattle of the water-kettle lid. "Never saw a man yet that couldn't eat five times a day, with lunch besides. 'Specially on the first day of thrashing."

Chuckling, Johnny splashed the dipper into the pail. He came to put an arm about Lilice and pat her stomach before he darkened the doorway, going back to the engine.

Sophie pushed the knife through the sausage. "That Johnny! He's got it sitting behind the ears." Her lips pursed. "I'll carry the basket out, or Johnny can. It's bad, you hefting heavy things now."

"Johnny?" Lilice glanced up from buttering the slices she had cut. "He's much too busy. Threshers——"

"Busy!" Sophie snorted. "He wasn't too busy to find you in bed." She laughed through all her bigness. "Just like a man-critter. You'll have to handle him with a curb bit. I made Clymy do the work before I had Irvie. I didn't lug in a stick of wood or a bucket of water. Them menfolks! If they want their fun, they can take care of the kids, too." Her knife poised over a link.

Deep in a thought of her own, Lilice wasn't paying attention. "Before your babies came along——" she placed four disks of sausage on a buttered slice, covered them with a second slice, cut the two crosswise—"did you ever get scared about—well, did you worry whether the baby'd be—what sort of person, crippled or—or——"

"With Clymy to watch over, I didn't have time." Sophie nibbled a fragment of sausage from the knife point. "Such a worry I had before Irvie was born. I thought his head would surely have a dent in it. I fell over a bucket one morning. Landed squawk on my belly."

"I—I didn't mean quite that." Lilice piled the sandwiches. "Did you ever wonder if—if people could see on the baby what it's—it's folks were like or——"

"Drat it!" roared Sophie. "I knew the minute I turned my back I'd forget the cake." She rushed to the oven. "When you've got three, four kids hanging on your skirts, you take trouble by the day, and forget tomorrow."

"I—I s'pose so." Lilice laid the knife aside. In a quick gesture, half of dread, she crowded a fisted hand up against her breasts.

Johnny paused for a step on the porch. His eyes crinkled and his nose twitched. Nothing like that smell, he thought—hot grease and smoke and thrasher's dust. It was better than pasture clover in spring. It was like the odor of frying meat to a stomach flat with hunger. The engine filled him with an almost kinesthetic delight . . . the flash of the governor balls . . . the polished stroke of the piston . . . gray blur of the flywheel . . . the up-and-down motion of the belt. It made the blood thump in the head. How it *chug-a-chugged* its smooth way through bundle after bundle of his good crops. His were better than most, that year. The Hessian fly, which had "stung" the growing stem on many farms, had not pestered him.

That self-feeder—bundles falling with a metallic rustle and snap on the slant of the carrier . . . bundles sliding one by one up the incline, heads first, into the hacking knives . . . the convulsive shaking of the butt ends under the knives (like rat by dog) . . . the bundle gone into the shadowy throat where the cylinder whirled.

Nevertheless, in the days that would follow, Johnny would have a queer notion that he'd left something behind he'd never see again. For a long time he couldn't get used to looking up and seeing, not the three dark figures bending over the tables, but the long underslung jaw of the feeder poking toward him. In the blaze of new metal, sun lances would strike his eyes. Gone were the cutters' tables at which he and Jackie Marchen or Snoose ("Snoose, my friend Snoose") had stood and hacked the bands, dreary hours together. Gone the feeder's table where Heinie used to stand; and before Heinie, Herky Morrison. Never again would three men (or a man and two kids) sweat themselves green in front of the cylinder.

On this day, however, he was proud of the feeder running so smoothly. And they said a machine couldn't feed so evenly as a man could by hand. Besides, it saves me three men's work and that much pay, he said to himself, or it wouldn't be worth a lip of snuff.

Over the cookies and sandwiches at lunchtime Mr. Peiser announced, "I'm gonna plant me more wheat next year. That self-feeder, that's the slickest thing yet."

"You better plant yourself a couple acres of hay," cautioned Mr. Dunkel. "And get yourself some decent livestock. You'll be ahead in the long run."

"Sure, but there's money in wheat, 'specially when she's thrashed early." Mr. Peiser's whiskery cheeks lengthened over a mouthful of coffee. "Used to be, I had to wait until the snow flew before a rig came, and half my stacks greened out and spoiled. But what can you do? This year it's different. Cripes, my grain'll be in the granary long before Thanksgiving."

The farmers nodded. A kind of excitement, the excitement of hard cash made quickly, ran the circle round.

Johnny kindled at their glowing enthusiasm. "Betcha life," he said. "I'll get a bigger rig if you fellers plant more wheat. The bigger the machine I got, the faster I'll thrash, and the less waste of time you have to take. Thrash you out by the end of October; earlier, maybe." Dissent struck sparks from agreement as they talked about it.

Alb pried his sandwich apart and ate a disk of sausage. Then he pushed a single slice far into his mouth. Before he bit a half-moon from the edge he felt a thought coming, changed his mind and removed the bread. "'Member how we used to come to August Breckmeyer's late in the fall?" he asked, absently regarding the semicircle of teeth marks in the butter and the space where his dogtooth had been. "Breckmeyer's horses and cattle always got loose and tore his stacks to hell; manure all over everything, bundles and all, freezing hard. We'd have to feed that mucky stuff to the separator. Sheetin' Judas, those frozen horse balls would shoot from the cylinder teeth like a slug out of muzzle-loader. Knock you flatter'n a pancake. I 'member one time a feller named Eddie Longheimer, he couldn't talk plain, sorta lisped. He got hit in the head; knocked him silly. Well, he picked himself up and started swearing. 'Desus Chwistopher, Gwod dummit, who in hell's shootin' cwaps awound heah?'"

The men guffawed over their cups. The women stared primly at the lunch basket. "'Pears like that's all past now, feeding at the table." Alb lifted a cup of coffee in the direction of the self-feeder. "No more cut fingers or busted knuckles because a bandcutter got careless and his knife slipped. No more spitting out chunks of dirt from the dust there by the cylinder. Sheetin' Judas, no."

Johnny emptied the last of his coffee into the grass. The grounds stained the side of the cup a hazelnut color. He arose. "Let 'er go, boys," he ordered.

The men obeyed, recognizing authority, however much they might resent it. There were hasty final gulps. A pitcher dallying with a sandwich squeezed the crust between his teeth; his cheeks bulged squirrelwise. The men unlimbered themselves from squatting positions. Pants were hitched up, escaping shirttails recaptured and thrust under belt bands, suspenders readjusted. Mr. Schimmel slipped his watch from a breast pocket. "Yesiree, Johnny. Right on time, reg'lar as *tick-tock*."

They went back to their forks or bags of grain, feeling the push of command. When Johnny Black spoke, the crew jumped, though more than one restive pitcher grumbled. Even the farmers moved faster. "Toot, toot, start up," the whistle screeched. Threshing, begun that morning, continued.

From the doorway Lilice waved good-by to Sophie rattling away in her buggy. Good old Sophie! Lilice leaned a cheek against a jamb. Threshing finished here and Johnny gone. A rooster crowed, his shrillness beating stridently against the quiet in the yard. Where the rig had puffed was emptiness now, silence roughly accentuated by the queerness of seeing the straw pile bulge near the barn not far from where the stacks had stood. In the yard was the jet-black line of the ash pile where the engine had been. Straw pile and ash heap, the one as large as the other was small.

Loneliness like a mist of cold slid over her until her heart seemed to sink below her apron strings. The cows, in from the pasture, lumbered awkwardly in the straw, tossing hornfuls over their backs. They kicked wildly at the tickle on their hides. The bull pawed at the ground, a lowing bellow riding under a cloud of dirt and chaff that rose above his shoulders. A chicken peered tentatively at the ash pile. Its white feathers against the black coals were like a fist of loneliness digging into Lilice's throat.

"What a silly I am!" Tears rubbed under her lids. (She'd parted the curtains when Johnny was leaving and watched the tail of smoke and the red end of the separator out of sight, a cry choked behind bitten lips, so that Sophie wouldn't know.) "What a silly!" Yet now that Sophie was gone, the snap of the fire under the rattling pan in the kitchen stretched the quiet until she put her knuckles hard against her teeth. "I can't help it," she moaned. "I can't help it. Johnny, Johnny, be careful." Quickly she ran into the bedroom, sobbing wildly over the sleeping Robin.

12

Blurred as they were and mixed with the shadows, afterward Lilice was sure that she could have put her hands on those hours when dread began to simmer and bubble like water in a pot, dragging her into wakefulness at night so that she clutched desperately at the empty pillow. If Johnny were at home, she whimpered forlornly in his arms, unsoothed by his comforting. "What in the world, Leesa? What ails you?"

They were in Mary's Hill to see Young Doctor Wilson the rainy afternoon Bory Tetzell waddled up to them. Dr. Wilson hadn't said when to expect the baby but guessed Christmastime. "You've nothing to worry about, Mrs. Black," he had assured her. (Nothing to worry about, thought Lilice mournfully.)

They were in the street again, their heels thumping on the board sidewalk when Tetzell lurched from the swinging doors of a saloon. Lilice drew back, her lips parting. She saw him stumbling through the mud, drunk and threatening.

"Two rigs, huh, Johnny Black?" he blustered, coming nearer. "And you hafta send one up my way? Drive me out business. Is that it?" His shoulders swung.

"You damn right, Tetzell." Lilice heard Johnny speak clearly and coldly. She caught his arm and felt the muscles tight and corded, a solid lump against her fingers. "If you want to take it that way, take it," Johnny was saying. "I've got a couple of figures yet on your score. They're going to be wiped out."

She saw the scar jerk.

"You get your bitchin' rig outta my territory, or there'll be trouble," Bory shouted.

"Try and stop me." Johnny's breath hoarsened. He hitched forward impetuously, despite Lilice's frantic tugs at his arm. They mustn't fight, they mustn't fight—the thought clanged in her mind.

"My rigs go where they damn please. Neither you nor anybody else is stopping me." Johnny's voice was loud.

In a haze of fear she saw Bory gather himself. She realized that Johnny crouched at her side . . . knew before a blow fell how fists would fly and kicks would be aimed at stomach or crotch. Knuckles against Johnny's teeth, the blood rilling down over his lips, his sweet, hard-pressing lips . . . Johnny's body grunting under Tetzell's swift kicking toe, that body her groping hands knew so well, muscle and rib. She felt agony in her own flesh. She saw Bory start forward. She must stop him . . . must stop him.

Blindly she flung herself forward between them . . . sensed Johnny's shout and his hand to pull her back . . . was tangled in Bory's rough clutching hands bumping against her shoulder, his pawing hands . . . the twitching scar . . .

Something almost metallic vibrated in the bones of her head, against her teeth, over her lips. Out of a momentary blackness she thought, I screamed. I'm going to again. Then water was trickling into her mouth, wetness was at her forehead, and Johnny was murmuring, "Leesa, you all right? You scared me so, I——"

"Where——" she asked fearfully, stirring in his arms.

"Tetzell? You needn't be afraid." In relief he grew sober, seeing the folks gathering around them. "He was so drunk he couldn't fight. Lornas took him away. Come on, let's get out of here."

On the way home, "Johnny?" she questioned. "Is Heinie taking the rig into Bory's—well, his territory?"

"Look, Punkin. There's not many rigs in these parts and there's miles of stacks," he said. "Plenty of room for all. I'm not stepping on anybody's toes. But more and more rigs are coming, that's surely so, and I'm aiming to get ahead of them."

"You'd get even with Bory if you could, wouldn't you?" she probed.

"He's a stinker who ought to be greased out," he exclaimed violently. "Nothing but——"

"Then it is spite. Johnny," she pleaded, "can't you thresh some place where——"

"Now, Punkin. Don't you get your hair down." He patted her hand. "I'm nowhere near Bory's runs. He's just sparking for trouble. Don't you worry. I can take care of myself."

Don't you worry, echoed mockingly in her head. Don't worry . . .

She didn't hear about the fire until he came home one night for a tub of grease. "Heh, Lilice," he yelled boisterously as he tramped in, all grins while he rough-and-tumbled her hair. "How's Robbie?" He tried to keep back of her shoulder.

But she saw it, the red welt like a ribbon across his forehead, the black wavy hair crisped away. "Johnny," she cried chokingly, her hands going to the burned place.

"Huh?" He pretended she was pulling his hair. "Hey, that's my bull curls. You want to tear——"

"Johnny, your head," she cried in such stifled agony his mirth vanished.

"Nothing to get excited about." He led her to a chair. "Thursday afternoon, when it was so windy, we had a little fire at Breckmeyer's. The last stacks, luckily. A spark must have flew over. Anyway, all of a sudden, it was burning. I got the separator out. Paint is blistered a little and some of the belts ain't much good, but that's all. Breckmeyer's grain is safe, except those two last stacks and the straw pile. That burnt."

"Johnny, I'm—I'm all sick inside me." Her hand trembled on the fire-touched skin.

That night Lilice mixed her restless sleeping more than once with letting her fingers rest lightly on the flame-kinked hair. She wondered what had really happened at the Breckmeyers', for Johnny evaded all her questions.

That season Johnny's second machine under Borman and Heinie Beer-wagon threshed deeply into North Pockerbrush near the Loon Lake country. The folks there slept uneasily, knowing how Bory Tetzell raged over his glasses of whisky in the saloons in Mary's Hill. "That bastard," Tetzell threatened. "I'll ride him out on a greased fork handle, damn him. Him and his self-feeders."

But Lornas quieted him. "There's threshing enough for our little rig; more than enough," he cautioned.

"Sure, if you want the leavings. But he's horning in here further and further." Bory grabbed another whisky. "For three cents, I'd set a match to——"

"Shut up," Lornas cut in swiftly, glancing around. "Course, if Black's rig comes closer——" All the fox in his countenance came out. "If he comes closer——"

After the Tetzells had gone, the bartender said, "Well, the shoe's on the other foot. Used to be, Tetzell bullied every farmer around here. He used to bully the small thrashermen, too. Now he's up against something he can't buck, I guess."

That season Johnny clucked in satisfaction over his account books. In two years I'll get me another rig, bigger and better, he promised himself. Guess I'll hire a man to do the farm work, too. No sense me plowing and seeding when I've got all this thrashing business to do.

Farmers were planting more wheat and making money, and he was helping them make it. True, they were buying more cattle and pigs, and planting more oats and barley and hay, and hauling cans of cream to the creameries and cheese factories instead of churning butter: these things put money in a farmer's pocket, too. But this Johnny ignored as being small potatoes.

One thing he couldn't ignore and that was the disturbing strangeness which enveloped Lilice like a cloak (or a shroud) these days—a kind of withdrawal from him that brought the sweat to his hands. When I can't come to her any more, I'll—— He breathed hard as if he'd been running.

It bothered him more than he could say, despite the fact that it wasn't anything so tangible that he could have dragged it box-fashion into the open. Sometimes he thought guiltily, I must be wild, getting such notions into my head. When she sits there, learning the kid to say grace or the Lord's Prayer, she's as good as a Bible to me. I'd have gone bugs lots of times if she hadn't pulled me out of it.

At other times, watching her, he shivered. It was there. He couldn't deny it. And the knowledge made his sleep uneven. She's like an arm or a leg to me, or supper when I'm hungry, he told himself. If anything happens to her, I'd—I'd—— Well, I might as well be buried too.

Sighing in a satisfaction that was marred with worry, he slanted his pencil over the account book. Breckmeyer. What was it he'd been about to do with Breckmeyer? Oh, yes. Breckmeyer. He bent down. His eyes crinkled. Swiftly he drew a line through the sum Mr. Breckmeyer owed him for the threshing. In the margin he wrote "Paid." His pencil came up. Tough when a feller's burnt out like that. Nearly burnt out anyway, he thought, shaking his head. He put the account books away.

Not until Christmastime did Lilice learn from Mr. Dunkel those things about the fire which Johnny kept to himself. Mr. Dunkel drove in one day to pick up the bags of feed Johnny had ground for him.

That winter Kurt and Mr. Dunkel were exchanging ideas about feed mixtures which they were trying on their blooded calves. "By jippers, Dunkel's got a reg'lar recipe for the feed he uses," Mr. Nussbaum told Mr. Schadel.

Realizing that there was money in "custom feed grinding," Johnny bought a feed mill and a gasoline engine and ground the barley, oats and corn hauled to him by Kurt and Mr. Dunkel, and later by other neighbors.

On this cold and glittery day, after he'd loaded the bags, Mr. Dunkel tramped the snowy path to the house.

"Come in and warm up." Lilice opened the door. "Johnny said you could see him later about paying. He had to see Norton in Mary's Hill today."

While Mr. Dunkel thawed the shivers from his body and winked at Robin clinging burdocklike to his mother's skirts, Lilice busied herself awhile before she asked abruptly, shrinking as if from pain but determined to endure it rather than uncertainty, "That fire at Breckmeyer's—it was a bad one, wasn't it? Johnny won't tell me much, though I've asked and asked. He——"

"Whoop-Jinny-and-fall-down!" boomed Mr. Dunkel. "Bad? There was the stacks all fire and the pitchers running and Alb climbing from the separator. Johnny, he backed the engine around. Never see the beat the way he got that engine back end to the separator. He would have pulled the separator out backward but there was a mess of fences and a small shed in the way. He had a long cable hooked to the engine. 'You take 'er,' he yelled at the fireman. 'When I holler, give 'er hell.' Well, he dragged the other end of the cable to the separator. There was fire all over everything, seems like. But he, the damn fool, he walked right into it."

Lilice's knuckles were white, her brown eyes depths of intensity that faded and then grew strangely pointed in her white face . . . hands of fire dividing into fingers of flame and reaching out, curling hot around Johnny's face, his mouth, his black hair. Suddenly she was sure something snapped, a tight cord, but whether inside or outside her mind, she wasn't sure. And then she heard it . . . on the edge of her mind . . . a sucking noise like water swirling in a pool, sucking, sucking. . . .

"—there he was." Mr. Dunkel's voice scattered the sound. She heard him continue like someone listening to a story told in a distant room. "He hooked the separator to the engine. But some bundles slipped. The wind kicked fire all over him. He got out all right. His clothes was afire here and there. Whoop-Jinny, that's a fool for luck, that man of yours!"

Time and again while the world began to tip south and days lengthened and her flesh sagged with coming birth, she'd say, "Now I know what mother meant. Waiting and waiting for something *not* to happen. I'm glad threshing is finished for another year—for another year."

Sometimes an unbearable fear seized and shook her. She felt dread concerning this life which kicked violently, animal-like against her apron band. It was flesh of her flesh, blood of her blood. But what of the dark caverns in her being, past which her mind tiptoed hastily and in fear— would the shadows haunting there, would they lie embedded in this new and untouched body?

That winter, before Richard was born, her mother died and so bereft Lilice of strength even to weep that Johnny hardly moved from the house more than to feed the animals and bring in wood and water.

"She just stopped breathing, Mother did," Adam told them. "Life just tires some folks out, I guess." He sighed as a man does, deep and hard, his arms full of loneliness for his son, his head full of Lena's nagging.

By the hour Johnny sat beside Lilice, Robin on his knee, hushing her. "You mustn't grieve so, Leesa-Punkin." He stroked her hair. "For the baby's sake, you must be strong. I've heard tell, if a mother frets and worries, the child is puny and sicklike. I hope it's a girl," he added generously.

Her eyes flew open. "I'm scared, Johnny," she cried. "Scared to have another baby. I won't have another baby—ever. If it should be——"

"What are you saying?" He put Robin down roughly, the male being irked at being deprived of that which it regarded as sacred. He bent over her. "For a long time I've noticed it," he said, his expression gentle. "Sometimes you're so queer, my heart crosses over in me."

She had no word for him, denial or solace.

Sophie was there to help Richard into a world that inside was warm with firewood and soapy water and soft flannels, but outside was snapping cold and black, though stars held the twinkle of moon over snowflakes.

"She's as good as a doctor." Johnny admired the firm way Sophie washed the baby on her lap.

"When you got three, four kids—" she chuckled, washing space by foamy space this new and tender budling—"you get plenty of practice."

From her pillow Lilice waited with the impatience of the hungry for food. There was a needlelike gleam under her lids, sharp and shiny as polished metal.

Sophie might have noticed it, if she hadn't been chattering with Johnny. She brought the child. "There you are, Lilice."

Lilice's eyes closed so that the gleam hid in her lashes. A smile curved over the tense way her fingers burrowed hastily under the covers. There they closed tightly.

The moment Sophie's back vanished from the doorway and the sound of a kettle on the stove mingled with Johnny's kitchen chatter, Lilice raised the covers beside her. Her white face grew tenser; a yellowish hue tinged her cheeks. Cunning winked in her eyes. Her fingers hesitated; moved eagerly as if to rip aside the cloths but became irresolute, fearful of what might be revealed. Almost doglike then she scratched and pawed until the bands and the garments were removed and the baby lay bare, nakedly red-skinned and whimpering softly before her. Her breath coming raggedly, she peered and poked at the scrawny, wriggling mite; rolled him over; lifted arms and legs. Nothing.

Letting the tightness in her throat rush away in a sob, she drew him hungrily to her breast, as though to relieve a pressure there. She began to laugh wildly but without sound, except for the rustle of starchy bedclothes; laughed until the sharp wild gleam and the cunning melted iciclelike into the clear water of relief and spent intensity and understanding. It was clean flesh, this smallness in her arms. Not blemished. It was pinkish as a boiled crab and squirming like a fistful of angleworms, but clean and sweet as apple meat, or the white heart of seed kernels, tenderly rose-petal under the skin.

More than once those winter days while Johnny rigged up the gasoline engine to a circle saw and sawed a neighbor's pole wood into summer's firewood, Lilice scrutinized the baby. A barb of uneasiness remained in her flesh. Often when Robin waddled about on steadying two-year-old legs her eyes flew comparingly between this mite on her knees and the boy romping among his blocks. Robin was firmly yet slenderly built and his hair was black and curly. So like Johnny's. If only this newest born (Richard Rose they named him) were as large as Robin and as perpetually into the corners of mischief. Between this moment and that day, how much the flesh might have to bear.

She wished desperately for Johnny's sake that she were Sophie—Sophie, who had received each new child with as little dubiousness of mind and heart as she did a harvest of grain in the field or a yellow pumpkin in the garden.

It was in spring while Johnny's wheat tied the promise of full ears into the green twists of stem and blade that Lilice found the roughened skin and the tender scab on little Dickie's knees. She was bathing him and he was grabbing lustily at air. She rubbed a knee. Where the cloth had gone she saw the slightly thickened and crimsoning skin. As though she wouldn't believe this to be more than a smutch, she rubbed again. He whimpered. The flesh raised in a kind of protest; the pinkness deepened as if blood ran no more than the thickness of a moth's wing away.

Then she noticed the same roughness on the other knee, on his waving elbow, on the other elbow. Frantically she swobbed at the places until his whimpers merged into loud complaint. Something like ice chilled her. There was more of the scab between his toes. But it really didn't mean anything. Not anything at all. Most kids had skin ailments. Sophie said so. She ought to know. A dab of ointment, and tomorrow (or the next day) not a white scale would remain. She wouldn't tell Johnny this. No, not now. Later. She scrubbed diligently over the baby's cries.

The scabbiness clung. It will disappear soon, she thought, her heart throbbing slowly. Tomorrow or the next day . . .

Johnny's wheat parted the blade into green stems; reached ankle-high; crept up to the tallness of a knee and pushed from its folded sheath the tender lance of the ear, lightly green as young willow leaves. Lilice watched young Dickie lose his boniness and round into solid flesh. The raspy skin remained. She scrubbed the blemishes with nothing for her haste but his bitter cries and the slow insistent growth upon his joints. (A slow unhurried weight gathering in her own mind.)

As his wheat paled in the ear, the stem and blade taking on yellow, Johnny listened carefully (for once) to Kurt's enthusiasm about a wind stacker. With interest mounting until he was sure he had developed the idea himself, he decided next year he'd get a wind stacker on a new outfit. Three Black rigs on the Pockerbrush roads.

Lilice kept her silence until the Sunday they visited the Humbers. With Clymy and Johnny safely away to inspect Clymy's pigs, Lilice said, "Look at this, Sophie," and pulled down the black stockings on Dickie's legs. "His knees there."

It was good to hear Sophie brush the worry aside with laughing. "Na, that? A little ringworm, or eczema." As good as hearing the running squirrel feet of rain on the shingles after a spell of dry weather. "Ya. Sophus had a big one on his arm. It's nothing to worry about."

"But this—this is on elbows and knees."

"It could be anywheres," Sophie said. "You try sulphur and lard. Rub it in good. See if that don't fix it in a jiffy."

Lilice heard her gladly. The horses seemed poky-slow, going home. That night, dribbling sulphur over the table in her nervousness, she kneaded the yellow dust into the lard. She rubbed the soft joints with ointment but did not touch with hope the hard case of doubt growing deep inside her.

For the rest of that year (while Johnny's wheat was heavy first in the ear and then in the bundle, was hauled and stacked and threshed), Lilice yellowed saucers of lard with sulphur and sent Dickie into yells by her vigorous applications. The skin became no tenderer, the scales no smaller.

She told Johnny finally. He agreed with Sophie. "Are you fretting over that, Leesa?" He poked at her chin playfully. It was only a skin ailment, he insisted. Time and healing sulphur would remove the blemishes. But they won't . . . they won't: the notion rang in Lilice's head.

That threshing season Young Abner Heberstadt, owner of a hundred and twenty and chuck full of the prickle ash of youth (Mr. Dunkel said) kicked over the traces and demanded that Johnny reduce the price he charged for threshing a bushel of wheat. With the self-feeder, Johnny had less help to pay; no sense charging so much.

Johnny trembled with an anger he couldn't quite understand. This trampling upon his authority. "Nothing doing," he glowered.

Heberstadt remained stubborn. He backed out of the run and refused to have Johnny's rig on his yard. "I guess I can find another machine. I don't have to kiss anybody's butt."

Johnny clamped his jaw in a twist of rage. "We'll have to take in a notch or two of Young Abner's belt, I think," he told Alb. With extreme care and much generosity he managed to get the neighbors surrounding Abner into a new threshing agreement. Before Young Heberstadt knew, he saw Johnny and the Buffalo Head on one side of him and Heinie Beerwagon and the Red Star on the other side. His neighbors were threshed in a hurry. With a sinking weight under his jacket he glanced at his own settings. His stacks remained the only ones unthreshed in a dozen lean miles.

Johnny laughed grimly when he heard how Young Abner ran to Tetzell and begged of Bluber. Both had jobs and were busy. Bluber was too far south anyway. Tetzell said, "Catch me moving my rig ten, twelve miles for a setting or two of grain. Hell, no. Though if I could do that Johnny Black a dirty trick, I'd move a hundred miles through mud."

Most of the farms were black with plowing while Abner's stacks, still unthreshed, were turning green. He heard his neighbors brag about the high prices they were receiving at the elevator. His cows broke into the settings. With tossing horns they ripped bundles from the stacks. He built a fence to keep them out. Not until Hubbel Martin, who lived in the Half-Moon Lake country, came by with his red "coffee mill" (so Alb called it) and agreed to thresh the stacks did Young Abner finally bring his wheat to the granary. What loss he had he kept to himself. He remembered Johnny with more than a sour look.

Perhaps it was for this reason that some of the farmers came early and arranged for next year's threshing so briskly. Johnny's chest and his ego bulged like a stack. He decided, "I guess that'll teach 'em not to balk me, damn 'em."

Kurt warned him, "That was a skunky trick to play on Heberstadt."

"Who's asking you to run my business?" Johnny flung at him, instantly bristling up. "Young Abner had it coming. If he——"

"You think you're pretty well on top of the heap, don't you, Johnny?" Kurt surveyed him with a coolness that made him uncomfortable. "Maybe you are. You've got the best rig in these hills. But if you think that gives you the right to be lord over the farmers——"

"Who's lording over the farmers?" Johnny demanded angrily. "I'm as fair and——"

"If you think you can boss them forever, you're crazy," Kurt interrupted. "Other machines are going to come in. And they'll have self-feeders and wind stackers. You'll have to have more than that to——"

"I'm getting a new rig next fall," Johnny snarled the words. "With a wind stacker."

"S'pose you do?" Kurt shrugged. "Then what? Can't you see? You can't buck against the whole country. You've got to——"

"I'll have three rigs out thrashing," Johnny said truculently. "Let anybody try to get in."

"Johnny, times are changing. If you don't change your attitude——" Kurt shifted a leg heavily. "Folks have got to get together. There must be co-operation. This cutting each other's throat, it belongs way back in the dark ages. We've got to co-operate——"

"I'll co-operate," Johnny said acidly. "I'll co-operate my way." He eyed Kurt belligerently. Kurt hadn't changed much. More weighty in ham and shoulders; slower in his walk and mouthier in his speech. Kurt was always butting into affairs none of his making. Yet you never knew what he was really thinking; you never knew where you had him. You had a feeling though, that Kurt knew where he had *you*.

Kurt hadn't married. He surveyed the girls in town and at church as if he were like Time, proud and aloof, unattached to the dusty trivial crawlings on the earth. "I can wait," he seemed to say. "I can wait a long while." But his eyes held a queer glow when he looked on Lilice.

"You know, Johnny," Kurt was saying. "One of these days you'll go down a peg or two, and you won't know what hit you, or where it came from."

Flexing his arms (strength that could grab two sacks of wheat by the ears and hoist them into a wagon box), Johnny grinned. "You want to try it?" he asked tantalizingly. For answer Kurt swung on his heel and left.

There was grumbling among the folks that year, however much Johnny may have been unaware of it, or pretended he was unaware. "A damn good thrasher, the best, that Johnny Black. But cripes, what a tough nut to deal with! . . . I wanted him to get at my oats first. I needed the feed. But no. He said, 'I thrash wheat first.' Nothing I could do. . . . A feller ought to have a rig of his own. This licking the thrasherman's butt . . . Ya, but you gotta admit he makes the straw fly. I'm making money for once." Sometimes folks muttered "Yes" when they had "No" between their teeth.

For the remainder of the season Johnny was tossed between a kind of exulted arrogance when he thought of his rigs and bitter rebellion when he thought of Lilice. This shaking grape-sweet and yarrow together. More than one time she brought him to a standstill beside his work, oilcan dribbling in his fist. He'd be so far bound in the immobility of thought that he'd lift a wrench and forget what he meant to do with it. Or he'd walk from separator to engine, and return to hear Alb chortle, "Judas, I thought you went for the concave wrench. That's a punch you're carrying."

"Huh?" Johnny would wave the tool, peering at it as though awakening from drowsiness. "Devil, so it is," he'd mutter and trot back to the engine again.

There was almost hurry in the way he came back to the rig after a rainy spell at home. His steps quickened as he approached the engine. (Let the shadows lie huddled at home.) He hustled into shouting to get the threshing started again. Not until he had the engine's sway in his bones and the smell of hot grease in his nostrils did the disquiet that hung about him leave. Once the machine was in motion, he felt relief like clean air in his lungs.

It was good, mighty good, sitting on the toolbox, to lean against the driver and feel richly in his shoulders the engine's gentle to-and-fro surge and sway, mixed as it was with a kind of up-and-down-ness. It was a motion as remote as the restless swell that lifted the amoeba under the ancient Cambrian sea, a motion as old as the first plowman's winnowing his grain from the chaff. Up, forward, down, backward . . .

That winter, after its first shocked wonder, the hills and valleys bellowed with laughter over the news that Gatha Blumen went and married Lornas Tetzell after all. "He was always hanging around her 'specially at the dances," Mrs. Peiser told Lilice. "And would you believe it, he got her to say 'yes.' Well, I never!"

Although the Pastor, rightful indignation stiffening every whisker in his beard, flung the law and the prophets at them, reducing their defiance to hangdog gravity, he married them. After all, they were members; they confessed their misdeed and vowed to live a better life (which privately he doubted). He read the service.

They returned from the ceremony shamefacedly smirking and a little proud of their neighborhood importance. ("Such a bold-mannered hussy," scolded Aunt Phrena.) At the shivaree folks twitted Lornas, "Well, you got yourself a kid in the bargain."

His face lean with slyness, Lornas admitted, "That's in the bargain, all right. As long as I started me a family back there four, five years ago, I thought I might as well go on where I left off." Which brass-bold talk so startled the younger boys they nearly forgot to bang the washtubs and clang the rolling colters they brought, and toot the horns they carried.

That winter Johnny packed Lilice and the kids and his possessions and left the Krumlich place for the Redick farm just north of Clymy Humber's. "Moving, moving," Lilice fretted over the boxes and bales and packages. "Just for once, I'd like to get into bed and be sure it wouldn't be carried away before morning." She wrapped a water pitcher. "Why, there are cups and saucers I haven't unpacked from the last time we moved."

"We'll leave the dirt behind anyway—" Johnny laughed—"and start with a new broom at the new place—our place. This is the last time we move, Leesa."

Leave the dirt behind, Lilice said inwardly. Oh, if we could only leave ourselves behind and start fresh! So much we'll take with us.

"It's been longer than I thought," he told her ruefully. Then he grinned. "Take a look at that." He flourished a rustle of papers in front of her nose. "Our farm at last, bought and paid for. You can sign there, missis."

Sighing Lilice gathered the waste papers and wrappings from the emptied boxes. A home of their own at last. A house all of frame. The other two had been of log (Whiteland's) or of log-and-board (Krumlich's). But this one was clapboarded on the outside and plastered and finished inside, even to the four rooms upstairs. Not a log in the building to harbor the squeak and scurry of mice, to shift lime dust upon the floor.

It was a huge square house with a living room in front, and a kitchen and a bedroom at the back. A long porch shaded the living-room windows. A wide staircase led upstairs. The house was roomy with many windows to the yard and the garden where, Mrs. Redick said, "There are lots of flowers in summer. I won't grow such pansies in town, I'm sure of that." From her porch Lilice could wave to Sophie hanging clothes in the Humber yard, the distance across the snowy road was no farther.

Patiently sometimes, fretfully at other times, she tried to spread feathers of hominess over this new nest where Johnny surveyed his two hundred acres and the big red barn pridefully; where Robin's helter-skelter tumblings demanded arnica and plaster; where Dickie's elbows and knees grew from pink to pepper-and-salt gray. After a while gravel-colored flakes began to appear on his legs. Lilice looked at them wildly sometimes so that for an afternoon she was nervous and upset, full of bitter scoldings and sharp-edged words.

The barn was large enough to hold nearly all the hay Johnny could cut in the meadows. It was high in the gables and shadowy under the roof-tree where among the crosspieces that supported the roof a hay fork rattled on its track. "Thirty-five feet from the cupola to the floor," Mr. Redick had bragged. On the wall near the sliding door at right angles to the alley-way was a covered ladderway like a stair leading upward to the eaves. "I don't like to climb ladders," said Mr. Redick. "Makes me dizzy. Up this I can go easy when the hay is high." And Mrs. Redick said, "Now I don't mind if the chickens lay eggs up in the hay."

Johnny snorted scornfully, "Worse than a pair of kids."

At the end of the alleyway dividing the loft was a large square trap door which led to the horse stalls and the cowbarn below. Above the trap door towered the post of one of the crosspieces.

"You watch out, Robbie. Don't you go tumbling down the hay chute," Lilice warned.

For that spring and summer Johnny planned to hire one of the Whiteland boys to do most of the farm work. He himself had his hands full up to the elbows, keeping the two rigs in repair and the circle of threshing runs intact. He strode from barn to granary, his mouth large with plans. "Another rig this fall, Punkin," he told her one day. "With a wind stacker."

"But Johnny," she worried, "we'll be buried in debt."

"Not so deep we can't keep our ears clean." He grinned at her. "Wait till you see the latest self-feeder. The way it cuts the bands. Why, it beats the one I've got all hollow."

Sharp edges . . . knives . . . I don't want to see them, thought Lilice. The glitter of knives . . .

The red snouts of peonies were rooting through the winter crust of flower beds the day Mrs. Peiser and Sophie came over. It was May and the weather warm. Lilice served coffee. They were having doughnuts and talking. Sophie was agreeing, "Ya, the Pastor, he gets meaner every day. A man is like that. The older, the crabbier."

Dickie crowed on the floor, his brown eyes lifted in curiosity. Lilice came from the kitchen with more doughnuts. She saw Mrs. Peiser bend over Dickie and heard her say, "Why, that looks like—it certainly looks like something Anna Krumlich was telling me a boy in Loon Lake had. He was fifteen or so, she says. He had horny scabs all over his body. He was marked for life. Doctors don't know a thing about it."

Marked for life . . . marked. Lilice heard the plate knock sharply on wood and realized that her hand was heavy on the table. She couldn't remember how she got there. Doughnuts spilled from the plate. Mechanically she put them back.

Sophie turned and saw the dead look veiling Lilice's eyes. Quickly she arose. "No, no more doughnuts, Mrs. Black," she said formally. "I've got to run now."

"But you said you had lots of time," protested Mrs. Peiser, her nose titillated by the scent of the unusual.

"I clean forgot something." Sophie answered brusquely. "I'll have to 'tend to it. You come along, Mrs. Peiser. It's just a little way over to my house. Did I show you the dirty joke book I took from that Haber boy? He was reading the stories to my Sophus."

"Ain't he a dratted boy?" Mrs. Peiser's mouth curved hopefully. "You burnt it, the book, I s'pose?" And when Sophie shook her head, Mrs. Peiser, a fresh smell tantalizing her nostrils, gathered her wraps. "Course I wouldn't have it around, but as long as you've got it——"

Slowly, with no more haste than a shadow creeping up a wall, the clock ticked the moments of Lilice's staring at the baby on the floor. He gurgled at her and tried to curl his fingers around a crumb of doughnut fallen near a chair. Her eyes felt itchy. There was a curious dustiness in them, as if moisture had dried and only salt remained. And over the salt, flickers of light seemed to dart and play. . . .

Sophie stormed back an hour later. "I got rid of her." She bustled into the kitchen. "That woman can smell a manure pile over in the next township." She pretended not to see how Lilice huddled in a chair, stirring sulphur into lard; nor the yellow dust spilled on the table, nor the package torn hastily, not unfolded. "If she'd stick to her own——"

"I guess I knew it all along," Lilice said quietly. "I s'pose it had to come."

"Don't you let Mrs. Peiser upset you. That woman blabbers at both ends," Sophie snapped bluntly. "I still say it's ringworm. You keep on with the sulphur and lard."

"I'm going to a doctor, Sophie. I've got to know." Lilice put the saucer down. "I've got to know."

"Doctor!" mocked Sophie. "They can find your pocketbook quicker'n what ails you."

"I've got to know," Lilice repeated woodenly.

"But s'pose he——" Sophie paused, for once uneasy.

"Yes." Lilice rubbed the yellow dust on her fingers. "Yes. S'pose he——"

The water kettle bubbled loudly.

All the way back from Mary's Hill she had a feeling that if she relaxed her grip on the lines for an eyewink, a swell of blackness would rush up her spine and swallow her. Whether the horses trotted or were snaffle-gaited she couldn't have told. Her fingers were white and bony, so hard she pressed the leather. Vaguely she was aware of Dickie leaning against her on the buggy seat, solemnly regarding the tails of the horses and struggling manfully with his cap.

No, she mustn't think about Young Doctor Wilson, the wolfishness of his long nose. She drove into the yard. The reddish stems of peonies were over ankle-high. Johnny, she saw, was in the farther field with the Whiteland boy. Good. She could get into the house before he spied her, before the blackness welled up wavelike to engulf her. She wouldn't unhitch the horses . . . there wasn't time. . . .

Quickly she stepped down, swung Dickie into her arms and fled to the house, the blackness like a dark gown rushing after her. Banging the door behind her, she ran into the bedroom and flung the door shut. There. It was outside.

Sitting on the bed, she pulled the stockings over Dickie's knees. She let the dark patches fill her eyes. . . . That doctor: the way he'd looked at her, beat her, pounded at the walls of her head. Oh, not with fists. No, but with words; no, not words: meanings of words. These cut and bruised more than simple bone or knuckle.

She heard the doctor's voice booming from a corner: "Wish I could suggest a remedy, Mrs. Black." . . . He suggest a remedy . . . hardening of the skin tissue . . . itch—ichthy—what was it he called it? Ichthyosis . . . rare, yes, but it occurs . . . well, sulphur and lard will do no harm . . . no harm; no good either, he means . . . skin like a turtle's back . . .

Without tears she let the blackness open the door and enter; slide close to her. So long she had stood against what howled in her mind. So long she had struggled against what was now crawling slimy as an eel into plain sight. How often she'd scolded herself for folly. Yet how many times she had come back to regard her thought now defiantly, now fearfully. Here it was out. "Done in secret . . . clear as day." Aunt Phrena was right, then. The Pastor, too. If she'd been brought up in sanctity, this wouldn't have happened . . . she wouldn't have sunk into Johnny's arms that night so long, so bitterly long ago, the night of Adam's wedding. A decent girl wouldn't have behaved like that . . . a girl like Gatha wouldn't . . .

But Gatha had a baby, a shame baby at that. And long before her marriage. Yet her baby was ringletted and pretty. No marks on her . . . because Gatha was recorded on the books of the church. She'd been forgiven by the congregation and the community. Or had she? She went to the dances as often as before; oftener. Waltzed with other men as much as with Lornas; more, they said. When you belong, much is forgiven you. . . .

But she, Lilice Black, that once was named Rose—she could look over the fence and yearn. . . . Was she leading Johnny down a long and crooked path, away from what was right? On Sunday mornings, content with her nearness, he'd merely grin and pull her closer to him. Because of her he didn't bother to go to church at all . . . he really didn't belong either any more. . . . That was charged to her; that and this other bane: her children . . . Ernst dead . . . Robin lightly touched . . . Dickie dreadfully. The next child . . . the next . . .

She heard the sucking noise again. It was as if water swirled. On the edge of her consciousness she *felt* more than saw the black whirlpool gliding circlewise, slowly, slowly. It was like thick water, or oil—thresher's oil. On its farther edge a boy was running, a boy with arms outstretched to her, entreating her, it seemed. His face was a mask of anonymity but his voice came to her: "Lilice, Lilice," so clearly that she started up. . . .

There was Dickie owlishly peering at her. "It's like a dream," she said half aloud. She realized that there was wetness on her cheeks, cleansing wetness. "A horrible dream." Exhausted she lay back, one hand going out to the boy. Tears ran from the corners of her eyes. They rilled into the crooks of her ears. She felt limp. Let what will happen, happen. I'll do it . . . it must be found in Johnny's church . . . he must go back . . . I'll see the Pastor . . . the water . . . the wine . . . the bread . . . there I'll find it. But not this, not this to the innocent. She groped for Dickie's arms. Let Johnny come back. Let Johnny . . .

13

Those next years were the heavy-stemmed years, had Johnny but known it; five in a row with the ear pointed with the kernel, plump as a woman's breasts in milk, the head low-hung with grain. They were the seasons without locust and weevil in the land before the time of the short-crop years. True, there were invaders thrusting their blighting jaws upon the yield—Hessian fly in the wheat stem and rots in the corn joint; a patch of grasshoppers on this ridge and crickets on the next; floods in the Valley and late frosts wilting the crisp white blossoms of apple and plum. But these were small worries, localized to handkerchief-sized areas. They were hardly noticed in most places, scarcely at all in the Pockerbrush hills. These were insignificant worries compared with the fungus of despair creeping over the landscape of the heart and of the mind.

Sometimes in the rush of an afternoon Johnny would look upon the Golden Bird, his latest engine, and could hardly breathe for the smothering tightness in his lungs—a tightness that was all exultation, proud-winged as the bird with the haughty neb and the spreading pinions raised there on the front door of the engine. He stood beside Alb on the feeder head of the separator at other times. Through the dust that rose from the clashing knives cutting the bands, he observed the engine. Under his soles he could feel the grunt-and-grind of the cylinder. Vaguely he heard the sound of rustly thudding as the bundles landed on the inclined carrier, tossed there by the pitchers. But these were inconsequential. Through the smoke of rust and dirt and the noise of gear and wheel he peered at the engine.

No one in the hills had ever seen such driver wheels! Higher than most men were tall, as wide as a young man's chest, they had a forest of spoke rods raying from the hub to the rim. And the rims, to make traction complete, were implemented with crooked lugs or cleats that ripped the sod and left a trail in the farmer's yard so deep, the scars remained to the following spring.

And the lofty thrust of the smokestack. It was of the latest design with screens to catch the least firefly of a spark that might wing flame to the dry sheaves. ("No cinder'll get through," the agents assured the thresher-men. But fires still roared through stacks, and separators smoked down to bony iron.)

And the auxiliary tanks! One in front, two in the rear. And all the newest devices for converting the least amount of straw into the greatest amount of steam pressure at the piston. There were three whistles on a single stem, a triad of gleaming brass and shrilly blended sound by which he could shriek across the hills, "Johnny Black is starting! Johnny Black is through for the day!" Right to the minute. Seven in the morning. Twelve o'clock noon. One o'clock starting time. Any minute of the evening dusk for stopping. Why it was getting so, Alb Hukelpoke swore, the women complained if they didn't hear the dinner or the supper whistle! And Mr. Schimmel said he always had correct time in fall.

On clear mornings Johnny often heard Heinie Beerwagon's whistle, for Heinie was running the Red Star this season and Marty Borman the Buffalo Head. Johnny grinned while he listened to Heinie's friendly, single-voiced call ringing over the hills, "Toot toot—toooot-toot: How are you this morning, you old dirty belly?" And Marty's two-tone reply came from a place four or five miles away, "Toooot-tootoootooot—toot: Starting up fine as a mosquito silk. How's your old lady?" Sometimes they muffled their whistles into hoarseness and together taunted Bory Tetzell or John Bluber, if these rivals happened within hearing distance: "Sowbelly, sowbelly, cockleberry thrasher," in a scornful whistled language grown familiar over the years.

The neighbors would halt their late chores and slap their thighs. "Na ya, seems like Tetzell's getting it in the neck again. Hee, hee, hee."

And at his rig Bory would grab a pitchfork and swear, the scar jerking, and Lornas would grin, coiling like a clock spring, the fox in him licking from his eyes.

Now and again a more sinister melody flung its demands across the ridges in these seasons: a dozen short toots and a handful of longs, imperative, breathless with urgency: "Fire in the separator! Fire in the separator. Quick! Quick! Quick!"

Ah yes, the whistles! No wonder the fireman likes to polish them into sun-returning brightness.

The improved clutch in the wheel—oh, that engine had a catalogue of excellencies as large as Montgomery Ward's! As many unfolding doodads to tickle a man into wonder as a woman possessed. If only once he could get Lilice to step onto the platform, to put a thumb on the steering wheel. Just once. But no. She never would.

By the hour he sat on the engine, outer muscles lax, inner senses alert. Below him the fireman shoved the wads of straw into the fire or stood twisting at the singed hair on his forearm. Sometimes Mr. Dunkel came to brag about his timothy crop: "Worth just as much as wheat." Or Mr. Muri leaned against a tank, sucking powerfully at his pipe and giving up in disgust. "By t'under," he'd say, pulling the stem from the bowl. "Plugged oop. Ya shure, I fix her." He'd hold the stem under a pet cock and let white steam whistle through the curved tubing.

"That's what gets 'em sweet and clean." Mr. Dunkel would approve the lusty smacks with which Mr. Muri afterward lipped the stem. Nodding, Johnny let a slow grin widen his mouth.

There was the new separator! He had bought it the year he'd moved

Lilice and the kids to the Redick place. Over it Alb poised like a king-fisher listening for a grumble or a growl that meant trouble, a clogged sieve or a choked rake. He poked his fingers into corners alive with motion in order to catch the sting of a hotbox. (Now and again, however, Alb yawned tiredly. "You know, Johnny, I got my eye on a little place south of the Diemer hills. This thrashing business—— Sheetin' Judas, I'm purty near tuckered out." "Aw hell, Alb." Johnny laughed at him. "As long as you can wiggle, you'll hang around a sacker and a blower.")

It was a big separator, all right; big enough to keep three men on a stack busy; four men, Alb maintained. And there was the new grain elevator with its automatic weigher hiccuping the bushels into a long tube that conveyed the grain to the wagon or to the sack. It measured and weighed each bushel and registered in one wild burst of sliding panels, jerking arms, clupping noises and grinding chains. Gone was the tally box and the half-bushel galvanized measure which used to be drawn past the prong of the register and so counted up the bushels with a musical click.

"Whoop-Jinny, how I did like to hear that tally box go clinking on the half bushel!" Mr. Dunkel used to remember wistfully. "When prices were good, every clink meant a half dollar. But you got to depend on milk and butter and calves now, not wheat."

Never again would Mr. Haber slyly heap up the galvanized half-bushel basket and then try to press it down again, in order to get full measure and then some. Wheel and sprocket smoothly and swiftly told the sum of the bushels now, unhurriedly, accurately, efficiently.

To be sure, at first the valley distrusted the elevator. "What? That thing weigh my grain?" yelped Mr. Schimmel. "And have me short by a hun-dred bushels? Mein Gott, no! I'll stick by the half-bushel measure." Not until he'd seen the weigher deal out fair and honest measure a dozen times over did he give in, though grudgingly. Once or twice, hoping to surprise the gadget in an inaccuracy, he swooped down on the grain wagon with his galvanized basket and let it run full, to sample the measurings. Half a bushel, all right! Peevish with reluctance to admit defeat, he finally gave up and accepted the machine's iron reckonings.

It was the wind stacker that raised a devil's twister of commotion. All his years Johnny remembered how the cylinder hum of the separator had dominated the threshing season. Day after day its locust whine had chafed the weary nerve. Not even the *chug-a-chug* of the engine obscured it. But now it was lost, submerged in the roar of the wind stacker. With an undu-lating boom, the blower fan hurled the straw and chaff up the long pipe and out into the current-shifted air, to fall into a heaping pile. From the rear of the separator the hollow metal tube stuck up like an arm raised at a slant; like an ear of corn slanting upward from the stalk.

On afternoons or evenings when the wind slowed to a touch on a cheek, or to nothing at all, the loud humming of the wind stacker or "blower" filled the valleys and ridges with a sound that brought farmers to a standstill on their "buggy plows," so new and strange it was: like thunder in snow-banked January. (It made Lilice put fingers in her ears, as it whined its way through an open window and into the kitchen. Once in desperation she banged the sash down.)

Men like Mr. Bachmann, who had spent God-numbered hours of chaff and dust in the straw pile, whooped when they saw the blower. "About time we got some help. The Lord took pity on the strawstacker at last." No more wallowing in soft yielding fluff that clogged the legs and left you for days with a feeling that you walked on a feather bed.

But the folks had other notions about the wind stacker. They bellowed resentment, suspicious of waste. They nearly smashed the threshing circles Johnny had so purposefully built. That's the way it went, he thought. No matter how careful you were, it was the unexpected that tumbled your plans. For a week after the men came running with the battering-ram of a log, he had stared holes into the dark curtain of midnight, and was more disturbed than he liked to admit.

The folks grumbled, "Contraption like that! A feller sweats half a year to raise a crop and the damn thrashers blow it into the straw pile. No siree. Not for me." Such gabble. He heard it everywhere, in the frogs croaking in the ditches even.

"You fellers are talking through your hats so fast it's a wonder they stay on your heads," he'd protest.

"Ya?" They'd point skeptically. "That fan there. It sucks the wheat right off'n the sieves; right out of the cylinder, by cripes. Nope."

"That blower won't pull a feather off a hen's eye," Johnny insisted. "I tried it out."

"Jippers, man, I wasn't born yesterday," one or another would say. "The whole front end of the separator is going to be pulled through the blower one of these days. No, I'll stick by the old straw carrier."

"Judas Proost, come and see for yourself!" shouted Johnny. But his exasperation was tinctured with uneasiness.

Never had he known such a thorny belligerency in the farmers. Even Mr. Peiser couldn't restrain dubiety. "I've been hearing about them wind stackers. Blow the grain in the straw. But what can you do?" he grumbled. "Irv Rancher, he that lives near Fergus—he was telling me about one of them contraptions. He saw it used on a neighbor's place. He says the straw pile was so green by Thanksgiving you could have mowed hay on it."

"Not only that," Mr. Fleischer continued the opposition; "that fan, it chews up the straw so that it's all chaff. Even the cows won't eat it."

But Alb and Heinie stood by Johnny. So did the nearest neighbors, those in the first ring. Whatever their inner qualms, they relied on him and swallowed their objections.

The distrustful and the detractors came in a fighting mood. They found the rig in motion, bundles flying into the cylinder. From the blower pipe they saw a tail of yellow straw, ragged and fuzzy-edged, curling like the arched feathers of a rooster over the growing straw pile. They prowled about the heap, kicking aside straw and chaff, hoping to uncover grain. And when they did find a kernel or two, they howled triumphantly and brought the damning evidence in a rounded palm.

"Devil grab it!" Johnny shouted at them in the booming of the stacker. "The straw carrier used to waste more than that, and you know it."

They did know it but continued to prowl. They opened the door in the side of the machine opposite the blower fan and saw the blur of iron and straw and chaff. Above and to the right of the fan they beheld the straw curling from the straw racks, twists and folds of it. Below these racks they saw the rocking ends of the shakers or shoe, jerking forward, backward, kicking the chaff ahead of it. They saw chaff and straw join in the whirl of the fan and vanish from their probing eyes.

They watched Alb thrust his arm in under the shaker and catch a fistful of broken stems and chaff. When he gestured them to do likewise, they followed in timorous example, eying the blower as if they expected a dragon jaw to snap their flesh to the elbow.

"Might suck a feller right through," one said cautiously, jerking his hand back. "Just as I thought," he crowed and piddled in his palm a single kernel of wheat. "Wastes grain by the peck."

"It might suck a feller like you through," Alb derided. "You're all wind anyway. But there ain't a bit of suction in there."

Johnny, standing near, overheard the man. Exasperatedly he waved to the pitchers. "Hold 'er up for a speck, fellers," he shouted. The pitching stopped. When the separator ran empty of straw and the sieves were clean of chaff, Johnny dragged his wallet from his pocket. "Damn it all, keep your eyes on this," he ordered. From the wallet he took a bill. "Here's ten dollars. I'm gonna lay that bill on the shoe here. If the blower fan as much as sucks it to the edge there, you can have the damn money."

Swiftly he placed the bill on the rocking edge of the shoe. It moved with the metal and the wood. The fan roared below. If their glances had been silver tacks and their eyes hammers, the men would have nailed the oblong of paper down, they peered at it so breathlessly. The bill remained where Johnny had placed it. It rocked with the shaker. Once under a current of air from the cylinder, it raised slightly. The men pursed their lips to squeal triumphantly. But it settled back.

"Sheetin' Judas!" Alb gasped. "I thought sure, there goes ten bucks."

"That satisfy ya?" Johnny pocketed the bill. "Or do you want to crawl in yourselves and lay on the shoe?"

They wolfed around, convinced against their wills, but truculent still. They connived in secret. They'd fix that Johnny's blower contraption.

They tried to fix it the day Johnny was threshing at Mr. Whiteland's. He and Alb were standing on the right hand—the belt side of the separator. There was a shout from Mr. Dunkel on the grain wagon. Wheeling, Johnny saw the men and acted in one motion.

There they came, four men bearing a small log, its pointed end aimed straight at the curve of metal enclosing the blower fan. A wild yell on his lips, Johnny lunged forward. He butted against the shoulder of the man nearest him.

The man stumbled. His wavering steps threw the others off balance. The pointed log angled off slightly, not enough to clear the blower but enough to scrape the edge and dent the shell. For a moment there was a tinny sound of iron scraping metal.

It was lost in the shouts of men. The attackers dropped the log and piled into Johnny and Alb. Fists flew. Two men drove Johnny against the separator. They were trying to thrust him head first against the blower wheel and its flapping belt. But from the wagon Mr. Dunkel threw an armful of sacks. Their dustiness enveloped one of the men. Blinded, he released his hold on Johnny and staggered back.

Mr. Dunkel jumped down. As if he had a calf before him, he lifted a small club of wood and struck the man across the head. The man dropped, limp as a gunny sack.

Johnny recovered himself and swayed in fierce encounter with the other man. The grain tenders came running. So did the pitchers, their forks gleaming. . . .

For a while, the four men were circled by angry threats. "Take off their pants and douse 'em with oil. Ride 'em on a pitchfork handle." The men cringed. They were torn and bleeding. One of them held his head in his hands.

"Shut up, you fellers," Johnny shouted. He wiped the blood from a cut lip. His shoulder hurt. "There'll be no greasing-out here," he said, remembering Bory and the crew on the flats. He told the four men, "You skunks, you get."

They "got." Threshing continued. What grumbles there were, were said in private. Johnny smiled grimly. From that day on, the threshing runs remained intact. That is, they did for these autumns, at least.

Taken together, engine and separator, it was a heavy rig, though he would have denied this hotly. Too heavy. The wheels cut deeply into the greensward of the farmers' yards. On steep hills where the smoke of the engine whitened with gathered strength, they gouged through the solid tops of roads and left holes, sand-filled and crumbly. For weeks afterward the neighbors complained about torn-up roadbeds. Wagons and buggies lurched crazily when the wheels struck the rough places.

"Let them damn thrashers keep in the fields," some folks said. "Costs us enough taxes now to keep up the roads."

"Build yourselves decent roads instead of these cow paths," Johnny told them, "and the wheels won't cut through."

"Danged if I'm gonna get a backache working out my poll tax so's that Johnny Black kin have a road for his thrashing rig," one or another growled at the church or at the store. The town board scratched its head and nibbled its fingernails and did nothing worriedly.

There was trouble about the bridges, too. Why, there were only two or three in the hills that didn't send a feather of fright tickling up Johnny's back every time he crossed them. That one called Drywash Bridge, for instance. That was an important span. Once across, either way, he entered miles of threshing. But the girders creaked and groaned, no matter how many planks Alb laid before the wheels. Let a beam crack—— He didn't dare talk about it! Lilice was worried enough, as it was.

The town board did nothing except warn him, "If you tear down the railing, Johnny Black, you'll have to put it up again." Put it up again! Down near Fergus a rig had crashed into a creek and killed the engineer. There had been a lawsuit and the township there had paid twice as much as would have built a dozen bridges; or so the folks said.

When the supervisors here heard about it, they called a hasty meeting at Toffman's store. All they did was post warnings. "Johnny, you cross that bridge at your own risk," they said. His own risk! A bunch of pimpled butts, that's what the town board was, he decided.

Ah, but that was a beauty of a thrashing rig, taken all in all, he thought over and over, glad to feel the rub of the engine's surge against his back, voluptuously against his shoulder bones. That separator. That engine. Pretty as a wheat field, tawny ripe, with the heads bowing in the middle of the field where the wind blew on them, standing quiet in the breathless corners.

Sometimes in the dusk-cool quiet of an evening he let the stillness after the rush of threshing fill his ears and slack his muscles. (Especially was this true in those years just before the short-crop season when he could look back and see how the years had slid past and left him.)

With the crew gone to the barn and the farmer finishing his chores, Johnny often came alone to the engine. And in the silence, under a moon as thin and crescent as the mark left by a thumbnail pressed into flesh, he heard wagons rattling over the stony roads as the neighbors rumbled homeward. A vesper sparrow complained sadly, three notes and a trill in a minor key, over and over. The moon poked one pointed silver horn into a cloud.

Echoes over the hill. The thought moved like a finger in his mind. But now he didn't try to dodge the words. For a moment he regarded their memories steadily. ("Snoose, my friend.") And a deep loneliness seeped through him, loneliness for the past, for his sons, Robin with his black wavy hair, Dickie, the horny-skinned Dickie, brown of eye as—as Lilice. Loneliness for Lilice, the old Lilice.

Here he had this good new rig and she wouldn't as much as look at it. During the late fall (the rig at home and ice-quiet), when a hood of early snow lay over the separator and the whistle cord sagged in knots of snow on it (like popcorn kernels on a string which the kids hung on the Christmas tree), she kept the granary between her and the rig, in order not to see its somber shape. And when all three rigs were housed for the winter, she hurried past them as though the engines were dark monsters in the cave of their shed, ready to snort flame and roar at her.

Where were the dimples that used to button her lips back in a smile? She's a skinful of—of—oh, I don't know, but she gets me going, he used to think, coming home eagerly, even when a shadow darkened the well of her eyes. But now, now, in his arms sometimes she trembled and drew away, as though shrinking from his flesh—or from herself. She cried often, and her tears cooled his ardor. For all his asking, she had little to tell him.

He'd sigh hugely, full of unhappiness for her, but hurt with frustration, too. Devil grab it! When a feller can't come to his wife any more—he'd grumble mournfully.

This which was happening to Lilice before his eyes and he helpless—in the months of snow-heaped winter, in the spring and in the summer of ripening, it was no more than a cloud, or the vapor of a cloud. But always in the middle of July it settled down on her like a dark mist. Now it seldom lifted.

He remembered that it had taken bitter shape and form—— Let's see.

Yes. It must have been the year they moved to the Redick place, four years before. That was the summer he'd bought the Golden Bird, the summer Lilice had taken Dickie to see Doctor Wilson.

Little Dickie. Funny about that poor kid, too—big for his age, with a twinkle like a sun-struck ripple in the brown deeps of his eyes, Lilice's eyes. Lilice taught him the Ten Commandments and the Lord's Prayer and grace before meals; and the darn little bugger, he'd blabber the words with one eye on a piece of meat or a breast of chicken, to see that Robin didn't put a fork into it before he did. Lilice would complain bitterly, "Johnny, make him mind. Acting like that. He's as bad as you are." (Lilice scolding and crabby.)

A moody feller, Dickie was; shy as a swamp veery at times, bawling for nothing at all, it seemed. He wouldn't so much as take his shoes off, as Robin did in summer, or his pants to go wading. And bawled against unbuttoning his clothes when Lilice wanted to scrub him on Saturday nights. Little wonder that he was bashful, with all those hard, scaly patches on his knees and elbows and feet; even on his chest and back. He'd try to hide his hands with the cracks in them when company came.

Poor little bugger! Nothing to be done, the doctor said. A rather unusual skin disturbance, though not rare. Unusual skin disturbance, hell. But he'd outgrow it, like calves did the scabs. It was a matter of time. Well, sure, Dick would outgrow it. Kids outgrew anything, especially pants and shirts. No sense in Lilice's fretting over him, or crying out sometimes, "I can't bear it. I can't bear to see him hide himself, like that." Stewing over something nobody could help . . .

14

It was the year after they'd bought the Redick place that Lilice spoke up over the supper table. "Tomorrow I'm going to see Pastor Steuber, Johnny."

He choked over a piece of fish. "Lilice—" he began.

"He's got to give me instruction in Catechism. For confirmation."

"Lilice." He cleared his throat. "Are you wild or something?" The boys were owl-eyed; this was beyond their two-and-four-yeared comprehension. It was summer then and warm. "Really, Leesa, what do you——"

"I know." She put a second helping of potatoes on Robin's plate. "Confirmation instruction is for kids, not for grownups."

"Oh, no. Hattie Melder was confirmed last year, and she's thirty, at least. But you——"

"I'm too old?"

"You'll never be too old for anything," he said, grinning crookedly. Inwardly he quailed at the rapt determination hardening her lips. "I pay my church dues," he said. "You can go any time you want to." He couldn't say, "I hope this does some good. I don't like it, my wife gawped at like a confirmation kid in knee pants."

"We have been staying away from the church a long, long time." She poured milk into Dickie's cup. Her voice was level but the reproach he felt in her words stopped his protests.

"I'll hitch up and drive you over," he proposed hastily.

"No, you have work to do on the—the separator. Repairing sieves or something," she reminded him dully. "You said so yourself."

"Heck, ya," he admitted, shoving his plate aside. "But that can wait for——"

"No. I'll attend to this," she monotoned. "This I must do for myself, Johnny," she added strangely, her voice low. "I'll take Dickie. Robin can stay with you."

Baffled, in alarm, he let her have her way, hearing in her words an echo of that night long ago when the Haber boy had come with the news of her father's death and she had said, "Please don't," when he'd tried to help her. As he stared at her, he had a queer feeling now (as then) that she stood alone, a space of distance between them he couldn't cross; and was irked again at the thought.

The rest of that summer and into autumn, there was much cackling in the nests of old women. "Na ya, that Lilice Black—she's taking Catechism from the Pastor. On Saturdays she drives over. . . . It takes some people an eternity to come to their senses . . . she always was a smarty. The Pastor, he'll trim her down a peg or two . . . hee, hee, hee."

". . . well now, she's got more gumption than most folks . . . she was in church last Sunday and Sunday before; brings her kids, too, nice, wellbehaved kids. And last Sunday that man of hers was along. He always sits in the pew like he was on a thrasher. . . ."

"I ain't listening to a word against Lilice Black." Sophie threatened Mrs. Peiser with a soup spoon. "It's her own peace of mind she's hunting for. That's her business."

Restively Johnny heard the echoes of this chatter. He didn't mind going to church, if that would quiet Lilice. And it might silence clacking tongues. He paid his church dues. (He noticed that after he paid them, there was less talk about his not appearing at services.) "I can always nap. And—who knows? I might hear a good sermon once. I wish they'd put cushions on the seats, though."

What blistering rods the Pastor laid upon Lilice, he heard by indirection and by hindsight, after it was all over. For Lilice kept her Saturdays dark. When the threshing season began, she left Robin with Sophie. Sometimes at Sophie's urging, Dickie too stayed at the Humber house on Saturday forenoons.

Johnny would come home to find her with a catechism in one hand and a skillet in the other; or he'd find her in the rocking chair, reciting the exposition of the Sixth Commandment with slow and dreadful emphasis, this her song to lullaby the sleepy-lidded Dick.

"Well," he'd joke her, "what did the Pastor rumpus about today? Did he knock you over the head with Matthew the last?"

Beyond the face she made at him, she reported only, "He read Sodom and Gomorrah today." Whatever her own feelings, in those days she cooked his meals and darned his socks, as before, and pricked the conscience of his children with the needle of right and wrong. Whatever may have bubbled corrosively inside her (whatever humiliation burned her cheeks, whatever harshness was thrust blazing into her mind), she let no more salt than was necessary drop into his bread, nor bitterness rot the comfort of a day at home. His meals never failed him. Only his bed cooled and left him restless.

At first she was so gravely happy, her laughter rang with the boys', as if this were expiation, and in present subjugation she was conscious of future triumph, the victim redeemed and justified. It was as though she were saying, This is the dark valley, Johnny, by which I come at last to you.

That the Pastor was gratified with such meekness (however much Lilice may have bitten her lips red to hold back hot denials at his probings) was revealed in a sermon. He spoke about the Ten Commandments and indicated how the jawbone of the law drives the unchurched sinner to earnest repentance and a seat in the fold. What an example for those who filled the pews each Sunday and yet were themselves defiled by the pitch of iniquity!

The congregation took the hint if not the advice and rattled inquisitively. Observed Mr. Dunkel, "The older the Pastor gets, the sourer. Did you see how red his face got today? Like the wattles of a rooster. He'll have a stroke yet, getting so mad and scolding so hard."

The congregation couldn't help noticing that in these years, when he sermonized on the evil ways of threshers, and he did each fall, the Pastor chose one of the Sundays after his own grain was safely out of the stack and in his granary. He had delayed his anger ever since one late September when Johnny insisted on threshing the church stacks on Sunday. Let the Pastor sputter; Johnny was in a hurry to finish a circle of jobs so that he could begin in Turkey Hollow on Monday.

The Pastor preached and Johnny threshed the Pastor's grain forty rods away. The noise of the rig boomed through the open windows until the metal voice triumphed over the mortal one; until the Pastor broke off in the middle of a "fourthly" to say, "Elder Norton, the decorum of this service is being disturbed. Will you be good enough to shut out that—that blasphemy?"

In sweltering closeness, the rumble of the machine not entirely dispatched, the sermon hurried into its "fifthly" and "sixthly." Thereafter Johnny was usually a dozen farms away before the Pastor hammered a text on the evil sweat of Sabbath labor.

"I don't believe the Pastor does it a-purpose, though," averred Mr. Nussbaum stoutly.

"No," sneered Alb Hukelpoke. "Course not. Sheetin' Judas! What you s'pose the Pastor would do if Johnny didn't thrash his little horse piles?"

"He don't have to thrash on Sunday, does he?" snapped Mr. Nussbaum.

Alb only bit off a hunk of Indian Twist for reply.

Lilice went to the church and studied Bible history and Catechism. But after Thanksgiving there was less mirth and longer moments of abstraction, a dish or a mop idle in her hand. Her fingers were light as moth wings on Dickie's skin. Some days she'd be gay, and the boys racketed with her like a nestful of crows in the swamp. On such a day Robin smashed her prized soup tureen. Howling before she laid a hand on him, he held his hands on his seat, ready to be spanked. But she sat with him for half an hour, talking so quietly that, little as he was, he never forgot that day.

There were other days, however, when gloominess dark as the shadows in the ravine swept over her. She had brittle, meaningless smiles then. Her hands were swift and slapping hard. So Robin found, and for no more reason than accidentally dropping a bite of cooky into his glass of milk. Her finger marks on his cheeks were red welts of impatience and bitter inner disquiet, as if doubt and uncertainly roared her into distraction.

One night near Christmas as she and Johnny were going to bed, Lilice huddled among the quilts. "I don't think—I can stand it till spring," she choked. "He says I can be confirmed then. But——"

"What's he been saying now?" Johnny was beginning, firing up in rage, feeling that all these months of frustration were somehow the Pastor's fault and longing to heap blame upon him.

"No, no, no, Johnny," she cried. "It's not him exactly. It's—it's what we talked about before. Pain and suffering and no mercy anywhere. Ma used to say that God was kind and understanding and forgiving. If you made a mistake, it would straighten itself out by and by. But I don't know. Even when I was little, I couldn't see much kindness. Pa so broken and Ma tiring herself. That really never straightened out."

"Hush, Punkin. You're getting yourself all upset." He sat beside her, trying to pull her close to him.

"No, Johnny." She moved away fretfully, going on: "All the Pastor can talk about is punishment. If there is any hope for you, it isn't worth anything, you have to suffer so much before it's yours." She drew back the covers. "Even in church we sing that we're no better than worms. What's the use of it all then?"

"I know." He sighed. "I've gone through all that. Sometimes I feel like I got a shell on me thicker'n the lining of the firebox."

They lay quiet at last like children in a dark forest too weary to be fearful over being lost, and sank to sleep, tired with asking but not answering questions that mocked them in the darkness under the ceiling. . . .

Before spring brought the first bluebird she gave up. "I can't do it, Johnny," she cried. "I can't."

"Nobody's asking you to, Leesa," he consoled her. "I guess we can get along."

"One more word about the sins of Adam," she sobbed, "and I'll throw his books into the stove. I'd just as soon not hear another sermon. I'll stay home and take care of you and the kids."

That spring while bellwort unfolded in the woods and violets blued in the grass, she washed and scrubbed and aired the house as if she were ridding herself of more than a winter's accumulation of dust and spiderwebs. But the impressions of those flinty tablets of instruction remained. As if her mind were still in the Pastor's study though her body was in her own house sweeping a corner, she'd hear that gravelly voice: "Be ye holy, for I am your God . . . the soul that sinneth it shall die . . . depart from me, ye cursed into everlasting fire. . . ."

Once in desperation (she remembered) she had tried to bring a cool tip of mercy into this scorching vengeance. "But, Pastor," she had protested, "isn't the Christ merciful? Look here where he says, 'Come unto me, all ye who are weary and heavy-laden and I will give you rest . . . him will I in no wise cast out . . . Blessed . . .' "

With no gentleness he had taken the volume from her. "What you have read, that is indeed the blessed gospel," he had said. "But first comes the law. When the law has been applied and the sinner sees the awfulness of his sin, and the stubborn heart is chaste and broken; one may say, it is in sackcloth and ashes, then we will let the healing gospel bring its comfort."

"How long the law?" she cried. "And if you yourself break before it comes to heal? How long must you——"

"Na ya," he answered. "As long as you can say that, your pride still keeps you in condemnation. . . ."

All the scrubbing of walls and windows, all the swabbing with a paint-brush to bring a new surface to her house, did not hide the stain left in her thought. Neither could she silence the reminder, What now? What now?

Without ever admitting a flicker of his notion, Johnny was vaguely glad when Lilice gave up the catechetical instruction. In spite of all his trying, he had never been able to grin back jokingly or indifferently when this or that farmer thumbed him slyly in the ribs. "Na, Johnny. Who's got the pants on in your house now? Your old woman? She gets the law fresh from the Pastor and lays it down, I hear."

He'd grin crustily. Not that he cared, he assured himself. But the notion of a public ceremony and his wife gawped at by the congregation—well, a feller that owned the biggest and best rig in a dozen townships, who was asked by practically all the folks in the hills to do their thrashing for them—well, Judas, it—it wasn't "seemly." It was the only word, and one of the Pastor's at that, he could think of just then.

His chest expanded, however, and the shirt tightened across the heavy muscles whenever he remembered his three rigs *chug-a-chugging* in the ridges. For two years his were the only rigs booming with wind stackers. Now of course Tetzell had one and so had Bluber. Folks no longer stopped in the furrow to listen to the smooth, *rum-rum-rumming* sound drifting from a hill or filling a valley.

He'd show them how to make money, now that he had a chance. He had no intention of lowering the price per bushel he charged in threshing, even though he had five or six men less in his crew. Nevertheless the farmers were complaining about the "damn thrashing outfits, so big they're like a circus." The crews were becoming synonymous with unnecessary largeness. "He had a family big as a thrashing crew. . . . I cooked me supper enough for a bunch of thrashers."

That fool of a Tetzell had reduced his rates, hoping to increase his runs. But his rig was small compared with the Golden Bird. Most of his earn-ings were slopped down his throat in the saloons. And this in spite of the fact that his rig was mortgaged up to the feeder and that Norton held the mortgage. At the end of his threshing season he was as poor as at the beginning, folks said.

One big job worried Johnny a little and that was Norton's. Always he had hurried the work in order to move to Four Oaks Farm. The figures he wrote in his book after he'd finished there lifted the blood in his veins. But common talk had it that Norton's fancy-edged shares in the oil wells and gold mines weren't worth so much as the gilt in their seals. Norton, they said, was turning a penny over twice these days before he laid it on the counter. If that job failed . . .

Oil wells and gold mines, Johnny thought. No, there was more money growing on the stem in a field, rich and unfailing, than in get-rich-quick schemes. You could depend on separators and engines. These would be necessary as long as a farmer scratched a rill of wheat or barley or flax into his seedbed. Big machines to thresh more acres faster.

"Big machines, eh?" Kurt said once when the threshing at Uncle Herm's place had been finished—Kurt's farm now. "You really think you're the only hog in the trough, don't you?" He spoke bluntly. "Charging such high prices."

"What the devil is it to you?" snapped Johnny, his bristles instantly beginning to ruffle. "The farmers get their stacks thrashed out faster than ever before. There's hardly anybody left unthrashed by the tail end of October. And they get a clean job, too. They make money. I got three rigs in the belt and that costs a hell of a lot to run. Money, it goes like oil in an oil cup."

Kurt paid little attention to him. He pursued his own notion. "I've been reading about tractors. They're going to demonstrate them in Mary's Hill before long." He screwed his brows up tantalizingly. "That's what we need. If we could get a small engine, small enough to get around but with plenty of power for farm machines, that would be something."

"Judas Proost!" Johnny couldn't help his exasperation. "A small engine! How you gonna get power out of a small engine? You need power and more power; and the more power you need, the bigger your engine's got to be. That's the only thing makes sense." He spat. "Machine-shop man says those tractors bog down as fast as they're put in the field."

Kurt, dropping the subject as fruitless, switched to one he knew would irritate Johnny. "What are you going to do with your rigs when the farmers quit planting wheat?" There was a calmly appraising look in his eyes, something of derision, too. "Diversified farming——"

"Diversified my heifer's ears!" exploded Johnny. "You still think you can farm out of a book, don't you? Well, put this in your fist and hold it.

As long as there's a good price for wheat, farmers'll plant it and I'll thrash it. You and your experiment stations!"

There was triumph in putting Kurt back on his haunches. Kurt still drove him within an inch of hauling out a fist and striking that heavy mouth. Kurt irritated him because Kurt might be right. He had been before. No one did Johnny regard with a more doubtful uneasiness. Let Kurt gabble, he thought belligerently. I can handle him. I can handle him or Tetzell or anybody.

That autumn there was trouble in the north. For months Tetzell had smoldered beside his rig, checked in all but drunken threats by the slippery-tongued Lornas. But even Lornas sometimes unleashed the fox on his lips.

"You're gonna have trouble with them buzzards," Alb warned Johnny.

"Tetzell?" Johnny laughed. "Bory's getting so fat he needs a two-wheeled cart to carry his belly."

"It's that sneak-faced Lornas," Alb said. "Aw sheets, Johnny, I'm quittin' thrashin' one of these days. Trouble shortens a man's life."

"And let Lornas stick a pitchfork into me?" Johnny clapped Alb's shoulder. "You know you wouldn't do that."

At first there were only threats from Bory and his crew. But as the Red Star and the Buffalo Head pushed their smokestacks nearer and nearer the Loon Lake country, "accidents" began to trail both rigs. A farmer lost a setting of grain. Wild flames crackled in the pit of dawn. Heinie was blamed for a spark that set it roaring despite his oath that he had "capped" the smokestack with a galvanized pail and had swashed water on every coal.

A small wooden bridge over what was no more than a ditch, and dry at that, collapsed when Marty crossed it. The rig was hauled out. The delay was short. But nerves became frazzled and profanity arched like heat lightning among the crew. Before he climbed back onto the engine, Marty stared a long time at the splintery gouges on certain posts and underpinnings. "Heck, I knew that bridge was ready to fall," Marty reported to Johnny. "It looks to me, somebody helped it along with a crowbar or a stump puller."

"Hang on and watch," said Johnny.

One Monday morning nearly every boxing on Heinie's separator ran "hot." Several burned out. "I can't figure why all of them should heat at the same time," Heinie growled.

The separator man pointed at a smear on a boxing that wasn't oil or grease. "That looks like linseed oil," he said. "You pour that stuff into an oil hole and all hell won't keep your box cool."

"Linseed oil." Wrathfully Heinie flung a wrench aside. "Why the dirty——"

On another morning the Buffalo Head "foamed." The steam pressure fell. The engine dragged in its wheels. "Acts like a pitcher with the 'thrasher's runs,'" the fireman said. But Marty, wise in tricks of rival firemen, said, "Some bastard put soap in the water." He ordered the tankee, "Spill 'er out on the ground." In a corner of the emptied tank they found a gelatinous square of soap. "Just as I said. Some dirty goose-wiper is having a busy night. I'd like to lay my hands on him," Marty threatened.

(At home Lilice told Mrs. Peiser, "Yes, I heard about it," and gazed at the empty thresher sheds as if their shadows were a dark space between herself and Johnny she could not cross.)

Thereafter at night sometimes both Heinie and Marty slid from the haymow and prowled about the rigs, a wrench or a neck yoke handy for an intruder. They found no more than an owl disturbing the dark tide of the night.

Folks began to say that more than accident was stalking two of Johnny's rigs. Over the first incidents Johnny had kept silent when the neighbors talked with him. But when a small box of "safety" matches was found among the bundles in Heinie's run, Johnny grew tense and expectant. By the sheerest wink of an eye, the pitcher had caught sight of the little box. What flame would have snapped had the cylinder teeth ripped those powder-tipped sticks into the straw-filled concaves, Heinie refused to imagine. Though Johnny made no accusations, lacking actual proof, the crews on the Red Star and the Buffalo Head rumbled loudly that the Tetzell outfit, descendants of the kennel anyway, and illegitimately at that, were guiltier than hell.

For a week they set guard. A pitcher yawned his way through the night on Heinie's machine, keeping a sharp watch with a length of pipe ready. Johnny waited, prepared to join Heinie. "You run the outfit, Alb, if I do go away," he said.

At Johnny's place Lilice went to bed each night prepared to have fists on the door banging her into harsh wakefulness. "Don't let me wake up and find him hurt," she pleaded. The boys looked at her, all eyes from fright, and glanced at each other.

And then it happened. A pitcher on Heinie's machine, slouching on a blanket on top of the separator one night, opened his eyes wide at a skulking form that crept in the shadows below him. With a yell as wild as a bobcat's yowl, he leaped down upon the intruder. So hasty was his plunge, he knocked the man limp and still, and himself breathless. His yell brought the men running, buttoning pants and slipping up suspenders and dragging feet solidly into shoes as they came.

The man was one of Bory's crew. They doused cold water on him until, snorting wetly, he sat up. He had matches and wads of paper in his pocket. In spite of his squeals, they tore his clothes off, splashed oil on his shivering nakedness. They dumped him into a mound of barley chaff and then rolled him in a pile of ashes. Choking and gasping, he struggled helplessly in their hands. They sent him over the fields at last, coal-black, oiled, lathered with prickly chaff, without a stitch on him. They hastened him with kicks and the prodding ends of fork handles. "Get back to Tetzell's outfit."

Johnny arrived home to find Lilice quivering. "Johnny, you aren't going to meet Bory?" She caught his arm. "If you get hurt, I don't know——"

"I'm not meeting anybody," he soothed her. "And I'm not going to get hurt. But I'm not hiding under the bed at home either, if anybody is looking for me."

"All you think of is a chance to settle your score with Tetzell." Lilice bit back the tears. "You never think of me."

"Never think of you!" he echoed bitterly. "It's because I can't stop thinking about you, that's why I won't have people jabbing their thumbs at me and calling me yellow."

Lilice watched him go. Nothing she could say. What next? What next? Then in a haze that sprinkled dust motes upon her sight, she saw the thresher, a monster with open jaws to swallow all she loved. And in the muddle of her thought, pain and suffering became mixed with the roar of the blower, sheaves of agony for the teeth of the cylinder. What shall I do? What?

One evening two weeks later when most of the crew of the Red Star were at Toffman's store to get the kinks out of their weary muscles, and the remainder were in the farmer's barn, joking before slumber, Heinie was in the field where the rig stood ready in the setting. The fireman and the separator man were with him. He was mending a belt. The rig, set a good quarter of a mile from the farmer's yard, was fading into dusk. Suddenly the shadows in a near-by hazel copse broke into a dozen handkerchief-masked figures. Before Heinie and his two helpers knew, the men were upon them. Two went at the separator, their fists full of matches; two at the engine, sledges swinging in their grasp. The rest dived at the three who stooped over the belting.

The attack was short. Heinie managed to grab up a neck yoke. The jingle of iron rings cracked into silence when the wood struck. Heinie felt the flesh of a body yield. Then the neck yoke was torn away. He succeeded in catching two heads in his wide-spread hands and knocking them together. He heard the hollow melonlike sound as nose and mouths were bashed one against another. But a fist below his ear shattered his firm hold on the world. . . .

When it was over, Heinie was trying to get up and falling back, the stickiness of blood clouding his vision and the fierce heat of flame reddening his cheeks. The fireman lay as one dead, and the separator man, escaping by agility no less than miraculous, was running through the woods as if cougar and timber wolf were pawing at his heels. The separator was more scarlet in flame than it had ever been in paint. Long red manes waved brightly from the feeder. The knives were coldly black against their crimson hues. And the teeth of the cylinder were dulling at the abrasive touch of fire. On the hazel copse scarlet streamers flickered, and the shadow of Heinie wobbling to his feet and falling again was incredibly black and grotesque.

The engine was a wreck of smashed tubing and wheel, bent and broken castings, shattered doors. They attached one end of a hose to an auxiliary tank. With a wooden plug they corked the other end and thrust it into the firebox. They ran for their lives. What heat remained in the firebox soon burned the rubber. Water sprayed on the still-hot walls. There was a dull explosion. The firebox door, ripped loose, shot through the air.

The farmer and three of the crew, running wildly over the stubbles, found Heinie dragging the fireman away from the burning separator. With each tug at the body he grunted as if he pulled at his own vitals. Of the masked men there was no sign. They had plunged back into the night again. . . .

Next day Johnny let the sharp edges of ruin and the smoldering pile sink into his consciousness. He kicked at the cylinder. The teeth were blackened and flecked with blue heat scales, fit only for the threshing of ashes now, not the husk-headed heart of grain. The spearator was no more than a wisp of gray smoke.

And the Red Star! His first engine. Sweat of his body and flesh of his bones had been the polishing cloth to make that throttle so shiny, the rim of that steering wheel so bright. That lever, worn in its fastening—the strength of his sinews had eaten away that iron. But it was the knotting muscles of his determination that had subdued the live vital element in this bludgeoned hulk, subdued it, and out of this one had made three. Now it sagged there, a wounded giant, splintered and cracked, its thews wrenched from its body and hanging crazily. He could have wept, if fury had not dried his tears.

"Devil grab it!" he shouted into the empty field and left the bones of the Red Star where they lay. He drove to Mary's Hill; ordered another outfit, one as big as the Golden Bird. "No son of a bastard is going to burn me out of business," he told the machine-shop man. "Just as soon as Heinie can use his arm, back on the road we go."

The crews of the Buffalo Head and the Golden Bird continued threshing without a break, although they spat in their work-horny palms and were ready with pitchfork and neck yoke to spread over the fields into the Tetzell crew and roll them flat; they said they would, let Johnny as much as wink.

But Johnny grunted them into remaining where they were. Sweat and profanity were the better part of their valor—for him, the more lucrative part. "When I need you, I'll whistle," he promised them. "Until trouble gets really bad, your job is getting these stacks into the machine. I'll take care of Bory."

After a week in the hospital, the fireman returned, dented and scarred, but yearning to break the skulls of those who had injured him. Johnny fired the separator man. "You could have stayed with the rig." He unsnapped his pocketbook.

"But them fellers—" the separator man cringed—"they had clubs. I wasn't gonna get my head cracked."

"Heinie stayed and so did Pete. They didn't run. They're thrashermen from way back. You——" Johnny pulled several bills from his pocketbook. "A good crack in your head, and some of the yellow would run out. Here's your money."

"There was a dozen or more against us three," pleaded the man. "We couldn't——"

"I can't stop to clean underpants every time there's trouble and somebody in my crew fills his drawers. You got your pay. Dust down that road."

Anger burned Johnny as fiercely as the flames that had devoured the Red Star. "I'll settle you for this, Bory Tetzell, or Lornas, or whoever the hell it was. Once and for all, and there won't be much left to wipe up either," he raged.

It was Mrs. Peiser who brought the news to Lilice. "Heinie is laid up and the fireman is in the hospital. The rig is burned to the ground, three stacks of grain with it."

"Johnny?" Lilice voiced her first thought before she realized that Heinie, not Johnny, engineered the Red Star.

"He wasn't there," Mrs. Peiser prattled. "But Tetzell is laughing fit to die. Says, ain't it funny what can happen to a thrashing rig? Mrs. Schimmel told me. Na, such a man. He says it ain't the last that might happen to Johnny Black either. And Mrs. Edgely, she says Johnny, he's so mad, he could bite himself."

Lilice heard the chatter dimly through a harrow of dull, hurting fear that was dragging through her mind. She said good-by to Mrs. Peiser as though she were a tightly wound toy unwinding. If the spring snaps——

"It's a big country. There's room for both you and Tetzell here," she begged Johnny when he came home.

"No there ain't." Johnny put aside her hands at his shoulders. This time he wasn't to be persuaded. "A man who sneaks up and burns my rig? There's not even elbowroom here for me and him."

"Johnny," she coaxed, her voice level to hide the quiver in it, "couldn't you take your rigs into the Valley, or down south?"

"And be as yellow as Tetzell?" Johnny demanded. "Not if I lose all three rigs."

"If you'd think of us here!" she moaned. He wouldn't listen. As though to dissaude him, she yielded to his importunities almost violently that night. Eagerly responsive, he accepted them as part of his manhood's necessity. Next morning, breakfast eaten, his purpose as unshaken as rock, he went his way.

She let the egg harden on the plates. Dry-lashed she gathered Robin in her lap. She couldn't trust herself to touch Dickie. So it was happening before her eyes and she mouse-helpless to stop it. Sparks of cunning began to dance in the brown wells of her eyes. The thresher—yes, that was it. A heap of cinders though it was, it demanded of her still. It demanded Johnny. She must save him . . . he must return to the fold of the white sheep. "Robin, Robin." She swayed backward, forward, scaring the boy until he held his breath in terror. "Nothing is ever forgotten. You have to pay for everything. Pay . . . pay. The Pastor said so. Aunt Phrena said so. I wouldn't listen. It's the thresher. A big red thresher, Robin; coming like a huge grasshopper . . . coming for him and he won't listen. . . ." The sparks whirled under her lashes.

15

Tenseness, singing tight as a fiddlestring, pulled at the voices and the steps of the folks that season. It came out in short clipped phrases, in quick alertness of heel and toe, in the way an eye shifted, avoiding the blame of taking sides, although most of the people favored Johnny Black. Setting fire to a man's rig, that was as bad as burning a farmstead. Of course, a thrasher wasn't quite the same as a farmer. Then too, Johnny Black had gone mighty near Bory's territory, practically singed Bory's whiskers. But burning a man's rig was too much.

"What we need," Kurt said at Toffman's store, "is a lot of small rigs. Let the farmers own them, say three, four of them together. Then you wouldn't have these scraps. You can depend on it, when there's trouble, the farmer gets the worst of the bargain."

But the folks, as ready to say "Amen" to the last part of Kurt's opinion as they were to guffaw at the first part, had distracted ears for anything but talk about Johnny's new rig and how a week after the fire he had deliberately threshed a setting under Bory's nose. "By jippers, *in* his nose, you might say," Mr. Nussbaum averred unbelievingly. "Madder'n a basket of hops, too, Johnny was." There'd be a row, sooner or later, nobody doubted that.

It came on a drizzly Thursday night. For several days not a pitchfork had moved, not a tooth crushed through the concaves because of the rain. Oat kernels, lodged in the moist corners of the tank wagon, were beginning to sprout. Those members of the crews who hadn't scattered to their near-by homes and farms were rough-tempered with loafing, their toes out for excitement. Some spent their time and their earnings over the bars in Mary's Hill.

That night the saloon was pushing-full of tankees and pitchers. There were strawstackers from the old machines. The mirror behind the bar, half the building long, was alive with overalled and dirty-shirted men, bearded faces. Johnny's men mingled with those from the flats and north of Mary's Hill. Whiskered lips opened to shout, "Set 'em up. . . . Come on, Lafe, you old son of a heifer, have another. . . . Betcha three schooners to one I can hist a barrel of wheat into a wagon box with my bare hands. . . . Aw, hell. . . . You oughta see how we thrash on Johnny's rig; three thousand bushels a day like a damn. . . . Ya don't say. Why, over on our rig . . ." The air was smelly with long-dried sweat, manury boots and slopped-over whisky. Overhead the new electric lights in their clear bulbs were so bright, when you looked at them, they left green spots in front of your eyes.

His scar red with drink, Bory was hunching over a glass. He swaggered at the bar. Lornas stood near him, a glass untouched at his finger tips. The Tetzell crew was knotted into a small group near by but apart too.

Bory was saying, "Nobody from Pockerbrush is going to run me out of the country," when the swinging doors creaked inwardly and Johnny walked along the bar. He was bareheaded. His black hair, still wavy though years and sweat had curbed its tumbles somewhat, glinted in the mirror. Heinie was with him and Marty Borman.

Without checking a lift of heel or a bend of knee, he plowed through the gathering. Silence in a wave flowed from his pushing way until quiet rolled into the corners. The chips on a poker table clicked loudly. "Three of a kind," a player said noisily. A bartender removed three bottles from the bar in a scuttling hurry.

Johnny walked toward Tetzell. Without waiting for Bory to put his glass down, Johnny's flat hand shot out. He slapped him—struck the jaw where the scar was a red slash. Whisky spilled over Bory's hand and on the pine of the bar. There was a dull hush, bored at by not so much as a small worm of noise. Lornas dipped his finger tips into his glass and touched his nose lightly, inhaling once deeply. The Tetzell crew pushed forward.

"Damn you," Bory screamed. He made for Johnny.

In the circle that swirled aside as if a finger milled a hollow in the sand, Johnny waited, light on his feet as thistledown. A cold ferocity brimmed over in him. "I'm going to lace your face wide open, you crooked-nosed devil," he chanted to himself. Heinie and Marty were at his back; the rest of his crew began to crowd in.

Bory came punching, as though, in a wild flailing of knuckles, he'd sweep Johnny to the floor. But drinker's fat and thresher's exhaustion slowed him. Through the tangle of enraged, unthinking, grasping arms, Johnny struck once, twice, again. Each time he thought queerly of Snoose.

Bory hunched aside. This wasn't the kid he'd known on the flats. This wasn't the half-grown squirt with his first threshing rig; this was somebody man-grown, skinful of hate, whose eyes were shining beads, bright as a grackle's with enmity; whose hands were curved for a windpipe.

Once more Bory surged forward. This time he broke through. Johnny tasted the blood of a glancing right. But, fists notched with hate out of the past, he knocked Tetzell backward. Each blow was tipped with venom. It was a poison that cascaded icy cold through Bory's flesh. Old. Getting old, that's what he was. Too old to handle a threshing crew. After this he'd never again see men draw aside when he stepped forward as men now did when Johnny Black appeared. And his kid, who he hoped would be a thresher one day, his long-legged kid, would be ashamed of his father.

He sagged. That's what Johnny Black wanted to see: Bory Tetzell, the once big thresherman, beaten to the knees. That mocking voice: "Come on, Bory, you prick-eared, dirty-bottomed, backhouse-seat-presser, you. Where's your guts? Between your legs? It's been a long time, settling this score, Tetzell. Why don't you get Lornas to back you up?"

Bory felt the fight slipping from him. Fear punctured his brag and left it flabby as his belly. "I got enough," he croaked.

At that moment Bory's crew, threading among the crowd until they surrounded Johnny, pressed in. At Heinie's wavering shout, Johnny flattened against the bar. His foot shot out; his fists flailed. For a while he made a space of safety about him, twice the length of his arm, which no one dared to cross. For a while. Then Lornas was facing him.

"Made up your mind, didn't ya?" Johnny's words came throatily. "This ain't schooltime now, Lornas. Why don't you sick Mosey Fritz on me?" Then the animal in them rushed out. High and shrill came the foxsnicker of Lornas. They crouched in front of one another; bobbed and shouldered grotesquely like worshipers before the god of violence. Fists snapped forward, knuckles squashed against noses. Hands grabbed at arms. They grappled. Fingers clawed into mouths. Claws groped for a windpipe. Blood made the skin slippery. Blows thudded, hard bone on dully resonant flesh; breathing hoarsened like enraged animals'.

Tetzell's crew waited, tense for the moment when they could trip Johnny, or kick him between the legs, or ram a bottle against his shoulder blades. In this swirling melee they scarcely dared interfere. Heinie watched, the wrench under his coat sweaty from the tight clasp of his hand. Marty stood beside him, a long cold chisel in his pocket. Johnny's men gathered, pushed forward. But the Tetzell men stood between.

Johnny was too busy to worry about thrust or attack from the circle. Slowly and steadily, as though a virus of antipathy were cording his muscles, he was slicing Lornas to ribbons. Lornas may have had cunning for his aid, but Johnny had the years' accumulation of hate long deferred. He jabbed through Lornas' guard, straight to jaw, to lips, to cheekbones—mercilessly, efficiently, each blow a salve for those he had once received. The leathery wheezing, the gulpy breaths, the slight moan when a knuckle bit at a nerve-tender spot in Lornas' body—these were like pungent relish to Johnny. For this he would have lost a mouthful of teeth, endured the plaster cast of a dozen broken arms.

Then Lornas went down. Instinctively he rolled over on his side as if expecting Johnny's leaping feet to crash into his belly. That's what you'd do to me, if I were down, Johnny thought swiftly. You low-tailed skunk!

Tetzell's crew lunged at Johnny the next instant. For a moment Johnny felt their clawing hands—hands that got one in the way of the other. Then Heinie was there, yelling. For this Heinie had waited. His wrench struck at jaws and faces. This for a blow he'd received, this for a kick he'd got. There was the sound of cracking bone. Marty was there, the cold chisel slashing. There would be scars to commemorate this fracas.

Johnny's men flung themselves into the squabble. Like grass fire in high wind, fight spread from wall to wall, corner to corner. Two bottles and a chair crashed into the mirror. Slivers of brightness fell. Pieces of silver hung at odd and chance-placed angles. The fight raged in mirrored fragments.

In a boat-shaped splinter Heinie slugged a Tetzell man who was choking Johnny. The wrench was tinged the color of freshly squeezed strawberries.

In a jagged diamond the Tetzell fireman mauled Marty Borman to the floor.

Two shattered pieces hung side by side, a space of wall between them. In one a Tetzell man had his teeth clamped on the ear of Johnny's tankee. They struggled to the edge of the reflection and vanished into nothingness; reappeared in the other fragment. Now Johnny's tankee had the nose of the Tetzell man in a tight fist hold, jerking and twisting. They fell backward off the edge of the glass.

Most of the fight was scattered and broken . . . fist raised high into sight and lowered, raised and lowered, redder with each stroke . . . half a face leering through blood . . . a bottle lifted in an upper mirror shard, vanished, reappeared in a lower splinter, smashing on the head of an antagonist . . . arms and heads waving without bodies . . . bodies swaying and falling without heads . . . the jumbled mirror going dark as the electric bulbs were smashed out one by one. . . .

When it was over, the Tetzell men, in disfavor at the start, had to be helped from the saloon. There would be no threshing in Bory's run for a couple of days, no matter how much the sun dried the stacks, so beaten and mauled was the crew. The saloonkeeper swore he'd bolt his door the next time a rainy spell set in. "Damn the thrashers anyway! I'm going to get me a shotgun next year."

Marty took Heinie's place in the hospital for a couple of days and was achy for a week. Heinie pointed joyously to a cut on his own lip. He had jabbed many a face for this, his only casualty and his badge of valor. Johnny limped badly. One eye was as dark as the purple iris growing near the creek. His lips felt like a slice of pounded beef.

When she saw him, Lilice sank into a chair, her knees all jelly. She was up in a moment, her murmurings half scoldings, half endearments. Without knowing how, she swabbed him with arnica and liniment, smeared salve on his pummeled lips, and cried dully over him, as if her tears were squeezed from a hurt too deep to be called by name.

She hushed the boys' whimperings. After Johnny had returned to the rig, she recounted to them day by day the awfulness of hurting your neighbor. Sometimes she pulled a word to a halt, only half of it spoken. Her stare would fix and a queer sparkle flash through the brown depths of her eyes.

But Johnny strode about the rig with a new authority in his step and voice. Folks hopped a little faster when he gave an order, as if in his command they heard the lash of a whip. That autumn he fell into argument with Amos Timmerman over the threshing rates.

"You charge too much, Johnny. I can't pay that," Amos protested. The threshing was about half finished then. Amos' stacks were open to the bulge.

"That's my price," snapped Johnny. "You know that."

"I know. But jiminy, man." Amos kicked at the grass stubbornly. "I got mostly oats and barley and hay this year. Hardly no wheat. And that price—why, I might as well give you the stacks."

"That's my price," Johnny simmered hotly. "Take it, or I'll pull out."

"It's too high." Amos faced him squarely. "Too damn high. And there's lots of fellers here feel like I do."

"That so?" Johnny's elbows crooked into belligerency. He glowered, his fists ready. Then he spun on a heel. "I guess we can get along without you," he flung over his shoulder.

Not until he heard the whistle screech "Stop!" and saw Johnny send the engine forward and the belt slip off did Amos plod over to beg, "You ain't going to pull out on me, Johnny."

"What the hell you think I'm doing? Getting ready to play marbles?" Johnny flung a hose aside, fury like ice masking his face.

"I've got most of my cash money for the winter in those stacks, and my feed for the animals," Amos pleaded. Sweat dotted his greasy forehead. Despair sagged in him as he remembered Abner Heberstadt. "Cripes, I got six kids to feed. I'll pay your price."

"Like hell you will." Johnny stomped up on the platform. "All I care, you can rake up pignuts and haul 'em into the granary. Couple 'er up," he yelled.

The rig left the yard. Smoke thinned to a sharp odor lingering among the buildings. Amos Timmerman looked at his stacks, or what remained of them. Their bellies lay open to rain or snow.

It was late in the season before Johnny gave in to Amos' desperation and allowed Marty Borman and the Buffalo Head to thresh the damp-stained sheaves. By that time most of the bundles were spoiled. The grain was "granary-burned" before Thanksgiving. The kernels had a grayish hue; a pinch of them, chewed, left a taste that was like the smell of mice, so that you spat quickly and longed for a drink of cleansing water.

Thereafter, not only the crew members but also the owners of farms put hurry in their knees when Johnny spoke. They'd answer "yes" with a kind of irritation at the sharp-shod way he ordered, "There's a quartering wind today. We better pile your straw over there," when they really wanted it elsewhere. They'd tear down fences with a reckless use of crowbar and hammer because Johnny wanted it so, and then, irked by their subservience, they would regain superiority by yelling at their sons, "Go get that scoop shovel, like I tell you, or I'll lick hell out of you"; or they'd bawl at the hired man, "By cripes, what am I paying you good board and keep for—rootin' your butt in the grass? Hitch up that team for me."

Nevertheless, there was much hidden grumbling among the farmers, the rim of the talk gathering wheel-like around Kurt. There was much Sunday truculence after church about what this man was going to do, and that man was going to say to Johnny. "I'm going to tell him a thing or two, by gollys-nach-a-mal!" one would threaten. And another, "He ain't gonna ride me piggyback, I'll tell you that." Such talk melted to weekday's subservience by Monday. Only Kurt lifted a strong, determined voice.

Triumphant, Johnny grinned over the steering wheel, thinking about Amos Timmerman. "That'll show 'em," he exulted. No use in denying it, he had his world by the tail and was swinging it, or pretty nearly so. The best thresher in the country, he had more rigs and more jobs than anybody hauling a tank wagon. The farmers were not far from their knees to get his outfits to thresh in their yards. Everybody in town hailed him by his first name, called him "Mister." And Bory Tetzell had had a taste of his knuckles. Though I'm not finished with that cow-licker yet, Johnny added to himself. It was a good autumn.

Yet, for all that his head was thrown back exultantly and his teeth, less milky now, were still white against the red of his lips, there was a small echoing place of loneliness aching in his satisfaction, fill his days with activity and pride as much as he liked. It was a lonely restlessness not even Lilice could touch with hands or thought. Oh, Judas, he sighed more than once. If only, if only Snoose were waiting at the end of a path and I could tell him all about this! Judas . . .

16

Robin was seven and Dickie past five the late summer Lilice went to the meetinghouse. Only a week or so remained for the wheat to "sweat" in the stacks before threshing. Summer was drying in the pods of autumn.

This Sunday morning had the brightness of June in the clean arch of the zenith. Here and there "popcorn" clouds, as Robin called them, bulged in shifting folds and billows. Johnny puttered at the Golden Bird.

Fresh in knee pants and blouses as white and starchy as Lilice's hands could scrub and iron them, the boys came trotting over the yard. Forgotten was Lilice's warning, "Now you stay out of the dirt for once, or you'll be messy when we get to Aunt Sophie's house." They romped over the grass.

"You kids heard what Ma said." Johnny lifted a hammer reprovingly. "I'll give you each a nickel if you stay clean till this afternoon."

A drift of cedar waxwings throbbed their clear notes overhead. He glanced up. The birds settled in the pin-cherry bushes beyond the pasture gate. His face softened in a rush of memory. "Haven't thought of them in a long time," he muttered. "Haven't had time." At an impulse that made his lips twitch, he laid his hammer on the toolbox. "Wonder if they still do it. Come along, kids." He held out his hands; then, remembering, wiped them on his handkerchief first. "I'll show you something."

As they reached the gate, Johnny pointed. "Keep your eyes open." On a slender limb among the late pin cherries, they saw a handful of birds, olive-backed and greenish-breasted, with flaunty topknots, a red spot on each wing and a tip of yellow on their tails. The crimson fruit on long stems (like scarlet-headed pins stuck into the soft wood of the twigs) hung about them. For a while the birds twittered and bobbed heads. But as Johnny and the boys watched, one bird picked a scarlet berry, turned it in his neb, passed it to his neighbor, who held it a moment before he stretched his neck and offered it farther. Along the row of beaks the scarlet berry passed, backward and forward. "And not one will eat it," Johnny told the saucer-eyed boys. "They'll drop it after a while. Snoose showed me," he added softly. They went back to the yard.

Thoughtfully Johnny screwed at a bolt, his mind alive with a flutter of wings and Snoose crouching in the underbrush over a bird's nest, Snoose in May touching the white legs of the Dutchmen's-breeches. What a big feller Snoose would be by now. He'd have kids, his and Em'ly's, big enough to play with Robin. Johnny caught his breath sharply.

He'd forgotten the boys when childish yells in blame and in dispute arose. He straightened quickly and wanted to laugh but frowned darkly instead. There they were, ladling grease from the grease bucket. They had shingle splinters for spoons and a board for a skillet. With chips for pieces of bacon they were frying breakfast so vigorously that their white blouses were splashed with dark widening smudges. Robin was paddling Dickie with an oily shingle. The grease spattered.

"Now you fellers'll catch it," Johnny prophesied, although he was not far from laughter. "I've a good mind to cut me a willow stick and——" He stopped.

Lilice stood there, how long he didn't know. On her face was a stiff, set expression that chilled him. "Now the thresher is going to take my babies too." She spoke in a queer throaty way. "I s'pose you are training them, Johnny, so they'll be good engineers and firemen." She went to the boys. They hung back before her strangeness. "Come." She took their hands firmly. "You were so nice and clean. I'll have to scrub you now. Only, I'm afraid water won't wash the grease off. It's deeper than skin. Come."

They trotted beside her reluctantly. Over her shoulder, firmly as if what she uttered had been in the mind for a long time, she said, "I'm not going to Sophie's this afternoon. Mr. Erdman is holding special services at the meetinghouse. I'm going there."

"Lilice, what in the world!" he cried, terror starting the cold sweat under his arms.

"You needn't come," she said quietly, as if this were talk about the mending of his socks. "This is for me, too."

The words, bringing with them the deadly echo of Lilice's study with the Pastor, frightened him as much as her queerness. Thoughts ran wildly to his lips, none was spoken. His head was as full of scurry as the ant heap Robin had upset only the day before. "Leesa, what is it? You are so——" He swallowed.

"Dinner'll be ready soon." Such calm indifference staggered him into silence. Helplessly he watched her go.

"What brought this on?" he groaned. Could it have been the saloon fight? The way she'd fretted over his bruises. But no; that was months and months ago. Mrs. Edgely had visited yesterday. Vaguely he remembered Lilice's mentioning the service. But it couldn't be that either. Why had Lilice stared so fixedly at the black grease smudges on the kids' blouses? Black oil stains . . .

He threw down his hammer and went to the house, dreading what he might find. His knees unhinged in the weakness of relief when he saw that whatever shadow had clouded her eyes before was gone now. As though nothing had happened she bent over the water kettle, pouring water into a basin. Happily, Robin strutted his nakedness; Dickie withdrew shyly.

Even though there were few smiles to break the gravity of her expression, the staring, immobile mask of cunning was gone from Lilice's face. He wanted to ask, "Leesa, tell me, what is this?" But for this while of respite he gabbled, he didn't remember what—gabbled as if he'd had too much pieplant wine: anything to crowd away the dreadful shadow of a thought slinking into his head—the thought of Mr. Dunkel and his wife.

They got ready to go to the meetinghouse. Johnny's dissuasions Lilice never heard, for all the attention she paid them. Finally Johnny hooked up the team. He went with misgivings. He remembered the outpourings at the Edgelys', dim and far away, and yet freshened in later years by what Aunt Phrena reported. Those promises of grace. The wild tales of evil-doers redeemed with visible signs of wonder. This would be a fine lapful of gossip for Mrs. Peiser to carry around. But if this would quiet Lilice . . .

·17

Lilice opened the door. The meeting was already loud in song. I'll find it here, the word to say to the thresher, she thought. This must be for Dickie's sake, too. She hesitated on the threshold which separated the church proper from the anteroom, the Sunday-school room. Johnny and the boys were behind her.

She entered. The house of Erdman (as the Pastor scornfully called it once in Mr. Nussbaum's presence) was long and rather narrow. At the front a railing from wall to wall was broken at the aisle by a gateway to a space beyond. Beside this opening Brother Erdman's hymnbook swayed as he beat the tempo. He kept a watery eye open for late-comers, a smile for their welcome. He hadn't changed much (Johnny decided). He was still energetic, commandingly dulcet, pink-cheeked, friendly. But the years had drawn their crow's-feet upon his eyes, too. There were flabbiness about his jaws and slackness in his backbone as if easy grace had sapped a vital artery.

Lilice steered the boys to a pew, Johnny following uneasily, feeling that he'd been caught tiptoeing in a stranger's house. After she'd settled the boys and brushed the hair they'd ruffled in jerking off their caps, she leaned forward eagerly. Here it could happen, something wonderful could happen; it could happen to Johnny, to her, but most of all to Dickie.

There weren't as many folks present today as she'd expected, considering that this was a special outpouring. The devout were there, however: Mr. Watters, the Habers (though Lena and Adam weren't), the Belsens. The Belsens had recently found God, they said. They were putting all their care on the Lord, they told the neighbors. They never worried about any-thing. They had found God. ("Ya, and they ain't done a lick of work since," the neighbors grumbled. "They're so far in debt, it sticks through the roof.") But the Belsens were happy.

Lilice gazed wraptly. Not in the Pastor's stony house but here, under the roof of promise, here indeed the ice that lay between her breasts would melt, here she could find that peace and calm that awakens tears—tears deep-welling and unsoiled to bring sweetness to her house, to cleanse the flesh of Dickie, to redeem that mad ecstasy she had permitted long ago.

Tears to blot from her brain an ugly, smoky, oily shape, a booming, devilish howl. Tears.

Then Brother Erdman was enjoining his flock to walk beside the cool waters of mercy. "Come, come, it is all prepared for you," he yearned, his voice flowing, the pinkness in his cheeks intensifying. "Yes, indeed. Yes, indeed. It is prepared for you in the blood of the Lamb. There is no time to think. Close your eyes and accept this. Wash yourself, sinner. From the crimson flood you will step white as the driven snow." Water trickled down his cheeks easily now, as if he no longer needed the spur of excitement but were drained involuntarily at the first glow of pity.

Johnny shifted on the bench, itchy with impatience and scorn. But Lilice felt a queer stirring at the sight of his tears. Pain rose in her throat. His gentle exhortations were like hands at her elbows, urging her forward. "Come, come, my brothers, my sisters, and rest in the arms of Jesus. He will wipe away your sorrow. Don't stop to argue with yourself. Come."

She watched a girl sidle up and slip through the gateway, a young girl with a hunted look, who fell to her knees, then lay outstretched on the floor. Others joined her. An elderly woman went forward, a jacket on her arm. Carefully she spread the jacket before she knelt, slowly and creakily.

Lilice watched them. It must be there, beyond the railing. Uncertainly, for she sensed nothing like the touch of flame in her bosom, Lilice fluttered on the edge of the pew. Then she arose without knowing how. She felt Johnny grab at her sleeve and heard his horrified, "Lilice, you mustn't; it's— it's not decent."

She pulled away and almost ran to that gateway into the space beyond. Brother Erdman smiled. She stumbled rather than knelt; was aware of unyielding wood against her knees, against her hands, against her forehead until she buried her face in an elbow.

She heard moans at her side. She longed to cry out but her tongue was dry, stricken and dumb, her heart unquickened, withered, responding no more than a fistful of clay. Quickless, withered. No tongue of fire, no froth of ecstasy, no voice crying from the rooftree. Only the dust on the floor and at her side the girl with the hunted look moaning, "Jesus, Jesus," and the elderly woman on the jacket muttering not far off, "I am forgiven, I am forgiven."

Dully she arose. She crept back to the pew, to an angry-lipped Johnny and a pair of scared-faced boys. Let Johnny be mad, it doesn't matter now. What did matter?

Johnny let her have the edge of his glare. The hymn started. Scornfully Johnny noted how fast and tripping it was, almost like a waltz tune. It was familiar too, but he couldn't place it. One could step that off at a dance, he thought, savagely content with the blasphemy. Then he realized that Mr. Watters ahead of him, lost in singing, had forgotten himself and was beating time with a heavy heel. Uncle Herm was right. Slop religion. Glancing furiously at Lilice, he leaned across the boys. "I'll get the horses ready," he growled urgently. "You can come when you've had enough of this."

The service ended. Mrs. Edgely came to say, "How de do, Mrs. Black. I'm glad you came. You look peaked, child. You must come often. You've no idea how good it is to find God. What you really need is a good 'whoopin',' as my brother used to say. Shouting and singing and halle- lujahs and God's glory." She bobbed away. It must be good to have the faith of Mrs. Edgely. Glory of God.

And there were Mr. and Mrs. Belsen who had found the Lord. Such happiness shone in their eyes that Lilice was pricked with a barb of envy. These two old people, why, they looked as if they had found the innocence of children again.

Sighing, Lilice led the boys into the aisle. Ahead of her, slow-moving as one who has been granted the boon of time, was the elderly lady with the jacket, she who had muttered, "I am saved, Lord." The woman's husband, a sourish-featured man as old as she was, was asking jovially in a low tone, "Well, Ma, you feel better now?"

"Oh, Pa, you come next Sunday." Her face glowed with benediction. "I feel so—like I could scrub fifty floors and sing a hallelujah besides."

"That's fine, Ma." He craned toward his wife, seriousness in his tone. "Abbie can come home then, can't she, Ma?"

"Abbie?" At once the mask slipped from her face. It turned waspish. "I won't have her set as much as a foot in my kitchen again. Disgracing me."

Lilice regarded the neck of the elderly lady, wondering whether the words she'd heard held meaning or were something hissed out of a night- mare. She tried to hurry those in front of her. She must get out of here and into the bright air and the untainted sun. She stepped into the ante- room. There over the top of a small thicket of feathers and sprigs of leaves and red cherries on the women's hats was the door. Then she saw the girl again.

She was sagged against a window, weeping as one whose hope is tooth- gnawed as a bone. Pity tugged at Lilice's heart. "Poor thing! It takes a lot of trouble to cry as hard as that," she murmured.

Folks sharpened glances on the girl but were too considerate to pry into her grief. Mrs. Haber leaned toward Mrs. Watters and whispered audibly, her look at the girl significant, "That's the one. She and that Karley boy, you know. He sneaked off to Canada." They pushed ahead.

With the boys close to her Lilice groped her way to the door. Where was forgiveness? she prayed. Nothing in this house of testimonial regret that she could take for bread. Nothing but crumbs in the Pastor's flame-tongued solace. Before what altar stumble next? How long?

". . . till thou hast paid the uttermost farthing." Was that the Pastor speaking or was it part of the roil that spilled discoloration into her mind? ". . . the uttermost farthing."

Outside Johnny waited impatiently. He flipped the lines to hurry her. There were stiff backs and tight lips on the road home. Shaming me in the sight of people, is what Johnny wanted to think. But he couldn't. The uneasiness of that morning was too vivid.

Lilice attended Erdman's services twice that early autumn. Mrs. Edgely fluttered about her. But Aunt Phrena said unexpectedly, "You let her alone, Abigail Edgely. It's a hard way she has to go, that Lilice, Johnny's wife." Her words were less harsh than usual. Thereafter when she spoke of Lilice, she always said, "Lilice, Johnny's wife, you know."

After the third service, to Johnny's silent relief, Lilice went no more. She put the Book upon the shelf. She saw autumn redden the oaks. Wide-eyed, she began to listen for the hum of the thresher.

18

Something about that autumn flaming on the ridges like brush fire stirred brews of excitement in Johnny. The peat-smoke-and-damp-leaf smell was sharp in his nose. When the valley blued with haze and the wild grape frosted on the vine, pungent in the morning, his heels had a quicker lift, as if the season's husk, full-eared with life but as yet untouched by germination, were a preparation for what was to come. The harvest is at once graveyard and birthing bed, decay and earth change. The snap of a cold morning put haste into his bones—hurry to move, as though whatever tracks he made in the dust might be his last.

"We'll drive over to the shop on Monday," he told Alb one evening. Two weeks before he had hauled the Golden Bird and the separator to the blacksmith shop. He had a notion about steadying the bolsters with extra braces. "Get yourself ready bright and early. The tankee and Pete will be waiting for us."

"All I need is a pair of suspenders to hold my britches up and a chew of Indian Twist, and I'm ready," Alb chortled. "But next year—— I'm warning you, Johnny. Next year I'm gonna move to that place southeast of the Vildvogels', on the other side of the Diemer Hills."

"When I see you there, I'll believe it." Johnny laughed.

They were in grumbly moods when on Monday they arrived at the shop, however. "That bridge over the dry wash, it wiggles like frog eggs," Johnny said to the men slouching on the nail kegs. The tankee and the fireman were there. "If I get my rig across and back home, I'll stay there and you fellers can thrash your stacks with a club and a sieve."

During the past year there had been a jumble of talk about the bridges. For three Sundays the supervisors had stayed away from church, they were so bullied by those who wanted new spans and those who didn't.

"I've moved my wheat and potatoes and heifers across that bridge all these thirty years," insisted Mr. Blumen, "and I'm damned if I'm gonna vote more money out of my pocket just so's Johnny Black can pull his thrashin' rig across—ya, and beat somebody out of a couple of bushels, too."

"Cripes, yes." Amos Timmerman joined the protest. "I sweat myself wet, fixing roads last year because he bellyached about the low grades. We repaired all the main town lines in the last three, four years. Got pretty good roads now." There were plenty of folks chewing their cud in agreement with him.

But there were those, not necessarily of Johnny's opinion, who expostulated, "We need a new bridge. Somebody's gonna get hurt there. The planks are so rotten, if you take a breath, you're liable to break through. Besides, Johnny Black's the best thrasher around. If we don't get him, we're liable to lose money. A new bridge won't cost so awful much. Even if it ain't Black's rig, somebody's thrasher has got to get across the river. . . ."

The pro and con of the argument so nullified the sermons that the Pastor showed by text and chapter how idle gossip will waste the rich kernel of the service. If more decorum wasn't observed, he threatened to plant shrubs and flowers in the space before the church where after services many a hot debate had trampled the grass into bare hard soil.

About the bridge nothing had been done. Johnny got no more than a throaty haw-and-hum from the men gathered at the shop this day. "Put more planks on her," they advised comfortably, watching the blacksmith and the sparks like fireflies wink from the anvil as the hammer struck. "She'll hold." They were much more interested in talk about Norton, since that was hearsay and therefore much more titillating. "They say Norton's oil stocks ain't worth the match to set them afire. . . . Johan Peiser told me Norton wants to sell his land now."

"I never seen such a bunch of flat butts in my life," Johnny flung at them bitterly. "Sit and gossip like old women. I saw Norton not long ago. He would have told me." But he was uneasy. He'd have to find out about this.

He was ready to pull the separator home when the Pastor drove up to the shop, his buggy whiffling, to have his team shod.

"Na, the thresher is ready to start again," the Pastor greeted him, alighting and handing the lines to the blacksmith. "The yield is excellent this year. But I don't see you in church very often, you lazybones."

The Pastor's tone scratched Johnny's ire to the surface. "I pay my church dues," he said curtly. "And I do more work in one day than the Herr Pastor does in a week."

"Na ya," admitted the Pastor, withdrawing turtlewise into the shell of his dignity. "In physical labor, yes. But in the performance of God's work——" He broke off to follow another thought. "Your wife. She was very eager in study. She had understanding, too; very near the light. I don't see her at services. She——"

"You should know why better than I do." Mounting the platform, Johnny looked down on the Pastor, this elevation a length of space to embolden him. The fireman stood beside him. Alb was on the separator. "There wasn't much comfort Lilice got from you," Johnny went on bluntly. "I can tell you that. Hard words——" He reached for the throttle. He braced himself for the Pastor's sharp reply.

Silently for a moment the Pastor regarded Johnny's lean figure bent over the steering wheel. When he answered, his tone was so subdued that Johnny halted his firm grasp on the lever. The Pastor said slowly, "By that you mean I am unforgiving. I have heard it before." There was a deep sadness in the way he spoke. "Sometimes I wonder, I wonder if—— But no. It is written. It cannot be otherwise." His back stiffened. "You young fool," he said slowly and distinctly, "what do you know about harshness? It is to myself that I have been harshest." He swung on his heel and marched into the shop, his black coat merging into the dusk that hovered over the anvil and the forge.

"Hah," exclaimed Johnny, taken aback but laughing. "It doesn't take much to rile him."

But Alb said, "That's the first time I ever saw the Pastor with a bigger frog than he could swallow."

They started. At Toffman's bridge they had no difficulty, though Alb growled, "Sheetin' Judas, I saw that stringer buckle like a fiddle bow." But when they came to the bridge over the dry wash, there was trouble.

"I don't like the looks of her at all," Alb warned, putting down the last plank. Uneasily he glanced at the steeply sloping sides of the dry wash. It wasn't particularly deep, a dozen feet at the most and ten yards across. But the creek bed was scattered with rocks. An engine smashing down there—— "She'd explode sure as thunder," he muttered. "I don't want to be around when the pieces fly."

North of Loon Lake an engine had tipped over into a gulch, he remembered. The engineer had been trapped and scalded to death in the live steam—"like a Sunday rooster in a pail of boiling water; only the man was alive." Aloud he said, "The way she wobbled when we came over two weeks ago——"

"If she holds coming over, she'll hold going back." Johnny helped uncouple the separator. "Run that cable back," he ordered the fireman. "We're going across."

Afterward Alb said he held his breath when the Golden Bird *chug-a-chugged* onto the bridge. ("I held it till the wind cracked in my pants.") No sooner had the front wheels rolled half a dozen feet, than the timbers began to tremble ominously. Johnny's hands gripped the wheel. Not a ripple of whatever he felt marred the firmness of lip and cheek. But a tremor rattled his spine. He stared straight ahead, as if his gaze were a grappling hook fastened to the opposite trees and his mind a winch by which to pull the rig and himself to safety.

Suddenly there was a splintery crash, a roar of smashing timbers. The Golden Bird lurched sidewise. Dust arose like smoke from an explosion. Planks tipped at an angle. A length of railing suddenly rested upon the governor. The smokestack sank away so that in a startled second Johnny looked down at its top. He saw the huge unwieldy bulk of the engine behave like a feather-weighted toy as it hung suspended in that interval of time and space where the ordinary-dimensioned laws are in abeyance and unexecuted. The front end swayed lazily downward in a tangle of leaping wood. A quarter-ton driver spun crazily as if the hand of the wind devil had a finger on the rim. The governor belt, unlooped, necklaced gaily through the air and wrapped itself about the spoke of the flywheel. The cap of a grease cup flipped into the air, somersaulted dizzily, and flopped neatly back into place. The whistle shrieked as though the engine screamed its fright, although no hand pulled the cord. Planks split with lazy jaggedness. A rough-edged board rose swimmingly into the air, graceful as a fish after bait, poised alertly and crashed its snout against the back of Johnny's head. . . .

When sight and sky and the tankee's scared face returned to their proper places minutes later, Johnny found himself among the rocks of the dry wash. Blood wet his neck. He heard a groaning near by. Farther away there was a shush of steam.

"You all right?" the tankee asked shakily. "Sure and by rights, about now you ought to be asking for your harp. The fireman's leg is broken."

"Aw sheets," came Alb's voice not far off. "Takes more'n a bridge to stop a thrasher."

Johnny struggled up. Dizziness began to settle like roiled water. He saw the fireman stir.

"That crazy Alb," the tankee said. "He pulled both of ye out of the wreck, and me scared to death the boiler would explode. Then he jumps down and puts a cold chisel in the pop-off: lets the steam out. Says it keeps the engine from exploding and——"

"Aw sheets, hang a chain on your tongue, feller." Alb bustled up.

Johnny shook his head to clear the fog from his eyes. There would be a time to grab Alb's hand in gratitude. But not now. Not now when the Golden Bird lay among the rocks in the matchwood of the bridge, her drivers higher than her flywheel, her front wheels bent.

He shut his eyes. It would take block and tackle and a week of frenzied sweat, dawn to late dark, to lug the engine from the dry wash and repair what had been broken or damaged. A week or more behind time. He was not far from tears of futility.

19

As in other years Johnny started the threshing run at his place that season. Yesterday they had begun in the morning. Today they would finish. They were threshing the oats when the accident occurred.

For more than a week now Heinie and Marty had been at work. Their whistles were shrill in the dusk. The sound reminded Johnny how late he was, and behind in his work. Since the trouble at the bridge he had flung himself at wheel and lever, at tankee and pitcher, curses scorching his mouth, his fingers it seemed of the same metal as his wrenches. Now he was crowding the hours with sweat. But always ahead of him, barring his hurry, lay the dark promontory of night to stop his progress.

He had no time for the fireman's leg to set. "I've hired another man," he said.

The Golden Bird, shorn of some of its pristine sleekness, chugged angrily over the bundles flung to the separator, it seemed. Except for a dent here and a battered spot there, a bend in a spoke or a nick in a casting, no casual eye would have guessed that it had recently wallowed among the rocks of the dry wash. With measured care Johnny had applied paint to scratch and scraped place, and grease to the new parts to give them that oil-soaked and trustworthy appearance which betokens for many folks, not the new and untried, but the proved and reliable. Yet to his ear, lifted like a rabbit's, there was a labored breath to the chugging and a rattle in the piston. "She ain't like she was," he mourned to Alb. "She grunts, it seems to me, and that's not the way she used to sound. I'll get a new one next year."

"Sheetin' Judas, I can't hear a thing wrong, Johnny," Alb consoled him. "She's breathing sweet as a milkmaid waiting for the hired man."

In the house Lilice had piles of cookies ready, white and dark, sugared and plain; raspberry pie for dinner; veal roasting in the pan; rice pudding with raisins for supper; green beans sliced for cooking; prune sauce and fried potatoes for breakfast; piles of biscuits and loaves of bread cooling their fragrance into crispness. Even Sophie, aproned to her chin, conceded, "That's the nicest thrashers' fixings I've ever seen, Lilice. But then, a man's stomach, it's like a barn door. Always open."

Yet as Lilice shooed the flies from the table this afternoon or tried to brush aside the chaff stuck in the screen door, she'd stop suddenly, her eyes clouding, and wonder, Why am I doing this? They'll be hungry again. Nothing ever stops. Not hunger nor pain. It just goes on.

And though the crew spoke in the haymow after meals about how silent and peaked-looking Johnny Black's wife was these days ("She goes around like she was walking in her sleep"), they all agreed that her meals would set a belly rumbling after only one sniff. "Cripes, I wish my old lady would make pie like that. . . . Yep, and didja notice the pretty little marks on the crust? Tastes better that way. . . . Of course, even slops would taste good after that Mrs. Krumlich's meals. Her biscuits—you could knock a pup's ears down with them. And what she has for coffee! Wrings out the dishrag and calls it done."

"Judas, Mis' Black, that was good cake," Alb had sighed regretfully at dinner, almost tempted to lift the plate and lick it clean. "Mrs. Edgely had something mixed together she called 'shoo-fly pie'——"

"Soufflé pie, Lilice," Sophie interrupted him laughing. "It's her own recipe. You take the whites of eggs, sugar and cinnamon, and whip 'em up. You take your pie——"

"Pie, eh? Cake, that's what it was," Alb growled scornfully. "Damn poor cake, at that."

And over the praise and the smacks of satisfied lips, Johnny watched Lilice, grinning at her sober face, proud of her housewifery. If only there were company here all the time, so that nothing but laughter might be heard in these rooms! If no silence, thick with portent, might ever descend! He thought this as Robin would have.

By midafternoon Mr. Svensen at the granary had taken his third stick of snuff and was ready to grab a sack from the wagon. Alb and Johnny were waving arms and nodding heads in talk near the elevator, the sound lost in the roar of the blower. Only that morning the auger in the conveyer had plugged with grain. They vanished behind the wagons.

Mr. Svensen had scarcely lifted his first sack when yells punctured the smooth rhythm of the afternoon. Mr. Dunkel shouted at the fireman. The fireman leaped up and brought the rig to a squeak and a groan, the dust falling with the last stopped wheel.

Lilice ran to the screen door. The boys were playing threshing, half their attention on the machine in the yard. Robin was grunting, "Chug-a-chug-a, I'm the engine, Mama. Dick's the separator." She nodded absently at them.

Then she saw Alb helping Johnny. Her bones went dry; a movement forward was all pain. She tried to call, "Johnny," but her lips only formed the syllables; there was no breath left for agony. She heard Johnny shout, "Get 'er running, Pete. I'll be all right. You can't stop for me. We got to get the thrashing done. Dunkel, watch that separator. Alb'll be back in no time."

Lilice heard the suck and swish of steam (sucking at her brain), the squeal of gears, the low rumble of starting wheels, the chug-a-chug going faster, mixing with the sound of the blower hum rising to a level song (wheels rattling over her bones, over the ridges of her heart). The rig started again.

Then she heard Johnny telling her, "Nothing to get excited about. I'll be all right." She saw how white his face was, how furrowed his brow with pain, which all his grinning could not hide. He tried to conceal his hand by using Alb as a shield. "Get the medicine, Punkin."

Quickly she brought hot water and arnica and bandages. She was aware of Sophie talking with the two men. It was as if she were in a deep kettle and grayness bubbled into whiteness and whiteness simmered into grayness, and she crowded her way through whirls of cobwebs. She offered a cloud in a basin. Suddenly the grayness spewed forth crimson—crimson as the water where Johnny had plunged his mangled fingers.

"Don't know how it happened," she heard Alb explaining to Sophie. "Got his hand in the gears some way. The auger clogged again. That finger there, Johnny—the one with the ring—that looks kinda bad."

The ring. Lilice put her hand to her mouth but no cry lay there.

"Hurts like—hell, Alb."

"I know, Johnny."

"It's swelling, too, looks like."

"That's because of the ring, I guess. I hate to say this, Johnny, but that ring—it's got to come off."

The ring. The circlet of gold, promised in life, in death, binding her flesh to Johnny's. Torn off.

"Judas, Alb, I can never pull it over my knuckle. Swollen like a——"

"We'll have to cut her off then. I've got a pincer, Johnny."

The ring. So that's what the thresher wanted. Wasn't it ever satisfied? Bundles, bundles. Her father, Uncle Herm, Snoose. Yes, in a way, Ernst too, and Robin and Dickie. And Johnny, Johnny . . . first the hair burned, then the finger crushed, next the . . . next the body under the engine. "Now it is coming," she had said after the accident in the dry wash. "Next time he'll be under the wheels." But no, it wasn't to be as easy as that. The punishment of the thresher wasn't satisfied with the easy dissolution of the flesh. No, there was a more tedious way. It wanted the sweetness that bound Johnny to her in the bright strength of a gold ring . . . in sickness and in health . . . as long as you both shall live. . . . Was that the thresher roaring, or the Pastor? . . . "The uttermost farthing . . ."

Alb was saying, "Kinda tough on your wedding ring, Johnny."

Johnny answered, "It is a good fit, too. It couldn't be better."

Lilice, starting forward, cried sharply, "No, no, no. Don't cut it. It's my wedding ring. You might as well cut my heart, too."

They stared at the wild look pointing her cheekbones and screwing up her forehead, the stony brown eyes with the sparkle of cunning in them. Sophie dropped the cloth she was holding.

Lilice grabbed at the pincer. "Give it to me. I'll put it into the fire."

Alb held it away, gulping between amazement and uneasiness, "Mis' Black, it's got to be done, or his hand'll never heal up."

Johnny felt ice chilling his heart. "Sophie," he cried desperately, "she's— she's——" The pain left his hand and gathered in his throat.

But when Sophie put an arm about her, Lilice clutched the strong arms and sobbed as if a web of agony were tearing and the gray swirls were dissolving. Here was understanding rock in a weary land. Dumbly she heard the slight crunch as iron jaws bit through metal. She quivered at Johnny's harsh, convulsive breath. There were Alb's harsh gaspings and a tiny metallic thud as the broken band struck the floor, slid toward her and lay on its side.

Lilice hesitated, stiff in Sophie's arms. Then she sank to her knees. Her hands groped over the floor. Her fingers closed over the ring. She held it in her palm, a twisted promise of security. One side was raggedly severed, the edges nicked where the pincer had slipped. The other side was cut partly through, the two halves bent backward like a crude W. Tears slid down her cheeks. Her hands moved. The mutilated ring clinked gently against the band on her own finger. "Johnny," she whispered.

Johnny gazed at her as if a dreadful phantom had come to his house to mold his bread and sour the sweetness of his pillow. He was scarcely aware how Sophie bound his fingers. Alb shifted foot to foot, sorrowful, wishing he'd been spared this revelation of darkness hanging under a neighbor's rooftree.

20

That next week Johnny walked beside his rig as though blinded with the chaff and dust of threshing. He stumbled like a sheep ill with the grass staggers. He worked but his mind was back within the doors of his own house, worrying over Lilice, however much his flesh strode here and his tongue gave orders there. "Don't pile those bundles two deep, you pitchers. . . . I want that separator level, Alb. . . . I don't care how many wagons you use, Muri, as long as you get the grain away from the spout. . . ."

Sophie ran across the road and into Lilice's kitchen many times a day, he knew. The Whiteland boy remained as hired man. And Sophie's eldest helped with the chores. (At another time he would have marveled how Time had brought years to Sophie's children. The eldest, Sophus, had been confirmed the spring before.) He'd have to get an older hired man next year. The Whiteland boy was reliable but too young. Maybe he ought to have two hired men. A feller couldn't run a thrashing outfit decently and farm too.

He couldn't get out of his head the way Lilice had stared at the broken wedding ring in her hand. "Means a lot to women, I guess." To be sure, afterward she had been calmer, the queer look in her eyes fading. She had made the supper that night, although Sophie scolded and wanted to do it herself. Nevertheless, Johnny had asked Sophie, "You kinda pop in and see her once in a while, won't ya?"

Sophie patted his arm. "Don't you fret. She'll be all right," she comforted him. "She is stronger inside than you think. It is a fit that will pass."

What waked him in the night sometimes to blink at the knotholes of light in a barn roof or listen to the nerve-starting squeak of a mouse, he refused to recognize but crowded to the periphery of awareness. However, in a fortnight Sophie's prophesy appeared to be fulfilled. Lilice smiled again, a tight-lipped smile it is true, but smiled, albeit her mouth twitched now and again, pulled by those invisible threads that tangle out of a dark world inhabiting each of us, beyond any man's power to control.

She even went to a dance with Johnny on a rainy end of the week. She danced one waltz with him. Thereafter she sat dimly in a corner, this rhythm dangerously sweet to the flesh. It was as though she had passed a crest and for a while had regained a plateau of calmness.

Johnny's hand, still bound and awkward with two finger stalls ("cots" Sophie called them), throbbed fiercely when he bumped it, and that was a hundred times a minute, it seemed. He swore deep-heartedly at his awkwardness. "Glad it wasn't my right hand," he said. He scarcely bothered to exchange old bandages for new, they were soaked with grease and oil so quickly.

The rig moved to Mr. Peiser's. Ribbons of early plowing were black on the dusty yellow-brown of the stubble. One farmer had turned a square of earth about his settings, a black boarder for the dark gold of stacks.

Mr. Peiser had notions about tapping a keg of beer just as soon as the barley was threshed. Alb ran his tongue beyond his lips and against the edge of scraggly whiskers. "Sounds good to me."

Johnny warned the crew brusquely, "You fellers can fix up your thirst, if you want to, but no getting pig-eyed drunk. If you get thrasher's gut tomorrow, you can have your walking papers, too."

Nevertheless, a pitcher stole several palmfuls of sugar, the fireman brought a can of water hot from the engine, and Mr. Peiser dragged a bottle of alcohol from his coat. That evening the haymow rang with loudening voices. And though the sugar was gray with the chaff in the pitcher's pocket and the water tasted of the engine's bowels, they mixed hot punches and toasted the barley. The tankee, who had worked on the flats, began a tune:

> "The cook car stands by the dried-up brook
> But it's very damn little the cook can cook.
> Scrambled eggs three times a day
> A mess of potatoes and a fair cup of tay."

Let tomorrow bring its own worries.

By afternoon lunchtime the next day, the last stacks were down to butts. Johnny shuffled across the Peiser yard, his head turned over his shoulder. He had one eye on the pitchers, half of whom were sticking their forks down for lunch. The other half continued their work, envying those who had first chance at sandwiches and dark cake. Tomorrow they would have the first chance.

Johnny tightened his belt. In the shade of an elm Mrs. Peiser drew back the cloth on the basket as if she were uncovering a baby for a neighbor's admiring inspection. It was cool there. The main road lay beyond a narrow field to the west. The men trooped around the basket, some rubbing their dust-caked lips, others pulling at their ear lobes as if to scratch the sound of humming from their heads.

Mrs. Blumen held the coffeepot ready. There was a ripple of chat. Long hands, some white and soft as goatskin from sweat and leather gloves, some horny as turtle legs with calluses and oil, reached out for sandwiches. They paused for a moment of selection, butter or meat or jelly, then dived down for the catch. Cups rattled one against another as they were taken from the basket. Johnny stroked the handle of his absently until he noticed the grease smudges he was leaving. Very likely my face is as oily as my hands, he thought. A pitcher dangled his cup on a forefinger, impatiently hearing the gurgle of coffee.

Heedless of clean linen, Alb scooped up a sandwich as if he suspected it of evading capture. Chaff stuck to the grease caught in his hairy arms.

With a meat sandwich and a steaming cup Johnny sat cross-leggedly in the grass, facing the rig vigilantly. His first bite left a faint smear of grease on the bread. His first sip of coffee tasted of dust or grease, he wasn't sure which. He spat and wiped his lips before he continued eating.

For a serious moment of chewing (the blunting of the sharp edge of hunger) there was silence. Then talk bubbled up again. "Your hand bother you much, Johnny?" Mr. Peiser wanted to know. His throat muscles bobbed over the last of his sandwich.

"Not much." Johnny shifted his cup. "Wasn't much left of one finger when the doc finished with it. It's gonna be stubby to the knuckle. The other's gone to the nail."

"Tell ya what you shoulda done." Mr. Peiser settled himself solidly. "Best thing for a bad swelling is to kill a chicken, cut it in half, and wrap it right over the sore. The chicken's heat and the blood, that's the best thing for drawing out a soreness that I know." Johnny nodded.

"Gettin' your hand caught in the auger is bad enough," a grainman said. "But if a feller lost his balance and fell into the feeder, and the knives got him. Damn it."

"Feller was telling me," the tankee offered, his lips wet with coffee. "This happened near Mary's Hill. Or maybe it was on the flats. I dunno. Anyway, two pitchers got into a fight. One was a big feller and the other kinda small. Well, the big feller, he threw the little one into the feeder. The knives got him and the cylinder. You could see blood on the straw in the straw pile, they say. The crew hung the big feller. They took him back to the blower and hung him there."

Finishing his coffee, a pitcher hiccuped noisily and pulled a sack of Bull Durham from his pocket before he realized that this was lunchtime, not dinner, and that he wouldn't have time for a smoke. He'd better hurry to relieve his partners, or God knew what tricks they'd have ready for him in bed that night.

While they lunched, the engine chugged its smoke, the separator hummed, the blower roared, a tail of straw spread like peacock feathers under a freshening wind. Setting his half-filled cup of black coffee in the grass, Mr. Svensen dragged a knife from his pocket. Reaching up he clipped a twig off the elm. He put it in his mouth like a toothpick and chewed reflectively while from another pocket he drew his snuffbox.

As long as he'd known him, Johnny had been fascinated by Mr. Svensen's snuffbox. It was rectangular, slightly longer than a palm is wide and shaped like a soapbox. The brass of the cover shone dully from the rub of the pocket. It was etched with curlicues and scrolls and a name: Viktor Svensen. Inside the cover was a mirror. More than one time Johnny had seen Mr. Svensen grope blindly for that snuffbox when a barley beard or a bit of chaff had turned his eye red and watery. With a pocketknife he'd pry up the cover and with a cuff edge he'd rub the mirror vigorously to clear it of snuff grains. Holding it up just beyond his nose, he'd agonizedly roll his eyes this way and that to find the shaft of fire that flamed under his lid.

Now Mr. Svensen pried up the lid with the tip of the knife. Into the snuffbox he splashed a little of the black coffee. "Rum is best," he said, stirring the brownish snuff with a finger.

"It's a lasting flavor all right," Johnny agreed.

Mr. Svensen nodded. He took the twig from his mouth and twirled the chewed end in the snuff until it was coated with the soft brown grains. Anticipation ripe on his face, he poked it into his mouth. His eyes closed as the first ecstatic pungency bit his tongue.

"You fellers certainly like your snuff sticks." Johnny emptied the dregs of his cup and arose. He stood quietly a moment. He was thinking about Lilice when he heard it. *Chook! chook! chook!* Short explosive barks. He turned curiously like a dog at a new sound. The explosions bounced across the small field that separated the elm trees from the road. He winked to see better. There it crawled along, a snub-nosed, sawed-off engine, cold and unfriendly in his eye, spurts of dark smoke jumping from the exhaust and vanishing.

"Why, it's Jimmy Morrison," exclaimed the fireman. "He's got the tractor he and Kurt Barewolf talked about getting. Well, I'll be a double-damned——" The men came to their feet, dribbling coffee as they stood in wonder.

Beyond that shouting distance the tractor inched along. Johnny regarded it with the interest of one poking at a lizard. He saw the huge double flywheels, larger than the front wheels even; the canopy of corrugated sheeting; the water tank of shining metal with a tent-shaped screen above it; the drivers, as large as those on the Buffalo Head, rolling up the dust of the road; the sharp bursts of exhaust smoke. All that iron and only one man running it—the machine expert from Fergus. Jimmy Morrison was riding the separator. The steady *chook! chook! chook!*—an arrogant sound, chill, efficient, uncompromising. How different from the warm human cough of the steam engine.

Johnny nearly let derisive mirth rattle over his Adam's apple. "That hunk of iron!" he said. For an instant there lingered in his memory the echo of another sound—a long spear of shrillness hurtling over ridge and valley and Mr. Schadel saying, "Bory Tetzell's steam engine. A mess of iron like that." But it vanished as he noticed that the flywheels of the tractor did not run smoothly as the one on the steam engine did, but jerkily. The wheels seemed to hesitate with each turn, to lose speed, to wait for the rush of the next explosion in order to complete a revolution. So it seemed to Johnny.

Chook! chook! Steadily the tractor pulled its separator along the road. As it came to a slight downgrade it ran freer. The steady chooks were interrupted with pops and snorts and a sound of *Chook! swish-swish-swish—chook! swish-swish-swish* in the throaty rattle of valves.

The crew laughed. "Sounds like a feller snortin' and snorin' in a nightmare," jibed Alb.

"Big mess of iron," Johnny hooted. "How does he expect to get power out of that? Stinks so you can smell it clear over here." He returned Jimmy's wave with no friendliness. Just like Kurt, joining Morrison in a scheme like this. I'll show both of them, he thought angrily. "Come on, boys," he shouted to the men. "Can't stand gawping here. Got lots of bundles to pitch. It ain't likely the tractor is going to make it easier for us."

That night there was a swishing noise on the edge of his sleep. For the most part, if he was disturbed, it was over Lilice, and not over the *chook! chook!* of the tractor.

Part 5

THE SEASON OF
GRAIN IN THE HARVEST:
THE WHEEL AND
THE FLAME

THE PASTOR died that next winter. He thundered from the pulpit, "The soul that sinneth it shall die," his face purple-red with passion, his beard stiff as a brush, his fist emphasizing each word with a short thumping blow. He uttered "Amen" gravely, descended from the pulpit, entered his little cubicle and collapsed. He expired in sweaty gasps. "I have been—Thy—servant, Lord." His faith trembled on his lips to the final respiration.

That year had frost on the stem in May and ice on the dried blade in late August. But it was only prelude to the short-crop year following, when heat seared the ridges, when the grass was drought-clipped and as meager as the hair on a scabby hog. But this the Pastor never knew. He lived his closing days and laid the last rods of Jeremiah upon his congregation during the season of dividing blade and granaries heaped bin-full. Until Gabriel Ewig was installed, Pastor Aberhalt of Mary's Hill conducted the services.

How Gabriel Ewig became shepherd of the Pockerbrush flock, Johnny never rightly understood, for certainly Mr. Nussbaum could smell a freethinker a mile away. For two months there were church meetings, he knew; "congregational hair-pullings in the name of Christ," Mr. Dunkel said once. For a time acrimony peppered the talk of the flock. Neighbors wrangled fiercely. Mr. Schimmel, who for years had shared with Mr. Haber the meadow hay along the creek, grabbed his neighbor's beard and insisted, "If you go against me in this, by godfreys, you can get somebody else to help you put up your damned old sloo grass." All this bickering, as Aunt Phrena pointed out, came because the members, disagree though they might, were ardently seeking a shepherd to lead them by the still waters.

For a while Mr. Nussbaum (without yielding one-quarter inch from his position) feared the congregation might have to join with the one in Mary's Hill. Then the Pockerbrush church would remain empty, with echoes only disturbing the dust and the cobwebs. Pastor Aberhalt held services but could only come once a month. At the meetings he spread what oil of persuasion he could upon the tumbling waters.

At last it was announced. Gabriel Ewig had been chosen. The voice of God through a devout congregation called upon a shepherd to lead a Christian flock. Many at once recollected Ewig's sermon as a student years before, as if that were a criterion for praise or blame.

Kurt, however, malice pointing his observation, told Mr. Dunkel, "Betcha Ewig doesn't come of his own free will. From what I've heard about him, he's too smart to want to be buried in this hole of a congregation. He'll not stay long. Maybe he was too mouthy to suit the professors in the college, and they fixed him, huh?"

Even Mr. Dunkel was shocked at such heresy. "Whoop-Jinny, Kurt," he chided, "you ain't got no right to go as far as that!"

Not until spring brought tufts of new green on twig and branch, and the Dutchman's-breeches, stained with butter yellow, were hanging their white pantaloons stiffly starched and upside down above the pale sage-green leaves, did Ewig arrive to preach his first sermon. He brought his wife and two dogs. He had no children.

Johnny said, "Well, I'm glad that's settled. One preacher is as good as another, I guess."

But when Lilice heard that Ewig was unpacking his boxes and bails in the parsonage, she frowned, clearing the spiderwebs from memory. She wondered about him. It would be strange enough, the Pastor's rumble absent from the curved ceiling. Stirring over the recollection, she tried to bring back the day of the mission festival. All she could remember was Ewig's eyes, gentle eyes holding out friendliness like hands, and the kindliness of his face, tinged with sorrow and compassion. "I could talk to him, if I were in trouble," she had said that day. But that was long ago. To one who is parched in drought, the floods of other years bring little comfort.

The day she was at Sophie's to borrow the saleratus, Sophie reminded her, "You and Johnny don't want to miss the installation service." It was a warm day. Lilice had felt its waves against her throat as she came over the road.

"Sophie, you ought to chase me with a broom," she confessed. "Forgetting like this. I had saleratus on my mind when I drove to the store yesterday. I know I did." She wrinkled her brows. "Funny, though. It wasn't in the grocery box when I got home. Most things I wanted weren't there either." She waved a hand in front of her face as though brushing away a mosquito or a gnat that buzzed there.

Sophie took Lilice's vague smile in one wide glance. Silently she opened the cupboard door. "Pastor Ewig preaches his first sermon next Sunday." She measured out the baking soda. "You and Johnny don't want to miss the installation service."

"I remember he looked so friendly." Lilice brightened over a thought of her own. "Remember the mission festival sermon? He had such—oh, I don't know. You suppose he's changed?"

"Folks are going to fill that church. They're curiouser than a red squirrel about him." Sophie tied up the package. "You better start early."

From a window Sophie peered after Lilice. She saw her come to the road and pause, staring down the wheel-marked dust as though something, an echo or a shape, would appear soon, and she would give it welcome, whether pale rider or bright horseman. After a while she brushed her hand before her face again. Shaking her head she wandered up her own path.

"Poor Johnny!" whispered Sophie. "Poor Lilice!"

2

Gabriel Ewig was duly installed, black gown and all, by Pastor Aberhalt. The congregation squeezed into the last chair. The gallery creaked, so many crowded into the benches there.

The Johnny Blacks came, Johnny with new crow's-feet about his eyes. The boys were as immaculate as starchy blouses and ironed coat and pants could make boy flesh—boy flesh that is as restless and un-sit-still-able, as shifty as a puppy's tail. In spite of Johnny's frown, Robin kept slipping off the hard, polished seat. And Dickie moved uneasily, kicking softly at the pew ahead of him. He kept his hands in his pockets or behind his back—a habit he'd got into, as if he were afraid of laughter, should a neighbor catch sight of his cracked and dirty-looking hands. Both boys however had only to peek at Lilice across the aisle on the women's side, her pale face netted by a veil that fell from her hat, and they settled into splinter-stiff decorum.

Johnny was glad Lilice had asked to go. A heaviness lay on his house these days. Silence at the table was so like a weight that an unexpected word cut through it like a dull knife through sausage, raggedly, and with effort. More than anyone else, though without comprehension, the boys sensed the queerness behind Johnny's monosyllabic replies, the way he stirred the emptiness in his cup before he realized that he had finished his coffee; the set expression on Lilice's face and the manner in which she frowned, or avoided Johnny's pleading glances.

They felt the chill of this strangeness and talked about it, boy-fashion, after they were snuggling in bed. "Didja have to say the milk was sour?" Robin demanded one night, his head in the hollow of a pillow.

"I didn't know Ma was going to bawl," Dickie defended himself and began to sniffle. "Why does she bawl?"

"You don't know much." Robin shoved a knee up, disgustedly. "You sure don't."

Lilice said the day after she'd been at Sophie's for the saleratus, "The new minister is going to be installed Sunday. Maybe we ought to go."

With an alacrity that stemmed from as small a matter as the gladness of hearing her say "we," he rejoiced. "Sure, we ought to go. I'll have the buggy ready."

Lilice kept her hands primly crossed in her lap while Ewig received the staff of authority. But when she saw him kneel where Johnny and the congregation knelt on other Sundays, she leaned forward, watching intently. A pastor kneeling? Did Pastor Steuber ever bring his knees so near the earth, so near the humiliation of common folk? she wondered. No, no, not him. But this man bowed so low, she was afraid he'd tumble forward. And when he arose, were his hands white from the tightness with which he'd clasped them, or was this her imagination?

He stepped into the pulpit and began to speak. His face was older and his hair grayer, she thought. But his voice was as soft-spoken as she remembered it. And yes—there was that trick he had of putting his hand out, then in a wide circle slowly bringing it to his breast, as if within that arc he included all those who heard him, and more besides. But his eyes— yes, steady, friendly as a handshake to welcome you. Or was she only dreaming this?

His words suddenly came through her thick abstraction, threaded together, formed patterns of meaning. ". . . suffering. You have heard it said that suffering is a cross of God, laid on us in His infinite mercy and inscrutable wisdom for our edification and our spiritual betterment. I think the efficacy of suffering is vastly overrated. I admit exceptions always. But there are few people who become better Christians or better people because of anguish. Most of them become more warped and crabbed than they already are. Lives are damaged, hopes are deferred, sweetness is soured—all because of suffering. And we say God does this for our betterment. Actually, we're blaming Him. I believe the troubles we bear are of our own making. God does not place them on us, as if we were animals and He a mule driver casting about with heavy burdens for a likely beast. . . .

"Search your heart. There you will find the root of your cross. There you will find God. You will never find Him in the law. Theology is the legal aspect of religion and the least salutary. . . .

"There is a God-given courage to face suffering placed in your own heart. Find it. It is within you. No law applied from without will fortify you within. . . . If your inner strength is broken, woe upon you indeed. . . . Seek the inner strength. . . ."

There was to-do and commotion after the last amen. Folks went up to greet the new pastor, the men first and then the women, as was proper. Those who liked what he said stayed to put their praise into fumbling words (as Mr. Dunkel); those who disagreed (as Mr. Nussbaum) said curtly, "How de do?" and went into the hot sunshine to argue heatedly, or to say, "Didn't understand a thing. What's he talking about?"

Lilice saw Johnny push forward, the boys with him. Yes, that was as it should be. Johnny and his sons—this was their inheritance. But she, Lilice . . . Hastily she arose. Troubles are not placed on us as punishment— did the Pastor really mean that? If only it were true—— But no, no. It couldn't be. Delusion, delusion again. She couldn't go up there to meet him. He'd see right through her, see what lay darkly in her mind. Those searching eyes of his. But such friendly eyes. She ought to go up and shake his hand. . . . No, no.

She went outside to the buggy. Johnny and the boys found her there. "Lilice," he said, cajolery lightening his voice, trying to act as if no stares were hooking into his backbone, "Lilice, you can't go home without meeting Pastor Ewig. It is always a good idea to know the preacher. He——"

"You have met him. That is enough." Her voice was calm.

"Lilice, I told him you'd come. He——"

"You know I haven't finished the Catechism." Her fingers picked nervously at a button in the upholstery.

He stared at her. "That has nothing to do with it. I——"

"Shall I drive home?" Her tone was flat. "I'd like to hear him again, though."

He called to the boys. "Get in." Quickly he caught up the lines. Only the spokes and the hubs whispered on the way home.

3

That spring frost sparkled in May and the crops were late. Rains fell stingily. After showers the ground under the peony stalks was gray with dryness, so light they were. Hot winds sucked at the sponge of the earth. "Looks like a bad summer and a poor crop," the folks said.

That spring Mr. Schadel sold his farm and moved to Mary's Hill. Strangers hauled their truck into his yard. The blacksmith shop they turned into a pig house. The forge they pitched into a junk heap where the horsepower rusted to brownish decay and the old thresher with the bandcutting tables and the straw carrier sagged into rotting looseness.

That spring, to Johnny's regret, Alb Hukelpoke gathered his wife and his children and moved his possessions to a farm south of the Diemer Hills, neighbor to the Vildvogels. "I've had my peck of dust, and more," he told Johnny. "Judas, the barley I've shaken out of my drawers and the clean white sheets I've dirtied with my greasy underpants—— Nope, Johnny. It's like I said. Get yourself another separator man. I'm finished with thrashing."

Grumbling, Johnny began to measure likely candidates for the job.

That summer, Pastor Ewig was on everybody's tongue. "What kind of a preacher is that? I came on his yard and he was wearing overalls. . . . Ya, I know. He came to my place; he had an old workshirt on. Says he can't have a black gown in the garden; it brings cutworms. . . . Didja hear? He went to see Mr. Erdman. They're good friends, they tell me. . . . He wants to start a baseball team among the kids. Hee, hee, hee! He better stay home and study his Bible. . . . That feller knows more about the congregation than Steuber did in twenty years. . . ."

For all the talk, Pastor Ewig continued his way. He went to see Mr. Muri and Mr. Svensen. Since their church was miles away, he invited them to services. They came with their families. But little Mrs. Fleischer, a fierce birdlike woman of sixty-five, glared at the gallery where they sat. Shaking her head until her earrings jerked, she sputtered furiously, "Na ya, so it's come to this. Noreegians and Hottentots in our good church." She glowered at Ewig.

He pointed a sermon with a text, "My sheep are not of this fold alone." (The Muris and the Svensens hesitated about coming again; finally didn't.) He rounded up three or four members whose names had been dropped from the treasurer's book.

"They didn't like Steuber and so they quit coming," explained Mr. Nussbaum. "Jippers, I think it was an excuse, and a blamed poor one."

Pastor Ewig smiled. But when at a meeting of the elders he said that they ought to have an English service once in two months, he was of course going too far. The suggestion was voted down with unanimous, emphatic, thumping nays. Pastor Ewig's mouth was firm. "It will come, gentlemen; it will come."

He and Mr. Dunkel were bosom cronies at once. It was Mr. Dunkel who sold him one of his best blooded calves; cheap, too. "Na, that Dunkel. Next thing he'll crawl into the minister's pants," Mr. Fleischer said. But Dunkel and the Pastor went fishing together and the Pastor invited Dunkel to many a supper at the parsonage.

More than one person felt the lash of Ewig's tongue. When Mr. Nussbaum cackled glumly because the Lesters attended a service now and again (he who was suspected of living with a woman not his wife), the Pastor snapped, "Brother Nussbaum, do you think the gospel is preached only for Pockerbrushers?" He disagreed with Pastor Aberhalt of the Mary's Hill church, called him a "verbal inspirationist," whatever that was. It sounded bad to Mr. Nussbaum.

According to Mr. Dunkel, Ewig held queer notions about ministers in general and himself in particular. "I must make my own peace with God," Ewig said. "Many people, including preachers, act as if a pastor had a kind of insurance policy with God, maturing say at the age of sixty-five. . . . A minister's office is one of fearful responsibility. I tremble when I think of this. Suppose in our zealous ignorance we have been wrong and ourselves come under the final condemnation. Whose fall so great as his who in the pride of humility imagines he cannot stumble?"

Once Mr. Dunkel nearly bit off the end of his pipestem at the cold fury in Ewig's voice, speaking out of some rankling past only God and he knew. "I have attended ministerial meetings and been at places where the cloth convenes. Such jockeying for position, such pulling of strings puppeteer-like behind the scenes, such cutting of throats for personal advantage, such logrolling and horse trading—it is worthy of the best maneuvers in Washington. Theological politicians, that's what such preachers are. They seek high office and huge church edifices and large memberships so they may overawe minorities and write theological articles for the homiletics magazines and the church papers. About the inner spiritual quality of what they profess they know little and care less."

"I spoilt three matches getting my pipe lit," Mr. Dunkel told afterward.

And one day Mr. Dunkel said excitedly to Kurt, "Guess you were right. The Pastor ain't staying. He's leaving the church just as soon as he can fix up a deal with some college. He's going to teach there—philosophy, or some such thing, he calls it." All of this was reported by Mr. Dunkel, and therefore, as Mr. Nussbaum acidly pointed out, had to be taken with caution. "Jippers, Wilhelm Dunkel never got a thing straight in his life yet."

As for Ewig's sermons, about them there was no hearsay. Folks crowded to church that summer—"for the novelty," sneered Kurt. The Blacks went now and again, Lilice listening as though waiting for a miracle and not daring to hope.

Ewig preached: "Sometimes I think the Sermon on the Mount is too Godlike, too idealistic for everyday mortals who are satisfied with board and bed, a bottle on Saturday nights and a game of baseball on Sunday afternoons.

". . . Job faced the problem of suffering. He pleaded with God for knowledge to understand it. He wanted to *know*. And did he receive an answer? Not one. Not one. Perhaps the answer lies in Ecclesiastes: 'Vanity of vanities, saith the Preacher.' Perhaps it will be revealed on Judgment Day."

". . . How inevitable is the harvest and the threshing floor! It is as certain as the cool of evening. Whether the crop is locust-bitten or plump-kerneled, the thresher shatters the husk and releases the seed, or reveals the emptiness of the ear. Like Time, it threshes the one with as much indifference as the other. It never asks what the wind and the hail, what man and his joys or his tears have done to the head. And lo! the yield of the season (or of a life) is laid bare to the judgment of all eyes. Let a man be like a wise farmer who knows that planting time and growing weather and the hardening kernel are only preparation for the harvest. The harvest is all. By his yield is a good husbandman known."

Usually Johnny moved restlessly on the seat, as restless as the boys. One sermon however brought him into such quiet that he could have heard the blood throb in his ears. On the women's side, Lilice tweaked the end of her glove until it was threadbare. Both listened with hard intentness, Johnny with growing conviction, Lilice with doubting awe.

That was the Sunday Ewig said, "When can you be sure of the forgiveness of sin? Never look to the law for answer. Look within yourself. It is a matter of taking stock of yourself, preserving what seems the best, rejecting what is past and done. The courage to go on comes when a decision is made under God within us; and that is the miracle of freedom from bondage, the miracle of liberty."

After the service Ewig pushed forward hurriedly. In the schoolhouse he touched Lilice's arm. "Mrs. Black, I am very glad to see you. I've—we've been so busy getting settled, I missed you before. I want to know all of you very well. Please come again." His handshake was gentle yet firm.

Lilice tried to answer, couldn't, and left quickly. "Please come again . . . I am very glad to see you." The phrases echoed with the ripple of wheels homeward. They remained in the kitchen noise and in the taste of food in the days that followed.

Johnny decided at last, What Ewig said, it is what I have been thinking, church or no church. What is past is past. Nothing I can do about it. I guess *he* would want it so, too. (My friend, my friend Snoose.) But I'll never know, I'll never know.

Lilice, however, put the words of the Pastor away after a while. It is too late, she thought dully. Years ago it might have been possible, but not now.

4

In June the mornings of summer seem as many as pebbles in a creek, as many as the flowerets on the lilac bush, Lilice dreamed on the porch. They crowd around and against you like hazel sprigs when you shove through the underbrush. If you waste the dew and the anemone of one dawn, you can feel remorsefully light-souled again in remembering that twenty-four hours away there are more hours of earth scent and flower breath. So many to dream on in June. But in July, when the clatter of the binder sickle startles the afternoon's bee-busy quiet with a jagged edge, how few remain; the hum of the thresher, how near it is.

Then in mid-August one morning the wind from the southeast has an unfriendly bounce in it. You shiver and wish for an extra jacket. The damp hard smell of bog peat fills your nose. The odor of rain-soaked wood where brush fires have been wetted out is raw and acrid in your throat. In the silence left by south-flying birds the rattle of the kingfisher is a lonely sound. No longer does the balm of Gilead flutter his stiff summer green in the early dawn. (This year the dry weather spoiled its waxy sheen.) It droops its rusty leaves in the late-rising sun. There is a chill finality in knowing that shadows are long and growing longer by nine o'clock.

All at once an empty loneliness crawls spiderlike over you. Out of a kind of sadness you realize that flowering time is in the pod and the harvest far gone, the knots all tied and bundles flying into the slashing knives of the feeder. Mornings like yesterdays—why, they are so few, they can be counted finger by finger on a hand. There is almost pain in the way you gasp, "Summer, it's the end of summer already, and nobody here to watch it go. . . ."

A morning like this September one: ice in the slop pail near the door, the soggy bread in it frozen stiff, the mist of a chill night floating on the meadow, the thresher roaring through the frigid quiet so that it seemed the *raaza-raaza-raaza* of chain and shaker was no farther than the length of a field away. Mornings like these—there will be many of them, too many.

Lilice shaded her hand. Across the road Sophie's yard stirred with the play of children. Robin was probably there; Dickie too. They usually were. So many children playing there. She looked at the wedding ring on her finger. That band, it was the seal and the promise of life dividing from life, as grass did from grass, or the wheat from wheat. But not for her. She was not in the circle . . . a dark kernel dropped in the shadows, spouting eldritch stems. Oh, they could say it was happenchance, eczema, birthmarks, something for which no one could be blamed. She knew better, she who had heard the loud breaking of the wedding band.

That Pastor Ewig—did he really know? Or was he only talking?

That thresher—crushing the ring so that Johnny would be bound to her no longer, all the dear sweet strength of him. Hurting him even, tearing his fingers, as if to unseal the blight that lay in her flesh. His wounds had healed, yes. But at night when his hands groped over her breasts and she felt the knobby fingers, she'd remember the strong, unimpaired hands that used to slide possessively along her arm. She snatched his bandaged hand quickly above the covers that first time and laid it on her throat. But even when ecstasy dimmed sight and sound, and touch was life, she'd feel those stubby mutilations clawing at her shoulders. . . .

That Pastor—did he really know? Surely in this wide world, there must be some mouth of twisting flame to pronounce for her the oracle of salvation.

She opened the door and went inside. Today she must do what must be done. After this hour Johnny's warmth must lie far from her, she thought. She went to the bedroom, hers and his. His head had dented that pillow only two nights before.

She gathered her things quickly, as if fearful that a voice from the bed might shout at her, restraining her. She walked slowly upstairs. In the spare room opposite the boys', she hung her things and put on the dresser the hair curlers and the jar of cream. She brought what was a woman's until the bedroom downstairs seemed half empty. Up here the room seemed half full. For a moment she stood at the door, swinging it gently. No lock there, no key. She lifted a shoulder. Of what use keys against Johnny's solid shoulder? No, she had metal stouter than lock or key to bar Johnny's way.

She stood by the dresser. From a box she had carried into this room only moments before, she drew a small case. She opened it. Twisted and bent and marred, Johnny's ring lay there. Hastily, as though it were a traitor to her determination, she put her hand over it. Tears blurred her sight. She fingered the case. Slowly then she drew her own ring from her finger and put it beside Johnny's. Her finger tightened. She snapped the case and put it away. And so it was done. Never living flesh of hers to bear a stain. . . .

5

Johnny spun the wheel and steered the engine past Mr. Schimmel's barn. Mr. Schimmel himself pulled aside the last wire of the fence he'd taken down to let the rig into the barnyard. He waved at Johnny but there was less buoyancy in his greeting than usual. No wonder he wears a long face, Johnny thought, notching the throttle up a bit. Where Mr. Schimmel had six stacks this year, last year he had two settings and a half. "Three-quarter crop. Judas, what a year for cockleberries!"

The pond near the pigpen was iced with a bubbly green scum, wrinkling the nose with a dead-fish smell. Calves, wading into the water to escape the stinging flies, left behind them twisty paths of clear water. Their tails lifted and fell splashing back. In the woods near by the rain-bird shrieked his sultry water call in vain.

Threshing began, the wheat first, then the oats. From the pasture the cattle came in single file along the path, head to tail, until the smell of fresh straw and the boom of the blower excited them and they scattered. They galloped wildly up to the machine. The bell cow's *cling-k, clung-k,* ordinarily a harsh metallic sound, was like struck silver in the dull monotone of the separator's hum. The heifers and the yearlings skittered under the blower, tails high and kicking awkwardly at the scratch of chaff and straw, and the hard shaft of air tickling the hide along the ribs. The bull pawed and brumbled in the dust until Mr. Schimmel ran toward him with a pitchfork. He wheeled and headed for the pond, his herd following him.

A queer autumn, frosty enough to wear long underwear one day and July heat the next. Over at the Heberstadts' Jimmy Morrison's tractor was *chook-chook-chook-ing* clumsily. The belt twitched with every hoarse, explosive grunt, Johnny observed scornfully. Johnny was in no hurry to hide his glee when Jimmy got mired and had to be yanked out with a stump puller. Not much power in those Kerosene Annies, he thought. How a feller could sit near that stone-cold hunk of iron, that chamberpot of stinking gas and oil and rank corruption, he couldn't understand. At least, not when a feller could have a warm-sided straw-burner at his back, sweet with live steam and the sweaty heat of the boiler, so like a man's moist warmth.

There was in the engine (oil beading like perspiration) a movement and a physical being closer to his own flesh and bodily movement than to anything inanimate he had ever known. As Alb had said once, "The old steamer, she's the closest thing to being warm in bed with a woman that I know of." Johnny had to admit there was some truth stuck in the words. It was good to cup chin in hand and lean against the side of the toolbox, his eyes on the separator, the gentle rocking of the engine restful in his bones, and let the dust of the cylinder and his own half-shut lashes mix together into a kind of curtain against the whimperings of disturbance inside and outside his ears.

But a tractor, now. Cold. Mechanical. Something dead limping along in a sham of life. There were fellers, however, who hung on Kurt's lip and buzzed loudly at what they heard. They were the first to cry, "That's the kind of rig to have. You can thrash cheaper that way." Sure, and slower, Johnny thought savagely. Pants hangers, that's what they were. Like burdocks in a cow's brush, swinging when the tail swung. You never knew how they were blowing, hot or cold. Your friend today, your enemy tomorrow.

Like those Gizzard Lake folks, up north of Mary's Hill beyond Pockerbrush and just off the Valley. Two years before they raised a crop of wheat that grew like swamp grass, full-eared and plump, and nobody to thresh it. The settlement was fairly recent. Soil and the lay of the land were hardly those to encourage an unusual crop there. What threshing was done, had come at the tail end of runs when this rig or that veered from its road home to make an extra cent or two. But that year soil and rain joined to make a bumper crop.

It was Norton who told Johnny, "They got a good stand of wheat around Gizzard Lake." The wrinkles about Norton's mouth were an indicator of his worry. "Better take a look."

Johnny did and found the wheat heavy and the heads leaning with fatness. He sent Marty into that land. Marty ripped through stack and setting, hull and band, like the jaws of the fabled cricket shearing the twine. Johnny had to admit that money almost rilled with the grain from the spout of the Buffalo Head. He startled Marty with a bonus and praise ringing with heartiness. Even Alb Hukelpoke, who knew Johnny, thrasherman and thrasher boy, longer than anyone, would have scrabbled in his whiskers over such rare behavior.

But that was two years before. Last season (and this season too) Johnny had planned to steam the big rig into that country, along with Heinie's. He had driven up to Gizzard Lake in the spring wagon himself to gather this golden twinkle into his orbit. He was swamped with ire when the farmers refused. They slapped their thighs as though over a joke and told him, "No, we ain't got no use for your big runs. That's the truth, plain and stark naked. We can't depend on another crop like the one we had. We made good money and we're putting it into dairying and hog-and-feed crops. We can't afford your big outfits."

"Hee, hee, hee," tittered the neighbors when they heard. "That was a good one. Told Johnny Black to pull in his horns, they did."

"Independent as a hog on ice, huh?" said Bern Hartman, the separator man, new that year, when he heard about it.

"That's the way they acted," Johnny had to confess. Such wanton indifference to what he considered advantages ruffled his feathers more than he cared to admit. "And it was my rig went in there and thrashed their lousy stacks, so they could put money in the bank. Now, they tell me, 'To hell with you!' That's the thanks I get." In the warmth of anger he felt bitterly misused. "Just a bunch of shirttailed farmers up there," he consoled himself. "It's different here. Here I'm—well, I'm really the boss."

But even in the hills here this autumn there was a growling among the folks. It was a rib-chested complaint, rumbling up from uneasy depths, so that disquiet began to stir him, sluggish it is true, but kinky with ache nevertheless.

They said: "Ya, it's all right, thrashing with Johnny and getting the grain in the bins early. But with the prices he charges and all, if we don't get a better crop next year, when then? Or the price of wheat drops? I don't know what we'll do. . . . By jippers, if our crops were all wheat, it would be really bad. But I've planted mostly oats and barley, and there never was a good price in the market for that. . . . Cripes, I'm still scared of fire. Burn ya up, them engines will. . . . Aw no, not with the new screens in the smokestack. . . . Well, they're dangerous, I don't care what you say. They ain't safe like a gasoline tractor. . . . Guess that's right. . . . No, but I figure it would almost pay to have a couple of neighbors get together and buy a small rig; like Morrison and Kurt Barewolf. . . ."

He heard the murmur of dissension go from hill to ridge, from valley to bluff. He drove the crew the harder. Thrash faster, that'll keep their mouths shut. But he couldn't keep Kurt from talking ("Got his backsides hot with blabber," Johnny growled).

"It's crazy," Kurt was fond of saying, "rolling a heavy piece of machinery like Johnny's outfit over the roads and bridges."

"What about Morrison's tractor?" somebody asked. "It's a heavy outfit, too."

"It's just as crazy, but the engine is more economical," Kurt answered. "You fellers are paying for those big drivers—what are they, six foot high? Every time they tear up a road or break down a bridge railing, you have to dig into your pockets. The time is coming when neighbors will have to co-operate in small units for community interest."

The folks winked their eyes at these new-fangled notions. Kurt went on, "Remember what Horace Greeley said years ago?" (Nobody did; nobody there had ever heard of Horace Greeley.) With that fine sense of authoritative scholarship which can quote to its own purpose, Kurt unwrinkled a clipping and read, " 'This engine—' Greeley surely meant the tractor," he explained cryptically—" 'this engine will be driving a scythe before it within five years. The time must be at hand when every thrifty farmer will have such an engine of his own.' That's what a great man said," he finished and returned the paper to his wallet, lest anyone see that Greeley had spoken about the steam engine, not the tractor.

Folks listened, if they didn't understand, and bugged their eyes at Jimmy Morrison. Mr. Haber's son James was hinting around that as soon as crops were good again, he was going to get a tractor outfit. The machine-shop man told him that the machine companies were planning to manufacture in quantity tractors that weighed perhaps half as much as a steam engine; perhaps less. They'd be on the market soon.

Such gibblegabble was gravel in Johnny's craw. "I learned thrashing in the dust of the bandcutters' tables." He scowled fiercely, his thoughts bitter. "I got grease in my ears, learning how to run the engine. But nowadays, any pants cracker that can squirt oil in an oil hole thinks he can run a thrashing outfit."

Anger against Kurt, long and smoldering, began to spit and glower into rage. "If that bastard would keep his mouth shut!" Johnny gritted his teeth.

In one matter he had his way without opposition and that concerned the bridge over the dry wash. The town board had been lackadaisical until Johnny decided bluntly early that summer, "Either you build a new bridge and repair the others, or Devil take it, I'll stay on my side of the river."

After a session that was hot with dispute, the board tore down the bridge and constructed one of steel and concrete. It was finished just after threshing began. Johnny's rig was the first to cross it. The new span hardly creaked under the weight of both engine and separator.

Johnny felt a tickle of mirth sometimes, overhearing this or that neighbor who, a year before, had been vehement in protest, but now was smug in complacency. "Ya, about time we got a new bridge. That rickety old thing we had—why, the way the planks gave when I took a load across, I never knew when the stringers might break and throw me the whole shootin' match onto the rocks. . . . Sure is a nice bridge. Red, that's a color you can't miss. . . ."

Johnny bragged at the store the night before he moved to the flats, "If it hadn't been for me and my rig, you fellers would still be hauling your wheat three miles around. You'd never trust that old goat track."

But Kurt, jingling the trace chains he'd just bought, answered, "Oh, I don't know. We'd have built a new bridge anyway. With cream to haul and cattle and stuff, the time was ripe." His eyes flickered scornfully. "You and your old steamer! Can't you get this through your head? Do you think progress depends on *one* man? Or is held back by one man?

You're crazy, if you do. Time and necessity, those are the parents of progress."

All Johnny could say was, "Judas, what a lot a feller can learn from a book."

The neighbors listened, enjoying the set-to, although there was an embarrassed silence afterward. Most of them were not quite sure what Kurt meant. They could see that Johnny was angry. They clucked their lips. One or two relieved the tension by taking a pinch of snuff. Johnny left the store, irritated and defiant.

He was glad that some things were tangible enough to put between the two sides of vehement dispute. There was something solid about a fight, even with words. But there were other things that were not tangible, that were evanescent as moon shadows at midnight, that were like those nameless forms which creep over the distorted landscape of a dream, there and yet not there, against which the hard fist of reason is as futile as a curse flung to stay the whirlwind.

Any day he was prepared to brace himself against Kurt or Tetzell—the whole neighborhood, if that were necessary. But in the sad face of silence, before eyes that lost their deep brown when they became fixed and sharp with a determination that was cloaked from him—before these, his fingers balled tightly and then relaxed helplessly. The flesh of his palms was white under pressure, except where nails left their red marks.

He carried worry into the flats that season along with the tank and the tender.

Norton added to it by warning him, "'Times are getting tough for me, Johnny. Maybe you better not depend on me for next year."

"What!" Johnny peered at him. "I've thrashed here at Four Oaks year in and——"

"It's not that I ain't satisfied."

"Yours is such a big job, I could maybe do it for less," Johnny said recklessly.

"If I still got a farm." Norton smiled grimly; said nothing more.

Johnny's brow crabbed. If he lost the Four Oaks job——

One Saturday night he came home in rain to find the house dark and the dog woofing uneasily at his heels. Usually, Lilice's coal-oil flame sent a shivering glow of anticipation through his legs the moment he saw it from the hill slanting down to the yard. But not tonight. "Prob'bly tired and went to bed," he muttered with a show of being tremendously sensible. But the cold dread mocked him. What now? What's she up to now?

He put the horses in the barn and went to the house. He found the matches, struck one and lighted the lamp. Blinking in the sharp, yellow brightness, he went to the bedroom. The door was open. He entered. He couldn't believe the bed was empty. He put the lamp on the dresser, noticing how rectangularly clean and empty the scarf was. No bottles there, no jars, no china box which in the morning he could see in the mirror—a box with a cover on which a little china girl kissed a little china boy.

His sight dragged heavy as a stoneboat to the four-poster—Mrs. Rose's once. The spread was smooth as the grain-worn side of the feeder. Lilice fussed over as much as a wrinkle. The crease mark. Like a small ridge it divided the bed evenly, running squarely between the two pillows—two. . . . There was only one now.

"Lilice!" His voice exploded in the dank, crowding quiet. Mustn't yell. Wake the kids. "Lilice," he whispered. A board creaked. It was as loud as a dropped pitchfork. Then he called, "Leesa, Punkin."

"Here, upstairs." Her voice came muffledly through the space of walls and rooms.

He caught up the lamp. As he ran up the stairs, the flame darkened in the chimney, flared, almost choked in the draft of his haste.

"Here." Lilice's voice was dulled by the wood of the door. "Don't come in, Johnny. Sleep down——"

He didn't hear her. The knob rattled under his hand. The lamp crowded darkness behind the chairs and the bed. In the quick flood it brought Lilice into his eyes.

"Leesa, are we going to sleep—— In all the world, what——" He was trembling. There was fear in him now; fear in a black lump bulging against his ribs, big and hard enough to pull out of a pocket.

She blinked. "Go downstairs, Johnny." She spoke flatly. "Your bed is there." Her face was cold and white and almost unfamiliar. It was as though a stranger rested on that single pillow.

"Lilice." He put the lamp on the dresser. "I won't let you stay up here alone. You and I—we've never been apart, not once since we were married. And I'm not——"

"Three months," she interrupted him, stirring against the covers. "Nearly three months every year, your pillow is cold. I put my hand on it and it's cold."

"Leesa, I never——"

"You and Alb go off to see some machine man, or there's a farmer with forty acres of wheat. Never been apart," she repeated his words dully.

"But that's my work, my business," he explained as if to a child. "I'm a thresher and if I don't hustle around——" Breaking off, he moved as though to sit on the edge of the bed.

"Don't." Lilice raised up, wild-eyed at once. "Go downstairs. You must."

You must, she thought, or I'll never learn to deny you, and it will be worse, worse for you, worse for both of us.

"It's a terrible thing," he said slowly, "when a man and his wife must live in the house and be like strangers or visitors to each other."

"Man and wife," she echoed him bitterly. "Before we had a wedding ring——"

"I am not ashamed of what was honest." His tone was edgy for all his despair. "Can't you ever see that?"

"I am blaming nobody. There were two of us then. No need to blame only one. But it happened."

"Lilice——"

"Go downstairs."

"And leave you here?" In a sudden bitter anger, he stepped toward her, his arms curved out, as though to take her, covers and all.

She drew the quilt up to her neck. Her voice was calm, if tinged with scorn and faintly mocking. "I can't stop you from taking me downstairs. I know how big your muscles are. You could break me, couldn't you? Like a—like a little piece of straw." Her breath came faster. He saw the pulse leap in her throat.

"Oh, Punkin, Punkin!" Anguish roughened his voice. He sagged into a chair, his hands pressed against his face. His shoulders slipped forward. There was silence—silence rising like a wall, growing brick by patient brick. (So is the circle of a stack built . . . slowly and patiently, bundle by bundle.)

At last he rose, "You'll want the lamp," he muttered. He groped his way down the black length of the stairs to the bedroom, his room. In the darkness the windows were squares of gray light. Woodenly he unhooked his suspenders, unlaced his shoes, finally crawled into bed. The clock in the living room ticked holes into the minutes, exploded craters into the hours of that night. Sleep rubbed over him in broken segments. Once he reached out in the darkness for a warm shoulder and found the cool preciseness of sheets. Again in the forgetfulness of a drowsy moment, he slid his leg over where he could tickle her ankle with his toe. The darkness turned white in a rush of memory. Slowly he drew his leg up. . . .

Hours later he felt himself awakening and fought to melt again into the drowsy well of nothingness, tried to squeeze out the clear brightness against his lids. Desperately he struggled to catch the twisted cords of sleep trailing slowly over the edge of his consciousness. Despite his efforts they slipped away. He could feel their silky strands flow out of the corners of his eye before the glare of consciousness.

He lay wide-eyed under the shuttered lids. And in that gray dimness, a dimness sensitive as a nerve end, sight was the mirage of his imagination: Lilice was there beside him, warm as on a Sunday morning, her brown fists banging comfort into a pillow before her head snuggled there . . . Lilice poking a finger at his shoulder blades or tugging at the hair darkening his armpits. . . .

He got up fast then, and found work in the machine shed.

He returned to the rig on Monday and tied his back into knots of ache. He pulled off his shoes some nights as if they were skin and a part of his flesh. In the lanternlight he saw the bluish marks on his feet where oats and wheat had pressed against the bone. Like a felled ox he dropped into a bed of blanket-covered hay or straw, and scarcely heard a pitcher complain, "Dammit, it feels like I got a barley beard in my ear," and the tankee answer, "Better get 'er out. I heard where a barley beard went right through a feller's head, brain and all; come out the other ear. That's a fact and no horse balls." He heard and saw and did not care, glad that tiredness blotted away even the troubled face of Lilice.

<h2 style="text-align:center">6</h2>

So little rain dampened the corn shocks of autumn that Mr. Dunkel said, "Whoop-Jinny, if we don't get snow banks higher'n a fence post this winter, I hate to think about next year's crops." (This autumn's harvest scarcely gathered and already the worry about another season.)

The snow that winter when it drifted down finally was thin and powdery. ("Sugar snow," Mr. Nussbaum called it. "Usually comes in March, but now nothing else falls.") It was hardly deep enough to hold the track of rabbit and partridge. When they met, the neighbors slipped fingers under their belts as if to tighten their stomachs against inevitable leanness. They shook pessimistic heads.

For the first time since he put hand to the steering wheel, Johnny found only gloom in the columns of his account books at the reckoning time. Always before, especially in the last four or five years of long crops, he could thump a fist upon these leather-covered books, assurance in his breast, and without a qualm shoulder new obligations at the bank and the machine shop. But this year he saw his harvest gains sieve away into figures on the wrong side of the book.

Not this year could he write down the large settings of grain, the bulging yields of wheat and oats, upon which he had come to depend. Instead he had to write down small stacks and button-sized settings and a season of half crops.

Norton's was the most scraggly of the lot. It was hardly a quarter crop.

"We got hit bad," Norton told Johnny, wiping his fat throat. "Hardly any rain at all. You fellers in the hills got at least mosquito drizzle. Times is really tough for me." The gray on his head was thinning. Johnny regarded the accounts somberly.

And there were his engines, three of them smoking in valley and on ridge. And his separators, all the biggest in Pockerbrush (he was sure), all thirsty as the ground for oil and grease and repairs. If another year of meagerness came—— He shut the books quickly. Only in minutes of thought about Lilice did he remember how heavy his debt really was.

When the news buzzed in March that Norton had failed, Johnny felt as if the ground under his feet were slipping. "Looks like I got to hustle faster than ever now," he told Lilice, feebly turning this into a pleasantry. But to Heinie he said, "I can't believe it. Norton broke. It don't make sense."

"All them oil wells." Heinie spat. "They petered out. Now he'll scratch in the ashes for a nickel. He'll sell everything."

"I got my first job there," Johnny said softly.

"Norton's got Bory Tetzell scared witless," Heinie went on. "Any day now, Bory expects the sher'ff to get the rig. Bory can't pay a cent."

"Bory, huh? Norton holds a mortgage on his rig." Johnny cogitated. He began to laugh grimly. "That would really put the old badger on his chain."

A week later Tetzell sidled up to Johnny. They were in the Farmer's Store in Mary's Hill. "Who in hell you think you are, buying my mortgage off'n Norton?" He tried bluster.

"Are you talking to me?" Johnny turned on him swiftly. "I'm not your fireman." He swung back to the counter, answering the clerk.

"You got my mortgage?" Bory's voice moderated.

"Sure." Johnny spoke sidewise over his shoulder. He picked up the package of nails the clerk put on the counter. There was a grin on his lips but no mirth in his eyes. "How you like paying me the interest, Bory? I'll take it in cash." Barbs were in his taunt. "And when I need money real bad, you'll pay me in full, or the sher'ff will be out to see you." He left the store, the nails crunching metallically in his grasp.

Bory squinted after him, all his hard words drained away.

7

Spring blew in on a dry and dusty wind, no different from the warm days of latter-end winter, as wrung out of moisture as last fall's corn husks still rattling on the stalk. Leaves when they came were small and nondescript. The Dutchman's-breeches were scrubby and torn, their snowy pantaloons stained more with the brown of dryness than the butter yellow of promise. What rain fell, exploded single craters in the dust. It hardly wetted the tiny circular earth heaps which the cinnamon ants gathered mite by mite.

Johnny seeded the grain himself that year, hopefully fresh in the morning, wilted by sunset. He couldn't afford to hire the Whiteland boy; told him to come back for corn plowing and haymaking. No clouds knotted themselves into the deluge of thunder and falling drops. The short-crop year had come when the stem grew ankle high and broke into heads.

That spring Norton moved to a weather-beaten house in Mary's Hill. He grayed more quickly after that. A land company divided his farm and sold it in parcels to small bidders.

"Four Oaks Farm," Johnny mourned. "I s'pose they'll cut all the oaks down now. I had my first big job there." He didn't tell Lilice how disturbed he really was.

That spring Mrs. Dunkel died in the Fergus asylum; gave up the costly argument with life and died, "Gretel" on her lips, as if among shadows she'd find what she sought vainly among the figures of substance. And so she left the bleakness of lonely walls and the screams of those who, exiled from a bright citadel, wandered in the undergrowth of terror.

She was buried in the Pockerbrush graveyard. People flocked to the services. The benches overflowed and the gallery creaked with the push. "They come out of curiosity," grunted Mr. Nussbaum dourly. "By jippers, what a crowd at her funeral! She couldn't ever get that many to come to her coffee parties."

Johnny sat in a rear seat with the boys, Lilice beside him for once. Because of the gathering, decorum had been temporarily suspended and men sat with the women. As he bowed over his knees, he said to himself, "Nussbaum's right. They didn't come out of love for her, or for Dunkel."

He hardly dared glance at Lilice's still white face, or the way she pinched the finger where the wedding ring used to be. When he did, his lungs became so tight and airless, his nostrils thinned with each breath. Hopeful as it was and sweet with courage, the sermon was a droning mumble far away and unimportant beside that which sent the sweat into his palms. Not for the dead and the rank clove odor of carnations did the tears suddenly blind him; not for the dead did his shoulders bow forward so that Lilice, turning to him, crinkled her eyes, and then whispered, "You got a clean handkerchief? Here's mine." Not for the dead but for the living did he cry inwardly, Lilice, Lilice, don't leave me . . . don't leave me like . . . like . . . The muscles on his neck tightened against the collar.

It was that spring that folks began to say, "That poor Johnny Black's wife. Ain't she the peaked-looking one, though? Sakes and days alive! . . . Acts funny too. Not all the time. Just when she gets spells, seems like. . . . So Mrs. Peiser told me. Up at the store Mis' Black ordered groceries and when Toffman added up the bill, she says to him, strange and queerlike, 'Is that the uttermost farthing?' Did you ever hear the like? Well, Toffman, he nearly fell over a jar of pickles—the sweet kind I like so. Was he s'prised! Then she got red and scared-looking and says she's been poorly lately; had a bad headache. . . .

"Ya, and at church. She was there Easter Sunday. She just sat there, staring at the Pastor; didn't look at anybody else or say a word to anybody. . . . Ya, the crosses we have to bear . . ."

Two Sundays after the Easter service Pastor Ewig preached on the necessity of a calm spirit and a tranquil soul in order that life be rich. "Sometimes when I am sorely pestered by dogma and doctrine, and even the Beatitudes seem more for angels than for men, I am indeed comforted by the simplicity of the Psalms. Remember where it is written, 'Stand in awe, and sin not: commune with your own heart upon your bed, and be still. Selah.' All this worry and this commotion in which we live: automobiles and airplanes and a thousand new attractions daily. 'Be still,' says the Psalmist. 'Commune with your heart upon your bed.' Wrinkles come to your soul before they come to your face."

Suddenly Lilice saw that he was looking straight at her. She felt his gaze as if it were the sun on a cold day and she in a sheltered place. Hastily she turned away. Was he trying to trap her soul so that he could lay it bare to the congregation? Before the service ended she arose and hurried out. She waited in the schoolhouse until the amen had been said.

8

By the last of June the most hopeful glance no longer searched skies that were bronze as the feathers of a turkey gobbler. Each man regarded the weather-squeezed land with a sullen kind of acceptance. "This is a dry one, all right," they said. "The creek is down to moss and scum. Won't be much to thrash this fall, 'ceptin' thistle. I got a fine crop in my back forty. . . ."

Hot moisture-sucking winds moaned drearily over the ridges. Grain that had struggled ankle-high broke into head and seemed to wither where it stood, stem and sheath. Cattle stretched their necks and their tongues between the barbwire to lick up the last hint of green. A gray shadow lay over the pastures and pushed its way out in scallops between the fence posts—the embroidery of desperation.

Hay in the meadow was short except in the creek bottoms. What moisture clung to the roots there produced a good crop. Ordinarily Johnny would have filled his barn to the eaves and stacked the rest. But this year, careful of every spear, he had every cock hauled into the mow. It piled up. High under the rooftree where the hay fork rattled, sloo grass and tame grass cured and settled. Before long chickens cackled from nests under the crossbeams.

Robin, past nine now, climbed up and gathered the eggs, though many times when he was at the Humbers' and chores were forgotten in games of tag, Lilice herself went up the covered ladderway like a stair and found the hidden nests. It was fragrant up here among the tumbles of hay but warm.

Once she stood on the edge near a post with a crossbar on it, and looked down at the alley below and the open trap door leading to the cow barn. A smell of manure and mangers drifted up. She turned hastily away.

Thereafter she warned Robin, "Don't you get too near the edge now. Stay away. Or maybe I better get the eggs myself."

At harvesttime folks brought out their binders and the harvest began, if wrinkled stems can be called a harvest. Toadstools and puffballs lifted the solid ground of roads upon their rank, fleshy, cone-shaped roofs. It was as if the earth had a colic and vomited in her own way.

A kind of disease hung in the air, Mr. Dunkel said. Calves got scabby on legs and back, and cows ran nearly blind, their large moon eyes red and flecked with pus. Mr. Dunkel advised fish bone shaved into scrapings and powdered to dust. "Blow it in the eye," he suggested. But Mr. Peiser had a quicker remedy. "Just you chew up a good mouthful of Piper Heidsieck until she's nice and juicy, and spit it in her eye; that'll take the soreness off in no time."

Cattle nosed at the dried water holes. They chewed despondently on thistles. "Cripes, but Schimmel's livestock is thin," observed Mr. Peiser one day when he came by and found Johnny in the field, cutting oats. Clymy was reaping his barley across the road. Mr. Peiser went on, "Them cattle of his'n is so thin, they walk twice to make a shadow."

"I know." Johnny climbed from the binder. "Clymy's got a horse that's sore in the shoulders. Want to take a look at it?"

They met Clymy at a corner. The black was galled with collar burns, Clymy said.

"I'll fix that." Mr. Peiser nodded sagely. He glanced toward the house. "Any women around?" he asked, unbuttoning his pants. His ribs tightened with effort. He caught a palmful of water from his body. The horse stepped uneasily. Liquid spurted as Mr. Peiser slapped the palm against the blistered hide. "Whoa, boy. That'll fix you up."

Would rain ever fall again, folks wondered. Pastor Ewig preached on "Drought: Blessing or Punishment." To Mr. Dunkel's chortling delight and Mr. Nussbaum's horror, he indicated that cycles of rainless seasons might have a definite basis far removed from the chastening hand of God. "I doubt that this is punishment. But I suppose we need adversity, not to destroy us, but to stir us to greater effort. . . . Faith and courage are plants. No field produces which is left uncultivated. . . . Strange that we think a green field is a blessing and a withered field a punishment. It may be the other way around. . . .

"You have heard it said that a country wracked by war is under a judgment of God. That is indeed an egotistical observation. As if we understood God's universe! A country that enjoys prosperity and easy living and high standards may be in greater judgment of God than any miserable land ravaged with battle. Those who are bowed down may rise. But what can be said for those who stand in their pride—and fail?"

Said Mr. Nussbaum, "Talks so much about what he calls laws in the— the spiritual world. By jippers, how does he know?"

"If there's laws that bring up cyclones and dust storms," answered Mr. Dunkel, "why not laws that—well, that take care of faith and grace, and that other stuff?"

"Why not?" barked Mr. Nussbaum triumphantly. "I'll tell you why not. Because Pastor Steuber never even mentioned such things, and he was one that should have known. By jippers, that's why."

Mr. Dunkel looked at him, scorn on his wrinkling face, as if to say, "Well, what can you expect from a man who believes that scrub cows are better than full bloods, and thinks wheat is the only crop?"

Prayer and services for rain, held in Mary's Hill and in Fergus as well as in Pockerbrush, were followed by the eager expectancy of a shower. But the dryness continued. It lay like a hot smothering burden on the land. Man panted in his house and his beast panted in the shade of a rock.

On a sweltering afternoon Pastor Ewig drove into the Black yard. With something like panic sweeping over her, Lilice saw him stride up to the door. She dried her hands and brushed back her hair. Absently she noticed that he wore overalls and a blue work shirt like the Whiteland boy or Johnny, not the black gown.

Then he was shaking her hand. Curiously, it was he who was welcoming her, it seemed, not she him.

"Shall I call Johnny?" she asked. "He's in the back field. I'll call——"

"No, Mrs. Black. I came to see you."

His eyes held hers. Now it's coming. . . . I knew he came for this . . . now it is here at last. . . . The uttermost farthing . . . all the days I've hidden, they will be scratched into plain view . . . almost glad . . . what use to struggle? If she could sink through the floor . . .

She stumbled into words. "You have come to blame me. I know that. Pastors always do. I don't go to church often enough. I haven't joined. Johnny doesn't go often enough and——"

"Mrs. Black, I——"

"You might as well know. I was to blame, not Johnny. Our son Ernst—before we were married——" She stopped. Absently she waved her hand before her face.

Pastor Ewig watched her closely. Into the silence he said quietly, "I know all that."

"You——" She hadn't heard him aright.

"Of course I do. His birthday is in the registry." He smiled gently. "I know a lot about my parishioners."

"You know." Her throat felt tight.

"That was a long time ago."

"Aren't you going to scold me?" she asked like a child.

"Scold you?"

"Pastor Steuber did." Her voice broke. "I can't tell you——" She paused.

"Steuber——" Ewig checked his words, afraid to go on.

"It doesn't matter now," she said. She sat down weakly. "Nothing matters."

"But it does matter," exclaimed Ewig, slow anger burning his thought: Oh, Pastor, Pastor, smug and assured in God-blinded Pharaohlike smugness, for how much will you be held accountable?

"I never belonged," she said as calmly as if she were reporting the weather outside. "But I do know what is right and what is wrong. You must believe that."

"Of course, Mrs. Black." He sat opposite her. "Listen to me, Mrs. Black," he commanded all at once. "What has happened is past. It is——"

"No, no, no," she interrupted wildly. "It is here now. It will always be here."

"It is past," he said urgently. "It is past. You must be *convinced* of that."

"Talk is easy." She glanced at him with the amused tolerance of one who has tried all the answers and found them incorrect.

He said in slow earnestness she couldn't avoid, "Forgiveness arises in a conviction within ourselves. You won't find it elsewhere. We pray, and thereby we bring our faults and our needs into plain sight. We take stock of ourselves. Some things must be discarded. They belong to the past, terrible mistakes though they may be. We don't do those things again. Other things must be borne. From such examinations comes the courage to face the worst. It is so in small affairs; it is so in large." He searched her face.

"I don't understand." She put a hand to her temple. "We do that ourselves? Pastor Steuber said God——"

For an instant he hesitated, thinking, This is a stone to stumble on. This could make skeptics of us all. Then he said, feeling suddenly that his own conviction sounded all at once curiously like a mealy-mouthed platitude, "God is within us, guiding us; not outside us, shaking the hammer of the law."

"I don't understand." She arose. "I don't understand that. No, Pastor. It was good of you to tell me this. But it is not for me. It is too late."

"It is never too late." He stood beside her. "We are having Lord's Supper very soon. Bring Johnny Black and——" He hesitated, thinking, If this be blasphemy, let it be. Aloud he said, "Come yourself. Come and bring Johnny."

"Johnny, yes," she said. "But I cannot. I am too——"

"Bring Johnny then?" he insisted.

"Yes."

"You promise me this? You will bring Johnny?"

"I promise, Pastor."

9

Johnny swished through his fields, his heart shriveling with more than the ovenlike breeze drying the moisture from his skin. His heart seemed to squeeze against his ribs. He came to the yard one afternoon and stopped in front of the shed where his three rigs were sheltered. His eyes became black holes under the lashes.

Everywhere like a chorus of croaking frogs he heard the murmurs and complaints of the farmers. "My oats ain't more'n grass high. No use wasting twine. I'm cutting it with the mower. . . . Damn glad I didn't put in a kernel of wheat. If the worst comes to worst, I can cut my crop and put it up for hay. . . . It's a bad year, but it coulda struck me worse. I saved me a little money in the good years. Feed is short this year, sure; but my pigs and chickens, and the cream I sell to the creamery, that'll tide me over. It'll be nip and tuck, of course. Cripes, if I would have planted wheat now. . . . You know that Kurt Barewolf, he ain't such a dumb feller after all. . . ."

In Mary's Hill Kurt said one day, "There'll be smaller thrashing rigs by the carload before long. And not high-priced either. Just read the papers. Like one writer says, there's no sense in farmers paying a high price to thrash a bushel of wheat, just to support eight or ten tons of iron spitting oil and gasoline in all directions. There's only one thing crazier and that's the big, overgrown steam outfits that waste seventy per cent of the fuel and have to have a crew large enough to eat you out of the house. And that's surely so."

Winds of opinion swirled through the ridges, heated as the drought itself. Eddies of it swept around Johnny's ears, disturbing his sleep at night, those nights when sleep should have come to soothe his yearning for Lilice.

"Sure, they can talk smart," he said bitterly. "I'm the feller that thrashed their grain so they could make a little money. Now, what do they do? The bastards!" he fumed.

One day near the end of cutting grain, Heinie came to say, "Muri is dropping out of the ring."

"What!" Johnny sprang from the seat of the binder. "Not Muri?"

"Yep."

"If that ain't like a Norwegian," Johnny sputtered, wanting to pile blame on someone.

"Well, Edgely's no Noreegian and he's quittin' too," Heinie went on. "And that whole gang in Turkey Hollow, they're gonna get Jimmy Morrison's outfit. They say they got so little grain, it wouldn't pay to hire you."

"Hire me." Rage shook him. "The dirty horse's rosettes, I'll—I'll——" Johnny let the lines slip from his grasp. What could he do? A queer helplessness rolled over him. For a moment the dusty earth wavered in heat quivers before his eyes. Then his lips hardened. "It's Kurt. He's behind this. Shootin' off his mouth about gasoline tractors and smaller rigs." He gazed over the fields. "Wait a minute, Heinie," he exclaimed suddenly.

In a wild hurry, breathless and sweaty, he rushed into Clymy's yard. "Clymy, drop what you're doing, man. Climb onto my binder and finish my oats. I've got a hell of a lot of driving to do."

He flung harness on the ponies, hitched them to the top buggy and rattled off. He'd give them fellers a piece of his mind, a long thick piece. And Kurt, that blabber mouth, with his noise about big outfits . . .

He returned when the foxtail grass in the meadows, red with the fire of evening, was becoming more gray than silver with mist. His ponies clumped tiredly through the dust. He sat, lines in hand, his mouth set and worn with talk, wanting to curse, and finding himself empty of strength even for that. Words and phrases he'd heard all that afternoon, wrung from the grim lips of those who had put their trust in the earth, came back to mock him. They had the acrid savor of the future strongly in them.

". . . That's the way it is, Johnny. I'm not trying to buck you. I'm just up against it. I ain't got but a couple of hen piles this year. With your big machine, I might as well buy my feed at the store. . . ." Over and over that murmured complaint, with variations. "All the oats them horses eat. Horses is the eatingest sons of buzzards God ever threw a mess of guts into anyway. . . . The crews are so big . . . my wife says last year she didn't find an egg for two days, the thrashers stole 'em all, and scared the hens besides so they wouldn't lay. . . ."

He had found a group of farmers at the store (he recalled) and listened to their gloom. The same forlorn tales. Finally Mr. Blumen said without looking up, "Next year we're gonna start thrashers' meetings. Seems like a good idea when——"

"Thrasher meetings?" Johnny blurted out, knowing that Mr. Blumen's shaft was aimed at him.

"Kurt says——" began Mr. Blumen.

"Oh, Kurt says again." Johnny scraped a heel noisily against a cracker box, anger beginning to simmer.

"Pretty good idea he's got there," Mr. Blumen continued warmly, as if this had to be said. "Next July sometime, us farmers get to hold a meeting. By that time we can tell how things are looking, whether it's a bad year or not. And we can decide—well, what we want to do." Mr. Blumen finished lamely.

"Sounds like a nice hen party." Johnny let bitter scorn smear his words. "And what you think you're gonna do, scratch up a little hemstitching?"

"Us farmers, we're the ones that plant the grain, and we——"

"And who thrashes for you?" Johnny interrupted loudly. "I do."

"Sure, Johnny. But we farmers ought to have some say about the prices and when we start in the morning and when we stop and who goes in the ring and who——"

"And who sits in the backhouse longest, huh? You want the say in that too?" Johnny stormed, his fists ridging. "Judas Proost! Who do you think is coming to your little coffee meeting?"

"Look, Johnny. I've known you, boy and man, all your life. I don't want to stand in your way. But this is something that hits all of us. I don't——"

"Kurt Barewolf is coming to the meeting, of course." Johnny didn't heed him. His eyes were black glints. "Who else?"

"Well, as I say, us farmers, we're getting together." Mr. Blumen glanced uneasily at the neighbors bestriding boxes or kegs, or leaning against the counter. He saw how tense Johnny's arms were; knew what Johnny wanted him to say, and at last said it plainly. "And you thrashermen can——"

"Us thrashermen!" exploded Johnny, his lips whitening and half his forehead plowing into furrows of rage. "Us thrashermen can come too. We're invited then. Is that it? What you want us to do, crawl on our bellies?" He stood among them, his fists half raised. "There ain't a man here big enough to make me come. Or you want to drive me over with a bull whip?" His muscled shoulders swung as if he longed to smash a cracker box or rip down a shelf of sundries.

Mr. Blumen answered calmly, "That's for you to say."

"Devil grab it!" There was a shortness of breath in Johnny's lungs. He shivered as if ice had been laid on a bare nerve in a tooth. "Damn you!" he yelled suddenly.

For a moment he stood trembling in his rage. Then he swung on his heel and went—went out fast, "Or I'd have hit that Blumen," he told the blacksmith at the shop minutes later. "He's so dirty, that Blumen, he's got a two-colored shirttail. If he crosses my path once more, I'll hit him so hard, I'll jar his folks in the old country."

The blacksmith laid his hammer aside and stated bluntly, "Well, Johnny, in all my days of smithing, I've never seen the folks so determined. This drought has helped a lot. I've heard it said beside this anvil time and again. Folks have got the gasoline engines on their minds."

"Like Morrison's?" Johnny kicked over the nail keg he was sitting on and came close to the forge.

"Well, look." The blacksmith cleared his anvil of metallic flakes. "That tractor of Morrison's—you start her up and let 'er go. There's no fireman, no water monkey, no tank team, no ashes in the yard, no sparks flying from the smokestack. Morrison's got a separator man but, in a pinch, I guess Morrison could get along without one. He could run both engine and separator. Well, Jimmy will probably charge half of what you ask. Like Kurt says——"

"Kurt, Kurt." The bit of coal he held powdered in Johnny's hands. He dusted them on his pants. "Wherever I go, it's Kurt this and Kurt that. You'd think the sun rose and the sun set in his butt, the way people act."

Bitterly he flung from the shop. As he stepped outside, Bory Tetzell lumbered from his spring wagon. Johnny's eyes flickered. All the indignities of that day welded into a solid phalanx of determination.

"Tetzell," he barked, "you're just the man I want to see."

Bory stopped. He was unshaven and dirty-whiskered, all his swaggering gone into the flabbiness of one who no longer commands but occupies a lower seat. "What you want?" he demanded, some of the old truculence edging his voice.

"Money," Johnny said curtly. "Times are hard."

"You need money?" Tetzell peered at him as though this were a joke. "I need it worse'n you do."

"That's your business," Johnny told him. "Pay me by September first, or pay the sher'ff."

Bory sagged a little. "You just try it. You can't——"

"Oh, can't I, though." Johnny's lip curled.

Bory peered at him a moment, then said, "I'm getting along in years." There was cringing in his tone.

"No fault of mine," said Johnny. He leaned toward Bory. "I was young when you were old enough to know better. You dirtied me then. I can still feel your hands on my face."

Bory almost whined, deaf to Johnny's cold anger. "I'm getting so I can't thrash much any more. But my kid—I want him to run my rig. He's still too young, but——"

"I was young too," Johnny snapped. "Your fists didn't ask my age."

"September first," mumbled Bory. "Not much use starting up——"

"Get yourself another job." Malice quivered in Johnny's flat insistence.

"Another——" Tetzell blinked at his hands as one who, having handled a shovel all his days, is helpless without the wood in his grasp. "Another job——" He lumbered an ungainly way into the shop.

Pucker-lipped Johnny watched him. "I promised I'd break you some day, Bory Tetzell," he said. . . .

"And I could break him," Johnny muttered, driving along in dusk growing so deep his ponies were only blacker patches bobbing ahead of the dashboard. The ponies stepped up, smelling home and the barn with hay in it and feed in the mangers. "Devil, but I could break Tetzell like that." He snapped his fingers. But there was no triumph in the gesture. Quickly the thought came: "It was really Snoose he dirtied most." Somehow in this dusky ride homeward Snoose's humiliation and his own were curiously one.

He felt strangely helpless and deserted, as if he had built a hope on iron and found it wax. The echoes of that day were loud in his ears.

Some farmers, to be sure, were not daunted by drought nor lured by Morrison's rig. Their loyalty was sweet as honeycomb to Johnny—sweeter because he'd tasted it so seldom that afternoon. "We'll stick by you, Johnny," they had assured him. "Ain't got much time for a lousy stinking Kerosene Annie anyway. No power in them." Other farmers were indefinite, hanging him between their yes and no. Most of them he could not depend on, he was sure of that. Even Mr. Edgely spread his hands help-lessly. "You see how it is, Johnny."

There would be enough jobs to form a long solid run, he decided. And he could pick up odd farms here and there. (Odd jobs: he taking odd jobs.) But the big runs were smashed, for this year anyway. If he had Norton's job now—but that belonged to the past, too.

"When the rains come again," he dreamed wrathfully, "I'll get them fellers together again. And what I'll do to them! They'll crawl. Oh, Devil, how they'll crawl!" He slapped the lines down. "And that Kurt. He'd better keep out of my way, or I'll break him into pieces—little pieces, at that!"

One thought was like gravel in his mind, sharp-pointed and hurting. "Morrison's thrashing for maybe half price," the blacksmith had said. Over and over Johnny argued, as if the blacksmith were there and he were answering him, "Judas, the price of oil where it is and grease and repairs and hired help, I can't cut down a cent. Not a cent. I can't . . . I can't. . . ."

After he'd unharnessed and fed the ponies, he sat on the feedbox. (In years gone by, how he would have rushed in to Lilice!) His arms and legs were like untwisting ropes as he slumped against the wood.

10

That fall Johnny fired up only one rig, the Buffalo Head, the one Marty had run these years. The small outfit, he called it, although it was larger than Tetzell's or Morrison's or Bluber's. The new rig and the Golden Bird stayed in the shed.

Heinie left the steering wheel to become a separator man again. Marty Borman was out of a job. Johnny took back the fireman he had employed the fall before. But Marty, restless at home, couldn't stay away from the odor of the engine and came to hang around the rig. "A wife and kids is all right," he said. "But when I get my fill of them, I have a hankering for the steamer again."

Johnny was glad to have him around. As it turned out, it was Marty who ran the engine the day Johnny went to see about an extra job or two in Wilkins' Coulee township.

"You take 'er, Marty," Johnny said, almost shamefaced. "Maybe I can get a couple of hen piles over there."

He got the jobs, but he felt as if he'd bitten into a wormy apple. "Beg-ging for jobs!" he muttered. A queer lassitude sometimes gripped him these days, as though the languor of autumn's fading were on his bones.

The day he finished his own stacks and prepared to move the rig to the Peisers', the boys begged for a ride. "On the engine, Pa," they squealed. "We'll walk back."

"Not this time, kids," he said firmly. "You stay home and see that Ma don't get lonesome." He glanced heavy-eyed at the door of the house.

Grumbling and scowl-faced, Dickie with trembling lip, the boys went back to the straw heap near the engine. Reluctantly they resumed the game of playing thresher. Soon, their disappointment forgotten, they were deep in the game which adults play for keeps.

"*Chug-a-chug-chug*," mimicked Robin. "I'm the Golden Bird." He scratched straw over his knees like a dog.

"I'm the Buffalo Head," yelled Dickie. "Look at me. I'm engine and separator."

Johnny heard them. Quickly he grabbed for the throttle, his vision blurred. The bitter, bitter years of long ago.

Thereafter folks saw that which made them scratch their jaws. Johnny Black took his top buggy with the rig, ponies and all. A pitcher drove the team from farm to farm. Some folks grumbled over the extra feed for the ponies, until Johnny swore, "Devil grab it, I'll buy the oats from you, if you're that hard up." No more was said. In the buggy he carted buckets of oil, cans of grease and odds and ends. A good carryall, he said defensively. But folks soon saw that, let the wind of a rumor about a job rustle in somebody's talk, and he was hitched up and away in search of it. Most folks said, "Ya, that Johnny Black. He's got his nose deep in humble pie this year." But some said, "Serves him right."

Kurt was at the store the noon Johnny drove over to buy a length of chain. There was a crowd near the hitching rail when he came. Jimmy Morrison was threshing on the yard of the farmer who lived opposite the store. Momentarily forgetting the sweat of work in the novelty of being near scales on the counter, rolls of print on the shelves, lanterns and buggy bows under the ceiling, the men stretched the time before one o'clock in gawping and in horseplay. Most of them were gathered on the steps.

Kurt was among them, waving a pudgy finger under Mr. Edgely's nose. "The time is closer than you think. The farmers'll all join together in a union, the way the factory man does." He saw Johnny leap to the ground and stride toward him. His feet squared a little more firmly. Otherwise he paid no attention to Johnny. He didn't drop a syllable of his talk. "And when anybody squeezes the farmers with high prices, they'll strike back. They'll plant no more than they can use. They'll dump the milk into the ditch. Half a dozen farmers will own a rig together. They'll have to. I don't believe that tractors will ever be so cheap every farmer will have one of his own. But farmers will own them together. They'll——" He broke off suddenly.

The gravel flew under Johnny's crowding soles. "So you're telling the boys how to thrash, Kurt, are ya?" he said, his voice soft and repressed. "Want the farmers here to gang up so you can sick them on the thrashers, huh?"

"I didn't say anything about that," Kurt denied, facing Johnny stolidly. "I was talking about farmers in general, not these here in——"

"I heard what you said." Johnny coiled. "Maybe you want to answer this." His hand lashed out.

The flat smack across Kurt's mouth brought a gabble of protest from the crew so that Kurt, retreating no more than an inch, warned them, "This is our quarrel."

"You damn right it is." Johnny waited. "And something's going to be settled right now."

"What I've said, I've studied over and thought about a good deal," Kurt said, touching his lips. There was no anger in his voice, only a kind of pity. He spoke as formally as if he were addressing the Turkey Hollow Farm Club, organized that summer. "And I believe——"

"Here's a new lesson for you to learn, then." Johnny's voice tightened. Suddenly he struck, seeing that Kurt wouldn't. His fist was ridged with the hate that had its unforgotten roots in the winter of the calf squabble and in the autumn of pain near the creek, and all the warped and crooked memories that came between. All these whipped out in that onslaught.

Kurt swayed, buckled down to the steps. Blood trickled from a lip. He shook his head slowly like a dog in water. Carefully, like something huge gathering its strength, he lumbered to his feet. The men crowded around. A late-comer yelled to those behind him, "Hurry up. It's a fight."

Before Johnny could strike again, Kurt lunged at him. For all his bulk, Kurt's flailing arms scattered Johnny's defense. Hard knuckles rocked Johnny's head. There was the thud of bone on flesh.

Then Johnny recovered himself. He avoided Kurt's wild swings and his pawing hands seeking a hold. In that embrace Johnny knew from bitter experience what danger lurked. Stepping lightly away from Kurt's unwieldy attack, Johnny struck as calmly, as surely as if he had a maul in his grasp and were driving a post into the ground. All the taunts and all the torments, dammed up these years and fretting for release, broke loose now. It seemed almost as if he were fighting with steam in his fists against the squat ironness of Kurt. His knuckles bored into Kurt's face.

Suddenly Kurt fell. Johnny stood over him, his hands talonwise in their curving readiness. "Get up, Kurt." His throat was raspy. "I haven't finished with the lesson yet. I'd like to tear your gullet out." There was an elbowing in the crowd.

"Sure." The word puffed with the blood on Kurt's lips. He struggled to a sitting position. "You knocked me down. You've done it before. But what is it going to get you?" He wiped his mouth into a red smear. "You think you're fighting me, but you're not. You think you can change the neighbors by knocking hell out of me? Edgely there, or Heberstadt, or any of the farmers——" He went on, gulping with pain, "You think fists can scare them into running back to you for a thrashing job? What does a fight settle anyway? Nothing. It only starts something."

"I'll thrash in my own way and you're not going to boss me," Johnny raged. But a chill misted through the heat of his anger. Suddenly he was twelve again and pounding Kurt, trying to force a grunted "I got enough," from that heavy body, and failing. In a swift moment he realized he was failing now. Bitter ire like the taste of wormwood ran over his tongue.

As though he guessed what caused the shift in Johnny's eyes, Kurt said in a low grave voice, "It's not your way any more, Johnny." He spoke quietly. He gave no sign that a front tooth was broken and jagged in his mouth. "Times are changing."

"Not in thrashing," Johnny snapped at him. "Folks'll always need thrashers."

"Sure." Kurt pulled a handkerchief from his pocket. "But not——"

"If you think I'm going to change to a mess of stinking iron, you're on the wrong trail." Johnny turned away. "Before I do that, I'll take in saw-milling up north."

"You like that better?" A barb of malice returned to Kurt's tongue. Without answering Johnny strode toward the buggy, the chain forgotten. He felt as he had so often years before. Kurt back there, struggling up on his elbow and wiping his lips on the handkerchief, was the victor in this set-to, while he, Johnny Black, was the conquered. Rebelliously he faced the bitter truth that some things like deadly birth and the rattle of death, love and the sequence of happenings wrapped in the belly sheaths of Time, are no more to be disturbed than rock ledges in the pastures. They may be accepted finally but not moved an iota.

11

The Friday Johnny threshed at Mr. Schimmel's, Em'ly Morrison, Jimmy's wife, and her new baby were visiting at Sophie's. "We're going to call her Lucy," Em'ly chattered, her voice lively but her face quiet as though happiness had been stopped in the middle of a laugh. (Em'ly, sober-browed

and queerly old for her years, the sprout toughened in the bruising agony
of grief until it had bark before it had flower.) Her baby was a bundle
of pink chin and gurgles and frilly laces. "She's got a heat rash on her legs.
Ma says you know something for it."

"Don't know whether my cures are any good." Sophie glanced dubiously
through the window at the Black house. "This is what I use. It almost
never fails."

They had settled the matter of lard and sulphur. Sophie was giving
Em'ly a recipe for "bubble and squeak"—"that's one of Mrs. Edgely's prime
favorites. She's had it in her family for years. You take your cabbage and
cut it up fine; fry it in boiling butter a second or so, and then cover it with
cold meat; then you——"

The screen door opened and Lilice walked in. "Sophie, I'm going to
make egg-white kisses for the boys, for lunch."

Sophie regarded her anxiously. The words sounded like a joke. But the
face remained tight as a mask. A corner of a lip twitched a little. The
brown eyes were curiously flat, without depth. "It's awfully hot. I think
it's going to shower. I felt the wind at my throat." She spoke soberly. "I
must have run out of sugar. You got a cupful to spare? I'll have to find
the eggs. The hens are laying in the haymow again." She looked about as
if searching for something.

Before Sophie could answer Lilice saw the baby. The faded brown eyes
deepened, darkened, softened with such tenderness that a smile broke the
somber line of her mouth—a smile so clear of shadows that Sophie, watching her, caught at a chair back and could not swallow the tightness in her
throat for an instant. In that smile was the soothing, nourishing smile of
mothers who offer their breasts to the hungry nudging life in their arms.
For that moment all tenseness was gone.

"Let me have her, Em'ly," Lilice begged suddenly, eagerly, her arms outstretched before she spoke. Sophie started forward, a hand uplifted, then
stopped. Em'ly hesitated, mother searching mother, then nodded.

Lilice gathered the squirming, fist-waving bundle closely, feverishly to
her breast, her arms hungry for the touch of helplessness. "I never had a
baby girl," she murmured. "Mine were all boys. I could hug you, you little
blue eyes." There was such yearning in her face (the yearning of a love
repressed and denied, withering as young roots do in the drought-parched
ground) that Sophie abruptly turned toward Em'ly, loud with senseless
remarks.

Lilice never heard them. In mothering half-understood syllables she
cooed at the baby. "Blue eyes, little blue eyes. So like my Ernst's," she
whispered. The baby gurgled and thrust a fist against her chin. "I've got

no one like you to rock to sleep." Against her flesh, a warm baby fist moved, smooth-skinned, soft as the petal of a rose. Soft and pink, not rough and scabby . . .

A knotty splinter seemed to press into her head. Pain twisted in her throat. Abruptly she cried, "Here, Em'ly, take her." She almost shoved the baby away. "It's late, isn't it? First thing it'll be dark."

Em'ly took the baby, astonishment plain in her look. Lilice stood for a moment, twisting her hands, her thumb and forefinger groping as though to find a ring on her left hand. Em'ly fussed over the baby, uncertain how to take Lilice's behavior. Fumbling with a cuff, Lilice leaned toward Sophie, glanced slyly at Em'ly, and whispered, "There's a lot of cobwebs in your kitchen." Abruptly she turned and left the house.

Em'ly stared after her. "I wonder what came over her," she said. "Such a queer look." Then she added, "Why, she forgot the sugar."

"She'll be back." Sophie hid the pity in her eyes. No need for the neighbors to know more than they did, even Em'ly Morrison. "We all forget things now and then. But it's terrible the way she forgets. She'll put an egg out for a cake. A minute later, she'll look high and low for it, and it'll be right there, plain as plain, in front of her."

"She always was a queer one," Em'ly said fretfully.

Sophie bit her lips. "Don't think about it, Em'ly. Lilice, she's a very troubled woman."

12

They were just about to start threshing after dinner at Mr. Schimmel's that Friday. Johnny said, "Time to get rolling, I guess, Marty. There's damn little to thrash here and we might as well get it done. They say Hadell's got a pretty decent run of stacks south of town. I've a mind to go see him tomorrow. Maybe we can pull down there. Or pull for home." He reached for the whistle cord.

Mr. Schimmel dragged his thick-cased watch from his pocket. Just then the whistle screeched. "Start up!" He tapped the crystal smartly. "Na, by Gott, I'm a minute behind again." Carefully he set the hands.

Mr. Schimmel was blowing his straw into the barn this year. "Mine meadow is ya dry," he said. "I got to have some hay." The back of the separator was set not far from the barn wall. A space less than the width of a hayrack intervened. Only that morning a Haber boy, driving a grain wagon, complained about the cramped quarters.

The separator had hardly begun to hum and the blower hadn't yet attained its full-voiced roar when there were crashes and bumps. Johnny shut the throttle down. He came to the separator, glaring—"Like it was my fault," Heinie complained later.

It was a broken shaker arm and splintered boards. They wired and spliced and repaired, Johnny cursing softly. "Tinker's job." At last he growled, "It'll hold for the afternoon. I'll have to get a new iron, I guess. If Schlosser hasn't got a new one, he'll have to make one. I'll see that he gets the right angle. Hitch the buggy team," he ordered his tankee. "As long as I'm in town," he said to Marty, "I might as well drive down and see Hadell. Might be thin stuff he's got, but its thrashing anyway."

Marty picked up the casting. "See there?" He pointed to a rusty spot in the shiny silver of the break. "A flaw. Just a little flaw. That's what broke 'er up."

"Ya," said Mr. Dunkel sighing. "It ain't the big things. It's the little things that break us."

Johnny was half a mile down the road when he remembered. Forgot to tell Marty that the pop-off stuck again this morning. Well. The momentary restraint he put on the lines slackened. Marty knows how to run the old bitch, he consoled himself. Oh yes, he mustn't forget that box of Copenhagen a pitcher asked him to get.

The fields were gray stubble, wheat and rye and barley together. Usually oats stubble had a bronze color at this season. Now it too was dun-colored. In the northwest clouds banked up. They should hold rain, he thought. But we've said that so many times. Just fool's thunderclouds, I guess. He slapped the lines down impatiently. "Get along, boys." The ponies trotted most of the way.

At the machine shop he bustled around, his step clicking sharply on the concrete floor. "You got an iron like this, Schlosser?" he demanded. "Otherwise you'll have to make one for me. And I need it damn quick, too."

"Haven't got a new one, Johnny." The machine man squinted at the break. "But I guess we can make you one that'll be just as good."

"Fine. Get at it right away, will ya?" Johnny asked. "I'm driving down to Hadell's. I'll be back in an hour or so."

"I'll try to have it ready." Schlosser hefted the iron. "I hear you're aiming to sell one of your rigs."

"I?" Johnny gaped at him. "Who's been blowing that?"

"Oh, I just heard. You ain't aiming to get a tractor, huh?"

"Tractor!" Johnny snarled the word. "Not by a damn sight. When I can't drive a steam engine, I'll quit."

"Oh, sure, sure," Schlosser mollified him. "It's just something I heard." He continued, "I got a new tractor in the other day."

"Don't say. You want me to jig?" Johnny demanded crustily. But when he saw the tractor, his brows furrowed. "Who is going to buy that?"

"Nobody yet," admitted Schlosser. "But if there's halfway decent crop next year, I'm betting young Haber will be running it."

"That—that young horse's crupper?" Exasperatedly Johnny swung around. "The way thrashing goes these days, any squirt old enough to keep his pants from clogging gets himself a rig—a tractor rig at that."

"There's money in thrashing. You know that," Schlosser answered. "And where there's money——"

"Oh, Devil grab it!" exploded Johnny and headed for the buggy. He jumped in. His whip licked out viciously. The wheels rattled on the drive southeast. The ponies were in a sweat by the time he arrived at Hadell's.

Hadell had a cluttered-up yard, a sag-ended barn and a house so weathered Johnny wondered if a brush of paint had ever been slapped on a clapboard. "Like a dozen other farms in the Valley," he decided. "Rich as hogs one year, poor the next. Never know what to plan for, and so they don't plan."

Hadell's kids were playing threshing when he said "Whoa!" in the yard. They stopped and arose from their knees, regarding him curiously. One was a freckled-faced boy, dreamy-eyed and sandy-haired, he noticed idly.

Then Mrs. Hadell stepped out on the porch. . . . No, Hadell wasn't to hum; wouldn't be till late; she didn't know nothing about thrashing plans but she'd heard Hadell say the neighbors were getting another rig; maybe if he talked to the mister; nothing was really settled yet. . . .

"Oh, ya." Johnny felt strangely foolish and wondered if his cheeks were red. Begging like a tramp at a farmer's gate. "I see."

His eyes shifted about the yard. The boys had returned to their play, squint eyes still on him, should he produce anything exciting. He watched them.

They had grass tied into bundles and stacked in round piles. The sandy-haired boy was crouched down, his knees almost touching the bundles. Johnny felt his heart constrict. Then his ears were full of boy sounds. "Chook! Chook! Chook!" The sandy-haired boy let the exhaust of the tractor pop from his teeth. He scratched a thin pile of grass over his knees, dog-fashion. "Let 'er snort, boys," he said. He was dreamy-eyed over the threshing, engine and separator at once; dreamy-eyed as Snoose . . . as Snoose had been long years (the long lizard years) before. Snoose.

In a bitter rush out of those years, Johnny heard Snoose's chuckling voice leap over the plum hedge again: "Hum-r, hum-m-m, hum, gr-r-r, gr-r-r-r. G'up there, Jerus'lem." Dreamy-eyed Snoose and the growl of the horsepower gears. The cylinder hum of the old thresher with the bandcutting tables. And after a silence, Snoose's voice, "I see you standing there. Come on over."

Johnny's throat squeezed tight. Where were they now? Where bull wheel and tumble rod and gear? Lost. Scattered. Buried in grass, the wheels tied to the ends of rope and flung into water as anchors when the farmers went fishing. And the old separator—a mess of rotting boards, white with the fungus of decay. Sinking into earth. Forgotten. Why, kids didn't know what you meant when you talked about horsepowers and thrashers today. They were like Robin and the Humber boys. When they played at thrashing, it was "*chug-a-chug-a-chug-a*" over the straw bundles, scratching the harvest over their knees, the sound of the steam engine softly rolled between their lips.

But now—now it wasn't even the steam engine any more. No, it was "*Chook! Chook! Chook!*" The swift explosive bark of the tractor. Efficient. Ruthless. And *chug-a-chug*: would it fade with the echoes, too, as *hum* and *gr-r-r* had faded, uselessness, forgotten, the whistle clogged with the rust of shower and snow?

Before he could shout a loud denial to himself he heard the sandy-haired boy yell, "Bundles, there. Get the bundle hacks moving. *Chook. Chook. Chook.*" Even in the mouths of babes the coldly snapping iron crowded out the smooth exhaust of the steamers.

He felt old all at once; tired as if he hadn't slept for a week of Sundays; shaggy like a tree with its bark peeling. He drove quietly away.

In Mary's Hill he bought the box of snuff for the pitcher. The Farmer's Store smelled of leather and coal oil and sardines. He asked for the Copenhagen and laid out the money. As he glanced around he saw a small woman whose face he thought he ought to know. After a moment he remembered her. Regina Fleischer, Bory Tetzell's wife now, young-looking in spite of Bory's hard hands. She was talking with Mrs. Peiser. Johnny wondered why she looked as if she might burst out crying any minute. How he hated a woman's sniffles! Water in Lilice's eyes—it was enough to drive him from one end of his forty-acre piece to the other.

As he walked to the door she stepped forward. "When are you going to send the sher'ff, Johnny Black?"

"Huh?" He stopped, bewildered for an instant, then remembered the papers he had in the strongbox at home. "Oh, well, I——"

"You are going to have your way, aren't you?" Her voice was soft but he saw how her lips trembled. "Without giving us another chance. I hope you'll be happy over it." With a gesture that reminded him of Lilice, she went back to the counter.

"Judas!" he breathed, letting the door close behind him and going into the sunshine. "When a woman gets on a man's back———" He shook his head. Clouds were ink-black in the north. "Might get rain at that. I don't care if it does stop the thrashing for a day or so."

At the machine shop he had to wait half an hour for the casting. After a while of chewing on a grass stem, he sat near the doorway, staring moodily at the river. Once Schlosser came to say, "I'm getting it done as fast as I can, Johnny." He expected a rush of impatience.

Johnny said without looking up, "I know you are. I guess it just takes time and there's no use arguing about it."

With the casting repaired and in the buggy he took the road home. The leather in his fists was slack. Only now and again did he urge the ponies with a downward slap. His gaze roamed over the fields as though he'd been too busy with the harvest before and now saw them clearly for the first time. Wasn't too much to see except stubble. Why, two, three years ago, there would have been straw piles sticking up like bellies in the yards and in the fields: the light gold of wheat, the bronzy color of barley, the blond of rye, the rusty green of flax. Now there were hen piles, scraggy and small. They were more like haystacks the cows had rummaged at than anything else. One straw pile was polka-dotted with white chickens scratching busily. Many farmers threshed their straw into the barn, as Mr. Schimmel was doing. "It'll be as good as hay this year," they said.

A bee flew into the buggy. It bumbled zizzily against the top before it tried to get out through the panel of glass in the back curtain. It moved sluggishly, the languor of winter death upon it. When it escaped finally, the silence after its buzzing wings was thick and heavy. The quiet seemed heavier when he studied the cloud bank hanging to the north. The way it looked, rain might be falling on his place right now, a shower at least. It lay in that direction.

Regarded closely, there was a dark strength in that curtain of storm, the angry iris purple of its swelling folds intensified by the clear blue overhead, for where he drove, all was hot sun. If you cared to look closely. There were folks who wasted half an hour over the crags of a sunset. He couldn't do that; hadn't been able to. He was too busy. In all his years, and he was not yet past his mid-thirties, he could remember few times when he had stopped to listen to those hours that come with twilight and a neighbor's cowbell *tink-klinking* from a hillside—hours when body and soul pause to listen, it seems, and the rush of being is heard deep in the corners of the ears, if one waits. Few hours of quiet since Snoose. . . . He could think of Snoose quietly now.

What was it the Pastor had said in a sermon? "It isn't enough to walk quietly in your body. You must walk quietly in your mind, in your soul."

Well, let the Pastor worry about souls. Ministers had time for such stuff. Of course, maybe there was some truth in what the Pastor said.

When you stopped to think about it, here he'd scurried around like an ant on a hot stove these years. He'd sweat and been full of drive and had bragged over saying, "I've got them crawling to me now." But when the kernel was shaken from the chaff, what had he gained? What could he look back on sweetly and with satisfaction? Distrust and suspicion, he thought bitterly. "Farmers are my friends at thrashing time, yes; they'd kick my butt the rest of the year, if they dared." Blaming him . . . short measure, high rates, wasteful machines, dangerous sparks. Blaming him like Mrs. Tetzell today. Her face kept returning, its sadness reminding him some way of Lilice.

Well, maybe Kurt was right; maybe times were changing (the thought wormed its way into his mind.) Before long perhaps small rigs would purr in every farmyard, a couple of neighbors getting together to thresh their grain, and not caring whose rig boomed on the next farm. Tractors instead of horses plowing and seeding . . .

His laugh smashed the worming thought. No, no. He shook his head, as if denying somebody's assertion. It's just a fad. It'll pass like these devil-grab-it dances the young fry go to now; turkey trots and bunny hugs. I'll get my jobs back. All this will be forgotten. . . . He lulled himself into a kind of relief, as, time and again, he had when the engine was warmly at his back and rocking him into calmness.

How that cloud towered to the north! Would it rain at last, rain in the harvest after the root is dead and the sheaf threshed? But no. He could see lightness underneath the dark edge of storm. It was a shower only.

Rightly taken, there was a rugged beauty in those years gone by, he thought. Beauty in stacks of grain cut sharply in silhouette against a yellowing dawn; a billowing pile of straw drenched with the red of sun burning itself to ash of clouds; Lilice's smile. Yes, but it was beauty the weevils had infested: the straw piles, soggy after the first rain, bulged distortedly like beggars swollen with emptiness. Where stacks leaned and shed no misty shower, the wheat was tarnished with mildew. And Lilice's smile, how smashed and jagged what had once held all his mirth. "Years of the locust," he said, remembering a snatch of Pastor's Ewig's sermon.

He sighed deeply. What wouldn't he give for one hour of laughter with the Lilice of years ago, all the red of her lips, the honey gold of her hair, the sweet knot of mirth tied under the button of the dimple, the eyes half-veiled in crinkling friendliness—all of her here beside him and they going to visit a neighbor.

Suddenly, as if giving in to an insistent nagging, he snarled, "All right,

Tetzell, you can have your chance, and the Devil grab you." He half closed his eyes, squinted at the sky quizzically, as though he expected some-body's notice. Then he shrugged. Was that a roll of thunder he heard just then? No. It was a puff of wind perhaps. He clucked to the horses. "Gid-dap, boys." His head bowed over the lines. Lilice, Lilice . . .

From a turn in the road he saw the smoke. With a startled jerk he grabbed the whip and lashed its length across the horses. Then he saw flames throw their red scarves upward from the stacks and long ribbons curl around the separator of the Buffalo Head. Soon now the barn would catch.

To the north thunder rumbled. The edge of the storm was not quite overhead. A white shower fell no more than two miles away. But here the sun was hot and unclouded. No drop spattered to drown a spark.

He was running even before he touched the ground, it seemed. Marty had stopped the rig and started the engine forward. The drive belt slipped off the flywheel. It snaked crazily in its own momentum.

Pull the separator out backward, was his first thought. No, the barn's blocking the way. Got to get her out frontward. "Back 'er up, Marty," he yelled. "I'll get the cable." He ran to the tender.

Then Heinie was pulling at his shoulder. "Johnny, it's all afire. You can't get a cable hooked——"

"To hell I can't!" Johnny grabbed the hook of a heavy coil. "Leave the separator there? No stack fire ever got my rig yet. I'm not letting this one burn me out." He started away.

Heinie tried to hold him. "For God's sakes, man——"

"Get the canvases. Wet 'em in the tank. Hurry," grunted Johnny, drag-ging the twisted iron coil. "Drive the tank team close. We'll need the water."

"Johnny," pleaded Heinie.

"Hurry, damn it," yelled Johnny.

A pitcher came up. "She's done for. Might as well let her burn."

"Burn?" Johnny faced him. "Burn the Buffalo Head's separator?" he screamed in cold rage. "Devil grab you!" Suddenly he dropped the hook. His fist flashed; struck. The pitcher swayed to his knees.

Then Johnny was running again, dragging the cable behind him, run-ning forward, watching for a cleft, an opening in the cloud and the fire. There was the feeder sticking its jaw toward him; underneath it on the ground was the pole. He'd run in and with one swing of his hand ram the hook of the cable into the clevis there. . . .

He ran forward . . . bent down . . . clawed at the ground. An idle wind out of the north swirled into a gust, whipped between the stacks, blew long streamers of smoke-darkened flame over the feeder. They touched him. He arose as if to turn, got half up, fell. A slant of bundles, left unsteady by the pitchers (or by those who built the stack) poised for an instant of flame, began to slide. Heinie came running. Smoke bellied upward, torn by twists of fire.

13

For several minutes Sophie stood in the kitchen. Em'ly had gone. Mr. Musser had picked her up. Down the road she could still hear the rattle of the wagon. In the yard the kids were racketing in play. Three of them were shrieking. All well. If only one bellowed, she'd better hurry to box an ear and restore order. All well.

If only all were well with Lilice. She drew aside the curtains of the window north and gazed at the Black house. "None of my business, really," she muttered. But all at once, her bony jaw tightened. "Maybe it ain't neighborly, but it's got to be done." Taking off her apron, she shook her skirts tidily and smoothed her hair.

She didn't know what to say, once she stood in Lilice's kitchen. She rubbed her hands, fiercely uncomfortable.

Lilice was poking aimlessly at a page in a recipe book. "I haven't made kisses in I don't know how long," she said. Her manner was vague. "Johnny used to like them so——" She brushed a page. "I've got to wash my house. There's spiderwebs over everything. I——"

"Lilice." Sophie creaked into a chair as though she needed all her strength for what she had to say. "Lilice, you and Johnny, you ought to have another baby. Two or three of them. I tell you——"

Lilice stared at her. "What are you saying?" she began. A momentary resentment sparkled in her eyes. Then she cried vehemently, "No, no, no, Sophie." The resentment faded. "Never. That can never be."

"Why not? I know how rough a man is and how he gets mad when you say no," Sophie went on hastily as if garrulity pardoned her rudeness. "Darn a man anyway. He looks at a girl's waist and it's all he can do to keep from wiggling. He marries her. When her time comes and she's heavy on her feet, he begins to make sheep's eyes at the neighbor girls. But a woman, she has to stay with him. Everybody grins at her bigness. Instead of feeling sorry for her, that fool of a man grinds his teeth and acts like it was her fault. And no sooner does a woman have her baby and gets thin again so that her dress fits her once more, than that calf of a man can't wait. He——" She broke off abruptly. "Lilice, Lilice, I'm—I'm such a muddle-head. I don't know how to——"

"You can say what you please," Lilice answered dully. "I'll never have another baby. Never." Goaded by memories sharp as awls, she flung up her head crying, "You think I haven't got feelings? You think I want to see hands and feet growing scabby again? Reminding me day after day what we——"

The feel of Em'ly's baby still fresh and hurting in her arms, Lilice sagged to the table, no tears running . . . the agony laid bare . . . those years of good bread (flour from the solid kernel) soured with the wormwood of blighted joy . . . shame made endurable with false hope . . . all the futile clasping of hands before altars . . . Aunt Phrena's words . . . all the fearful regard for signs and portents.

Sophie listened, a finger and thumb pressing against a button on her cuff so hard, the flesh remained white and indented until she rubbed it. "Poor little kid! Only a woman could stand this. A man never could." Her voice was soft. "I thought I guessed most of this. But all these years." She stared unbelievingly. "Lilice, listen. You listen to me. I've had four kids. Some came easy and some tore me to the bone. I've watched 'em sick and I've watched 'em well. I've made Clymy into something I'm not ashamed of, little as he is. I know something about pain. And I've made mistakes. Oh ya, plenty of mistakes, big and small. Mean things. What I've done some nights with Clymy—I could get red in the face yet. But I won't. That's past. That's done. I've got enough trouble with today without worrying about yesterday."

"Oh, Sophie, if I could believe that." Lilice clasped her hands, one finger on the place where the ring had been.

"You've got to believe it." Sophie tapped the tablecloth with a knuckle. "As the Pastor said, nobody can tell you when a thing is past and you're done with it. It's got to come from inside you. When you can say, 'I won't do that again,' then——"

"I don't understand that," Lilice cried despairingly. "It is too easy."

"That's just what Ewig said last Sunday. We think our badness is so big we stumble all over our feet and never make any headway. When really it is simple. Like the sinful woman and how the Master wrote in the sand—— Oh, I don't know. You read it when you get time. John, somewhere."

"There's Lord's Supper soon," Lilice muttered suddenly, with curious intensity. "Johnny ought to go. He really ought."

"Sure, he ought to go." Sophie knitted her forehead, not sure of this new strangeness. "You mark this, Lilice. Between a man and a woman, there are some things even God can't help, not even if the Holy Ghost stood over them with a club."

"I can't think any more." Lilice lifted her hands despairingly. "I got to get the eggs for the kisses." Her voice broke. "Oh, Sophie, Sophie! ..."

For a long while after Sophie had gone, Lilice stared at her hands. "If it is true," the echo in her mind said. Slowly she moved about the kitchen. "The sinful woman ..." Quietly she entered the living room and brought the Book to the table. The pages rustled loudly into John. Yes, there it was. She read with fearful breath-held eagerness, "Woman, where are those thine accusers? Hath no man accused thee? She said, No man, Lord. And Jesus said unto her, Neither do I condemn thee: go and sin no more. ..."

Her fingers slipped from the smooth covers. "Neither do I condemn thee ... go ..." Could this be meant for her? So many times she'd read the words before, hungrily. But now—for her? The dreadful weight in her heart removed, the heavy band that crushed into her brain at times and spotted her sight—all these removed at last? "For me?" she cried, tears blurring the words. Her mind, like good soil in drought, seeded down yet impotent, which is brushed with faint moisture, stirred to the promise of growth but could not put forth sprout or curling root for the lethargy of a long rainless season.

She felt suddenly as though she were in the swing the boys had in the basswood, and were going up, the earth falling away, all the sweet green world in ridge and valley below her ... up ...

Far away she thought she heard a roll of thunder ... no, it was a whimper. Dickie. The swing descended. The green world vanished; the shadowy room closed around her. She was hot and sticky. Outside the world lay as tinder to the match. Dickie crying in the kitchen.

"I'm coming, Dickie," she called, letting the Book lie on the table.

She found him sitting by the screen door, his feet under him. His lips were puckered with the tears drying on his cheeks.

"It can't be that bad, Sonny," she said so brightly that he looked startled for a moment. Ma had been queerly nice all that day. If only she were like this always.

He muttered, "They went swimming. Robin and Sophus and the rest."

"And you——" She knelt beside him. The icicles began to grow in her breast again. Dickie ashamed to undress in front of the boys.

"Oh, Ma, they laugh at me," he whimpered and hid his face in her lap. "Irvie says I never wash myself. I do too, don't I, Ma?"

"Of course you do," she whispered. His whimpers came muffledly. She felt his hot breath through the cloth against her knee. Not for her, not for her, the blessed words. She heard the echo far away. Upstairs they must have been uttered.

"Look, Ma," he said, pulling at her arm. He stuck a foot out for her to see.

Her breath caught sharply. Gray it was and caked as if with the mud of years dried there, though only the night before he'd scrubbed patiently with soap and brush. Gray and cracked, and in the crevices the bright, vivid threads of blood squeezing through. . . . She put her hands to her eyes. Lies, lies . . .

"It aches so, Ma." Dickie scratched a rough place. "I couldn't sleep last night. And Robin kicks."

He mustn't cry, she thought, or I'll . . . "Dickie," she said aloud, tremulously. "Listen, Sonny. We'll make a batch of kisses, you and I. Run over to Auntie Sophie and get me a cupful of sugar. I must have forgotten it." Vagueness began to drift down. Lies, lies . . .

"And Robin can't have a single one, can he?" Dickie looked up.

Lies, lies, lies . . . "What did you say, Dickie?" Had she really spoken? Or had someone else?

"They buried the kitty." Dickie arose with her. "I heard her meow."

"The kitty?" she asked numbly. The kitty. What kitty? Kitty . . .

"The black one." He caught her hand. "They put her in a stone jar and covered her up. Robbie dug the hole. Irvie said the Lord's Prayer, only he couldn't remember nothing but the Power and the Glory. I told them you'd scold," he added virtuously, all his past seven years outraged. "I told them. They buried the kitty like it was the old crazy woman, Mrs. Dunkel."

"Crazy . . . kitty alive." She went quickly to the door, wondering who was calling from the cupboard, "What do you care, what do you care, lies, lies, lies? . . ."

"Come quick." She caught his hand. They ran to the garden. She wondered who had left all the sticks in the path today.

In a bed where the stumps of cabbages protruded like the stubby teeth of earth was a small mound. As she bent over it she heard a faint "Meow." She dug away the thin layer of earth, tore aside the cover of sticks. The black kitten jumped out, shaking the dust from her fur.

"My, but pussy is glad, ain't she, Ma?" Dickie stroked the arching back.

Lilice stared at the jar buried in the ground. She put her hand into it until she touched the bottom. Cool and quiet in there, under the canopy of darkness . . .

"Robbie found my willow whistle. He says it's mine, anyway." Dickie nudged her arm. "See? It's been in the ground all winter."

Silently she took the length of notched wood, a boy's whistle to call up April.

"See, Ma. The dirty old bark's nearly all gone." Dickie glanced at his feet. "You s'pose, Ma, if I buried my foot awhile, it would come out clean?"

"Dickie, Dickie!" she cried, hugging him to her. Suddenly she began to giggle wildly. (Was that the sound of water she heard?) What was it she was going to do? Wash the stairs this afternoon? Oh, no. Make a batch of kisses for the boys . . . for lunch. She'd have to get the eggs. "We'll have kisses, Dickie. A whole basket of them," she cried gaily. "Come."

"Will we?" he said doubtfully. But she pressed him against her. He looked at her, suspicious of her strained fixed mouth. "Can I go to Auntie Sophie's now?"

Lies, lies, lies, pounded in her head. She hurried through the gate. Far away, it seemed, Dickie was saying, "Look at that cloud. I guess it's going to rain, Ma." There were so many sticks in the path she scarcely paid attention to him. She entered the kitchen, blundered into the cupboard, found a cup, heard Dickie bang the screen door. "I'll come right back, Ma, and get the eggs for you." He was gone.

Not for her, the words, then. Sophie and her soft and easy ways. All that talk about what's past is done, and there's an end of it. But it didn't stay done. It came back; it would always come back. . . . And the Pastor and his sweet-spoken ideas. Lies, lies. Forgiveness? With Dickie crying over . . .

My, but this kitchen is dirty. All those cobwebs over the bread board. . . . I'll have to get the sugar . . . no, the eggs . . . in the henhouse . . . in the haymow. . . .

It was as though she were searching through curtains of endless dusk, each new one striking lightly across her eyes. But in the henhouse the bars on the windows were as black as night . . . one egg . . . put it in the basket . . . others in the haymow . . . dimness coming out of the sky . . .

My, that is a big black cave where the hay is left . . . hay walling up, up, into the cupola . . . shadows of the ladderway . . . if she could fly like the pigeons up there . . . why, she was almost flying . . . here she was airily under the rooftree . . . I'll spread my wings and fly down . . . I'm light, light as a feather . . . so many cobwebs here . . .

There was a nest, down near the edge where a post kept the hay from falling into the alleyway below. . . . Pesky hens, I'll just reach down . . . I could fly down. . . .

Something jolted her. Her arms closed instinctively around something hard. Dimly she realized that she was clinging to the post, hanging there, high up. A little pile of hay slid past her and fell down, down.

Then she heard it, the sound she'd known before: a sucking watery sound. From a corner of her eye she saw it, the pool, large and molasses-black, slowly circling, making a smutchy noise like thresher's oil pouring ... a sucking noise that seemed to whisper, "Let your fingers slip ... soft and cool and restful ... let your fingers slip. ..."

She'd go like the hay, only lighter ... light as a sparrow feather floating down that long stretch of hay wall to the floor, strike the floor lightly, float through the trap door, lightly on the concrete floor and the iron manger ends ... so many shadows in the cow barn below ... float into darkness ... darkness like that in the jar where the kitten was ... better so ... better so ...

"Let your fingers slip," whispered the pool. A rumbling wave rippled across it, like thunder under water.

Far away somebody yelled, or was it a shout in her own mind? No, no, there, there, on the farther edge of the pool, a boy was running, and flames were behind him like a wall, as of a house burning or a barn ... a barn ... reddening the oily, wheeling pool ... a boy running and waving his arms at her, his hair escaping under the rim of his cap, wavy hair, black and unruly. ... "Wait for me, Lilice; wait for me."

"Johnny, Johnny," she wanted to cry then, but couldn't for the cobwebs that choked her.

Then the slow swirl changed. It was a pool no longer but a wheel, large and grease-smudged with cogs like huge dogteeth, sharp and cutting. And the boy, no, it was a man, the man with wavy black hair was running straight into those knifelike edges. ... He'll die ... he touched them. ...

Everything flew into the burst of a great sun showering down streaks of crimson fire, and through them she was screaming, "Johnny, Johnny, I'll wait for you."

A dreadful clarity broke through what had been like lids on her eyes, or on her mind. She felt as though she'd endured a hill-rattling shock that was like a thunderbolt in a dry season or an icy blizzard after a long and feverishly arid season. There were no cobwebs now. Clear-eyed, awareness in every stiffening muscle, she clung desperately to the post. A draft of air, strong with the smell of manure and drying mangers, filled her nostrils. The trap door was open below her.

On the shingles above her was a rushing sound—rain after all, she thought; rain dashed in large splashes by the wind. A lightning flash ripped the dimness of the mow. Thunder hesitated a decent interval and roared.

She tried to catch a toe hold. Hay slithered past her. She waited through seconds until it swished on the floor below. Above her, the cross-bars of the post leaned like a head tiredly on one side under the slant of the roof.

I mustn't look down, I mustn't. She fastened her gaze on the crossbar and began to dig toe and knee into the hay, to climb slowly, with fearful gasps of breath. And through the muddle of drawing forward and sliding back and trying again, she kept thinking, Johnny, he's got to go to Lord's Supper. He's got to go.

Carefully, slowly, she pulled herself up, spear by spear of grass, it seemed. The rain splashed overhead. What's past is done, the Pastor said . . . walk quietly in your mind.

"Oh, please make it come true," she prayed as if someone were listening. "For Johnny."

She caught at the crossbar, dragged herself into a fold of solidness in the hay, and let her fear tremble in her limbs, the seconds of eternity behind her, bringing cold sweat to her limbs. . . . She mustn't lie here. Not now. There was a thing to do, and she had wasted the years already.

As she ran out of the haymow door, rain brushed at her face. She let it run down her cheeks. She hurried across the yard, thinking, Sophie must have kept Dickie because of the rain. It's only a shower after all. I wish it would rain hard.

On the porch steps she thought, Oh, Dickie, I've left the eggs in the mow after all. But she didn't stop. She entered the living room. No cobwebs now. Things were cluttered, but there were no cobwebs. She almost ran upstairs. From the drawer she brought the case and snapped the cover open.

There was her wedding ring, so long absent from her finger, it seemed. The mark of it no longer remained on her flesh. And beside her ring was Johnny's, twisted, broken. Quickly, as one who has little time to spare, she took her ring and slipped it onto a finger, over a knuckle, screwed it into comfort. For a moment she laid it against her cheek.

With Johnny's ring in her hand, she went downstairs. She hesitated as she turned the knob of Johnny's bedroom—their bedroom, as if Johnny were within, listening. Then she opened the door and stepped inside. She sat on the edge of the bed. Her hand closed. She felt the sharp metal of the broken ring press into her hand. It was good to feel.

From where she sat she saw in the mirror the separate loneliness of a can of shaving talc and a bottle of toilet water. Johnny's, her presents to him, though he seldom had time for such niceties. "Years of the locust." A phrase of the Pastor's repeated itself in her mind.

She opened her hand. There lay the rings, almost touching in her palm. Tears blurred her eyes and through the blur the rings blazed golden with sudden light. Outside the thunder muttered into distance. Hardly a drop was splashing.

She scarcely dared look into the mirror. As though fearful of what she'd see, she crept around the bed and approached the dresser. For a long time she stared at the image, as if it were strange to her, as if she'd been on a long journey away from herself, and returning, hardly recognized this chin, this tired mouth, these pale cheeks, the weary depth of the eyes. "So long," she whispered. "So long. If he wants me——"

Suddenly she buried her face in her arms and sobbed bitterly. "Don't be lonely any more, my dearest. Oh, Johnny, come home."

Through a window rose the spring freshness of earth newly sprinkled with rain. She scarcely heard the bump of the screen door and Dickie's loud, "I got the sugar, Ma. The rain's over. Aunt Sophie sent a jar of raspberries with cream."

14

They laid him on the drought-cropped grass. A moan puffed his lips. It might have been Lilice's name. There was no other sound from him. The sun shone brightly. The edge of storm rumbled away. The heat of the flaming barn was searing. Numbly Heinie kept rubbing a piece of the burned cloth he'd picked up from the ground. Marty folded and unfolded the drenched canvas. Mr. Schimmel came up. As if unaware of destruction in his barn, he pulled his watch out. "The rig. It stopped at forty minutes till five," he said hoarsely. "Forty till."

And Time the great cylinder whirled, slow in its swiftness, swift in its slowness, ripping the seed from the hull, and the seed falling. . . .

From the engine came the hiss of steam; from the separator a dull crackling. But Johnny lay as if earth were a good shoulder on which to rest. A knee was a little crooked. Then they saw that one fist was clenched tight. When they pried the fingers open, a scattering of wheat, golden, unseared by flame, rolled over the callused flesh and fell to the ground.

ACKNOWLEDGMENTS

THIS project was largely facilitated by a University of Minnesota Regional Writing Fellowship. I am under a feeling of deep obligation to Miss Helen Clapesattle, then acting chairman, to Dean Theodore C. Blegen, chairman, and to the members of the Committee.

I am indeed grateful to D. L. Chambers, of the Bobbs-Merrill Company, adviser, friend and patient guide; to Miss Grace Lee Nute, of the Minnesota Historical Society, and her assistants, for permission to read the Society's copies of the Dartt papers, the Murray, Barrick and Rollins diaries and the Begbie letters; to Miss M. Hrebek of the Edison Institute Museum; to J. I. Case Company and E. R. Durgin for invaluable prints and historical background; to Belle City Manufacturing Company and International Harvester for catalog material; to Allis-Chalmers, Minneapolis-Moline, and other implement companies; to Miss Selma Hogenson, Miss Lora Crouch and Miss Catherine Schoenmann for untangling research difficulties; to President Lawrence M. Stavig and my colleagues at Augustana, especially the members of the English Department and Professors I. B. Hauge, Stanley Olsen, Albert Tollevs and O. Tonning, for settling knotty problems.

Many people kindly searched the crannies of their memories for details regarding the threshers. I am sincerely thankful for their aid. For large measures of information I am indebted to Alva E. Miller, himself a thresher on the horsepower rigs; to the Emil Votrebek family; to Carl Kugler who sang for me some of the old thresher songs; to James O. Berdahl for the Berdahl memoirs; to Martin Tew for his privately printed *Autobiography;* to Albert and Mattie Duenow and the D. S. Danielson and George Duenow families for suggestive incidents.

I have no way to express my gratitude to my mother, who remembers the threshers vividly; to my brother Julius and his wife LaVerne; to the William O. Knights, Jr. and the H. C. Duenows, Raymond, Mel and Floyd; to my colleague H. M. (Pat) Blegen and his wife Anne; to Orin and Del Lofthus, friendliest critics of the University of South Dakota, who listened while I read; to Mr. and Mrs. Henry Hahn, Sr. They know what they know.

Augustana College
Sioux Falls, South Dakota